CRIMSON
IN
TRIUMPH

For Finn —
on your twenty-first
birthday

with love from
Mom & Dad

CRIMSON
IN
TRIUMPH

A PICTORIAL HISTORY OF HARVARD ATHLETICS, 1852–1985

Joe Bertagna

A Terry Catchpole Book

THE STEPHEN GREENE PRESS
Lexington, Massachusetts

First published in 1986 by The Stephen Greene Press, Inc.
Published simultaneously in Canada by Penguin Books Canada Limited
Distributed by Viking Penguin Inc., 40 West 23rd Street, New York, NY 10010

The author wishes to thank the Harvard Varsity Club and the Department of
Athletics of Harvard University for their cooperation and support while
researching and writing this book.

Photo credits appear on page 367.

LIBRARY OF CONGRESS CATALOGING IN PUBLICATION DATA
Bertagna, Joe.
Crimson in triumph.
"A Terry Catchpole Book"
Includes index.
1. Harvard University—Athletics—History.   I. Title.
GV691.H3B47   1986   796′.07′117444   85-27175
ISBN 0-8289-0573-8

Printed in the United States of America by
The Murray Printing Company, Westford, Massachusetts
Set in Garamond Book Condensed
Book design by Mary A. Wirth

With Crimson in triumph flashing
      'Mid the strains of victory
Poor Eli's hopes we are dashing into blue obscurity.
Resistless our team sweeps goalward
      'Mid the fury of the blast;
We'll fight for dear old Harvard
      till the last white line is passed.

           —Raymond G. Williams '11
              "Harvardiana"

ACKNOWLEDGMENTS

"So, you are writing a history of Harvard athletics," said my friend. "Exactly how many volumes are you planning to produce?"

The question was asked somewhat mischievously, for Harvard's rich athletic history could indeed fill volumes covering the period of 133 years chosen for this book. Fortunately for this writer, a pair of handy volumes already existed.

This project would have been virtually impossible for one author were it not for the existence of two books covering Harvard's athletic accomplishments from their 19th-century beginnings through 1963. The period 1852–1922 was described in *The H Book of Harvard Athletics,* edited by John A. Blanchard '91 and published by the Harvard Varsity Club in 1923. The years 1923–63 were given full coverage in *The Second H Book of Harvard Athletics,* edited by Geoffrey H. Movius '62 and also published by the Varsity Club (1964). Beyond the respective editors, the many contributors to these *H Books* must be acknowledged, particularly the 19 alumni who wrote the individual chapters of *The Second H Book.*

The post-1963 wins and losses have been chronicled in great detail through another Varsity Club publication, "News and Views," a newsletter produced weekly during football season and monthly thereafter by Harvard's Sports Information Office. In a way, the real heroes of this production are the many sports information directors who have served Harvard over the years, preserving documents and photographs and, in the process, preserving Harvard's athletic history. Special thanks go out to the directors, W. Henry Johnston, Baaron Pittenger, Ron Cantera, Dave Matthews (my boss from 1977 to 1978 and whom I succeeded in 1978), Jim Greenidge, and the man whose office I invaded frequently in search of a stat, a photo, or a date, Ed Markey. He couldn't have been more helpful. And while we're thinking of the sports information world, a tip of the hat is directed toward the assistants over the years, particularly Jean MacIver, John Powers, Bob Donovan, Pat Walsh, and Mark Bergeron.

Nearly 100 people were interviewed during a year and a half of research. This group included past and present coaches, athletes, and administrators, as well as fans who simply watched generations of heroes wear the H proudly. The fans who read this history may be dismayed to occasionally find a favorite halfback or forward left out. That, I'm afraid, was unavoidable. But with a deliberate focus on the post–*H Book* years, the pages should be reasonably complete.

Finally, there was the inner circle of advisors and counselors who kept a frequently distracted author on schedule. Will Cloney '33 and Dave Mittell '39, key figures in *The Second H Book* and friends of Harvard athletics of the first degree, were always there to provide direction, answer questions, and locate a comma I had somehow misplaced. The Varsity Club, a constant in virtually all historical treatments, lent valuable support through the efforts of Bob Pickett, John Arnold, and Walter Greeley. Jack Reardon, Harvard's capable Director of Athletics, kept all athletic department doors and resources open. My sincerest thanks go out to copy reader Peg Anderson who caught more inconsistencies than I care to admit. And

both publisher Tom Begner and editor Terry Catchpole managed to instill confidence in the author, particularly in the early days when the project had yet to take full shape.

While photographers' contributions are noted in the back of the book, special thanks must go to Tim and Karen Morse, friends and professionals, who solved every copying problem and provided some of their best work as well.

Maybe there should be one more blanket acknowledgment, one directed at the thousands of men and women who created the stories told on the following pages. And along with the champions and all-stars, include those who worked and cared just as much without a moment in the spotlight. This book is about them all. This book is for them all.

Joseph Bertagna
Londonderry, New Hampshire
Summer, 1985

Contents

CRIMSON
IN
TRIUMPH

Harvard and the Ivy League

When the last regular-season game of the 1980 Eastern Intercollegiate Baseball League had been played, Harvard found itself deadlocked with Cornell and Yale atop the league standings. To break the first three-way tie in EIBL history, the teams met at Army's neutral field for a weekend play-off.

As the play-offs were set to begin, so too were final exams at Harvard. And among those scheduled for a three-hour exam on the play-off Saturday was Harvard's freshman shortstop Brad Bauer. In the past, Harvard's Administrative Board had allowed athletes to take their exams on the road, under the supervision of a coach or an administrator from the site of the competition. But those same authorities also had the right to keep a freshman on campus for his first set of year-end finals. Such was the right exercised with All-EIBL shortstop Bauer.

The decision caused a minor stir among those close to the baseball team. How could Harvard do such a thing? Didn't they care about winning? The controversy died down after Harvard beat both Cornell and Yale on that Saturday, with substitute shortstop Paul Chicarello going

5-for-8. Credit Harvard's depth with curtailing an interesting debate.

The story of the detained shortstop never made headlines. It was simply business as usual at an institution where baseball players, even all-star shortstops, are treated as students first and athletes second. And that is a philosophy that Harvard and its Ivy League brethren have been trying to follow since they introduced college athletics to this country more than 130 years ago.

To be completely accurate, this credo has not been faithfully adhered to for the entire 130-plus years. It can be argued that the same schools that took up the fight against excesses in college athletics were the very schools that created the problems in the first place. In the early days of this century, it was Harvard that hired the first professional coaches, recruited the first ringers, played professional teams, and with the construction of Harvard Stadium, introduced big-time athletics to America.

So it was only fitting that in 1954 Harvard and seven other schools (Brown, Columbia, Cornell, Dartmouth, Penn, Princeton, and Yale) should band together to lead the way once more by signing the Ivy Group Presidents' Agreement. This document stated that "emphasis upon intercollegiate competition must be kept in harmony with the essential educational purposes of the institution." With that agreement, the Ivy League was born.

The term "Ivy League" had been coined by Caswell Adams of the *New York Herald Tribune* some 20 years before and represents a philosophy that has been frequently discussed but seldom understood. One of the most direct interpretations of Ivy League goals was voiced by Tom Bolles, the former Harvard athletic director, who was influential in the formation of early league policy. Said Bolles in a 1955 Harvard football program:

> The Ivy League believes that the entire control of the valuable program of intercollegiate athletics must be under the jurisdiction of the President and Faculty. It believes that athletics are good for students. But it insists that athletics must be kept in perspective and that students are students first and athletes second.
>
> The League has no quarrel with its many friends in intercollegiate athletics. It is not asking that any other individual college or group subscribe to its policies. It does not believe that all other institutions are less ethical in their athletic policies.... Nor do the Ivies feel that they themselves have reached perfection in their operations. Ivy members are quick to acknowledge that they themselves are responsible for starting, many years ago, practices which grew into evils. But adhering strictly to the belief that control of the athletic program belongs in the office of the President and that only true amateurs and bona fide students participate, Ivy League members are convinced that they are not only improving intercollegiate athletics, but in reality saving them.

Two of the biggest misconceptions about Harvard and the Ivy League are that the Ivies have tried to force their philosophy on others and that they are not concerned with athletic excellence. Evidence suggests the contrary to be true.

There are plenty of people associated with the Ivy League—administrators, coaches, alumni—who indeed feel that they and they alone have found the proper way to run an intercollegiate athletic program. But the Ivy way has always been to lead through example. Representatives of Ivy League interests have frequently made speeches and written articles espousing the virtues of college athletics Ivy-style. But speeches and other public pronouncements hardly constitute an attempt to force the Ivy approach on the rest of the nation.

On the contrary, it can be argued that more often than not others have wanted to impose their will on the Ivies. That has frequently been the case at the annual convention of the National Collegiate Athletic Association. Harvard and the Ivies have frequently taken a stand for institutional autonomy, not forcing all schools, big and small, to come around to one way of doing things.

In 1966, for example, the NCAA convention passed a rule upholding the 1.6 grade point average as a standard for incoming student-athletes. Though such a standard should not have been formidable to Ivy athletes, the league opposed the ruling. Its grounds: that each school should determine the academic qualifications of its incoming students. Nearly 20 years later, the issue before the NCAA convention was recruiting, and exactly who could contact prospective student-athletes and when. Legislation passed in the early 1980s struck hard at the Ivy League, and both their use of alumni and their various admissions schedules.

As for the charge that the Ivy schools are not concerned with athletic excellence, one only need look at the Ivy League teams that advance to national championship play. Harvard has won national titles in crew and squash with some frequency, has sent four baseball teams to the College World Series, and in 1983 saw the hockey team finish second behind Wisconsin in the NCAA finals.

Ivy athletes continue to dot the rosters of various Olympic and professional teams. Recent National Football League rosters have included Pat McInally and Dan Jiggetts of Harvard, Gary Fencik of Yale, Nick Lowery of Dartmouth, John Woodring of Brown, and others. Among the National Hockey League's recent Ivy grads are Mark Fusco and Neil Sheehy of Harvard, Bob Brooke of Yale, Darren Eliot and Brian Hayward of Cornell, and Carey Wilson of Dartmouth. Major league baseball includes even more Ivy graduates than do these sports.

While the argument that the Ivy League is not concerned with excellence is a weak one, there is another charge that is more legitimate. That is that the Ivy League is not attracting as many outstanding athletes as it once did. Granted, Ivy schools still draw exceptional athletes who earn individual honors and go on to higher levels of competition. But they do not attract top-notch athletes in numbers sufficient to make their football, basketball, baseball, and track teams, for example, competitive against teams outside the league.

The sports that Ivy teams excel at nationally seem to be those played by relatively few colleges (crew, squash, ice hockey). It has been ten years since Harvard's last appearance at the College World Series, and the record of

Ivy football teams in nonleague play has been startling. From 1980 through 1984 Ivy football teams were 30-80-2 outside the league. Dartmouth, a perennial Ivy and regional power only a decade earlier, was 0-14.

If Ivy schools are not attracting as many outstanding athletes, it is not because they do not want them. In addition to the fact that academic standards remain extremely high, there is one problem that is more serious than ever—finances. Rising costs have hit hard at the middle class, perhaps the best source of tough, motivated athletes. In the mid-1970s the cost of attending an Ivy League school was less than $6,000 annually, and when a partial financial aid package fell short of the needed amount, loans were available at interest rates of 3 percent.

Ten years later the cost is over $15,000, loans are more difficult to obtain, and more than a few Ivy coaches are losing prized recruits for one reason only: They can't afford to turn down athletic scholarships from outside the league. The effects of this phenomenon are seen in the nonleague results and provide one more reason for Ivy teams to set their seasonal sights on one realistic goal: winning the Ivy League title.

FROM CHAOS TO CONTROL

There was a time when being the best among the Ivies meant being the best in the country—no matter what the sport. Today, aside from sports with limited participation, such as crew or squash, that is no longer the case. There are now two worlds, big-time sports and the rest. Sometimes the line between the two is undefined. But in some cases it is quite sharp, as in 1982 when NCAA legislation divided Division I football teams into 1A and 1AA. Among the criteria that left the Ivy League with the reduced status of 1AA were stadium seating capacity and annual attendance figures.

Ivy teams might still set the Ivy League championship as their primary goal, but aside from football national aspirations are rarely far behind. League athletic directors must insure that the pursuit of both goals remains balanced.

The Harvard philosophy has been to allow teams to strive for their highest potential. That means that although national championships are not the stated goal of a program, the university and the Department of Athletics will not prohibit a team or individuals from competing at the national level if their regular-season success brings them the opportunity.

At Harvard, the job of seeing this philosophy through falls to the director of athletics, and since 1977 that position has been held by John P. Reardon '60. Reardon, a former undergraduate football manager, is the fifth man to serve Harvard in that capacity, carrying on a tradition inaugurated by William J. Bingham '16 in 1926. For different reasons, the tenures of Bingham and Reardon have been the most taxing of the five regimes. Bingham, as the first athletic director, had to define the job. Reardon, as the athletic director facing the rebuilding of the school's athletic plant and the implementation of women's athletics, faced unique problems. Both passed their tests with flying colors.

For a complete history of Harvard's athletic administration prior to and up through Bill Bingham's 25-year tenure, one should read the opening chapter of *The Second H Book of Harvard Athletics.* The book's editors have painstakingly traced the development of Harvard's athletic policy and identified the key figures in that evolution. For the moment, a condensed version of that history is in order.

When Harvard entered the world of intercollegiate athletics in the 19th century, the operation of the early teams was left in the hands of undergraduates. Students selected coaches, usually on an annual basis, and students were responsible for the financial operation of the programs.

In 1874 the Harvard Athletic Association was formed, made up entirely of undergraduates, who ran every aspect of the Harvard athletic program. By 1882 a series of potential problems had surfaced, most notably lengthy schedules, the hiring of professional (i.e., paid) coaches, and the use of athletes who were not full-time students.

And so in June of 1882 President Charles W. Eliot '53, a former Harvard oarsman, appointed three faculty members to the Committee on the Regulation of Athletic Sports. This committee, composed of Charles Eliot Norton, Horatio S. White, and Dr. Dudley A. Sargent, is believed to be the first such body to oversee college athletics.

Although the baseball team's 28-game schedule of 1882 (19 on the road) had been the most pointed reason for the committee's birth, it soon became apparent that the subject of amateurism was of much greater concern. There were hardly any eligibility rules at the time, only that an athlete must be enrolled in some department of the college.

At the same time that schools sought to limit their athletic programs to legitimate student-athletes, two other problems surfaced, increased violence at football games

The role of the college athletic director changed dramatically from the days of Bill Bingham '16 (right) and Jack Reardon '60 (below). Bingham, Harvard's first director, served from 1926 to 1951 and saw the transfer of power from alumni to his office. Jack Reardon became Harvard's fifth athletic director in 1977 and presided over the complete overhaul of Harvard's athletic facilities and the implementation of the women's sports program.

and the growth of gate receipts from university contests. Suddenly, the games were more than just an outlet for students. They had become a source of considerable amounts of money, and the university was concerned with the potential for abuse in the operation of its athletic program.

Accordingly, in 1888 a new committee was organized, with more representatives from more constituencies and with more clearly defined goals. This committee was made up of three faculty members, three alumni, and three undergraduates. According to its constitution, the committee was assigned "entire supervision and control over all athletic exercise within and without the precincts of the University, subject to the authority of the faculty."

The establishment of this Athletic Committee brought the alumni into the action, and within five years their role would increase. During this period a number of Alumni Advisory Committees had sprung up, assisting the still student-run teams. In 1893 the Athletic Committee formally took control of the teams from the students and placed it with the alumni. This step, for a while, was successful.

Over the next decade, Harvard took the lead in establishing new eligibility guidelines. Among the Harvard practices adopted by other schools were the banning of freshmen and graduate students from varsity play and the one-year residency requirement for transfer students.

The one issue that Harvard and the rest of the nation's colleges had greater difficulty with was football's brutality. The matter peaked in 1905, when Harvard's head football coach Bill Reid was among the college representatives summoned to the White House by President Theodore Roosevelt '80. With a clear mandate from Roosevelt, the football leadership set out to save their game. At Harvard, that meant saving the game from extinction, an option favored by some of the Harvard faculty members.

The construction of Harvard Stadium in 1903 had made such a drastic measure unlikely. To make sure, Reid and Dean LeBaron Briggs set up a committee of alumni to investigate football rules reform and insure the game's survival in Cambridge. When football's national leadership convened in 1906, the Harvard group's ideas were responsible for many of the subsequent changes in the game.

By the time A. Lawrence Lowell succeeded Charles W. Eliot as Harvard president in 1909, two sides had formed within the Harvard community over an athletic battle that, to some extent, still rages today. On one side were those alumni whose main concern was Harvard's athletic success, and who insisted on better coaching, better athletes, and more games. On the other side was the Harvard Corporation itself, endorsing reductions in the athletic program.

With increasing gate receipts and revenue potential came increased pressures to win. Lowell was concerned with this trend and also with the general state of Harvard's athletic administration. The Athletic Committee and, more significantly, the Alumni Advisory Committees provided too many sources of influence and power. Missing was control, which one central source could bring.

One story that circulated at the time spelled out the problem. When asked if he would consider taking a job at Harvard, one established crew coach of that period said, "You haven't got a thing to say for Harvard athletics. The alumni run the show, and everybody knows it. Under your system, a coach doesn't stand a chance—he loses a few contests and he gets the ax. No wonder you have such a great turnover on your coaching staff. Nope, I wouldn't come to Harvard—not even if you offered me $100,000 a year."

The problem was soon resolved. President Lowell convinced Bill Bingham to become the first director of athletics in 1926, but only after Bingham was assured that he would answer to the faculty, not the alumni. Bingham, a former track star and coach, tested the system in his first year, overruling both the football and crew advisory committees on the matter of selecting head coaches. The new director's actions led to a number of alumni resigning former positions of power, just as Lowell had hoped. A short time later Bingham abolished the advisory committees altogether.

Under Bingham, the modern athletic department was created. Harvard would not allow athletic scholarships nor could Harvard coaches travel for the purpose of recruiting athletes. The former would become league policy when the Ivies were born; the latter remained a Harvard policy into the late 1970s.

It was also under Bingham that Harvard's extensive intramural program was born. Launched with the construction of the river houses in 1932, the program grew first under Dolph Samborski (later director of athletics) and then under Floyd Wilson. By 1985 more than 4,000 undergraduates were participating in 36 different intramural and recreational activities.

The maturity and success of the Harvard Athletic Association were not without their rough spots. In the early days, the HAA was totally dependent upon its own ability to raise revenues, and in the 1930s it found this increasingly difficult to do. After World War II, Harvard's athletics-for-all program was operating in the red and had to be bailed out by the Faculty of Arts and Sciences. Beginning with the 1945–46 season, the HAA deficits ranged from $91,000 to $153,000 over a five-year period. In 1951, future deficits were estimated at more than $300,000 annually.

At this point, Harvard authorities realized that the athletic department not only couldn't support itself but, more important, shouldn't have to. As Provost Paul Buck said at the time, "The director of athletics should be an educational officer, not a representative of the entertainment business."

So changes were promptly made in the operation of Harvard's athletic program. The corporation in 1951 turned the old HAA into the Harvard Department of Athletics, with its budget controlled by the Faculty of Arts and Sciences. Replacing Bill Bingham as director of athletics would be Tom Bolles, the head coach of heavyweight crew.

Bingham's "resignation" was not altogether a happy situation. He had long advocated relieving the athletic interests of the burden of raising their own revenues. But he did not see eye to eye with Dr. James B. Conant, Harvard's president since 1933, on just how this should be done. And so in February of 1951, Bingham was asked to resign. It came as no surprise to Harvard insiders when the fiery, outspoken Bingham was replaced by the quiet, reserved Bolles.

The changing of the guard took place amid a different yet not unrelated controversy. Harvard's athletic fortunes, particularly on the football field, had taken a nose dive. When the 1-8 football season of 1949 was followed by a 1-7 campaign in 1950, Harvard's entire athletic future was called into question. The debate, carried out among alumni as well as in the local media, produced opinions ranging from outright abolition of athletics—as the University of Chicago had done in 1939—to going after prospective student-athletes more aggressively than ever before.

The result was a new effort to define exactly where the student-athlete fit in at Harvard. Provost Buck, at a press conference on March 11, 1950, took the first step toward making that definition clear when he said, "We shall continue to play the same game of football. We are not going the road of Chicago. . . . We want athletes at the college because we believe in a balanced student body. Such men contribute to Harvard life."

Other, more substantial steps soon followed. That same

month, the Financial Aid Center was established under the direction of John Munro '34 to bring all forms of financial aid—scholarships, loans, and jobs—together under one office and make them available to all Harvard students, including athletes. Two years later, when Wilbur J. Bender succeeded Richard Gummere as chairman of the Admission and Scholarship Committee, the stage was set for an even more dramatic step for Harvard athletics.

Bender's ideas on attracting quality student-athletes to Harvard did not involve lowering standards. His method was simply to articulate the role of athletes in a given entering class, and to involve Harvard alumni in directing these people toward Cambridge. "There was a very real danger that we would become so lopsided, so narrowly intellectual, so brittle and precious and neurotic that we would cut ourselves off from the mainstream of American life and seriously diminish the contribution we could make to the country," said Bender.

In his final report as dean of admissions, Bender wrote, "Let's have some other students to help hold the place together, students who are intelligent without necessarily being 'intellectuals.'"

What this approach begat was an effort to identify good students who could contribute more than their intellectual prowess to life at Harvard. Some have referred to these students as the "happy bottom quarter," students who are content to pursue a specific activity at college, such as athletics, even if one price they pay is finishing in the bottom quarter of the class. Clearly, however, many athletes were to graduate with honors and the bottom quarter was peopled with many nonathletes.

Tom Bolles served as director of athletics from 1951 to 1963, a tenure that saw the Ivy Group Agreement signed and the league goal articulated. Thus, in a matter of a few years, the athletic structure of Harvard and the Ivy League were established and solidly so, as the tumultuous and historic Bingham administration was followed by the three quietly productive regimes of Bolles, Dolph Samborski (1963–70), and Bob Watson (1970–77).

Samborski, Harvard '25, developed and directed Harvard's intramural program for 35 years before his seven years as director of athletics. In January of 1970, Watson '37 became Harvard's fourth athletic director when he relinquished his position as dean of students, a title he had held with distinction since 1958.

The heart of Harvard's athletic life is the Dillon Field House at Soldiers Field.

THE REARDON YEARS

During the 1970s, Harvard's ability to provide athletics for all faced two new challenges. The first emerged with the realization that the university's athletic facilities, once the best in the nation, had become an embarrassment. The other came about through the absorption of Radcliffe College's athletic program into the Harvard Department of Athletics. Fortunately for Harvard, it had an individual who could handle both problems: Jack Reardon.

When Reardon was named Harvard's fifth director of athletics in September of 1977, he had already served his alma mater for more than ten years, most notably as associate dean of admissions and financial aid for Harvard and Radcliffe. Reardon's administrative skills had been honed at Harvard as undergraduate manager of the 1959 football team and at Pennsylvania's Wharton School, where he earned a master's degree in business administration.

His involvement with the matter of Harvard's athletic facilities began long before he settled into his third-floor office at 60 Boylston Street. "When I was in the admissions office," he later recalled, "I was afraid we were going to lose good applicants—not just good athletes, but students in general—whose judgments on Harvard could be affected by the sorry state of our athletic plant."

By the early 1970s, it was apparent that something had to be done quickly and carefully. Others had made facility proposals to the Harvard Corporation a decade earlier, but those attempts fell on deaf ears. Not only were their

cost estimates unrealistic, but the proposals did not answer the questions that the corporation was sure to ask: How would these proposed new facilities be endowed, and what would be the priorities in assigning their use?

From his position in admissions, Reardon was familiar with both the needs of the athletic program and the realities of the Harvard community. With the help of the athletic department, he was in a perfect position to devise a plan that not only met those athletic needs but could also gain approval from the Harvard administration.

"From the beginning, our attitude was, 'What do we have to do to get this built?' " said Reardon. "To sell it in this community, we knew we had to make sure that everyone understood that the athletic department was planning for the needs of the entire Harvard community. Certainly, the intercollegiate program would have a major priority, and alumni who gave strong support to the intercollegiate program were among the major contributors."

By February of 1974 Reardon had approval from Harvard president Derek Bok and the corporation to prepare plans. In June, Dr. Chase Peterson, vice-president for alumni affairs and development, appointed Reardon to head a special fund-raising effort for the improvement of Harvard's athletic plant. Dr. Peterson's leadership and support through all stages of this effort were vital to its success.

Harvard's concern for the needs of the entire community was evident from President Bok's statement announcing the project, comments that stressed that "the steady growth of interest in athletics and physical exercise,

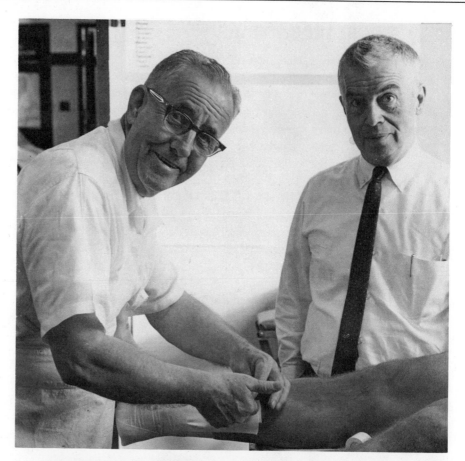

In addition to housing medical facilities, equipment, and coaches' offices, Dillon has always been the place to visit old friends, like trainer Jack Fadden (top) and former equipment manager Jimmy Cunniff (bottom, left).

especially on the part of women, faculty, and graduate students, has placed severe strains on our facilities."

Reardon's task was clear. He realized that his effort would go nowhere without the right individual to chair the fund-raising drive. The already difficult challenge would be compounded by the Harvard Campaign, a five-year, university-wide fund-raising operation that put restraints on how the athletic interests could raise their money.

Reardon had the man in Albert Hamilton Gordon, class of '23. He was a friend of Harvard athletics who would later become cochairman of the Harvard Campaign. By August of 1974 Reardon had convinced Gordon to spearhead the athletic facilities effort.

The university made it tough by insisting that the athletic drive raise enough money not only to build the facilities but also to endow the operation of the buildings. But the challenge was met, and on May 15, 1976, ten years of construction and renovation began with ground-breaking ceremonies at Soldiers Field. The day recognized months of work on the part of Reardon and representatives of both the development office and the Department of Athletics, the latter represented by Director of Athletics Bob Watson and Associate Director of Athletics Baaron Pittenger.

By 1985 Harvard's entire athletic plant had been affected by the change. The price tag for the decade of activity: $33 million. While there were donations of all sizes, the project was keyed by a handful of individuals whose major gifts made all the difference. One such benefactor was Jack Blodgett, a classmate of Al Gordon's who had retired from a successful career in the lumber business. Blodgett, who did not play sports at Harvard, knew about the state of Harvard's athletic facilities and wanted to do something about them. He originally wanted to build a basketball facility, having been convinced, and rightly so, that Harvard needed one badly. But basketball was not the number-one priority under Harvard's plan. Phase I would produce a new pool and an indoor track, facilities that could maximize community use. And so Harvard's Olympic-sized pool is named for John W. Blodgett, Jr., class of '23.

Phase II originally called for a new hockey rink and the conversion of the Watson Rink into a basketball facility. When the cost of building a new rink went out of sight, Watson Rink was renovated to become the Alexander H. Bright Hockey Center. The renovation met all skating and hockey requirements better than the proposed new facility and at less than half the cost. Basketball needs were subsequently met when, through an innovative renovation,

the old Briggs Cage became a multiuse facility in 1982. The $3 million renovation included a unique Astroturf carpet that could be installed over the wood basketball floor in a matter of minutes, allowing baseball, lacrosse, or other sports to run an indoor practice session.

The individual facilities are described in greater detail in the chapters that follow, but the table below gives an idea of the scope of this entire rebuilding project.

Year	Facility	Building or Renovation Cost
1978	Blodgett Pool Gordon Track and Tennis Center	$10.7 million (new)
1979	Bright Hockey Center	3.0 million (renovation)
	Dillon Field House	1.5 million (renovation)
1982	Briggs Athletic Center	3.0 million (renovation)
	Harvard Stadium	9.0 million (renovation)
	Beren Tennis Courts	0.3 million (new)
1984	McCurdy Track (outdoor)	1.0 million (new)
1985	Indoor Athletic Building	4.0 million (renovation)
	Total Cost	$32.5 million

One unexpected item on the final tally was the $9 million put into Harvard Stadium. A variety of studies conducted on the structure indicated that if Harvard did not act quickly to replace the concrete seats and the steel supports beneath, the Stadium might be lost within 15 years. The price tag for saving the 79-year-old Stadium was 30 times the original cost of building it in 1903.

Among the many beneficiaries of the improved facilities were the woman athletes who were to give Harvard athletics a new look beginning in 1974, the year that Harvard accepted the responsibility for the operation of Radcliffe College's sports programs. People are careful not to use the word "merger," as Harvard College and Radcliffe College have not officially merged. But in a number of areas, most significantly the Harvard-Radcliffe Admissions Office, there are all the signs of the two institutions being one.

Up until 1973 the Radcliffe athletic program had been ably run by Mary Paget. Among the more developed Radcliffe intercollegiate programs were basketball, crew, field hockey, sailing, swimming, and tennis. Within the next decade, a dozen new sports would be added and the budget for women's athletics would increase from $60,000 to $700,000.

The biggest impetus for this growth came from the federal Higher Education Act of 1972, Title IX of which mandated equality in the funding of athletic programs at educational institutions receiving federal aid by prohibiting discrimination on the basis of sex. At Harvard, and elsewhere across the country, women's athletic programs blossomed almost overnight.

The progress was not always smooth. To female undergraduates in the mid-to-late 1970s, it was frequently a battle just to gain access to certain facilities at reasonable hours, under qualified coaches. Often the coaches were qualified but their commitment was part-time.

By 1984 most of the problems had been ironed out and nearly 600 women were competing on 33 teams in 18 intercollegiate sports. Another 1,000 women were involved in 16 intramural sports. Improvements were evident in the areas of coaching, equipment, and schedules. Round-robin Ivy League competition had been established in a number of sports and, beyond regular-season play, a number of Harvard women's teams were experiencing some of the extras that the men had enjoyed for so long, including competitive trips abroad, such as field hockey's visit to Great Britain in 1980, soccer's trip to Holland in 1984, and lacrosse's excursion to Australia in 1984.

Perhaps the most important change came in people's attitudes toward woman athletes at Harvard. The reluctance to accept the women as bona fide competitors was painfully evident in many quarters during the early years. Some male critics scoffed at the skill levels in certain women's sports and noted how many women could arrive at the school with no prior experience in a sport and go on to earn four varsity letters. Those critics forgot how male athletes at Harvard, long after a sport's first decade, could pick up swimming or crew or squash and go on to become intercollegiate champions. Those occurrences are documented in the pages that follow.

Some of the criticisms seem humorous now. Take the example of the old-timer who hated seeing women's sports written up in "News and Views," the athletic newsletter published by the Harvard Varsity Club. The gentleman wrote to the newsletter's editor saying, "I think it's great that they are playing sports. I will provide financial contributions to help them along. I just don't want to read about it."

• • •

CONTINUING THE CAUSE

The pages that follow cover 133 years of Harvard athletics. There are a few constants amid these years of continuous change. It is a story of opportunities, of leadership, and of people.

The real challenge in running Harvard's athletic department comes in providing for the nine-letter winner as well as the recreational athlete who simply wants a place to jog, play tennis, and have a game of pick-up basketball. With 41 intercollegiate sports and another 36 intramural sports, Harvard does a pretty good job at meeting the challenge.

Two activities underscore the incredible record of athletic participation at Harvard. One is found on the Charles River. "I've always felt that one of the most amazing examples of what we're doing is the house crew program," says Floyd Wilson, director of intramurals since 1968. "We've got forty-four different crews, and I can't think of any other activity at Harvard that gets people up at six in the morning like this does."

The other, more celebrated example is visible on the Friday before the annual Harvard-Yale football game. Each year some 500 undergraduates take part in tackle football, touch football, and soccer against their Yale counterparts. It is a spectacle unmatched anywhere in the country and, as John Powers '70 of the *Boston Globe* has observed, allows the undergraduate population to "grab a piece of the rivalry."

Through programs like this, Harvard continues to provide leadership through example. At the same time, critics continue to chip away at the role they perceive Harvard to assume. "Harvard does things right," said one Boston sportswriter, "but do they have to keep telling us about it?"

Jack Reardon has an answer: "If you see yourself as an educator, you almost have a mission to speak out and raise real questions that no one else is asking. Should freshmen play high-powered varsity sports? What are the potential problems with athletic scholarships? The only solutions being offered nationally are little more than control mechanisms. No one is raising the important philosophical questions."

And so Harvard and its Ivy brethren continue to do so. Through the years, Harvard has been blessed with individuals who have provided leadership at crucial times in the school's athletic history. In 1905 it was Bill Reid. From 1926 to 1951 it was Bill Bingham. Since 1977 it has been Jack Reardon.

"Jack Reardon has a good sense of what he is all about," observed Jim Litvack, executive director of the Council of Ivy Group Presidents from 1974 to 1984. "Jack was never afraid to see a vote of athletic directors come out seven to one against him, because he always knew what he wanted and he stood by it. Frequently, events would prove him right, and after a while, you didn't see so many seven-to-one votes any more. It was as if people were saying, 'Well, if Jack feels that way, maybe I better think about that a little more.' "

Jack Reardon is an example of what Harvard's greatest strength has always been: people. Perhaps more to the point, that strength has been found in the diversity of people at Harvard. There was a time when the stereotypical Harvard athlete was a prep school product who came to Harvard for a multisport career and went on to become a doctor, a lawyer, or a stockbroker. But all that has changed.

The modern Harvard athlete is as likely to come from a public school as from a private school. An age of specialization, for better or for worse, has replaced the day of the multisport star. And although Harvard continues to produce its share of doctors, lawyers, and stockbrokers, the Harvard letter-winner surfaces in a variety of careers, many of which are connected with the world of sports.

Consider Dr. William Southmayd, former Harvard football captain and leader in the field of sports medicine. Or Ed Durso, shortstop in the class of '75, who serves as counsel in the office of baseball commissioner Peter Ueberroth. And then there is Ric LaCivita, soccer and baseball letter-winner, who serves as a leading producer of college sports events for CBS-TV.

These are just a few of the Harvard people whose undergraduate careers are highlighted in the 14 chapters that follow. For all the attention they deserve, it is a shame that another set of heroes can't be afforded the same space. These are the behind-the-scenes Harvard people who served these athletes and, indirectly, the Greater Boston sports community.

How many sportswriters, looking for the real stories, stopped by Dillon Field House to see equipment managers Jimmy Cunniff and Chet Stone? How many aging alumni, sore from a weekend of tennis or skiing, made an early-morning visit to Dillon for therapy, coffee, and a sermon from trainer Jack Fadden? How many neighboring schools—colleges and high schools alike—sought advice and relief from Harvard people like Ticket Manager Gordon Page and Business Manager Fran Toland?

These people never threw a pass, never scored a goal, and never broke any records. But because of people like them, hundreds of others could. Together, they make up the rich history of Harvard athletics.

A new and increasingly common scene at Soldiers Field: A former Harvard letter-winner returns to watch his daughter in varsity competition. Here, Walter Greeley '53, MVP of the first Beanpot Hockey Tournament, chats with daughter Jenny '85, voted 1985 Ivy League Player of the Year in lacrosse.

CHAPTER 2

Football

The argument continues today. Which teams played the first college football game? Was it Princeton versus Rutgers in 1869? Or Harvard versus McGill in 1874?

Neither game may ever receive universal acceptance as the first, but one thing seems clear. Were it not for Harvard University, millions of Americans might now spend Super Sunday watching a professional soccer championship on their television sets.

The word "football" has been used at various times and in various countries to describe any number of games. Today, we can reduce this history to three games played in the United States: soccer, rugby, and football.

Although the Chinese have some earlier claims, the accepted history traces a soccerlike game from the Greeks to the Romans to the British. This game was played exclusively with the feet until 1823, when a maverick at the Rugby School named William Webb Ellis picked up the ball and ran with it. From that rebellious start grew the game named after Ellis's school, rugby. With this dangerously abbreviated history, we introduce the two games that, with constant amendment, were called football in late 19th-century America: association football (soccer) and rugby.

Advocates of the former first met in the 1869 Princeton-Rutgers contest. Those who allowed some handling of the ball had their first collision in the 1874 Harvard-McGill encounter.

From these games and those that followed came Percy Haughton, the end around, Barry Wood, ticket scalping, offside, Harvard Stadium, the forward pass, Amos Alonzo Stagg, the NFL, Bear Bryant, zone defenses, Dick Clasby, tailgate parties, Vince Lombardi, the Heisman Trophy, Pete Rozelle, bowl games, the flea flicker, the AFL, Frank Champi, the 2-point conversion, Joe Restic, Monday Night Football, the USFL, and Super Sunday.

Lest the connection between Harvard and today's Super Bowl remain foggy, consider this: When Princeton, Rutgers, Yale, and Columbia drew up the first intercollegiate football rules in 1873, Harvard was invited to participate but declined. The rules adopted were those resembling today's game of soccer.

Harvard continued to play its own game which, while

still primarily a kicking game, did allow a pursued player to pick up the ball and run with it. Had Harvard attended that 1873 meeting and gone along with the others, who can say that Super Sundays past wouldn't have found Joe Montana and Dan Marino kicking a round ball down a wider field?

SHOWING AMERICA THE WAY

Football in one form or another appears to have existed at Harvard long before the historic game with McGill. Dating back to the 18th century, the first Monday of the new academic year brought about some sort of interclass clash. At first it was wrestling, later football. A poem written in 1827 by Reverend James Cook Richmond, then a Harvard senior, refers to an annual football contest between freshmen and sophomores. And, writing 28 years later, an unidentified member of the class of 1859 describes the interclass contest in these terms:

> 3rd September, 1855: Tonight the usual football game took place between Freshmen and Sophomores. The latter beat as usual, both on account of their superior numbers, and also on account of their greater confidence. Before the first game was over I was knocked down by a blow on the jaw, which for several days was somewhat swollen. The Sophs beat each time. The students then all joined in the game. Freshmen and Juniors, Sophomores and Seniors, and the result was the same as in the previous games. Rings were then formed, Auld Lang Syne sung, all the classes cheered,—and thus ended the football game.

As the event degenerated from a football game to a fight with a football thrown in for effect, a movement to abolish the annual game was organized. That effort proved successful when the faculty committee voted on July 2, 1860, to ban the annual freshman-sophomore "game."

The faculty continued to allow the more civilized, informal football that was played during fall afternoons after classes. This activity, interrupted by the Civil War, grew more organized toward the end of the 1860s.

At the same time, a form of football was a popular pastime in many New England prep schools. The rules of the game, known as Boston Football, allowed for some carrying and even dribbling ("babying") of the ball but still emphasized kicking. When many of these prep school athletes found their way to Harvard, their desire to continue playing football led to the first organized football

group on campus. In the fall of 1872 the Harvard University Football Club (HUFBC) was established. This took place after the students successfully petitioned President Eliot on this matter in 1871.

The club's first order of business was to codify the rules of the game, which at that point had never been formally written down. Though organized for on-campus activity—one class playing against another—the club would also have to deal with the matter of competition against organizations outside the school.

This possibility was realized in 1873, when the HUFBC was invited to join representatives of Yale, Princeton, Rutgers, and Columbia at a convention in New York to organize a football association based upon common rules.

Aware that the convention would certainly adopt the other schools' rules (which did not allow the use of the hands in passing, dribbling, or carrying the ball), Harvard declined the offer and was widely criticized in the process. It was a tough decision for captain Henry Grant of the HUFBC, but the club's desire for intercollegiate play was met in 1874, when Harvard answered a challenge from an institution to the north.

1874–1900: On May 14 and 15, 1874, Harvard hosted Montreal's McGill University in history's first "real" college football games. Playing under rules closely resembling those of rugby, Harvard won the first game by three touchdowns to nothing; the second game was a scoreless tie.

Harvard's first American opponent was Tufts, which it played twice—in the spring and again in the fall in 1875. The teams split the pair of games.

On November 13 of that year the first of what was to be more than 100 games with Yale took place in New Haven. Playing under rugby rules, with a few concessions made to Yale, Harvard prevailed by four goals and four touchdowns to nothing. Ten days later representatives from Harvard, Yale, Princeton, and Columbia met in Springfield to form the Intercollegiate Football Association, with Harvard's playing rules adopted as standard.

From 1875 to 1884 Yale and Princeton established themselves as Harvard's most difficult opponents. While the crimson were 47-17-6 in this period, 12 of the losses came against Yale and Princeton.

Trouble surfaced as Harvard entered its second decade of football. On December 2, 1884, Harvard's Committee on the Regulation of Athletic Sports recommended to the faculty that football be dropped at Harvard because of

As successful as they were stylish, Harvard's 1876 varsity had the school's first perfect record at 4-0.

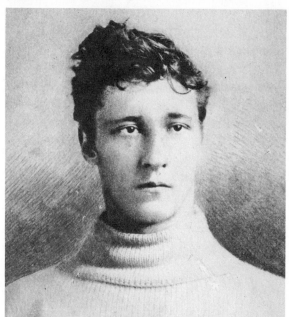

Marshall ''Ma'' Newell was a four-time Walter Camp All-American at tackle, from 1890 to 1893. He is one of 17 Harvard men in the National Football Foundation Hall of Fame.

increased violence on the playing field. Said the committee, "The nature of the game puts a premium on unfair play, inasmuch as such play is easy, is profitable if it succeeds, is unlikely to be detected by the referee, and if detected is very slightly punished."

The following year the faculty abolished football for the 1885 season. It was the only time other than the two world wars that football was ever interrupted at Harvard.

In 1886 football returned to Harvard and with it the start of systematic coaching, as team captain William Brooks '87 appointed F. A. Mason '84 as coach. The appointment of both A. J. Cumnock '91 and George Stewart '84 as coaches in 1890 marked the installation of Harvard's first coaching staff. The 1890 season was a tremendous success: Harvard went 11-0, outscoring the opposition by 550-12 and winning its first victory over Yale in 12 attempts by a 12-6 margin.

From 1891 to 1893 Harvard lost only three games, but all three losses were to chief rival Yale. The 1892 game featured the flying wedge, brainchild of Harvard assistant

Lorin Deland. Quarterback Bernie Trafford gave the ball to Charley Brewer, who followed a wedge of players into the Yale line. The move created headlines but no points in a 6-0 Yale win.

In 1893 Harvard's secret weapon came in the form of new leather uniforms, each costing $125, from a Park Street tailor. Yale won again by 6-0.

Despite losing four-time All-American Marshall Newell to graduation, Harvard was again undefeated (11-0) going into the 1894 Yale game. For the fourth straight year, Yale ruined Harvard's perfect season, this time by 12-4. The game was marred by violence sufficient to cause the two schools to suspend competition in football for two years and baseball, crew, and track for one year.

With Yale off the schedule in 1895 and 1896, Pennsylvania and Princeton became the spoilers. Harvard again put together strong seasons, but the record against the Quakers and Tigers stood at 0-4.

W. Cameron Forbes '92, who never played football at Harvard, took over as head coach for the next two years and was 21-1. The second of his teams was known as the Coaches Eleven, since five team members went on to coach at Harvard. They were Ben Dibblee, Bill Reid, John Farley, Percy Haughton (all head coaches), and Charlie Daly (assistant at Harvard, head coach at West Point).

Following the 1898 season, Forbes was injured in a fall from a horse and was replaced by Ben Dibblee. The two-time All-American halfback led Harvard to records of 10-0-1 and 10-1, with both the tie and loss to Yale.

1901–18: Harvard enjoyed a 23-game win streak during 1901 and 1902, the winning ways ending with a Yale victory in the 1902 finale. In the last home game before Harvard Stadium was opened, in 1903, Glenn "Pop" Warner brought his Carlisle Indians to Cambridge on Halloween and gave Harvard one big trick. Forming a wedge on the second-half kickoff, the Indians seemed to be setting up a return for deep man Johnson. One would-be Indian blocker, Dillon, was easily swept aside by Harvard's Carl Marshall but continued to run down the field. Upon reaching the end zone, Dillon pulled the football from under his shirt for a touchdown. Harvard had the treat, however: It won, 12-11.

Harvard's next home game was on November 14, when Dartmouth helped to christen the Stadium. Dartmouth, 0-18 against Harvard at that point, won 11-0.

Brutality in college football became a national issue over the next two years. When the *Chicago Tribune*

reported that the 1905 season produced 18 football-related deaths and 159 serious injuries, a public debate ensued. Responding to the situation, President Theodore Roosevelt, a Harvard man himself, summoned college representatives to the White House to discuss ways to save the game. Included in this group was Harvard's head coach, Bill Reid. Said Roosevelt, "Brutality and foul play should receive the same summary punishment given to a man who cheats at cards."

The second of two December meetings, with officials from 62 schools in attendance, produced the Intercollegiate Athletic Association of the United States. Five years later this group would become the National Collegiate Athletic Association.

In January of 1906 members of this group met with Yale's Walter Camp to consider rules changes that would diminish the violence in the game. The major change to emerge was a rule that would allow for the forward pass.

Fullback Bill Reid '01 became head coach the fall after he graduated and led Harvard to a 12-0 record. He returned for two more seasons in 1905 and 1906.

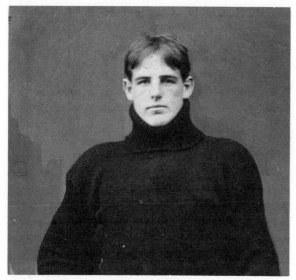

The first Harvard coach to serve beyond three seasons, Percy Haughton '99 led Harvard from 1908 to 1916. The former All-American tackle ran up a record of 71-7-5 (.886), the best in Harvard history.

More than 70 years after his last successful kick, Charlie Brickley still holds Harvard's field goal records. Below, the Everett native demonstrates the proper technique for the dropkick he used so well from 1912 to 1914.

The group had considered widening the field, but the opening of Harvard Stadium, whose field could not be widened, was a key factor in killing that idea.

Meanwhile, on the field Harvard continued to struggle with Yale. The team was 17-4 in 1905–06 but was twice shut out by Yale (the fifth and sixth straight times).

All-American and captain Francis H. "Hooks" Burr made his most important move in 1908. That's when he selected Percy Haughton '99 as head coach. At a time when head coaches normally stayed on for one or two years, Haughton served nine seasons and compiled a record of 71-7-5, best in Harvard history. His 9-0-1 first year included seven shutouts and broke the losing streak with Yale.

From 1909 to 1911, Yale continued to play the nemesis in three otherwise successful seasons. The three games with the Elis produced an 8-0 Harvard loss and two scoreless ties and compounded the fact that Harvard had not scored on Yale in nine of the last ten games.

Finally in 1912 Haughton put it all together in a 9-0 season capped by a 20-0 domination of Yale. Captain Percy Wendell was one of nine members of this team who would earn All-American honors before graduating.

Another future All-American, sophomore Eddie Mahan, scored on a 67-yard run in his first varsity game, a 34-0 win over Maine to open the 1913 season. Mahan, who

would become a three-time All-American, paced Harvard to another 9-0 record. In a 15-5 victory over Yale, Charlie Brickley kicked a school record five field goals.

By this time it was clear that Haughton had moved Harvard past the Yales and Princetons. Only Pitt challenged the Crimson for football supremacy in the East, as this young coach won while never ceasing to learn.

"He never hesitated to take what was good from other systems, styles of play, or ideas," said Lo Withington, captain of the 1910 team. "He recognized the greatness of [Walter] Camp and the Yale system based on sound fundamentals and superior line play. He did not hesitate to borrow deception from [Pop] Warner, discipline from Army, power of Pennsylvania guards, nor passing skills displayed by any opponent."

Seniors H. R. "Tack" Hardwick and Stan Pennock earned their second and third All-American selections respectively in 1914 in a 7-0-2 season. They were joined by Brickley, Mahan, Walter Trumbull, and Fred Bradlee in a year that ended with a 36-0 thrashing of Yale.

A 10-0 loss to Cornell in 1915 snapped Harvard's 33-game unbeaten streak, the only disappointment in an 8-1 season that finished with the worst beating of Yale in the series history, 41-0. In 1916 Harvard started off at 7-1, outscoring the opposition by 171-0 in the wins; but season-ending losses to Brown and Yale closed out the illustrious career of Percy Haughton, as World War I interrupted Harvard football for two seasons.

An admirer of Haughton's, Notre Dame coach Jesse Harper once said, "Here was a great coach, not merely a good one. . . . He was colder than an iceberg, harder than granite. But he was brilliant—a natural leader. He was to football what General Patton was to our armies."

CONTINUING THE TRADITION

1919–34: After the war, former All-American guard Bob Fisher took over as head coach. His first season was the best of his seven, as an 8-0-1 Harvard team went to the Rose Bowl and defeated Oregon, 7-6, on Fred Church's touchdown and Arnie Horween's kick. Running back Eddie Casey was named All-American for the second time, having previously received the honor before the war, in 1916.

After an 8-0-1 record in 1920, the team was a combined 8-7-1 over the next two seasons. Despite the team's disappointments, halfback George Owen, a nine-letter winner, was twice an All-American.

Running back Eddie Casey '19 had the distinction of earning All-American honors both before and after World War I.

Arnold Horween '20 replaced Fisher as head coach in 1926. A member of the Rose Bowl team and captain of the 1920 squad, Horween started slowly at 3-5, including an opening-game loss to tiny Geneva College, 16-7.

In the next two years, Harvard could only come up with 4-4 and 5-2-1 seasons, despite the presence of such backs as Art French, Dave Guarnaccia, and Joe Crosby. Then came 1929. Harvard football took on a new look in many ways that year. First was the addition of heavyweights Michigan, Florida, and Army to the schedule. Then there were the 19,000 new seats in the steel stands that closed up the open end of the Stadium. Finally, there was Barry Wood.

Perhaps the greatest athlete ever to wear a Harvard uniform, Wood began writing his story in the 1929 Army game, when he came off the bench to salvage a tie for the Crimson. With his team down 20-13 in the fourth quarter, the young reserve quarterback entered the game to throw a 40-yard touchdown pass to Victor Harding and then kick the tying point.

Wood and two-time All-American Ben Ticknor were the big names at Harvard in 1929 and 1930, Horween's last years as head coach. Opponent Yale's answer to Wood was Albie Booth, a talented back whose career in New Haven paralleled Wood's in Cambridge. In the first varsity meeting between the two, Booth was hurting and Harvard won, 10-6. In 1930 Booth was healthy but held to just 22 yards rushing in a 13-0 Harvard win.

Perhaps the best game of all was the pair's last, a 3-0 Yale victory decided by a Booth field goal late in the fourth quarter. The loss ended Harvard's bid for a perfect season as well as the football careers of two collegiate legends.

A 7-1 record in 1931 marked the coaching debut of Eddie Casey, whose four-year tenure went rapidly downhill, with seasons of 5-3, 5-2-1, and 3-5.

Harvard's Bowl Game

Charlie Chaplin sat on the Harvard bench. So did Douglas Fairbanks. This was the big time, the Rose Bowl. And Harvard made the most of its first and only bowl appearance.

On January 1, 1920, Harvard defeated Oregon, 7-6, in the Rose Bowl at Pasadena, capping a brilliant season for Coach Bob Fisher and his All-American back Eddie Casey. This was a team that outscored its opposition 217-19 in nine regular-season games. The only blemish on the record was a 10-10 tie with Princeton.

Harvard's first, and last, postseason appearance preceded by three years an agreement between the presidents of Harvard, Yale, and Princeton that

prohibited teams from their institutions from participating in bowl games in the future.

A five-day train trip brought the Harvards from Cambridge to Pasadena. Along the way, Coach Fisher would organize impromptu practice sessions on small town streets while the train refueled. It was the best way to keep his 22-man squad in shape for the showdown ahead.

Arriving in California on Christmas Day, the team had a week to prepare for Oregon. Harvard would enter that game without full contact work since defeating Yale in Harvard Stadium, 10-3, on November 22.

The Rose Bowl was a physical game, played almost entirely on the ground. Harvard threw just five passes, Oregon only two. Ironically, two passes caught by Eddie Casey set up Harvard's winning touchdown.

Oregon opened the scoring in the second quarter but missed the extra point attempt. Later in the same quarter, Harvard mounted an eight-play, 55-yard drive that was keyed by those Casey receptions and a 25-yard run by Arnie Horween. The final 15 yards were covered by Fred Church, whose touchdown tied the game. Horween's kick gave Harvard the lead and ultimately the game.

The 70-degree heat in the Rose Bowl was a far cry from the wintry conditions the team had left behind in New England. The climate particularly took its toll on the half dozen players who went the full 60 minutes.

But in the end, after two Oregon field goal attempts had been blocked and a third hurried wide, Harvard's defense saved the day. Only the clock prevented Harvard's one bowl victory from being more convincing: The gun sounded with the Crimson on Oregon's 1-foot line.

. . .

Barry Wood

During the last decade, American football has borne the brunt of severe criticism. It has been forced to face charges of "overemphasis" and "commercialism," and the "grind" of daily practice, the danger of serious injuries, and "ballyhoo" publicity have been widely condemned. These "evils," as described by the critics, have caused many people to lose faith in the game and to join in a cry of protest against it. The man who watches an occasional game from the stands, listens to radio reports, or reads the accounts in the Sunday newspapers has no way of judging the validity of such charges; he sees the football world only from a distance and knows little about what goes on behind the scenes. Yet he cannot be unconscious of the storm of criticism raging about modern football, and very naturally he takes sides according to his personal views, oblivious of the fact that he is not fully qualified to pass judgement.

These words could have been written in the past few years, in a newspaper editorial or a television broadcaster's script. They were, in fact, written in 1932, when Barry Wood included them in the preface to What Price Football?, his intelligent defense of the game he loved and played so brilliantly.

Barry Wood was perhaps Harvard's greatest athlete. He won ten varsity letters, nine major H's—three each in football, hockey, and baseball—and one minor H for being named to the Harvard-Yale tennis team that competed against Oxford-Cambridge for the Prentice Cup.

A first team Grantland Rice All-American in 1931 and a member of Phi Beta Kappa, Wood graduated summa cum laude from Harvard and went on to attend Johns Hopkins Medical School. After graduating in 1936, Wood was professor of medicine at Washington University in St. Louis, physician in chief at Barnes Hospital (also in St. Louis), and later a research specialist at Johns Hopkins Medical School. He died of a heart attack in 1971.

For all his athletic accomplishments, Wood is best remembered for his football heroics, particularly against Army and Yale.

One of Harvard's greatest two-way players, All-American Barry Wood '32 earned ten letters at Harvard, three each in football, hockey, and baseball, and one in tennis as a member of the Prentice Cup team (Harvard and Yale combined) that met Oxford-Cambridge.

Against Army, Wood fashioned his first head-lines as a sophomore, when he came off the bench to throw a 40-yard TD pass and kick the extra point that tied the Cadets, 20-20. As a senior, Wood led two touchdown drives that put the Crimson up, 14-13. Then, with Army's Paul Johnson sprinting for an apparent game-winning score, defensive back Wood caught the would-be hero from behind to preserve the Harvard victory.

Wood's four games with Yale were highlighted by his rivalry with Yale's great Albie Booth. While the Wood legend was being established in Cambridge, Booth was matching every headline in New Haven. Both were talented backs who made their teams go. And both were dropkick specialists, the last of the great ones.

For three years in this head-to-head battle, Wood came out the winner. As a freshman, Wood kicked the winning point in a 7-6 Yardling victory. In their sophomore year, Wood's toe again provided the margin of victory, in a 10-6 Harvard win. And in 1930, when the two went at it as juniors, Wood's two touchdown passes to Art Huguley beat Yale, 13-0.

But in 1931, Albie Booth got the last laugh. Harvard entered the game having won seven straight and was looking for its first perfect season since 1913. Yale had a good team, but the Crimson were decided favorites.

The game was a struggle from the start, and late in the fourth quarter the teams remained deadlocked at 0-0. With Harvard stopped once more by the Eli defense, Wood set up to punt from his own 30-yard line. He never got the kick away, as Yale's Jack Wilbur burst through the Harvard line to block it.

In his final minutes of Yale football, Booth avenged three years of frustration against Harvard. He began by hitting split end Herster Barres for 20 yards to put Yale within range of a Booth dropkick. Two running plays were smothered by the Harvard defense. And so on third down, with time running out, Booth dropped back and calmly kicked a field goal that gave Yale a 3-0 victory.

• • •

Dick Harlow's 11 years as head coach (interrupted by World War II) were the longest in the first 90 years of Harvard football. A collector of rare birds' eggs as well as a master of football, Harlow was appointed as a curator at Harvard's Museum of Comparative Zoology.

1935–44: In 1935 Dick Harlow became the first non-Harvard man to coach football in the school's history. Don't think that wasn't a topic of discussion after his first two clubs went 3-5 and 3-4-1.

Gradually, Harlow's many talents, particularly with defenses, became evident. His 1937 team surrendered only 19 points against the likes of Army, Navy, Princeton, and Yale. On the field, 60-minute players like Alex Kevorkian and Ken Booth made the difference.

Football historian Tim Cohane recognized one key element of Harlow's defenses: "Harvard's football teams of the '30s were pioneers of stunting in their defensive line play. By looping or slanting just before or at the snap of the ball, they were never where they were supposed to be when opponents tried to block them."

Offensively, Harlow was blessed with running backs Torbert Macdonald and Vernon Struck. Against Princeton, a team Harvard had not beaten in the last three years,

Struck carried the ball 33 times for 233 yards and three touchdowns. Harvard won, 34-6.

In 1938 two streaks—four losses followed by four wins—made for an odd season. The losing streak was halted by Macdonald's 182-yard, three-touchdown effort, which beat Princeton. In the finale a .500 season was salvaged before 60,000 in the New Haven rain when Frank Foley and Macdonald authored an 80-yard drive in the fourth quarter to beat Yale, 7-0.

Only three regulars returned for another 4-4 season in 1939. The new people on defense must have known their stuff, since all four wins were shutouts.

Harlow's defenses continued to shine in 1940, a year that produced an odd 3-2-3 record. The three ties displayed that defense in scores of 0-0, 6-6, and 10-10 against Princeton, Army, and Penn, respectively.

A more satisfying performance came in a 28-0 pasting of Yale. Captain Joe Gardella scored two touchdowns, and a 78-yard punt return by Fran Lee added another.

After two shutout losses launched the 1941 season, Harvard went 5-0-1 down the stretch. The Crimson defense excelled in Ivy wins over Dartmouth (7-0), Princeton (6-4), and Yale (14-0), the Dartmouth win being the first in nine attempts and Harlow's first ever.

Keying Harvard's defense was Endicott "Chub" Peabody, whom *Boston Globe* sportswriter Jerry Nason dubbed the Babyface Assassin.

In 1941 Peabody, a future governor of Massachusetts, became Harvard's first football All-American since Barry Wood in 1931 and the last until Pat McInally in 1973. An alert, combative type who played with a killer's instinct, Peabody commanded a respect enjoyed by few players of any era. Indicative was his capturing the 1941 Knute Rockne Trophy, awarded annually by the Touchdown Club of Washington, D.C., to the country's outstanding lineman.

World War II intervened after the 1941 season. Harlow remained in Cambridge for the 2-4-1 season of 1942, but junior varsity coach Henry Lamar took over Harvard's unofficial program for the next two seasons. Harlow went overseas, and when he returned after the war, neither he nor Harvard football was quite the same.

• • •

The Babyface Assassin

Harvard football has launched many an ex-gridder from the Stadium to the political arena. For example, old teammates Ted Kennedy and John Culver were U.S. senators together while Torbert Macdonald, a star running back from the previous decade, was serving in the House of Representatives.

These are just three of the many who made the transition from one type of battlefield to another. While it may be a matter of debate which of these fellows gave the most to his party and his country, there is little doubt as to which player turned politico was the best on the field.

Former Massachusetts governor Endicott "Chub" Peabody was a bona fide All-American who played for Dick Harlow from 1939 to 1941. The handsome yet brutally tough guard earned the nickname the Babyface Assassin for his effective physical style.

Harvard welcomed Peabody from the Groton School, which was founded by his grandfather, the Rev. Endicott Peabody, school headmaster for 55 years. Arriving in Cambridge in 1938, the young Peabody was an impressive 6-foot, 160-pounder. At least he was impressive at the freshman level, but his size worried the varsity staff that would inherit him.

The summer before his sophomore year, Peabody was encouraged by assistant coach Henry Lamar to add some bulk to his frame. And so the varsity hopeful went to work on his strength. By the fall he had gained 25 pounds and increased his neck size from 14 inches to 17. He was ready for the varsity schedule that included the likes of Army, Navy, and Michigan over the next three years.

Peabody was a standout from the start. The recurrent memory from the Peabody years is that of a bone-jarring hit that freed the football from an enemy running back. One of the most memorable of these plays came in the 1941 game against Navy at the Stadium. Navy was 4-0 and a heavy favorite entering the game. Harvard, 1-2 but improving, was considered to be in over its head.

Navy coach Swede Larsen had a deep squad, with perhaps no one more talented than All-American back Bill Busik. It was a meeting between Busik and Peabody that wrote the story of this game. Stopped by the Navy defense in the second quarter, Harvard was forced to punt.

When Endicott "Chub" Peabody (left) was named All-American at guard in 1941, he was known as the Baby-face Assassin. Twenty-two years later, he was known as governor of the Commonwealth of Massachusetts, serving from 1963 to 1965.

Fielding that punt was Navy's Busik, but not for long. Breaking through the Navy blockers, Peabody first hit Busik so hard that the ball popped loose, then made the recovery for Harvard. The Navy All-American was taken out of the game, which eventually ended in a 0-0 tie.

Navy's Larsen was overwhelmed by the play of Peabody. After the game, the coach remarked, "There is the greatest guard I have ever seen, and I've seen a lot of them."

Harvard went on to win the remaining four games of its schedule and of Chub Peabody's career. Peabody earned his All-American berth that season, some 20 years before another major triumph, his election as governor of Massachusetts in 1962. After stepping down from politics, he had the pleasure of watching his son, Bobby, play varsity football at Harvard in the mid-1970s. Fittingly, the younger Peabody received the Henry Lamar Award, named after the former Harvard assistant, for dedication to the football program.

1945–47: Football returned to regular status at Harvard in 1945, but the schedule indicated otherwise. Such irregular opponents as New London Sub Base (18-7 winners) and King's Point (defeated by 28-7) dotted the schedule, and traditional Ivy foes Dartmouth and Princeton were missing.

A tougher schedule was met by a tougher Harvard squad in 1946. Dick Harlow's machine was operating at high efficiency and finished at 7-2, with Rutgers and Yale spoiling not unrealistic hopes for a perfect season.

The offensive skill positions made most of the headlines, with the likes of fullback Vince Moravec, halfbacks Chip Gannon and Cleo O'Donnell, end Wally Flynn, and placekicker Emil Drvaric. The defense had its heroes as well, particularly in the secondary, where Jim Noonan and Gannon excelled. Each entered the record book by intercepting three passes in a game, Noonan against Coast Guard, Gannon against Yale.

The success of 1946 put expectations on the succeeding team that it couldn't meet. Dick Harlow, battling both failing health and growing team discontent, would finish his Harvard career following the 1947 season.

Harlow's final team struggled through a 4-5 campaign that included losses to Dartmouth, Princeton, and Yale. Perhaps most painful was a 47-0 drubbing at the hands of the University of Virginia, a team Harvard had beaten in all eight previous meetings, which included seven shutouts.

Adding to the atmosphere of that Virginia game was an incident involving Harvard tackle Chester Pierce. It appeared that Pierce's participation at Virginia would make him the first black player to play in an intersectional game below the Mason-Dixon line.

Sometime prior to the game, officials from Virginia's athletic department, fearing that ugliness could possibly develop from Pierce's presence, telephoned Harvard athletic director Bill Bingham and suggested that Pierce be kept at home. Bingham's response was simple: Harvard comes with Pierce or not at all. A few days later Virginia officials tried again, but Bingham stood his ground. It was reported that the Virginia players took a team vote that unanimously recognized Pierce's right to compete.

The 1947 Harvard football team had a small but tough end by the name of Robert Kennedy '48 (second from right in front row). He would display that same toughness in public life as U.S. attorney general and U.S. senator from New York.

Regardless of such an action, it was Bill Bingham's unwavering position that made the difference.

The Cavaliers' good will stopped with that vote, and the game was a one-sided affair marred by a number of injuries, including Vince Moravec's broken kneecap. His brilliant Harvard career was ended in the third week of his senior year.

Also over was the brilliant career of Dick Harlow. He should be remembered as the Renaissance man who was innovative on the football field and at the same time was an avid student of biology. Specifically, he was an associate in Harvard's Department of Zoology, and in 1939 President James B. Conant named him Curator of Zoology at Harvard's Museum of Comparative Zoology.

This was a man who grew rare gentians and rhododendrons at his summer gardens in the Poconos and cultivated six species never grown before in the United States. His collection of rare birds' eggs reached 850 and was valued at $40,000.

The excellence of Dick Harlow's early teams stands out in Harvard football history. And that should overshadow the disappointments of his later years, after he had

returned from the war having lost 50 pounds and in ill health. Harlow grew difficult for his players to deal with and was never the same man he was before going overseas.

Adding to the problems was the fact that the postwar teams were a mix of young undergraduates and war veterans, all playing at a time when campus interest in football was at an all-time low. It was not an easy time for the coach or his teams.

The Dick Harlow to be remembered is the coach who, up to that point, had served more seasons (11) than any coach in Harvard football history.

1948–49: Harvard looked to Michigan for Harlow's successor and came up with Arthur Valpey, a former Wolverine star and then an assistant coach. Valpey's two years produced a combined 5-12 record and enough disappointment to make his tenure a brief one. Following the 1949 season, with a year left on his contract, Valpey took the head coaching position at Connecticut.

The 1948 season was memorable for some individual moments. Against Holy Cross, Hal Moffie returned a punt

A familiar sight to spectators at Harvard Stadium over the years has been the oversized drum of the Harvard University band (shown here in a 1948 photo). Equally familiar have been the band's topically irreverent halftime shows, which have both amused and offended thousands annually.

yards for a score and piled up 137 total return yards in a 20-13 win. Both statistics remain Harvard records. Captain Ken O'Donnell finished his career with 15 interceptions and 347 interception return yards. These marks also remain in the Harvard book.

The success of 1948's final games, including a 20-7 win over Yale, could not be carried into 1949. A shocking 44-0 loss to Stanford on opening day ruined Harvard's first trip to the West Coast since the 1920 Rose Bowl. It was a tough, physical game on a hot afternoon and left a number of Harvard regulars on the injured list, many for the remainder of the season.

The resulting 1-8 season, punctuated by a final game 29-6 loss to Yale, brought Harvard football to the lowest point in its history. Newspaper columnists joined Harvard alumni in asking not only "What happened?" but "Where does Harvard go from here?"

Some blamed the coach. But before that discussion could go too far, Art Valpey left Cambridge and headed for Connecticut. It was lack of talent, according to others. Harvard was "champion of Middlesex County," said the *Boston Herald*'s Bill Cunningham, "only because she didn't meet Arlington High School this season." More constructively, the *Boston Globe*'s Jerry Nason suggested that the competition had gone out and found better talent while "Harvard stood still."

Similarly disappointing seasons in other sports led to discussions of Harvard's entire athletic program. So, in a backhanded way, the agony of the 1949 season soon brought about a new approach for Harvard athletics. The value of the student-athlete began to receive greater appreciation. Harvard alumni rallied to attract better athletes. And in a few years the results would show up on the field. But it would still take a little time.

Harvard Stadium

It is the one visible link to Harvard's athletic past. And in many respects it embodies all that Harvard athletics stands for. More than 80 years ago, it was the first and it was the best. And while others have come along and done things bigger, none have done better.

Harvard Stadium connects early Harvard with today's Harvard. It was home for Hamilton Fish and George Owen just as it was home for Vic Gatto and Joe Azelby. Charlie Brickley's kicks were good there. So were Jim Villanueva's. And as often as Eddie Casey found its end zones, so too did Dick Clasby.

When fire destroyed a section of Harvard's old wooden bleachers in 1902, the football community thought it was time for a football facility commensurate with Harvard's status in the sport. President Eliot, concerned with the growing violence dominating the game, felt otherwise.

Fortunately for the football faithful, President Eliot listened to Ira Nelson Hollis, a professor of mechanical engineering and chairman of the university's Athletic Committee. Hollis wanted to see a stadium built, knew how it should be constructed, and convinced Eliot that it was a good idea.

That problem swept aside, one other emerged: financing. With just $75,000 available through the Athletic Committee, the project would need a major benefactor in order to become a reality. Enter the Harvard class of 1879, which would be celebrating its 25th reunion in the 1903–04 academic year. The reunion class was willing to help, and the university responded with a challenge: Match the existing $75,000 and construction of a stadium will follow. The class raised $100,000.

And so on June 22, 1903, following a Harvard-Yale baseball game, the remaining wooden bleachers at Soldiers Field were torn down and work began on America's first large and permanent sports arena.

Professor Hollis modified some architectural drawings first produced by George B. deGersdorff from a design by Professor L. J. Johnson. Also assisting this team was J. R. Worcester. The reinforced concrete structure that emerged from their labors was as much an architectural wonder as a sports phenomenon. Those marveling the most were the critics who felt that concrete could not survive a New England winter.

The Aberthaw Construction Company completed the project in four and a half months, an accomplishment made possible by locating a minifoundry right on the site. The foundry produced 4,800 concrete slabs, which would become seats, and these slabs were transported by a small railroad that was built on the grounds.

When it was all over, the cost of the project was just under $320,000. That may have seemed like a lot of money in 1903. But consider this: When a new yet modest press box was built above the home stands in 1981, the price tag was $375,000.

The first game was played on November 14, 1903, when Dartmouth came to town and prevailed by 11-0. That was hardly an auspicious opener, as Harvard had never lost to Dartmouth and of its 18 previous victories, 16 had been shutouts.

Said the Harvard Bulletin:

> It was an uninteresting game. The University team had the ball but a few minutes. Several of the Harvard players were not in first-class shape as they had recently recovered from tonsilitis. . . . LeMoyne's punting was distinctly bad and Captain Marshall's work at quarterback was, as it has been all season, very slow and generally unsatisfactory.

Harvard's Stadium fortunes would improve over the years, as the home team would win close to 70 percent of its contests up through the 1984 season.

Not only did this facility affect the Harvards, it also played a major role in how everyone played football. When brutality in college football peaked in 1905, the game's future was on the line. President Theodore Roosevelt, a Harvard man himself, made it clear that the game's leaders had better take action to clean up the sport. With Harvard's head coach Bill Reid and Yale's Walter Camp leading the way, college representatives met in New York in January of 1906 to come up with some answers.

Among the more revolutionary proposals dis-

Two views of America's oldest reinforced concrete stadium. Above: Harvard Stadium with steel stands that were removed in 1951. Below: A full house in 1984, when the Stadium turned 81 years old.

cussed at the meetings were widening the field of play and introducing the forward pass. Among the reasons cited by those opposed to increasing the width of the field was the fact that such a measure would be virtually impossible at Harvard Stadium, the sport's new showcase. For this and other reasons, the leadership scrapped plans for widening the field and instead introduced the forward pass to the game.

Although football has been the Stadium's main tenant over the years, other sports have found their way within those ivied walls. One of the first was ice hockey, which played games on rinks that ran from sideline to sideline.

In the summer of 1971, with the football field ready for new sod, the Stadium was the site of a polo match. Later in the decade, women's championships in field hockey and lacrosse graced the turf. And perhaps the grandest event of all took place in the summer of 1984, when the preliminary round of Olympic soccer unfolded at the Stadium.

During the summer of 1982 Harvard Stadium underwent a multimillion-dollar renovation, which primarily consisted of replacing all the concrete slabs (which make up the seats) and reinforcing the steel supports beneath them. The new seats are no kinder to the backside on a cold, autumn Saturday. But the revitalization project should insure a gala 100th birthday party in 2003 for the grande dame of American sports arenas, Harvard Stadium.

• • •

1950–52: The selection of Lloyd P. Jordan as Harvard's 21st head coach of football was a surprise to many. Few questioned Jordan's qualifications, but many wondered why he would be interested in the job. At the time, Jordan was in his 18th year as head coach at Amherst, where he also served as director of athletics. Jordan, who assumed the Harvard post at the age of 50, would remain in Cambridge for seven seasons.

Jordan would coach some of the best remembered individuals in Harvard history. Three teams in the middle of his tenure would forge winning records. But in the end, Jordan could not claim a winning record against any of his Ivy foes.

The 1950 team struggled as much as its predecessor, finishing at 1-7 after dropping the first six games. Harvard scored a single touchdown in four of its first five games and was blanked in the other. Finally the efforts of a diminutive passer named Carroll Lowenstein put Harvard in the victory column. That came in a 14-13 win over Brown, when the 145-pound Lowenstein fired touchdown strikes to Fred Ravreby and Gil O'Neil. Earlier, in a 63-26 pasting by Princeton and Dick Kazmaier, Lowenstein had set a school record, throwing for 258 yards.

Harvard football, now reeling from a two-year mark of 2-15, was dealt another blow in the summer of 1951. The steel stands that had expanded Stadium seating capacity in 1929 were dismantled as maintenance costs were up and attendance was down. It was another unsettling sign of football's plight.

With the emergence of Lowenstein and the addition of a couple of highly touted sophomore backs in Dick Clasby and John Culver, the 1951 season held promise. But things did not go as planned. First Lowenstein was called off to military service after the second game. Two games later his replacement, Warren "Red" Wylie, broke his arm.

With these and other misfortunes, the squad went 3-5-1, but this was still a step up from preceding campaigns. The season's most memorable victory came when Bob Hardy blocked a punt to produce a safety and the difference in a 22-21 win over Army. The Cadets had won by 49-0 the year before.

Also of note was a season-ending 21-21 tie with Yale. The Elis had taken the last two games from the Crimson, and when they went up 14-0 in this match-up, a third straight seemed likely. But the next three scores were Harvard's. First Clasby hit Paul Crowley before halftime to make it 14-7. Then John Ederer, a reserve back for most of the year, took off on an 83-yard touchdown jaunt that tied the score. Harvard finally grabbed the lead when Fred Drill picked off a pass and returned it 20 yards for another score. It remained for a late Yale rally to tie the score at 21-21, where it ended.

The 1952 season brought Jordan's first winning campaign, a 5-4 record that featured five wins on the year's first six Saturdays. That hot start was followed by three Ivy losses in which the enemy piled up 110 points.

The season included some brilliant individual efforts. Twice Dick Clasby ran for 175 yards, against Dartmouth in victory and against Brown in defeat. John Culver, later a U.S. senator from Iowa, had an even more impressive effort against Springfield, as he scored three touchdowns while piling up 174 yards.

There was Clasby's 96-yard touchdown against Wash-

CRIMSON BOMB THROWERS!

Two of Harvard's most notable football players from the 1950s are the subjects of this Bob Coyne cartoon. Carroll Lowenstein and Dick Clasby gave Harvard unusual offensive depth at a time when, as the cartoon indicates, Harvard and other New England colleges received significant media attention.

ington University of St. Louis. And there was Jerry Blitz returning the opening kickoff 93 yards for a touchdown against Princeton.

Clasby finished the year with 950 yards rushing in 205 carries, both school records that would not be broken for 30 years. (Jim Callinan bettered the marks in 1981.)

The Harvard cheering all but stopped on the last weekend, when Yale took a 41-14 affair, the worst Harvard beating in that series since the 1884 game. Adding insult to injury was the appearance of Yale manager Charlie Yeager, who caught a pass for the final points and became part of the lore of The Game.

1953–56: The improvement continued in 1953, when Harvard went 6-2, stopped only by 6-0 losses to Columbia and Princeton. Carroll Lowenstein was back from the service, and the Clasby-Culver duo was back for its third and final year. Of equal importance to this team was center Jeff Coolidge, an iron man who made 60-minute performances routine.

After two early wins, the Crimson were stopped by Columbia, losing the ball three times inside the Lions'

yard line. The Stadium's 50th anniversary provided the setting for a 20-14 win over Dartmouth. Then came Davidson and a remarkable day for Lowenstein.

The books say that he only completed six of nine passes that afternoon. But the same books say that five of those completions were for touchdowns and the half dozen aerials totaled 268 yards. Dexter Lewis, Harvard's lacrosse wizard, caught TD passes of 63 and 51 yards, Culver grabbed another for 55 yards, and Bill Weber and Frank White had 38- and 36-yard touchdown catches respectively. If this wasn't enough, Lowenstein ran 8 yards for another score.

With Culver, Clasby, and Coolidge all sidelined by injuries, it is little wonder that Princeton had its way. What is surprising is that the Tigers took 57 minutes to score in this 6-0 game.

The season ended on a high note when the Crimson blanked the Elis, 13-0, before 65,000 in the Yale Bowl. Appropriately, Culver and Clasby led the way, combining for 200 yards on the ground in 43 carries.

Despite the loss of key players, the 1954 squad forged a 4-3-1 record that was just a few plays away from an even better mark. The three losses were by a combined 13

From football to politics: Classmates John Culver '54 (No. 34, above) and Edward 'Ted" Kennedy '54 (left) in their playing days. The two U.S. senators (right), flanking Kennedy's son Patrick, get together on the occasion of Culver's 1978 induction into the Harvard Varsity Club Hall of Fame.

points and came in the first four weeks of the season. As some talented underclassmen matured, the team came together late. The last four Saturdays produced a 3-0-1 record and included the first win over Princeton in eight years and a thrilling 13-9 win over Yale.

Sophomores such as Matt Botsford, Tony Gianelly, Jim Joslin, Ted Metropoulos, and John Simourian had been coming along with each game. This group combined with a few veterans to make the 1954 Yale game memorable.

A third-period Yale touchdown had combined with an earlier safety to give the visitors a 9-0 lead entering the final quarter. On the first play of this period, Harvard capped a 72-yard march when Gianelly scored to put Harvard on the board. Later in the quarter, an 80-yard drive ended when Frank White hit Bob Cochran with a pass that Cochran bobbled and then secured before sprinting the final 16 yards to the end zone.

That would close out Jordan's last winning season, as the 1955 and 1956 teams went 3-4-1 and 2-6 respectively. The first of those seasons produced a pair of Ivy wins, over Columbia and Princeton. Against the Lions, three different players—John Simourian, Matt Botsford, and Jim Joslin—threw touchdown strikes in a 21-7 triumph. The 7-6 win over Princeton was the most satisfying of the year and resulted from a fumble forced by captain Bill Meigs. A Joslin–to–Dexter Lewis touchdown pass followed the turnover and secured the victory.

The season ended with a 21-7 loss to Yale, in which Harvard's only score was a Walt Stahura touchdown pass to Ted Kennedy, later the U.S. senator from Massachusetts.

The 1956 season was the first for official Ivy League play. Captain Ted Metropoulos, an outstanding leader on and off the field, was named to the first official All-Ivy team. It was the high point to an otherwise painful postseason.

THE YOVICSIN YEARS

1957–60: Harvard football was not in its healthiest state when the faculty committee decided to pick up the remainder of Lloyd Jordan's contract in 1957. The next step was to find a replacement who could turn things around.

To the surprise of most observers, the committee named the young head coach at Gettysburg College, John M. Yovicsin, as Harvard's 22nd head coach of football. Handsome, articulate, and highly regarded, Yovicsin was nevertheless an unknown in Cambridge. Few anticipated

that his tenure would be longer than that of any of his predecessors.

Yovicsin's record at Gettysburg, his alma mater, had been 32-11 in five seasons. It would take him a couple of years to get on the high side of the .500 mark at Harvard, but when he did it would become a habit.

The first Yovicsin team went 3-5 after a promising 3-2 start. Manpower problems surfaced after a physical game with Princeton, as the Tigers rallied from a 14-20 deficit to a 28-20 win, and the Crimson lost six regulars to injuries. Ivy losses to Brown and Yale also pointed up lack of team depth in general and quarterback problems in particular. Robert "Shag" Shaunessy earned All-Ivy honors at tackle, and sophomore back Chet Boulris showed indications of greatness to come.

The 1958 season provided more signs of improvement than the 4-5 record might suggest. The 1957 squad had been outscored 180-78, but this team turned those numbers around to read 149-99 in the Crimson's favor. Dramatic evidence of improvement can be found in results against archrivals Dartmouth and Yale. Losers by 28-0 and 54-0 scores respectively the year before, captain Shaunessy's squad claimed 16-8 and 28-0 wins against the Big Green and the Elis.

One key for the Crimson was the emergence of a quarterback in sophomore Charley Ravenel, "the Riverboat Gambler," from Charleston, South Carolina. Ravenel wasn't big and wasn't fast, and his arm wasn't exactly a cannon, but he was a leader who got the job done.

With Ravenel's leadership and Boulris's brute force, the Harvard backfield was always dangerous. These two, who tied for the team scoring lead, had plenty of support from the likes of split end Hank Keohane and fullback Sam Halaby, whose 85-yard touchdown run against Brown ranks as one of the top ten runs from scrimmage in Harvard history.

The Shaunessy-led defense played a major role as well. Perhaps its best moment came in the 28-0 win over Yale, when the Crimson held the Elis to just 12 yards rushing and 23 yards in the air.

The 1959 season, the first of ten straight winning seasons for John Yovicsin, saw a 6-3 record that could easily have been even better. Cornell won 20-16 on a 76-yard pass play with 24 seconds left; Dartmouth's 9-0 win was played in rain and mud; and Brown took a 16-6 decision on the strength of a 40-yard interception return for a touchdown and the Bruins' first field goal in ten years.

Although the defensive line was perhaps the 1959

An early Yovicsin backfield (left to right): halfback Larry Repsher, quarterback Charley Ravenel, fullback Sam Halaby, and halfback Chet Boulris. Each back won three varsity letters, and Boulris was twice a first team All-Ivy selection.

squad's greatest strength, the secondary featured such stars as defensive back Jim Nelson, who returned an interception 77 yards for a touchdown in an early-season 20-6 win over Bucknell.

There were big plays on the other side of the ball as well. In Harvard's 35-6 win over Yale at New Haven (an 8-6 game through three quarters), Chet Boulris hit Hank Keohane with an 85-yard touchdown pass, still the longest pass play in Harvard history.

Ravenel repeated as Harvard's leading scorer in 1959, and senior Boulris put his scoring feats in the record book by finishing his career with 112 points. Boulris ranked second in career scoring at that time behind Charlie Brickley and even today, with the great offensive stars who have followed, he remains sixth in Harvard scoring totals. Repeating on the All-Ivy team, Boulris was also named to the Ivy Team of the Decade.

The 1960 Harvard team began the season with captain Terry Lenzner's squad listed as a preseason Ivy League favorite by some prognosticators, but a pair of knee injuries kept those expectations from being met. After a 13-6 win over Holy Cross in the season opener, Harvard endured a painful Saturday against Massachusetts a week later, a 27-12 loss compounded by the loss of quarterback Ravenel, whose banged-up knee would keep him out of the lineup until the season finale. While sophomore Terry Bartolet and junior Ted Halaby assumed the quarterbacking chores, more frustration arrived when damaged knee ligaments sidelined captain Lenzner for much of the year.

1961–64: The script was reversed in 1961, when the loss of 16 seniors to graduation dimmed hopes at the start of the season. But when it was all over, Harvard had a piece of the Ivy title.

Captain Pete Hart's team dropped three of its first four games—including a costly league loss to Columbia—and the low expectations remained unchanged. But when Dartmouth visited the Stadium on the season's fifth Saturday, things changed dramatically.

Credit the defense for the reversal. Bob Boyda's interception set up one score. Mike Sheridan's fumble recovery set up another. And Bill Swinford's interception preceded a third. The touchdowns came from backs Bill Grana, who scored one, and Bill Taylor, who had a pair. The result was a 21-15 win over Dartmouth and a new outlook on the season.

The Dartmouth game began a five-game win streak that carried through the end of the season. The defense yielded but 19 points in the final four games, the toughest being a 9-7 win over Princeton that knocked the Tigers from first place in the league standings.

The memorable play from the Princeton victory was sophomore quarterback Bill Humenuk's bootleg from 2 yards out, which produced Harvard's only touchdown. With Ivy wins over Penn and Brown sandwiching the Princeton win, only Yale remained between Harvard and a share of the Ivy crown.

Two first-quarter scores just 80 seconds apart launched Harvard to a 27-0 victory. Both scores resulted from fumble recoveries in Yale territory, one by Pete Hart and the other by Dick Diehl. Taylor and Grana scored those first touchdowns, and when it was all over, Columbia—beaten once by Princeton—and Harvard shared first place.

The 1962 squad stumbled off to a 2-3 start before back-to-school shutouts of Penn and Princeton launched another fast finish. Four straight wins gave Harvard another 6-3 season and second place in the Ivy League.

Captain Dick Diehl anchored the young 1962 group up front, while the offensive backfield was filled with the likes of Mike Bassett, Bill Taylor, and Bill Grana. The Bassett-to-Taylor passing combo provided two of the longest scoring strikes in Harvard history. Against Dartmouth, in a 24-6 defeat, the pair combined for an 82-yarder that was the first touchdown against the strong Green defense all year; and later, in a 31-19 win over Brown, the tandem hit on a 76-yard TD play that was one of four touchdowns scored by Taylor during the afternoon.

The 1962 season was the first of four straight in which Harvard would suffer just two league losses yet finish painfully shy of an Ivy championship. Of all the near misses, 1963 was the most painful.

Guard Bill Southmayd, later a leader in the field of sports medicine, was captain of the 1963 team, which began the campaign with a win over Cornell. Next, the Lions of Columbia traveled to the Stadium for a game that would come back to haunt Harvard when the season was over. The game ended at 3-3, with John Hartranft's 22-yard field goal providing the only Harvard points. But six fumbles had conspired to help prevent a Harvard victory, and the tie was ultimately to cost the Crimson a piece of the Ivy title.

This was a topsy-turvy season that saw Harvard, behind quarterback Bill Humenuk, end Dartmouth's 15-game win streak, then be upset by Penn, 7-2, and then come back to upset Princeton, 21-7.

Finally it came down to Yale at the Bowl. The game was originally scheduled for Saturday, November 23, but the day before it was to be played, President John F. Kennedy '40, a Harvard Stadium spectator at the October 19 Columbia game, was assassinated in Dallas.

The Yale game was moved to November 30, and the extra week of waiting seemed to take its toll on the Harvards, as Yale prevailed, 20-6. Twenty years after the game, halfback Scott Harshbarger remembered that week clearly.

"It happened very gradually, but the assassination

definitely had its effect on us. It was a depressing type of atmosphere that for some subtle reason, and I'm not sure of the connection, hit us harder than them. I'm convinced that we would have beaten them had we played that first Saturday. But when the game rolled around, we were flat and they did a job on us."

All year long Harvard had been a ball control team that took command of the line of scrimmage. On that Saturday, Yale owned the line and the game. When Harshbarger scored in the first period on a 38-yard pass from Mike Bassett, things looked good. Or did they?

"When our most successful plays were passes coming to me, I knew we were in trouble," recalled Harshbarger, who caught eight that day. "That was not our game plan."

The next three scores were Yale's, one in each of the final quarters, and the Elis had a 20-6 win. Harvard finished 5-2-2 overall and 4-2-1 in the league, a half game behind cochamps Dartmouth and Princeton (5-2), two teams Harvard had beaten. The team's strength, the offensive line, was recognized when captain Southmayd (guard) and Brad Stephens (center) were named All-Ivy.

A third-place finish followed in 1964, when Harvard went 6-3 overall, 5-2 in the league. This team was much like its predecessor, as it was seventh in the league in offense but second in defense (the 1963 team was sixth and third respectively).

The 1964 season will perhaps be remembered most for a statistical oddity: The team's first five games against Ivy League opponents were shutouts—three for Harvard and two for the enemy.

For the first time since 1956, Harvard won its first two league games, 3-0 and 16-0 over Columbia and Cornell respectively. The game with the Lions matched their brilliant quarterback Archie Roberts with Harvard senior Tom Bilodeau, Jr., a halfback for two years and the son of one of Harvard's greatest baseball players. It was Bilodeau who won the duel, thanks to Maury Dullea's field goal. In the Cornell game the most memorable play was John Dockery's 104-yard interception return for a Harvard touchdown. That remains an Ivy record for Dockery, who went on to win Super Bowl rings with both the New York Jets and the Pittsburgh Steelers.

Following those happy shutouts came one of the most painful losses of the Yovicsin era. Before a regional TV audience and a packed Stadium crowd, Harvard was humbled by the Indians of Dartmouth, 48-0. Nothing went right for the home team, who somehow bounced back to blank Penn, 34-0, the following Saturday. The fifth shutout in the string went to Princeton, 16-0, with kicker Charlie

Harvard Football in the White House

In the early 1960s Harvard football had friends in high places. President John F. Kennedy, Harvard class of 1940, occupied the White House, but the Kennedy connection to football went beyond those friendly games on the White House lawn.

Jack Kennedy did not play varsity football at Harvard but won his freshman numerals in 1936 and a minor H a year later as a member of the JV team. That year, he suited for three games as an end, the position his younger brothers would play. (President Kennedy's athletic record at Harvard also included participating in three freshman swim meets in 1936–37, without receiving his freshman numerals. In 1938 he was a member of the winning crew in the McMillan Cup Atlantic Coast Invitational Sailing Championships. Among the other crew members was his older brother, Joseph P. Kennedy, Jr., '38.)

Robert Kennedy '48, JFK's attorney general, earned a varsity letter as a senior when he was a starting end for two weeks. His season was cut short in that second week during a scrimmage, when he broke his leg colliding with an equipment cart. He remained healthy long enough to catch a 6-yard touchdown pass from Kenny O'Donnell in Harvard's 52-0 win over Western Maryland.

United States Senator Edward M. Kennedy '54 also earned a single varsity letter as an end. At 6 feet 2 inches, 200 pounds, Teddy was the biggest of the brothers and also had the most successful playing career. He caught two touchdown passes as a senior, one in a 21-7 win over Columbia and the other in a 21-7 loss to Yale.

Three other football letter-winners were frequent visitors to the Kennedy White House. Perhaps the most successful on the gridiron was Representative Torbert Macdonald '40. Captain of the 1939 team, halfback Macdonald scored 15 touchdowns in three varsity seasons and also lettered in track and baseball. He was the president's Winthrop House roommate.

Forging an equally impressive career record was Ken O'Donnell '49, special assistant to the president under JFK. Harvard captain in 1948, two years after his brother Cleo had held the

President John F. Kennedy '40 sits between Senator Edmund Muskie (left) and Postmaster General Lawrence O'Brien (later commissioner of the National Basketball Association) during the 1963 Harvard-Columbia game at the Stadium. Just over a month later, the president was assassinated in Dallas.

same title, O'Donnell was a two-way player, best remembered as a defensive back. He still holds Harvard records for interceptions in a season (8) and a career (15).

Another who made the Harvard–White House connection was Chuck Roche '50, a talented punter and back, who served as vice-chairman of the Democratic National Committee. He was one of the few to earn four football letters, picking up his first as a 17-year-old freshman out of Winchester High School in 1945 (freshmen were eligible that year).

• • •

Gogolak doing the most damage (three field goals and an extra point).

After a win over Brown, Harvard clinched third place with a most satisfying win over Yale before a capacity crowd at the Stadium. Trailing 14-12 at the start of the fourth quarter, Harvard reversed matters dramatically on the period's fifth play, when sophomore halfback Bobby Leo scampered 46 yards for what proved to be the decisive score in an 18-14 Crimson win.

It was a gratifying finish for Leo, a highly touted running back out of nearby Everett High School. Even though he had scored two touchdowns in his first varsity game (a loss to Bucknell), a leg injury suffered the previous summer in a baseball game hampered Leo much of the season. More would be heard from him later.

1965–67: The 1965 team again finished third in the Ivy League, and again the defense bested the offense by allowing the fewest points in the league. The 5-2-2 season started nicely with three straight wins. Two Bobby Leo touchdowns and three Dave Poe interceptions paced a 17-7 win over Holy Cross. Tom Choquette scored twice and the defense did the rest in a 33-0 blanking of Tufts. And in the Ivy opener against Cornell, a 21-6 win, it was senior Walt Grant scoring twice, including a 65-yard dash. Grant would go on to lead the Crimson in rushing for the third straight year.

But the next four weeks produced 0-2-2 results, even though the defense allowed just five touchdowns. The defense continued to shine in 17-8 and 13-0 wins over Brown and Yale that closed the season.

Four years of being close finally paid off for Harvard in 1966, when there were almost as many Ivy League champions as nonchampions. Harvard finished a strong 6-1 in the league in 1966. But so did Dartmouth and Princeton. Here's how it happened.

After scoring just 120 points in 1965, the 1966 Crimson came up with 109 on the season's first three Saturdays. The emergence of southpaw Ric Zimmerman at quarterback had a lot to do with the scoring blitz, as did the arrival of sophomore back Vic Gatto and the continued devastating play of veterans Leo and Choquette.

The win streak went to six and included a satisfying 19-14 win over Dartmouth, winner of ten straight Ivy games and at least a share of the league title in each of the last four seasons. The Harvard triumph was made possible by 275 yards rushing from Leo and Gatto and two fourth-quarter scores. The last score, a 1-yard dive by

"The greatest back I ever coached." That's how John Yovicsin described Bobby Leo when the halfback finished his playing career in 1966. Winner of the George Bulger Lowe Award as New England's best player that year, the Everett native set a Harvard career mark of 5.5 yards per carry over three seasons. In each of those years, he scored the winning touchdown against Yale.

quarterback Zimmerman, capped a seven-minute, 80-yard drive and left less than two minutes to play. Yovicsin had high praise for Zimmerman after the game.

"Ric called a great series that exploited every possible Dartmouth weakness. He watched the clock so well that Dartmouth had no time left to mount a sustained counteroffensive after we scored."

Harvard's streak was snapped two weeks later at Princeton, when the Tigers marched 93 yards in the final quarter to post an 18-14 win. Since the Tigers had been beaten by Penn earlier in the year, Harvard, Dartmouth, and Princeton were tied with a loss apiece.

The league leaders played perfectly over the final two weeks, none more so than Harvard. With 24-7 and 17-0 wins over Brown and Yale respectively, Harvard ended up outscoring its opposition by 231-60, the widest margin since the 1920 team.

Bobby Leo was All-Ivy and the team scoring leader for the second straight year. His 827 yards were second only to Dick Clasby's 1951 season total at that point, and his career total of 1,629 was also second to Clasby. Leo's knack for performing under pressure was emphasized by the fact that he scored the winning touchdown in three straight Yale games. Joining Leo on the All-Ivy team were safety John Tyson, middle guard Stan Greenidge, linebacker Don Chiofaro, defensive tackle Dave Davis, and offensive tackle Steve Diamond (for the second time).

Big things were expected of captain Don Chiofaro's 1967 squad, and when the team opened with four impressive wins, everything seemed to be on schedule.

First came Yovicsin's most lopsided win, a 51-0 rout of Lafayette that was dubbed the Ric and Vic Show when Ric Zimmerman threw three touchdown passes and Vic Gatto ran for 103 yards. And that was just in the first half!

The numbers weren't as gaudy when Boston University was taken by 29-14 the next week, Tom Wynne's three interceptions highlighting the effort. When Harvard scored its most Ivy points ever in a 49-13 romp over Columbia, big plays were the order of the day. There was Wynne's record 51-yard field goal. There was Ken Thomas's 91-yard interception return for a touchdown. And there was a Zimmerman–to–Gary Strandemo touchdown pass that covered 72 yards. The fourth consecutive 1967 win was a 14-12 squeaker over Cornell that saw Harvard score all its points in the first quarter, then hold on as the Big Red rallied.

On the season's fifth Saturday, Harvard hosted Dartmouth in what may be the second most memorable contest of the 1960s. Two teams brought perfect Ivy records to a packed stadium on a sunny afternoon. And the battle that followed was a classic.

Dartmouth, paced by its brilliant quarterback Gene Ryzewicz, dominated early and took a 20-0 lead into the fourth quarter. Then suddenly, within a span of seven minutes, Harvard scored three touchdowns. Vic Gatto tallied twice after his new backfield mate Ray Hornblower had first put the Crimson on the board. With Wynne's three kicks, the score was Harvard 21, Dartmouth 20, with just under eight minutes to play.

It's a long way from Harvard Stadium to Coal Miner's Daughter. *But that's the journey Tommy Lee Jones made. The motion picture star was an All-Ivy guard on Harvard's 8-0-1 team that shared the 1968 Ivy title with Yale.*

As the clock wound down to just 1:07 remaining, Dartmouth faced a fourth and 6 on the Harvard 8-yard line. When Pete Donovan's field goal attempt went wide to the left, the Harvard crowd exploded. But the joy was short-lived, as an offside call gave new life to Dartmouth. On his second attempt, with the ball on the 4, Donovan's kick was good and Dartmouth had a 23-21 win.

"It was a depressing feeling after that one, but we really didn't play real well," remembered Gatto, who scored his late touchdowns despite being knocked cold on the second-half kickoff.

Two other games stood out that year, as the Crimson, 2-3 over the final five Saturdays, finished 6-3 overall, 4-3 in the league. En route to a 45-7 victory against Penn, quarterback Zimmerman completed 14 of 17 passes, including a record nine receptions for Carter Lord. (At season's end, Yovicsin would call Lord "the finest end I've ever coached.")

Then, in the season finale against a Yale team that would finish 7-0 in the league, Harvard rallied from a

17-0 first-half deficit to go ahead 20-17 with three minutes left. But Yale, led by quarterback Brian Dowling, took just 49 seconds to regain the lead.

With more than 68,000 fans watching in the Yale Bowl, Dowling sent split end Walt Marting deep and went for it all. Harvard defensive back Mike Ananis went for the interception and slipped on the wet turf. The result was a 66-yard touchdown pass that put Yale up 24-20 with 2:16 to play. Prior to that pass, Dowling had more completions to Harvard defenders (five interceptions) than he had to Yale receivers.

Harvard got the ball back long enough to mount one last drive that went the length of the field only to be stopped by a fumble on the Yale 10-yard line.

The loss was particularly rough for the Harvard defense which, besides those five interceptions, had pressured Yale's Dowling to the point that he connected on only 5 of 20 passes. Yet he was victorious despite the subpar performance.

"This game had the same range of emotions as the Dartmouth game but hurt more because we really played well against Yale," recalled Vic Gatto. Playing particularly well were Zimmerman (14 of 29 for a record 289 yards) and Lord (nine catches for 188 yards and a record sixth touchdown on the season).

The game marked the end of brilliant careers of a number of seniors, most notably quarterback Zimmerman, split end Lord, and linebacker Chiofaro. Lord and Chiofaro were All-Ivy choices, and team MVP Zimmerman had to settle for second team behind Yale's Dowling.

The quarterback was not second to his coach, and that was clear following the final game. "I told Ric in the locker room that no individual had done as much for Harvard football in my eleven years as he had," said Yovicsin.

Also earning first-team attention were halfback Gatto, guard Al Bersin, defensive end Bob Hoffman, and safety Tom Williamson. That made six selections from a team that tied for fourth in the league at 4-3. Bersin and Williamson pulled off a rare and impressive double later that year when both won Rhodes Scholarships.

1968: Then there was 1968. Captain Vic Gatto's team first took the field in a series of preseason scrimmages and, according to Harvard's "News and Views" newsletter, did so "without looking particularly impressive." The description was recalled when, trailing 20-12 in the fourth

He was best remembered for his final score, a touchdown reception that brought Harvard closer to Yale in the famed 29-29 tie in 1968. But Vic Gatto was a three-year star, and holder of Harvard's career rushing record. His success as a player was followed by an equally successful coaching career.

quarter against Holy Cross, Harvard had to rally for 15 final-quarter points to take a 27-20 season opener.

When Gatto's running paced a 59-0 demolition of Bucknell, the team's stock rose considerably. And, after a 21-14 win over Columbia launched the Ivy season, the team was said to be "maturing."

Over the next five Saturdays, the maturation process was completed. The offense was paced by the running of Gatto and Ray Hornblower and the big pass receptions of a mammoth (6 feet 4 inches, 240 pounds) sophomore tight end named Pete Varney. Directing the attack was quarterback George Lalich. Defensively, the team allowed a touchdown or less in each of those five games and through six league games had given up a total of 41 points.

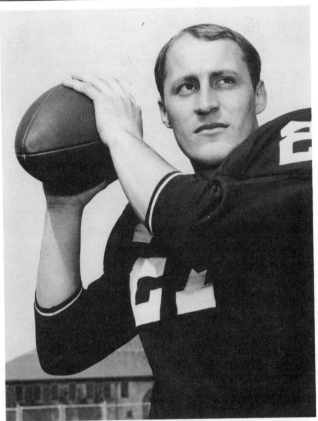

For eight and half games in 1968, Everett's Frank Champi was a back-up quarterback. Coming off the bench to rally Harvard in the second half against Yale, Champi turned 42 seconds of action into a career. He would give up football in the early weeks of the 1969 season.

The Miracle of 1968

There has always been something special about a Harvard-Yale game at Harvard Stadium. The teams have regularly been the league's best and with the game, or rather, The Game coming at the end of each season, the possibility of drama is heightened.

But there is something else. Something special. No one has captured this better than Roger Angell '42, the New Yorker fiction editor and contributor, who once wrote:

I come back to the Game, year after year, not so much for the sport as for a feeling of renewal. It has become a rite, and its capacity to move me does not have much to do with the final score or even with the pleasures of meeting old friends there, before the kickoff and after. It has something to do with the turn of the seasons; winter begins here, every year, when the gun goes off and the last cries and songs are exchanged across the field. . . . The Game picks us up each November and holds us for two hours and then releases us into the early darkness of winter, and all of us, homeward bound, sense that we are different yet still the same. It is magic.

Angell wrote those lines in 1978 on the occasion of the tenth anniversary of the most magical of all Harvard-Yale games, the 29-29 tie of 1968. What happened on November 23 of that year has become part of American sports lore.

For the first time since 1909, Harvard and Yale were meeting with perfect records. It would prove to be the only time in the history of the two schools that both teams remained undefeated at season's end.

There was 8-0 Harvard, led by its superb running backs Vic Gatto and Ray Hornblower and a defense that had allowed just 27 points on the five Saturdays preceding The Game '68.

And there was 8-0 Yale, a one-touchdown favorite, who had destroyed Ivy opponents behind the league's two big names, quarterback Brian Dowling and halfback Calvin Hill. Dowling was the guy who had not lost a game since the seventh grade, the soon-to-be-legendary "B.D." from a campus comic strip that would later become "Doonesbury." Hill was simply a dominating tal-

Since this success was being matched stat for stat in New Haven, Saturday, November 23, 1968, featured an Ivy rarity. For the first time in 60 years, Harvard and Yale would bring perfect records into the season finale.

Legions of sportswriters and football fans have replayed this game countless times since some 40,000 people walked out of Harvard Stadium late that afternoon. It was a less than memorable game until it concluded with college football's most memorable 42 seconds.

Outplayed and trailing by 29-13 late in the fourth quarter, Harvard, behind reserve quarterback Frank Champi, rallied for 16 points in those final seconds to "beat" Yale, 29-29. Both teams finished at 8-0-1 and shared the Ivy League crown.

For the third year in a row, Harvard had six All-Ivy selections, as Gatto, Harvard's career rushing leader, repeated and shared the honor with punter Gary Singleterry, safety Pat Conway, linebacker John Emery, defensive end Pete Hall, and guard Tommy Lee Jones (who went on to become a major motion picture star).

ent and would be the National Football League's Rookie of the Year the following fall.

Ticket demand, always high for this event, was unprecedented. The Harvard ticket office had to stop filling class orders with the class of 1949. Scalpers were getting $200 a pair for the few ducats that were floating around at game time. Everyone anticipated a great 60 minutes of action.

It didn't happen. Yale dominated play from the start, jumping out to a 22-0 lead by 7:24 of the second quarter. Harvard was flat. And the game offered little indication of its eventual immortality.

Harvard coach John Yovicsin needed to shake up his offense and did so by replacing season-long starter George Lalich with back-up quarterback Frank Champi late in the second quarter. Champi had been a standout at nearby Everett High, the same school that gave Harvard Bobby Leo '67. In his three Yale games, Leo had scored three winning touchdowns. Maybe this other kid from Everett could do something.

On his first possession Champi directed a 12-play, 64-yard drive that ended when he hit split end Bruce Freeman with an 8-yard pass. A bad snap from center botched Richie Szaro's PAT attempt, so the scoreboard read 22-6 at halftime.

Despite Champi's success, Lalich started the second half and again Harvard went nowhere. When Yale fumbled the ball on the ensuing possession, Champi returned to the lineup. Three plays later, fullback Gus Crim scored from the 1 and, with Szaro's kick, it was 22-13.

Before the Harvard faithful could get too excited, Yale regained its control of the game and pushed the lead to 29-13 four minutes into the fourth quarter. On the Harvard side, people began fumbling for their car keys and heading for the exits.

And why shouldn't they? The Elis, behind a quarterback who had never lost a game, were in full command. Their 16-point lead could have been even greater had they not fumbled five times.

By the fourth quarter Harvard was playing without its three offensive leaders. Gatto had pulled a hamstring early in the game and despite attempts to return was on the bench for most of

the second half. Hornblower, gamely running on an injured ankle, left the game for good after the first play of the final quarter. Lalich had to watch his understudy try to move the team.

With less than four minutes to play, Yale was deep in Harvard territory, threatening to score again. Suddenly the football popped loose from Yale's Bob Levin, and Steve Ranere recovered for Harvard on the Crimson 14. The clock showed 3:31 to play. Yale would never get the ball back.

To fully comprehend what happened in those final three and a half minutes, let alone the final 42 seconds, one must look at each of the plays that gave Harvard its final 16 points. Few Hollywood scripts have so strained the imagination.

TIME REMAINING: 3:31
SCORE: Yale 29, Harvard 13
Ball on Harvard 14

—John Ballantyne takes pitch from Champi, loses 2.
—Ballantyne gains 17 on reverse. First down.
—Champi pass to Ballantyne fails.
—Champi sacked for loss of 12. Yale holding penalty. First down.
—Champi pass to Freeman fails.
—Champi pass to Freeman good for 17 to Yale 30.
—Champi pass to Crim fails.
—Champi sacked for loss of 8. Third and 18.
—Champi back to pass, bobbles ball, laterals to tackle Fritz Reed, who gains 23 yards. First down at Yale 15.
—Champi passes to Freeman for TD.
—Champi PAT pass to Varney incomplete. Yale penalized for interference.
—Crim from 1 for two points. Time of score: 14:18.

"We had practiced those onside kickoffs all year," recalled Bill Kelly, a sophomore from Reading, Massachusetts, back in 1968. "The key was to kick the ball on the top so it would bounce twice on the ground and then into the air. The kickoff came to my side but it didn't bounce right, and I thought, 'Uh-oh, this isn't what we practiced.' Then the Yale player fumbled, and I saw the ball lying on the ground with no one around it. I thought, 'This is amazing, all I have to do is fall on it.' "

TIME REMAINING: 0:42
SCORE: Yale 29, Harvard 21
Harvard Kicking Off

—Ken Thomas onside kick recovered by Bill Kelly on Yale 49.
—Champi scrambles, gains 14. Yale face-mask penalty. First down on Yale 20. Time left: 0:32.
—Champi pass to Freeman fails.
—Champi pass to Jim Reynolds fails. Third and 10. Time left: 0:20

"We were in the same situation the year before in New Haven," Vic Gatto would later recall. "We were on the Yale 10 with about a minute left and tried our fullback, Ken O'Connell, up the middle. He got hit hard, fumbled, and we lost the ball and the game [24-20]. In 1968, we called the same play in the same situation."

—Fullback Crim on draw up the middle for 14. First and goal from the 6. Time left: 0:14.
—Champi back to pass, hit for loss of 2. Time left: 0:03.

"Flank Vic left," Yovicsin told Champi. "Then roll right and throw back to Vic." As Champi rolled right, he could not find Gatto on the other side of the field.

"I remember just this tunnel of noise," re-called Gatto, "and it was as if time had slowed down. I knew I was free, but I didn't want to wave because I didn't want to call attention to the fact that I was open. Then Champi threw to me, and the ball came so slow and big."

—Champi pass to Gatto in corner of end zone for TD. Time left: 0:00.

When Yovicsin had given Champi the final play of regulation, he also told him how to get the extra points. So, with two quarterbacks who had won 16 games watching from the sidelines,

The Miracle of '68 is complete: Sophomore tight end Pete Varney clutches the ball after receiving a 2-point conversion pass that ties Yale, 29-29. Harvard, down 29-13 with less than a minute to play, scored 16 points in 42 seconds to ''beat'' the Elis. (Dick Raphael photo courtesy of Sports Illustrated.)

Champi went to the line of scrimmage for the season's final play.

—Champi pass to tight end Pete Varney just inside goal line is good.

Time Remaining: 0:00
Final Score: Harvard 29, Yale 29

1969–70: The contrast between 1968 and 1969 could not have been sharper. Yovicsin's best record was followed by his worst, as the 1969 squad went 3-6 overall, 2-5 in the league.

The year began well enough with a 13-0 win over Holy Cross, the tenth game without a defeat for the Crimson. But from that point the team struggled through a 2-6 spell that saw Columbia and Penn the only victims.

One of the defeats was well remembered for a couple of statistical notes. In a 41-24 loss to Cornell, Harvard defensive back Neil Hurley intercepted a pass and returned it 102 yards for a score. On the other side of the field, Cornell fans cheered All-American running back Ed Marinaro, who gained 281 yards on the ground that day. (He was later to star in the successful television program "Hill Street Blues.")

The 51-0 win over Columbia was notable for a number of reasons. It featured a 27-point fourth quarter fashioned by reserves; it came following a painful 13-10 loss to Boston University; and it came days after quarterback Frank Champi announced his retirement from football.

Champi, the hero of the previous year's Yale game, had lost his enthusiasm for football. His decision caused quite a stir in Boston.

"Football has lost its meaning for me," said Champi at the time. "I've been thinking about my relation to the game for a long time . . . several years. I kept asking myself why I was playing. I wasn't doing it for publicity, for pride, or for the thrill of victory. I wasn't getting any of those things from it. I can't take it seriously enough any more."

The season ended with a strong defensive effort but still a loss, 7-0 in New Haven. One of the standouts that day was linebacker Gary Farneti, who was to be elected captain of the 1970 team, Yovicsin's last. The coach had undergone open heart surgery in 1965 and had been beset by medical problems in subsequent years. Doctors finally convinced him that it was time to retire.

The team's remarkable turnaround in 1970 was a fitting way for Yovvy to exit. Confidence was restored early in the season when Northeastern and Rutgers fell handily on the first two weekends. Sparking the revival was a pair of sophomore quarterbacks, Rod Foster and Eric Crone. Foster was the crowd pleaser with the shifty moves and breakaway speed. Crone had the arm.

When Columbia grabbed a 28-21 victory, doubts resurfaced. But the team bounced back the following week with a thrilling 27-24 win over Cornell, thanks to Richie Szaro's 28-yard field goal with eight seconds to play. Another key was Harvard's banged-up defense, which held together long enough to "limit" Ed Marinaro to 151 yards (down 130 from the year before).

When undefeated Dartmouth waltzed to a 37-14 win at the Stadium, the 3-2 Harvard team was at a crossroads. The Ivy League title was out of reach, and so the question became: Could this group finish strong and send Yovvy out on a happy note?

The team responded by winning four straight and finishing 7-2 overall, 5-2 in the league, good for second. It was a team without a big star that got a little help from everyone each Saturday. In a 38-23 win over Penn, Yovicsin stuck with one quarterback and Foster responded with his best day. Sophomore halfback Ted DeMars had his best outing, too, as he ran for 139 yards. In the 29-7 win at Princeton, the defense put on a show, picking off five passes and recovering three fumbles, Jack Neal, Chris Doyle, Rick Frisbie, and Spencer Dreischarf led the defensive unit along with captain Farneti. Crone was at quarterback in the 17-10 win over Brown. Eric completed 14 of 18 for 196 yards, Harvard's best passing attack of the year. That left Yale.

John Yovicsin's last game, against a favored Yale team, was played with second place in the league at stake. A loss or a tie and the spot belonged to Yale; a win and the teams shared second.

Harvard went up 14-0 with two second-period scores. Crone hit Ted DeMars with a 7-yard TD strike and ran the other in from 8 yards away. Szaro's two kicks would prove crucial.

Yale answered with 10 points in the third quarter, and the score remained 14-10 until the game's closing seconds. That's when Yovvy's party was nearly spoiled and Eric Crone earned a dubious nickname.

Harvard had stopped Yale's final drive on the Harvard 20 with little more than a minute to play. Using just two plays, quarterback Crone killed all but a few seconds of that time. On third down Crone ran back into the end zone as time expired and held his arms up in celebration.

Yale's Ron Kell fought through the spectators in the end zone to make the tackle, actually more of a bear hug. With that, Yale registered a safety to make the score 14-12 and end the game. Had Kell knocked the ball out of Crone's hands and recovered it in the end zone, Yale could have snatched victory from defeat and End Zone Crone would have had more than a nickname to live with.

For John Yovicsin the game was the end of 14 seasons

at Harvard, the longest tenure of any Harvard football coach at that time. His record was not just one of time but also of achievement: His mark of 78-42-5 (.644) is the third best winning percentage among Harvard coaches who have coached for more than three seasons.

A Difference of Style

One was called conservative, even dull. The other was called imaginative, an innovator. Both were winners.

John Yovicsin served as Harvard's head football coach for 14 seasons (1957–70), longer than any of his predecessors. With the conclusion of the 1984 season, Joe Restic, the man who followed Yovvy, equaled that mark. The two men could not have embraced more contrasting philosophies. Yet their 14-year records were startlingly identical.

JOHN YOVICSIN		JOE RESTIC
14 (1957–70)	Years	14 (1971–84)
78-42-5 (.644)	Overall Record	77-48-5 (.612)
59-36-4 (.616)	Ivy Record	60-34-4 (.633)
6-8-0	vs. Dartmouth	6-7-1
6-8-0	vs. Princeton	6-6-2
8-5-1	vs. Yale	6-8-0
3 shared	Ivy Titles	3 shared, 1 outright

Once you get past the numbers and examine how the records were achieved, all comparisons end.

When John Yovicsin came to Cambridge in March of 1957, he had a definite assignment: Return winning football to Harvard. In a way, his task was defined when the Ivy Group Presidents' Agreement of 1954 established the goals of an Ivy football program: Be competitive in your own league.

What has been called formal league play began in 1956, Lloyd Jordan's final season as Harvard head coach. Jordan took a half step toward the kind of respectability that the Harvards sought from their football program. Yovicsin went the distance.

"Defense, kicking, and offense." Those were the stated priorities of this young coach plucked from his alma mater, Gettysburg College of Pennsylvania. And that is actually how it was done.

Yovicsin did not seek out the Harvard job. It was on the recommendation of former Harvard coach Dick Harlow that the university sought Yovicsin. The climate of his early years was reflected in a story that Yovicsin enjoyed telling on the postseason banquet circuit.

"One night in the early weeks of our first season, I was driving home from practice. I'm going through Newton and there's so much Harvard football on my mind that I'm not paying attention to driving. I get pulled over by a Newton police cruiser and a policeman approaches me. He asks for my papers and he looks at them. 'Are you really John Yovicsin, the Harvard football coach?' he asks. I assure him I am, and he says, 'With the problems you've got, you don't need this ticket.' And he let me go with a reprimand."

That first year began with significant defections from the program, including all of the centers listed on the depth chart. But the final story was not written by those who dropped out.

"The kids who stayed with us in 1957 are the ones who made Harvard football what it was for the next ten years," said Yovicsin, "players like Bob Foster and [captain] Tom Hooper."

That first Harvard team contained just four seniors on it. Yovvy's final team in 1970 contained 27.

From the beginning, one of Yovicsin's strengths was his selection and use of assistant coaches. This was a lesson he learned from Lefty James, a former coach at Cornell.

"A coach first must be an organizer," said Yovicsin. "He has to deal with a huge squad and a big staff. The nature of the game forces him to detach himself from the players. They are closer to the assistants than they are to the head coach."

Not only did Yovicsin's assistants help him, but the head coach helped them, many moving on to head coaching positions. This list included Jim Lentz (Bowdoin), Foge Fazio (Pittsburgh), Roger Robinson (Cortland), Pat Stark (Rochester), Alex Bell (Villanova), and Tom Stephens (Curry). Even some of his players became coaches, most notably 1968 captain Vic Gatto (Bates, Tufts, and Davidson).

After two losing seasons, Yovicsin engineered

ten straight winning campaigns that included three shared Ivy League titles. And this tall, thin, angular man did it in a way one would have expected from someone who neither smoked nor drank nor cursed. He was conservative.

"We were always well coached in fundamentals. We could block and tackle as well as anyone," recalled Scott Harshbarger '64, a Yovicsin half-back who went on to become the district attorney of Middlesex County. "And since we rarely had the explosive back, we went with a conservative, ball control offense. And, yes, sometimes it was dull to watch."

Yovicsin's critics went further. "Yovicsin hasn't recognized the existence of the forward pass," alumni would lament. "Harvard is a team that can be depended upon to play the percentages," said one Yale scouting report.

Yovicsin, whose Gettysburg teams were known for their passing, never fully agreed with the knock on his offense. "You had to go with the material you had at the time. And when we had passing quarterbacks, we used them."

Left-hander Ric Zimmerman was his best and is the only Yovicsin quarterback to remain among Harvard passing leaders. The role of the quarter-back and the forward pass would change drastically when Yovicsin's successor paced the sidelines.

Though their coaching styles were different, John Yovicsin (top left) and Joe Restic enjoyed almost identical success in back-to-back tenures covering nearly 30 years.

Joe Restic had no program to save when he came to Harvard in 1971. He simply had to live up to his advance billing as an innovator. By the end of his first Yale game, when he sent his quarterback in motion, he had done just that.

Restic's offense even had its own name, the Multiflex, which reflected its multiple sets and flexible options. The Harvard and Boston sports communities were intrigued with this Villanova graduate who came to Cambridge from Canada's pro football league. If his offense had a unique title, so should the coach, and Harvard Magazine obliged by dubbing Restic "the radical theoretician of Soldiers Field."

"The offense should be the aggressor," said the new coach. "The one advantage we have is surprise. You have to come out and confuse them [the defense], make them hesitate."

The Restic philosophy continued on the other side of the ball. "Our style is to capture the line of scrimmage, get across, and force a big loss or a fumble. We play defense in an offensive way."

No longer could teams depend upon Harvard to play the percentages. Quarterbacks would go in motion. Tight ends would go in motion. Quarterbacks would share the backfield with other quarterbacks. Three receivers would be wide to the same side. It was different, it was fun, and it was successful.

The Multiflex includes so many sets and allows so many variations that a detailed explanation of exactly what it is would require a small booklet. But that, according to its architect, isn't necessary anyway. People only need to understand the system's major objectives.

"It doesn't matter what defense a team throws at us. Every defense has a weakness, and our system allows us to take advantage of that weakness, every week, without being limited by a set offensive system. And the system allows us to tailor our offense to the talents of the individuals we have at a given time."

And so a Larry Brown could set passing records, a Jim Callinan could set rushing records, and a Donnie Allard could operate the best option of the Restic years. The system made the players, but at the same time the players made the system.

Restic's pride in his offense would surface regularly, particularly when professional football hyped new trends in its game. "The Redskins sent the tight end in motion in the 1983 Super Bowl and everyone said it was an innovation. Then the pro teams went to the one-back offense, the H back, they called it. That was a new idea. We were doing those things in 1971."

Like Yovicsin, Restic endured a pair of average seasons before enjoying arguably his best years in the mid-1970s. Three 7-2 teams, led by three different quarterbacks, displayed Restic and his offense at their best. Jim Stoeckel came close to a title in 1973. Lefty Milt Holt's final game heroics gave the coach his first piece of a championship. And Jim Kubacki, another southpaw, led Harvard and Restic to their first and only undisputed Ivy League crown in 1975.

With those titles and the cochampionships in 1982 and 1983, Restic and his system were proven winners. Still, like Yovicsin before him, the coach had to deal with critics. No one complained that Restic was dull. But when there were too many years between titles, the alumni questioned Restic's ability to win the games that mattered to them. In the five years from 1977 through 1981, Harvard went 3-10-2 against Dartmouth, Princeton, and Yale.

When this period ended with a 28-0 loss at Yale, the second straight shutout loss to the Elis, the ranks of the disenchanted grew. Critics attacked the Multiflex as more myth than machine. All that motion led to excessive penalties and fumbles, they said. The system put too great a burden on the quarterback, they said. And when starters were injured, five of them in 1979 and three of them in 1980, the back-up players couldn't run the show.

"A lot of people never really understood the system," countered Restic. "They would see the quarterback fumble the ball coming out from center and say, 'Oh, it's the Multifex.' That sort of thing happens in every offense."

When the criticism peaked after the 1981 season, Restic responded in the most convincing way he could. He won pieces of two more league titles and prepared for a record-breaking 15th season in Cambridge.

THE THINKING MAN'S GAME ARRIVES

1971–72: On January 4, 1971, Harvard found a successor to Yovy in Joe Restic, a former assistant at Brown and Colgate who came to Harvard from professional football in Canada. A Villanova graduate, Restic had earned a reputation as an innovator while head coach of the Canadian Football League's Hamilton Tiger Cats.

"I believe in a thinking man's game," said Restic when he met the press in Cambridge that January, "Harvard athletes like to play a thinking man's game."

And so a new era began for Harvard football. Restic made an immediate impression upon all who listened to him that January afternoon. He would quickly show how his love for that "thinking game" would materialize on the football field.

Restic's first two teams labored through 5-4 and 4-4-1 seasons before a trio of 7-2 squads grabbed middecade headlines. Understandably, the 1971 squad started slowly.

Holy Cross ruined Restic's opener with a 21-16 victory despite nine receptions by junior Rich Gatto (Vic's brother) and a blocked punt for a score by captain Dave Ignacio. Restic's first victory came a week later when Northeastern fell, 17-7.

In the Ivy opener, Ted DeMars ran for 132 yards and two touchdowns in a 21-19 win over Columbia. But subsequent losses to Cornell (21-16) and Dartmouth (16-13) left Harvard at 2-3. In that Cornell game, Ed Marinaro ran for 146 yards to put his three-year total against the Crimson at 578.

Against Dartmouth, a bid for victory was denied when Ted Perry's field goal with two seconds left stunned the stadium crowd. The boot also ruined a brilliant debut by sophomore quarterback Jim Stoeckel, who hit on 20 of 37 passes for 230 yards.

From that point the team went 3-1 to give Restic a winning season his first time around, ending with a 35-16 win over Yale. This one was put away in a span of three minutes and 12 seconds—from 12:29 of the first quarter to 0:41 of the second—when Harvard scored 21 points and never looked back.

First came Crone-to-Gatto for a touchdown. Then, following a Mark Steiner fumble recovery, Crone threw to split end Denis Sullivan for another TD. Finally, as he had done in the season opener, Dave Ignacio blocked a punt for a Crimson touchdown, this time with Jack Neal

recovering the ball. Bruce Tetirick made all three extra point conversions (he had five on the day) and Harvard led 21-0.

This game also introduced the Yale Bowl crowd to signs of things to come. The Restic offense, soon to be dubbed the Multiflex, put on a show. On that Crone-to-Sullivan touchdown pass, Harvard had two quarterbacks in the backfield. Rod Foster lined up behind the center but went in motion. The ball was snapped shotgun style to Crone while Foster sprinted out on a pass route. Looking first to Foster, Crone then turned and hit Sullivan 29 yards downfield for a score. It would not be the last of such innovations for the Multiflex.

In 1972 only a tie with Dartmouth kept Harvard from repeating its overall and Ivy records of 1971. After a victory over Columbia in the Ivy opener (20-18), captain DeMars ran for 119 yards and three touchdowns, as Harvard beat Cornell, 33-15, to go 2-0 in the league.

A 21-21 tie with Dartmouth didn't seem to hurt matters. The defense did the job that day, as Kerry Rifkin recovered a Dartmouth fumble off a punt for one touchdown and a Mike McHugh hit on the Dartmouth 2 caused another fumble, which led to another score.

But Harvard didn't have it down the stretch, dropping three of its last four games. Penn's 38-27 win was the Quakers' first at the Stadium since 1958; Princeton created a 10-7 nightmare in the mud; and Yale, down 17-0 three minutes into the second quarter, rallied to win, 28-17.

That Yale game featured two senior backs who went out in glory. Harvard captain Ted DeMars opened the scoring with an 86-yard touchdown jaunt in the first quarter, the longest touchdown run in The Game's 89-game history. DeMars would finish his career with a 153-yard day. On the other side of the field, Yale's Dick Jauron watched his team falter early. Then he broke one for 74 yards and a score in the third quarter and added a 1-yard plunge for a second TD later.

1973–74: Each of the Harvard teams from 1973 through 1975 compiled a record of 7-2. But the net result of each team's efforts differed significantly.

The 1973 squad sprinted to a 4-0 start, allowing just three touchdowns on those four Saturdays. The offense was directed by quarterback Stoeckel, who found a favorite target in split end Pat McInally. From opening day, when he grabbed eight passes, McInally was a dominating presence on the field.

The win streak was snapped by—who else?—Dartmouth, who frustrated the Crimson, 24-18, at the Stadium. Dartmouth scored all its points in the first half, and although Harvard had a 15-0 advantage over the final 30 minutes, it wasn't enough. That made five years without a Harvard win in the H-D series.

On the following week Harvard fashioned its most satisfying win of the year, a 34-30 thriller at Penn. Jim Stoeckel completed 27 of 48 passes for 291 yards, all Harvard records. Ten of those tosses were caught by McInally, including one for a 30-yard TD with a minute and a half to go and just two minutes after Penn had taken the lead.

Wins over Princeton and Brown followed, the latter a memorable 35-32 affair in Providence in which Harvard trailed 0-13 early and 28-36 late. But heroes emerged in the form of reserve fullback Phil Allen, who gained 112 second-half yards, and McInally, whose 13 receptions set a school record.

The Brown win sent a Harvard team that was 5-1 in the Ivy League (tied for first with Dartmouth) to New Haven to face a 4-2 Yale squad (tied for third place with Penn). The trip couldn't have been less pleasant, as Yale outgained Harvard 523 to 232 in total yardage and 35-0 on the scoreboard. And it all happened in a rainstorm to boot, causing one Harvard season ticket holder to comment, "Never have nature and art so coincided."

Quarterback Jim Stoeckel earned All-Ivy status and became Harvard's first Ivy League Player of the Year. "Jimmy was a great play-action type," said coach Restic. "He had a great understanding of what we were trying to do each week, to exploit a defense's weaknesses, and he gave us that part of it which gave us an edge on the field."

Joining Stoeckel on the first team were split end Pat McInally, offensive guard Bill Ferry, defensive tackle Rob Shaw, and safety (and captain) Dave St. Pierre.

The 1974 team showed how one team's 7-2 record can be better than another's. This team won a share of the Ivy title in a race that was decided in the season's final minute.

Harvard started at 3-1, the only loss a 24-21 stumble against Rutgers at the Stadium. The three wins were engineered by quarterback Milt Holt, halfback/place-kicker Alky Tsitsos, and split end McInally.

Holt, the Hawaiian quarterback with the white shoes, was a gambler and a tremendous athlete. What endeared him to his coach was his ability to adapt week after week. "Milt could break all the tendencies and go against the odds," Restic later recalled. "I could adapt with him right on the sidelines, which made it difficult for a defense to know what we would do, even if they studied us."

On the season's fifth Saturday, Harvard ended the Dartmouth jinx and took a tense 17-15 win at Dartmouth. It marked the fourth time in 92 years that the game was played at Hanover's Memorial Field (20,000 capacity). This game will be remembered for many things, not the least of which were Joe Sciolla's diving deflection of a last-second Dartmouth pass and the all-around performance of McInally.

Already Harvard's leading receiver, the 6-foot 6-inch Californian added six catches and 76 yards to his totals—but that was only half the story. While his hands produced those numbers, his feet boomed six punts of over 45 yards, and only one of his four kickoffs was returned past the 20.

Wins over Penn and Princeton gave Harvard a 5-0 Ivy mark with two games to go. Perhaps thoughts were on Yale and title hopes when Brown came to the Stadium and shocked the Crimson, 10-7.

That created a matchup between 5-1 Harvard and 6-0 Yale, with nobody else a factor. Little wonder that 40,000 fans packed the Stadium to see the battle.

And what a battle it was. The 29-29 tie of 1968 had those famous 42 seconds, but this was a far better game from start to finish. Undefeated and untied Yale took advantage of four Harvard fumbles to go on top 13-0 in the second quarter. But Harvard clawed back, and two Holt touchdown strikes made it 14-13 for Harvard at the half.

It remained that way until early in the fourth quarter, when another Harvard error, a bad snap on a punt attempt, gave Yale the ball on the Crimson 15. The Harvard defense stiffened and the Elis had to settle for a field goal and a 16-14 lead.

That was the score with just over five minutes remaining and Harvard taking over on its own 10-yard line. Nine runs, four completions, and one incomplete pass later, Milt Holt called Harvard's final time-out with the Crimson facing second and goal on the Yale 1-yard line and a minute left to play.

"At that point, Milt was out of it," recalled Restic. "He had taken a shot to the head and was not thinking clearly. I put up one finger and he saw two. I put up two and he saw three."

Restic realized he had time for perhaps two plays. He had just one concern.

The Stadium's second most famous finish took place in 1974, when "Pineapple Milt" Holt led Harvard the length of the field in the closing minutes and dove in for the winning score. The victory over Yale gave the Crimson a share of the Ivy title with the Elis.

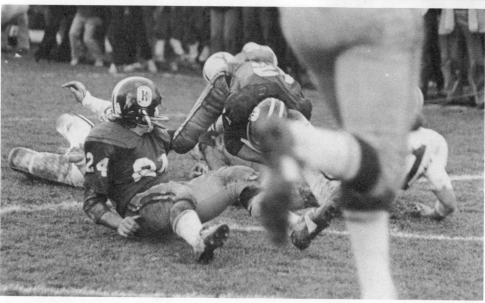

"I kept telling Milt to make sure he did not get trapped on the field with the ball in his hands. We had no time-outs. We called a rollout, and I remember asking him to repeat to me what we were going to do."

Holt returned to the field and lined up for one more play from scrimmage. That's all he would need. Rolling left with an eye toward would-be receivers in the end zone, "Pineapple Milt" saw no one open. And so the southpaw cradled the ball in his left arm, followed the blocks of Steve Dart and Tommy Winn, and sprinted into the end zone with 15 seconds showing on the clock. Alky Tsitsos made the placement and Harvard led 21-16. To this day, Holt does not recall much about that final drive.

The closing seconds proved uneventful, and Harvard and captain Brian Hehir savored a piece of the Ivy title. It was a fitting conclusion to the year when Harvard celebrated 100 years of football, the "real centennial," as it was called.*

On the All-Ivy team, McInally and Rob Shaw repeated as split end and defensive tackle respectively, with Pat also being named All-Ivy punter. Joining them on the first team were center Carl Culig, offensive tackle Dan Jiggetts, and quarterback Holt.

Pat McInally

Pat McInally did not understand it. Sitting in the Eliot House bedroom of teammate John Hagerty, the sophomore split end was baffled.

"I don't know why they don't use me more. A team ought to exploit its strengths." Pretty heady stuff from a sophomore who had yet to make his mark on the varsity. Within a year, however, the comment made all the sense in the world.

Pat McInally came to Harvard from Villa Park, California, a 6-foot 6-inch headliner who could catch and kick footballs. He did both at Harvard, earning All-Ivy honors as a punter and split end and as a receiver was All-American as well.

"Loose, relaxed, as good as he wanted to be," is how Joe Restic described him. "When I think of him, I think of him making so many great

---

* Princeton and Rutgers celebrated the centennial of their 1869 "first game" five years earlier. The Harvard centennial commemorated the Harvard-McGill series of 1874, played under rules more closely resembling those of modern-day football.

catches in key games that spelled the difference for us."

He was a star from his first freshman game, when he scored the first time he handled the ball, through Harvard and into the National Football League, where he was still punting for the Cincinnati Bengals in 1984.

It wasn't just the end result that distinguished McInally. It was his Southern California style as well. He talked and he produced.

There was the Penn game of 1973, a come-from-behind 34-30 Harvard win. At midweek, McInally warned one writer, "You know, after this game Saturday, your fingers are going to burn those typewriter keys." He then went out and caught ten passes, including a one-handed, 30-yarder in the corner of the end zone that won the game with a minute and a half remaining.

These were fun years for football fans in Cambridge. One hundred years of Harvard football had never before produced a duo as dynamic as split end McInally and his bomb-tossing partner, quarterback Milt Holt. There was the gawky McInally, shirttail sticking out, socks drooping, leaping out of a pack of defenders to pull down a game-saving pass. And there was Holt, "Pineapple Milt" from Hawaii, scrambling in the backfield in his white shoes and making the big play time and again.

Taking passes from Holt and his predecessor, Jim Stoeckel, McInally set all the Harvard receiving records: 13 catches in a game (shared), 56 in a season, 108 in his career. He remains 35 receptions ahead of his nearest rival in the last category despite catching only six passes as a sophomore, the year he felt that his strengths were not exploited.

What makes McInally's records even more significant is that many of the catches came when they were most needed. Like that catch at Penn. Or the 13 he grabbed two weeks later in a 35-32 win at Brown. Or the six passes he caught against Yale in his final game, a 21-16 win at the Stadium that left the two rivals tied atop the Ivy standings.

One reception produced Harvard's first points after Yale had gone ahead by 13-0. The last two catches of the game, and of his Harvard career, came during the dramatic drive that began on the

Harvard's first All-American since 1941 was split end Pat McInally '75. The colorful receiver and punter went on to a professional career (right) with the Cincinnati Bengals of the National Football League.

1975–76: The 1975 squad had a tough act to follow but did so without a hitch. The first potential problem appeared to be finding a replacement for Pineapple Milt Holt, but this puzzle was solved early.

In the season opener, an 18-7 win against Holy Cross, Joe Restic found his leader in another southpaw, junior quarterback Jim Kubacki. Although playing with a dislocated finger on his passing hand, Kubacki threw for 104 yards and ran for another 151. At once, Kubacki established his trademarks: versatility and playing in pain.

The following week, a couple of other trademarks surfaced in a 13-9 upset loss to Boston University. Restic's multiflex was a thing of beauty when operating on all cylinders, but when there were problems, particularly early in the year, it often seemed to self-destruct. So it was against the Terriers, when the team amassed 112 yards in penalties and lost four of eight fumbles.

In a 35-30 win over Columbia, Kubacki set a single-game total offense mark with 310 yards, 236 of them in the air. This was a game in which Harvard scored 28 points in the second quarter and led 35-17 at halftime.

Crimson 10 with 5:07 to play and ended with Milt Holt's game-winning touchdown with 0:15 showing on the clock.

From the days of Milton Academy's Barry Wood to Groton's Chub Peabody, the leaders of Harvard football always had character and talent. With Hawaii's Pineapple Milt Holt and California's Pat McInally, the new leaders had character, talent, and a new brand of showmanship that Harvard had never seen before.

There may have been better teams. But none were more fun to watch.

• • •

Nine minutes into the third quarter, the score was 35-30 and stayed that way.

The passing attack was showcased the next two weeks, when Cornell and Dartmouth fell by 34-13 and 24-10 scores respectively. Against the Big Red, Jim Curry caught nine passes for a record 214 yards. With Dartmouth keying on Curry, tight end Bob McDermott hauled in three touchdown passes to pace that win.

Another Kubacki injury, this time a shoulder banged up on Penn's artificial turf, affected the next two games. At Penn, placekicker and back-up quarterback Mike Lynch came off the bench to direct a 21-3 win. But things didn't go as smoothly at Princeton.

The Tigers raced off to a 24-0 lead through three quarters before Harvard, behind third-string quarterback Tim Davenport, put 20 points on the board in just seven minutes. But that's where the rally stopped, as Princeton prevailed 24-20.

At this point, Harvard was 4-1 in Ivy League play, tied for second with Yale behind first-place Brown (4-0-1). The task was clear: Sweep Brown and Yale and the Ivy title would be Harvard's.

The setting was perfect in Providence. With Brown's first sellout in 43 years and a regional television audience watching as well, Harvard and a patched-up Jim Kubacki destroyed the Bruins, 45-26. Kubacki had not worked out all week. In fact, he did not get the green light to play from trainer Jack Fadden until the morning of the game.

Kubacki was 13 of 15 for 222 yards by halftime. With fullback Neal Miller and halfback Tommy Winn pacing the ground game, Harvard gained 476 yards on the day.

"This was our offense at its best," Restic later said. "Everything we did worked. For years after the game, every time I saw Bud Wilkinson [former Oklahoma coach] and Keith Jackson, who broadcast the game, they always referred to that game as the best of Ivy League football."

That left Yale. Again. This time a win would give Harvard its first outright Ivy championship since the league formally began play in 1956. And this time the game was in New Haven.

The contest marked the 100th anniversary of that first H-Y affair in 1875, but it would be remembered as more than a historical footnote.

Yale went ahead 7-0 in the second quarter in a game that was dominated by defenses. While the Elis were containing Kubacki and company, Harvard's defense was at its stingy best. One key matchup put Harvard defensive back Bill Emper on Yale receiver Gary Fencik. Fencik, who would go on to a fine professional career as a Chicago Bears defensive back, was held to one reception all afternoon.

Harvard's running game finally broke through in the second half, when Tommy Winn gained 52 yards, 30 of them on a third-quarter drive that knotted the score at 7-7. Winn scored from the 2 and Lynch added the point after.

Late in the fourth quarter, with the game still tied at 7-7, Harvard started one last drive. The ground game continued to do much of the work, Winn and Miller usually looking to run behind the blocks of captain Danny Jiggetts, a future Bears teammate of Yale's Fencik.

But the drive's big play was a pass, a fourth and 12 cliffhanger from Kubacki to McDermott that kept things alive. Finally, the game came down to a 26-yard field goal attempt with just over 30 seconds to go. With Joe Antonellis snapping and Tim Davenport holding, Mike Lynch made the kick that had more than 65,000 in the Yale Bowl on the edge of their seats. When the ball just made it over the crossbar, Harvard's first outright championship was sewn up.

When postseason honors were announced, Harvard's talented offensive line was recognized, as tackle Jiggetts and guard Kevin McCafferty were All-Ivy choices. Joining them were quarterback Kubacki, cornerback Emper, and adjuster (a Restic term for a type of defensive back) George Newhouse.

With most of the key offensive heroes returning, the 1976 team had reasonable hopes of a successful title defense. Kubacki, Winn, McDermott, Curry, and Lynch were all back on offense, and captain Bill Emper led a veteran defense.

But on the season's fourth Saturday, the rain, the mud, and Cornell punter Dave Johnson changed the scenario. With Harvard leading 3-2 (yes, 3-2) in the third quarter, Johnson took a bad snap on a punting situation and ad-libbed a 75-yard gallop down a muddy sideline for a touchdown. The game ended that way, and Cornell had a 9-3 shocker.

The team regrouped quickly to take a 17-10 thriller at Dartmouth. This one went down to the wire, as linebacker Tommy Joyce stopped Dartmouth's sprinting quarterback Kevin Case at the 2-yard line on the game's final play.

The glee was short-lived. Brown won by 16-14 the following week in a game virtually given away by the Crimson. In addition to four fumbles and two interceptions, Harvard gave up 75 yards in penalties and perhaps title hopes as well.

Not all of Harvard's heroes were on the offensive side of the ball. Above, defensive back (and captain) Bill Emper saves an apparent Dartmouth touchdown with a well-timed leap.

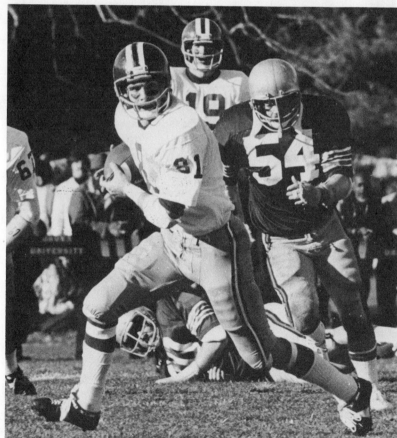

One key to Harvard's 1975 championship was the play of Bobby McDermott (81) right. Always the man with the clutch reception, McDermott graduated as one of Harvard's all-time leading receivers. His life ended tragically in 1978, when a fire engulfed his Boston apartment.

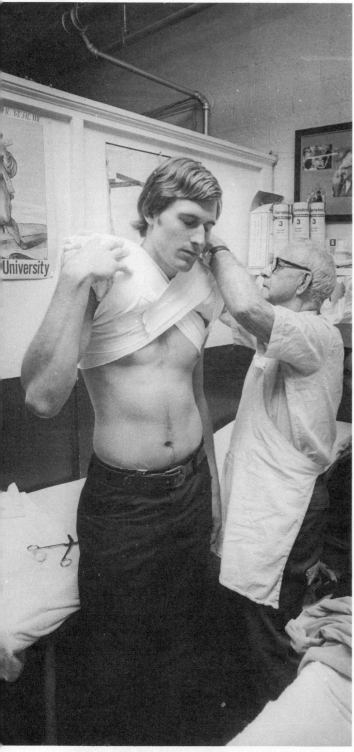

Harvard's oft-injured quarterback Jim Kubacki gets special attention from Jack Fadden, legendary trainer for Harvard and the Boston Red Sox. Kubacki, who quarterbacked Harvard to the 1975 Ivy League title, later received the John P. Fadden Award, presented annually to a senior who overcomes physical adversity.

Harvard played take-away the following week, when the Crimson beat Penn, 20-8. With pressure applied by junior defensive ends Bob Baggott and Russ Savage, Harvard recovered three fumbles and made a record six interceptions, two by defensive back Andy Puopolo.

When Yale came to the Stadium for the season finale, there were warm memories of the previous two classics. And when Russ Savage returned a first-quarter interception 74 yards for a score, a third pleasant memory appeared to be in the making. But the rest of the game was all Yale, as the Elis took a 21-7 win and shared the league title with Brown.

The game closed out the careers of some great individuals who added their names to the Harvard record book. There was tight end Bob McDermott, who tied Pete Varney as third leading receiver in Harvard history. Finishing as third leading scorer by kicking was Mike Lynch. Then there was Tommy Winn, the diminutive halfback, who finished as fourth leading rusher and fifth leading receiver at that time. His senior year was a picture of consistency as he ran for 68, 84, 76, 79, 75, 84, 79, and 95 yards in eight of the team's nine games.

Finally there was Kubacki. Playing injured for virtually his entire career, the left-handed quarterback became Harvard's career total offense leader when he gained 16 yards on the final play of that Yale game. Beyond the statistics, he displayed as much leadership on the field as any who have worn the Harvard uniform.

"He got the maximum out of his abilities, overcame great odds, and was simply a winner," said Restic.

Offensive standouts McDermott and Winn earned first team All-Ivy status, while the defense put four players on that squad: Joining cornerback Emper, a repeat selection, were linebacker Tommy Joyce, tackle Charley Kaye, and end Bob Baggott.

An unhappy footnote to this team followed with the deaths of two of its outstanding players. Following the team's break-up dinner in November of 1976, defensive back Andy Puopolo was stabbed during an altercation in downtown Boston. He died just over a month later. And in 1978, Bobby McDermott, the talented tight end who came up with so many big plays in his varsity career, perished when a fire swept his apartment just outside Boston.

• • •

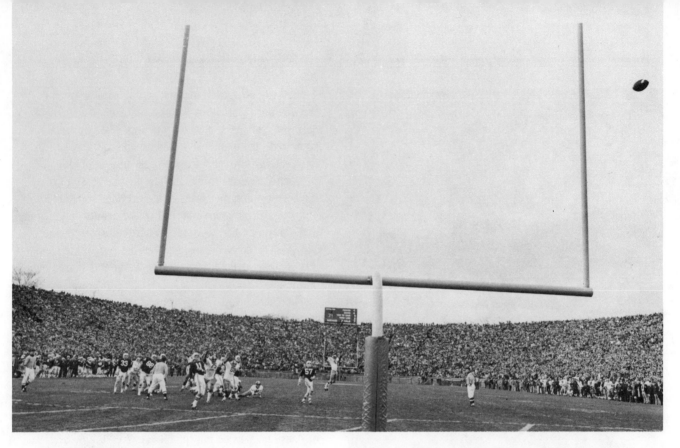

Harvard's Own Title

Since the Ivy League began play in 1956 through the 1984 season, eight Harvard football teams have been able to call themselves Ivy champs. But only one, the 1975 squad, won the title outright. Despite this feat, that team often takes a historical back seat.

"More people tend to recall the undefeated 1968 team because of the 29-29 tie, or the 1974 team led by Milt Holt," according to Mike Lynch, the reserve quarterback and placekicker who became a hero in 1975. "Both of those teams beat Yale at home dramatically. But our club, who won it all, had its great moment in New Haven."

Lynch, later an accomplished sports broadcaster in Boston, played a major role in that 1975 showdown at Yale. Harvard and Yale entered the game tied atop the Ivy standings at 5-1. Entering the season's final quarter, the teams were tied on the scoreboard at 7-7.

"Late in the fourth quarter, Jimmy Kubacki led us on a seventy-two-yard drive, the key play of which was a fourth-and-twelve pass to Bobby McDermott that kept us going," recalled Lynch. "When we got down to fourth and four from the nine, it was up to me."

It took 100 years. But when Mike Lynch's field goal attempt split the uprights at Yale in 1975, the Crimson had their first undisputed Ivy League title.

There were 66,000 people in the Yale Bowl that day. All of them had seen Mike Lynch miss a 42-yard field goal attempt in the second quarter. This time they had a chance to see him attempt a 26-yarder with 38 seconds remaining on the clock. All that was riding on it was Harvard's first unshared Ivy League title.

"Joe Antonellis made a perfect snap, Tim Davenport held, and there was no question in my mind that it was good," recalled Lynch with pride.

There was a certain symmetry to that winning effort, one not lost on Lynch.

"Along with Kubacki and Davenport, I had my eyes on the starting quarterback spot, and we all became pretty close in the middle of competition. What made that win even more special was that we all contributed: Jimmy brought us close, Timmy held the ball, and I made the kick. That made it all the more special to us."

And the result of their efforts made the 1975 football team all the more special in Harvard football history.

1977–79: The closing years of the 1970s could not match the success of the 1973–76 period, as records of 4-5, 4-4-1, and 3-6 completed the decade. But individual efforts that equaled those of any period highlighted these years.

Captain Steve Kaseta's 1977 team lost its two nonleague games but sprinted to a 3-0 Ivy start. In one of those nonleague losses, a 38-21 defeat by Colgate, split end Jim Curry hauled in a record-tying 13 passes and Brian Buckley was 20 of 40 for 250 yards in one half. Three quarterbacks—Buckley, Burke St. John, and Larry Brown—were used in that game as Restic searched for a replacement to Tim Davenport, a senior, who was lost for the year with an opening-game neck injury.

Restic found his man in junior Larry Brown. A star pitcher on the baseball team, Brown proved to be just the leader that Restic's Multiflex needed.

"People told me that Larry Brown would never be quarterback," said Restic. "And then he went out and set records."

In the season's biggest win, a 31-25 mastering of Dartmouth, Harvard gained 277 yards on the ground as Brown led drives of 65, 76, 71, 75, and 76 yards. In a 34-15 win over Penn, Brown set a Harvard single-game passing record of 349 yards. A good piece of that yardage came in TD strikes to Curry of 51 and 79 yards.

In 1978 the 4-4-1 mark was a half game better, but the Ivy record dropped to 2-4-1. Again, the team was 3-2 after five games but stumbled down the stretch.

Two offensive players distinguished themselves throughout the year, halfback Ralph Polillio and quarterback Brown. Polillio led the team in rushing and receiving, while Brown set single-season records for passing and total offense.

The season's biggest win was, for the fifth year in a row, Dartmouth. But perhaps the best-remembered game was a tough 35-28 loss to Yale in the Stadium.

Yale led by 35-14 as the fourth quarter started, but Brown and his rifle arm were not through. In the final game of his career, Brown threw for 301 yards and four touchdowns to become Harvard's all-time passing leader. The last two of those TD strikes went to Rich Horner and John Macleod, to make the score 35-28 with six minutes remaining in the game.

Restic found two great quarterbacks in Jim Stoeckel '74 (top right) *and Milt Holt '75.*

But on this tenth anniversary of the 29-29 affair, there would be no miracle finish. Yale never let Larry Brown touch the ball again, as the Elis kept possession for the final 5:51.

The 1979 campaign could have been titled "The Agony and the Ecstasy," for it was made up of two clearly defined acts.

The season started innocently enough with a 26-7 win at Columbia behind new quarterback Burke St. John, an able successor to Larry Brown.

Then the roof caved in. St. John went down with a knee injury in a loss to Massachusetts. His replacement, Mike Buchanan, broke his jaw in a loss to Boston University. *His* replacement, Mike Smerczynski, sprained an ankle in a loss to Cornell.

A Restic team with quarterback problems is a team in trouble. This squad, which had started the year without ineligible quarterback Brian Buckley, lost four more starters and, in the process, lost six straight games.

It was following the sixth loss that the *Boston Globe* ran a major story titled "Trouble by the Yard," an examination of Harvard's football woes that looked well beyond injured quarterbacks. Written by John Powers, the article suggested, among other items, that Harvard was simply not attracting the same level of athletic talent it once did.

The team reacted emotionally. The combination of the article, the schedule, and the law of averages resulted in a 41-26 explosion against Pennsylvania on the season's eighth Saturday. Everything went right for Harvard, which was paced by three touchdown passes from a rehabilitated St. John to Rich Horner. Both players would earn All-Ivy status.

In this season of troubles, Horner quietly became Harvard's third leading pass receiver, behind McInally and Curry. His 40 catches in 1979 also marked the third best season ever for a Harvard receiver.

If the horrors of the losing streak defined Act I of this season, the final two weeks marked Act II. As enjoyable as the Penn win was, it could not compare with what followed.

The Yale Bowl was packed on November 17 to see an 8-0 Yale team host a 2-6 Harvard squad. In 1968 and again in 1974, Harvard teams had spoiled a Yale bid for a

You need a good quarterback to lead Joe Restic's Multiflex: two of the best were Jim Kubacki '77 (top) and Larry Brown '79.

perfect season. But those were strong Harvard teams and the games were in Cambridge.

Little matter to the 1979 Crimson, who carried the emotion over from week eight in Cambridge to week nine in New Haven. Behind a "Star Is Born" effort from sophomore fullback Jim Callinan, Harvard pulled off a 22-7 upset of Yale to conclude the most successful 3-6 season in the school's history.

"If I ever had a team whose character was reflected in one game, it was that team and that game," Restic would say later.

Yale, which had given up an average of just 65 yards a game on the ground, saw Harvard rush for 64 on the opening 17-play, 74-yard TD drive. Callinan gained most of those yards, and it was Callinan who caught a 23-yard TD pass later in the quarter to make it 13-0 Harvard. The team never looked back.

The defense shared the glory that day, causing a veteran Yale offense to fumble six times. Defensive back Jon Casto recovered a pair of those fumbles as he was joined by linebackers Matt Sabetti and Bob Woolway and All-Ivy end Chuck Durst in a superlative team effort.

1980–81: Picking up where its predecessor left off, the 1980 team started quickly and was 4-0 early until another string of quarterback injuries surfaced. The team was exciting on both sides of the ball. Fullback Callinan was the most powerful running back the program had enjoyed in years. Southpaw Brian Buckley looked smooth at quarterback. And a former high school phenom from Los Angeles named Ron Cuccia had made the switch from quarterback to receiver with a great deal of fanfare.

On defense, an aggressive secondary and a veteran line provided cause for optimism. One player who stood out was captain Chuck Durst, an All-Ivy defensive end whom defensive coordinator George Clemens called "the best I've coached in thirty years."

Wins over Columbia and Holy Cross paved the way for the season's most satisfying triumph, a 15-10 victory at Army in the renewal of a series that had been dormant for 29 years. Four interceptions—two by Rocky Delgadillo—and a pair of touchdowns by Buckley paced the victory. Known more for his passing, Buckley showed some fancy footwork with his two scores, one a 67-yard dash and the other a 1-yard plunge.

But the artificial surface of Michie Stadium was both kind and cruel to Buckley. Following his early-game

Jim Callinan celebrates the beginning of one of Harvard's greatest upset wins ever. That was 1979's 22-7 win at Yale, engineered by Callinan and a stingy Harvard defense. Entering the game, Yale was 8-0, Harvard just 2-6.

success, the senior quarterback suffered a knee injury and left the contest in the last period.

With junior Mike Buchanan at quarterback against Cornell, Harvard won its fourth straight, 20-12. But in a monsoon at Dartmouth on the season's fifth week, there was a strange sense of déjà vu.

First, Buchanan suffered an ankle injury and was replaced by Mark Marion. When Marion failed to move the club, Ron Cuccia came in, and the flashy sophomore got things going. But a pulled hamstring shortened his stint, and Marion reentered to finish up. The result was a 30-12 Dartmouth win.

Following a loss to Princeton, Buckley returned to the lineup to toss two TD strikes in a 17-16 victory over Brown, the first of three straight wins for the Crimson. After William and Mary and Penn fell, The Game '80 was to be played for the Ivy League title.

The defense performed well against Yale, but the

When the Harvard-Army series was renewed in 1980 after a 30-year lapse, the Harvard defense put on a show. Keys to the 15-10 Crimson victory were defensive linemen Chuck Durst (72) and Dave Otto (94), above, *and defensive back Rocky Delgadillo (17), who takes off with the first two interceptions.*

offense managed only 130 yards in a 14-0 defeat, and the Ivy championship belonged to the Elis. The defensive unit, molded by Coach Clemens, was recognized with the naming of cornerback Delgadillo and end Durst as first team All-Ivy selections. Placekicker Dave Cody joined them.

In the record book the 1981 season seems very ordinary. The team's 5-4-1 record developed in three phases. First came an up-and-down 2-3 start, followed by a promising 3-0-1 stretch, and then a 28-0 loss to Yale, the second straight shutout by the Elis.

Former schoolboy standout Ron Cuccia was now running the offense, and the showy Southern Californian was brilliant at times and frustrating at others. He moved the team best when he simply gave the football to fullback Jim Callinan. The hero of the 1979 Yale game enjoyed a record-breaking season, few afternoons showcasing his

talents more than the Princeton game, in which he ran for 190 yards on a record 34 carries.

Against Penn, the senior fullback gained 188 yards on just 15 carries and scored on runs of 66, 68, and 9 yards. He also caught six passes for 86 yards in Harvard's 45-7 waltz.

His final carry of the day produced that 66-yard touchdown and also broke Dick Clasby's 30-year single-season rushing mark. Callinan, with 994 yards at that point, had bettered Clasby's 950.

The 1981 Harvard-Yale game had the makings of a great one. Harvard was 4-1-1 in the league and Yale was 5-1. Harvard had Callinan and Yale had Rich Diana. But in the end Harvard had little to cheer about, with Yale a 28-0 victor. While Diana scored twice, Callinan was held to 60 yards, numbers good enough to make him Harvard's first 1,000-yard back. The actual total was 1,054, shattering Clasby's old mark.

Callinan made All-Ivy along with two men who opened holes for him, offensive tackle Greg Brown and offensive guard Mike Corbat. For the second straight year, cornerback Rocky Delgadillo was a first-teamer as well.

The on-field results in 1981 had been successful by most standards, 5-4-1 overall and 4-2-1 in a balanced league. But whispers suggested otherwise. Alumni worried aloud about those two Yale shutouts. Whispers grew louder in the spring when a group of disgruntled seniors went public with some complaints, for the most part directed at Joe Restic and his manner of dealing with individuals. Campus and Boston papers picked up the story, and soon wire services made it national.

Others on the team spoke out in defense of the program, and the issue quickly fell from the headlines. Restic, clearly bothered by the publicity surrounding the incident, answered back in a most effective way. His 1982 and 1983 teams went out and grabbed a share of the Ivy title.

1982–84: The 1982 season may go down as the Year of The Call. It was also the year that the University of Pennsylvania returned to the Ivy League's upper echelon. The two stories are not unrelated.

The season started with a 27-16 win over Columbia fashioned by a pair of quarterbacks, Don Allard and Ron Cuccia. Allard had shown flashes of brilliance in two years of reserve roles. Cuccia, a natural with so much potential, had spent his Harvard career in search of the right stage to perform on.

The fate of these two individuals and the team was determined on the season's second Saturday, when the University of Massachusetts fell by 31-14. On that day, Donald Allard, Jr., son of former Boston College and Boston Patriot quarterback Donald, Sr., completed 18 of 29 passes for two scores and a school record 358 yards. On that day, Cuccia became a wide receiver.

After missing the Dartmouth game (a 14-12 Big Green win) with a shoulder injury, Allard returned against Princeton and threw for 231 yards in a 27-15 victory. It was Harvard's first win over the Tigers since 1976 and kept the Crimson in Ivy contention at 3-1. It also allowed the defense to shine, particularly the secondary, which picked off 6 of Brent Woods's 56 pass attempts.

While Allard was creating most of the headlines, the

On April 21, 1981, Harvard Stadium received some unwanted out-of-season attention when the press box was destroyed by fire. The rebuilding cost more than the stadium itself had cost nearly 80 years earlier.

defense was quietly producing some superstars. The linebacking tandem of Joe Azelby and Andy Nolan, when healthy, was the league's best. The secondary, which picked off six more passes in a 34-0 blanking of Brown, had mastered big play defense with style. Perhaps the flashiest of this group was cornerback John Dailey, who had six interceptions in a three-week period against Princeton, Brown, and Holy Cross. Dailey would also set single-game and single-season records for punt returns before he was through.

The Holy Cross game further established Allard's leadership abilities, as he engineered a 24-17 upset against a strong Crusader eleven. All he did was throw for 150 yards and run for another 112 yards, 44 of those on a second-quarter touchdown dash. Mike Ernst's 4-yard TD plunge won the game with 17 seconds showing on the clock.

The Holy Cross victory brought Harvard to Philadelphia tied for first with the revived Quakers of Penn. Just how revived they were became clear when it was 20-0 for Penn entering the fourth quarter.

But in classic Ivy fashion, Harvard came to life in a big way. In a span of seven and a half minutes, Allard fired TD strikes to Pete Quartararo and Steve Ernst (Mike's brother) and watched Mike Granger run in another score from the 4. Jim Villanueva's three placements were good, and with a minute and a half to go, it was 21-20, Harvard.

However, Penn wasn't through. Using all the remaining time, the Quakers moved into Harvard territory and faced a 38-yard field goal attempt on the game's last play. With no time left on the clock, Dave Shulman's kick went wide and it appeared that Harvard was the victor.

But the celebration stopped abruptly—and emotionally—when a referee's flag indicated roughing the kicker. The Harvard sideline, most notably Joe Restic, was incensed. The feelings grew worse when Shulman, given a second chance from the 27-yard line, made his kick good and gave Penn a 23-21 victory.

Restic smoldered for a week, publicly challenging the official's call and showing game films to the media. At one point, he went so far as to suggest that Penn relinquish the victory.

"I can still see our kids in the dressing room after the game," recalled Restic, three years after the incident. "Total devastation. But the thing that stands out in my mind is how they were strong enough to come back and beat Yale for a piece of the title."

The two-year scoring drought against Yale ended with the most points ever scored by a Harvard team against the

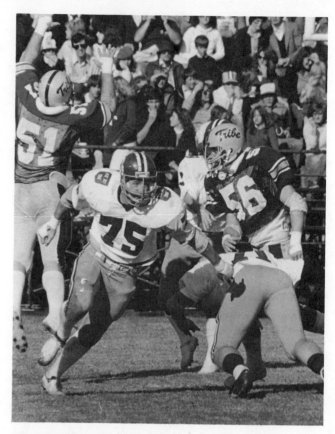

Recognition came to Harvard's offensive line in 1982 when Mike Corbat (75) was selected to the Division 1AA All-American team as an offensive guard.

Elis, as Harvard breezed, 45-7. While seven different players scored points for the offense, the defense enjoyed its finest moment, holding Yale to a minus 12 yards rushing and just 116 yards in total offense.

The game will also be remembered for the ingenuity and timing of some students who weren't in uniform and, in fact, who didn't even attend Harvard or Yale. A group of MIT students made national headlines when a giant black balloon that they had buried under the playing field sometime before game day emerged from under the turf during the first half.

Activated by remote control, the mysterious object rose from the ground during a break in play and soon had everyone's attention until it burst to a large round of applause. If the game had not been so one-sided, the incident might not have been received so lightly.

Making the day even more memorable for Harvard was late news that Cornell had upset Penn to create a three-way Ivy tie between Harvard, Penn, and Dartmouth.

A record seven Harvard players grabbed first team All-Ivy berths. The workers were rewarded as offensive linemen Mike Corbat and Greg Brown were joined by defensive ends Pat Fleming and Joe Margolis, middle guard Scott Murrer, adjuster Lou Varsames, and linebacker Joe Azelby, later a Buffalo Bills draft choice. Corbat was also chosen on the Division 1AA All-American team.

Though left off the All-Ivy squad, quarterback Allard left his name in the record books. His 1,870 yards of total offense set a new Harvard standard, and his overall leadership was recognized when he shared the William J. Bingham Award with hockey's Mark Fusco as the top athlete in his class.

The 1983 team survived a Jekyll and Hyde start to finish strong and grab another share of the Ivy title. Replacing skill people, particularly at quarterback, seemed to pose the squad's biggest problem.

Kicker Jim Villanueva, split end John O'Brien, and running backs Mark Vignali and Steve Ernst were the offensive mainstays of this team. Vignali was capable of the big effort, as evidenced by his 39-carry, 172-yard performance against Army, a 24-21 Harvard win.

When Dartmouth beat Harvard for the fifth straight time, the quarterback situation was still unsettled. But signs of hope emerged that afternoon from the late-game efforts of senior Greg Gizzi. The unheralded reserve directed Harvard's final touchdown against Dartmouth and earned a starting assignment against Princeton. With that adjustment, the season turned.

Gizzi led Harvard to a pair of wins over Princeton and Brown that made Harvard a sudden Ivy contender. Against the Tigers, Gizzi threw for 143 yards, ran for 87 more, and scored two TDs. At the same time, senior Steve Ernst was emerging as a major offensive force, rushing for 115 yards against Princeton. At Brown, these two combined on a 69-yard screen pass with 58 seconds remaining to pull out a 17-10 thriller. Ernst ran for 101 yards in that one.

A hard-fought 10-10 tie against undefeated Holy Cross kept up the momentum before a grudge match with Ivy rival Penn. The emotions of the previous year's controversy came into play in a sweet 28-0 verdict for Harvard.

"This was a tribute to all the people who took part in both games," said Restic. "I told them after the game that in my estimation, the scoreboard read, 'Paid In Full.'"

The defense, led by linebackers Joe Azelby and Andy Nolan and the likes of Morgan Rector, Mark Mead, and Barry Ford up front, continued its season-long brilliance that day. Offensively, Ernst had another 100-yard game and Gizzi scored another pair of touchdowns.

Next was Yale and all the hoopla of the 100th game in the series. The pregame festivities included 66 former

Co-winner of the 1983 Bingham Award as the school's top athlete was quarterback Donnie Allard. The Winchester native's 358 yards against Massachusetts in 1982 set a Harvard single-game passing mark.

Harvard and Yale captains parading on the field and having the game ball delivered by parachute. All of this happened on a sunlit day before some 75,000 spectators who paid $20 per ticket. Harvard thus shared in the Ivy League's first million-dollar gate, a far cry from the $70 Harvard brought back from New Haven in 1875.

Once the game started it was clear that Harvard was the superior team, but the Crimson had trouble proving it on the scoreboard. The defense smothered the Yale attack—the Elis had minus 22 yards rushing in the first half—but the score was 7-7 entering the fourth quarter.

Finally, Harvard broke through with 9 points in the

Linebacker Joe Azelby (50), above, *was drafted by the Buffalo Bills of the National Football League after leading Harvard to Ivy League cochampionships in 1982 and 1983.*

fourth quarter to take a 16-7 win and a share of the Ivy League title with Pennsylvania. In the end, it was a game won like so many others that year: Gizzi ran for 97 yards and threw for 94 more; Ernst picked up 113 yards on the ground; and the entire defense was superb throughout.

Team MVP Ernst joined some elite company, as his 761 yards rushing ranked fourth behind the best seasons of Jim Callinan, Dick Clasby, and Bobby Leo.

All-Ivy recognition went to six players. Offensively, Ernst was joined by tackle Roger Caron and placekicker/punter Jim Villanueva (recognized in both areas). Linebacker Joe Azelby, cornerback Mike Dixon, and end Mark Mead represented the defense.

The title was Penn's alone in 1984. The Quakers made sure of that when they dismantled a good Harvard team, 38-7, at Franklin Field. This Harvard team, led by the running of Robert Santiago and Mark Vignali, was the first to go 5-0 in the league since the 1974 squad. But in 1974 the team finished at 6-1 and shared the league crown. The 1984 edition stumbled twice, first to Penn and then to Yale (30-27), to end the season empty-handed.

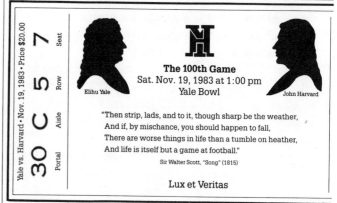

The Harvard-Yale football game, The Game *to the Harvards and Yales, has always been a big event, as reflected in these tickets. Note the effect of inflation, as 1894 ticket (left) sold for $2.50 and 1983 ticket, for the 100th meeting of the schools, sold for $20.*

Ice Hockey

In March of 1983 a talented Harvard hockey team arrived in Grand Forks, North Dakota, for the 36th annual NCAA championships. For many of the players it was an eye-opening experience. Not so much from any on-ice happenings but from the way the Harvards were received in the West.

As one local columnist put it in his tournament preview. "And then there's Harvard. I don't recall anybody asking for a lawyer!"

Harvard University, for better or for worse, has certainly produced its share of lawyers in over 350 years. It has also produced its share of outstanding hockey teams and individuals since 1895, when American ice hockey began in New England.

IN THE BEGINNING THERE WAS HARVARD

Those pundits in North Dakota were obviously unaware of the relationship between Harvard and the game so many

claim as their own. In the beginning there was Harvard. And its contributions to amateur ice hockey in this country continue to the present.

To be exact, the beginning was January 19, 1898. On that day Harvard hosted Brown University in what is generally considered to be the first intercollegiate ice hockey game ever. The site was Franklin Field in Boston, and the final score was Brown 6, Harvard 0. The visiting Bruins enjoyed a clear territorial advantage, outshooting Harvard by 21-2 in the contest. Keeping the score down was Harvard's first hockey star, "goal tend" Fred Russell '99, who came up with 15 saves for the Crimson.

In its account of the historic contest, the *Brown Daily Herald* attributed the Harvard defeat to "lack of headwork and method." No, the press has not always been kind.

For the record, be it noted that this was not the first time Harvard and Brown had competed on ice. The historic hockey game was preceded by two years of ice polo between the schools. (Ice polo was a wide-open game, played with a hard rubber ball instead of a puck. There were no limits to the rink, nor were there any offside rules.) In 1895 the Harvard Ice Polo Association was formed by F. S. Eliot '95 and J. W. Dunlop '97 while a similar group was being organized in Providence.

In February of 1896, Brown defeated Harvard by the score of 5-4 in an ice polo game on Spy Pond in Arlington. A year later the Bruins prevailed again, this time at Roger Williams Park in Providence. The score was 5-0.

1898–1918: Attracted by the faster game of ice hockey played in Canada, the Harvard Ice Polo Association became the Harvard Ice Hockey Association in 1898. The first team was formed that year, losing 6-0 to Brown in college hockey's inaugural game.

Those college teams played a game quite different from today's. There were seven men to a side, as four forwards skated in front of two defensemen (known then as the point and cover-point) and the goalie.

Evidence suggests that the game was every bit as rough as the worst of what might be seen today. Equipment was in a constant state of development and improvement, with Harvard in the forefront of a number of innovations.

Influencing many of the changes was the man who dominated much of Harvard hockey's first two decades, Alfred Winsor '02. Winsor was a member of the 1901 and 1902 teams, being elected captain of the latter. Upon graduation he became Harvard's first head coach and compiled a record of 124 wins and just 29 defeats from 1902 to 1917.

As it was in other sports at that time, Yale became the chief hockey rival early. Harvard's first meeting with Yale took place on February 26, 1900, at the St. Nick's Rink in New York. It was a black-tie affair for Harvard and Yale followers. Yale won, 5-4.

That same year Harvard's first outdoor rink was constructed on Holmes Field near the site of the present law school. Yale and Princeton enjoyed the benefits of the St. Nick's Rink, but Harvard would struggle with a number of facilities before enjoying its own.

In 1901 a rink was built at Soldiers Field, but the players preferred the Holmes Field facility and continued to play there. Two years later Harvard Stadium was built, and the hockey players could at least enjoy their first indoor locker facility. A pair of rinks were constructed with their length running from sideline to sideline and the Stadium became the home of Harvard Hockey for seven years.

Finally, in 1910, the first Boston Arena was built and, like chief rivals Princeton and Yale, Harvard had an indoor facility to call home. Perhaps the best Crimson player of this early period, S. Trafford Hicks, was graduated that year.

On March 14, 1913, the Athletic Committee voted to make ice hockey a major sport. A year later, the committee recognized Harvard's pioneer hockey players and chief rival Yale with the decree that "the Hockey H be awarded to all men who have ever played for Harvard against Yale."

One of the most memorable games of that period took place on January 24, 1914, when Harvard hosted Princeton and the legendary Hobey Baker at Boston Arena. Tied at 1-1 after regulation time, the teams battled through more than 40 minutes of overtime before a spare forward for Harvard scored the game-winning goal. He was Leverett Saltonstall '14, later the distinguished governor and U.S. Senator from Massachusetts, who banged home a rebound off the stick of classmate Paul Smart, later an Olympic gold medal winner in sailing.

Winsor's Harvard coaching career came to an end after the 1917 season, when World War I interrupted college athletics. He later resumed his coaching and directed the U.S. Olympic hockey team at Lake Placid in 1932, gaining a silver medal when Canada nipped the United States 2-1 in the final.

Among his many contributions to the game, Winsor was the first to pair his defensemen side by side. He explains:

In the first years, the two defence players stayed fairly close to the goal, one behind the other, and the first man used to skate out at the attacking man combination with the intention of checking them with his body or stick. If the first man, the "cover-point," missed, the second man, or "point," tried his luck. This method was found very faulty as the clever dodger had a chance to dodge each man consecutively and the defence had no chance whatever to stop a clever passing game. Gradually the defence was widened out until the "point" and "cover-point" were playing side by side or parallel. This move was a very great success and it became almost impossible for one opponent to get through and the passing game had to be very accurately executed in order to be successful.

1919–45: The postwar hockey team had to make a couple of adjustments. First, the original Boston Arena was destroyed by fire, putting Harvard hockey outdoors for the next three years. Second, Alfred Winsor was gone.

But the team returned in a big way, going undefeated in

The styles were different, but this Harvard hockey team (above) shared future teams' reputation for excellence. With a 3-0 record, the 1901 squad fashioned the first of Harvard's seven undefeated seasons.

When Harvard Stadium was completed in 1903, the hockey team had its first campus facility with locker rooms.

1919 behind the captain and coach Robert Gross '19. A senior forward on this team was Alexander H. Bright, later an Olympic skier, for whom the present Harvard rink is named.

Bill Claflin took over as head coach in 1920. His four-year record of 29-8 would include 6-0 and 8-1 advantages over Princeton and Yale respectively.

The 1921 season was good to Harvard. Yale was beaten by 7-0 and 13-1 scores, thanks to goalie Jabish Holmes '21 and classmates Ned Bigelow and Francis Bacon, and a new Boston Arena was constructed.

A year later a major rules change made hockey a six-man game, as the fourth forward was dropped. Harvard's best in this period was George Owen, a future Boston Bruin, who dazzled opponents en route to a nine-letter career (football, hockey, baseball). On Owen's suggestion, Claflin tried a new tactic in 1923. During games the coach would rest an entire forward line at a

Left: *Nine-letter winner George Owen (shown in the University Club uniform) went from Harvard to the Boston Bruins, where he was team captain.*

Right: *Coach Joe Stubbs poses with his star forward and captain John Chase. Chase, a member of the U.S. Olympic team in 1932, served as Harvard's head coach from 1942 to 1950.*

time instead of resting just individuals when they were tired. This practice was soon adopted throughout college hockey.

In 1924 Ned Bigelow became Harvard's fourth head coach. One of his best was Clark Hodder, a future Harvard coach himself. Hodder the player is best remembered for his amazing display of stamina in the final Yale game of his senior year. It was on February 25, 1925, that defenseman Hodder played all 90 minutes of a tough 1-0 overtime loss to the Elis.

With the 1927–28 season, Joe Stubbs began his 11-year rule as head coach and inherited the senior class of captain John Chase '28. Chase, the captain of the 1932 U.S. Olympic hockey team, later coached Harvard. His three playing years saw Harvard go 9-4, 10-1-2, and 9-2-1, records that included six straight wins against chief rival Yale.

College hockey enjoyed immense popularity entering the 1930s. Nowhere was this more evident than on March

1930, when Harvard met Yale at the Boston Garden. With 14,000 spectators on hand, the two teams battled to a 2-2 tie before a city curfew suspended play.

The rules changes continued the next year when the forward pass was introduced to the game. Prior to the 1931 season, players could only advance the puck by carrying it forward, and all passes had to be lateral or backward.

The leading player of this period was John Garrison '31, later a member of the 1932 and 1936 Olympic teams and coach of the 1948 squad. He would eventually be inducted into the U.S. Hockey Hall of Fame. Harvard's great all-around athlete and ten-letter winner Barry Wood earned his third and final hockey letter in 1932.

The new game of the 1930s put the goalies on the spot. And Harvard had one of its best ever in this period. On December 22, 1933, goaltender Paul deB. deGive '34 recorded 70 saves in an 8-1 loss at McGill. This effort was completed only after the game was halted for 40 minutes as deGive had his face stitched up.

In 1936 forward and captain Fred Moseley led Harvard to a 14-4 mark and two wins over Yale for the first time in eight years. It was the following year's team that set the standard for the period. Harvard was 15-1 in 1937, the only loss a 7-2 defeat to McGill at the Montreal Forum. Canadian universities like McGill and Toronto were proving to be among Harvard's toughest rivals at this time.

Clark Hodder returned to Harvard as head coach for the 1938–39 season. The best remembered contest from

John Garrison earned a spot in the U.S. Hockey Hall of Fame as a Harvard standout, a playing member of the 1932 and 1936 Olympic teams, and coach of the 1948 Olympic team.

his inaugural season was the finale, a 7-3 win over Yale at Boston Garden. Austie Harding closed out his career by playing 58 minutes and scoring four of the last five goals of the game. Brothers Goodwin '43 (a goalie) and William '46 (a winger) would follow Austie to Harvard, and Goodwin would captain the 1948 Olympic team.

Following that 15-1 team of 1937, Harvard hockey suffered a minidrought. That ended in 1942, when captain Greely Summers led Harvard to its first winning record (10-9) in five years.

Hodder stepped down in mid-season in 1942, and John Chase took over. Chase's first full season was a smash, as the Crimson outscored the opposition by 150-54 en route to a 14-3-1 campaign. The tie was a standing-room-only affair at the Boston Arena on February 20, 1943, against Dartmouth, the era's leading hockey power. Dartmouth had won 33 straight, including two against Harvard earlier that season.

Just as Harvard hockey seemed ready for a renaissance, World War II put an end to college athletics across the country.

• • •

LEARNING AND WINNING WITH COONEY

1946–55: Nearly 180 candidates turned out for practice when the 1946–47 season began. A different sort of rebuilding process took place with 18-to-21-year-old undergraduates joined by 24-to-26-year-old war veterans. Progress was slow as the five postwar years produced an even .500 record, 51-51-2.

Up to this point, every Harvard hockey coach had been a former Crimson iceman. In 1950 all that would change in a big way.

The 1949–50 Harvard team finished a 10-8 season with a 2-1 win over Yale. It was a fitting finale for John Chase, who completed his coaching tenure with that game. The war had complicated his task, but the Harvard program had moved within striking distance of the game's best teams once again.

The remainder of that distance would have to be traveled by a new coach. And when the selection process began, few anticipated that some very traditional people would tab a very untraditional candidate. In the spring of 1950 Director of Athletics Bill Bingham announced that Harvard's new hockey coach was Ralph "Cooney" Weiland, a former player and coach in the National Hockey League. Weiland's hockey credentials were impeccable. As a player, he once scored 43 goals in 44 games while leading the 1928–29 Bruins to their first Stanley Cup. A member of Boston's second Stanley Cup team in 1938–39, Weiland went on to coach the Bruins to their third cup success in 1941.

But a non-Harvard man as head coach? And a former pro at that? This marriage was going to need some time.

"The first year I came to Harvard," Weiland later recalled, "I was right out of the pro circles. It was quite different, the whole concept of hockey. Kids were very puck conscious. They didn't know too much about playing position, and it took me a better part of the year to change things. Most of them thought they could score the minute they got the puck. One guy would go as far as he could with it, then another guy would pick it up and go as far as he could with it, and so on."

Weiland and Harvard learned how to get along through two building-block seasons with 12-11 and 8-11 records. Then things picked up with the 1952–53 season. Captain Walt Greeley '53, along with Amory Hubbard '53, Normie Wood '54, and a strong group of sophomores, led

Harvard to an 11-5-1 record, two losses coming at the hands of Ivy Champ Brown.

One highlight of the successful campaign came on back-to-back nights in December. That was when a pair of victories, 3-2 (OT) over Boston College and 7-4 over Boston University, gave Harvard the first Beanpot championship. Brad Richardson '53 had 36 saves in the final and tournament MVP Greeley had the hat trick.

At the time, the Beanpot Hockey Tournament was considered little more than another Boston Arena doubleheader for area schools Harvard, Boston College, Boston University, and Northeastern. When it moved to the Boston Garden the following season and only 711 people watched the opener, it seemed even less significant. By the time the 30th Beanpot was played in 1982, it was simply the most successful in-season college hockey tournament in the country.

The 1953–54 squad went 10-11-2, but the numbers were deceptive. Captain Normie Wood and company lost 8 of their first 11, including 6 straight out west to Minnesota, Colorado, and Denver. After Christmas the team went 7-3-2 and signaled greater successes to come.

One of the reasons for the second-half surge was the late arrival of a former schoolboy star by the name of Bill Cleary. A local phenom out of Cambridge and Belmont Hill, Cleary came to Harvard in the fall of 1952 and immediately made his presence felt. As captain of the

freshman team Cleary scored 36 goals and 35 assists in the Yardlings' 15-1 season.

But when it appeared that this talent would leap to the varsity, he was ruled academically ineligible for the first half of the 1953–54 season. Following midyear exams, Cleary immediately made up for lost time. After a slow start, a goal and an assist in wins over Dartmouth and Brown, Cleary scored ten goals in the final six games of the season. Six of the goals came via hat tricks against Princeton and Yale. In two games against Yale, 3-3 and 5-5 stalemates, Cleary had five goals.

The ties evened the H-Y series for the year, but the Crimson took the league title on points. It was the first of eight Ivy championships under Cooney Weiland's direction.

The 1954–55 season ranks with the best that any Harvard team has ever enjoyed. The brilliance that Bill Cleary revealed over 8 games the year before would go on display for a full 21-game season. Charlie Flynn '56 would emerge as an All-American goaltender, and captain Scott Cooledge '55 would lead Joe Crehore '56, Mario Celi '56, Terry O'Malley '57, and others to a 17-3-1 mark and Harvard's first NCAA tournament appearance.

The team's only losses came at the hands of Boston College (later avenged twice), McGill, and eventual NCAA champ Michigan. The regular season brought a Beanpot championship, an Ivy League title, and a national scoring title for All-American Bill Cleary.

Cleary's 42 goals and 47 assists gave him 89 points, a national record at the time and one that remains a school mark. He scored 6 against Providence, 5 against Northeastern, 4 against Princeton, and hat tricks on three other occasions. After being shut out back-to-back by St. Lawrence and McGill early in the year, Cleary scored at least 1 goal (34 in all) in each of the remaining 15 contests.

Unlike many high scorers, who feed on the weaker teams on a schedule, Cleary was there when it mattered. In the NCAA tournament, he had two goals in the 7-3 opening-round loss to Michigan. In the consolation game, Cleary's three goals provided the margin of victory in a 6-3 win over St. Lawrence. No Harvard team would better this third-in-the-nation finish until the 1983 squad finished second.

Bill Cleary scores another goal despite being tightly checked. The leading scorer in the nation in 1955 with 89 points, Cleary went on to play in both the 1956 and 1960 Olympic Games and became head coach at Harvard in 1971.

But of all Billy Cleary's college goals, none is more fondly remembered than the one that so dramatically ended the 1955 Beanpot final. With time running out in regulation play, Harvard held a 4-2 lead over defending champ Boston College. It was a lead that vanished in a minute and nine seconds when BC captain Dick Dempsey scored a pair of goals, the latter on a power play with just six seconds to play.

The momentum was with the high-flying Eagles as they began overtime with Harvard still shorthanded. It was in this setting that Cleary created another memory for the 6,000 Boston Garden fans. Killing the penalty effectively, Clearly stole a loose puck and raced in alone on BC goalie Chuck D'Entremont. With the quick deke that rarely failed him, Cleary slipped the puck past D'Entremont for the unassisted goal that won the title. With seven goals and four assists in the tournament, Cleary was an easy MVP choice.

Cooney Weiland

In January of 1985 a reunion of former Beanpot Hockey Tournament participants was held at Harvard's Bright Hockey Center. Each of the four schools was represented by a score of alumni over 30 years of age, and even a few Beanpot coaches returned. One of these was an 80-year-old gentleman who took the train up from Florida.

"Cooney, what's your pregame strategy going to be for this tournament?" someone asked the man.

"To keep quiet," snapped Cooney Weiland with a grin.

Ralph "Cooney" Weiland. There he was, 14 years after his retirement, recreating the memories. Wearing that old hat, trench coat, and dark-rimmed glasses. Breaking everyone up with short, snappy comebacks.

The image of Cooney that lingers is that of a real character. He was the guy who forgot his own players' names. He was the guy, concerned about Boston University's Dick Rodenheiser, telling his players to "watch that Eisenhower." He was the coach who eschewed pep talks and simply opened the gate and let his boys play.

But it is an image that, while not altogether inaccurate, undercuts the genius of the man. This was a National Hockey League Hall of Famer, a Stanley Cup winner as both player and coach, who entered a strange new world and continued his winning ways. At Harvard, Cooney won 315 games over 21 seasons. And he did so by being more than just a character.

"He was hard to get to know, and he didn't say very much," remembers Bill Cleary. "But he taught us a lot about life and a lot about hockey. He really appreciated the skill and beauty of the game and taught me the way it should be played. Fifteen years after I followed him, I still used his drills at practice."

Tim Taylor, captain of Cooney's 1963 ECAC champs and later head coach at Yale, recalls Cooney's way of preparing a team.

"Whenever I think in terms of Cooney, I think

Ralph "Cooney" Weiland as a member of the Boston Bruins in the 1930s.

Coach Weiland in his familiar spot on the Harvard bench, from which he directed the Crimson to 315 victories in 21 seasons.

His manner was rough to young players who could not figure him out. Conversations were brief or nonexistent. When a mistake was made on the ice, there were no scenes, no tongue-lashings. Cooney would make one well-timed remark and it would stay with a player.

Like the time the sophomore goalie responded to a bad day at practice by heaving his stick into the old Watson Rink balcony. Cooney skated toward the young goaltender, who braced for a verbal assault. Without stopping or establishing eye contact, the coach said simply, "Can't play goal without a stick," and continued past the crease.

"People thought he was unemotional," said Cleary. "But they didn't understand him. The wheels were turning all the time. He always saw something in a hockey player that no one else did."

Some of Cooney's friends held a party for him in 1985 when he turned 80. Just how much the "wheels were turning" became clear when it came his turn to speak. He recalled names and situations that revealed how much he took in during his years at Harvard. *

Harvard became a part of this old pro. And he became part of Harvard.

• • •

of our teams in the early sixties. I remember practicing, how frustrating it was. It was impossible just to score a goal. We practiced the Cooney Weiland way, with a lot of back-checking. You'd get in a game, and it was an entirely different world. Then you'd realize how right Cooney was."

He was a conservative coach who stressed individual skills and fundamental team play. He did not like the changes that affected the game after his retirement. Speaking in 1977, six years after leaving Harvard, Cooney said, "I'm not knocking it, but they've taken the skill out. Anybody can shoot the puck into the corner, race for it, and scoop it in front of the net. I like to see one-on-one. Today, there's so much confusion in front of the net that by the time the goaltender untangles himself, someone has poked it in. I've never seen so many goaltenders on their backs. You don't know half the time who has scored."

1956–59: With the success of the 1955 team, it is little wonder that the Harvard following could barely wait for the 1955–56 season to unfold. Bobby Cleary '58, Bill's brother, led a strong sophomore class to the varsity ranks, and there seemed no limit to what Weiland's sixth team might accomplish.

But the team suffered a major blow early when Bill Cleary was once again ruled ineligible to compete. Instead of thrilling college crowds, Bill Cleary moved on to international play as a member of the 1956 U.S. Olympic team. He never shared the Harvard ice with brother Bob, though the two would team up in 1960 to win Olympic gold at Squaw Valley.

With captain Charlie Flynn in goal, Harvard won its third of five straight Ivy titles en route to a 15-10 season in

---

* *Following a brief illness later that year, Cooney Weiland passed away on July 3, 1985.*

1956. No small contribution was made by the sophomore class, which included John Copeland, Lyle Guttu, Bob McVey, Bob Owen, Dan Ullyot, and the younger Cleary. Cleary and Mario Celi were named to the first formal All-Ivy team.

The highlight of the season was the opening of the Donald C. Watson Rink, Harvard's first indoor hockey facility. The rink was first built in 1954 and operated as an outdoor rink for a season. But the New England weather necessitated immediate improvements.

With an effort organized by Alec Bright '19 and made possible by a gift from John W. Watson '22, the enclosed rink was finished early in 1956. On March 7 of that year, Princeton visited Cambridge for the dedication game. The Tigers were a fitting opponent for the occasion since their Hobey Baker Rink, built in 1923, was college hockey's first indoor rink.

The game lived up to the occasion, as a late goal by John Copeland gave Harvard a well-earned 2-1 victory.

The 1956–57 Crimson team set new standards for Harvard hockey. With a record of 21-5, the team set a single-season win record that lasted 18 years. All six players forming the 1957 All-Ivy team were from Harvard: Cleary, Guttu, and Paul Kelley '59 up front, Copeland and Owen on defense, and captain Jim Bailey '57 in goal.

Bobby Cleary emerged as a star on the national level, being named All-American and winning the national scoring title with 36 goals and 37 assists for 73 points. In the Harvard record book, those 73 points were second only to brother Bill's 89 points in 1954–55.

The 1957–58 team survived a stormy start, losing 8 of 11, to finish 18-10-1 and win its fifth straight Ivy title and another Beanpot crown. After those early losses, 6 to the best of the West, Harvard engineered a 17-game unbeaten streak that showcased the unparalleled class of '58.

As juniors and seniors this group never lost an Ivy League game, an accomplishment seriously jeopardized in their final Dartmouth game. Eddie Jeremiah's Dartmouth team came to Watson Rink in late February and seemed in command when the score read 4-2 for the visitors near the end of the game.

Late goals by Cleary and McVey, the latter with goalie Harry Pratt '59 pulled from the nets and Harvard on a power play, tied the score at 4-4. That is how the game ended, leaving Harvard's streak intact.

Bob (left) and Bill Cleary pose during a quiet moment at Squaw Valley in 1960. Harvard's brother act led the U.S. Olympic team to its first hockey gold medal.

Bob Cleary earned All-Ivy honors for the third straight season, while classmates Guttu and Owen made it two straight. Cleary also earned All-American honors for the second straight year in winning another national scoring title. This effort, 31-41-72, meant that three out of four titles had been won by Clearys.

The 1958–59 squad continued Harvard's winning ways, though not to the extent of its immediate predecessors. The team went 12-9-4 but saw its five-year hold on the Ivy crown broken by an undefeated Dartmouth Squad. The lone Harvard entry to the All-Ivy team was senior forward George Higginbottom, who won the league scoring title.

Harvard Icemen in the Olympics

Harvard has played a major role in the development of amateur hockey in the United States going back to the late 19th century. Nowhere is this more evident than in the records of the Winter Olympic Games.

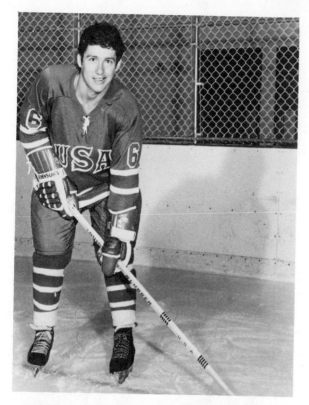

Twenty years before 1980's Miracle at Lake Placid, another U.S. hockey team shocked the world with a gold medal victory at Squaw Valley. That roster featured four Harvard players, including team leading scorer Bill Cleary.

Below is a listing of Harvard men who have made their contributions to the U.S. Olympic team.

Teammates at Harvard, Dan Bolduc (left) and Ted Thorndike teamed up again in 1976 at the Olympic Games at Innsbruck.

HARVARD HOCKEY IN THE OLYMPICS*

YEAR	SITE	NAME	HOMETOWN
1932	Lake Placid	John Chase '28	Boston, MA
		John Garrison '31	Newton, MA
		Alfred Winsor '02 (coach)	Boston, MA
1936	Garmisch-Pártenkirchen	John Garrison '31	Newton, MA
		Frank Stubbs '32	Newton, MA
1948	St. Moritz	John Garrison '31 (coach)	Newton, MA
		Goodwin Harding '43	Brookline, MA
1952	Oslo	Bob Ridder '41 (manager)	St. Paul, MN
1956	Cortina d'Ampezzo	Bill Cleary '56	Cambridge, MA
		Bob Ridder '41 (manager)	St. Paul, MN
1960	Squaw Valley	Bill Cleary '56	Cambridge, MA
		Bob Cleary '58	Cambridge, MA
		Bob McVey '58	Hamden, CT
		Bob Owen '58	St. Louis Park, MN
1976	Innsbruck	Dan Bolduc '76	Waterville, ME
		Ted Thorndike '75	Chestnut Hill, MA
1980	Lake Placid	Jack Hughes '80	Somerville, MA
1984	Sarajevo	Mark Fusco '83	Burlington, MA
		Scott Fusco '85	Burlington, MA

* Information courtesy of the Amateur Hockey Association of the United States (AHAUS).

1960–63: The decade of the 1960s was a strong one for Harvard hockey. The best years were at the beginning and at the very end, interrupted by a brief period of disappointment.

Beginning with the 1959–60 season, Harvard put together five seasons that averaged better than 18 wins a year. It remains arguably the best five-year span of Harvard hockey's modern era.

The first of those teams was captained by Mike Graney and compiled a 16-7-1 record that included the Beanpot title. Three of the losses were to Ivy opponents, which effectively cost the league championship. Making their mark and serving notice for the future were eight sophomores, led by goalie Bob Bland '62 and forwards Dave Grannis '62 and Dave Morse '62.

The record improved to 18-4-2 in 1960–61, as the Crimson ended Dartmouth's two-year hold on the Ivy title. Harvard's defensive strength was reflected in the three Crimson representatives on the All-Ivy team: goalie Bland and defensemen Bob Anderson '62 and Harry Howell '63.

This was a season that started with three painful losses in the first month. Those were at Clarkson and St. Lawrence by scores of 6-5 and 2-1 respectively, and at the Rensselaer Polytechnic Institute Christmas Tournament by 5-3 to RPI. The club then put together a 12-game winning streak that ended in the Beanpot final. That was a 4-2 BC

win before 13,909, the first Boston Garden sellout for college hockey in 30 years. It was also the first of many Beanpot sellouts on Causeway Street.

The game that put Harvard into the final is worthy of mention. The Crimson trailed BU by 2-1 with two minutes remaining when Ted Ingalls caught fire. Two quick goals by the senior forward gave Harvard a 3-2 win and a spot in the final.

The 1961–62 team kept things on the upswing with a 21-5 record that matched the 1957 mark. Ivy League and Beanpot championships resulted from this powerful squad's efforts.

With Bob Bland and Godfrey Wood alternating in goal and Harry Howell and All-American Davey Johnston (later the president of McGill University) on defense, it is little wonder that the team allowed only 54 goals in 26 games.

Up front a new magician was added to the ranks. He was a sophomore from Edmonton, Alberta, named Gene Kinasewich. Having accepted some expense money when he played junior A hockey in Canada before enrolling at Harvard, Kinasewich was ruled ineligible to compete on Harvard's freshman team. Before the start of his

Dave Johnston (4) displayed his leadership qualities as an All-Ivy defenseman at Harvard and later as president of Montreal's McGill University.

sophomore season, the 1961–62 campaign, the Ivy League Committee on Eligibility reviewed his case and gave him the go-ahead to participate.

With this new weapon Harvard outscored opponents 125-54 and set a school record with five shutouts on the season. One of those was a 5-0 blanking of Boston University in the Beanpot final.

The Kinasewich decision wasn't the only off-ice verdict to affect this team. As the season wound down, Harvard's Faculty Committee on Athletic Sports issued a statement declaring that despite its record, Harvard would not be a candidate for the NCAA Tournament. The committee's statement reflected disapproval of western teams whose rosters strained the definition of the word "amateur."

While the NCAA championships were ruled out, Harvard did accept the chance to play in the first tournament offered by the Eastern College Athletic Conference. Harvard hosted Army in its first ECAC playoff game and survived a squeaker when Dave Morse won it in overtime, 2-1.

In the semifinals at the Boston Arena, Harvard raced to a 5-2 lead before the game and season collapsed. Eventual champion St. Lawrence scored four goals in just over two minutes to steal a 6-5 victory. The Crimson regained their poise in the season-ending consolation game, a 2-0 blanking of Colby.

Shortly after the season ended, a magazine article kept Harvard hockey in the news. The story, inaccurately reported, reopened the matter of Gene Kinasewich's hockey past. As a result of the misinformation, the athletic directors composing the ECAC Committee on Eligibility once again ruled Kinasewich ineligible.

The matter was eventually resolved, but not before Kinasewich missed a few games at the start of the 1962–63 season, perhaps Harvard's greatest to that point.

Almost all of the key performers returned from the previous year's 21-5 squad. This one would go 21-3-2, capturing its third straight Ivy title and first ECAC championship. Four players made All-Ivy. There were Davey Johnston, a repeater on defense along with Harry Howell, who had made it as a sophomore, and first-time entries Tim Taylor and Godfrey Wood.

Championship form was displayed early when the team took the Boston Arena Christmas Tournament with wins over BU and Colorado. The latter was a 3-2 overtime affair captured on Bill Lamarche's game-winner.

The Clarkson-St. Lawrence swing through northern New York once again proved too much to overcome, and a 3-1 Beanpot final loss to Boston College added the

season's other setback. From that point the Crimson won their remaining five regular-season games and hungrily awaited the ECAC play-offs.

In the ECAC opener at Watson Rink, Harvard prevailed over Colgate by 5-3 to earn a date at the Boston Arena with Clarkson. The Golden Knights had prevailed by 4-3 in Potsdam in December, but this March rematch went to Harvard in a 6-4 come-from-behind effort.

Then came the final. Hollywood couldn't have scripted this one any better. On one side there is BC the 3-1 conqueror of Harvard in the Beanpot final, led by the red hot-line of Billy Hogan, Paul Aiken, and Jack Leetch and the goaltending of Tommy Apprille. On the other side is Harvard, the 20-3-2 Crimson led by the likes of Kinasewich, Taylor, Howell, Wood and two-time All-American Johnston.

Oh, yes, if any more drama is needed, add the fact that Cooney Weiland is but one victory shy of 200 career wins with the Crimson.

A capacity crowd of 5,900 rocks Boston Arena as the game seesaws its way to the end of regulation time. The score is knotted at 3-3 when the overtime period begins.

Nearly five minutes into overtime, the drama's final scene reveals Gene Kinasewich racing down the right wing past two fallen Eagle defenders. Cutting across the goal mouth, Kinasewich pulls the puck from his backhand to his forehand and deftly slips it through the legs of goalie Apprille. The drama is over.

Kinasewich had been in the news for most of the year but not always for the reasons he would have preferred. Now, with the last rush down the ice, he created a final headline he could savor.

Gene Kinasewich

At times the affair was downright ugly. The talented hockey player with the number 13 on his Harvard jersey would be warming up in some opposing team's rink when the voices would be heard.

"Hey, Kinasewich, who's paying you to play tonight?"

They called him a professional. They ruled him ineligible, not once but twice. But he came back. Not once but twice. And his name was finally cleared after everyone heard the whole story.

Gene Kinasewich was born on August 8, 1941, in Edmonton, Alberta. He was the second youn-

gest of 13 children, orphaned when both parents died when Gene was ten years old.

Juggling school with a job to help support the family, Gene found time to develop considerable hockey skills. This talent led him to the Edmonton Oil Kings, a junior A hockey team, where he played during the 1957–58 and 1958–59 seasons. With an eye on college hockey down the road, Gene refrained from signing a professional contract. He did, however, accept expense money. For his first year with the Oil Kings, he received $450. The next year it was $702, for a total of $1,152.

Meanwhile, Gene's older brother Orie was attending Colorado College and describing his intense and talented younger brother to Jim Lombard, a Colorado freshman who was from the Boston area. Lombard, who later transferred to Harvard and became the hockey manager, took an interest in the younger Kinasewich and helped steer him toward Harvard by way of Deerfield Academy.

Even before Kinasewich enrolled at Harvard, the Ivy League eligibility committee ruled that he, should he come to Harvard, would be ineligible to compete on the varsity hockey team. He had taken money as a hockey player. He was a professional.

Eligibility battles with Ivy League and ECAC administrators were neatly put to rest by the time Gene Kinasewich scored the overtime game-winner that beat Boston College and gave Harvard its first ECAC championship, in 1963.

Although he received scholarship offers from Colorado and Michigan, where he would have been allowed to play, Kinasewich chose Harvard. That's where he wanted to receive an education. And so he arrived in Cambridge in September of 1960.

In September of the following year, impressed with the character of this young man from Edmonton, the Ivy League reversed itself and allowed Kinasewich a new hockey life. He was ruled eligible to play and helped lead Harvard to a 22-5 season that included the 1962 Beanpot championship.

But the administrators struck again in the spring of 1962. This time it was the ECAC Committee on Eligibility that denied Kinasewich the right to play because of "his receipt of excessive expense allowances, i.e., payments over and above out-of-pocket expenditures."

The same rule that handcuffed Kinasewich included a small passage referring to "exceptions" when circumstances were unusual. Gene's story *was presented to the ECAC again, with Kinasewich himself invited to speak on his own behalf. A few games into the 1962–63 season, Kinasewich was allowed to play once more.*

All of this adds special meaning to the events of that wondrous season. In a year of on-ice triumphs, none was more memorable than the final game of the 1963 ECAC tournament at the Boston Arena, with Harvard and Boston College fighting for the title. In overtime. George Frazier, writing for the Boston Herald, *told the story best.*

> *Now, on this midnight in this madhouse, you suddenly knew that this was how it would have to end. Now you knew that there could be no other way—that any other ending would be an indignity. This way, so suspenseful and storybook that hearts stopped beating, was inevitable. This was the hurrah for man's hope—so fit and proper that anything else would seem trite and contrived. For if ever there was a moment of truth, this was to be it. And then, with the hands of the clock standing at four minutes and forty-nine seconds of the "sudden death" overtime period, he shot the puck past the goalie into the net and the red light flashed on and the game was over. Any other way and all our bright dreams would have been smashed to smithereens.*

· · ·

1964–68: A successful ECAC title defense seemed unlikely in 1963–64, for graduation losses were heavy. But captain Kinasewich had some returning support, particularly up front, with the likes of Ike Ikauniks, Billy Lamarche, Barry Treadwell, and Baldy Smith.

An 11-2 start had the Harvards smiling, but matters soured with three straight postexam losses. Included in that trio was a 3-2 double overtime loss to BU in the Beanpot and a loss to Cornell at Watson Rink that snapped a 21-game home winning streak.

The good start reserved a playoff appearance, but it was a brief one. After a snowstorm traded a scheduled plane trip for a ten-hour bus ride to Clarkson, the team arrived in Potsdam at 1:30 A.M. on the day of its ECAC quarterfinal round game. The contest went to the Knights by 6-4, and the season was over.

Also over was the illustrious career of Gene Kinasewich, who led the squad in scoring, earned All-Ivy and All–New England status, and at the time was second only to Bob Cleary as career scoring leader.

With that 1964 campaign one of the strongest periods in Harvard hockey history came to a close. Ten straight winning seasons would be followed by a rebuilding period that covered three losing years.

It was apparent early in the 1964–65 season that goal scoring would be a problem. In January the team's leading scorer, Dennis McCullough, had but nine points. Still, with goalie Bill Fitzsimmons holding the fort, Harvard remained competitive.

With some talented sophomores up from a 14-4-1 freshman team, captain Bobby Clark hoped to halt the skid in 1965–66. A slow start included the first loss to Princeton in 12 years and a significant 5-4 overime win over Cornell. It was significant because it would be the last Harvard victory over the Big Red until 1971.

When the season ended, Cooney Weiland had endured consecutive losing seasons for the first time in his 16 years at Harvard. It was also the first time since 1902 that Yale had defeated Harvard three times in one season.

The rebuilding assignment came to an end in 1967. For the first time in three years, Harvard took a winning record into January and remained a contender for the Ivy title into February. Leading the attack were juniors like Kent Parrot, Ben Smith, Bob Carr, Bob Fredo, and Jack Garrity. This young team also got some mileage out of impressive sophomores like goalie Bill Diercks and forwards Dwight Ware and Bobby Bauer, Jr., son of the former National Hockey League great.

A final-week sweep of Yale grabbed second place in the Ivies and the first ECAC berth in three years. A 6-2 loss to top seed BU ended the season, but the climb back to the upper echelon was completed.

The 11-12 mark included three losses each to Cornell and Boston University, the East's top two squads. These opponents in the similar red-and-white uniforms would be Harvard's most intense rivals over the next ten years. While older alumni continued to see Yale as the archenemy, the players realized that the Elis were no longer the power they once were. The Big Red and the Terriers were in a different class and if Ivy, ECAC, or Beanpot titles were to be won, these were the opponents who would have to be overcome.

The 1967–68 squad started at 5-0 until a jolting 9-0 loss to Cornell at Watson Rink brought the team to earth. With just 11 saves in that one, Cornell goalie Ken Dryden had little to do that night, but more would be heard from him later.

A midseason slump still left the squad at 9-5 through exams, with Parrot, captain Garrity, and sophomore Jack Turco leading the scorers. By Beanpot time, a seven-game win streak had elevated the Crimson to second in the East, and title hopes were very much alive.

But those guys in red and white spoiled the party again. A 7-2 loss to Dryden and Cornell gave Harvard another second-place Ivy finish, and 4-1 and 6-3 losses to BU in the Beanpot and ECAC tourneys cost the Crimson those titles.

The 15-9 season was the last one for the talented class of '68, who engineered Harvard's hockey revival. Bob Carr set a Harvard record for defensemen with 28 points, and Parrot finished as Harvard's third leading career scorer at the time.

1969–71: During the next three seasons, many talented players took the ice for Harvard, but one of them was in a class by himself. In 70 years of Harvard hockey, there may have been more purely talented players. But no one was ever as inspirational a leader on or off the ice as Joe Cavanagh.

When this Cranston, Rhode Island, native joined the varsity in 1968–69, he had already opened a few eyes. His line with left wing Dan DeMichele (a high school teammate) and right wing Steve Owen was the highest scoring freshman line ever. That success continued into the early months of their sophomore year.

Led by this trio Harvard started fast, averaging eight goals a game in December. By midseason the club had a 14-4-1 mark that included Harvard's first Beanpot title in seven years. Tournament MVP Cavanagh was the key as BU fell in the final by 5-3.

While the Crimson overcame one rival, the team in Ithaca continued to have its way. Led by goaltender Dryden, Cornell took both meetings with Harvard, 8-4 and 6-3, as well as another Ivy title, its fourth straight.

Seeded second behind the Big Red, Harvard hosted New Hampshire in the ECAC quarterfinals. Down 3-1 early, the Crimson rallied and prevailed 4-3 on Bobby Bauer's overtime tally.

Then it was on to the Boston Garden, where three goals and two assists from Cavanagh led Harvard past Clarkson, 8-6, in the semifinals.

In the final, Harvard met up with Cornell for the third time that season. The new setting had little effect on the results, as tournament MVP (and future Montreal

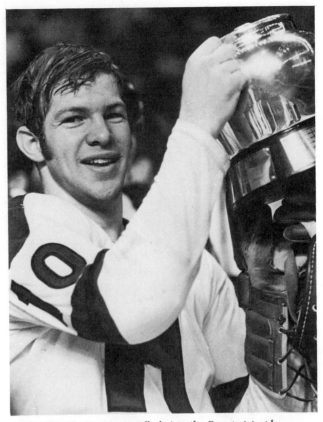

Captain Bobby Bauer proudly hoists the Beanpot trophy after Harvard captured top honors in 1969. The Crimson have won the 'Pot eight times in the first 33 years of the February classic.

Canadien) Dryden led the Big Red to a 4-2 win and the ECAC title.

The appearance in the final earned Harvard a trip to the NCAA championships in Colorado Springs. In the opening round the Crimson hopped on top-seeded Denver with a goal just 28 seconds into the game. But that was the high point, as the Pioneers won the contest 9-2 en route to the title.

The consolation game provided one more highlight in this memorable season. At the end of regulation play, Harvard and Michigan Tech were tied at 5-5. And although MTU outshot the Crimson by 9-1 in the ten-minute overtime that followed, the score remained tied. Senior goalie Bill Diercks was spectacular, and when defenseman Chris Gurry won it in the second overtime, Diercks had 47 saves and Harvard was the No. 3 team in the nation.

Injuries at the start of the 1969–70 season kept Harvard at less than full strength. A fractured ankle to

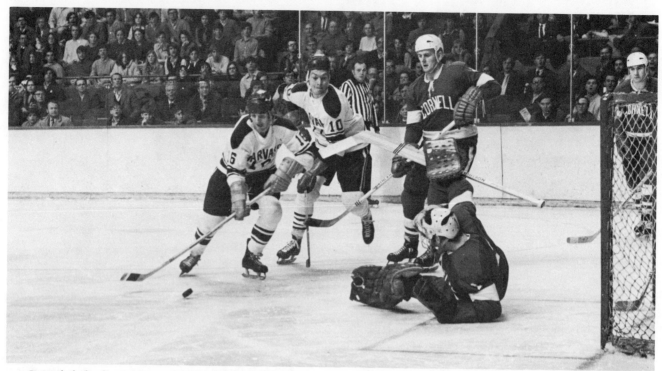

DeMichele broke up the top line, and a shoulder injury to another left wing, senior Ron Mark, disrupted another wave.

With sophomore Tommy Paul filling in capably for DeMichele, the new Cavanagh line led Harvard to a fine 16-9 mark at the end of the regular season. A loss to BU stopped a Beanpot defense, and two more losses to Cornell (who would go 29-0 on the year) foiled Ivy chances again.

That record was good enough for another ECAC appearance, this time at Boston College for a quarterfinal matchup. BC was led by Tim Sheehy, a talented forward out of International Falls, Minnesota, who was, with the possible exception of Cavanagh, the best player in the East.

Despite the presence of these superstars, the game belonged to Harvard's Jack Turco and George McManama. Turco, a senior forward from Melrose who had led Harvard in scoring as a sophomore, tallied five goals in a 10-5 Harvard victory. Linemate McManama, a senior from Belmont who had played both up front and on defense in his varsity career, assisted on seven Harvard goals. Both accomplishments remain ECAC tournament records.

The Boston Garden semifinal between Harvard and Cornell was a classic. When Harvard went up 3-1 early, it marked the first time all year that the Big Red had trailed by two goals. Early in the third period the score was 5-3 for Cornell, but Harvard stormed back to tie on a

Sophomore Bobby Havern, of Arlington, is denied from in close by Cornell goalie Brian Cropper. The Big Red became Harvard's chief rival in the late 1960s and early 1970s. The two schools won all ten Ivy titles from 1966 to 1975.

DeMichele slap shot and a beautiful individual effort by sophomore Leif Rosenberger.

The rally stopped there as a Cornell power-play goal in the third period kept the Big Red undefeated with a 6-5 win. The next night Cornell won its fourth straight ECAC title with a 3-2 win over Clarkson.

The 1970–71 season attracted attention from the start. It would be Cooney Weiland's 21st and final campaign behind the Harvard bench, and an important milestone in that career was expected early. Cooney entered the season with 297 victories, and the talent on his final team insured that his 300th win would not be long in coming. The Cavanagh-led seniors provided the heart and soul of this team, but in the end a trio of sophomores would play a major role in one more championship for Weiland.

First-week wins over Northeastern and Dartmouth made it 299 and counting. When BU came to Watson Rink for the next contest, manager Max Bleakie had the 300th party waiting in the wings. The game was a beauty, with Steve Stirling (later head coach at Providence and Babson) leading the Terriers and Cavanagh inspiring the

Harvard hockey's first three-time All-American was Joe Cavanagh of Cranston, Rhode Island (above). The inspirational Cavanagh led Harvard to the 1971 ECAC title in Cooney Weiland's last year as coach.

Crimson. It ended at 4-4, and Bleakie's refreshments went back on ice.

Number 300 arrived three nights later with a 5-0 blanking of Brown. Goalie Bruce Durno, who had four shutouts in his first seven games, would later record a fifth to tie the mark set by Wood and Bland in 1962.

Cavanagh continued his magic but paid a price in the process. At one point in early January he played with a broken hand and with 12 stitches in his head. At exam break his point total (29) equaled the number of stitches he had acquired that year. At no time did the many injuries ever curtail his effort.

By Beanpot time the team was 12-4-1, all four losses by one goal and two of them in overtime. The most bitter of that quartet was a 5-4 heartbreaker at Cornell. To this day Harvard players will swear that two goals were stolen

Two of the most explosive lines in Harvard history played together for the championship year of 1970–71. Seniors Steve "Cooch" Owen, Joe Cavanagh, and Dan "Monk" DeMichele (top, left to right) paced the team early, while sophomores Bill Corkery, Bob McManama, and Dave Hynes (left to right) caught fire during the ECAC Tournament.

from them that night. Cornell's superb goalie Brian Cropper even admitted after the game that he indeed pulled one out of the goal. But when Cornell scored in overtime, little of that mattered. For the seniors, it was the closest they would come to defeating their number-one nemesis.

As Weiland's last regular season wound down, a Beanpot loss to BU and a second loss to Cornell saw two title hopes fade. That left the ECACs. A wild, penalty-filled opening round 4-3 win over Brown set up a rematch with the favored Terriers in a Boston Garden semifinal.

It was during this weekend that three sophomore forwards came into their own and became household words with the college hockey crowd. Quickly dubbed the Local Line, Dave Hynes (Cambridge), Bob McManama (Belmont), and Bill Corkery (Arlington) shared the ECAC spotlight with the DeMichele-Cavanagh-Owen unit.

The result was a 4-2 win over BU, with the game-winner from another sophomore forward, Jay Riley. The key to the victory was Harvard's staying out of the penalty box the entire evening and thus never giving the Terriers' vaunted power play a chance to perform.

The following night may not have been as artistic, but it got the job done. Led by three goals from tournament MVP Hynes, Harvard overcame a 4-2 deficit to defeat Clarkson, 7-4 for the ECAC title and Weiland's 315th career win.

It would prove to be Cooney's last, as Harvard's NCAA appearance in Syracuse produced frustrating 6-5 and 1-0 losses to Minnesota and Denver. The opening-round loss to the Gophers was particularly painful, as Harvard had a 5-4 lead and a power play in the closing minute of regulation. A shorthanded goal with nine seconds left sent the game into overtime, where Minnesota eventually won it.

With the season's end, two Harvard legends received well-earned attention. Joe Cavanagh became Harvard's first three-time hockey All-American and garnered every other honor a college player could be awarded. His career stats, 60-127-187, left only Bob Cleary ahead of him for total points, and his assist total remains a Harvard standard for three-year players. He would drop back to defense when injuries disrupted the team. He would often play hurt with no discernible change in style. He was the money man who produced in the clutch.

Then there was the coach. In 21 seasons Cooney's teams won eight Ivy titles, five Beanpots, and two ECAC championships. The totals were 315-174-17. The crowning touch was his selection as national coach of the year by his peers in his final season.

Love Story

"In an instant, we were hugging and kissing. Me and Davey Johnston and the other guys. Hugging and kissing and backslapping and jumping up and down (on skates). The crowd was screaming. And the Dartmouth guy I hit was still on his ass. The fans threw programs onto the ice. This really broke Dartmouth's back. We creamed them 7-0."

Hugging and kissing? Jumping up and down? Even in the Ivy League, players don't hug and kiss and jump up and down. Then who is saying all these things?

Those are the immortal words of Oliver Barrett IV, one of the sappiest players never to have played for Harvard. Well, actually those are the words of Erich Segal, Harvard class of '58, a track man turned Yale classics professor turned camp novelist. Writing a successful novel means never having to say you're sorry.

The novel was Love Story, *a smash at bookstores and later at the box office. It was a simple story of a well-bred Harvard hockey player who falls in love with a terminally ill Radcliffe woman of modest means. She dies and he goes on to make movies with Barbra Streisand. Or something like that.*

It was in November of 1969 that Paramount Pictures set up shop at Watson Rink for three days of shooting. Only a few seconds of hockey scenes would survive the editing room, but it took 30 hours in the rink to produce those fleeting seconds.

The script called for parts of two games to be staged, one against Cornell and one against Dartmouth. The two Ivy foes provided game uniforms for Harvard varsity and freshmen players to wear, and Bill Cleary, then the Harvard freshman coach, supervised the hockey scenes with Paramount representatives.

Bill also served as stunt man for actor Ryan O'Neal, a Californian with little experience on ice skates. It was Cleary, with blonde wig sewn into an old leather helmet, who flashed across the screen as Oliver Barrett. It was O'Neal, filmed from the waist up, who stood knock-kneed on close-ups.

The novel made plenty of references to real people and places at Harvard. There was Davey

The big kid in the middle (7) is actor Ryan O'Neal, alias Oliver Barrett. O'Neal took time out from the 1969 filming of Love Story *to pose with members of the Harvard freshman team who served as extras in the filming. They are, from left, Phil Shea, Joe Bertagna, Mark Riley (brother of Jay and a future Boston College iceman), Bob McManama, Dave Hynes, Charlie Olchowski, Jay Riley, Jim Thomson, and Bob Muse.*

Johnston's name quite clearly. And Jimmy (Cunniff) and Richie (Dwyer) were equipment room chums of young Oliver. Other references were less clear. Was the fictitious Gene Kennaway supposed to be Gene Kinasewich? We'll never know.

There was certainly never an Oliver Barrett, "All-Ivy, 1962 and 1963," as the book says. Oh, there may have been some that fit his description and background. But there was one clear sign that Ollie never really donned a Crimson uniform.

A Harvard hockey player would never say, "We creamed them 7-0."

. . .

CLEARY TAKES CHARGE

1972–73: As had been the pre-Weiland custom, Harvard turned to one of its own to direct hockey's future in Cambridge. Bill Cleary, the former Harvard and Olympic hero, succeeded Cooney Weiland in 1971, after serving stints as freshman and assistant varsity coach. As a player in the 1950s and as a college referee in the 1960s, Cleary left his own mark on the game of hockey. He would waste little time leaving his imprint as head coach.

The 1971–72 team was young, with captain Tommy Paul joined by just a few contributing seniors. Ten juniors formed the heart of this team, with the Local Line leading the forwards and classmates Kevin Hampe and Doug Elliott pacing the defensemen. Between the loss of the Cavanagh group and the appearance of a new coach, the early season would be telling.

The team opened strong with an 11-3 win at Pennsylvania and a thrilling 4-4 tie at BU's newly opened

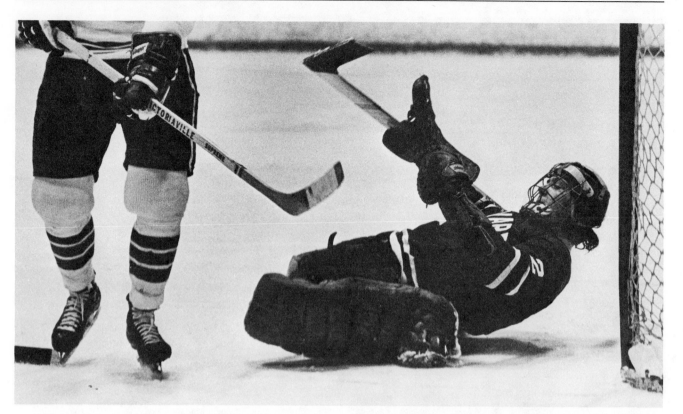

Walter Brown Arena. Then came a little excursion to West Point.

Following a 5-2 win over Army, Cleary imposed a team curfew, which was sidestepped by eight players. Learning of this. Cleary suspended the eight for the next game, which happened to be against Boston College, Cleary's biggest rival. With eight JV players in the line up. Harvard went over to McHugh Forum and took an emotional 6-4 win from the Eagles.

Discipline established, the team posted a pre-exam ECAC record of 9-1-1, which included a 6-4 win over Cornell, Harvard's first defeat of the Big Red since 1965. But four straight postexam losses brought the club down to earth before a late-season surge grabbed home ice for the playoffs.

In the quarterfinals Bill Corkery's overtime goal gave the Crimson a 6-5 win over Clarkson and another trip to Boston Garden. There BU took a 3-1 win that effectively ended a 17-8-1 season.

The 1972–73 season was both a major success and a major disappointment. Captain Hampe's team went 17-4-1, the best Harvard record in a decade, and finished the regular season tied with Cornell atop the ECAC ladder. But each of the games that was not won deprived the team of a championship.

With the Local Line back for its third season and a

The author comes up with a glove save against Pennsylvania in 1972 Ivy League action. Before turning to the typewriter, Joe Bertagna was a varsity goaltender from 1970 to 1973 and led the Ivy League with a 2.45 goals-against average in 1971–72.

healthy influx of talented sophomores, great things were expected of this group. And when they raced off to a 7-0 start, the expectations were being met. The last of those wins was a 4-2 thriller against Michigan Tech before 13,000 fans in Detroit's Olympia Stadium. The win gave Harvard the Great Lakes Tournament championship and top spot in the national rankings.

But the team was unable to maintain this level of play and, hampered by the midseason loss of Dave Hynes (ineligible), it let the season slip away. Two losses to Cornell cost the Ivy title, and an 8-3 drubbing by BU lost the Beanpot. Seeded second in the ECAC tournament, the Crimson were upset at home by Clarkson, 7-4, in the opening round.

Individually, Bob McManama earned All-American honors, as Hynes had the year before, and his third All-Ivy berth. Joining him on the first team was Ivy scoring champ Corkery. With their illustrious careers over, McManama, Hynes, and Corkery ranked third, fourth, and seventh in Harvard career scoring.

"These guys were all talented centers when they came here, and they just fit together perfectly," said Cleary. "David was the shooter, Billy was good around the net, and Bobby was a classic center. But beyond all the talent they had, you've got to remember how hard they always worked on their game."

1974–75: With ten seniors graduated, the 1973–74 team had a new look. After early trouble the new combinations clicked and brought Beanpot and Ivy titles to Cambridge.

Junior center Randy Roth was the best of six strong junior forwards, and his effort in the Beanpot established him as one of the best in the East. After an 11-6 rout of BC, Harvard met BU in the final. Roth had two goals against All-American goalie Ed Walsh, the second with just under three minutes left to win it 5-4.

The Ivy title was made possible by snapping the Lynah Rink jinx. Cornell had not lost to Harvard at home in ten years, and they hadn't lost to anybody at home in the last 44 games. That ended when Harvard beat the Big Red by 7-4 in February.

Entering the ECAC play-offs, this team that had been 6-7-1 at one time boasted a 17-8-1 record. Much of the success had to be credited to the defensive corps, which included cocaptain Mark Noonan, Ed Rossi, Steve Janicek, Dave Hands, and All-Ivy Levy Byrd.

It seemed to make little difference to this team when Providence jumped out to a 3-0 lead after four minutes of the quarterfinal game. The last nine goals belonged to Harvard, and it was on to Boston Garden.

RPI was easily dispatched, 7-2, and that left a rematch with BU for the championship. Roth scored two more against tournament MVP Walsh, but it was the Terriers' title by 4-2.

Finishing second in the ECAC meant another Garden appearance in the NCAA championships two weeks later. Harvard drew top-seeded Michigan Tech and had the Huskies on the ropes, 3-0, after just eight minutes of play. It was 5-3 Harvard early in the third period, and Harvard had visions of its first appearance in the NCAA final.

It was not to be. Two Tech slap shots tied the game in regulation, and at 0:31 of the overtime the Huskies won it.

"That was one of the greatest games I've ever seen a Harvard team play," said Cleary. "I remember one of the Tech players came over to me after the game and said he had never seen a team who could skate like that. He knew that his guys didn't deserve to win it."

The 1974–75 season ranks with the best in Harvard history. The juniors who had carried the team the year before were now seniors, and they had plenty of help. The biggest addition to the team was sophomore goalie Brian Petrovek, who would earn All-American honors.

Just how good was this team? They sprinted to a 13-0 ECAC start that included a 7-2 December rout of a strong BU team. They beat a good Vermont team 10-1 in a game long remembered for the opening three-minute blitz when Harvard scored four times.

The Ivy record was 12-0 with the first sweep of Cornell in a decade. At times the team seemed able to turn on the scoring whenever it wanted. A case in point was a late game with Yale. Trailing the Elis 2-0 with three minutes left, Harvard came back with goals by Kevin Carr, Leigh Hogan, and Dave Gauthier to make it seem like just another night's work.

The offensive explosion was a trademark of this team. In the ECAC quarterfinals against Clarkson, Dan Bolduc had four goals, two of them six seconds apart, three of them in 3:22. Harvard won it, 10-5.

This team was also noted for its speed, with the likes of Bolduc, Kevin Burke, and Paul Haley. But as had been the case so many times in the past decade, the Terriers of Boston University ruined the fun. In the Beanpot, BU reversed December's 7-2 embarrassment, and at the ECACs the enemy prevailed by 7-3.

That left another NCAA appearance, this time at St. Louis. With an unappreciated sense of déjà vu, Harvard jumped ahead of top-seeded Minnesota by a 4-2 score through two periods. In the end it was 6-4 for the Gophers and another disappointment.

The final mark was 23-6, a school record for wins, with Roth and Petrovek named All-American, the second such honor for Roth. The All-Ivy team featured this pair along with sparkplug forward Jim Thomas and defenseman Eddie Rossi.

Randy Roth (142 points) and classmate Jim McMahon (109) finished as Harvard's fourth and tenth career scoring leaders. Ed Rossi set Harvard and Ivy records for assists by a defenseman in a season and tied the career mark.

1976–81: Another cycle was just about completed and a temporary descent loomed ahead. The 1975–76 team could not chalk up the gaudy results of its immediate predecessors but left a mark of its own.

Freshmen became eligible in Ivy play that year, and

Harvard would benefit with the arrival of George Hughes. A former schoolboy star out of Somerville and Malden Catholic, Hughes would lead Harvard in scoring in each of his four varsity seasons.

Seniors like captain Kevin Carr and Paul Haley provided offense, and goaltender Petrovek's record 650 saves did the rest. And despite struggling at or below .500 much of the year, the team grabbed the seventh seed for the ECAC play-offs.

That meant a trip to Durham, New Hampshire, to meet the Wildcats of UNH. The host team led 1-0, 2-1, and 3-2, but Harvard kept tying things up. Led by an inspirational effort from captain Carr, Harvard finally won it, 4-3.

That in effect was the season for the Crimson. In the next game BU knocked Harvard from the ECACs for the fourth time in five years.

A Beanpot title made 1977 a year to remember. Another win one, lose one season seemed to be going nowhere when those two February Mondays brightened the picture. A 4-2 win against BC and the Eagles' stellar goalie Paul Skidmore put Harvard against heavily favored BU in the final.

It was a battle of All-American goalies, with Petrovek going against the Terriers' Jim Craig, whose performance on the gold medal–winning Olympic team in 1980 would add new meaning to the word "hero." When the battle was over, it was Petrovek with the MVP award and Harvard with the Beanpot. The score was 4-3 for the Crimson, with Jon Garrity, former captain Jack's brother, scoring the winning goal.

"The thing I remember most about that Beanpot was that we had run into some injuries and I brought up Lyman Bullard from the JVs," recalled Cleary. "He was a senior who had never played varsity hockey before, but he was an athlete. I saw that in his varsity soccer efforts. Doesn't he go out and get a goal in one game and an assist in the other? He got as much out of that Beanpot as any Harvard player ever had."

The only late-season event was Bill Cleary's 100th win, a 5-3 decision over Yale, making Cleary just the second Harvard coach to reach that plateau. For the first time since 1967, there would be no ECAC playoff appearance.

That development soured the accomplishments of the Hughes brothers. Leading scorer George was joined by freshman defenseman Jack, the ECAC Rookie of the Year.

Five seasons would pass before Harvard enjoyed a winning record. Results and morale would drop sharply, particularly in the 1978–80 period. The record in this stretch was a combined 27-47-4, bottoming out in 1978–

In between the Clearys and the Fuscos came the Hughes brothers, Jack (left) and George. Younger brother Jack was ECAC Rookie of the Year as a defenseman in 1977 and later a 1980 Olympian. Center George led Harvard in scoring in each of his four seasons, 1976–79.

79, when Harvard went 7-18-1 and just 1-8-1 in the Ivy League. Contributing to this dismal performance was the fact that Harvard practiced and played on the road while Watson Rink was being transformed into the Bright Hockey Center.

On November 10, 1979, the Alexander H. Bright

Hockey Center was dedicated before a game with the 1980 U.S. Olympic team. Built on the site of the Watson Rink, the new Bright Center was one of the most beautiful hockey facilities in the East. For the players, the new rink ended 25 years of dressing in Dillon Field House and putting skates on in Watson's cramped skate rooms. A modern, carpeted locker room embraced the team beneath the rink's 2,850 new seats.

On opening night Harvard was blanked by former Terrier Jim Craig, 4-0, in a game that was a sign of things to come for both teams. The Olympians would go on to make history at Lake Placid, while Harvard would stumble through an 8-15-3 season.

But those numbers did reflect a half step upward on the rebuilding ladder. And much as the class of '68 had halted Harvard's last decline, the class of '83 would return Harvard hockey to greatness.

There were 13 freshmen on that 1980 team, the best of the lot being a redheaded defenseman from Burlington, Massachusetts, named Mark Fusco. He would lead Harvard in scoring and be named ECAC Rookie of the Year. Before he was through, he would be Harvard hockey's first four-time All-Ivy and second three-time All-American.

The 1980–81 squad played like a .500 hockey team much of the year and finished at 11-14-1, another step up that ladder. But on two February Mondays, the team played like a champion.

The opening round of the Beanpot produced a 10-2 mauling of Northeastern, a good team that had won the 1980 Beanpot, the school's first. That led to the championship final against Boston College.

The Eagles were a strong team led by a good goaltender in Bob O'Connor. But it was Harvard goalie Wade Lau who stole the show in a 2-0 Crimson triumph. Bill Larson's eventual game-winner made it a tense 1-0 game for much of the evening. When Dave Burke scored on a final-minute slap shot, two things became clear. Harvard had a Beanpot, and the drought was over.

. . .

A Long Way From Spy Pond

After more than half a century, Harvard hockey owns a building befitting the role played by the Crimson in the annals of this intercollegiate sport and Harvard athletic history.

—Leonard Fowle '30

Leonard Fowle, the esteemed sportswriter at the Boston Globe, made this observation back on March 7, 1956, when Harvard dedicated its first indoor hockey facility, the Donald C. Watson Rink. It was a simple structure by today's standards, concrete block walls with bleacher seating for the most part. But it was a major step forward for Harvard hockey at the time.

Those were the days before Bobby Orr captured Boston, before metropolitan and private rinks popped up in virtually every suburb. For the most part, Greater Boston schools used the Boston Arena on St. Botolph Street. Occasionally, a trip to the Skating Club in Allston was necessary. Or maybe even Lynn Arena.

It wasn't a satisfactory situation for a group of Harvard alumni who thought it important that the hockey program have its own facility. Surely, other schools would move in that direction, and being the first could boost the attractiveness of the program to young hockey players.

The first positive step was taken by the Harvard Corporation in 1953 when it provided $250,000 for the construction of an "open" outdoor hockey rink. That facility was constructed but proved to be vulnerable to New England winters.

So the Working Friends of Harvard Hockey came into being, the brainchild of former goalie Dave Mittell '39 and organized by icemen Alec Bright '19 and Greely Summers '42. Their goal was simple: to raise $350,000 to enclose the outdoor rink. When the effort stalled some $100,000 short of the needed sum, John W. Watson '22 came through with a gift in the name of his brother, Donald C. Watson '16.

Donald "Dumpy" Watson was one of Percy Haughton's best quarterbacks, directing the Harvard attack in both 1914 and 1915. To hundreds of Harvard hockey players from 1956 to 1979, he

was the man whose photograph graced the wall just inside the heavy doors to Watson Rink. Countless players with stick and skates in their arms had to open those doors, pass the picture of Don Watson, and put on their skates in the small rooms beneath the rink balcony.

It was a familiar routine, perhaps a nuisance to some by the late 1970s. But it was a far cry from the early days of the century, when Harvard players had to search for a frozen pond in Cambridge or Arlington or beyond.

In those days it wasn't just a walk from Dillon Field House to Watson Rink. It was a trolley ride to Fresh Pond or Spy Pond or maybe even a nameless pond in Concord. Coats and stones served as goalposts, and much time was spent hunting for pucks lost in the woods or chasing down others that scaled beyond imaginary boundaries.

Such was the situation in the first decade of Harvard hockey. Soon, crude rinks were constructed near the law school and down at Soldiers Field. And then came the rinks in the Stadium.

But Watson Rink ended all of that. For 24 seasons, this was the stage for Harvard's best winter drama. It was the place to be on a cold Saturday night when guys named Cleary or Johnston or Cavanagh could entertain or amaze or inspire. It was watching Cooney Weiland battle Snooks

The Watson Rink balcony crowd rejoices after a Harvard goal. Next page: *The 1980 U.S. Olympic team joins Harvard in dedication ceremonies for the opening of the Alexander H. Bright Hockey Center in November of 1979. The Bright Center was built on th site of the old Watson Rink.*

Kelley. It was standing next to the skate room and giving the guys a pat on the back as they walked out to the ice. It was a reserved and loyal alumni following in the balcony caring just as much as the raucous and mischievous students in Section 19 behind the far goal. It was holding a hot chocolate, pulling on gloves, and wishing it was just a little bit warmer.

By 1978 Harvard's hockey program was outgrowing Watson Rink. And so a $3 million renovation process began, which increased seating from 1,500 to 2,850, widened the ice surface by 5 feet, and increased locker and storage facilities, among other improvements.

As John Watson had done 23 years earlier, Horace Bright '17 provided the major contribution that made the renovation possible. And on November 10, 1979, the new facility, named after Horace's younger brother Alec, was dedicated with a game between Harvard and the 1980 U.S. Olympic team.

Alec Bright was a hockey player and skier at

Harvard whose efforts to support those programs throughout his life were unequaled. He was a hockey player of modest skills at Harvard who improved in his postgraduate years with the Boston Hockey Club and BAA team. His career as a competitive skier also prospered after graduation, as he was a member of the U.S. Olympic ski team at the age of 39.

When the Alexander H. Bright Hockey Center opened, fans could look upward at the same ceiling that graced the Watson Rink. It provided a sense of continuity, as did the name of Alec Bright, who played when there was no Harvard rink, who helped build the first rink, and who will be remembered throughout the life of the second.

• • •

THE WINNING RETURNS

1982–83: The 1981–82 hockey season extended Harvard's comeback, as the Crimson qualified for postseason play for the first time in six years. An 11-1 pasting of Dartmouth, first win over the Big Green in three years, opened the season and signaled what was to come.

It was a season that started slowly and forced Harvard to finish fast. After a 5-3 loss to Ivy leader Yale on February 20, the squad was 7-8-2 in the ECAC and, to qualify for post-season play, had to sweep its last four games and hope that someone else could knock off Yale. And this was a team that had won back-to-back games only once that season, and at one stretch went eight games without a win.

At least these final four games were at home, and the first was against Northeastern. Trailing 3-2 after two

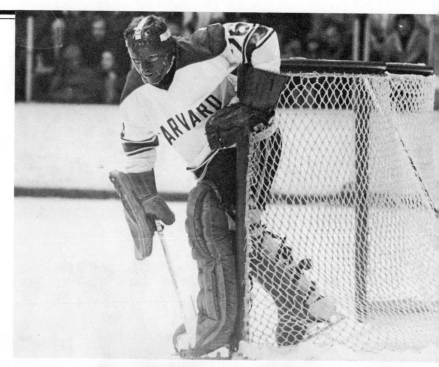

Harvard goaltending records were established, in succession, by All-American Brian Petrovek (right), Wade Lau (27) (bottom left), and Grant Blair (29).

periods, the Crimson exploded for four goals in the third for a 6-3 win.

Next on the list was a Friday-Saturday special with Princeton and Cornell. With goaltender Lau putting on a clinic, Harvard swept the pair by 10-0 and 7-0. Suddenly Harvard's hockey team was a big story. And just as suddenly, playing a major role in that story was a group of Harvard students who filled three sections of the Bright Center.

Harvard hockey crowds had never been known as wild

or even excitable. There was always that blend of polite alumni, parents, Greater Boston hockey types, and maybe a handful of creative students. Neither Watson Rink nor the Bright Center had ever been known to terrify an opponent. But in February of 1982, that changed as Harvard students turned out in unusually large numbers to support the team that had captured their fancy.

Following the double shut outs, Harvard received a gift. Dartmouth defeated Yale, 4-1, in Hanover, to put Harvard in the driver's seat. All the Crimson had to do was beat that same Dartmouth team in Cambridge and the ECAC's Ivy Region title was Harvard's. And that meant a home ice berth for the playoffs.

With those new fans serving as a seventh player, Harvard took a crowd-pleasing 7-4 win over the Big Green that ended that six-year playoff drought.

The madness continued into Harvard's fifth straight win, a 2-0 ECAC quarterfinal decision over Boston College. That game will long be remembered for Jim Turner's game-winning goal, a 60-foot shot that appeared to be going off the boards and behind the goal until it ricocheted off an official's skate and into an empty Eagle net.

Next came the semifinals against the ECAC's No. 1 seed, Clarkson. This was the same Clarkson squad that had belted the Crimson, 8-1, back in January.

Outshot by 14-5 in the first period, Harvard trailed only 1-0 thanks to the continued brilliance of goalie Lau. But the next seven goals, five of them in the third period, belonged to Harvard as the Crimson shocked Clarkson, 7-1. The offensive stars were defenseman Neil Sheehy, who scored a hat trick, and Jim Turner, the quiet forward, who continued a late-season binge with two more goals.

That victory, Harvard's sixth straight, would be the team's last. Northeastern took the final by 5-2 and then, in a two-game total-goals series, Harvard was stopped in the NCAA quarterfinals, 6-1 and 4-3, by Wisconsin.

Harvard's Fusco brothers enjoyed postseason attention as defenseman Mark was named All-Ivy for the third straight time and All-American for the second year in a row. Freshman forward Scott won the Ivy scoring title and was named Ivy League Rookie of the Year while joining his brother on the All-Ivy team.

The 1982–83 hockey season can take its place as the best in Harvard history. It was a team that began the year with high expectations and, despite losing captain Greg Olson with a broken ankle for most of the year, it lived up to its potential.

The team would finish at 23-9-2, winning the school's

Coach Bill Cleary and sidelined captain Greg Olson celebrated Harvard's 1983 ECAC championship victory over Providence at the Boston Garden. The team finished second in the nation—Harvard's best finish ever—after losing the NCAA final to Wisconsin, 6-2.

third ECAC title and finishing second in the nation, Harvard's best finish ever.

Entering the season Harvard's strength seemed to be its depth, most of which was found in the senior class. But finding a successor in goal to the graduated Lau appeared to be a problem.

That problem was solved with the emergence of freshman Grant Blair. Alternating with classmate Dickie McEvoy at first, Blair took over at midseason and played like a veteran. By year's end he had the lowest goals-against average in the country and was voted the Ivy's top rookie.

The team started fast, paced by special teams success. The Crimson power play hit on 40 percent of its opportunities early, and at one time the team had scored more shorthanded goals (six) than the opposition had power-play goals (four).

The ECAC playoffs began at the Bright Center when second-seeded Harvard hosted seventh-seeded RPI. This RPI team was considered an offensive machine, but Blair and a veteran defense easily dismantled the machine in a 5-1, 4-2 sweep, sending Harvard to the Garden again.

In the semifinals, third seed New Hampshire took a 3-1 first period lead against a flat Harvard team. And then, in what Bill Cleary later called "as good a period of hockey as any of my teams have played," Harvard exploded for four goals in three minutes to take the lead and, in effect, the game. The surprise offensive star in this flurry was defenseman Mitch Olson, who scored a pair, one on a dazzling, defense-splitting individual effort.

The final score was 6-3 and set up a final game match-up with top seed Providence. The Crimson had bested the Friars by an 8-5 score earlier in the season at home. But that would provide no guarantee for continued success.

Each team scored a single goal in the second period after a scoreless opening stanza. When Scott Fusco scored early in the third, Harvard had a slim 2-1 edge. Then, at 18:31, that newly developed offensive weapon Mitch Olson finished off a two-on-one to give Harvard some breathing room. The final was 4-1, Olson was tourney MVP, and Harvard had its third ECAC crown. The comeback was complete.

The triumph earned Harvard home ice for the NCAA quarterfinals on the following weekend. The team's depth was on display as the Crimson edged Michigan State in a two-game total-goals series. Junior Rob Wheeler, a former varsity tennis star who first came out for hockey at the start of the season, set up two key goals in Friday's 6-5 win and then scored the tying goal in Saturday's 3-3 deadlock. That was enough for Harvard to take the total-goals series by 9-8 and advance to the Final Four in Grand Forks, North Dakota.

At the NCAA championships Harvard hockey enjoyed some of its finest moments ever. On Friday afternoon, before Harvard's semifinal matchup with Minnesota, defenseman Mark Fusco was named the winner of the Hobey Baker Memorial Award as the nation's best college hockey player. The first easterner to win the award, Fusco made the entire East proud with dazzling performances at both the afternoon press conference and the evening hockey game.

The game was a struggle, with Harvard enjoying leads of 1-0 and 2-1 before Minnesota took a 3-2 lead into the third period. It was during these final 20 minutes that more than a few western skeptics first took Harvard seriously. And when the period was history, goals by Scott

Fusco, Phil Falcone, and Jim Turner had given Harvard a 5-3 win.

The subsequent 6-2 loss to Wisconsin in Harvard's first NCAA final did little to tarnish the record of this memorable season. Mark Fusco took every honor imaginable, and brother Scott, whose 33-22-55 was Harvard's seventh best year ever, joined him on both the All-Ivy and All-ECAC teams. Also recognized for his efforts was Bill Cleary, who was named national coach of the year by his peers.

He was a four-time All-Ivy and a three-time All-American, but the honor that distinguished Mark Fusco from the pack was the 1983 Hobey Baker Memorial Award as the best college player in the country. Fusco, later an Olympian and a Hartford Whaler, was the first easterner to win the coveted award.

Mark Fusco

Freshman eligibility made it possible. But Mark Fusco still had to earn his four All-Ivy selections. No other Ivy player has equaled that record.

And through the first five years of the Hobey Baker Memorial Award, no easterner other than Fusco had won that prestigious honor. Given to the top college hockey player in the country, the award is named for the former hockey and football standout at Princeton.

"Mark was not very big but he controlled a game out there," said his coach, Bill Cleary. "I don't think I ever coached a kid who wanted to win more than Mark."

Cleary's admiration for Fusco may have stemmed from more than what the defenseman did on the ice. The coach may have seen a similarity between the Fusco brothers (Mark and Scott) of the 1980s and the Cleary brothers (Bill and Bob) of the 1950s. All four players followed a Belmont Hill School-Harvard-Olympics path and all were remembered for their competitiveness as well as their talent.

For all his individual honors, the older Fusco may well be remembered as leading the class that pulled Harvard hockey out of its worst slump in decades. The class of '83 turned things around at Harvard and put three players into the pros: Fusco (Hartford), Neil Sheehy (Calgary), and Greg Britz (Toronto). Their results at Harvard and visibility afterward made the program more attractive to those who followed them.

HOBEY BAKER MEMORIAL AWARD WINNERS*

1981	*Neal Broten, Minnesota*	
1982	*George McPhee, Bowling Green*	
1983	*MARK FUSCO, HARVARD*	
1984	*Tom Kurvers, Minnesota-Duluth*	
1985	*Bill Watson, Minnesota-Duluth*	

• • •

* Selected by the Decathlon Athletic Club of Bloomington, Minnesota.

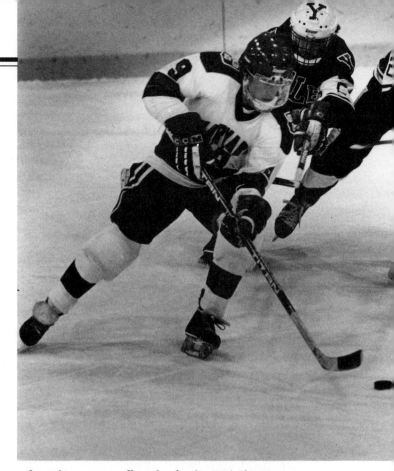

After taking a year off to play for the 1984 Olympic team, Scott Fusco returned to Harvard and was named ECAC Player of the Year in 1985. His 81 points were second only to Bill Cleary's Harvard record of 89 in 1955.

1984–85: Graduation losses strapped the 1984 team from the start. And when Scott Fusco joined brother Mark on the Olympic team, matters worsened.

Still, captain Ken Code, the only veteran defenseman, did a good job at leading the returning icemen to another shared (with Cornell) Ivy League title. Scoring goals was this club's problem, as leading scorer Brian Busconi had 18 points (compared with Scott Fusco's 55 the year before).

The clear-cut team hero was goalie Grant Blair, whose own stats improved while Harvard's goal production went from 177 to 84. He shared Ivy League Player of the Year honors, while freshman defenseman Butch Cutone shared the Ivy Rookie of the Year award.

Scott Fusco returned in 1984–85 and so did Harvard's offense. Teamed up with junior Tim Smith and freshman Lane MacDonald, Fusco had a banner year. His 34-47-81 season was second only to Bill Cleary's Harvard record of 89 points and earned him All-Ivy and All-American status. He was also selected as the ECAC Player of the Year.

His value was reflected in the season that his linemates

had as well. After a 2-3-5 season the year before, Smith was 31-22-53 in a year in which he set an ECAC mark by scoring a goal in 13 straight games. MacDonald, son of the former NHL veteran Lowell MacDonald, set freshman marks for goals and points with 21-31-52.

"Scotty was every bit as competitive as his brother Mark was," said Bill Cleary, "Off the ice they were different, Mark more gregarious, Scott on the quiet side. But they both possessed that incredible desire to win."

Typical of Fusco's year was his effort in the ECAC semifinals against Clarkson. The score was knotted at 1-1 with just over a minute to go and overtime a likely possibility. Suddenly Fusco, hampered by a bad back the latter part of the season, cut around Clarkson's All-American defenseman Dave Fretz and sent a backhand to the far corner of the net. The goal, with 59 seconds remaining, sent Harvard to the ECAC final for the third time in four years.

The wins stopped there, as eventual NCAA champ RPI took a 3-1 victory, breaking a 1-1 tie with two goals in the game's final four minutes. Harvard advanced to NCAA play but lost a pair of tough 4-2 decisions at Minnesota-Duluth.

This team took its place in Harvard history with a share of a fourth straight Ivy title and a third NCAA berth in four years. They would have made Alfred Winsor proud.

THE WOMEN TAKE THE ICE

1977–81: Unlike the pioneering efforts of their male counterparts, women's hockey at Harvard emerged relatively late. Brown University, Harvard's opponent in the first collegiate men's game, is generally given credit for organizing the first significant women's hockey program at the college level, in the mid-1960s.

Not until the fall of 1977 did women's hockey get its start at Harvard. It was then that a group of undergraduates approached men's hockey coach Bill Cleary about the possibility of starting a women's hockey team. Cleary responded by convincing his first goalie, Joe Bertagna '73, to take an interest and help get the program started.

The first women's team operated as a club sport. This important distinction kept significant funding from the program and put the burden squarely on the participants. If women's hockey was to have any future, the first team would have to show interest early and maintain it through a full season.

The team was given two hours of practice each week

and a schedule of eight games. A budget of $500 allowed for the purchase of some equipment, but most of the gear came from the players themselves or from equipment manager Chet Stone, who channeled a few pieces from the men to the women when possible.

Harvard's first team was led by captain Lucy Wood, a field hockey player who had gained earlier attention as the first woman to play intramural hockey at Harvard.

After a month of practice, the team played its first game on December 10, 1977, when Boston University played host to the historic contest. Despite three goals from Tania Huber, BU rallied to take a 4-3 victory. History should note that the coach of record for this first game was the team's assistant coach, John Christensen. Sports information duties sidelined Bertagna, so Christensen, a JV player from Waterloo, Iowa, coached Harvard's first game.

Each of the season's eventual three victories was somewhat tainted. On December 11, the team defeated a town team from Nashua, New Hampshire, 4-2. Later in the season, with high school girls in goal, the team fashioned wins of 3-0 and 7-2 over Boston University and Ithaca College.

The season ended at 3-5, with the major accomplishment being the maintenance of a sufficient number of participants out on the ice all year. The athletic department recognized the accomplishment and awarded the team varsity status beginning in 1978–79.

The second year brought new challenges. The team had to prove that it deserved varsity status and do so under taxing conditions. The Watson Rink was to undergo yearlong renovation, which put all Harvard hockey teams on the road. For the women, that meant 6:15 A.M. practices in the semicovered Buckingham Browne and Nichols Rink across from Soldiers Field. Led by captain Alison Bell '79, the team did an exceptional job under the conditions.

The first legitimate win came in January when Harvard traveled to Hanover and beat Dartmouth, 5-3, with Huber scoring four goals. Another key to the team's steady improvement was the play of Nelia Worsley '79, a senior goalie who immediately garnered the nickname "Gump," though the former NHL legend was no relation.

Late-season success, including a 3-2 win over Yale, earned Harvard second seed in the Ivy League tournament. Harvard lost both tournament games, ending up fourth in the league, and finished its first varsity year at 6-11-1.

At the conclusion of the season Bertagna stepped down to devote full time to his duties as Harvard's sports

information director. He was followed as coach by Rita Harder, a former standout player at Brown.

Harder's two seasons continued the slow but steady progress both on and off the ice. The 1979–80 team was 4-13 but fashioned a significant 5-3 win over Boston University in the consolation game of the Women's Beanpot. It was the first tournament win ever for Harvard after two years of Beanpot and Ivy tournament disappointments.

The 1980–81 team set a record for wins in a 7-12

What a difference four years can make! Harvard's first women's hockey team (top) paved the way for the championship teams that followed, like the 1982 Beanpot titlists.

season that featured a pair of 2-1 overtime victories against Yale and Dartmouth. Seniors Lauren Norton, an All-Ivy defenseman, and Sara Fischer, the leading goal scorer, became Harvard's first four-year players.

1982–85: Women's hockey at Harvard didn't fully blossom until the arrival of head coach John Dooley in the fall of 1981. Dooley brought 20 years of boys' high school and men's college coaching experience to a program that was just starting to attract some talent. The combination made the 1981–82 season a turning point.

The team compiled a 15-6 record that included a memorable Beanpot championship. It was during this tournament that the program matured and the first superstar emerged for Harvard women's hockey.

In a pair of one-goal victories, sophomore goalie Cheryl Tate put on an MVP performance that brought the Beanpot to Cambridge. In the opener against Northeastern, Tate had 67 saves in a 3-2, five-overtime classic. Even with Tate's brilliance, all would have been for naught if not for classmate Sue Newell's breakaway goal that sent everyone home. In the final against defending champ Boston University, Liz Ward's two goals and Tate's goaltending produced a 2-1 win and the first championship of any kind for Harvard women's hockey.

Junior forward Diane Hurley rewrote most of the offensive records with a 23-24-47 season that paced the team's offense.

The success continued into 1982–83, when Harvard went 11-8 after a slow 4-5 start. Again the Beanpot was the season highlight, as Tate's second MVP performance produced 12-0 and 2-1 wins over Boston College and Northeastern.

Tate repeated as a first team All-Ivy choice, while a new offensive threat emerged in leading scorer Kathy Carroll.

The 1983–84 season brought no championships but once again displayed the skills of seniors Tate, Hurley, and Carroll. Tate earned her third straight All-Ivy berth, while Hurley and Carroll shared virtually all offensive records.

Hurley's 23-20-43 season gave her a career total of 65-46-111, career marks for goals and points. Carroll's 23-27-50 earned season records for most assists and points as well as the career assist record.

Dooley and Harvard made it four straight winning seasons when the 1984–85 squad went 13-9-1. The big story of this season, and most likely for seasons to come, was the play of Julie Sasner. The freshman from Exeter, New Hampshire, was Ivy League Rookie of the Year and set a Harvard record for goals with 25. And that was as a defenseman.

The first superstar of women's hockey was goalie Cheryl Tate, three times a first team All-Ivy choice and twice Beanpot MVP.

CHAPTER
4

Heavyweight and Lightweight Crew

If you have ever visited New Hampshire's Lake Winnipesaukee in the summer, you know it can be very beautiful and very crowded. It is a popular spot for tourists who like swimming and boating by day and dining and summer theater by night.

But back in 1852 the crowds had not yet discovered Winnipesaukee and there were those with an interest in making that sort of thing happen. To be specific, the Boston, Concord & Montreal Railroad was eager to succeed in that area of New England and welcomed any event of substance that could attract crowds along their railroad lines to that region.

It was in this context that Mr. James N. Elkins, superintendent of that railroad, first proposed a rowing regatta to one Dr. Whiton, whose son happened to be rowing at Yale. Yale's James M. Whiton '53 approached Harvard's Joseph M. Brown '53, and the result was a race between Harvard and Yale on Lake Winnipesaukee on August 3, 1852, financed by the Boston, Concord & Montreal Railroad.

Thus began not only intercollegiate rowing in this country but intercollegiate athletics in general. That 2-mile race on a beautiful New England summer afternoon was the first athletic contest between two universities this country had ever witnessed.

The railroad people were pleased at the large crowds that traveled to Lake Winnipesaukee (at the time called Winnipissiogee) to witness the historic event. Included in the gathering was presidential nominee (and later U.S. president) Franklin Pierce, a native of nearby Hillsborough.

The Harvard people were happy as well. Their boat, the *Oneida,* finished 4 lengths ahead of the Yale's *Shawmut* and 8 lengths ahead of the *Undine,* Yale's second boat. The Harvard boat was manned by six members of the class of 1853, including race organizer Brown at coxswain, and three members of the class of 1852, including Harvard's first victorious stroke, Thomas J. Curtis.

On that day, Harvard was best, and in the years since few have been able to make that claim as often and as convincingly as the men who have rowed for Harvard. The

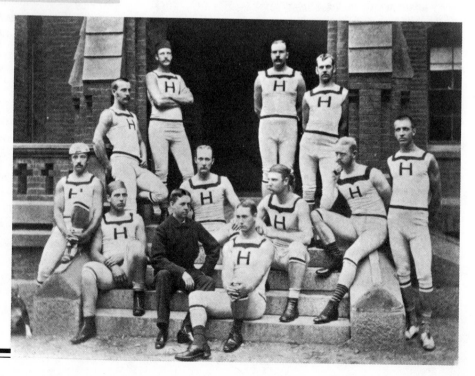

REGATTAS

ON

LAKE WINNIPISSIOGEE!

THE BOAT RACES BETWEEN THE CLUBS OF

Harvard and Yale Colleges!

Will take place as follows, in the morning and afternoon of each day.

At Centre Harbor, Tuesday, August 3d.
At Wolfboro', Thursday, August 5th.

The following boats will contend for the prizes:

ONEIDA, from Harvard University. Uniform Red, Blue and White.
UNDINE, from Yale College. Uniform White and Blue.
SHAWMUT, from Yale College. Uniform White and Red.
ATALANTA, from New-York, but manned by students of Yale College. Uniform Blue and White.

These Boats were built at a great expense, and their crews are disciplined in the most perfect manner. They carry eight oars to a boat, and are from 35 to 40 feet long. The Races will consist of several one mile heats, and the ground has been so selected that any number of spectators, however large, will obtain each an equally good view with the other.

PRIZES will be publicly presented to the winners.

MUSIC by the CONCORD MECHANICS' BRASS BAND.

☞ Arrangements have been made with the Boston, Concord & Montreal Railroad, to run special trains between Concord and Warren and the Lake on the morning and afternoon of the days of the Regatta to accommodate persons going and returning on the same day.

Fare in the special Trains HALF PRICE. The regular trains run as usual, giving persons from connecting roads an opportunity to witness the Regatta in the afternoon of each day.

N. B. BAKER, for the Committee of Arrangements.
July 28, 1852.

men of the *Oneida* began a glorious tradition of hard work and success that Harvard's heavyweight oarsmen now share with lightweight rowers and a successful women's rowing program.

Rowing is the ultimate team sport. While an outstanding individual can frequently make the difference, more often than not it is the group of rowers working as one that ultimately leads to success.

The sport is uncluttered by the excesses that creep into so many others. Since the emphasis is on the group, not the individual, there are no horror stories of recruiting abuses in rowing. There are no efforts to define a rower's worth through individual statistics. And there are no all-star teams subject to second-guessing.

There are no arenas or stadiums to fill, so putting spectators into seats is of no concern to the sport's participants. But it is an expensive sport, and that limits its participants to a relatively small number of schools, primarily in the Northeast and on the West Coast.

Not surprisingly, Harvard and Yale dominated the early years of rowing, each with its own period of preeminence. Harvard captured 18 of the first 25 meetings with Yale from 1852 to 1885, a time during which Harvard was generally considered the sport's best. Yale assumed a leadership position until the end of the century, when Cornell and then the University of Washington, in Seattle, enjoyed their glory years leading up to World War II.

• • •

College athletics was just an idea when the poster above was first tacked up. It became a reality when the advertised event, a crew race between Harvard and Yale, took place on "Lake Winnipissiogee" (Winnipesaukee) on August 3, 1852. Harvard's Oneida won the historic race.

The 1879 Harvard crew strikes a pose in the uniforms of the day. While many athletic programs were yet to be organized at Harvard, this group represented the 27th year of rowing for the Crimson.

ONE RACE BEGINS IT ALL

1844–85: The first Harvard boat club was organized by Horace Cunningham '46 and his classmates in 1844 when they purchased the school's first boat, the *Star,* and rechristened it *Oneida.*

Two years later members of the class of 1847, in their boat the *Huron,* defeated the *Wave* out of Boston on the Charles River. It marked the first race ever for a Harvard crew against an outside opponent.

In these early years before the historic race at Winnipesaukee, many clubs were organized, but when the Ariel Club crew had a misunderstanding with the Boston police along the Charles, the faculty put a halt to all rowing clubs except the Oneida. This was the only active club when Yale's invitation came in 1852.

After that first win over Yale, three years passed before the next challenge came out of New Haven. That challenge was successfully met on July 21, 1855, in Springfield.

On October 3 representatives of the various class crews met to form the Harvard University Boat Club. One of the club's first acts was to purchase a university boat.

In 1856 a house was built for the university boat near the site of the current Weld Boat House. It served its purpose until 1869, but boats had to be moved inside Appleton Chapel during the winters.

It was in 1858 that a couple of Harvard men took one step that would affect all future Harvard athletes whether they ever touched an oar or not. Charles W. Eliot, later president of the college, and Ben Crowninshield purchased red handkerchiefs for the crew to wear as uniform caps at the first college regatta in Springfield. They became the basis for the first Harvard colors.

When a Yale man drowned just days before the race, the regatta was canceled. The very next year, Harvard won the first Intercollegiate Regatta, which featured only Harvard, Yale, and Brown. Caspar Crowninshield '60 stroked this crew and the 1860 regatta champion as well.

From 1860 to 1871 the Intercollegiate Regatta involved only Harvard and Yale. Gradually, more colleges become involved until 13 institutions were represented in 1875. The standard shell for this period was a six-oar without coxswain.

Over the years Harvard oarsmen have made a name for themselves around the world. Harvard's first international competition took place on August 27, 1869, in England, when a four-oar crew from Oxford captured a 4½ mile race from Harvard.

The technology continued to change in these early years. In 1872 a major innovation came when the sliding seat was introduced. Previously, rowers had leather in the seats of their trousers and slid on a greased bench.

Throughout all of this time Harvard remained the country's top crew, but Yale's ascendancy loomed. In 1876, after a five-year hiatus, the two schools renewed their annual dual race. On June 30 of that year, the Harvard-Yale Regatta became an eight-oar event and the distance was established at 4 miles, where it remains today. In the first race at that distance, Yale was the victor.

One of Harvard's strongest periods came to an end in 1879 with the graduation of William "Foxey" Bancroft, stroke of the last three crews, and oarsmen Fred Smith and William Schwartz. Harvard still managed to prosper, taking 3 of 4 Yale races from 1882 to 1885. But beginning in 1886 Yale rebounded, winning 11 of the next 12 meetings.

1886–1930: Beginning in 1886, Yale dominated rowing for aproximately 20 years. From 1886 to 1905 the Elis won 18 of 20 dual races with Harvard and by 1901 had tied the series at 20 wins apiece.

It has been suggested that the lack of one, single head coach at Harvard in this period spelled the difference between Harvard and Yale. While Yale succeeded under Bob Cook for two decades, Harvard went through a regular changing of the guard as captains held the right to select coaches.

In 1899 Yale's mastery was interrupted when Harvard, behind junior stroke and captain Francis L. "Peter" Higginson, snapped a six-race Eli win streak. Harvard was unable to repeat the next year as Higginson, again captain and stroke, broke his leg just days before the race. Yale won and began another streak of six straight wins.

On October 20, 1900, Harvard began using the Newell Boat House, a gift from the Harvard Club of New York in memory of Marshall Newell '94, a seven-letter winner in crew, football (All-American), and track. It remains the home of the men's rowing program.

In 1905 and 1906 Oliver Filley matched Higginson's two-year stint as captain and further contributed to the program with the hiring of James Wray as Harvard's first professional coach. Wray guided Harvard's rowing fortunes from 1905 through 1915, besting Yale in 7 of 11 meetings.

Taking a page from the opposition, Harvard ran off its

Harvard's 1914 JV heavies approach the finish line at the Henley Royal Regatta en route to capturing the Grand Challenge Cup. It was the first time in history that an American crew had prevailed at the most prestigious rowing event of the day.

own six-race win streak against Yale between 1908 and 1913. John Richardson '08, Roger Cutler '11, and Alexander Strong '12 were among the stalwarts of this period.

At the conclusion of the 1914 rowing season, Harvard entered its junior varsity boat in the Henley Royal Regatta in England. To the surprise of many, the Harvard boat won the Grand Challenge Cup, the most prestigious event of the competition and of the rowing world at that time. The victory marked the first such triumph by an American crew.

Wray completed his tenure in 1915, and Robert Herrick, with more than a little assistance from William Haines, assumed command. After World War I interrupted the program for two years, Haines returned with even greater influence through 1922, although Herrick retained the title of coach.

During the decade of the 1920s, Harvard rowing struggled, and nowhere was this reflected more than in its coaching situation. Five different men assumed the head coaching post in this period while in contrast, Yale prospered under one man, Edward Leader, well into the tenure of Harvard's sixth and seventh coaches in this period.

R. Heber Howe '01 served in 1922, followed by the one-year stint of the Vesper Boat Club's Frank Muller, whose crew failed to win a single race. Ed Stevens, who had learned his craft at Cornell and the University of Washington, remained for two years, but freshman coach Bert Haines replaced him in 1926. Haines opted to go back to the freshmen, and Ed Brown '96 took over in 1927 for three years.

Brown's crews had some of the best individuals of this period, most notably Geoffrey Platt '27, John Watts '28, and Forrester "Tim" Clark '29. Despite captain Clark's presence in 1929, the crew lost all its races.

In 1930 the sixth coach in nine years arrived in the person of Charles Whiteside. While the varsity enjoyed mixed results in Whiteside's first year, Bert Haines was molding an undefeated freshman crew whose members would dominate Harvard rowing until their graduation in 1933.

The Cup Races

With the Eastern Association of Rowing Colleges Regatta—the Eastern Sprints—looming at the end of each season, the remainder of Harvard's schedule is framed by a number of cup races. In 1933 the Compton Cup was inaugurated in honor of the former president of MIT Dr. Karl T. Compton. This race features Harvard, Princeton, and MIT each year.

That same year, the annual competition between Harvard, Penn, and Navy was waged for the Adams Cup, named in honor of Charles F. Adams, Harvard '88 and former secretary of the navy. The oldest of the cup races is the Harvard-Yale meeting for the Sexton Cup. This was introduced in 1925 and was named after Lawrence E. Sexton, manager of the Harvard crew of 1883.

In 1965 a fourth cup race was introduced, the annual battle between Harvard and Brown for the Stein Cup. This cup, named after Walter J. Stein, Brown class of '17, was won by Harvard the first 19 years for which it was competed. Brown, under former Harvard lightweight coach Steve Gladstone, finally ended the streak with back-to-back wins in 1984 and 1985.

In addition to frequent early-summer trips to the Henley Royal Regatta, Harvard's heavyweights have found themselves in two other regattas of note. The San Diego Crew Classic has become a semiregular season opener for Harvard and others. And in recent years the best crews from the country have met in Cincinnati in June to determine a national champion. Harvard's first visit to this fledgling event was a successful one by 1983's national champs.

• • •

1931–45: In his second year in charge, Whiteside took three veteran oarsmen and added six members of the class of '33 to produce Harvard's first undefeated season since 1908. Sophomores Gerard "Killer" Cassedy (stroke), Robert Saltonstall (No. 7 oar), W. Benjamin Bacon (No. 6), Malcom Bancroft (No. 5 and grandson of Foxey), Waldo Holcombe (bow), and H. Hamilton Bissell (cox) took and held their seats in the varsity boat for three straight years. To fully grasp the depth of talent in this one class, one should know that there were four others from the class of '33 in the JV boat and one more in the third varsity as well.

Neither of the next two crews was able to match the success of 1931 despite the fact that 7 of the 8 oarsmen were constants from that class of '33. By 1933, including the JV boat, 13 of the top 16 oarsmen in the school were from that one class. In all, 14 classmates would win 30 major letters in rowing by graduation.

Not surprisingly, talent was thin for the next two years. Despite the efforts of Sam Drury, stroke both years and captain the latter, Harvard's results were unimpressive.

Much like the sophomores had done in 1931, the sophomores of 1936 started a revitalization of Harvard rowing. With stroke Spike Chace '38 and captain Raymond Clark '36 providing leadership, Harvard survived Whiteside's less than satisfying final year, one which ended positively with a win over Yale.

In 1937 a new era began for Harvard crew when Director of Athletics Bill Bingham announced the hiring of Thomas D. Bolles as the new crew coach. Bolles had been freshman coach at his alma mater, the University of Washington, since 1927. He brought with him another Washington product, Harvey Love, to serve as Harvard's freshman coach.

Bolles arrived with some definite plans to change Harvard's stroking style. His chief aim was to "develop some semblance of a straight line drive." Commenting on his predecessor's technique, Bolles said to crew historian Thomas C. Mendenhall:

> His style of rowing included a sudden drop with the body at the catch followed by a sharp swing up of the hands and body. This, coupled with a tendency to miss water—which was inevitable inasmuch as when fresh, the oarsman would get more water than he could handle—caused a bounce in the boat during the drive, with resulting loss of speed and a "heavy" boat on the catch. This, of course, would be especially pronounced at the higher cadences generally used in the short races.
> My secondary aims were: to break the arms sooner on

the drive in order to "flatten" out the release by completing the arm pull simultaneously with the leg drive; to achieve the body angles during the first one-half of the recovery (not the last); to keep the backs "comfortable" both during the drive and the recovery, rather than rigidly or artificially straight or arched in; and, on the drive, to keep the power "on" unwavering and uniform, thus eliminating a catch that was so hard that the bodies could not continue it evenly throughout the drive.

With captain and coxswain Edward H. Bennett, Jr., '37 providing leadership, Bolles's first crew had a strong season, losing one race, by one second, to Navy. Bolles's second crew, with Spike Chace at stroke for the third straight year, produced Harvard's first undefeated season since 1931.

Cornell, Harvard's chief rival of the period, prevented another undefeated season in 1939. But that blemish was more than overcome by Harvard's second triumph at Henley. The varsity boat appropriately won the Grand Challenge Cup on the 25th anniversary of the 1914 crew's victory, which coincided with the 100th anniversary of the Henley Regatta itself.

Harvard's success continued with a single loss in 1940, to Cornell once more, and undefeated campaigns in 1941 and 1942. Two sophomores emerged in 1941 and played major roles in these perfect seasons, Darcy "Bus" Curwen at stroke and David Challinor, Jr., at No. 7 were regarded by Bolles as the best stern pair he ever coached.

Curwen was elected captain for 1943 but never rowed under that title, as the war curtailed official rowing at Harvard until the 1946 season. Following the 1942 campaign, both Bolles and Love entered the U.S. Naval Reserve.

• • •

The Man in the Gray Felt Hat

Back in 1951, page 521 of the Harvard Alumni Directory listed the name of Thomas D. Bolles along with the classification, "Grad. '37-41." Bolles, who made the transition from crew coach to athletic director at Harvard that year, never did receive a degree in Cambridge. The directory's notation reflected his five years in pursuit of a PhD. in history at Harvard.

Still, Harvard claimed Bolles just as the University of Washington had. It was at Washington that Bolles earned his AB in 1926 and master's in 1936. And it was at Washington that Bolles developed his greater love, not for history but for rowing.

He had been introduced to the sport through his older brother Harry, an Olympic candidate as a Navy plebe in 1920 (he was a spare on Navy's Olympic eight). Three years later the younger Bolles was rowing for the Washington freshmen.

After graduating in 1926 Bolles began his coaching career with a rowing club in Havana. A year later he returned to Washington as freshman coach to head coach Al Ulbrickson, Bolles' classmate. Just as Miami of Ohio would produce a stream of college football coaches later in the century, Washington was developing a reputation as a source of great rowing coaches. "The mother church of 20th-century rowing," said crew historian Thomas C. Mendenhall.

Yale was smart enough to lure Ed Leader in 1923. Penn signed up Rusty Callow in 1927. And after he had won eight Pacific Coast championships in his nine years with Washington's freshmen, Harvard beckoned Tom Bolles.

Between 1937 and 1950 Tom Bolles had all the numbers that mattered: 61-15 overall, twice a winner of the Grand Challenge Cup at Henley (1939 and 1950), and of greater importance to some, just one loss to Yale.

History should credit Bolles with lending stability to one area of Harvard's rowing program that had never quite solidified: coaching. The Yales and Cornells and Washingtons had dealt with this problem directly and, in turn, ruled the first three decades of the 20th century.

But Harvard floundered. The undergraduate

When he stepped down as head coach of crew in 1951, Tom Bolles succeeded Bill Bingham as Harvard's director of athletics.

captain selected the coach up through World War I, and that prevented continuity of command. With the alumni running the crew program, conflicting philosophies further restrained Harvard from moving in one direction, and as late as 1923 there were as many as 11 coaches on the staff.

The first step toward rectifying the situation came in 1926, when Bill Bingham became Harvard's first director of athletics. Control of athletics would be taken from the alumni, and a strong, single administrator would be heard.

When Bingham hired Bolles ten years later, the rowing world heard him loud and clear. While it is difficult to assess how many head coaches Harvard had in its first 8 years of rowing, there have only been three since 1936: Bolles, Harvey Love, and Harry Parker. It is not surprising that Harvard's winning percentage in those 50 years approaches 80 percent.

On a more personal level, Tom Bolles is remembered as a great teacher. The words often associated with him are "quiet, dignified, and pleasant." And he was patient as he introduced new techniques to the Harvards, changing their stroking style and always advocating a low stroking rate.

The warmth felt for this thin, balding man in the gray felt hat was captured by Bob Stone, Bolles' captain in 1947, who delivered the eulogy at a special memorial service in January of 1979. Speaking of his coach, who died of a heart attack in December of 1978, Stone said:

"His voice, when coaching, was firm and inspiring. When we were dead beat in a time trial, he would tell us to 'bring it up from our toes.' When we were finishing a long piece from the Basin to Newell with about a mile to go and everyone exhausted, his long-remembered words through the bullhorn were, 'Now's where it counts! Now's where it counts!' When one of his better late forties crews was having a downstream time trial in New London, his voice from the coaching launch was telling them they were ahead of the course record; he knew they were tired, and with a bull voice said, 'Now call on your ancestors!'. And on occasion, he would give great whoops of delight through the megaphone. . . . He was a gentleman, articulate and thoughtful, whose presence exuded leadership and who, by example, showed how we should conduct our lives."

. . .

1946–58: After the war the coaches returned to find that the talent was thin the first time around. Part of the problem was alleviated when freshmen became eligible for the 1946 season (a temporary change). That resulted in Michael Scully becoming the first rower to earn four varsity letters since coxswain Merry Blagden '09

It was an uninspiring season for Harvard, who won but one race, a 1¾ mile event against Yale. In the first Eastern Association of Rowing Colleges (EARC) Regatta—the Eastern Sprints—Harvard finished ninth.

Bolles turned things around quickly. A number of war

When the Charles River has frozen over, Harvard oarsmen have turned to the indoor tanks at the Newell Boat House, as in this scene from the late 1940s.

veterans returned for his 1947 boat, including Bob Stone, who was elected captain. Two of Harvard's best, Jud Gale and Frank Strong, were underclassmen who led Harvard to a successful year marred only by another loss to Cornell.

That setback was avenged twice, first when Harvard won its first EARC Regatta and next when the Crimson were best in the Washington Regatta in Seattle. That victory had special meaning, as it was a homecoming of sorts for Bolles, whose crew rewarded him with a world record time of 5:49 over the 2,000-meter distance.

The quest for perfection came up painfully short in each of the next three seasons. Again, it was Cornell doing the damage in 1948 but again Harvard had its way at the Eastern Sprints.

In 1949 Harvard beat Cornell in Ithaca and an undefeated season seemed in the cards. But Yale pulled off a stunning upset in New London by a little over a second to give Bolles his only loss to Yale in his 12-year tenure.

Both Cornell and Yale fell to Harvard in 1950, the year

that Bill Leavitt became the fourth Harvard coxswain to be elected captain. But MIT took the Sprints, by one-tenth of a second. That disappointment was quickly forgotten when Leavitt's crew won the Grand Challenge Cup at Henley.

In 1951, Tom Bolles's final crew lost the Compton Cup to Princeton and the Sprints to Yale but also claimed dual race victories over Navy, Cornell, and Yale. That last race, in New London, concluded an illustrious career that saw Bolles's crews win more than 80 percent of their races. To be exact, Bolles's winning percentage was .868. In contrast to this, Harvard's pre-Bolles percentage going back to 1852 was at .587. Although his efforts on the water came to an end in 1951, his contributions to Harvard did not, as he succeeded Bill Bingham as Harvard's director of athletics in 1951.

There was little doubt as to who would succeed Bolles. Harvey Love, the competent freshman coach who arrived with Bolles in 1937, took over as head coach in 1952. He had the immediate benefit of a two-year veteran at stroke in Louis McCagg, Jr., who was elected captain as his father, Louis, Sr., had been in 1921.

Unfortunately, Love's first season produced only a win over MIT and a Compton Cup win over MIT, Princeton, and Rutgers. The competitive highlight of the season took place, in effect, after the season. That was the August 3 reenactment of the first Harvard-Yale race on Lake Winnipesaukee. True to history, though unlike results in New London two months earlier, Harvard was the winner.

More mixed results followed in 1953, but the season ended nicely with a victory over Yale at New London, Love's first such triumph and his last until 1959.

Despite various success, the period from 1954 to 1958 was plagued by two major disappointments: Yale fashioned a five-race domination of Harvard, and the EARC Sprints championship continued to elude the Crimson. After three titles in the first four years of the regatta, Harvard would go empty-handed for the next ten years.

1959–62: All the disappointments were forgotten in 1959. Coach Love and captain Townsend Swayze inherited four promising sophomores from Bill Leavitt's last freshman crew (he went on to become head coach at Rutgers). The best from this quartet was a much-heralded schoolboy phenom out of Middlesex by the name of Perry Boyden. To add incentive to the season, it was announced at the start that should this crew perform well, they would go to Henley for the 45th anniversary of Harvard's first success in that regatta.

Three Harvard crews who claimed victory at Henley get together in 1959 for this group shot. Back row, left to right (1959 heavyweights): Peter Binney, John Ellefson, Townsend Swayze, Jerry Jones, Kenneth Gregg, Torry Everett, James McClennen, Perry Boyden, Barrows Peale, and Manager Robert Goldstein. Middle row (1914 Henley crew): Sen. Leverett Saltonstall, James Talcott, Henry Meyer, Harry Middendorf, John Middendorf, David Morgan, Louis Curtis, stroke Dr. Charles C. Lund, and coxswain Henry Kreger. Front row (1959 lightweights): John Noble, Jonathan French, Michael Christian, Mark Hoffman, Melvin Hodder, Lloyd McKeeman, David Richards, Tony Goodman, and Mario Bryan.

With Boyden leading the way at stroke, Harvard put together an undefeated season, its first since 1942, and earned the right to enter Henley. The record remained intact, as the Grand Challenge Cup was brought home for the fourth time.

In 1960 Perry Boyden was elected captain as a junior, the 12th Harvard man so honored (5th in the century). His crew started quickly, winning three races, before Cornell and Pennsylvania prevailed in the Sprints and Adams Cup competition respectively. The season ended positively when Harvard finished 27 seconds ahead of Yale at New London.

Once again in 1961 the standards set by the 1959 crew could not be matched. But Boyden met a personal goal in becoming the first varsity stroke to beat Yale three times in New London since Gerry Cassedy in 1933. And he did it in style with a 29-second margin of victory.

Boyden's talent was recognized by the college when he was named a recipient of the William J. Bingham Award, symbolic of the top athlete in the school. Boyden shared the award with quarterback Charley Ravenel and became the first rower so honored since the award was initiated in 1954.

When Harvard defeated BU and Rutgers in a 1-mile race to open the 1962 season, few expected that not only would it be Harvard's final victory of the season but also

Victorious stroke in three races against Yale and captain of both the 1960 and 1961 boats, Perry Boyden was named Harvard's top athlete as a senior.

Harvey Love's last career victory. On January 14, 1963, after attending a luncheon meeting of the Friends of Harvard Rowing, Love suffered a heart attack and passed away later that afternoon.

Love served Harvard as freshman and varsity coach for 27 years, a tenure surpassed only by Bert Haines, who served in a variety of roles from 1920 to 1952. Love's varsity record could not compare with that of Tom Bolles, the dominant figure of the era. But his contributions over nearly three decades were embraced and appreciated by those close to the program.

1963–67: With the death of Harvey Love, Harvard turned to a relatively new face on the scene, freshman coach Harry Parker. The 27-year-old Penn graduate had just two year's experience with the freshmen, so his first title was that of acting head coach for the 1963 season.

If Parker was a less than traditional choice for coach, two-year veteran Nick Bancroft was an ever so traditional captain. His father (Malcom '33), grandfather (Guy '02), and great-grandfather (William "Foxey" '78) all rowed for Harvard.

Parker won his first two races on the Charles but then stumbled against his alma mater and was eliminated from the Sprints early. That left a date with Yale, which produced an upset victory for Harvard. It was the first of an incredible 18 straight wins over Yale for the "acting head coach." More than a few of those varsity wins capped off Harvard sweeps, freshman and JV boats already victorious. That would send a broom up the flag pole at Red Top, the training quarters along the Thames in Ledyard, Connecticut, where Harvard crews prepared for the annual Yale race.

Harvard's rowing history has had so many golden periods that it is probably unwise to search for the best. But the five-year span from 1964 to 1968 must comfortably challenge any other. It is a period bookended by crews seeking to accomplish what no Harvard crew had ever done: represent the United States in the Olympic Games. One crew failed and the other succeeded. What both shared with the other three crews of this period is an unblemished record against college competition, a streak that actually began with that Yale win in 1963 and continued until 1969.

Rowing's powers-that-be determined that beginning with the 1964 season, all intercollegiate races would be rowed at 2,000 meters, with the exception of Harvard and Yale's traditional 4-mile affair. This put the colleges at the same distance as the prestigious international regattas and the Olympics. Harvard found this to its liking, as Parker's second crew breezed through an undefeated season, including an EARC Sprints victory before 10,000 spectators on Worcester's Lake Quinsigamond.

The real goal of the season, however, was the summer's Olympic trials. Though the United States had been represented by a college crew in every Olympics since 1920, no Harvard crew had ever earned that distinction. The 1964 crew believed itself to be the best collegiate crew in the country. And events at the Olympic trials at New York's Orchard Beach Lagoon proved the Harvards right. They finished ahead of collegiate challengers California and Yale, but they lost to the Vesper Boat Club of Philadelphia by four seconds.

Because of the trials, the varsity boat did not attend Henley, the junior varsity going instead. That crew was joined by another Harvard junior varsity, the 1914 Grand Challenge Cup winner, who returned to celebrate its 50th anniversary. All nine members of the 1914 boat and the squad's manager were on hand for the festivities. The 1964 JV boat was not so fortunate, as it was eliminated on the regatta's opening day.

Another perfect year followed in 1965, prompting a *Sports Illustrated* cover story to proclaim Harvard the world's best crew. Sharing that admiration for Harvard was Penn coach Joe Burk, Harry Parker's mentor.

"There are other crews in the country just as strong, just as smooth, but Harvard's better," said Burk. "This is the greatest American crew there has ever been, college or club."

Before history so ordains the 1965 boat and no other, one should remember that the crew was basically the same as 1964, when seven men went on to the Olympics (four plus cox, two spares). Both crews should share in the praise generated by the *Sports Illustrated* piece, a direct result of two early-season wins in which Harvard broke course records by 20 seconds.

Why this Harvard crew was so much better than the rest was a topic of discussion all season. And this was a season in which Harvard's closest victory was its 2½ length win over Cornell at the Sprints.

It was their Swiss Stampfli shell, some said. It was their European-influenced stroking technique, said others. Perhaps it was their English oars. But maybe it was just an excellent group of rowers. Said Harvard track coach Bill McCurdy, an admirer from Soldiers Field, "Those boys could win most of their races pulling an old barge with broomsticks."

At the Sprints, varsity, JV, and freshman boats prevailed, with the varsity posting the largest margin of victory (9.7 seconds) in the 19-year history of the event. The margin of victory against Yale was an even more impressive 39.4 seconds.

This was a group of men who took a serious, businesslike approach to rowing. They would later be known as Harry's Crew, that group whose nature was most like its mentor's.

The consistency of this crew, stroked by Geoff Picard and averaging 6 feet 4 inches, 188 pounds, led *Sports Illustrated*'s Hugh Whall to observe, "It's hard when watching to believe the men are mortal and not metal." But they were mortal, at least at Henley, where Vesper eliminated the Crimson in the first race.

The academic year ended on a high note when captain Paul Gunderson received the Bingham Award as top athlete in the school, the second rower so honored. Gunderson, like many Harvard oarsmen to follow, had never rowed competitively until he arrived in Cambridge.

A major reason Harvard would develop so many champion oarsmen out of raw athletes was the presence of Ted Washburn '64, Parker's first coxswain, who became freshman coach in 1965. Through the 1985 season, the just slightly intense Washburn had produced ten Sprints champions and had consistently provided the

varsity boats with well-prepared talent. Whereas most programs suffer from the regular departure of freshman coaches, Washburn's long tenure saved Harvard from dealing with this problem and kept a sense of continuity at Newell Boat House.

When the varsity's third straight undefeated season was completed in 1966, the seniors looked back at never having lost to another college crew in their varsity careers. The next two classes would be able to make the same claim.

In 1967, Harvard became the first school to win four straight Eastern Sprint titles. The crew remained busy during the summer, first at the Pan American trials and then at various national and international regattas. The Pan American trials brought Harvard and Vesper together again at the Orchard Beach Lagoon, site of the 1964 Olympic trials. This time Harvard emerged the victor, and the crew later won the gold at the Pan American Games in Winnipeg.

No Harvard crew had been able to represent the United States in the Olympics until this 1968 boat did so (from left): Paul Hoffman, Art Evans, Curt Canning, Andy Larkin, Scott Steketee, Fritz Hobbs, Steve Brooks, Cleve Livingston, and Dave Higgins.

What It's All About

You watch the football players on a fall Saturday, and your thoughts are fragmented. You wonder at the concentration of the receiver who hauls in a pass amid three defenders. You wince at the contact that the linemen endure on each play. You envy the quarterback who seems so sure, so much in command.

Now you stand alongside the Charles River and you watch Harvard's oarsmen at work. You've heard all the stories. You've seen them running up and down the Stadium steps as you've driven on Storrow Drive. You've heard about them breaking the ice on the Charles in March. And you've seen the pain in their faces after they've rowed 4 miles in the June heat at New London.

The thoughts are not fragmented now. You don't see them as individuals. Stroke as quarterback, and so on. You just look out on the water and see nine parts to one machine. And you wonder. What do they think about before a race? What keeps them from letting up? How do they mesh so well? What drives them to work so hard?

Occasionally, the oarsmen address these questions, prompted by a curious reporter from the Harvard Crimson *or the* Boston Globe *or* Sports Illustrated. *It is difficult not to be intrigued by a Harvard oarsman.*

Most college athletes are asked about a particular game or a play or an opponent. With oarsmen, the questions go beyond the event at hand. There is that fascination, that "why do you do it?" angle that separates their endeavor from the rest.

Here, through selected observations of Harvard oarsmen from their competitive years, is a look at the inner battles that each rower faces, in the season and in a race.

David Weinberg '74, coxswain, on the start of the year:
"The fall is a pretty exciting time. I've always enjoyed the fall. The squad is a squad. No one's ego is being fed. No one's ego is bent. As the winter comes along, you start thinking a little more about the racing season. You have to. It takes a deeper motivation then. Once you start to get past midterms, you get really cranked up. From February until Harry selects the boats, people start to compete on an individual basis. There's a group competitiveness." (To John Powers '70 of the *Boston Globe*)

Tiff Wood '75, on the individual battle:
"Initially, the commitment is to make the boat. There are those who are sure of it. But you can never count on being in the varsity boat. Up until you're on the water, you're concerned about making yourself better. You think about who you have to beat. But you think about making the boat first. I've always approached it in a very individual manner. I feel very much alone. I feel very much it's me, possibly, against all eight in the other boat. Harry's selection process accentuates that, too. It becomes very much a race of you against the other guys. I say, 'I've got to make the boat go.' It's not, 'We've got to make it go.' " (To Powers)

Art Evans '69, on motivation:
"For me, it's competition—trying to make a higher boat and staying there." (To Roger Angell '42 of the *New Yorker*)

Fritz Hobbs '69, on motivation:
"Well, I know what I get out of rowing. I like winning. We're winners and I like to win. And then, I guess, that you meet such a great bunch of people." (To Angell)

Jim Tew '66, on the start of a race:
"As with most athletes, oarsmen must prepare themselves for a race by achieving a balance of fear and confidence. A tendency toward one extreme or the other will produce bad results: A panicky crew cannot row well, an overconfident crew will not row hard. Practices will go well or poorly, depending on how the boat feels at the time—but as the race draws closer, a good crew will have achieved an emotional equilibrium, a sense of irrefutable logic. 'If we row our best, we will win. At least I'm almost sure we will.' " (As written under special by-line in the *Boston Globe*)

Curt Canning '68, on fighting fatigue in a race:
"The body of a race reaches out and grabs an oarsman. He cannot avoid the consciousness that what is happening must continue and continue and continue until the distance is covered. It makes him want to slow up a little or go easy or save something. But he can't." (As written in the *Harvard Football News*)

Andy Larkin '68, on the challenge of rowing:
"There are no stars in this. No quarterbacks or .300 hitters. Each person in a shell rows alone, but the only glory comes as a unit. And it's hard. People keep asking me, 'What's so hard about rowing?' and I point how tough it is to learn to hit a golf ball two hundred yards

down the fairway. You know how many books there are about that? Well, rowing is getting eight guys to hit a drive two hundred yards at exactly the same instant, and doing it over and over again, faster and faster, even when you're all at the absolute end of your physical capacity." (To Angell)

Curt Canning '68, on the end of a losing race:
"When I slumped into that semiconscious mist after the finish line, none of the exultation that facilitates recovery was present. We had finished fourth." (In the *Harvard Football News*)

Gregg Stone '75, on the meaning of "winning" in the Harry Parker era:
"To the layman, winning means finishing before, or scoring more points than, the competition. We, however, did not put in those hours, those miles, those summers in small boats, those winter weekends on cross-country skis in order to just finish ahead. We trained, competed with each other, and raced to be the very best ever, to win by as much as possible, to beat not only college crews, but also national crews. The 'winning' came not at the end of a race, for most races were merely a stepping-stone to the ultimate goal, but at the end of a season or perhaps a career." (To the author for this book)

• • •

1968–71: Sights were realistically aimed at 1968 and one more shot at an Olympic berth. That year turned out to be Harvard's fifth straight undefeated season and included another Sprints title, two wins over chief rival Pennsylvania and a 44-second drowning of Yale.

But it was all a prelude to a summer trip to Long Beach, California, and the 1968 Olympic trials. How much were the Mexico City games on the rowers' minds? Coxswain Paul Hoffman '68 arrived in Cambridge as a freshman with a travel poster of Mexico, a reminder of where he wanted to be four years later.

Harry Parker remembers the first race of 1967, when he kept three sophomores out of the varsity boat. "All they said to me was, 'But Coach, how can we go to Mexico if we're not in the top boat?' They weren't concerned with the race at hand. I was keeping them from reaching their goal of competing at the Olympics."

At the July trials Penn figured to be Harvard's chief rival, and when the finals got under way, those two college crews battled for the honor of representing the country in Mexico City.

Despite two losses to Harvard earlier in the year, Penn, with a realigned crew, took an early lead, and it looked as if the Quakers might pull off an upset. If the race had been 1,900 meters long, they would have. Harvard surged at the end and forced the judges to refer to photographs of the finish. The technology revealed Harvard the winner by less than a foot, and that was enough to send the Crimson to the Olympics.

Between the July trials and the October games, five members of the crew caused a minor stir when they came out in support of Olympic demonstrations planned by black athletes. Specifically, captain Curt Canning, captain-elect Cleve Livingston, Paul Hoffman, Scott Steketee, and Dave Higgins called a press conference at Kirkland House to formally declare their support for the Olympic Project for Human Rights, the brainchild of Professor Harry Edwards, of San Jose State.

In retrospect, the athletes' statement was simply a show of support for a group of their fellow athletes, and one that bound no other members of the crew.

"Because we do not know what specific form the black athletes' demonstration will take, we do not consider ourselves tied to any specific action. It is their criticisms of society which we here support."

Those who were less supportive of such tactics found the rowers' involvement a distraction and something to point a finger at when Harvard's fall showing was disappointing. Fighting equipment repairs, high altitude, stomach disorders, and a strong field, Harvard finished sixth when the Olympic finals were rowed in Mexico City that October.

"I have never seen any athletes put as much work and energy into a single event, before or since, as these guys did for the trials," said Parker. "But it was a clue to what followed. It was as if their bodies would not allow them to be injured or sick until that goal was reached. As soon as it was over, a number of them came down with problems."

The Harvard-Pennsylvania rivalry continued unabated over the next two years. And the Quakers finally got the upper hand in 1969 when they ended Harvard's undefeated streak at 34 intercollegiate races. Some 10,000 spectators turned out on the banks of Philadelphia's Schuylkill River to see Penn take the Adams Cup race by a little over six seconds.

Penn would repeat that Adams Cup victory the next year in Cambridge as well. But in both years, Harvard would get the last laugh with EARC Sprints titles, running its Sprints streak to seven straight years.

The Adams Cup continued to elude Harvard, but in 1971 it was Navy, not Penn, that grabbed the honors. This time there was no late-season redemption, as Navy captured the Sprints as well.

The Summer of '68

By the summer of 1968, young men had rowed for Harvard University for 116 years. In that time Harvard oarsmen had accomplished just about everything affordable in the world of amateur rowing. Everything except representing the United States in the Olympic Games.

From 1920 to 1960 the United States was represented by a college crew at the summer games. But none of those nine crews was from Harvard. In 1964 Harvard proved to be the best college crew in the country. But they finished second to Philadelphia's Vesper Boat Club in the Olympic trials. As the 1967–68 school year opened, Harry Parker's oarsmen had one goal in mind: Be second to nobody at the Olympic trials in July of 1968.

The 1968 intercollegiate season was a breeze for Harvard. It brought a fifth straight undefeated season, the fifth of seven straight EARC Sprints championships. Everything was right on schedule.

But the summer's challenge would be different. Many in the Harvard boat learned that lesson the previous summer through a heavy diet of international competition. After winning at the Pan American Games, another undefeated Harvard crew finished fourth behind New Zealand, Australia, and West Germany's Ratzeburg in an international race in Canada. From there, it was a pair of second-place finishes, behind New Zealand at Philadelphia and behind Ratzeburg at the European championships in Vichy.

The Harvards learned that they were capable of losing. At the same time, as Harry Parker pointed out, "The total experience made this crew realize it was equal to the best in the world." And it had still been five years since another college crew had beaten Harvard.

This was a veteran crew, but in rowing the

word "veteran" has a special meaning. Seven members of the boat, including coxswain Paul Hoffman, were returnees from 1967. But only Steve Brooks, the boat's lone sophomore, who had rowed at Noble and Greenough, had any previous rowing experience before Harvard.

The others may not have been rowers, but they were athletes. As a group they had earned 39 letters in 12 different high school sports. That versatility was reflected in junior Fritz Hobbs, a member of Harvard's national champion squash team and No. 4 on the varsity boat.

But the only skill that would matter in the summer of 1968 was how well they could move Harvard's Stampfli shell, the Louis B. McCagg '22, against the country's best. And by the first week of July, it was clear exactly who the best were.

On June 29 Harvard defeated 1964 nemesis Vesper by 5.8 seconds at a race in Orchard Park, New York. Just five days later an improved Pennsylvania crew defeated Vesper by 7.0 seconds and looked good doing so. Whereas Harvard had to close fast to beat the club boat, Penn led right from the start and simply built on its lead.

Harry Parker, Penn '57, was wary of his alma mater. Harvard had beaten the Quakers twice in the spring, for the Adams Cup and at the Sprints. But this was a different boat, strengthened by the addition of a freshman and a sophomore who had not been with Penn's top boat in the spring.

Arriving at Long Beach for the Olympic trials, Parker did not hide his concern. "It [Penn] is a good, strong crew, very fast, and it's done a tremendous amount of work," he said. "I don't think our experience makes much difference at this point."

Parker had more reason to be concerned after the initial heats. In the first, Penn set a course record of 5:56.1, beating Vesper by a length. In the second, Harvard breezed past Washington and the rest of the pack, winning by 2 lengths. But the Harvard time was 6:03.3.

Penn, preparing to meet the reigning champs of college crew, sensed it had pulled even with Harvard. All the records and the history meant nothing. As the Quakers' Gardner Cadwalader said before the race, "I say this race is going to be just guts. I think we're invulnerable."

The 2,000 meter course at Long Beach Marine

Here's how close Harvard came to missing those 1968 Olympics. Approaching the finish line at the trials (above), Harvard (dark jerseys) strains to catch Pennsylvania. Race officials were forced to refer to sequential photographs (immediate right) of the finish to determine a winner. After a seven-minute delay, the scores on the blackboard (far right) told the story of Harvard's narrow victory.

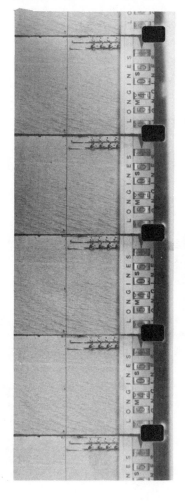

Stadium had been built for the 1932 Olympic trials. Thirty-six years later, its waters would send America's best to Lake Xochimilco in Mexico for the 1968 games.

The race that determined Harvard's fate took place on a windy Sunday afternoon. It was a strong tail wind, one Parker felt would help Penn. Everyone agreed it would guarantee remarkable times.

"This is the first time that four American crews who have all done better than six minutes for the two thousand meters have ever faced each other," noted Vesper coach Dietrich Rose. "It will be a race to remember."

Convinced that any advantage Harvard once enjoyed had been erased by Penn's new personnel and the conditions, Parker's prerace appraisal to his crew was blunt. There was nothing separating Harvard and Pennsylvania. Whoever went out and rowed the hardest would win.

"Our hope was to stay close through the first

five hundred, hold their margin through the second, begin to move on them in the third, and go past them at the finish," Parker opined. And it pretty much happened that way. Barely.

Penn started fast and led Harvard by 1.4 seconds after 500 meters. The lead was the same at the halfway point and upped slightly to 1.5 seconds at 1,500 meters. Harvard had not been able to move on the Quakers during that third 500.

With 500 meters to go, the Harvards were still confident that their final sprint would catch Penn. They could not have cut it any closer. As the two shells approached the finish line, it was clear that Harvard would need every meter to complete its pursuit. And when the line was reached, Harvard and Penn appeared dead even.

With exhausted oarsmen trying to regain their breath, judges examined photographs of the finish. The Harvard side worried that Penn's Pocock shell, 3 feet longer than the Harvard Stampfli, might have nosed across the line first. "Seatways, we were there," said captain Curt Canning, "but there was the matter of the length of the bow."

After seven agonizing minutes, the public address announcer made it official: Harvard was going to the Olympics. When the official photos were brought to Harry Parker, he beamed and simply said, "Beautiful."

The blackboard listed the times as Harvard 5:40.5 and Penn 5:40.7. A look at the Longines photo finish revealed that the margin was even less: 5:40.55 to 5:40.60. Both times beat Penn's course record, set two days earlier, by 16 seconds.

October's story in Mexico did not have the same happy ending. The international field, broken rigging, and some under-the-weather oarsmen combined to leave Harvard in sixth place at the Olympic Games. It was a disappointment to the men who made up Harvard's first Olympic crew. But it did not detract from what they had accomplished.

They remain a part of Harvard history:

Bow	—	Dave Higgins '69
No. 2	—	Cleve Livingston '69
No. 3	—	Steve Brooks '70
No. 4	—	Fritz Hobbs '69
No. 5	—	Scott Steketee '68
No. 6	—	Andy Larkin '68
No. 7	—	Captain Curt Canning '68
Stroke	—	Art Evans '69
Cox	—	Paul Hoffman '68

1972–76: Perhaps motivated by 1971's lack of glory, Harvard rowers rebounded with another five-year stretch of domination. In the period 1972–76, Harvard's only setbacks were the 1972 and 1973 Sprints, each of which was won by Northeastern. The remaining events gave Harvard a 26-0 race record, with three EARC titles (1977 would make it four in a row).

At the heart of this success was an extraordinarily deep class of 1975. They were, for the record, Blair Brooks, Dick Cashin, Rick Grogan, Ron Shaw, Al Shealy, Gregg Stone, Tiff Wood, and Ed Woodhouse. As freshmen, seven of them made history as members of the first freshman boat to compete at Henley. Not only did they compete, they won the Thames Challenge Cup in July of 1972.

As members of the varsity they suffered only one defeat in three years, the 1973 Sprints. And outside Harvard, four of them (the entire port side) rowed on national and Olympic teams.

Preceding page: *For two weeks each spring Harvard's heavy-weight crews call Red Top home as they prepare to meet their Yale counterparts on the Thames River* Above: *When freshman, JV, and varsity boats sweep their races, a broom is run up the flagpole at the Ledyard, Connecticut, site.*

As juniors their legend grew, and they became known as the Rude and Smooth, a reference to their style off and on the water. It was not so much that they were rude individuals in a societal sense. But in a sport in which even the best are accustomed to quiet anonymity, these talented athletes allowed their personalities to emerge, most notably in the brash, outspoken stroke, Al Shealy. And the press, never quite sure how to cover the sport, found something new to pick up on.

But Shealy wasn't just a product of his clippings. He may have been the best stroke Harry Parker ever had. Explaining the difference one individual can make, Parker paid tribute to Shealy. "The sum of the eight rowers does not equal the chemistry of the boat. The stroke is the guy who has the most impact on that chemistry. He lets the crew become a boat and not just eight people," said Parker. "Shealy was almost a perfect stroke. He had a beautiful feel for setting the right rhythm to a boat. He really knew how to race, how to get everyone right to maximum speed, and when to exploit that."

The entire group enjoyed a proud moment when one of their own, Dick Cashin, was selected top male athlete in the school in 1975. A resident of Djakarta, Indonesia, where his father was a foreign service officer, Cashin had the distinction of winning national championships in two sports, squash and crew. That crew claim came about through victories over Washington and Wisconsin, the best in the west, in 1974 and 1975.

With graduation taking half a dozen stalwarts out of the 1976 boat, expectations for that season were anything but high. The resulting 5-0 season, with Harvard's third straight Sprints title, provided Harry Parker unique satisfaction. He took particular delight in the performance of senior stroke Ollie Scholle.

"He was strong, very aggressive. And in his own way, he was as good as Shealy. Clearly, he was the making of the '76 crew."

The Rude and Smooth

There are two versions of the story. In one of them, an elder oarsman is said to have watched Harvard's 1974 crew in action and been struck by their performance, on and off the water. Speaking to some of the athletes, the gentleman commented on how smoothly they rowed but also expressed his opinion that their manners had been

The most celebrated and possibly the most talented of all Harvard crews was this 1975 contingent (from left): Al Shealy, Ron Shaw, Dick Cashin, Hovey Kemp, John Brock, Tiff Wood, Blair Brooks, and Gregg Stone. Kneeling: *Cox Bruce Larson.*

somewhat rude. In the other version, Sports Illustrated's Dan Levin drew the same conclusion. Either way, Harvard's 1974 and 1975 championship crews would come to be known as the Rude and Smooth.

They were loose, refreshing, and ever so confident. And they had every reason to be. Seven of them (Blair Brooks, Dick Cashin, Ron Shaw, Al Shealy, Gregg Stone, Tiff Wood, and Ed Woodhouse) had made history at Henley as freshmen when they capped an undefeated season by winning the Thames Cup by 5 lengths. As juniors, they won a national title by whipping Wisconsin and then Washington on their home courses, and with everyone gunning for them the next year, repeated with victories over the best of the West, Midwest, and East.

But what would distinguish them from so many other dominating Harvard crews was their collective personality. It was, at least as it was picked up by the media, the personality of its stroke, Al Shealy.

"I'm very proud of what I've done," Shealy told

a writer for the Harvard Football News, the weekly game program. "And I'm never humble about it. You work at crew for such an incredibly long time—it's a real butt-busting process—without any kind of reward. So when you finally do get a payoff by a win, there's an awful lot of pride involved."

When pulling away from an opponent, Shealy would punctuate the moment by offering a rude, "So long, baby," to the enemy, usually the lesser opponents, as Harvard's shell sprinted smoothly toward the finish line. It became his trademark and did not exactly endear him to the opposition.

Shealy attracted the attention of writers who adored quotable characters. At the start of the 1975 season, when Harvard won at San Diego, Shealy told a writer from Sports Illustrated that "a month from now, we'll be unbeatable." As oarsmen around the East were busy clipping the article and adhering it to boat house bulletin boards, Shealy and crew continued the work on the Charles that would make the brash prediction come true.

Their phenomenal success on the water should have been enough to gain recognition. But college sports rarely get much attention in the springtime unless there's a special hook. For the Rude and Smooth, their personality was the hook.

And so it was reported that their boat was called the George S. Patton *because of Shealy's love for Patton and military history. We learned that they called their big wins "horizon jobs" because the opponent's shell would seem to drop below the horizon. And it was also alleged that at the 1974 break-up banquet, two oarsmen from the varsity boat and one from the JVs streaked the gathering.*

It seemed that the group's initial delight in its reputation was tamed somewhat at the end. The outrageous quotes were still sought but less likely to emerge. Maybe the Bomber (Shealy) and the Brain (Shaw) still called Harry Parker the Weird One, but it was not to gain attention. The crew members were just being themselves and that, for the most part, meant that they were working hard to be the best.

That should not be lost amid the fun with their style. Their two years on top put an end to a slide that saw Harvard blanked at the Sprints for three seasons. Al Shealy was perhaps Harvard's best stroke ever. Shealy, Cashin, and Dave Weinberg '74 were part of the crew that won the gold for eight-oared heavyweights at the 1974 world championships, the only U.S. eight to do so in 20 years. Gregg Stone and Tiff Wood became national sculling champions, Stone from 1977 to 1979, Wood in 1983.

The individual accomplishments go on. Rick Grogan '75, the JV stroke, pushed his crew faster than many varsities in that period and was also the stroke of the U.S. lightweight eight that also won a gold medal in 1974. John Brock '77, the only sophomore on the 1975 boat, and Hovey Kemp '76, the only junior, also rowed on national and Pan American teams.

These were the reasons that the oarsmen from the mid-1970s distinguished themselves from the rest. The rude was fun to read about. The smooth should never be forgotten.

• • •

1977–81: It was around this time that the focus began to switch from Pennsylvania to Yale. Sure, it was Penn spoiling the 1977 show with an Adams Cup win, avenged at the Sprints much like the 1969–70 scripts. But suddenly it was Yale winning the Sprints in 1978, the first of two straight and four in six years.

Yale coach Tony Johnson appeared ready to break Harvard's—and Harry Parker's—domination of the Elis. In 1978 and again in 1979 Yale, fresh from its Sprints triumphs, was the favorite in New London. But each time, in memorable races, it was Harvard getting the upper hand.

In 1978 Yale rowed the first mile faster than any it had rowed all year. And it still had 3 miles to go. It also had Harvard unfazed by the pace, staying close despite the oppressive heat taking its toll on No. 6 man George Aitken.

"The race was essentially won at the mile mark," remembered Parker. "Dave Bogosian set an unbelievable pace for us, and although they were determined to move on us they couldn't. The race essentially ended there, and the rest was a matter of struggling home without Aitken falling out of the boat."

In 1979 there was talk that Harvard was slipping. Beaten three times the year before, Harry Parker's crew was being second-guessed when the season opened at the San Diego Classic. But the victory was Harvard's.

"You don't know what it's like to lose, until you've lost for Harvard," said Charlie Altekruse, the boat's no. 4 man. "Everyone always talks about the winner of a race. But if Harvard loses, then everyone talks about that. So we had a score to settle."

At New London, Harvard won again in what may have been the best H-Y race ever. It was a larger (by 15 to 20 pounds per man), more powerful Yale boat, stroked by John Biglow, against a smaller, equally determined Harvard crew, stroked by Gordie Gardiner.

Yale exploded at the start and led by nearly a length just a half mile into the race. Harvard tried to close the lead but Yale, and Biglow, would respond to deny them.

"Watching the race, I got the impression that he [Biglow] himself was determined not to let Harvard win. For three miles, we'd gain, they'd counter. And he appeared to be doing it all by himself," said Parker.

Finally, in the last half mile, Harvard's eight oars overcame Biglow and the others. Harvard would gain three seats, Yale would gain two. Harvard would gain two, Yale one. In the end, it was Harvard winning by just over two seconds in a 4-mile race.

With the Yale program continuing its progress, Harvard

pulled a double stunner in 1980, knocking off top-seeded Yale at the Sprints and again on the Thames. The Crimson's streak against Yale had reached 18.

But it was not 18 and counting. For on May 31, 1981, Yale put an end to the streak. All three Harvard boats were swept, and an 18-year nightmare was over for the Elis. Yale's victory started its own streak, which reached four in 1984.

1982–85: The 1982 season started on a somewhat down beat as Harvard finished fifth in San Diego. But in the various cup races that followed, Harvard was back in top form and took a 4-0 record into the Sprints.

This success earned Harvard top seed for the Sprints, a mild surprise since Yale had beaten Harvard in San Diego and had rowed well all year. Yale then made the seeding committee, and Harvard, look bad with victories at both the Sprints and New London.

The next season would be different. Despite losing the Compton Cup to Princeton on Lake Carnegie, Harvard was the team to beat when the Sprints arrived. This crew, stroked by Andy Sudduth, wanted to be compared to Parker's best. Sudduth had stroked the world championship crew for Parker in the preceding summer. A year later he would earn a silver medal on the U.S. Olympic boat.

But in 1983 the collegiate national championship was the prize Sudduth and his crew sought. At the Sprints, Harvard came close to that goal with a victory by two-tenths of a second over Brown. That earned Harvard an automatic berth in the second annual Cincinnati Invitational Regatta. This event brought together the best crews in the country to crown a national champion.

So in June of 1983, Sprints champ Harvard went to Cincinnati to battle the likes of Yale (who took its third straight from Harvard earlier in the month), Pacific Coast Conference winner Washington, and Intercollegiate Rowing Association champ Brown.

When the race began on Harsha Lake, Washington and Yale jumped out to an early lead. After the first 500 meters, Harvard began to pass Yale but Washington remained comfortably ahead.

With 800 meters to go, Washington had open water on the Crimson and appeared set to make a mockery of the event. But Sudduth and company went to work, and with 12,000 spectators enjoying the closing rush, Harvard caught its western foe at the line. Another national champion returned to Newell.

This 1983 crew, stroked by Andy Sudduth, earned its place in Harvard history when it won the national championship at the Cincinnati Invitational Regatta. Sudduth, a native of Exeter, New Hampshire, also won a silver medal at the 1984 Los Angeles Olympics.

The joy that was 1983 could not be sustained in 1984. Losses to Brown and Navy during the year followed a fifth-place finish at San Diego. In the final big events, Harvard finished fourth at the Sprints and lost its fourth straight to Yale.

Much had changed in college rowing since Harry Parker took control of Harvard's fates in 1963. One of the most significant changes was the rise of a number of challenging crew programs in the 1980s. No longer could the gang at Newell pay special attention to just one or two dangerous opponents.

But while there has been change, there has also been one constant. In 22 years Harry Parker has always found a way to meet new challenges. And the time to fear him most is when Harvard's strength is questioned.

So it was in 1985 when Harvard, a loser to Navy and Brown in the early going, rebounded to leave everyone else behind at the Sprints. And this crew was not finished. For the first time since 1980, Harvard defeated Yale on the Thames, and two weeks later the Crimson success continued with victory in the nationals at Cincinnati. In July, the biggest prize of all, Henley's Grand Challenge Cup, was Harvard's.

Once again, Harvard was number one.

Harry Parker

It has appeared every time a Harvard heavyweight crew has done something special or was expected to. That is, it has appeared often. "It" is the stock Harry Parker feature.

The story begins with a summary of Harvard's incredible racing record since 1963, the 18 straight wins against Yale, the undefeated streaks, the Sprints titles, and the rest. It proceeds to tie these accomplishments to the man with the heavy jaw and thinning blond hair, Harry Parker. So far, so good.

The focus suddenly becomes the man's personality, his style. Imposing, dominant, proud, tough, alert, intelligent, distant, subtle, competitive, and intense. These descriptions came from a single story on Parker. And they don't even cover the nouns. Like mentor, enigma, myth, and mystique.

More than anything, the stock Harry Parker story centers on this mystique, the notion that there is something magical to the way Parker affects those around him, most directly his oarsmen and those who row against him.

"I am moved to rise when I hear his name mentioned," one rower has reportedly said.

Another oarsman, commenting on the effect of a good word from Parker after a race, said, "It's almost as if God had said it."

Then there was the time late into Parker's tenure at Harvard that he entered himself in the senior division of the annual Head of The Charles Regatta under the name T. Lazarus, the man who returned from the dead.

"I think there's been too much of a focus on my personality," says Parker, adding, "observations which may or may not be accurate." And the mystique continues.

For the most part, the observations are right on the money. And Parker has never made any effort to deny them. That's not really his concern. But the fascination with Harry's persona has directed attention away from his real contributions to Harvard's rowing success. When pressed to talk about his role, and only when pressed, he identifies four areas in which he has made a difference.

"I have a good, sound sense, technically, of what effective rowing is and I believe I can teach people to row well, technically.

"I spend a lot of time thinking about training methods, not just theoretically, but how a crew can make the most of these methods and how I can be sure our crews are well conditioned.

"I've worked very hard at being able to pick crews, which is very difficult. Yes, seat racing has told us a lot, but too much has been made over that.

"And I think we've made good use of proper equipment, shells, oars, rigging, and so forth over the years."

As coach for Harvard and various Olympic squads, Harry Parker has affected amateur rowing like no other individual in the history of the sport. In his first 23 seasons at Harvard, he had a phenomenal record of 95-15 with 14 Eastern Sprints championships.

Few people in the rowing world would argue with Parker's assessment. Most would put forth that Parker has done these things sooner and better than anyone else. Parker himself simply concedes, "Well, we got a little jump on people."

That "little jump" began in 1963 when Parker, then a 27-year-old freshman coach, succeeded head coach Harvey Love, who died suddenly in January of that year. Beginning with an upset of Yale in the season finale, 6 years would pass before Harvard would lose to a college crew, 18 years before it would be Yale.

Parker was introduced to rowing at Pennsylvania by the Quakers' legendary coach Joe Burk. It is not coincidence that the same stream of adjectives used to describe Parker over the years had previously been directed to Burk. Both established themselves as stern, no-nonsense technicians.

After graduating from Penn in 1957, Parker took up single sculling and was national champion in both 1959 and 1960. That led to a fifth-place finish at Rome's Olympics in 1960 and eventually a spot on the Harvard coaching staff.

The young coach quickly earned a reputation as an innovator. Admiring the success of European crews, Parker began advocating stroking techniques embraced by West Germany's Ratzeburg crews and others. Convinced that the role of conditioning had been underappreciated, Parker demanded a year-round commitment with more intense year-round training. Then came changes in the rigging, new shells, new oars, and so forth.

Still, overshadowing all the things he did was the manner in which he did them. Specifically, the Parker legend became his ability to get his oarsmen to perform their best through a seemingly silent rapport. Thus was born the mystique.

"Harry lets you go through all the thinking processes on your own," said No. 4 oar Charlie Altekruse in 1979. "He's rarely explicit. The information is never pushed on you, but somehow he still imparts what you need for a good, hard race. He plants it in your mind and it starts to grow. He makes you think, or maybe he lets you think, and you come out a better oarsman for it, and a better person too."

With the media, indifferent to rowing for the most part, Harry could be even less explicit. Countless journalists, struggling to master such phrases as "open water" and "catching a crab," were further frustrated by Parker's reticence. Many a postrace press conference found Harry describing a 2,000-meter battle as "fun" or a "nice row."

Somewhere in the late 1970s, it is alleged, Harry changed. He smiled more. He spoke to reporters in full sentences. He was less intense.

What did not change, for the most part, was Harvard's success and the rowing world's respect for Harry Parker.

"It may be a dumb thing to say," offered Harry Parker in May of 1985, "but I don't win races."

Harvard's record of 95-15 in Parker's first 23 seasons at Cambridge says otherwise.

• • •

THE LIGHTWEIGHTS KEEP IT GOING

Though difficult to pinpoint, the acceptance of lightweight crew as a legitimate sport in this country seems traceable to the year 1919. That's when the American Rowing Association finally accepted the notion put forth by Pennsylvania coach Joseph Wright.

It was Wright who argued that too many potential oarsmen were being kept out of the sport by their inability to compete with men who outweighed them by 30 or 40 pounds. At his urging, a new lightweight classification was devised, limiting an individual's weight to 155 pounds, and the average weight of a crew to 150 pounds. (These numbers were subsequently increased by 5 pounds in each category.)

If all lightweight rowers owe Joe Wright their thanks, then Harvard's lightweights should be indebted to Bert Haines, later to become Harvard's first great varsity lightweight coach. Haines's efforts in the spring of 1921 organized lightweight rowing at Harvard. At that time a number of freshman boats made up the lightweight program. A year later, those freshmen continued as sophomores under William Haines, Bert's uncle, while Bert remained as freshman coach.

1922–36: The early years of Harvard lightweight rowing brought progress but no major glory. On May 20, 1922, Harvard competed in its first triangular race, finishing third behind winner Princeton and runner-up Yale. In 1923, captain Elliott Perkins' crew recorded Harvard's first lightweight win ever, over MIT on the Charles, before finishing second to Yale in the Big Three (Harvard-Yale-Princeton) race.

The progress continued as Harvard finally won that race in 1924 and again in 1925. Each of these victories came under a different coach, as Fred Newell followed Bill Haines in 1924 and was replaced by Fred Spuhn a year later.

In 1926 the race with Princeton and Yale became the Goldthwait Cup Regatta, in honor of Vincent B. Goldthwait '24, who had drowned following his sophomore year at Harvard. In the first 60 years of Goldthwait Cup competition, Harvard has triumphed 33 times.

From 1926 to 1928 Harvard's only victory came against the Kent School of Connecticut, though the books show Harvard the Goldthwait Cup winner in 1927. That triangular never took place, as Harvard and Princeton were warring over some less than sportsmanlike activities on the football fields. Harvard was credited as the Big Three winner because it had finished ahead of both Yale and Princeton at the American Henley Regatta in Philadelphia.

Harvard's first strong lightweight crew took the water in 1929 under coach Fred Sullivan '27, a former heavyweight cox for the Crimson, and captain Frederick "Chic" Farnsworth. This crew went undefeated against collegiate competition and won its first Joseph Wright Trophy (competed for since 1927), symbolic of the best lightweight crew in the East.

The 1930 crew marked a transitional period: It wasn't quite as good as that 1929 boat, but its two victories equaled the total Harvard would amass in the next six years. In that period, Harvard's only wins came over MIT in 1932 and over both Cornell and MIT in a three-way race in 1935.

This 1939 Harvard lightweight crew captured the Wright Trophy, symbolic of lightweight rowing supremacy, seven years before the first EARC Regatta.

1937–52: The first 15 years of lightweight rowing at Harvard featured four different coaches. The next 15 saw one. When Tom Bolles and Harvey Love arrived in Cambridge in 1937 to guide heavyweight fortunes, Bert Haines' new duties became the heavyweight freshmen and lightweight varsity. Both programs were blessed.

Haines won his first two races in 1937 before coming up short the rest of the way. But considering the previous six years' record, it was a significant accomplishment.

That only served as a prelude to Harvard's first dominating period in lightweight rowing. From 1938 to 1940 Harvard lost but one race, finishing second in the Wright Trophy race in 1938. Besides Haines, stroke Vincent Bailey was the other constant on these three crews, which remained the standard for future Harvard oarsmen.

The 1938 crew began a streak of seven straight Goldthwait victories and became the first Harvard lightweight crew to compete at Henley. After defeating the Henley Rowing Club in the first race, Harvard lost to Connecticut's Kent School, the eventual Thames Cup winner.

The 1939 crew captured the Wright Trophy, the first of three straight for Harvard. Vincent Bailey captained this crew and repeated as captain of 1940's undefeated boat.

The only blemish on the 1941 crew's record was a loss to MIT by two-tenths of a second. And in 1942, the last season of rowing before the war, Harvard won two early races before finishing third in the Wright Cup race.

Bert Haines' first six years as head coach firmly established Harvard as a lightweight rowing power. After the war, he picked up right where he had left off, producing undefeated crews in 1946 and 1947 and a strong but once-defeated boat in 1948.

The strength of the 1946 boat became evident to all on June 1 when heavyweight coach Tom Bolles, impressed at what he had seen on the Charles all season, chose the varsity lights to row the JV heavyweight race against Yale. The lights beat Yale's JV heavyweights by 5 lengths.

One highlight of this season came in the new premier event of the schedule, the Eastern Association of Rowing Colleges Regatta, which Harvard won and with it the Wright Trophy.

The 1947 boat drew its strength from captain and stroke Howie Hall, youngest of three brothers in that boat and perhaps the best oarsman in the program since Vincent Bailey.

Haines had mixed success with his final five crews, but none reached the heights of the 1946 and 1947 boats. No

Bert Haines served Harvard lightweight rowers from 1921 to 1952. He was varsity coach from 1937 to 1943 and again from 1946 to 1952.

more EARC titles came his way, and after winning the Goldthwait Cup for the seventh straight time in 1948, Harvard lost its grip on that trophy until Haines' final try in 1952 proved successful.

As coach of both the heavyweight and lightweight freshmen and the lightweight varsity, Bert Haines served Harvard rowing for 32 years, the longest tenure of any coach in more than 130 years of rowing at Harvard. Because of those various duties, particularly his involvement with freshmen, he proved to be a strong influence on virtually every oarsman who competed for Harvard in that period.

1953–68: Following Bert Haines' long tenure, ten different coaches directed the fortunes of Harvard lightweight rowing over the next 15 seasons. The string of part-timers began with three one-year terms put in by Ted Reynolds '50, Leroy Rouner '53, and C. Diederich Wilde '53 from 1953 to 1955.

Then in 1956 a third member of the class of 1953 took

charge and affected the most change around Newell Boat House. The Reverend H. O. J. "Joe" Brown, a former pupil of Bert Haines, ran the lightweight show for three years and launched one of the peak periods in the program's history.

It was a building process, as Brown's crews had marginal success in 1956, lost only to Princeton in 1957 (twice, by less than two seconds combined), and then went undefeated in 1958, the first of three straight perfect seasons.

By this time two new cup races had been introduced to the lightweight season. The annual race with Dartmouth and MIT was fought for the Biglin Bowl, a gift from Dartmouth's rowing alumni. And in 1958 Harvard and Navy competed for the first Haines Cup, presented by Mrs. H. Herbert Haines in memory of Harvard's beloved coach, who had passed away earlier in the year.

Harvard swept the cup races and advanced to the EARC Sprints, where it was favored to win for the first time since 1947. It did—barely—as Cornell finished just one-tenth of a second behind. As Harvard swept the freshman and JV races, it ended a perfect season for varsity, JV, third varsity, freshman, and second freshman boats. All that was left was the varsity's trip to Henley.

This crew featured some of the most talented individuals in the program's history, most notably the stern pair of Mark Hoffman and Mike Christian and three-year coxswain Mario Bryan, considered the best ever by some. Christian had the distinction of rowing for three perfect crews from 1958 to 1960. Later he would continue his post-Harvard rowing career at Cambridge University along with Hoffman.

The 1958 trip to Henley was a successful one, the first of three consecutive Thames Cup victories. To capture this first one, Harvard had to sweep Twickenham Rowing Club, the Kent School, Washington and Lee School, and, on the final day, the Royal Air Force and the Thames Rowing Club.

Included in the memories of that trip are Mike Christian's recollections of the popular coach Reverend Joe Brown, who wrapped up his Harvard coaching career. Writing in *The Second H Book of Harvard Athletics*, Christian said, "Those who rowed for and knew Joe at Henley will never forget him, off to address an elderly English ladies' church alliance, wearing his clerical collar and black shirt beneath a white Harvard rowing blazer with crimson piping."

Brown's successor, Laury Coolidge '58, had the unenviable task of following this perfect season. He responded with two perfect seasons of his own. After much jockeying around of personnel, Coolidge found the right combination to accompany stroke Tony Goodman, and the result was a regular-season sweep punctuated by a 2-length victory over Dartmouth at the Sprints, the last of those races to be held on the Charles River. (Worcester's Lake Quinsigamond would become the home of the Sprints, with the exception of 1975–77, when the regatta was held on Princeton's Lake Carnegie.)

At "Harvard's Henley," as it would be called, the lights repeated in the Thames Cup while the heavies took the Grand Challenge Cup. But the path to this title was somewhat more difficult than the year before. After victories against Crowland Rowing Club and Oriel College, the Harvards nearly met their match in Oxford's Isis Boat Club. Having gone up early by 2 lengths, Harvard was passed at the halfway point, the first time in two years a Harvard boat had been passed.

With a half mile to go, stroke Goodman kicked it up and Harvard's final sprint proved successful. That left final day victories over Boston's Union Boat Club (coached by Joe Brown) and London University to take home the Thames Cup again.

In 1960 Harvard again breezed through all comers at home and returned to Great Britain for a third triumph at Henley. The word upon arrival was that the Isis Boat Club was tired of these Yanks having all the fun and that they had put together some sort of super boat to spoil Harvard's bid. When pairings were drawn out of a hat, sure enough Harvard drew Isis for the first race.

The challengers were tough but not tough enough. After a race-long battle, it was Harvard pulling ahead to win by three quarters of a length and the rest of the regatta was somewhat less challenging.

After one more Sprints title in 1961 under new coach Kingsbury "K. C." Chase, Harvard watched Cornell become the crew to beat for most of the 1960s. The Big Red prevailed at the Sprints in five of the next six years, sharing the 1962 honors with MIT and Navy, and letting Harvard slip in under coach Bill Weber in 1966.

Harvard returned to its rotating coaches system after Coolidge left the program. Beginning in 1961, it was Chase, Coolidge again for a year, Fred Cabot '59 for two, and Dave Richard '61 and Bill Weber for a year each. Besides winning the 1966 Sprints, Weber's one crew also won at Henley, highlighted by two come-from-behind victories against the London Boat Club in the semifinals and the Isis Boat Club in the finals. Both British crews averaged close to 180 pounds. Weber had rowed at MIT and he was followed by another non-Harvard man, Bo Andersen, a former Dartmouth oarsman who became the lightweights' first full-time coach since Bert Haines.

In 1968 Andersen's second and final year, Harvard again won the Sprints and began a series of incredible streaks. The most modest of these was the varsity string of five Sprints wins, seven in eight years. The more remarkable involved the sub-varsity boats as well.

Each year at the Sprints, the Ralph T. Jope Cup is awarded to the college whose lightweight varsity, junior varsity, and freshman boats score the highest combined point total. It is an award that recognizes an entire program, not just the varsity boat. Beginning in 1968, Harvard won the Jope Cup 13 consecutive years up through 1980. Making this possible was the even more phenomenal record of Harvard's junior varsity, which won 14 straight Sprints titles from 1967 to 1980.

That 1968 varsity race received some notoriety because Harvard was very nearly eliminated in the morning heats on Lake Quinsigamond. Seeded first in all three lightweight events, Harvard was meeting all expectations until the seat of No. 4 man Fred Fisher jumped its slide early in the varsity heat. Fisher tried to row with his left hand and deal with the seat with his right. After three strokes, Fisher lost control of his oar, which flipped up and damaged the back post of the shell's rigger.

As a result Harvard finished last, eight seconds behind Princeton. Andersen protested the result, noting that rowing rules allow a race to be restarted when a boat suffers equipment damage in the first 30 seconds of a race. The referee had ordered Harvard to continue racing at the time of the accident, but after a lengthy meeting among regatta officials, Harvard was allowed to enter the afternoon finals as a seventh qualifier.

The decision was not universally popular and would have been less so if Harvard's new lightweight reign were not just beginning. By the time the varsity race began, the freshmen and JVs had already won handily. Just 400 meters into the varsity race, Harvard had open water and went on to win by a length over Penn.

Back in the pack was Cornell, the lightweight power Harvard seemed to be dethroning. The Big Red would delay that coronation slightly by upsetting Harvard twice in the early summer of 1968, first at the American Henley in Philadelphia and then at the real Henley's opening day. Harvard's reign would follow soon enough.

1969–71: The Jope Cup results previously noted give a pretty good indication of Harvard's consistent depth over a dozen or so years. It may seem dangerous to pick a best crew from all of these, but one group does stand out.

The 1969–71 crews rank with the 1958–60 Henley winners as the best in Harvard lightweight history. The beneficiary, and molder, of these talented oarsmen was Steve Gladstone, a 1964 Syracuse graduate who stayed around Cambridge for four near-perfect seasons before launching a successful heavyweight coaching career at Berkeley.

Gladstone arrived at a time when Harvard's heavyweight crews of 1967 and 1968 were being hailed as the school's best ever. He would soon have the local sports world buzzing about his lightweights.

In 1969 Gladstone's first crew featured four sophomores, including two gems, stroke Dave Harman and No. 7 Dick Moore, who would never lose a college race in their varsity careers. Their efforts recalled that other great stern pair of Hoffman and Christian from the 1958–59 boats.

This boat, like the previous four, entered the Sprints undefeated. It then came through with Harvard's first successful defense of that title in nearly a decade. The finish line scene found Harvard symbolically all alone, with open water separating the victors from the remaining five finalists, all of whom were within a half length of each other.

But there was still work to be done. This crew avoided the first-day elimination at Henley that its predecessor had suffered. But a loss to Leander in the semifinals sent Harvard home without any championship hardware.

The headlines and whispers really began with Gladstone's 1970 crew. It wasn't just their winning, but how they were winning. Four lengths over MIT, 3½ over Princeton, 3 over Yale, and so on. And some of their times were faster than heavyweight crews rowing on the same mornings.

"It's really an emotional group," Gladstone would say.

Preceding page: Perhaps Harvard's best lightweight crew ever, the 1971 varsity earned the name Superboat for its dominance throughout the 1971 season. Front row: Coxswain Fred Yalouris, Second row (from left): Bow Phin Sprague, No. 7 Dick Moore, stroke and captain Dave Harman, No. 6 Chuck Hewitt, No. 5 Jim Richardson. Third row: Coach Steve Gladstone, No. 3 Ephraim King, No. 4 Tony Brooks, No. 2 Andy Narva; manager John DioDato.

"I've never seen so many aggressive, competitive people in a boat. And they have the equipment to back it up. . . . Sometimes they scare even me."

At the heart of this group was junior captain and stroke Harman. He was able to get the boat off to early leads and then pull it ahead even farther. "He's an amazing stroke," Gladstone said at the time. "He has the ability to move the boat, and he has a killer instinct on the water."

With their gaudy record behind them, Harvard's 1970 crew entered the Sprints determined to show that they still had not peaked. And at Worcester they put on a show. Their 6:03.3 in the heats compared favorably with many heavyweight times. And their 6:06.7 times in the finals not only beat second-place Yale by nine seconds, it was the fastest final in history for a lightweight crew.

There was no Henley trip in 1970. That was saved for 1971, the year of Superboat. That was the name bestowed upon Gladstone's third crew by Harvard's publicity office. The coach was wary to accept the title, but the facts made it clear. Everyone returned from the 1970 boat, and even then the coach wasn't satisfied, as he found room for sophomores Andy Narva and Ephraim King in the varsity boat.

The early results were predictable: Harvard was undefeated in pre-Sprints competition for the seventh straight year. But the margin of victory averaged an unheard of 17 seconds. On a day when Columbia was beaten by 7 lengths on the Charles, Superboat's time was better than both the Brown and MIT heavyweights who were on the river that day.

At Worcester, a 6.4-second victory in the heats was the boat's closest race all year. In the afternoon finals, the margin was a more characteristic 14-second job over Columbia. Without a legitimate lightweight challenger in sight, Superboat sought out the heavies.

The 1971 rowing season was a perfect time to provide an answer to an age-old question: How would a great lightweight boat do against average heavyweight boats? The heavyweight ranks had not produced a dominant boat that spring, and perhaps the time was right for Harvard's lights to issue a challenge.

Lightweight crews had frequently competed against heavyweights at Henley and had done well. But it was not common for such competition to take place elsewhere. The venerable Intercollegiate Rowing Association Regatta at Syracuse would not allow Harvard to enter against its heavyweights, but the Pan American trials, to be held two days later in Syracuse, offered no such resistance.

"A great lightweight crew will not beat a great

heavyweight crew," said Gladstone before Syracuse. "But a great lightweight against a good heavyweight? That's something different. I think we've got a chance."

As it turned out, Gladstone's crew performed admirably at the Pan Am trials, finishing fourth in opening-round trials and second to Brown in a second-round repechage. That was good enough to earn a berth in the final six, but in that competition, the lights finished last.

There were no disappointments at Henley, where Harvard was a double winner. After drawing a bye, the varsity lights swept four races to take home the Thames Cup, and at the same time a Harvard four without coxswain swept five races to take the Wyfold Challenge Cup, giving Harvard the first double for an American crew in ten years.

For the record, the men who comprised Superboat were stroke Dave Harman, No. 7 Dick Moore, No. 6 Chuck Hewitt, No. 5 Jim Richardson, No. 4 Tony Brooks, No. 3 Ephraim King, No. 2 Andy Narva, bow Phin Sprague, and coxswain Fred Yalouris.

The Wyfold Cup winners were Howie Burnett, Kim Kiley, Al Kleindienst, and Scott Baker.

1972–85: As the 1972 crew season opened, Harvard's lightweights were on the spot. The Crimson's last lightweight varsity regular-season loss was 32 races ago, in April of 1964. Since his arrival in 1969, Steve Gladstone had never lost to an American college crew. By the time his fourth and final season at Harvard was over, he had kept his record clean.

This would not be a year of flashy victories. Gladstone juggled personnel, settled for things like nine-second victories, went 4-0, and won an unprecedented fifth straight Sprints title. The coach left Harvard at 16-0, with four wins at Worcester and one at Henley. He went on to become a successful heavyweight coach, first at Berkeley and then at Brown. In 1984 Gladstone led the Bruins to their first win over Harvard after 19 straight Stein Cup losses. He made it two straight a year later.

Gladstone was followed by John Higginson '62, captain of Harvey Love's last heavyweight varsity and grandson of Francis "Peter" Higginson, '00, one of the great figures in Harvard rowing history.

Higginson served for six years and produced a 22-3 record, winning four Sprints titles and finishing second in two others. There were no superboats in this period, but there was plenty of depth. From varsity through third

varsity, the Higginson years were noted for solid rowers who simply went out and won.

Higginson's deepest class was the class of '76, which featured three-year stroke Ned Reynolds and classmates Bob Leahey, John Kiger, Mac Heller, and Gil Welch. Their bid for three straight Sprints titles was stopped when Penn upset the previously undefeated 1976 boat.

"We hadn't seen Penn that spring," said Higginson, "and they went out and rowed a great race while we rowed an okay race."

Higginson's final two seasons featured a 7-1 record and two more Sprints titles. Kevin Cunningham and John Pickering were the keys to these crews, which featured a number of oarsmen who had spent time on third and second varsities before finding their way to the top boat. These sub-varsities were a source of pride to the coach.

"The JVs were always a very exciting element to the program," said Higginson. "They just kept on winning, and you unconsciously found yourself giving them a lot of attention without ignoring the varsity in any way."

Under Higginson and his successor Peter Raymond, the JV lights ran that incredible Sprints streak to 14 straight years. Raymond, a former Princeton oarsman, directed the Radcliffe program for two years before turning his attention to the men's lightweights for the same amount of time.

His first year produced a 3-1 boat that finished third at the Sprints with a senior-laden crew. The highlight of the year was a postseason trip to Japan to compete in the Japanese National Championships, a regatta that would determine which Japanese boat would represent Japan in the world championships. Harvard, the only foreign boat invited, won the event to provide the seniors with a special graduation present.

With a new combination for the start of 1980, Raymond's second crew opened with two straight losses, the first time Harvard had lost two regular-season races in 26 years. Raymond made a few changes, beat Coast Guard and Navy in the Haines cup, and faced a turning point at Princeton.

"Both the varsity and JV boats went down to Princeton and rowed exceptional, tough races against Yale and Princeton, each winning by about a second. And they just carried it over to the Sprints."

The early-season loss to Cornell was avenged nicely at Worcester, where Harvard beat second-place Cornell by 6 seconds and fifth place MIT by 18.

"We had to decide what to do with Courtlandt Gates,

Lightweight coach John Higginson '62 accepts the trophy for winning the 1975 Eastern Sprints title. A former heavyweight captain, Higginson compiled a 22-3 record, with four Sprints victories, from 1973 through 1978.

who had been our stroke. Do we keep him or move him to the JVs? We ended up moving Kevin Gaut to stroke and Courty to number four, and they both came through beautifully."

Raymond, like Higginson before him, opted out of the coaching field on a high note. His successor, Bruce Beall, opted for the Gladstone example of hopping from the lightweight world to that of the heavyweights, but not before he became the sixth straight Harvard lightweight coach to win the Sprints.

Beall, an accomplished oarsman out of the University of Washington, was Harvard's lightweight coach for five years, from 1981 to 1985. His best boat was his only Sprints winner, the 1982 crew that went 3-1. The one loss came in the Goldthwait Cup race which Beall called "the most exciting race I've ever seen."

Yale got the win in a time of 5:32.0. Both Harvard and Princeton were clocked in 5:32.5. At the Sprints it was a different story, as Harvard nipped Princeton by a second and Yale by three. It wasn't just a big win for Beall and his lightweights, it was a big win for Harvard rowing in general. Harvard heavyweights and lightweights frequently dominated the Sprints, but in 1981 and 1982, that lightweight victory was Harvard's only triumph in Worcester.

After earning a spot as a sculler on the 1984 U.S. Olympic team, Beall coached one more season at Harvard before accepting the position of heavyweight coach at MIT. It was time for a seventh coach to continue the lightweights championship streak.

ROWING FOR THE BLACK AND WHITE

In 1976, two years after Harvard's Department of Athletics assumed administrative control of Radcliffe athletics, the captains of the Harvard-Radcliffe teams took a vote. The question at hand was, "What shall we be called, Radcliffe Athletics or Harvard Women's Athletics?"

At the time, one could pick up the sports page and find "Radcliffe 8, Yale 1" under tennis, and "Harvard 3, Tufts 0" under field hockey. It was mildly confusing, and the resulting vote made it slightly less so. Slightly? All teams voted for "Harvard" except one. So ten years later, all women's teams in Cambridge wear Harvard on their jerseys except the Radcliffe crew.

The rowers were not simply being stubborn. They had a very real reason to maintain the name under which they gained early visibility and respect for all women athletes on campus. That came about from the national championship won by Radcliffe's 1973 heavyweight crew.

The crew story began in the fall of 1970, when Martha McDaniel made a trip to Weld Boat House to teach herself how to row. By the spring, the energetic Radcliffe freshman decided to put an eight together for some intercollegiate competition.

There weren't any experienced rowers on hand, but borrowing a concept the men had used successfully for years, McDaniel sought out the best athletes she could find. One of those was All-American swimmer RoAnn Costin.

"We had a couple of swimmers, a skier, a trained dancer. People who knew about training and competition," Costin recalled. "And then we went out and finished third at the nationals down at Old Lyme, Connecticut."

That third-place finish may have said as much about the state of women's rowing at that time as it did about the effort of this first Radcliffe boat. But still, nothing should be taken away from this group, working out in an old men's heavyweight shell, who launched the intercollegiate rowing program at Radcliffe.

Assisting that first crew were Garrett and Hope Olmstead, who took time to coach the crew but no compensation for their efforts. The first hired coach was John Baker, a former Harvard oarsman, who led the program to its great moment in 1973.

After finishing second in 1972 at the Eastern Association of Women's Rowing Colleges championships (the Sprints, actually called the New England championships at the time), Radcliffe and Baker approached the 1973 season with hopes of winning it all. Still, this would be a boat with just one experienced rower, captain and stroke Charlotte Crane. And by Sprints time, there would be five freshmen in the boat, including cox Nancy Hadley.

The spring season was a strong one, as Radcliffe won four of five races, losing only at Princeton by a second. All of that was redeemed at the Sprints, when Radcliffe beat Princeton (which finished fourth behind Connecticut College and Williams) by 16 seconds.

In June, Baker's crew competed at the national championships and beat the country's best college and club crews, earning the right to represent the United States in the world championships at Moscow later in the summer. There, the dream season ended, as Radcliffe finished in the back of the pack.

There are those who scoff at the attention given this championship crew on the grounds that women's rowing was underdeveloped at the time. They will point out how less-heralded crews, a year or two down the line, were far superior to 1973's titlists. And after Radcliffe's poor showing in Moscow, a fate suffered by virtually every U.S. women's crew in those days, the camp system was inaugurated to select a stronger national crew.

Such criticism, while close to the mark, has been an unfair shot at what these people accomplished. "They were the best eight in the country," recalled Carie Graves, a Wisconsin rower who competed against Radcliffe in 1973 and later became Radcliffe's head coach in 1978. "They worked hard for it and had to beat the likes of Vesper Boat Club as well as the colleges. It's tough to take that away from them."

Radcliffe won Sprints titles again in 1974 and 1975, further establishing the reputation of the Black and White on the water. But it wasn't just the winning that led the crew to keep the Radcliffe R on their shirts, it was also the support that the college directed their way.

Radcliffe president Matina Horner was helpful in the crew's fund-raising efforts, which purchased necessary equipment and financed the Moscow trip. As a result, the first Radcliffe shell was named in honor of President Horner. It is safe to say that Radcliffe's involvement with the rowing program was more far-reaching than with the majority of other women's sports, many of which were born after Harvard's athletic department became involved.

The Sprints victories stopped in 1975. Radcliffe crews continued to improve, but so did the competition. The early boats out of Weld had been organized before Title IX legislation gave women's athletics a boost at all colleges. So Radcliffe had gotten a jump on the competition.

Peter Raymond, a former Princeton oarsman, followed Baker as Radcliffe head coach and went 9-1 in two seasons, finishing third and second in his Sprints efforts. When Raymond took over the Harvard men's lightweight program, Carie Graves took charge of the women.

Graves was one of the finest rowers the United States ever produced. Instrumental in launching the program at the University of Wisconsin as an undergraduate, Graves stroked the Badgers to the 1975 national championship. Outside Wisconsin, she stroked the United States to a stunning silver medal finish at the 1975 world championships and then was the No. 6 oar on the Olympic bronze medal boat at Montreal in 1976. Both of those boats were coached by Harvard's Harry Parker.

Graves further entrenched herself in rowing history by becoming the first woman to serve on three Olympic eights, as she made the 1980 boat, which did not compete in Moscow, and the 1984 boat, which won the gold at Los Angeles.

The best of her six Radcliffe crews was the 1980 boat, which was 4-0 in the spring and second at the Sprints.

"That was a very strong group, primarily extraordinary athletes, not extraordinary rowers," recalled Graves. "Anne Benton and Tory Laughlin had rowed extensively, but the others, like Jenny Stone for example, were simply great athletes who took up the sport seriously when they arrived."

Stone's father (Bob '45) and brother (Gregg '75) had rowed for Harvard, and she followed their example. She also excelled in field hockey and squash, earning ten varsity letters in her four-year career. Athletes like Stone continued to gain visibility for their sport even after the championships stopped coming. They did so by carrying on the tradition of hard work begun by the 1971 pioneers.

The white R on black shirts has identified Radcliffe rowers on the Charles and elsewhere. While other women athletes chose to compete as Harvard teams, the rowers, such as the undefeated 1976 crew at top, preferred to keep the Radcliffe name under which the program gained prominence in the early 1970s. Head coach of Radcliffe from 1978 to 1983 was Carie Graves, the first woman to row on three Olympic eights (1976, 1980, and 1984).

That meant sticking to the type of grueling practice and training regimen that the men had made famous. The first crews followed exactly the same program of running, training in the tanks and on the ergometer, and double workouts that their male counterparts were known for.

One difference emerged in the occasional multisport star who combined her rowing with other pursuits. Fritz Hobbs '69 and Dick Cashin '75, who pulled off the crew-squash double, were oddities on the men's side. Frequently, the women who doubled up, like ice hockey goalie Nelia Worsley '79, would overlap their respective workouts.

As Coach Graves pursued her third Olympic berth, and a degree from Harvard's School of Education, Radcliffe turned to Lisa Hansen (later Lisa Stone when she married oarsman Gregg Stone) in 1984. At the time, eight full seasons had been completed since Radcliffe's last Sprints title.

There was no single power dominating the women's rowing world in this period. In those eight years there had been five different winners and no one was victorious in consecutive years. Radcliffe was the most consistently competitive program, as evidenced by the fact that no other crew had qualified for the finals of the Sprints in every year since the competition began in 1972.

The women have also produced lightweight crews since 1975. Much as the 1973 heavyweights have had to defend their accomplishments, so too have the Radcliffe lights. The record books show that from 1977 through 1985, the Radcliffe lights finished no worse than second at their Sprints and won the title five times (1977, 1980, 1982, 1984, and 1985).

But the nagging fact remains that there are very few competitive lightweight crews in existence. The value of finishing second is undercut when there are only two competitors in the race. The available competition is inconsistent, as evidenced by the nationals. In 1982 Radcliffe won the national championship in a race that featured only Radcliffe, Smith, and MIT. In 1985 Radcliffe beat a single opponent, Oregon, in the final.

Still, as one veteran crew watcher remarked, "It's not their fault there's few takers on the river. They just go out and beat whoever's around."

CHAPTER 5

Track and Cross-Country

"These guys today are unbelievable. Why, some of them will pick which meets to gear up for and they'll sit out other ones. The idea of missing a meet just wasn't talked about. I mean, if you missed a meet, it was because of a death in the family, and even then it had better have been your mother or father."

It was not always easy to tell whether Bill McCurdy meant everything he told you. But speaking about the modern athlete in general, not necessarily the Harvard athlete, three years after stepping down as Harvard's track coach in 1982, McCurdy was obviously disappointed in what he saw developing.

"They're getting away from the team concept. The focus is too high now, on the Olympics or the personal best."

Could the athletes of whom McCurdy speaks ever relate to Paul Withington of the class of 1912? Withington, a Harvard track captain of modest talents, once finished dead last in a 2-mile run during a meet that Harvard went on to lose badly. Despite the fact that he had become ill during the running of the race, Withington was distraught

that his Harvard team had been trounced and that he had not contributed even a single point to the cause.

Withington's shame led to his appearing in the IC4A championships two weeks later wearing a plain white t-shirt rather than his Harvard shirt with its familiar H. In his opinion he had been an embarrassment and did not deserve to wear the H until he had redeemed himself. In that IC4A race he did just that by winning in a time of 9:24.4, a new Harvard and intercollegiate record.

Withington's performance was an individual triumph made possible by his commitment to the team. It is the loss of this relationship between the individual and the group that Bill McCurdy laments.

"The irony here is that the athlete can do more when he has a cause. And the team is a cause. They'll accomplish more things when they are working for a team than they could possibly do as an individual working for himself."

Each Harvard generation has had its Paul Withington. Perhaps the gesture has changed. But there has always been the individual with a particular goal who has struggled and succeeded in a way that touched all observers. Sometimes the needs of the team have served as catalyst. For others, the motivation has arisen from personal reasons not always revealed.

Harvard track has been blessed with brilliant performers one remembers for their strength, their grace, or their intensity. There have been those without a wealth of talent who have turned four years of struggle into one day of redemption. And there have been those whose effort was equal to the rest but who never enjoyed that day in the sun.

The motives may have changed for some. But the level of accomplishment has remained high for more than a century.

Ellery Clark

For all of the great athletes to grace Harvard's track program in recent years, few can compare with Ellery H. Clark '96, one of Harvard's first and most versatile track greats. His exploits spanned two decades, first at Harvard and later with the Boston Athletic Association.

Clark first gained prominence as a Harvard junior when he scored in 18 events in five important meets. "When the points he won from throwing the shot beat Pennsylvania, the Penn track team gave him a cheer," according to his son, Ellery Clark, Jr., '33.

After he left Harvard, Clark's versatility remained on display, as he set records for the BAA while competing in 21 different events over a competitive career lasting 21 years. At age 33 he won the New York Athletic Club high jump, and at age 56 he captured two Amateur Athletic Union (AAU) 1-mile walks. He also penned four books on track and field.

But of all the accomplishments that filled Clark's career, none can compare with his efforts in the 1896 Olympic Games in Athens. Winner of both the running long jump and the high jump, a double never equaled, Clark holds a lofty position in Olympic history. Yet there was a time when Harvard threatened to prevent that history from being written. Clark's son explains:

"In February of 1896, the BAA asked my father to represent them at the games in Athens. Harvard president Eliot was not enthusiastic about the revival of the games and opposed Harvard's direct involvement. But on March 4, Dean LeBaron Briggs granted approval with expected conservatism. His letter, in part, said, 'May I ask you not to emphasize unduly the Harvard side of your athletic position. . . . You go, as I understand it, in the capacity of a B.A.A. man, and the fact that you are a Harvard man is, so to speak, accidental.' "

Clark competed in Athens along with William Hoyt '98. History shows that a third Harvard undergraduate took part in those 1896 games. James B. Connolly '99, a freshman at the time of this excitement, requested permission to compete from the dean's office and was denied. Connolly went anyway, paying his own expenses, and won the hop, step, and jump.

Connolly never returned to Harvard, but 50 years later he was awarded a varsity track H by the Harvard Athletic Committee. Upon receiving the award, Connolly used no more than ten

One of Harvard track's first superstars, William Schick set a record in the 100-yard dash (9.8 seconds) that lasted from 1902 to 1963, when Aggrey Awori ran 9.7.

words in offering a terse "thank you" for such overdue consideration.

Clark was forever grateful to Dean Briggs for the way his request was handled. His feelings about those 1896 games were eloquently stated in his 1911 Reminiscences of An Athlete.

Nothing could equal this first revival. The flavor of the Athenian soil—the feeling of helping to bridge the gap between the old and the new—the indefinable poetic charm of knowing one's self thus linked with the past, a successor to the great heroic figures of olden times . . . there is but one first time in everything, and that first time was gloriously, and in a manner ever to be remembered, the privilege of the American team of 1896.

. . .

A CENTURY OF ACHIEVEMENT

1874–1919: The earliest recorded efforts of Harvard men competing in a track meet date back to the spring of 1874, when four undergraduates took part in a meet in Saratoga, New York. This historic yet less than official happening took place months before the formation of the Harvard Athletic Association, the first organized track body at Harvard, in the fall of 1874.

By the following year intercollegiate track in the Northeast was gaining in popularity, and in 1876 the Intercollegiate Association of Amateur Athletics of America was born. The IC4A, as it is known today, still sponsors major championships for eastern schools in cross-country, indoor track, and outdoor track.

Harvard's early track fortunes were reflected in its IC4A success. From 1879 to 1892 the Crimson won 11 of 13 championship meets. And throughout this period Harvard track was organized and financed completely by undergraduates.

The top performers of these early years were Evert Wendell '82, William Goodwin '84, and Wendell Baker '86. Wendell and Goodwin saved some of their best efforts for the IC4A championships. Wendell earned six IC4A victories in the 100-, 220-, and 440-yard races over a three-year period, while Goodwin swept the 880 and mile in three consecutive meets.

As Harvard track entered its third decade, the competition stiffened and the Crimson were unable to continue their domination. Still, the program prospered as the start of a new century approached. George Fearing '93 was one who kept Harvard among the best. His high-jump mark of 6 feet 2¼ inches remained a Harvard record for 46 years.

For all the great track accomplishments in Olympic history, no one has yet equaled the double victory by Ellery Clark in the running long jump and high jump, set in 1896 at the games' renewal.

Harvard track had unusually high visibility in 1896, when four athletes with ties to Harvard participated in the renewed Olympic Games in Athens. Ellery Clark '96 and William Hoyt '98, winners of three events, were two Harvard undergraduates representing the United States at the games. They were joined by Thomas Burke and James Connolly, whose Harvard affiliations were somewhat qualified. Burke, a student at Boston University Law School at the time, received a Harvard degree as a special student five years after the games. He won both the 110-meter dash and 400-meter run. Connolly was a Harvard freshman denied permission to compete by the Harvard dean. As a result he left Harvard, never to return, and paid his way to Athens, where he won the hop, step, and jump.

With the added benefit of professional coaching, Harvard track continued to prosper into the 20th century. James G. Lathrop became Harvard's first track coach in 1885 and remained on the scene for 15 years. After the 5-year tenure of John Graham, manager of the U.S. Olympic squad in 1896, Lathrop returned to Harvard for 5 years before W. F. "Pooch" Donovan took over in 1909.

Harvard remained strong throughout this period. Of all the individual heroics in these years, four accomplishments stand out. First are the efforts of William Schick '05, a sprinter without equal in his day. In the most important meets of his time, the IC4As and the Yale dual meet, Schick was virtually unbeatable. He won the 100- and 220-yard dashes in the 1904 and 1905 IC4A meets and won the same events in all four of his meetings with Yale. In 1902 Schick ran the 100 in 9.8 seconds, establishing a Harvard record that stood for 61 years.

Four Harvard men joined distinguished company when they set a world record at the 1914 Boston Athletic Association Games. Roderick Tower, Francis Capper, Bill Bingham, and William Barron were the record-setting relay team that covered a 1,560-yard course in 3:03.

And then there were the achievements of Westmore Wilcox and Ned Gourdin. Wilcox's time of 48 seconds in the 440 set a Harvard record in 1915 that lasted until Jeff Huvelle's 47.6 in 1968. Gourdin did him one better. His 25-foot 3-inch long jump in the 1921 Harvard-Yale versus Oxford-Cambridge meet is still a Harvard record.

1920–49: Harvard track suffered its first real decline following World War I. Results against archrival Yale were always a good barometer of any Harvard team in the early 20th century, and by this standard Harvard fared poorly. Yale took six of seven meets during the 1920s, a decade in which Harvard fortunes improved toward the end.

Bill Bingham, just four years out of Harvard, became head coach in 1920, and with him came two experienced men as assistants, Eddie Farrell and Jaakko Mikkola. They stayed on to assist Bill Martin, who assumed head coaching duties for the 1922 season, and eventually took over the head position in successive tenures. Farrell restored success to Harvard track from 1923 to 1936. Mikkola was head coach from 1936 to 1952.

Farrell's early years were blessed with outstanding middle-distance runners. The trio of John "Soapy" Watters, Willard Tibbetts, and Ellsworth "Red" Haggerty dominated the 880-yard, 2-mile, and mile events respectively, as Harvard won both the 1926 and 1927 indoor IC4A titles.

Willard Tibbetts (114) turns it on down the stretch to catch Loucks of Syracuse and win the 1925 IC4A cross-country championship in record time. The two men had battled for a mile before Tibbetts's sprint over the last 50 yards brought him the title.

Tibbetts (1925) and Watters (1926) also established themselves in cross-country, winning back-to-back IC4A cross-country championships as well.

Despite these successes, the class of '26 endured one nagging disappointment. As freshmen and again as seniors they suffered identical losses to Yale by the score of 67⅔ to 67⅓.

Moving into the 1930s Farrell enjoyed more consistent success. Again, using Yale as the standard, Harvard's 8-5 record against the Elis in both indoor and outdoor meets reflected the improvement.

Some of the more memorable efforts came early in the decade, like the world-record performance by the mile relay team at the indoor IC4As of 1930. This quartet included Vernon Munroe, Francis Cummings, Vincent Hennessy, and Eugene Record, perhaps the most talented of the group. In addition to his quarter-mile heroics, Record was an undefeated hurdler in his career, winning the high hurdles in three straight outdoor IC4As and the 70-yard indoor hurdles twice.

The 1931 cross-country team earned its place in Harvard history with an IC4A team championship, the first since 1912 and last until 1976. Runners continued to dominate Harvard track throughout the decade. One of the best was Pen Hallowell '32, Gene Record's classmate and a standout in both the mile and half mile.

Another pair of classmates, Milton Green and Norm Cahners of the class of '36, were Farrell's last superstars. Each competed regularly in three events, and frequently the pair accounted for six wins in a single afternoon. Green's events were low hurdles, high hurdles, and broad jump; Cahners was master of the 100-meter dash, 200-meter dash, and the hammer throw.

The field events produced standouts around this time as well. Both Bob Hall '36 and Bob Haydock '39 established new high-jump standards after George Fearing's 6 feet 2¼ inches survived for 46 years. And Richard Johnson '36 became the first Harvard man to throw a javelin 200 feet.

In 1936 Jaakko Mikkola took over the program. The coach of Finland's Olympic team in 1920 and 1924, Mikkola coached the great Finnish miler Paavo Nurmi, whose exhibition mile in May of 1925 filled Harvard Stadium.

Mikkola's first superstar was another fine runner, James D. Lightbody, Jr., '40. Son of a four-time Olympic medal-winner, Lightbody excelled at 600 and 880 yards. He made his name not only by establishing records but

Sam Felton swings into his last turn for one more winning toss. A member of the 1948 and 1952 Olympic squads, Felton held the Harvard hammer and discus records while an undergraduate.

also by an electrifying kick that pulled out many a victory at the tape.

Following World War II, Harvard track began another serious decline. Still, the efforts of Sam Felton rose above the troubles. Felton, who had the distinction of competing for both Dartmouth and Princeton during the war years, set Harvard records in the hammer and discus and earned a berth on the 1948 and 1952 U.S. Olympic teams. A member of the class of '48, Felton made his best international showing with a fourth-place finish at the 1948 Olympics in London.

1950–59: As the 1950s approached, all was not well with Harvard track. Jaakko Mikkola, a kind, beloved figure at Harvard for nearly 30 years, was overseeing a program that had grown soft. As one member of the class of 1955 recalled about his freshman year, "Varsity meets were held without anyone really being sure which athletes would show up."

From 1948 to 1950 Yale enjoyed some of the most

lopsided victories in the recent history of the series. And in 1949 the combined Harvard-Yale squad that faced Oxford-Cambridge was virtually all Yale.

Adding to the situation was the failing health of Mikkola, who underwent a serious operation in the fall of 1951 followed by a heart attack in the spring of 1952. The squad responded with an undefeated outdoor dual meet campaign in 1952, which ended with the second straight upset of Yale, this one by the largest margin in 13 years, 83-57.

Two weeks after that victory, Mikkola succumbed to his illness. His freshman coach of three seasons, Bill McCurdy, was named to take over the role of head coach.

It was not by chance that Bill McCurdy arrived at Harvard at this time. Athletic director Bill Bingham had brought the Stanford graduate into the program for a very definite purpose. Bingham had met the future coach in the armed forces, where McCurdy was a physical education instructor. The no-nonsense McCurdy, later the coach at Springfield College, impressed Bingham as the right man to return discipline to the Harvard track program.

It did not take long for McCurdy's influence to be felt. The task he faced was underscored by one incident in his first year.

"We used to do plenty of timed quarter miles in preseason, and the upperclassmen didn't take to these very well," said McCurdy. "I remember one of the seniors coming up to [Bob] Rittenburg, who was a sophomore at the time, and saying to him, 'Just remember. We don't do these very hard.' Rittenburg was incensed. He just went out and won them all but seemed to worry that his times could have been better if he had been pushed."

The contrast between the old and the new could not have been clearer. Bob Rittenburg, a member of McCurdy's last freshman team and first varsity, recalled that incident well.

"I was bothered a little bit. I was a workhorse type, accustomed to working three hours a day. I didn't feel right if I didn't have to drag myself off the track."

McCurdy's philosophy meshed well with that of Rittenburg and the other members of the class of '55. This would be the transition class, the one that set the standards for future McCurdy trackmen.

The first loud message was sent in the 1954 outdoor meet with Yale. This was a Yale team that had won the indoor IC4As and the indoor Heptagonal meet (Ivy League plus Army and Navy) after beating Harvard badly. They were undefeated in dual meets entering Harvard Stadium and would later win the outdoor Heptagonals.

But on May 4, 1954, on a rainy afternoon, Harvard pulled off a major upset that in retrospect seemed to launch the McCurdy era. As would happen so many times over the next three decades, the key to victory was McCurdy's use of personnel.

"From the start, he ran a program that involved numbers," said Rittenburg. "This may not have helped the stars in the program, but it was consistent with his philosophy. He arrived here as if he was a professor coming to teach a class. He had to treat everyone the same."

One of the numbers involved on that rainy May afternoon was Al Wills, a sophomore chosen to run the mile though he had not done so all year. Against Yale men who had won the IC4A mile and half mile, the unheralded Wills started fast and caught the Elis napping. By the time they realized Wills was for real, it was too late. He stole the mile and started Harvard on its way to a 72-68 upset.

McCurdy's touch carried over to cross-country the following fall, when Harvard enjoyed its first undefeated season since 1939. The indoor and outdoor seasons nearly followed suit, combining for a 6-1 record, the only loss being a close indoor decision to Yale.

This was the final season for the class of '55 and the likes of Rittenburg, Rennie Little, Alan Howe, and Carl Goldman, all letter-winners for three years. Little, often overshadowed by Rittenburg's exploits, frequently provided key points as anchor on the relay team.

But it was Rittenburg who provided the most spectacular moments of this period. Starting as a freshman, when he scored 19½ points in five events against Yale, Rittenburg lived up to all the expectations he brought with him from Boston Latin, where he was a much-heralded schoolboy star.

By the time he was a senior, his feats were increasingly hard to believe. There were three firsts and a second against Dartmouth. Then came five firsts against Brown. Finally, against some real competition at Yale, he scored 26 points in a meet that Harvard won by two-thirds of a point.

New heroes emerged for Harvard track as the program continued to gain strength through the rest of the 1950s. Cross-country began to steal the spotlight through the efforts of contrasting standouts.

First there was Pete Reider, the diminutive yet cocky Californian first heard from as a freshman, when he set a course record at New Haven in the rain. McCurdy's memories of Reider went back even further.

"In the days when we couldn't contact prospective

students, Reider was someone we could write to because he wrote us first. I'll never forget that guy, having the nerve to write and ask if we had a track program. Then he shows up, announcing his arrival by walking into my office and saying, 'I'm Reider. Where's McCurdy?'"

In addition to being dominant in cross-country for three years, Reider led indoor and outdoor success as the first Harvard man to regularly run both the mile and 2-mile events.

In contrast to Reider was the 6-foot 4-inch Dyke Benjamin, plagued by injury for three years only to win eight straight cross-country meets as a senior in 1958. Benjamin set a course record in the Heptagonal cross-country championships and went on that year to set a Harvard 2-mile record and an American 4-mile record.

Two other standouts of this period were Joel Landau and Richard Wharton. Landau followed Reider's tradition of running in a number of events. His most spectacular efforts came as a junior, when he set Harvard records in four different events and also took four firsts against Yale.

Wharton was one of McCurdy's favorites. "Two things stand out about Wharton. The first was his versatility. He was a winner in cross-country and also helped upset Yale indoors with a victory in the two-twenty. I also remember seeing him lead the others in a spontaneous victory lap after our first Big Three win indoors at Yale."

The great 1954 upset of previously unbeaten Yale was set in motion by Al Wills's upset of Yale captain Mike Stanley in the mile. Harvard's young coach Bill McCurdy would make a habit of beating Yale in his 30-year career.

Bob Rittenburg was another factor in that 1954 upset in the Stadium. No Harvard trackman has ever had a better day than Bob Rittenburg did at Yale in 1955. The Harvard captain won both hurdles, both jumps, and was second in both sprints in Harvard's 70 ⅓ to 69 ⅔ win over the Elis. Rittenburg was named Harvard's best athlete in 1955.

Rittenburg's Day Against Yale

Reading about track exploits can make one dizzy from all the numbers, all those times and heights and distances. It can be numbing to the point that no single accomplishment can be separated from the rest.

Still, every once in a while, someone does something that stands out from the pack. The numbers are different. You remember them. On May 21, 1955, Harvard captain Bob Rittenburg produced some numbers that Harvard people still talk about.

To begin with, the opponent was Yale and the meet was in New Haven. Next, the final score was unusually close: Harvard 70⅓, Yale 69⅔. In this context, it's easy to understand why people remember that Bob Rittenburg provided 26 of Harvard's points that day.

For the record, Rittenburg's points came from winning both hurdles and both jumps and finishing second in both sprints.

"It was typical of the guy," according to Coach Bill McCurdy. "We had planned to have him in the high jump and the two hurdles. Then he brought up the hundred. He never said anything before the meet about the two-twenty. Then during the meet, he made that suggestion. I asked him if there'd be a conflict with the two-twenty, and he said there wouldn't. Of course, there was."

Rittenburg cleared 6 feet in the high jump on his first try while on his way over to the start of the 220. The almost cavalier way he cleared that height seemed to take its toll on the Yale jumpers, who failed at that height even though they had consistently cleared higher levels in other meets.

"I was a dual meet competitor. My entire focus was on contributing to success in the dual meets," Rittenburg would later observe. "What made those twenty-six points important to me was the fact that we needed every one of them to win the meet."

Rittenburg had arrived at Harvard as a scholastic champion of national calibre. A native of Dorchester, Rittenburg attended the Boston Latin School and gained prominence through BAA and Knights of Columbus meets at the Boston Garden.

He was also a national AAU champion (60-yard hurdles and high jump) in the major event now known as the Eastern States Championships.

His city background provided all the preparation he would need for intercollegiate track. "I think I was toughened by that environment. I mean we ran in school basements, old armories, anywhere we could."

Rittenburg's day against Yale, one of the last meets of his brilliant career, stunned just about everyone, with the possible exception of McCurdy. He had seen the efforts that made such an afternoon possible.

"He got better because he worked harder than anyone else. After everyone else was long gone after practice, he always ran one more quarter."

And on one spring day in New Haven, all those extra quarter miles made the difference.

• • •

1960–63: Harvard's heralded runners received much of the attention in Bill McCurdy's early years and later. Of equal importance were the points gained from the field events. This was the domain of Ed Stowell, a former runner for McCurdy at Springfield who became assistant coach in 1956.

Stowell soon became an invaluable yet unsung member of the program. Dwarfed by the indomitable presence of a McCurdy, Stowell simply went about the business of producing champions in a way that few noticed.

"Ed was never fully appreciated," McCurdy would say later. "He was at his best at meets, where he had a confident, almost rabid enthusiasm when it got down to competition."

In the early 1960s Stowell put together one of Harvard's best field event teams. In Stan Doten and Ted Bailey, Stowell had two standouts in the hammer who broke the school mark six times in two years. In 1962 Bailey was the NCAA champion.

Tom Blodgett was another of Stowell's early stars. As a senior in 1961 Blodgett accounted for 15 points in the high jump, pole vault, and both hurdles as Harvard upset Yale, 73-67. Mark Mullin, the Ivy League's top miler, was another key to this win.

Yale remained a special date on the Harvard schedule, though the new life McCurdy breathed into the program had made upsets less possible than a decade earlier. The IC4A meets had become just a little out of reach and had been replaced by the Heptagonal championships as the major postseason event.

Using the Heps as a measuring stick, two distinct periods stand out in the 1950s and 1960s. The first came in 1956–57, when Harvard won consecutive Heptagonal titles in the three running seasons—outdoor, cross-country, and indoor—beginning in the spring of 1956. Next came perhaps Harvard track's golden era, from 1964 to 1970, when McCurdy's men dominated all three seasons. In a seven-year stretch, Harvard won 13 Heptagonals, finishing with a sweep of all three events in both 1969 and 1970.

Harvard took indoor and outdoor Heptagonal titles in 1964 and again in 1965. These team successes were preceded by one of the most extraordinary individual performances in the 1963 indoor games. Aggrey Awori, a sophomore from Uganda, became the first person to win

An entire program takes pride in the selection of one of its members as winner of the Bingham Award, symbolic of Harvard's best athlete. Mark Mullin, accepting the 1962 award from athletic director Tom Bolles, was the third of eight trackmen to win the honor from 1955 through 1979.

Beginning in 1962, Harvard took four of the next five indoor Heptagonal titles thanks to such performers as (from left) Aggrey Awori, Art Croasdale, and Chris Ohiri. Awori was the outstanding performer of the 1963 meet, when he became the first triple winner in the history of the event. He shared the honor two years later.

three separate events when he captured the broad jump, the 60-yard dash, and the 60-yard hurdles. Later in the year, Awori again made headlines when his 9.7 seconds in the 100-yard dash broke William Schick's 61-year-old record. That remains a Harvard best.

1964–70: There were a variety of heroes in the 1964 Heps winners. Indoors, Awori and Nigerian Chris Ohiri were one-two in the broad jump. Ed Meehan and Keith Chiappa did the same in the 1,000 meters. And coach Stowell produced the first of his great high-jumpers in Chris Pardee, whose 6 feet 9 inches won the IC4As that year.

Outdoors, Harvard was phenomenal. The 103-46 beating of Yale was the most one-sided ever, and the Heps win was the school's first outdoors in eight years. Ohiri turned in the most spectacular performance as he added 2 feet to the Harvard triple jump record, which had been set in 1893.

Awori and Ohiri received a good deal of publicity, particularly Ohiri, who was arguably the greatest soccer player in Harvard history. Both arrived at Harvard at a time when the Ivy League was sponsoring special programs for African students. "They were exceptional athletes. But for all they accomplished, I don't think we saw them at their best," was McCurdy's assessment. "They were older than our undergraduates and arrived here with full competitive careers behind them."

The following year the Crimson were even more dominating, as they were a combined 12-0 indoors and outdoors. Indoors, Awori, now a senior, won the Heptagonals' Outstanding Performer award for a second time. As he won the broad jump for the third straight year, he shared the spotlight with hurdler Tony Lynch and 2-miler Walt Hewlett. Hewlett had been the mainstay of the cross-country team for two years and as a sophomore finished 16th in the Boston Marathon. (It should be noted that the field for that 1964 event was just 350.)

The success continued in the spring. Harvard was heard from at the IC4A championships, where Jim Bakkensen became the school's first two-time winner with his second discus title and Lynch tied a record in the 440 hurdles.

In 1965–66 Harvard again went undefeated indoors and outdoors in dual meets, but it lost the outdoor Heps by a point to Army. Indoors, Chris Pardee was the meet's top performer as he set a Harvard record with a high jump of 6 feet 10¼ inches. Perhaps the most significant individual honor went to Tony Lynch, who earned the

1966 Bingham Award as the top athlete in the school. He was the fourth track man to be so honored, following Bob Rittenburg, 1955; Dyke Benjamin, 1959; and Mark Mullin, 1962.

During the 1966–67 indoor season, Harvard saw its dual meet streak snapped at 29 straight wins. And after three straight Heptagonal titles, Harvard saw another streak end as Army took the meet.

But no one saw any long-term problems with the program. New talent kept pouring in. While the indoor and outdoor squads missed out on Heptagonal triumphs for two seasons, the cross-country program stole the spotlight.

Beginning in the fall of 1967, Harvard cross-country put together seasons of 9-0, 10-0, and 10-0. Four straight Heps crowns were taken (from 1939 through 1966, the Crimson had won only two cross-country Heptagonals). In all, Harvard won 33 straight dual meets from 1967 to 1970 and produced a parade of outstanding harriers, including Doug Hardin, Jim Baker, Royce Shaw, Keith Colburn, Dave Potetti, and Tom Spengler.

The first and perhaps best of these was Hardin, of whom McCurdy said, "Hardin had an interesting philosophy of training. He'd say, 'Training only makes it easier to do. You still have to go out there and do it.'"

Hardin set new standards as he became the only Harvard harrier to win individual Heptagonal honors twice. His battles with Yale's Frank Shorter, winner of the 1972 Olympic marathon in Montreal, highlighted the 1967 season. McCurdy considered that year's squad the deepest, and nowhere was it more evident than in a victory over Northeastern in which Harvard took the first seven places.

Harvard could boast depth indoors and outdoors as well. Launched by their fall success, the distance runners continued to shine over the rest of the year. There was Royce Shaw, whose 4:03.4 mile as a freshman was the fastest ever by an Ivy Leaguer. There was Doug Hardin's 8:48.8 for 2 miles, another Ivy best and still a Harvard outdoor record.

But possibly the best trackman of them all was Jim Baker. The lanky native of Northfleet, England, consistently scored in the 880, the mile, and the 2-mile run. His specialty was the mile, and his 4:00.2 at the outdoor IC4As remained a Harvard and New England record until 1985.

Dubbed Mr. Magnificent for his style and results, Baker finished his career in a meet against Yale in which he won the mile and 2-mile events and placed second in the 880, all in a period of 80 minutes. Two weeks later he became

The outstanding performer of the 1966 Heptagonals—Harvard's third straight victory—was hurdler Tony Lynch (top). Lynch won Harvard's 1966 Bingham Award.

All-American Walt Hewlett '66 (left) was one of a long line of Harvard harriers to capture the Heptagonal cross-country championship. Hewlett's individual title came in 1964.

One of Great Britain's classiest gifts to Harvard was Jim Baker '68 (above right), whose 4:00.2 mile at the 1968 IC4As remained a Harvard and New England record until the spring of 1985.

The only Harvard man to win back-to-back Heptagonal cross-country titles was Doug Hardin '69, who pulled off the double in 1967 and 1968. Keith Colburn's 1969 title made it three straight for the Crimson.

Yale's Frank Shorter (below, right) went on to greater fame as the Olympic marathon champ in 1972, but on this 1969 spring afternoon it was Roy Shaw who captured the Heptagonal mile.

track's fifth Bingham Award winner as the school's top athlete in 1968.

Meanwhile, Ed Stowell was making sure that the field events were carrying their share of the load. In 1968 Steve Schoonover became the first Harvard man to clear 16 feet in the pole vault, and the next year Dick Benka rewrote shot put records. His 61 feet 3¾ inches indoors and 59 feet 8¼ inches outdoors remain Harvard records.

Stowell took particular pride in his first NCAA champions since Ted Bailey won the hammer throw in 1962. These were back-to-back winners of the weight throw in 1969 and 1970, Charles Ajootjian and Ed Nosal. This period also produced national champs out of the

Nearly 20 years after his college career ended, Dick Benka '69 still holds Harvard's shot put records.

2-mile relay team in 1968 (Jim Baker, Royce Shaw, Trey Burns, and Dave McKelvey) and Keith Colburn (track's sixth Bingham winner) in the 1,000-yard run in 1970.

Up through the 1968–69 season, the home of Harvard's indoor program was Briggs Cage. The dark, dirt-floor facility was more suitable as a place for the baseball and lacrosse teams to get a jump on their spring seasons when Soldiers Field was covered with snow.

"To survive in Briggs Cage and be good was a sort of survival of the fittest," said McCurdy. "Working out in that facility toughened those guys."

"Those guys" got a new facility in the Edward Farrell Track Facility, which eventually opened in January of 1969 although it was dedicated a year later. Perhaps it was coincidence, but Harvard regained its Heptagonal titles for the next two indoor and outdoor seasons after moving into "the Bubble," what was then the world's largest air-supported structure.

Taking a Stand

During the 1969–70 season, events outside the world of athletics made their mark on the Harvard track team. First came the matter of Jack Langer, a basketball player at Yale.

Langer had competed in the Maccabiah Games in Israel in August of 1969, and as a result he was declared ineligible and Yale was placed on probation by both the NCAA and the Eastern College Athletic Conference.

Yale knew that allowing Langer to compete in Israel would bring this sort of reaction but forced the issue to underscore the absurdity of a running feud between the NCAA and the AAU.

Sympathetic to the Yale situation, Harvard's track team, behind the leadership of junior Ed Nosal, prepared a formal protest of the NCAA and ECAC action.

Nosal saw the NCAA championships as the perfect forum at which to voice dissatisfaction with the NCAA treatment of Langer and Yale. To gain support for his idea, he wrote the following letter to captains of eastern track teams during the 1969–70 indoor season:

With the belief that the NCAA exists to benefit the athlete, I find the NCAA and ECAC action

against Langer and Yale irresponsible and unacceptable. . . . Yale should be praised, not condemned, for its courage in protecting Langer's right to participate in both the Maccabiah Games and Yale athletics. In order to show support for Yale's position, I propose that all Heptagonal and IC4A athletes placing in the NCAA championships wear Yale T-shirts or jerseys to the award stand.

No other school supported Nosal's proposal. But at the 1970 NCAA Indoor Track and Field Championships at Detroit, three Harvard men stood on the award stand wearing blue Yale jerseys. They were Nosal and Keith Colburn, winners of the weight throw and 1,000-yard run respectively, and Skip Hare, third in the long jump.

Coach McCurdy was quietly supportive of the gesture, while Harvard administrators kept their distance. Said McCurdy, "That was something the guys came up with on their own. But I was in favor of it all the way. And now we are responsible for an NCAA rule: You must wear your own jersey at a meet. That's the sort of thing the NCAA worries about."

The Harvard conscience was stirred once more in the spring over a more serious issue. When four students were killed at Kent State in May during a demonstration against U.S. involvement in Cambodia, a national student strike was organized. Four days later, Harvard was scheduled to compete in the Heptagonal championships.

Army and Navy withdrew from the meet, and the Harvard athletes, with their Ivy brothers, had to decide what action to take in the middle of this crisis, which reached deep into every college campus in the country.

"The problems on the campuses and in Southeast Asia really bothered all of us," said captain Keith Colburn. "When the nationwide student strike was called, we then became confronted with whether or not to compete."

The Harvard response was two-fold. Some athletes, like star runners Royce Shaw and Dave Potetti, chose to join student demonstrations in Washington, D.C., that weekend. Others attended the meet and stood beside Ed Nosal as he read a statement prepared by the Ivy captains that condemned U.S. involvement in Cambodia and the deaths of the four students.

After the reading, the meet was held and Har-

When Ed Nosal stepped to the awards stand at the 1970 NCAAs, he had traded his Harvard H for a Yale Y in protest of the NCAA's treatment of Yale's Jack Langer. Langer, an Eli basketball player, had lost his eligibility because of participating in the Maccabiah Games.

vard won its second straight outdoor Heptagon-als. But it was a victory whose taste was less than sweet.

• • •

1971–73: The Golden Era was over. After sweeping those indoor and outdoor Heptagonal meets for 2 years, Harvard would go 13 years before winning another in March of 1983. The competition was catching up, though Harvard trackmen continued to improve, establishing new school records in all but a few events during this same period.

The cross-country arm of the program enjoyed some of the best moments of the early 1970s. Captain Tom Spengler paced the 1970 squad to a Heps crown, and Ric Rojas led Harvard to a tie with Navy in the 1972 meet.

In addition to cross-country success in 1972 and 1973, Rojas also set a school record outdoors at the 3-mile distance. Still, he never reached all the expectations placed on him until after leaving Harvard, when he became a world-class distance runner.

"He was a pure long-distance type," offered McCurdy. "It's not surprising how he blossomed after leaving college. He was free of the tensions and pressures of school. All that stuff got in the way"

One reason for this and later cross-country success was the preseason training camp held at Groton, a half hour northwest of Boston. McCurdy took his troops away from Cambridge for a couple of weeks before school began in September. It allowed intense training and a chance for team camaraderie to develop. It was special.

"For more of those guys, it was the greatest experience of their lives," said McCurdy. "It brought together a small group with common abilities and will power. And after two days they hated every bit of it. But it had its effect, upon their performances and beyond. I remember one of my captains, Mark Meyer. The first thing he did when his parents visited Harvard was to bring them out and show them Groton."

One squad that was well prepared by the rigors of Groton was the 1976 group. Peter Fitzsimmons and Jeff Campbell were the leaders of a supporting cast that worked hard but were often undermanned. This was a 4-4 team that made history when, to the surprise of just about everyone, they captured Harvard's first IC4A title since 1931.

"These guys were rewarded for doing all the hard things," said McCurdy. "Week after week, they worked

Ric Rojas had a moderately successful career at Harvard, then blossomed into a world-class distance runner after leaving Cambridge in 1974.

hard and got beat. They went out hard every time whether it was a practice or a meet. And that's not easy when you have a full schedule and you're getting licked all the time."

Harvard grabbed the 5th, 7th, 11th, 20th, and 92nd spots and needed every point to edge out Villanova. And no one else was more important than that No. 92 man, Rocky Moulton.

Said McCurdy, "The key, though he probably didn't know it, was Moulton. He was way back in the pack and just did what he was used to. And that was running tired and passing people in the back. And he passed enough people and just finished high enough to give us the points we needed to win it all."

Another of cross-country's golden moments was created by John O'Brien Murphy, the Harvard leprechaun who was the individual winner of the 1979 Heps. Murphy, who had not won a single race that fall, surprised a few people. But not McCurdy.

"Talk about psychology! When Murphy believed he could do something, watch out. He had no right to do some of the things he accomplished."

Indoors and outdoors, the opening years of the 1970s produced a number of standouts in a variety of events. Speedsters Baylee Reid and Nick Leone set records at 100 and 600 yards. Jim Kleiger did the same in the pole vault, topping out at 16 feet 6 inches. And Vincent Vanderpool-

Wallace set new standards in the long jump and triple jump.

But the best-remembered event of this period, and of the short-lived Bubble, was the 1,000-yard match-up between Harvard's Bob Clayton and Boston College's Keith Francis in the 1973 Greater Boston Championships. Entering the race senior Clayton and freshman Francis were the country's top two in the event.

"We talked before the race and decided it was pretty much between us," Clayton would say after the race. "I knew he was the type of runner who takes the pace out and overpowers everyone. So I wanted to get out fast and follow him because I felt I could outkick him if it got down to a one-lap thing."

It indeed became a "one-lap thing," and Clayton's kick caught Francis at the wire in a time of 2:08.0, the fastest in the world that year. It was the single most electrifying event in the four-year history of Harvard's inflated indoor track facility. On December 21, 1973, the Bubble literally burst after being pounded by high winds. That returned Harvard indoor track to Briggs Cage for six more seasons.

1974–79: As the 1970s wound down, the preeminent figures of Harvard track came from the field events. First there was a high-jumper without equal. Then came a pole-vaulting artist.

The high-jumper was Melvyn C. Embree of Ann Arbor, Michigan. Mel Embree had all the gaudy statistics and records and much more. He won 42 of 44 meets; was Heptagonal champion indoors twice (1975 and 1976) and outdoors three times (1974, 1975, 1976); was IC4A champ indoors and out in 1976; and set every Harvard,

Heps, and IC4A record. His best efforts were 7 feet 2¼ inches indoors and 7 feet 3¼ inches outdoors.

Embree made national headlines when he beat then world record holder Dwight Stones at the 1975 Millrose Games in New York. Later, he earned a spot on the 1976 U.S. Olympic team.

His performances were noted as much for their style as their results. Embree, whose mother was a ballet instructor and father a one-time member of the Baltimore Colts, combined the grace of the former with the strength of the latter.

What stood out to Bill McCurdy was the quality of selflessness. "In an Olympic year, some guys would have left the team to concentrate on their specialty. Mel wouldn't do that. Instead, risking a possible injury, he would practice a number of events, just in case we might need points from him to win a dual meet."

Ed Stowell was as proud as he was busy in those days. In addition to Embree, Stowell brought along two other standouts in this period, Ed Ajootjian, a Heps winner in the weight throw and an IC4A winner in the hammer, and John McCulloch, another superior high-jumper. In fact, McCulloch jumped 7 feet 2½ inches in earning a trip to the Olympic trials.

"McCulloch's success can be directly attributed to Stowell," said Bill McCurdy. "If a guy was good, Stowell wouldn't let up, wouldn't get off his back. And one of the

Mel Embree enjoyed a banner year in 1976, when he won Harvard's Bingham Award and earned a spot on the Olympic squad at Montreal. His jumps of 7 feet 2 ¼ inches indoors and 7 feet 3 ¼ inches outdoors are Harvard bests.

reasons that Embree jumped so high was that McCulloch was so good. He pushed Mel farther."

What Embree did to Harvard's high-jump standards, Geoff Stiles did for pole-vaulting marks. Together, they were track's seventh and eighth Bingham Award winners (in 1976 and 1979 respectively).

Stiles had never topped 14 feet when he was competing as a freshman. But he kept establishing personal bests, highlighted by two major victories, the IC4As as a junior (16 feet 4 inches) and the NCAAs as a senior (17 feet 3 inches). The latter height is the Harvard indoor record. His 16 feet 10 inches at the NCAA trials in 1979 remains the outdoor mark.

As the decade came to a close, the field events continued to produce winners. In addition to Ajootjian's strength in the weight throw, there were his teammate from Providence Classical High School, Tom Lenz, in the hammer, and Joe Pellegrini, a school record holder in the discus who went on to a brief career with football's New York Jets.

But the 1980s would return runners to prominence, and one of them may have been the best the school had ever seen.

McCurdy

McCurdy. That's how his athletes referred to him. Not Coach McCurdy or Coach or Bill. Simply McCurdy. His athletes enjoyed a unique relationship with this teacher. And the teacher had a theory about that.

"I really don't know how I coached. But I think I meshed with the athletes because I was young, maybe not in age but in the way I could work out with them and do the very things I talked about."

What made McCurdy's relationship with his athletes even more unusual was that his athletic philosophy was based first and foremost on hard work. The concept of pushing oneself to new limits comes up time and again with McCurdy.

Speaking on Harvard's new track: "To work hard, you need a protective track. It doesn't prevent injuries. It just lets you accomplish more before you are injured. A measure of a coach is how many people he doesn't hurt."

Speaking on today's training theories: "Today, coaches practice to exercise what you already know you can do. It's a cautious approach. I believed in pushing yourself hard to discover what you can't do."

And when he recalls his favorite teams, those with ability to perform when tired, the philosophy comes through frequently.

"I remember my first cross-country team. They weren't very good, but they went out and surprised everyone by winning the Big Three title. And they did it because they had worked very hard and got used to running tired. John Bidwell set a suicidal pace in the first mile. Everyone knew he wouldn't be a factor at the finish. But as a result of the pace he set, our guys, who had worked on performing when tired, came on at the end and pulled off the upset."

While acknowledging his role as taskmaster, McCurdy always downplayed his reputation as a psychologist. Others disagreed.

"We were at cross-country camp at Groton, and Thad McNulty asked McCurdy how many push-ups

The only Harvard man to win an NCAA pole vault title was Geoff Stiles, who set a school mark of 17 feet 3 inches in winning the 1979 indoor title.

the coach thought he could do," recalled Adam Dixon. "McCurdy's reply was, 'One more than you.' So Thad did thirteen, and McCurdy did fourteen. A week later, Thad came back and did eighteen. McCurdy did nineteen. A few days later, Thad did twenty-three and McCurdy did twenty-four. What I enjoyed about this wasn't how Thad was pushed to do more push-ups. What I find illuminating is that I am sure that when McCurdy started this, he didn't know how many push-ups he really could do."

The respect that Bill McCurdy commanded was best summed up by former Yale coach Bob Geigengack during their years in competition. He said:

"Bill McCurdy is a top-flight individual in every way. He makes my life miserable because I cannot take a minute off to relax. When I do, I get my ears beaten in. He is a hard worker, competent, enthusiastic, and very obviously has the affection of his entire squad and the respect of all of his opponents. The happiest part of this relationship is that we both want most of all to beat each other, but sincerely and wholeheartedly wish to our friendly enemies success and victory against all other opponents."

• • •

For 30 years Harvard trackmen found a teacher and a friend in Bill McCurdy. He rejuvenated the track program in the 1950s and kept it successful through his final team in 1982.

1980–85: The records began falling in 1979. That's when Ed Sheehan set the Harvard mark for the 5,000-meter run indoors and out. From that point on, the middle- and long-distance records might best have been kept on an erasable board. Few of these standards lasted very long.

Part of the reason was the opening of Harvard's new indoor track facility in January of 1978. The uniquely banked running track immediately produced coveted results and was the talk of the track world. Harvard runners loved it. In 1981 the track officially became the Albert H. Gordon Track and Tennis Center, a tribute to one of Harvard athletics' more generous friends and more competitive senior runners.

The 1979–80 season showcased some of the period's best runners. At the Millrose Games in New York, Harvard's star quartet of Eric Schuler, Thad McNulty, John Murphy, and Adam Dixon set a meet record (7:31.2) in winning the 2-mile relay. In a special Boston-New York intercollegiate meet, Dixon's 1:51.61 was a new 880 mark.

And so it went every time out. McNulty set Heptagonal

records in the 1,000 meters in 1979 and in the 800 meters in 1980. Murphy, battling injuries constantly, was the 1,500-meter winner in the 1979 Heps. And then there was Dixon.

Adam Dixon combined intellect, style, and power. His name appears in the Harvard track record book seven times for various indoor and outdoor efforts at 800 meters, 880 yards, 1,000 meters, 1,500 meters, and 1 mile. And he was at his best when the spotlight was on him. His 1,000-meter time of 2:19.8, then an American record, came in the Big Three (Harvard, Yale, Princeton) meet of 1981. His 1,500-meter record of 3:43.89 came later that year in the IC4As. And his mile time of 4:01.3 was turned in at the 1983 NCAAs.

Dixon credited McCurdy's role as both teacher and motivator. The coach would suggest modifications to Dixon's style, and the star pupil would respond. "He taught me to relax, to run lightly. He would be aware if I was running too much from my shoulders, for example."

In 1981 Dixon was voted the outstanding performer of the Heptagonals. After a year away from school, he

Harvard point scorers came in all sizes in 1979–80. In the fall, 5-foot 8-inch John Murphy won the Heptagonal cross-country title, while 6-foot 2-inch Tom Lenz was a Heps hammer champion in the spring.

returned in 1983 to lead Harvard—and new coach Frank Haggerty—to the school's first indoor Heptagonal win since 1970, winning the meet's 1,500 meters for the third time.

At the end of the 1981–82 season, Bill McCurdy called it quits. He coached for 30 years and won 445 track meets in all kinds of places, under all kinds of conditions. Some coaches make friends without winning many championships. Others are successful with athletes who hate every minute of the grind. Few coaches, at Harvard or elsewhere, have been as successful and beloved as Bill McCurdy.

Taking over for McCurdy was Frank Haggerty '68, a former trackman who had scored regularly as a hurdler and member of the mile relay team. Haggerty would engineer a Heptagonal win in his first indoor season. In addition to Dixon, the standouts of the 1983 season were triple jump expert Gus Udo, hurdler Steve Ezeji-Okoye, and hurdler Dwayne Jones, all record-setters. They were major contributors to Harvard's victory in the 1983 outdoor Heps, the Crimson's first since 1970.

Haggerty and Harvard repeated their indoor Heps success in 1985. That win came as more of a surprise than the one two years earlier.

"We had a better dual meet record [in 1983] and had just killed Yale and Princeton in the Big Three meet," said Haggerty. "But in 1985, we were the ones who had looked bad in that meet and we had four dual meet losses."

Whereas the 1983 squad had depth, the 1985 entry prevailed with more first-place finishers. Those winners included Cliff Sheehan (1,500 meters), Doug Boyd (high jump), Mark Henry (triple jump), Steve Ezeji-Okoye (55-meter hurdles), and the distance medley relay team (Sheehan, Bill Barton, Jim Herberich, and Bill Pate). Sheehan, who also finished second in the 3,000 meters, was voted the meet's outstanding performer.

Later that year Sheehan made headlines despite finishing fourth in a race. The race was the Jumbo Elliott Invitational Mile at the Penn Relays, and the headlines stemmed from Sheehan's time of 3:59.2. With that effort the Westfield, New Jersey, native became the first New Englander to break the four-minute mile and in the process erased Jim Baker's 17-year Harvard and New England mark of 4:00.2, set at the 1968 IC4As.

Cliff Sheehan (below) became the first New England collegian to break the four-minute mile when he ran a 3:59.2 in the Jumbo Elliott Invitational Mile at the 1985 Penn Relays. Sheehan broke Jim Baker's 17-year-old Harvard and New England mark of 4:00.2 in the process.

Men's indoor track cocaptains for 1984–85 Steve Ezeji-Okoye (front left) and John Perkins (front right) hold the trophy as the Crimson celebrate another Heptagonal championship at Dartmouth's Leverone Field House.

Harvard athletic director Jack Reardon '60 (right) shares a laugh with Al Gordon '23, friend of all Harvard athletics and particularly track, at dedication ceremonies for the Albert H. Gordon Track and Tennis Center in December of 1981.

Adam Dixon

Adam Dixon was the type of athlete people talked about. A lot. People who did not normally attend track meets began coming down to Harvard's new facility just to see this graceful runner with the long stride and exciting kick. Mile or 2-mile. The 880 or 1,500, perhaps. Maybe the last leg of the relay. Whatever the event, Dixon brought something special to the competition.

"He was a most unusual individual in many ways," said Bill McCurdy, who continued to work with Dixon even after both had left Harvard. "He was brilliant, and when he arrived at Harvard, I didn't think track was particularly high on his list. It was just another thing he did well."

Dixon agreed with that observation. "No, track wasn't high on my list when I first arrived. But it became important because of McCurdy and because I liked many of the people on the team. We had a very good ethos as a group"

McCurdy and Dixon worked well together. The coach demanded that an athlete push himself. This particular athlete needed to be pushed.

"It's like reading about some woman who lifts a Volkswagen off her injured son. Who knew she was capable of such an act? This is what track is all about—the right physical response to the needs of a situation. You try to create the physical and psychological conditions in which that sort of phenomenon can occur. In this sense, I meshed with McCurdy. I was reluctant to work,

Harvard's computerized scoreboard lets everyone know who has been named outstanding performer at the 1981 indoor Heptagonals. Adam Dixon (right), who accepts the award from Jerry Kanter '51, set records in the 1,500 meters and as a member of the distance medley relay squad.

Adam Dixon strikes a pose before the start of a cross-country meet. Harvard's first freshman All-American, Dixon set eight different Harvard records in middle-distance events from 1980 to 1983.

and he served as a catalyst to get me to work hard."

The relationship between teacher and student is underscored by Dixon's recollection of his most satisfying race. "The best race I ever ran was the handicap race against McCurdy. Every year at Groton, McCurdy would give each runner a carefully calculated handicap of a set number of minutes and then he would race us. He knew everyone so well that the handicaps were often just what he would need to win." Dixon paused and then broke into a smile, adding simply, "My handicap was eighteen minutes and I beat McCurdy."

• • •

SPRINTING AT THE START

During the late 1970s, womens' track programs were born at the Ivy League schools, all attaining varsity status within two or three years of one another. Yet from 1979 to 1984, every Ivy championship track event was won by one of two schools, Harvard or Princeton.

Harvard's program was born in 1975, when graduate student John Jurevich assembled a club team. In the spring of 1976, athletic director Bob Watson made the program a Level II varsity under Robert "Pappy" Hunt, men's freshmen coach since 1968.

Pappy enjoyed immediate success, particularly in his first cross-country season. His first two fall squads swept Greater Boston and Ivy championships, and the 1977 group, elevated to Level I status, was undefeated in dual competition as well.

"That first cross-country team consisted of just six people," remembered Hunt. "And they went out and won the Ivies."

The six—Kat Taylor, Karla Amble, Sarah Linsley, Sara Robinson, Wendy Carle, and Judy Rabinowitz—included a future Olympian, but not a track Olympian. Rabinowitz became a world-class cross-country skier and competed for the 1984 U.S. Olympic team in Sarajevo.

In 1977 the program's first superstar arrived in Anne Sullivan, who routinely improved course records around the league by one minute or better. Her 14th-place finish in the cross-country nationals that year made her Harvard's first track All-American.

A transitional period approached for Harvard. The program's early runners were being joined by new, more experienced runners, such as Paula Newnham and Joanna Foreman. Whereas Cohasset's Sarah Linsley had little competitive experience before coming to Harvard, Great Britain's Newnham had been a nationally ranked runner who competed in the Commonwealth Games before crossing the ocean.

Despite this influx of talent, the next few years belonged to Princeton, in cross-country as well as the track and field seasons. After two years at Harvard, Sullivan transferred to Brown, where she competed successfully against her old teammates. Newnham, individual winner of the 1978 Ivy cross-country meet, was plagued by injuries for most of her career as was Falmouth's Foreman.

With Sullivan gone and Newnham hurt, Harvard needed a star to take her place amidst an already productive

supporting cast. In the fall of 1979, the need was filled when a gifted runner from nearby Cambridge High and Latin School enrolled at Harvard.

Darlene Beckford was a nationally ranked runner before, during, and after Harvard. She was Harvard's best in the fall of 1979, when Princeton was successfully defending its Ivy cross-country mark. But she was even better during the indoor season.

That was the year that Harvard hosted the Eastern Championships in its exciting new track facility. Equally exciting was Beckford, whose 4:32.3 mile set a national collegiate record, taking some 15 seconds off the previous mark.

As a sophomore Beckford kept up the pace. She was Harvard's top finisher in every cross-country meet in 1980, and in the indoor season she added records in the 400 and 800 meters to those she already owned in the 1,500 meters and mile. The year was topped off by winning the 800 in the nationals and earning All-American status.

This was a turning point for the track program and women's athletics in general. Programs were making the shift from developing athletes who happened to be there to recruiting those who were nationally recognized, in this case, ranked in high school.

As a member of a men's staff that could not recruit, Pappy Hunt did not have experience in this area. But he had an assistant who could help with the transition. "John Babington had competed against club teams when he coached the Liberty Athletic Club before he came to Harvard," said Hunt. "Coaches would tip him off to prospects and we'd contact them."

In 1981 Beckford, who had run for Babington's Liberty AC, no longer had to do it all by herself. She was joined by two runners who would lead Harvard to four straight Ivy cross-country titles and three straight undefeated seasons.

Jenny Stricker was a highly sought-after runner from Lincoln, Nebraska. She won her first Ivy cross-country meet. Kate Wiley arrived at Harvard from Toronto with slightly less attention but just as much potential. She won the Ivy cross-country meet the following three seasons.

The backgrounds of these three runners from the Midwest, Canada, and Cambridge High and Latin could not have been more dissimilar. But their contributions to Harvard track were of equal significance.

Beckford improved her 800-meter record, added one in the 600 meters, and earned her second All-American berth by winning the national mile. Harvard actually got three All-Americans out of that one event, as Stricker and captain Mary Herlihy finished fourth and eighth behind Beckford.

During their freshman year, Stricker and Wiley—both regional Academic All-Americans—added their names to nine records in both the indoor and outdoor seasons and began a string of Ivy, later Heptagonal, firsts that overlapped during their careers. Wiley's victories came at 3,000, 5,000, and 10,00 meters; Stricker's wins were at 1,500, and 3,000 meters.

"I don't really know why, but we always had distance runners," said Hunt. "I think it went back to McCurdy's ability to attract distance runners to the men's program. He always had them, too. So the women must have figured that Harvard was a good place to develop runners. I wish we could have gotten a few more sprinters, though."

The success of the middle- and long-distance superstars often overshadowed the accomplishments of the supporting players. The best of the sprinters that Hunt did get were Pat Gopaul and Kim Clermont, who set records back in 1977 that remained in the books eight years later, when virtually all other school marks had fallen.

Another to survive the program's development was shot-putter Kim Johnson, the first star of the field events, whose toss at the 1979 outdoor Ivy League meet remains a record. Johnson also won the Heptagonal shot put in 1981 and 1982, setting a meet record the latter year. Wendy Carle's javelin record of 128 feet survived from 1978 to 1985, when Jennifer St. Louis, sister of soccer All-American Sue St. Louis, threw over 141 feet.

One of Harvard's more versatile athletes was Ellen Hart, member of the Ivy champion soccer team, record-setting hurdler in her early years, and later the record-setter in the 2-mile and 10,000-meter events. She had been a high school All-American in cross-country, but other sports and injuries delayed her return to distance running.

"Ellen got back into distance running in her senior year," recalled John Babington. "Within seven months, she was fifth in the national ten thousand meters and third in an exhibition ten thousand at the 1980 Olympic trials."

That last effort, coming after the Moscow boycott had already been announced, earned her a spot on the Olympic team that never competed.

"She really was our first women's track Olympian," according to Hunt.

Hart later became a world-class marathoner after graduating from Harvard in 1980. Her time of 2:35.04 in the 1984 Olympic trials, some 15 minutes better than the world record of ten years earlier, left her in 11th place in that event.

Toronto's Kate Wiley was a runner for all seasons at Harvard but saved some of her best for the fall, when she won three straight Ive cross-country titles from 1983 to 1985.

Although Stricker and Wiley made the most headlines from 1981 to 1985, there were other major contributors. Cocaptains Kathy Busby and Grace deFries led the 1984 squad by example. Busby, who never ran competitively before coming to Harvard, set school marks in the 100 and 200 meters and registered a Heps win in the 400. The event for deFries was the Heps 800 meters, which she won twice indoors and once outdoors.

Perhaps the most diverse talent in the group was Mariquita Patterson, who set school records in the 55-meter, 60-yard, and 100-meter hurdles, as well as the long jump, pentathlon (hurdles, high jump, long jump, shot put, and 800—indoors), and heptathlon (pentathlon events plus javelin and discus—outdoors).

"She had an enormous amount of talent, but it was her determination that set her apart," said Frank Haggerty, men's and women's coach since 1983. "And it was not geared solely for herself. She was oriented to team performance and would compete anywhere she thought it could help the team gain points. That's why it was normal for her to compete in a minimum of four events each time out. If she had concentrated on any single event, she could have smashed records."

Not all athletes are preoccupied with their personal bests, as evidenced by Mariquita Patterson. Paul Withington '12 would have liked that.

Darlene Beckford

The crowds at Harvard track meets swelled in the early 1980s as sports fans—not just track fans—came down to the Gordon Track to watch two superstars, Adam Dixon and Darlene Beckford.

Both were middle-distance runners capable of the spectacular. Both were crowd pleasers who often remained with the pack before pulling out a victory with an electrifying kick. And both were record-setters described by their coaches with the same words, "very athletic and very intelligent."

In fact, were it not for their backgrounds, the comparisons might have been scarily complete. Dixon, a Portsmouth Abbey graduate from Wilton, Connecticut, came to Harvard some 60 years after his grandfather, W. Palmer Dixon, Harvard's Hall of Fame squash and tennis great.

Beckford, a graduate of Cambridge High and Latin, was a blue-collar, city product. Her biggest adjustments at Harvard came outside the world of track, where she was most comfortable.

John Babington was Beckford's coach before, during, and after Darlene's Harvard experience. Sandwiched in between his years with a local track club, Babington was Harvard's associate coach from 1979 to 1982, not coincidentally the years of Beckford's Harvard career.

"Darlene developed as a person and as a runner at Harvard," said Babington. "It wasn't always easy for her. While she was exceptionally bright, which was one of her major assets as a competi-

Just a year out of Cambridge High and Latin School, Darlene Beckford set a national indoor collegiate mile record and earned All-American status at Harvard.

tor, she was introduced to a new world at Harvard. And that was why she curtailed her running in the spring. She needed that time to devote to her schoolwork."

In addition to the social and academic pressures that Harvard can provide, Beckford faced a new athletic world. The year after she left Cambridge High and Latin, she was racing against Mary Decker in the Millrose Games, finishing fourth in the 1,500 meters in a race in which Decker set a world record.

"Darlene didn't mind working for things, a result of her being working-class Cambridge, born and bred," said Babington. This work ethic, combined with tremendous athletic ability and intellectual curiosity, kept Beckford improving.

"She was much more of an athlete than the average runner," observed Babington. "But she was certainly more intelligent than the average athlete as well. She constantly asked questions and revealed an unusual awareness of her athletic processes."

During her three competitive years at Harvard, Beckford earned All-American status in both cross-country and indoor track. She set eight individual Harvard records at distances ranging from 400 to 5,000 meters and was a member of two record-setting relay teams.

"Darlene was a racer, not a pacer," said Babington. "Her primary, almost exclusive, goal was winning the race."

When Babington left Harvard in 1982, Beckford returned to club track, finishing up her studies at Harvard at the same time. By 1985 she was one of the leaders of the invitational circuit, ranked among the country's premier middle-distance runners. Perhaps her biggest victory came in June of that year when she beat Zola Budd, the celebrated South African, in a 2-mile race.

For all she has accomplished, Darlene Beckford may just be warming up. She has paced her career more slowly than the average world-class runner. That may mean that following the plan of so many of her races, the best may be saved for the end.

CHAPTER 6

Baseball

When one thinks of baseball in the Boston area, one's mind turns, for better or for worse, to the Boston Red Sox. But there is an organization that has been playing baseball in and around Boston far longer than the Sox.

It was in 1862 that a group of Phillips Exeter Academy students enrolled at Harvard University and soon thereafter organized Harvard's first baseball team. Freshmen George Flagg and Frank Wright of the class of 1866 were the prime movers in this regard, for baseball had little if any history at Harvard, before their arrival.

The game itself has commonly been traced to General Abner Doubleday in 1839 or thereabouts. But a growing list of baseball scholars questions the general's right to credit for inventing the game, instead of finding its origins in simple English ball games. Regardless of Doubleday's role, it's clear that a game called baseball was growing in popularity in America during the years 1845–61.

If we could step back and watch a game from this period, we would find quite a few differences from today's product. We would see gloveless players throwing fielded balls at the runners and getting credit for an out upon making contact. Those same runners would be trying to reach stakes or posts sticking four or five feet out of the ground instead of bases. We'd see "strikers" called out not only if their batted ball was caught in the air but also if it was fielded cleanly on one bounce.

Pitchers were forced to throw underhand in a stiff-armed style similar to today's softball hurlers. Bending the elbow to gain velocity was against the rules.

And the games were quite gentlemanly. As Bill Reid '01 remarks in *The H Book of Harvard Athletics:*

> It must have been a great pleasure to attend these games where there was no constant "yapping" by the players and no overdone coaching, where the fair-minded spectators gave the visiting team a fair chance and where "rattling," the shame of our own game, was unknown. Enjoyable too to see the umpire respected and to know that the rule forbidding "anyone to approach or speak with the umpire, scorers, or players, unless by special request of the umpire" was honored.

The rules were changing quickly and would continue to do so long after Harvard's first team took the field in the spring of 1863. That field was the Cambridge Common, where General George Washington had taken command of the Continental Army 80 odd years before.

The 1899 Harvard baseball team was paced by three of the era's greatest athletes. In addition to their baseball skills, Ben Dibblee (front row, far left) and Percy Haughton (center of picture with hands crossed) were both All-American football players. Haughton went on to become head coach of football, as did Bill Reid (front row, second from right).

THE CRIMSON TAKE THE FIELD

1863–1919: The first decade of Harvard baseball was occupied with defining who would play where against whom. There were games with amateur teams, college teams, and professionals and trips to play them all that seem phenomenal by today's scheduling standards.

Harvard's first official game took place on June 27, 1863, at the Dexter Training Ground in Providence. Harvard, represented by the class of 1866, defeated Brown's class of 1865 by a score of 27-17.

On July 15, 1865, Harvard's win over a highly touted amateur team from Lowell, 28-17, brought home the Silver Ball, symbolic of New England supremacy. Four days later, on July 19, the first intercollegiate game involving a full university-fed squad (teams representing

single classes competed previously) was played. It was Harvard over Williams, 35-20.

When there is a first college win, there is usually a first college loss. That came on July 27, 1866, when Williams beat Harvard, 39-37. Harvard, whose previous losses were to professional and noncollege amateur teams, would not lose to another college for seven years.

Frank Wright graduated in 1866. That is notable because, with the exception of his last five games, Wright pitched every scheduled Harvard game for three and a half years.

As was the case with most sports at that time, Harvard baseball's big rival soon became Yale. The first meeting produced a 25-17 Harvard win on July 25, 1867. The game was held on Regatta Day in Worcester, a tradition that lasted into the next century.

One unusual aspect of the early schedules was the long trip. None were longer than 1870's 43-day summer odyssey to seek out the best competition in the country. The record on this July-August extravaganza was 18-8, with seven losses to professional teams. The toughest of these was an 18-17 affair with the Cincinnati Red Stockings, who trailed the Crimson by five runs entering the ninth inning.

The last quarter of the 19th century saw the game of baseball change rapidly and Harvard at the forefront of much of this change.

As baseball gradually allowed pitchers to throw overhand, Harvard's H. C. Ernst became one of the game's first curveball pitchers in 1876. The next year, Harvard's Fred Thayer, working with a Cambridge tinsmith, developed the first catcher's mask. Later, in 1884, another Harvard player, H. T. Allen, would be the first to use a chest protector. That device made its debut only after Allen tested it by having his teammates pelt him with baseballs at practice.

Around the turn of the century, Harvard baseball got a boost with major improvements in its playing field and coaching situation. First, in 1898, Harvard began playing its games at Soldiers Field. Previously the team had played on the Cambridge Common, the Delta (where Memorial Hall now stands), and Holmes and Jarvis fields (where Harvard Law School now stands).

Then, in 1900, Harvard received its first systematic coaching when E. H. Nichols '86 took control. His first three teams were 55-10, led by one of the best athletes of that time, Bill Reid.

Reid was a football star who coached Harvard after he graduated in 1901. One of his most remarkable baseball accomplishments was going errorless in the 1900 season as a catcher at a time when passed balls were recorded as errors.

Two standouts from this period are remembered through trophies that bear their names. Barratt Wendell '02 and Dana J. P. Wingate '04 were two of the era's better players, and both were killed in World War I. The Wendell Bat, symbolic of offensive production, and the Wingate Trophy, awarded to the team MVP, were established after the war and are still given to Harvard ballplayers today.

In 1910 the first paid coach arrived on the scene in former big-leaguer Frank Sexton. He lasted until the middle of the 1915 season, when a dispute with Harvard baseball's advisory committee cut short his successful tenure. Football great Percy Haughton '99 stepped in at that point, and along with another football All-American, H. R. "Tack" Hardwick '15, Haughton salvaged a successful season.

The next year, Harvard turned to another former big-leaguer, Fred Mitchell. He took over as coach for one season (he returned in 1926) and continued to keep Harvard among the stronger teams in the country. Among the more memorable games from 1916 was a 1-0 win over the Boston Red Sox in the season opener.

Harvard and the Red Sox had teamed up back in 1912 to make a little entry in the history books. That came about when the two teams opened Fenway Park in an exhibition game on April 9 of that year. The score: Red Sox 2, Harvard 0.

The top players in this prewar period were football hero Eddie Mahan and slick-fielding first baseman H. L. Nash. Nash went the full year without an error, a feat highlighted by his perfect handling of 15 chances in an extra-inning win over Princeton.

There were no errors for anyone over the next two seasons, as World War I stopped Harvard's baseball program.

A Letter to Mr. Spalding

Fred Thayer '78 earned six varsity letters at Harvard, four in baseball and two in football. But he is best remembered as the Harvard player who invented the catcher's mask.

How the young Thayer became involved with this undertaking has been documented in a letter he wrote in 1911 to one of baseball's early pioneers, A. G. Spalding. Spalding published Thayer's letter in America's National Game *a fairly complete baseball almanac at that time. It has subsequently appeared in* The Baseball Reader, *an even more complete collection of baseball writings, fact and fiction, published by McGraw-Hill.*

The following, in its entirety, is Mr. Thayer's letter.

116 Federal Street
Boston, May 18, 1911

My dear Mr. Spalding,
I am in receipt of your favor of the 9th instant. You shall have the facts in regard to the catcher's mask, and I think you can feel assured that the data are all correct.
In order to give you the whole story I shall have to ask you to go back to the year '76 that

you may know what the conditions were in Harvard Base Ball matters.

Thatcher was the catcher in the season of '76. He left college at the end of the year.

You will recall the fact that college nines especially had rarely more than one, possibly two, substitutes, and these were "general utility" men.

Tyng was the best all-around natural ballplayer of my time. He had played third base, center field, and helped out in other positions, including catcher, in the season of '76. In one or two games in which he caught behind the bat he had been hit by foul tips and had become more or less timid.

He was, by all odds, the most available man as catcher for the season of '77, and it was up to me to find some way to bring back his confidence.

The fencing mask naturally gave me the hint as to protection for the face, and then it was up to me to devise some means of having the impact of the blow kept from driving the mask onto the face. The forehead and chin rest accomplished this and also made it possible for me to secure a patent, which I did in the winter of 1878.

Tyng practiced catching with the mask, behind the bat, in the gymnasium during the winter of '77, and became so thoroughly proficient that foul tips had no further terrors for him.

The first match game in which the mask was used was on Fast day, in Lynn, against the Live Oaks, in April 1877. Thereafter the Harvard catcher used it in all games.

I hope this will give you the data which you wish. At all events it gives you the real facts in regard to the Base Ball mask.

*Yours faithfully,
(signed) Fred W. Thayer*

• • •

John Hammond, captain of the 1925 baseball team, earned nine letters at Harvard, three each in football, hockey, and baseball.

1920–35: Harvard baseball may have enjoyed its best days in the decade of the 1920s. This wasn't just a matter of on-field results, which were highly successful. But it was reflected in the attention the sport received from the media and the public in that period.

From the spring trips to the South in private Pullman cars, to the crowds at Soldiers Field sometimes reaching 10,000 or more, to the media coverage so lacking in today's college game, Harvard baseball was something special.

Perhaps the individuals involved had something to do with it. From nine-letter winners like George Owen '23 and John Hammond '25, to the diminutive sparkplug J. Clifford "Jeff" Ross '23 (5 feet 4 inches, 119 pounds), the players were a unique and memorable lot. Owen, Hammond, Lewis Gordon, and Percy Jenkins '24 were all three-sport athletes, and each captained a varsity team.

There was Dolph Samborski '25, later a Harvard coach and athletic director, and Johnny Chase '28, an Olympic hockey star who would go on to be head hockey coach.

And the opposition had some interesting characters as well. Princeton had Moe Berg, a catcher and shortstop who went on to the Red Sox and later a somewhat renowned career in military intelligence.

And what about that guy who pitched and batted third for Columbia? His name was Lou Gehrig, and he'd stick around New York to play ball a few years after graduation.

Memories live on from this period. There was the 1923 Yale game at Soldiers Field, witnessed by an estimated 12,000 spectators. Imagine the roar that echoed across the Charles when George Owen, facing a full count with two out and the bases loaded in the ninth, lifted a home run to win the game 8-7.

While Babe Ruth's run at 60 homers had the whole country watching baseball in 1927, Harvard had its own sluggers that year. The most memorable moment was Izzy Zarakov nearly matching Owen's feat by hitting a two-run shot with two out in the ninth to beat Yale 6-5.

It was also in 1926–27 that Bill Bingham became Harvard's athletic director. The first baseball schedule he arranged gave Harvard 32 games, the most since 1870. The Crimson met the challenge with a strong 25-6-1 record.

That was also the year that Briggs Cage opened at Soldiers Field. Modeled after the facility at Phillips Andover and named after Dean LeBaron Briggs '16, the Briggs Cage gave Harvard an effective indoor training facility, no small benefit from a spring team in New England.*

Perhaps the dominant figure of the late 1920s and early 1930s was Coach Fred Mitchell, who first came to Harvard for a one-year stint in 1916. Mitchell returned in 1926, after Harvard had suffered through three straight losing seasons, and stayed through 1938. He started with three straight winning seasons, in which the Crimson compiled a 58-23 mark.

Baseball in the 1930s never seemed able to match the heights of popularity enjoyed in the previous decade. But while the crowds grew smaller, the talent on the field suffered little.

Mitchell's 1932 squad was one of his best. Captained by Al Lupien, this team went 16-6-1 (the tie resulting from a suspended game that was never made up) and finished with three memorable games with Yale. The Elis took the first one dramatically when their multisport star Albie

Booth, who was suffering from tuberculosis, hit a game-winning grand slam in Yale's 4-2 win.

When the scene shifted to Cambridge, Harvard prevailed by 17-4 and 6-0 (with the incomparable Charlie Devens hurling the shutout) to close out the season. With that final game, Harvard's Barry Wood earned his tenth varsity letter and then was graduated summa cum laude the very next day.

After an outstanding collegiate career as a Harvard pitcher, Charlie Devens '32 went on to the New York Yankees during the Ruth-Gehrig era.

_____

* Briggs Cage became the Briggs Athletic Center in 1982, when a multimillion-dollar renovation replaced the dirt floor with a wood basketball floor that could be covered by a modern artificial turf carpet. This surface, which was rolled and stored under the court, could be positioned in less than 30 minutes, allowing baseball and other outdoor sports to practice inside when conditions demanded.

1936–45: Perhaps the two best ballplayers in Mitchell's final years were Tom Bilodeau '37 and Tony Lupien '39. Bilodeau, whose two sons would follow his footsteps, had been a schoolboy star at Boston Latin and Exeter. He showed remarkable flexibility in his Harvard baseball career, as he was at various times a first baseman, a second baseman, a shortstop, and a relief pitcher. Regardless of where he was in the field, he was always a slugger.

In both his sophomore and junior seasons, Bilodeau won the Wendell Bat and the Wingate Trophy. As a junior he captured the batting title of the newly formed (1930) Eastern Intercollegiate Baseball League (Ivy League plus Army and Navy) with a .422 mark. Only a shoulder injury suffered during the 1936 football season finally slowed him down.

While Bilodeau struggled with that shoulder, a sophomore named Ulysses J. "Tony" Lupien emerged during the spring of 1937. His performance that year led his teammates to elect him captain for 1938, although he would be just a junior. He responded by winning both the

Left: Two immortals chat before closing out their respective college careers in June of 1932: Harvard's Barry Wood (left) and Yale's Albie Booth.

Below: The 1934 Harvard squad poses with host team from Keio University in Tokyo. Harvard took two out of three games on that stop of the Japanese tour.

Tom Bilodeau's hook slide gets him safely to third in a 1936 Holy Cross game at Soldiers Field.

EIBL batting title and the Wendell Bat in each of his last two seasons.

Lupien signed with the Boston Red Sox upon graduation and later returned to the college ranks as head coach at Dartmouth.

One interesting feature of this period was the appearance of Japanese teams on the Harvard schedule. In 1931 and again in 1936, Japanese touring teams visited Cambridge. Between these single contests, Harvard embarked on a 60-day, 16-game tour during the summer of 1934. This trip took Harvard to Honolulu, Tokyo, Yokohama, and Osaka.

The team played well, winning 10 of the 16 games on this goodwill trip. Accompanying the team was a message from President Franklin D. Roosevelt, Harvard '04. It said, "It is believed that such athletic meetings as the one the Harvard boys will have with the Japanese universities will do a great deal to promulgate international friendship and understanding."

Seven years later, the two countries were at war. The 1943 season would be Harvard's last before the fighting interrupted business as usual. By this time, Floyd Stahl had come from Ohio State to replace Fred Mitchell as Harvard's coach.

Below: *College baseball in New England once drew sizable crowds, as this picture from the 1941 Harvard-Yale game in Cambridge reveals. The crowd didn't help the hosts, however, as Yale won, 3-1.*

Stahl, a master organizer and teacher who stood just 5 feet 2 inches tall, enjoyed his best season in 1939, his first year. With veterans like Lupien and Artie Johns, this team went 16-10, sweeping three games from Yale to end the season.

But matters worsened quickly, and the next two teams went 8-18 and 7-18. Stahl's only other winning campaign came in the war-affected 1943 season, when Harvard's abbreviated schedule included everyone from the Boston Red Sox to Fort Devens to both Andover and Exeter.

The game with the Red Sox, a 21-0 drubbing at the hands of the local pros, had its memorable moments. There was Tony Lupien, the former Harvard star turned Sox first baseman, hitting a grand slam on a two-strike pitch. And there was Crimson pitcher Bud Mains striking out Joe Cronin, Bobby Doerr, and Eddie Lake in succession.

Despite the outcome, the Harvard battery of pitcher Warren Berg and catcher Ned Fitzgibbons would later sign with the Red Sox, while Mains became a member of the Philadelphia Athletics.

Just as Berg and others were coming into their best years, the war disbanded athletics at Harvard. Two years went by before a 14-game schedule was played in 1946.

1946–54: After the war, Stahl remained for one more year, an abbreviated 5-9 campaign that failed to bring back the promise of the prewar years.

During the next two years, things got back to normal under the tutelage of Dolph Samborski '25, a former ballplayer who had spent nearly 20 years involved with freshman and JV teams as well as with intramurals.

The 1947 and 1948 seasons were quite similar. A 12-13 record was followed by a 12-11-1 campaign, and both years ended with memorable pitching duels against Yale. In 1947 Harvard lost a chance at the Eastern League title when Yale's Frank Quinn bested the Crimson's Brendan Reilly, 1-0, before 10,000 fans in New Haven.

It was Harvard's turn in 1948, when sophomore Ira Godin pitched a four-hitter to blank the Elis, 2-0, at Yale. This was a scoreless affair until the ninth, when football and basketball star Thomas "Chip" Gannon hit an inside-the-park home run, scoring Cambridge's own Johnny Caulfield ahead of him.

Samborski's brief tenure ended with the 1948 season, and Harvard once again turned to the pros. John P. "Stuffy" McInnis, the first baseman on Connie Mack's famed Million-Dollar Infield, became Harvard's new coach for the 1949 season and remained there for six years.*

McInnis was a beloved figure at Harvard. He could spend hours talking about the Babe or Ty, perhaps he would just lean against the batting cage and offer a tip or two to improve a young hitter's swing. There were no quick-paced, use-every-minute practice sessions that future teams learned from. But there was Stuffy and his wealth of experience.

These were somewhat frustrating years, dotted with brilliant individual performances but featuring only one winning season. Typifying the frustration was the career of Ira Godin, a hard-throwing right-hander who was the best pitcher of this period. In 1949 Godin was sensational all season long. In April he went the distance in a 17-inning, 6-5 win over Navy. In wins over Brown and Army, he struck out 12 and 14 batters respectively.

When the season ended, Godin had set a new Eastern League record with 83 strikeouts. His season ERA of 1.34 was a Harvard best. Yet due to lack of support from Crimson bats, Godin's record for the year was 5-7-1.

One of the best hitters of this period was outfielder and first baseman Johnny Caulfield. His .438 average won the EIBL batting crown in 1950, McInnis' only winning season. Caulfield went on to become an elementary school headmaster in Cambridge and a popular humorist on the Greater Boston banquet scene. His license plate brought back memories of that great year. It read: HAA-438.

It was during this period that Harvard's customary spring trips were canceled by the athletic department. Many alumni pointed to this development as a major reason for the program's post-war slide. Few people would point a finger at the popular McInnis.

When the coach stepped down after a 7-15 campaign in 1954, Harvard turned to Norm Shepard, head coach of Crimson basketball for the previous five seasons and also the JV football coach. Shepard's experienced background also included success as a coach at North Carolina and as an athletic director at Davidson. The veteran would turn things around almost overnight.

---

* The rest of the 1911 Philadelphia A's famed infield included Eddie Collins at second, Jack Barry at short, and Frank "Home Run" Baker at third. The closest McInnis came to this at Harvard was his 1953 infield, which included five varsity captains: first baseman Russ Johnson (baseball), second baseman Walt Greeley (hockey), shortstop Ed Krinsky (basketball), third baseman Tim Wise (skiing), and catcher Dick Clasby (football).

Beneath that cloud of dust is Harvard's Chip Gannon, completing an inside-the-park home run. Gannon's two-run effort was all that Harvard needed in a 2-0 win at Yale in 1948.

When he played first base for Connie Mack, he was part of the famed Million-Dollar Infield. But the closest Stuffy McInnis came to that a Harvard was when his 1953 infield consisted of captains of five Harvard varsities.

1955–63: The 1955 season launched a five-year period as strong as any in modern Harvard baseball history. Harvard averaged 16 wins a season in this stretch and combined was 80-36-1. Norm Shepard may have been one factor, but Harvard's depth of talent was the key.

The class of 1957 paced this resurgence. First baseman John "Babe" Simourian could deliver 400-foot home runs, often in clutch situations, and was a presence from his sophomore year through graduation. Shortstop Bob Hastings, perhaps the best all-around player on the team, became Harvard's first baseball All-American. He could hit for power and average while getting the job done in the field. Outfielders Matt Botsford and Dick Fisher were EIBL all-star selections who consistently hit in the .300s, and catcher Phil Haughey, a basketball standout, became the most improved player in this talented class.

While these men provided a steady offensive attack, a new pitching star emerged in each of their three varsity seasons. At first it was Andy Ward '55. Then came captain

Ken Rossano '56. Finally it was a pair of classmates in Bob McGinnis and Dom Repetto.

Repetto gained more than a little fame by defeating Yale three times in 1957. The right-hander allowed just 13 hits in 27 innings against the Elis, as Harvard duplicated a feat last accomplished in 1878. Yale had swept three from Harvard only once (1889) in the 90 years of competition to that point.

Despite all these heroics, the class of '57 never won an Eastern League title. That accomplishment remained for the unheralded 1958 team. Led by hockey star Bobby Cleary, this club combined clutch hitting, tight defense, and superb relief pitching to bring Harvard its first championship in 29 years of league play.

This team was loaded with former junior varsity players who, after being tutored on the JVs by player-turned-coach John Caulfield, made the best of their long-awaited varsity chances. Characteristic of this team were five one-run league wins that made all the difference.

First baseman Frank Saia, another Cambridge native, became Harvard baseball's second All-American. Sharing the spotlight with Saia were four EIBL all-stars, second baseman Cleary, outfielder Kent Hathaway, and the battery of pitcher Dave Brigham and catcher Johnnie Davis.

Few would have predicted that 1959 would be the last winning season until 1962. Paced by sophomore football stars Chet Boulris and Charley Ravenel, the 1959 club started and finished strong, enduring a brief midseason slump.

Boulris would hit .355 in his only varsity season before giving up baseball to concentrate on both football and his desire to become an ophthalmologist. That pursuit was appropriate for the All-Ivy running back, who struggled with vision problems himself. As longtime trainer Jack Fadden would say about Boulris, "He was a helluva hitter, but I don't know how he did it. I swear he saw three baseballs coming at him and just hit the one in the middle."

Boulris's retirement and graduation losses returned just five lettermen to the 1960 team, first of two straight losing campaigns for Coach Shepard. Lack of depth and pitching problems seemed to victimize these teams, both captained by Al Martin, an offensive spark plug for his two final seasons.

The losing seasons provided a disappointing end to the careers of Martin, Ravenel, and Dick Shima, all outstanding batsmen. But they also helped develop young players who would lead Harvard's next resurgence.

One such player was the 1962 captain, Dave Morse. This hockey star brought considerable skills to the baseball field as hitter, base runner, and shortstop. He was the team MVP as a junior but enjoyed even more the team's dramatic improvement in his final year.

That 1962 team compiled a 19-4 record, which resulted in Shepard being named New England's coach of the year. Seniors Tom Boone and Mike Drummey got offensive help from a trio of juniors, Gavin Gilmor, Terry Bartolet, and Dick Diehl.

Harvard won its fifth Greater Boston League crown thanks to a big day from Drummey, who would go on to hit .341. With the Crimson trailing 4-1 in the bottom of the eighth against GBL rival Boston College, Drummey laid down a perfect squeeze bunt to spark a four-run rally that put Harvard up 5-4. In the ninth, with two on and two out for the Eagles, Drummey made a diving stab of a shot down the third base line, and then, from a sitting position, threw to second for the force that won both the game and the GBL title.

In three years as Harvard's top pitcher, Paul Del Rossi '64 compiled a phenomenal 30-3 record with a 1.51 ERA.

His ability to hit the long ball gave John Simourian (right) the nickname Babe. Here Simourian poses with head coach Norm Shepard.

Despite these efforts by hot hitters and slick fielders, many of the 1962 headlines went to a hard-throwing sophomore pitcher named Paul Del Rossi. While Bartolet hit .374 and both Drummey and Gilmor batted .341, it was Del Rossi's 10-1 record and 1.40 ERA in his first varsity season that garnered team MVP honors.

To prove that his first season wasn't a fluke, Del Rossi went out and fashioned marks of 9-1 and 1.86 in 1963, when Harvard went 17-6. Despite the presence of this left-handed ace and the continued hot hitting of Gilmor and Bartolet, Harvard again failed to win the Eastern League crown. That would change in 1964.

As a defensive back for the New York Jets, John Dockery won a Super Bowl ring in 1969. At Harvard, he combined football with baseball and was MVP in the spring of 1965. Here, his speed produces a run against Northeastern in May of 1966.

THE ROAD TO OMAHA

1964–69: The 1964 Harvard team provided proof that you don't judge a squad by the number of returning lettermen it has. Only five such veterans returned from 1963, yet the resulting 21-2-1 record gave Harvard its best winning percentage since 1895 and its first team to win 20 games in 37 years.

There was little question who carried this club. Senior left-hander Paul Del Rossi finished his career in style, chalking up an 11-1 record to make him the first postwar New Englander to win 30 games in a career. His three-year stats were incredible: a 30-3 record and an ERA of 1.51.

Harvard's pitching staff had depth as well as an ace. Lee Sargent was 5-0, with a Harvard record ERA of 0.41. Andy Luther checked in with 4-1, and 1.96 numbers. Rounding

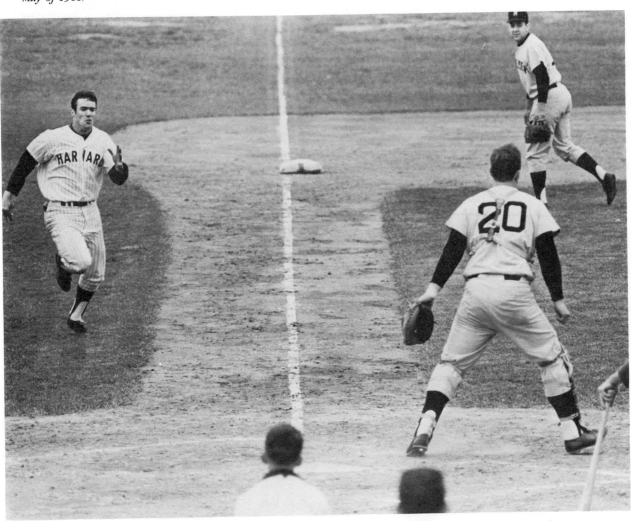

out the team stat leaders were batsmen Jim Tobin (.351), George Neville (.345), and Tom Stephenson (.340), who gave those pitchers runs to work with.

Following 1964's success, Harvard put together three successful but nonchampionship seasons that preceded greater things to come in 1968. Paving the way for that big year was the last half of the 1967 season. Sophomore pitcher Ray Peters went 9-3 on the year, twice struck out 16 batters in a game, and paced Harvard to seven straight wins to close out the year. Leading hitter Carter Lord, who also starred on the gridiron as the best receiver of the John Yovicsin era, batted .357. It was all table-setting for 1968.

In Norm Shepard's final year, Harvard won the EIBL title behind a balanced attack that saw all eight regulars hit between .269 and .320 overall. The biggest offensive numbers came from EIBL batting champ Dick Manchester, who hit .467 in league games.

But much as Del Rossi had done for the last Harvard champions, Peters carried this club. The junior All-American was 8-2, seven of the wins coming in league play. The

eighth was in the NCAA district championships against Boston University, and it helped send Harvard to Omaha for its first College World Series.

Harvard's first trip to Omaha established a pattern that would become all too familiar through the school's next three appearances out west. With bats going silent, Harvard lost to St. John's, 2-0, and to Southern Illinois, 2-1, in 11 innings.

Those losses did little to tarnish the season or career of retiring coach Norm Shepard. The 1968 New England Coach of the Year stepped down after a 14-season record of 218-108-4 for a .667 winning percentage.

Any chance that Harvard had of returning to Omaha in 1969 was pretty much canceled out by Ray Peters's decision to turn pro before his senior year. As he signed

The goose eggs on the scoreboard mean trouble for Yale as Ray Peters throws a one-hitter at the Elis in May of 1968. The final score was Harvard 9, Yale 0.

John Ignacio crosses the plate after hitting a home run at the 1968 College World Series in Omaha, Nebraska. Harvard has made four trips to the world series: 1968, 1971, 1973, and 1974.

with the short-lived Seattle Pilots, new baseball coach Loyal Park signed on with Harvard.

Park, a defensive backfield coach for John Yovicsin, was not new to Harvard. His was a fine baseball mind, and from the beginning Park teams earned a reputation for never beating themselves. The coach always made sure his teams were prepared.

His first club made a late run for EIBL honors but had to settle for a three-way tie at third. Senior outfielder John Ignacio gave Harvard another league batting title (.448), but catching most people's attention was a sophomore tandem of catcher Pete Varney and outfielder Dan DeMichele, whose .377 and .344 averages overall were one-two on the team.

1970–73: Around the time he started his second year in charge of Harvard's baseball fortunes, Loyal Park had to endure some occasional ribbing. The joke was always a variation of, "Loyal Park. Isn't that where the Patriots play their home games?"

After his second season, the jokes would subside as Park's 24-7 team made him somewhat more visible. This 1970 team became the second Harvard team in 42 years to win 20 games and did so by riding the bats of those multisport stars Varney and DeMichele.

There was the big (6 feet 4 inches, 240 pounds) tight end/catcher from North Quincy, Massachusetts, Pete Varney, whose ten home runs established a Harvard record and helped set a new team mark for RBIs as well. Varney had become a household name in Cambridge long before Loyal Park. After all, it was Varney's big hands that caught the tying points in 1968's fabled 29-29 football "victory" over Yale.

Varney received offensive help from 6-foot 3-inch left wing-turned-outfielder Dan DeMichele out of hockey-mad Cranston, Rhode Island. DeMichele was a member of Harvard's top scoring hockey line and went from leading goal scorer to leading hitter. He would win both the EIBL and GBL batting titles and finish with an overall average of .421, Harvard's best in nearly 40 years.

Five pitchers had between three and five wins each, with junior J. C. Nickens the best of the lot with a 5-2 mark and a 1.13 ERA. Nickens picked up two of those wins in relief as Harvard swept a doubleheader from Navy in a strong stretch run that just missed winning the league title. After a 1-4 EIBL start, the Crimson finished tied for second at 10-4.

The near miss of 1970 became the championship season of 1971. Varney and DeMichele continued to pace the hitters, and Park's pitching corps of seniors Nickens (7-1), Bill Kelly (7-2), Phil Collins (6-1), and sophomore Roz Brayton (3-0) had plenty of depth.

In the end, though, it was the phenomenal performance of Kelly that carried Harvard into the College World Series in Omaha. Prior to this season, Kelly was the kid with so much athletic potential who had forged but one memorable moment. He was the guy who recovered the onside kick in that 29-29 football classic. His hands made the play that allowed Varney's hands their moment.

But in the spring of 1971, Kelly lived up to all his potential and made that singular moment just a footnote. On May 1 Kelly bested Dartmouth ace (and future pro) Pete Broberg, 1-0, in ten innings. As if his pitching were not enough, his double drove in the winning run.

Two weeks later Kelly's two-hitter beat Cornell, 2-1, in a special playoff game to determine the EIBL champion. Then on Memorial Day, Kelly surrendered ten hits but prevailed over Massachusetts by a 2-1 score in the NCAA regionals. Typifying Kelly's performance was the eighth inning, in which UMass loaded the bases with nobody out. Kelly reached back and found what he needed to strike out the No. 4, 5, and 6 batters in the UMass lineup to save the day.

In Omaha it was Kelly again whose four-hitter gave Harvard a 4-1 win over Brigham Young, the Crimson's first world series win ever. But a pair of one-run losses to Tulsa (9-8) and Pan American (1-0) ended the season at 27-8, Harvard's winningest campaign in 108 years of baseball.

When the season ended, Varney and DeMichele signed pro contracts with Chicago's White Sox and Cubs respectively. Graduation claimed others, such as captain and first baseman Pete Bernhard and pitchers Nickens, Kelly, and Collins, who provided 20 of the team's 27 wins.

Such was the background as the 1972 season opened. This would not be a team with the offensive power or veteran pitching staff its predecessor enjoyed. But it would scrap and claw for production and ride the arm of Roz Brayton to another EIBL title.

Brayton had signaled great things to come in the 1971 season finale in Omaha. Fastballing his way to a no-hitter through 5 innings, Brayton was finally derailed by a couple of missed pitches that gave Pan American the 1-0 win. In April of 1972 he missed very few pitches, tossing four shutouts and setting a school mark of 40 consecutive scoreless innings.

The offensive load was shared by many; and whereas home runs carried previous Harvard teams, this club was more likely to beat you with a bunt, a stolen base, or a late-inning rally.

Captain Vin McGugan, who would win the Bingham Award as the school's top athlete, typified this club. Sure-handed at second base and leading the team in hitting, McGugan was also a whiz at base-stealing, going 16 for 16 in the club's first 18 games.

To the surprise of most everyone, the team finished at 30-9, setting new records for wins and games played. Perhaps most memorable of them all was a 3-2 playoff win over Cornell that gave Harvard its second straight EIBL crown.

Down 2-1 in the ninth, the Crimson rallied for two runs when sophomore Joe Mackey tripled home classmate Jim Stoeckel and scored the winner on senior Tim Bilodeau's single.

Strangely memorable were the NCAA regionals, where Harvard stranded 17 runners in a 4-2 win in 12 and then lost to the University of Connecticut, 8-5, in 16 innings. An 18-6 pasting of Northeastern was followed by an 11-2 loss to UConn, which ended the season.

Harvard returned to Omaha in 1973 and became the first team to win three straight EIBL titles. This team, like so many Harvard nines through the years, featured an array of multisport athletes, perhaps more than any other ballclub. Here's a breakdown:

FOOTBALL
Milt Holt, QB (pitcher)
Joe Mackey, DE (first base)
Barry Malinowski, DB (pitcher)
Keith Schappert, OG (pitcher)
Joe Sciolla, DB (outfield)
Jim Stoeckel, QB (shortstop)

ICE HOCKEY
Kevin Hampe, D (outfield)
Leigh Hogan, C (first base)
Jim Thomas, LW (infield)

BASKETBALL
Hal Smith, G (outfield)

SOCCER
Ric LaCivita, B (second base)

Alex Nahigian, coach of Providence College in the early 1970s and later Park's successor at Harvard, would recall these great Harvard teams. "I used to say to Loyal, 'You've got some talented kids. Who does your recruiting?' He'd say, 'The football coach, the hockey coach, the basketball coach.'"

This was a team with incredible pitching depth. Park could call on any of 11 pitchers with confidence. Starters from 1972 such as Brayton (8-2), Sandy Weissant (6-0), Mike O'Malley (4-2), and Barry Malinowski (3-3) returned, along with ace reliever Norm Walsh (6-1). Added to these veterans were sophomore prospects Milt Holt and Don Driscoll. As a result of these numbers, the fifth and sixth starters were named to the Greater Boston League all-star team.

The team had already won 30 games entering the NCAA district playoffs at Fenway Park, where a classic matchup loomed. It was Harvard versus chief rival Massachusetts. And it was left-hander Roz Brayton against left-hander Mike Flanagan, later an all-star with the Baltimore Orioles.

The game lived up to its billing, and the teams were tied at 2-2 in the top of the eighth. That's when shortstop Jim Stoeckel sent a Flanagan offering over the screen in left field to give Harvard a 4-2 lead it never relinquished. Two wins later, the Crimson were off to Omaha.

It was downhill from there as the team dropped a pair, 4-1 to Southern California (with future big-leaguers Fred Lynn, Roy Smalley, and Rich Dauer), and 8-0 to Georgia Southern.

The final mark was 35-5, two more records for wins and games played. The balance on this club was reflected in its top three pitchers and hitters. Senior Brayton (7-2), junior Mike O'Malley (7-0), and sophomore Don Driscoll (5-1) all had ERAs under 2.00. The top hitters were senior Hal Smith (.353), sophomore Ed Durso (.350), and junior Ric LaCivita (.333). Perhaps the unsung hero in all of this was captain (hockey captain as well) Kevin Hampe, baseball's second straight Bingham Award winner as top athlete in the university.

Enduring the Success

The phone rang in Fenway Park's dugout and when Harvard coach Loyal Park answered it, someone wanted to order a pizza. The call came, of course, from the free thinkers in Harvard's bullpen. This was 1973 and playing baseball for Harvard was fun. Most of the time.

Most of the fun came from winning, which Harvard did often in the early 1970s. And those daffy ones in the bullpen had a lot to do with it. When

In ten seasons as head coach of Harvard baseball, Loyal Park had an overall record of 248-93 and won the Eastern League championship five times.

not ordering pizzas from bullpen phones, or playing their own brand of hockey out in Soldiers Field's makeshift bullpen, guys like Norm Walsh, Tom O'Neill, Keith Schappert, and others put out the few fires left by an extraordinarily deep starting staff.

Harvard went to the College World Series three times in four years, 1971, 1973, and 1974. That first team had the big bats of Pete Varney and Dan DeMichele. The later squads could do a little of everything, but their strong suits, like those of most Loyal Park teams, were pitching and defense.

The man who groomed these teams was a dominating presence, for better and worse, for ten years at Soldiers Field. Coach Loyal Park made that decade both a success and an ordeal for Harvard baseball players.

He was a great college baseball coach. No one, even his harshest critics, ever questioned that. His teams were as fundamentally sound as any.

"Our practices were incredibly complete and consistent," recalled Leigh Hogan, a star first baseman on three Park teams. "Every practice was the same: bunting, bunt coverages, baserunning, situations, pitcher covering first, and so on. Every single day."

Many of Park's ballplayers went into coaching after Harvard. Varney, after a brief pro career, became head coach at Brandeis. Hogan and Walsh were successful high school coaches in the Boston area as was their teammate Rich Bridich in Milwaukee. Shortstop Jim Stoeckel briefly assisted Alex Nahigian before returning to his native Florida, where he worked with the Los Angeles Dodgers' Vero Beach farm team. As many of these coaches will admit, a trip to their own practice sessions would reveal a typical Loyal Park workout.

Park might allow the daffiness in the bullpen, perhaps sensing it relieved the tension and could help his teams win games. But he would not tolerate sloppiness at practice. If an afternoon workout grew ragged, he would call the team together at the mound, bang the fungo bat into the rubber, and berate his troops for their lack of precision. The routine grew familiar, but the message was picked up loud and clear.

But throughout the Park years, there were problems never too far from the surface. Players would show up for a road game only to be told by a manager that they weren't making the trip. Unnamed players, spoken of in a thinly disguised third person, were berated by the coach in front of the entire team. Pitchers who had fallen out of favor were left in games long after enemy bats had suggested otherwise.

As one player said, "His selection of personnel was always predicated on who would make us a

These two diamond stars are perhaps best remembered as key players in 1968's famed 29-29 football tie with Yale. Bill Kelly (left) recovered the crucial onside kick that eventually led to Pete Varney (right) catching the final conversion to tie the game.

better team. He was usually right as to who should play. But how he went about it was another thing."

When his Harvard years ended after the 1978 season, Park was still a successful baseball coach. And he remained in college athletics as a coach and administrator in a number of locales beginning with Salem College in West Virginia.

The comings and goings of coaches at both amateur and professional levels are frequently bittersweet. While the professionals are governed primarily by winning percentages and championships, college athletics, at Harvard and throughout the Ivy League, remain a people business. Unfortunately, people sometimes forget that.

• • •

Above: *The 1973 Bingham Award for the best athlete at Harvard went to Dedham's Kevin Hampe, captain of both baseball and hockey and a regular on eastern champions in both sports.*

Left: *Roz Brayton '73 put three strong years together in the early 1970s and signed with the Boston Red Sox after graduation. His 0.43 ERA led the Eastern League in 1972.*

Below: *Celebrating a fourth straight Eastern League title in 1974, pitcher Don Driscoll lifts second baseman Ric LaCivita, and third baseman Jim Thomas joins the fun.*

• • •

STAYING NEAR THE TOP

1974–77: Another 30-win season followed in 1974, and that included Harvard's fourth straight EIBL title and another trip to Omaha. This team's strength was pitching, as only two hitters batted above .300 (Leigh Hogan and Joe Mackey) and three players shared top home run honors with just a pair each.

Though the final mark read 31-9, as the season wound down there was considerable doubt about whether this team could keep the EIBL streak alive. With a 4-4 league record on May 4, mathematical elimination from the race was a distinct possibility. Enter the Big Three.

The Big Three were pitchers Milt Holt, Mike O'Malley, and Don Driscoll. Much like Bill Kelly had done single-handedly in 1971, these three combined to give one clutch performance after another to carry Harvard to glory.

It was Holt who tossed 2-0, 2-1, and 4-1 league wins down the stretch. It was O'Malley who beat chief rivals Princeton and Pennsylvania in the final week of the season. And it was Driscoll who shut out Navy and then beat Princeton in Harvard's third EIBL tie-breaking playoff game in four years.

Driscoll was perhaps the most intense of this trio. It was not uncommon for the hard-throwing right-hander to fan an opponent and then storm off the mound unhappy with himself because the pitch wasn't where he wanted it.

All that pitching put Harvard in the NCAA districts once more. And what happened there? Driscoll threw a one-hitter, Holt tossed a three-hitter, and O'Malley surrendered just four hits as Harvard outscored three opponents 18-2 to advance to Omaha.

Unfortunately, the trip west produced the same fate as so many previous visits: two games and two losses, to Miami (4-1) and Northern Colorado (4-2). The trip brought one historic moment. Leading off for the Crimson, second baseman Ric LaCivita became the first college player ever to use an aluminum bat, as the new items were introduced to the college game at this event.

It is interesting to note that five of Park's nine pitchers—O'Malley, Holt, Driscoll, Jim Harrell, and Norm Walsh—pitched 300 of the team's 349 innings, and all had ERAs below 2.50. O'Malley (1.09) and relief ace Walsh (3-0, 1.19) were particularly effective, as was team

batting leader Leigh Hogan (.352), who set a New England record for hits in a season with 55.

Harvard's EIBL streak was snapped at four when the 1975 team finished third while going a respectable 25-10 overall. It was a somewhat frustrating season, and the timely hitting of recent years could not always be found. In seven of the eight losses suffered by veterans Don Driscoll and Milt Holt, Harvard scored a total of seven runs. Somewhat more fortunate was the surprise of the staff, Mark Linehan, who went 7-1.

Leigh Hogan led the team in batting for the second straight season (.341) despite playing injured for most of the year. Classmates Joe Sciolla and Ed Durso also had productive seasons in closing out three-year careers that produced a 91-26 record.

When the 1976 team returned from its southern swing with an 11-2 mark, there were mixed reviews. Considering that the roster contained 18 freshmen and sophomores, these results seemed encouraging.

Some critics, though, questioned the legitimacy of the competition. Indeed, Loyal Park's Florida schedule had long been a topic of conversation among Harvard's baseball types. What did it mean to go 10-0 against the likes of West Virginia Wesleyan, Bethune-Cookman, Florida Presbyterian, and Embry-Riddle Aeronautical University?

The other side of the argument was that coming out of the snow of New England, a light schedule made some sense. And some of the names unfamiliar to Northerners, like Orlando's Rollins College, did indeed field strong baseball teams.

The critics were heard again when that 11-2 southern start was followed by a 6-16 northern finish. The resulting 17-18 season was Harvard's first losing campaign since 1961.

The brief skid ended in 1977, when the team bounced back with a 22-7 mark. Five freshmen won starting berths and helped lead the revival. Most impressive of this quintet was outfielder Mike Stenhouse, son of former Washington Senator's all-star pitcher Dave. The younger Stenhouse only batted .475 and knocked in 40 runs, both new Harvard records.

With senior Dave Singleton hitting .398 and freshman Mark Bingham at .383, this team produced three of the top ten batting averages in modern Harvard history.

On the mound, sophomore Larry Brown began to mature and posted a 4-0 record and 2.40 ERA. Those numbers would seem insignificant a year later.

1978–80: It is safe to say that the 1977–78 academic year was a good one for Lawrence Brown of Norwood, Massachusetts. In the fall, Brown won the starting quarterback spot on the football team and set a single-game passing record with 349 yards against Pennsylvania.

Then came the spring. Brown's right arm remained busy as he compiled a 10-1 record with a stingy 0.95 ERA. Those numbers were a major reason that Harvard returned to the top of the Eastern League.

Equally important was the second banner year of Mike Stenhouse. The smooth-swinging outfielder from Rhode Island put together gaudy numbers that included a .404 batting average, 36 RBIs, and a record-tying ten home runs. Stenhouse won the EIBL batting crown with an even .500 average and through two varsity seasons owned nearly every Harvard career and single-season record.

These superstars brought Harvard to the NCAA districts but no farther. Brown, winner of his first ten, lost his only game of the season to Delaware, 1-0 in a six-inning, rain-shortened heartbreaker. The next day St. John's prevailed 8-0, and just like that the team with five .300 hitters was blanked twice and the season was over.

Also over was the ten-year reign of coach Loyal Park. In that time, Harvard won 248 baseball games and lost just 93 while producing five Eastern League titles and three trips to Omaha. It was a record that few coaches could match.

But all was not rosy beneath the surface. Despite averaging nearly 25 wins a season, Park was not embraced by a large number of the athletes who played for him. He knew the game of baseball and his teams were well prepared. But a growing number of personality clashes with team members hastened his departure despite continued success.

In sharp contrast to the gregarious, back-slapping Park was his successor, Alex Nahigian. A quiet, warmly sincere man, Nahigian had been head baseball coach at Providence College for 18 seasons and had also been the linebacker coach at Harvard since 1975.

Nahigian inherited Brown, Stenhouse, and more than a few veterans from the 1978 championship team but got off to a slow start. After splitting its first six league games, this team won six of its last eight only to fall a game short of first place.

Brown won his first five, then lost a pair, and finished his four-year career with a 23-5 record. Stenhouse hit .395 and abruptly ended his Harvard career by signing

As a member of the Washington Senators, pitcher Dave Stenhouse once started an All-Star Game for the American League. But son Mike was pure hitter, perhaps Harvard's best. His .422 career average and .475 single-season mark are Harvard records. Like his dad, Mike became a major-leaguer (Montreal and Minnesota).

with the Montreal Expos and forgoing his senior year in the process. He finished as career leader in home runs, RBIs, hits, and triples, and batted a phenomenal .422 for his career.

Stenhouse's departure allowed classmate Mark Bingham to enjoy the spotlight by himself. As a freshman, in 1977, the tall first baseman had hit .383 and made just one error in 146 chances, but Stenhouse hit .475 and was flawless in the field. The next year Bingham hit .311 and made only one error in 249 chances; again Stenhouse hit over .400 and played errorless ball. Finally, as juniors, it was Bingham who led the team in batting (.403) and RBIs (36) while making just three errors in 339 chances. He received team MVP honors over classmate Stenhouse.

Stenhouse's departure allowed the class of '80 to receive plenty of attention in its final season in Cambridge. There was Bingham, never missing a game at first base in four years and committing just eight errors out of a record 1,094 chances (.992). He finished with career marks for hits, RBIs, at-bats, and put-outs as well, and his .346 career average was fifth best in Harvard history.

Second baseman Bobby Kelley fashioned a 20-game hitting streak en route to all-league honors, and captain Charlie Santos-Buch was the team's only .300 hitter overall, winning the EIBL crown with a .444 mark.

But in the end it was the surprise performance of pitcher Rob Alevizos that brought Alex Nahigian his first EIBL title. The senior right-hander carried an undistinguished 3-2 career mark into his final season and impressively won five in a row.

When the EIBL regular season produced a three-way tie among Harvard, Cornell, and Yale, it was Alevizos who launched Harvard's playoff sweep with a four-hitter against Cornell. And it was Alevizos in the regionals beating East Carolina to run his record to 7-0. But there were no more chances, as two NCAA losses to St. John's ended the season before reservations could be booked for Nebraska.

1981–85: With graduation claiming three-quarters of the infield, the best pitcher, and the best hitter, little was expected in 1981, and there were no surprises. Another Greater Boston League title was chalked up, but fifth place was Harvard's lot in the EIBL.

Only during a midseason win streak of four games did this club offer hope of performing the impossible. Two of those wins came in an impressive doubleheader sweep of Pennsylvania in which Harvard won the first game 6-5 after trailing 5-0, and the second 4-0 on a no-hitter by football captain Greg Brown.

But the next time out, Yale's Ron Darling, who went on to become a New York Mets standout, fanned nine and put an end to the streak. Harvard never won more than two straight the rest of the season.

The season did serve to launch a couple of power hitters on record-breaking paths. Sophomores Vinnie Martelli and Don Allard had 35 and 32 RBIs respectively. Both would rank among Harvard's best hitters before they were through.

Despite the presence of six .300 hitters (Bruce Weller, Martelli, Brad Bauer, Paul Chicarello, Ed Farrell, and

From 1980 to 1983 catcher and first baseman Vin Martelli knocked in 123 runs for Harvard, a school record. His power recalled the efforts of his older cousin, former Red Sox slugger Tony Conigliaro.

Allard) in the lineup, the problem was finding that stopper on the mound. The 1982 team had to settle for third place in the EIBL, tied with Brown and Penn in an odd year that left seven EIBL teams with records ranging from 9-9 to 7-9.

The next year, Harvard found the stoppers to go with the bats, and another league title resulted. How well did this team hit? Check out these scores: 14-3 over Boston College, 17-1 and 20-1 over Northeastern, and against those rivals from New Haven, 18-6 and 24-9. No previous Harvard team had ever scored 42 runs in two games against Yale.

In addition to impressive batting averages, this team had power. Never before had a Harvard lineup featured as many home runs as those provided by Farrell (8), Allard (7), and Martelli (6). By season's end, Allard's 21 total homers and Martelli's 123 RBIs were Harvard career bests.

But what distinguished this team from its third-place predecessor was the emergence of two pitching aces in senior hockey player Bill Larson (8-1) and sophomore Charlie Marchese (7-1). Their arms and their teammates' bats brought Harvard to a one-game play-off against Navy that would determine the EIBL champion and send that team to the NCAAs.

The game, played at Cornell's neutral site, went to Harvard by 10-1. But then the newly crowned league champs took four full games to score ten runs at the NCAA play-offs. Those quiet bats and Maine pitching ended Harvard's season in the districts once more.

The 1983 season may have been a hard act to follow, particularly with the graduation of the top four hitters, including record-setters Allard and Martelli and four-year starter Brad Bauer.

But the 1984 squad matched that club virtually step for step as new heroes emerged. This 28-6 club won the GBL and EIBL titles handily and produced some exceptional individual efforts. Outfielder Elliott Rivera set a new single-season mark with 44 RBIs; designated hitter Mickey Maspons (.491) and pitcher Charlie Marchese (4-0, 2.40 ERA) were the EIBL's statistical leaders; and outfielder Bruce Weller set new records for runs scored in a season (53) and a career (142).

This was a team that fashioned win streaks of six, eight, and ten games and lost only four regular-season games. Its other two losses came in its final two games at the NCAA regionals at Orono, Maine.

An explosive team that had rallied when it had to all year, Harvard spotted Seton Hall 5-1 and 6-3 leads in the opener at that tournament only to come back to win, 10-8. Then it was old nemesis Maine, the team that had ended the previous year's postseason hopes. Again Harvard fell behind, this time by 3-0 and then 4-1. Again Harvard came back, and the score was tied 4-4 in the ninth inning. As if the Black Bears needed any help with their ace pitcher Billy Swift (17 strikeouts on the day) on the mound, a rainstorm came along to further cool Harvard bats.

After a half-hour delay, the game was called in the 10th and continued on Sunday. There, in the 12th inning, Maine won it, 5-4, to give Charle Marchese his first and only loss of the season. The junior EIBL Pitcher of the Year finished with a 7-1 record, 14-2 over two seasons.

After 18 seasons as head coach at Providence College, Alex Nahigian became Harvard's head coach in 1979. Nahigian had already served the Crimson as linebacker coach for Joe Restic since 1975.

Harvard had to come right back out to play Seton Hall just 20 minutes later. The result was a sloppy (eight errors) 9-1 loss that ended a happy season unhappily.

Six players hit over .300 on this team, including All-EIBL selections Maspons, Weller, and shortstop Tony DiCesare. It was a group that pleased Nahigian and offered peace of mind. Only two starters were graduated, none of them pitchers.

Despite this experience, Nahigian's 25th team (7th at Harvard) started slowly at 6-6 before turning up the heat and winning 20 out of 22 games down the stretch, the most emotional of those perhaps Jeff Musselman's 2-1 no-hitter against Penn.

This month-long comeback was particularly notable in that Princeton, the EIBL leader, had finished its league schedule four weeks ahead of Harvard. That meant that the Tigers could sit back and watch as Harvard had to be perfect in its final six league games.

Harvard met that challenge successfully, only to be rebuffed by Princeton, 5-1, in a one-game play-off. The comeback of '85 would be a source of pride but no championship.

The Nahigian teams continued a tradition of Harvard baseball excellence that began in the late 19th century and never looked healthier than in the late 20th century. One statistic reflects this later success: From 1968 through 1984, Harvard won 9 of a possible 17 Eastern League titles.

After 3,000 games and 122 years, Harvard baseball was still on top of its game.

CHAPTER 7

Basketball

You couldn't get a seat. In fact, you couldn't even get through that last set of doors to see a speck of the hardwood floor. On February 7, 1964, Harvard's Indoor Athletic Building was sold out. The attraction was Princeton's basketball team and its celebrated All-American Bill Bradley, later the Rhodes scholar turned New York Knick turned U.S. senator from New Jersey. People came to see Bradley score points. And he did. Thirty of them.

As often as undergraduate public address announcer Jerry Kapstein (later a sports attorney of note) said the name Bradley, he also intoned the names McClung and Sedlacek. That's because Harvard's Merle McClung and Keith Sedlacek had 30 and 31 points respectively as Harvard shocked the Tigers, 88-82.

It was a great night for Harvard basketball. There were the crowd, the individual performances, and the victory that left the Crimson in a tie for first place in the Ivy League. That's the way it should be. That's the way it could be.

Unfortunately, that's the way it has seldom been. The big games before big crowds have been few and far between in the history of Harvard basketball. Yet the men who have played the game have worked as hard and been as dedicated as those in any program in the college.

Basketball has always taken a back seat at Harvard. Winter has been the time for ice hockey, at Harvard and in New England in general. That's a fact of life that has touched the basketball program in many ways. At New England prep schools, a major supplier of Harvard athletes for decades, hockey is the top winter sport. In the Boston area, before the Celtics made their name and even into their reign, hockey was the darling of the public.

And there are those who will argue that the people who can make a difference at Harvard have looked more favorably at the hockey program than the basketball program. Have the two sports' facility needs been addressed equally over the years? Have they both been assisted in attracting quality athletes?

Whatever the reasons, it is clear that Harvard has seldom had the basketball talent to mount a strong challenge to the Ivy's best. What is remarkable is how consistent the record has been. Aside from the 1920s, when the Crimson enjoyed seven winning seasons, every decade since has featured two to four winning seasons. No more, no less.

As a result of this overriding uniformity of results, the accomplishments of the good teams and great players that have dotted the sport's history have been all but ignored. There may not have been a Bill Bradley or an Ivy champ in the group. But there have been plenty upon whom history could have directed a little more light.

MEN'S BASKETBALL:
A QUEST FOR RESPECT

1900–19: There may be a simple explanation for everything. It seems that the first basketball team at Harvard was organized by a Yale man. In the fall of 1900, John Kirkland Clark, a Yalie attending Harvard Law School, convinced the Harvard Athletic Committee to acknowledge his yearlong efforts to legitimize basketball. On December 7, 1900, the committee officially recognized the sport at Harvard.

Clark did a creditable job with the young program, leading the first two teams to winning seasons. As rules regarding the use of graduate students (and freshmen) had yet to be invoked, Clark was a player-coach . . . with one exception. On January 26, 1901, when Harvard first met Yale in basketball, Clark declined to play.

Judging from department records, the sport enjoyed enough popularity to draw anywhere from 50 to 100 students to participate in the program. The largest source of appeal seemed to be the notion that the game would be a good off-season conditioner for football players. This was also the source of the game's first problem. Harvard Athletic Association records describe one contest this way:

> Gillies forgot himself in the closing minutes and ran down the court with the ball beneath his arm as if playing football. . . . There was much roughness on the part of both teams, especially in the second period. The College boys jumped among the spectators for the ball out of bounds like battering rams. . . . The game was a bit rough. . . . One player was picked up by his opponent on his back and tossed against the dumbbell rack along the side of the court. . . . Brown hit his head against the wall, towards the close of the game, and retired.

It was in 1902 that Harvard first got a taste of league play as a member of both the New England League and the Eastern Intercollegiate League, a forerunner of the Ivy League. Because of conflicts Harvard withdrew from the New England League after one season.

It was also in 1902 that basketball fortunes began to wane. Clark stepped down as his law school work was coming to a close, and Harvard suffered back-to-back losing seasons. And although the 1904–06 periods brought two winning records, there were signs that interest was lacking on campus.

During those seasons all home games were played in the afternoon instead of in the evening. The reasons offered for this were: "The public does not want to waste an entire evening at such a thing as a basketball game"; "It is more difficult to procure friends to accompany a fan to such a place as Cambridge for the night"; and "There is no necessity for a chaperone at an afternoon game."

In effect, the decision was an attempt to increase gate receipts, as all minor sports were responsible for raising their own funds in those days. The move had little effect, compounded by on-court happenings that produced records of 7-9, 4-12, and 1-7 through the 1908–09 season.

The result of the failing fortunes was the Athletic Committee's decision to abolish basketball, on May 11, 1909. With the announcement came the following reasoning: "The game has not flourished here, and is regarded by many competent critics as among the least desirable of athletic sports in this part of the country."

Eleven years would pass before basketball returned to Harvard on an officially sanctioned basis.

1920–45: During basketball's hiatus at Harvard, the game grew in popularity nationally. And so efforts were launched in the fall of 1919 to return the sport to Cambridge.

The program's resurrection was overseen by William H. Geer, Harvard's director of physical training, and Daniel J. Kelly, a member of Geer's department. These gentlemen, along with undergraduate Bernard Damon '20, set out on their task mindful of what led to the program's demise. Specifically, they hoped to curb the roughness in play, improve conditions in Hemenway Gymnasium, and make a Harvard basketball game an attractive event for spectators to attend.

After a year of on-campus competition, basketball returned as an intercollegiate pastime at Harvard for the 1920–21 season. Chosen to guide Crimson fortunes was

Edward A. Wachter, a native of Troy, New York, who had earned a reputation as a deadly shooter in professional basketball. He would make a smooth transition to coaching in becoming the most successful head coach in Harvard basketball history.

Wachter produced nine winning seasons in 13 years and remains the only Harvard coach to compile a winning career record (121-81). After a 9-10 effort the first time out, Wachter directed seven straight winning seasons. It would be 45 years before Harvard would again put together three winning seasons in a row.

Wachter was able to accomplish this despite a talent pool that was average at best. Dolph Samborski, the 1925 captain who later became director of athletics, paid this tribute to Wachter's skill:

"In addition to expert techniques in coaching, the success of Wachter's teams may be attributed almost entirely to his ability to judge and build character, and his sympathetic understanding of the individual. His tactful methods seldom failed to bring out the talent that may have been hidden."

Samborski was one of six players whom Wachter placed on his personal all-star team upon retiring in 1933. The others were Lew Gordon '24, William Smith '26, Jack Leekley '27, John Barbee, Jr., '28, and Thomas Farrell '31. With the exception of Leekley, all were team captains.

Wachter's efforts were appreciated beyond Harvard's ivy walls, a fact underscored in 1961 when he became the third professional ever chosen for the Naismith Basketball Hall of Fame.

Wachter's final two seasons saw a drop in Harvard's basketball fortunes and an accompanying decline in fan interest. This trend came about despite the construction of a new facility, the Indoor Athletic Building, in 1930.

Such was the climate when Wesley Fesler took over the program in 1933. The former basketball and football All-American from Ohio State was a winner as an athlete. And later, when he led his alma mater to the Big Ten football title and victory in the 1950 Rose Bowl, he was a winner as a football coach.

But as Harvard's basketball coach from 1933–34 to 1940–41, he could only manage three winning seasons in eight tries. It was after the first of these seasons, in 1936–37, that the program was elevated to major status at Harvard.

Perhaps the best statement on the talent level in this period was the fact that the 1939–40 team included seven players who did not start on their high school teams.

When Harvard's postwar teams produced records of 17-3 and 16-9, playmaker Saul Mariaschin was the team spark plug. The Brooklyn native enjoyed a brief stint with the Boston Celtics and was inducted into the Harvard Varsity Club Hall of Fame in 1980.

In the two years between Fesler's departure and the outbreak of World War II, Earl Brown took over the program. Despite fielding a team entirely under 6 feet tall except 6-foot 2-inch Bud Finegan, Brown pulled off a major upset when Dartmouth was beaten, 49-36 in 1942. That victory, by a team that would wind up 8-16, came at the expense of a Dartmouth team that finished second in the NCAA tournament.

Varsity baseball coach Floyd Stahl steered the program for three seasons, the first two on an informal basis due to the war. His third team, a slightly more formal ensemble, produced the most brilliant record of all.

1946–53: Floyd Stahl's 1945–46 squad was shaped by the wartime experience. Harvard, like many of the other Ivy League schools, had served as a breeding ground for naval officers during the war. The Navy V-12 and ROTC programs provided much of the talent for Stahl's two wartime teams, and it was a member of the ROTC program who led Harvard's first postwar team to a 17-3 record. (This record is sometimes listed as 20-3, but that includes three wins against the Chelsea Naval Hospital team.)

Wyndol Gray, captain of that 1945–46 team, was one of the best basketball players ever to wear a Harvard uniform. In his only Harvard season, Gray led the Crimson to its only NCAA playoff appearance. It was there that Harvard lost two of its three games (to Ohio State and New York University). The only regular-season loss was a 47-42 decision to Holy Cross.

Because of its outstanding record, this team has been considered by many to be Harvard's greatest. But an asterisk must accompany its place in history because of the war's effect on the schedule and personnel. Whereas the last official schedule in 1943 included the likes of Wisconsin and Michigan State and a full Ivy slate, the 1946 team played just three Ivy games and no national powers until the postseason tournament.

Gray, who went on to play professionally for both Boston and St. Louis, was a legitimate standout. But his was not a typical four-year stint at Harvard, since he had played at Bowling Green before entering the ROTC program in Cambridge.

No such caveat is needed for Saul Mariaschin, Gray's teammate, who went on to captain 1947's 16-9 squad under new coach Bill Barclay. Mariaschin was a clever ballhandler who later enjoyed a brief stint with the Boston Celtics until another clever guard named Cousy moved him out.

Chief beneficiary of Mariaschin's playmaking was George Hauptfuhrer, Jr., leading scorer as a junior on that winning team. Mariaschin and Hauptfuhrer remain the only basketball entries in the Harvard Varsity Club Hall of Fame.

The 1946–47 team was Harvard's last winning team for ten years. Barclay coached for two more seasons before Norm Shepard followed with a five-year tenure, and all of these teams finished below .500. As is often the case, the lack of team success has overshadowed the efforts of some of this era's top individuals. There was John Rockwell, the first Harvard player to lead the Eastern Intercollegiate League in scoring. And there was Ed Smith, a talented center who was drafted by the New York Knicks.

One of the best players of this period was Bill Dennis. The first Harvard man to score more than 1,000 career points (1,074), Dennis was one of a handful of New York–bred basketball players to arrive at Harvard in the early 1950s.

These players improved the talent pool but not the results. The teams simply didn't come together with any consistency, beating an opponent by a dozen points one night and losing by the same margin to the same team two weeks later. The most notable example of this came in the two games played with Princeton in 1953. On February 7 Harvard lost to the Tigers 83-53 in Cambridge. On February 23 Harvard traveled to Princeton and won easily, 71-49.

Norm Shepard relinquished his basketball duties in 1954 and went on to success as Harvard's baseball coach. At that time Harvard's basketball coaches were expected

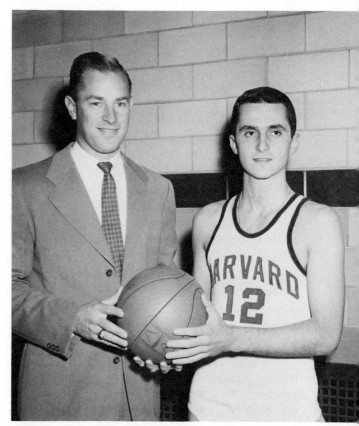

Harvard's basketball coach from 1954 to 1968 was Floyd Wilson, shown here with 1955 captain Roger Bulger. Wilson went on to direct Harvard's vast intramural and recreation program through the 1980s.

to take on more that one coaching assignment. All that changed with Shepard's successor, who served longer than any other head coach in Harvard basketball history.

1954–67: Floyd Wilson did his best. In fact, for 14 seasons Floyd Wilson did as well as anyone might have with basketball talent that was never quite up to the level of the Ivy League's upper echelon.

While the talent might not have been first division, the effort always was. And that was a source of pride to the Harvard coach.

"One of the best things about the kids I coached was the way they came through it all. It wasn't easy for kids who were achievers to go through that experience with no glory, no attention. And still to endure that sort of thing and go on to achieve again as doctors, lawyers, and so forth was tremendous."

Four of Wilson's teams finished on the winning side, with three of the winning campaigns coming between 1956–57 and 1959–60. The first of these was fashioned by the 1957 team, featuring six seniors who had gone undefeated under then freshman coach Wilson in 1953–54. Their 1957 record was 12-9.

Captain Bob Canty was the most productive of this group, finishing as Harvard's seventh career scorer at that time. Perhaps the best all-around athlete was Bob Hastings, who earned three letters in both basketball and baseball and was later selected for Harvard's Hall of Fame in the latter sport.

"There weren't any real superstars on this team," Wilson would later recall. "But from that freshman experience through graduation, they just hit it off as well as any team I had. They were really a close-knit group on and off the court."

Possibly the best player to emerge from this team was George Harrington, a diminutive guard whom Wilson called "pound for pound, the best basketball player of that period. He wasn't particularly big or fast but had a quick first step and was as smart as any of them on the floor."

As a junior in 1957–58, Harrington led Harvard to the best record of Wilson's years, 16-9. A third winning season came two years later, one that featured a pair of wins over archenemy Yale, something that had not happened since the war and would not happen again until 1971.

Harvard's winning year of 1963–64 was the first in four seasons and the last for seven more. That was the season of the victory over Bill Bradley's Princeton team and that was the season of Merle McClung.

The soft-spoken junior from Montevideo, Minnesota, became Harvard basketball's first All-Ivy performer since the league was formed ten years earlier. He averaged just under 20 points a game and failed to score in double figures only once. His 30 points keyed that upset of Princeton, and he had a record 39 in the finale against Dartmouth.

With McClung and three other starters returning for 1964–65, Harvard basketball faced unusually high expectations. But the team went 11-12 overall and 6-8 in the league, the second of three straight such Ivy finishes. McClung, who was awarded a Rhodes Scholarship that year, did not score as he had the previous year. But there was a good reason for it.

"We changed our offense in Merle's senior year, and it was a change that would not put him in as good a position to score," according to Wilson. "Typically, he never said a word about it but just continued to give his best. That's what he was like."

When McClung's numbers fell off, Keith Sedlacek's soared. As a sophomore, Sedlacek emerged with 31 points against Princeton. With the change in offense the next year, Sedlacek's shooting was put on display. Finally, in 1965–66, Sedlacek put on a show.

He may not have contributed in as many ways as McClung, but Keith Sedlacek could shoot a basketball. He did that so well as a senior that he set ten Harvard records, became Harvard's second All-Ivy selection, and also became the second Crimson player to win a league scoring crown.

For every Harrington, McClung, and Sedlacek, there were dozens who worked just as hard in this period but whose names have not entered the record books. Floyd Wilson recalled one player who represented this group.

"The captain of my 1955 team, Roger Bulger, had been chosen for a prestigious scholarship his senior year. Bulger was an average player who earned three letters on three losing teams. When we played Yale in the last game of the season, the head of the scholarship committee, Dean Delmar Leighton, decided to come to watch Roger. When Leighton first saw Roger, who was a small, not overly gifted player, he wondered about his decision. But when the game neared its end and it was apparent we were going to upset Yale, Leighton felt differently. Because when the crowd stood and gave Roger a standing ovation when he was taken out of the game, Leighton stood and clapped along with them."

Two of Harvard's big guns from the mid-1960s were Merle McClung (left, 5) and Keith Sedlacek (right, shooting). McClung, a Rhodes scholar, and Sedlacek, the 1966 Ivy scoring champ, teamed up in February of 1964 to lead Harvard to a major upset of Bill Bradley's Princeton Tigers.

1968–73: In the spring of 1968 Floyd Wilson became the full-time director of intramurals at Harvard, expanding a job he already had on a part-time basis. The new basketball coach was Bob Harrison.

A former captain at Michigan, Harrison enjoyed an impressive nine-year professional career that included five years with the Minneapolis Lakers (four world championships) and two each with the St. Louis Hawks and Syracuse Nationals. With the Hawks he was team captain and a league all-star.

What most impressed Harvard officials, however, was his coaching stint at tiny Kenyon College in Gambier, Ohio. Harrison's ten years at Kenyon had brought a struggling basketball program from obscurity to a top 20 ranking among small colleges. His last team went 23-5 and averaged more than 98 points a game. His arrival in Cambridge was said to signal a new era for Harvard basketball.

Harrison did not predict overnight results, but he did promise positive signs before his three-year contract would expire. Seasons of 7-18 and 7-19 taught him how complex his task was. But the events of his third year kept him an honest man.

Harvard's 1970–71 team compiled an overall record of

Coach Bob Harrison (right) *and assistant K. C. Jones* (center) *don't seem to be enjoying this action. Harrison served as head coach from 1969 to 1973, leading Harvard to an 11-3 Ivy mark in 1971, its best league showing ever.*

16-10 and an Ivy mark of 11-3 that was unprecedented, to say the least. Harvard's last winning record in league play had come in 1938, and the Ivy record of the 1969–70 team had been 1-13.

To understand this gem of a season, one has to understand events that transpired two years earlier. That's when an unparalleled recruiting effort brought to Harvard the best basketball talent in the school's history.

"I think it's safe to say that there had never been such a concerted effort to attract quality basketball players to Harvard as there was with that class of 1973, and there hasn't been a similar effort since," observed Floyd Wilson with the perspective of one who has had a keen interest in Harvard basketball since 1951, when he began as freshman coach.

Specifically, the recruiting focused on James Brown and Floyd Lewis, two talented schoolboy stars from the Washington, D.C., area. And that effort involved enlisting the services of two U.S. senators, Edward Kennedy and John Culver, both varsity football players in Harvard's class of '54.

Beyond Brown and Lewis, the superstars of the class of '73, there were seven others from the class who eventually made the varsity as sophomores. In fact, the depth was so great that an all-state performer from Massachusetts, normally a coveted recruit for Harvard, was sixth man on his freshman team.

With these nine sophomores joining senior captain Dale Dover in the fall of 1970, expectations were higher than ever for Harvard basketball. Two games in January added fuel to the fire. On January 7 Harvard led the nation's fifth-ranked team, Pennsylvania, 35-29 at half-time. The Crimson eventually lost that game but gained confidence from staying close. On January 9 Dale Dover's shot at the buzzer beat Princeton, 62-60, and a run at the Ivy title seemed possible. By the time it was all over, Harvard was second only to Penn, the best finish ever for a Crimson basketball team.

Lewis and Brown finished one-two in both scoring and rebounding, while Dover completed his career as Harvard's second career scorer behind Sedlacek. For his efforts Floyd Lewis was named to the All-Ivy first team.

With this start the young sophomores had realistic hopes of bringing home Harvard's first Ivy title. But it didn't happen. In fact, they were never able to match 1971's achievements.

The next two teams were winners at 15-11 and 14-12. But both Ivy campaigns, 8-6 and 7-7, failed to approach the success of 1971. And somehow, the most successful

James Brown '73 drives for two points against Yale. The classy forward, fourth in career scoring, went on to become a basketball broadcaster at the national level after leaving Harvard.

Floyd Lewis '73 lets go a jumper at the IAB. Known more for his rebounding, Lewis set a Harvard record with 343 rebounds as a sophomore and was a first-team All-Ivy selection.

period in Harvard basketball history became the most disappointing.

Nearly half a century had gone by since Harvard teams had produced three consecutive winning seasons. Never before had anyone earned three straight second team All-Ivy selections as James Brown had. Never had anyone grabbed more rebounds in a season than Floyd Lewis did in 1971.

But never had a group created so many expectations as well. More effort went into attracting them to Harvard. More pleasure was produced by their sophomore year. More was anticipated from the last two years, and it never happened.

New stars blossomed during this period as well. Jim Fitzsimmons, a transfer from Duke, averaged better than 24 points as a sophomore in 1971–72. Tony Jenkins's sophomore year saw him score more than either Brown or Lewis in 1972–73. But it wasn't enough.

After the disappointments were felt in 1973, Bob Harrison stepped down. He had seen Harvard through arguably its best period ever. But when all the goals weren't met, there was dissatisfaction among the players and he walked away.

As one observer to the scene said, "The problem was that when some of the players arrived, they actually thought they could compete for a national championship. When they couldn't even consistently compete for their own league title, the unhappiness set in. Their goals were unrealistic."

The new era of Harvard basketball was over.

1974–77: After the unfulfilled promise of the early 1970s, Harvard basketball slipped back once again. Seven losing seasons followed 1972–73, the first four constituting the career of head coach Tom "Satch" Sanders.

For 13 seasons Satch Sanders was a defensive stalwart for the great Boston Celtics teams under Red Auerbach. "Cool, poised, and soft-spoken" was how the Harvard releases described Sanders. He was admired by all who met him.

For all his success as a professional forward, Sanders's only coaching experience was limited to summer clinics. And of his assistants in this period, the most notable was his Celtics teammate K. C. Jones, later a successful head coach in Boston, who also had limited coaching experience at the time.

Add to this a sharp drop-off in talent and the resulting difficulties hardly come as a surprise. Sanders's first two seasons were virtual carbon copies. The 1973–74 club started off 4-10, losing seven games by a total of 13 points, before winning seven of its last ten. More impressive than the 11-13 overall mark was the 9-5 Ivy finish.

Lou Silver and Tony Jenkins, one-two in scoring and rebounding, were quality players in search of a supporting cast. Silver's All-Ivy selection was the fourth in Harvard history.

The same script was followed the next year. Silver, who would become a professional superstar in Israel over the next decade, averaged better than 16 points a game for the second year in a row. Junior Bill Carey, who keyed Harvard's late-season surge, had the unusual distinction of being voted both MVP and unsung hero by his teammates.

Sanders's last two years continued the trend of starting slow (3-10, 4-14) but late-season heroics couldn't make

After 13 years with the world champion Boston Celtics, Tom "Satch" Sanders (right) came to Harvard as head coach. Shown here with Director of Athletics Bob Watson, Sanders served for four seasons, from 1974 to 1977.

up the difference. It was a familiar story: Plenty of guys giving their all, but quality players hard to find.

Two coaches with professional backgrounds had not found the solution to the Harvard basketball riddle. It was time for a fresh approach.

1978–85: In July of 1977 Tom Sanders left Harvard to return to the Celtics as an assistant coach. Enter Francis X. McLaughlin.

Frank McLaughlin and Tom Sanders had one thing in common: They grew up in New York. But beyond that the resumes were quite different. The youthful McLaughlin played at Fordham, where he was graduated in 1969. Drafted by the New York Knicks, McLaughlin chose coaching over playing and served as an assistant at Holy Cross for a year.

He returned to his alma mater for a year, as an assistant to head coach Digger Phelps. When the Rams went 26-3 and finished ninth in the nation, Phelps accepted a new position at Notre Dame and took young Frank McLaughlin with him.

One of the best ballhandlers in Harvard history was Glenn Fine (23). Winner of a Rhodes Scholarship in 1979, Fine holds the Ivy League record for assists in a career, with 280 in 42 games.

It was after six years of recruiting for Phelps and Notre Dame that McLaughlin arrived in Cambridge. He was young, energetic, and optimistic.

"I had heard how bad things were at Harvard and how everything in the Ivy League was Penn and Princeton. Then, we went out and beat Penn my first year, and I said, 'Hey, this is easy. We just turned everything around.' It wasn't until later that I realized it was a fluke."

McLaughlin's optimism was tested early. He couldn't understand the negative attitudes. He couldn't understand why the crowds were so small or why the band played at hockey games but not basketball games. But he never stopped being the optimist seeing change right around the corner.

On the court, nothing seemed changed. Harvard started off at 4-10 for the young coach, though a better fate always seemed close at hand. Big man Brian Banks, a mystery for three years, seemed just one extra effort away from stardom. Little man Glenn Fine seemed like a magician in the backcourt, but he never knew what would happen once he relinquished the ball.

Then came that 93-87 upset of Pennsylvania, the undefeated Ivy leader whom Harvard had not beaten in the last 19 meetings. No longer was McLaughlin the only optimist around Harvard basketball.

The fluke, as McLaughlin would later call it, was the

highlight of a season that finished somewhat better than it began. The 11-15 record was hardly a disappointing start, all things considered. And when McLaughlin's second team opened at 3-2, including a road loss to South Carolina, everything seemed on schedule. Then came a 12-game losing streak that brought everyone back to earth.

But still the optimist saw reasons to be upbeat. "In the middle of all that, we played an undefeated Boston College team at the Boston Garden and lost a heartbreaker, 86-83. Glenn Fine got nineteen points, fifteen assists, eight steals and then learned after the game that he had won a Rhodes Scholarship. That said something good about the program."

Fine was the star of this 8-21 team. His supporting cast were role-players. Tom Mannix could shoot. Mark Harris, at 6 feet 8 inches, had to be the big man. And Bobby Hooft simply overachieved as an inside scorer. And then there was Donald Fleming.

Fleming was a natural athlete, the most graceful, potentially explosive player Harvard had welcomed since the days of James Brown and Floyd Lewis. He started slowly as a freshman but gave signs toward the end of the 1978–79 season that he could be something special.

Over the next three seasons Fleming led Harvard to 38 victories, equaling the most wins in any three-year period

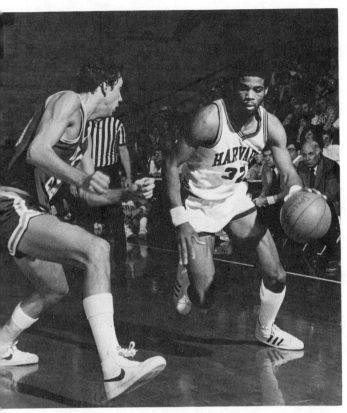

Donald Fleming '82 was the first Harvard player to repeat on the All-Ivy team and the only one to earn three first-team selections. When he graduated in 1982, he was Harvard's career scoring leader.

in Harvard history. In each season Fleming was a first team All-Ivy selection, the first Harvard cager to earn the honor more than once.

The best of these teams was the 1980–81 edition, which went 16-10, Harvard's first winning team in eight years. For the first time in years, there was some semblance of depth. Freshmen Joe Carrabino and Monroe Trout gave McLaughlin some size. Sophomore Calvin Dixon was a clever, sometimes too exciting point guard. Senior Tom Mannix was a superb outside shooter. And, of course, there was Fleming.

In his third season, Fleming led the Ivies in scoring and became Harvard's career scoring leader. As the first beneficiary of the freshman eligibility rule, he would shatter that mark the following season.

Once again, with expectations raised, disappointment followed. But this time it really wasn't fair. The ingredients for greatness were there until a series of injuries ruined what might have been. Frank McLaughlin capsulized it this way:

"After that one winning season, we really had a good

shot at putting a number of those years together. Then a bunch of guys got hurt in 1982, and we lost Carrabino [bad back] for the whole season that followed."

The "bunch of guys" included Calvin Dixon, Monroe Trout, and Ken Plutnicki, all key players, and limited the season's original starting five to just three Ivy games as a group. Still, that 1981–82 season featured an upset win over Princeton and saw freshman guard Bob Ferry follow Carrabino as Ivy League Rookie of the Year.

McLaughlin recalled the Princeton win as particularly sweet. "They had beaten us twenty-one straight when we finally beat them in overtime. The IAB was packed, the game was on regional television, and one of the broadcasters that day was James Brown, a member of the team that last beat Princeton in 1971."

One player who escaped the injury jinx was Don Fleming, who not only rewrote the Harvard record books but never missed a game in four years. His graduation, coupled with the back injury that sidelined Carrabino for the year, hurt the 1982–83 squad, McLaughlin's sixth.

This team went 12-14, dropping its final four games. But the big story was the opening of the Briggs Athletic Center, the new home of Harvard basketball.

"The new facility made a statement," said McLaughlin. "It wasn't just a nicer place to play or watch basketball, which was important. But it made a statement that there's a new commitment here. People care about basketball."

A lot of new things happened during the 1983–84 season. When Harvard lost a midseason thriller at home to nationally respected Duke, people took notice. The sports world was actually talking about basketball at Harvard.

When Harvard made its annual dreaded trek to Princeton and Penn, people did more than talk. They actually got excited and cared about this team that beat the first-place Tigers and lost in two overtimes to the Quakers. The win at Princeton was the second of the year over that archenemy to the south.

What all of this added up to was a couple of firsts: For the first time ever, Harvard had a shot at the Ivy title going into the final weekend of the season. On the same night that the hockey team was playing for its Ivy title at the Bright Center, the basketball team was battling for its Ivy honors just yards away at the Briggs Center. And for the first time, Harvard people cared about both.

"People at Harvard are like people anywhere else. They like winners. When we were in contention for the title late, we had new interest," said McLaughlin. "If we continue to do that, we'll continue to attract people's interest."

The fairy tale ended with a loss to Cornell and a

Guard Bob Ferry (left) and forward Joe Carrabino (right) made Harvard serious Ivy contenders from 1981 to 1985. Carrabino was the Ivy League Player of the Year in 1984, was twice first-team All-Ivy, and finished as Harvard's all-time scoring leader. Ferry, son of NBA great Bob Ferry, was three times a second-team All-Ivy choice and was Ivy Rookie of the Year in 1982.

second-place finish, matching Harvard's best ever. What made the near miss more painful was that Princeton, twice beaten by Harvard, won the title.

Joe Carrabino, healthy after a year away, had a banner year. Harvard's first Ivy Player of the Year, Carrabino was the big, powerful forward so often missing from Harvard's past. He also had a light touch, as indicated by his free-throw shooting, second best in the nation. The combination of Carrabino up front and Bob Ferry in the backcourt gave Harvard a quality one-two punch. But unlike the past, this year had a supporting cast that was not light years behind in talent.

Senior Ken Plutnicki had his best year ever. Freshman

Keith Webster and sophomore Arne Duncan matured early and gave hope for the immediate future.

It appeared that the Ivy championship drought would end in 1985. That's what many of the pollsters thought in making Harvard the preseason favorite.

When the team jumped out to an 11-1 start, the pollsters looked pretty good. Included in that streak was a sweep of Penn and Princeton on the road, something that no Harvard team had managed in the 74-year history of the program. Ironically, these victories came after the season's first loss, a 62-60 upset to Dartmouth at home.

"If we had won the Dartmouth game, we would not have won this one," said McLaughlin after the 77-75 win against Penn at the Palestra completed the sweep. It was Harvard's first win in that building in 16 years.

The team was riding the play of Carrabino and Ferry for the most part. But when teams keyed on these stars, the supporting cast came through. Such was the case in the 60-50 win at Princeton, when sophomore guard Keith Webster hit for 21 points.

This was a team like so many Ivy League squads, lacking a big man and thus pressured to do all the little things well. "It's Joe [Carrabino] and basically four guards," McLaughlin would say in midseason. "The key to our team is that we have very good shooters, passers, and ballhandlers. We make our free throws and play very good defense."

Harvard's very good shooters would go on to lead the nation in free-throw percentage for the second year in a row, but that was about the only place this team finished first. The second half record was 4-8, including losses to Penn and Princeton at home. The Ivy record was 7-7.

Carrabino, an All-Ivy repeater and an Academic All-American, finished his career as Harvard's all-time scoring leader. Ferry, second team All-Ivy for the third straight year, was third on that list behind Carrabino and Don Fleming. Carrabino and Ferry were both drafted by the National Basketball Association in June of 1985. Together, despite that still missing Ivy title, they brought a new respect to Harvard basketball.

Some said Harvard finally enjoyed depth. Some said the league giants, Penn and Princeton, had finally fallen a peg. Everyone said things looked brighter for Harvard basketball.

Raised expectations have always meant trouble for that star-crossed program. Perhaps caution should accompany the positive signs. But the law of averages, and the effort that has never been lacking, must surely pay off one day.

In Search of Respect

The setting was the Great Hall in Boston's fashionable Quincy Market. The event was 1979's $25-a-plate Harvard basketball dinner. The guest speaker was Bryant Gumbel, then an up-and-coming sportscaster for NBC.

All the extra touches—the locale, the price, the speaker—were just a few of the fringe efforts made by the Friends of Harvard Basketball in their never-ending efforts to boost the reputation of Harvard's long-maligned basketball program.

Harvard's basketball program was energized in 1977, when Frank McLaughlin became head coach. The former Fordham star and Notre Dame assistant won 99 games in his first eight seasons and brought Harvard basketball to a level equal to the Ivy's best.

One can imagine the disappointment when Gumbel began his remarks with an ill-chosen attempt at humor: "In preparing for this dinner, I tried researching information on Harvard's Ivy champions of the past. But there weren't any. And so I tried looking up Harvard's All-Americans from the past. But there weren't any of them either. And then . . ."

For more than 80 years, Harvard basketball has sought respect. On the campus, in newspapers, with after-dinner speakers, and elsewhere, the noble efforts to gain that respect have too often been ignored.

Just why basketball has struggled to produce winning teams and interested fans at Harvard is difficult to explain. What is clear, however, is that the sport's problems can be traced back to its earliest years. Basketball was recognized as an official sport at Harvard in December of 1900. Nine years later the sport was abolished for a variety of reasons, not the least of which was declining interest on campus. Not until 1920 was the sport revived, when national interest in basketball was on the rise.

Unlike so many other sports at Harvard, basketball in its early years was not in the forefront of national attention. The first college athletic contest ever was a Harvard crew race. The first college hockey game ever featured Harvard. It was a Harvard man who invented the baseball catcher's mask. And other teams were the best in their sport nationally in the early years.

Basketball could make no such claims. And so the seeds were sown for decades of second-class status as Harvard basketball tried to live up to the reputation of excellence so present in other Harvard programs.

The numbers say quite a bit. In the first 76 seasons of Harvard basketball, only 27 teams have enjoyed winning records. Only once since the 1920s (1971–73) has Harvard had three winning years in a row. No Harvard team from 1947 to 1970 compiled a winning record against Ivy opponents. And, as Mr. Gumbel so sensitively reminded us, no Harvard basketball team has ever won a league championship.

The respect came gradually in the 1980s. Frank McLaughlin saw it.

"When I first came to Harvard, we had a home game against Massachusetts," recalled the coach. "I called up the leader of the school band and asked if they would play at the game. He said, 'We don't play at basketball games.' By 1984 they were at all the home games and some of the away games."

That season saw Harvard picked to win the league, jump off to an 11-1 start in its newly renovated home, the Briggs Athletic Center, and grab a New York Times headline that said, "Harvard Basketball Gains New Respect."

One other sign was more important than bands and news clippings. Harvard was attracting gifted players. The starting lineup of the 1984–85 team boasted two players from DeMatha High School in Hyattsville, Maryland, long a producer of top-shelf basketball talent. Harvard had become a place that these standouts wanted to go to play basketball.

There's still space in the trophy case for some Ivy championship hardware. It may not be long before that space is cramped.

• • •

WOMEN'S BASKETBALL: A FAMILIAR STRUGGLE

It was back in 1973 that the Radcliffe basketball program was granted permission to use Harvard's Indoor Athletic Building one night a week. The IAB may not have been state of the art, but it was a far cry from the musty confines of the Radcliffe gym.

One night during that first winter of IAB use, a men's intramural team took the court during a Radcliffe practice. When the women protested an argument ensued, causing the building's custodian to enter the fray and settle the dispute. He shut off the lights.

Such was the state of women's athletics in the early 1970s. Ten years later Harvard women's basketball shared the renovated Briggs Athletic Center with the men's varsity. Practice and game needs were allotted equally. And no one ever thought to shut off the lights.

The women's program made the transition from Radcliffe to Harvard beginning with the 1974–75 season. It was a period of slow change for a couple of seasons.

"In 1975, the program seemed to have a recreational feel to it. It was basically the old program transferred to a new facility, the IAB," recalled Katherine Fulton, captain of both the 1977 and 1978 teams.

Coaching was part-time and, in effect, so were some of the players, who seemed to use basketball as a way to stay in shape for the spring season that followed.

"Many of our players had never played competitive basketball before coming to Harvard," said Fulton. "I played guard, forward, and center, and I was only five-eight."

Significant change began in 1976, when the starting lineup, annoyed at the lack of progress through two seasons of varsity status, threatened to walk out. The department got the message and responded for the start of the 1976–77 season.

That is when Harvard hired Carole Kleinfelder, the program's first full-time basketball coach. At the same time, the team got a full-time female trainer and an incoming class of talented athletes. The result was an 18-3 season, the most satisfying in the program's history.

Freshmen like Caryn Curry, Wendy Carle, and Leslie Greis led this team, which was primarily first-year players and two holdovers from the darker days, Fulton and Sue Williams. Williams was the program's first legitimate standout. A native of Tuba City, Arizona, Williams had played on two state championship teams in high school before coming to Cambridge. It would be nearly a decade before the program regularly attracted players with this sort of background.

That 1976–77 season with its stellar record was the last for Harvard as a Division II program. The schedule was upgraded the following year, and Kleinfelder's team struggled a little more but still turned out two more winning seasons.

"We accomplished a lot of what we wanted to do those first two years," said Kleinfelder. "We wanted to see if we could move up and compete, and we wanted to gain experience. I think we did both."

The class of '80 continued to shine. Curry, younger sister of football receiver Jim Curry, established virtually all offensive records, many of which survived well into the 1980s. Greis's 29 points against Pennsylvania in 1977 has been equaled but not bettered.

Despite the efforts of the top players, the supporting cast was generally thinner than the opposition's. As a result Harvard found it difficult to make significant progress within the Ivy League.

Beginning with the 1979–80 season, the program began a string of six losing seasons that bottomed out in 1984 when the team went 3-22. There were outstanding individuals, such as center Elaine Holpuch '83 and guard Nancy Boutilier '84, but very little depth. It was a problem for both Carole Kleinfelder and her successor, Kathy Delaney Smith, who took over in 1983–84.

By the end of the 1984–85 season, an 8-18 campaign, there were signs that women's basketball at Harvard was about to gain new respect just as the men had. Delaney Smith, a former Massachusetts Coach of the Year at nearby Westwood High School, began attracting the talent and depth that Harvard had always lacked.

Freshman Sharon Hayes led the 1985 team in scoring. Classmate Barbarann Keffer set a single-season record for assists. In all, the team had six freshmen, most of whom had been high school all-scholastics. That was a far cry from the days when starters learned how to play the game when they arrived at Harvard.

Harvard's women's basketball's first star was Sue Williams '77 (16), one of the few players to make the transition from the club sport days to varsity competition.

One of those freshmen is likely to be Harvard's first All-Ivy selection. All of them may help bring Harvard its first Ivy title. Then the change that began nearly ten years earlier will be complete.

Women's basketball hopes were raised with the hiring of Kathy Delaney Smith (center), who came to Harvard in 1983. Before arriving at Harvard, Delaney Smith was Massachusetts High School Coach of the Year at nearby Westwood High School.

Caryn Curry (left) and Wendy Carle, co-captains for 1980's team, pose in front of the IAB. Curry, sister of record-setting split end Jim Curry, set records of her own and graduated as career scoring leader. Carle was a multisport star, participating in soccer and track as well as basketball.

Swimming

It has already been documented how intercollegiate sports in this country began with an afternoon of rowing back in 1852. What also began that day was the all-encompassing athletic rivalry between Harvard and Yale.

While almost every Crimson team met its match in the Elis back in the early decades, few athletes suffered this fate so consistently and so late as the swimmers. From 1930, when competitive swimming was born at Harvard, through the 1971–72 season, Yale held a 37-3 edge over Harvard teams that were consistently strong.

Yale's domination was particularly clear in the standings of the Eastern Intercollegiate Swim League (Ivy schools plus Army and Navy). From 1946 to 1960 Yale captured 15 straight league titles. In the last ten years of that streak, Harvard frustration peaked, as once-beaten Harvard teams finished second to undefeated Yale teams nine times.

By the mid-1970s Harvard stopped looking at Yale from behind. From 1973 to 1985, it was Harvard's name on 11 of 13 league trophies. Yale was nowhere to be found.

The Harvard swimming story is one of dedicated teachers, inspired swimmers and divers, and state-of-the-art facilities. Such was the formula for success in 1930. So it was again more than 50 years later.

MEN'S SWIMMING: A HALF CENTURY OF EXCELLENCE

1930–59: The first three decades of Harvard swimming belonged to one man, Hal Ulen, Harvard's first coach and greatest teacher. Often undermanned, Ulen teams were always closer to the powerful Yale squads than anyone felt they had a right to be. That was particularly the case in 1937–38, when the former Syracuse coach led Harvard to back-to-back Eastern League titles.

Ulen's arrival in Cambridge was made possible by the completion of Harvard's Indoor Athletic Building in 1930. This would be the home of Harvard intercollegiate swimming, basketball, wrestling, and fencing, as well as

The 1937–38 Harvard squad made it two straight over Yale and two straight Eastern League titles thanks to the efforts of Olympian Charlie Hutter (front row, center). It would be another 24 seasons before Harvard would beat Yale again.

countless clubs and intramural sports. More than 50 years after it opened, the IAB continued to house all kinds of Harvard athletes, though it was no longer the jewel in the Harvard athletic complex that it once had been.

Hal Ulen had the dual ability to develop raw, inexperienced swimmers and, at the same time, guide his more talented athletes without tampering with their strengths.

"I look for four things in a new swimmer," Ulen once said. "They are flexibility of his shoulder and leg muscles, buoyancy, a sense of turning mechanics, and, especially, a fighting heart."

Ulen excelled at developing that necessary flexibility and teaching the skills needed to master the maneuvers of turning and starting. With a significant number of swimmers arriving at Harvard without previous competitive experience, Ulen often had his work cut out for him.

But there were superstars as well. And among those were Olympians Charlie Hutter '38, Ted Norris '49, Dave Hawkins '56, and Bruce Hunter '61. In these instances, Ulen's genius may have been what he didn't do.

"No two boys swim alike," he would say. "And if a fellow is making mistakes but breaking records, you don't change him."

The first of those record-breakers was Charlie Hutter, a super athlete who came to Harvard with very few thoughts about swimming. He became involved with Coach Bob Muir's freshman team in 1934 and quickly elevated swimming on his list of priorities.

By his sophomore year Hutter was a world-class swimmer. He won the NCAA 100-yard freestyle in a time of 52.9 seconds and later that summer competed at the 1936 Olympic Games in Berlin as a member of the winning U.S 800-meter relay team.

To the Harvard swimming family, those accomplishments paled in comparison to what he did the following season. Accounting for a third of his team's points, Hutter led Harvard to a 39-36 win over Yale, the school's first against the Elis and Yale's first loss after 164 consecutive dual meet victories.

Hutter's points came from his record-setting times in the 100- and 220-yard freestyle, which were somewhat expected, and his second-place finish in the 440 behind Yale's Peter Brueckel, which was not. Those final points decided the meet and, ultimately, the Eastern League standings.

Ulen was a master at developing inexperienced swimmers into champions. Two of his best products came out of the 1940s, Eric Cutler '40 and Ted Norris '49.

Eric Cutler came to Harvard from the Noble and Greenough School, where he took part in football, baseball, hockey, and track. Due to a shoulder injury, he decided to take up swimming at Harvard, and after missing his sophomore year due to polio, he broke pool and NCAA records as a junior.

"The boys respect him for more than the fact that he can beat them in the water," Ulen said of his prize pupil. Cutler later served Harvard as assistant director of athletics and went into the Harvard Hall of Fame in 1972.

Like Cutler, Ted Norris had never swum competitively before coming to Harvard. But Norris' story was even more unusual. As a result of a childhood accident, one of Norris' legs was shorter than the other. While taking Harvard's compulsory swimming test for freshmen, Norris was spotted by Ulen.

"He wasn't a swimmer. Or perhaps you should say he was an indifferent swimmer. I noticed him come to the pool two or three times before I approached him. 'Would you like to come out for the swimming team?' I asked. He seemed surprised and said, 'I couldn't make any team, the way I am.' I didn't even discuss his problem, and from that time on his handicap was never mentioned. But he came out for the team and worked as hard as any man I've ever known in my life."

Norris earned a spot on the 1948 Olympic team, an accomplishment that Ulen ranked "with the miraculous in sports." At the 1949 Eastern Seaboard Championships, the largest college meet in the East, Norris set a meet record in the 1,500-meter freestyle with a time of 19:40.06.

Another swimmer of note from this decade was Franny Powers '41, who followed Eric Cutler as team captain. He was Eastern Seaboard champ in 1941 in the 220-yard freestyle.

Ulen's swimmers stole the spotlight from his divers, but two of his best, Russell Greenhood '39 and Frank Gorman '59, were Eastern champs in both the 1-meter and 3-meter events. Greenhood was also the first diver to be elected captain of the squad.

Gorman, a Long Island native, continued diving after Harvard and became one of the world's best springboard competitors. His most memorable dives came in the 1964 Tokyo Olympics, where he won the silver medal.

Three of Ulen's best swimmers graced the 1954–57 teams. But despite their presence, the coach could not pull off that elusive third victory against archrival Yale.

Dave Hawkins '56 was the only Harvard athlete to earn four swimming letters before freshmen were made eligible for varsity competition. A member of the 1952 Australian Olympic team, Hawkins came to Harvard that fall and followed a strong freshman year by winning national AAU titles in both the 100-yard and 200-meter breaststroke. Harvard awarded him a major H for these triumphs. A year later he took two NCAA firsts in the 100- and 200-yard butterfly.

Classmate Jim Jorgensen never lost to his Yale opposition while earning three varsity letters. He was the

Few swimmers made head coach Hal Ulen as proud as Ted Norris '49 did in 1948. That's when Norris swam the 1,500-meter freestyle at the Olympic Games in London. Norris had entered Harvard without prior competitive experience, a childhood injury having left him with one leg shorter than the other.

East's best in the 220-yard freestyle in both 1955 and 1956 and became the first swimmer to win the Bingham Award as Harvard's top athlete. But perhaps the best freestyler of all was Chouteau Dyer '57.

"I knew as soon as I saw him swim that he was the most perfect swimmer I had ever seen at Harvard," Ulen said of Dyer. Holder of all Harvard sprint records at one time, Dyer won the 100-yard freestyle at the 1957 NCAA championships. Just four years later, this great athlete fell victim to leukemia.

1960–70: When Hal Ulen stepped down after the 1958–59 season, Harvard turned to his freshman coach of 13 years, Bill Brooks. Brooks would continue the tradition of excellent teaching over the next 12 seasons and win 87 meets in the process.

The best years of the Brooks era came early, when Harvard went 35-4 from 1960 to 1963, losing three of those meets to Yale. Brooks's sole victory against the Elis came in March of 1962; it was the first time Harvard had beaten Yale since 1938 and only the third time ever. Not coincidentally, the victory led to Harvard's third Eastern League title ever.

That success was made possible in a big way by a swimmer who wasn't there to enjoy it. Cambridge High and Latin product Bruce Hunter '61 was one of Harvard's greatest freestylers. His list of personal accomplishments touched all the bases: winner of four Eastern Seaboard titles, winner of two NCAA titles, and member of the 1960 U.S. Olympic team in Rome. Just about the only thing he didn't do was beat Yale.

But when that finally happened in 1962, the year after Hunter was graduated, he could point to his role in three years of bringing Harvard closer. From 1959 to 1961, the Yale victory margin was cut from 40 points to 17 to 9. Then in 1961–62 it was Harvard's turn, by the slimmest of margins.

Hunter may have been gone, but Harvard had enough talent to win its first nine meets that year. Perhaps the best of the lot was captain Bob Kaufmann, a freestyler who held Harvard records in seven different events. He had been a member of the 400-yard freestyle relay team that won the 1961 NCAA championship, along with Hunter, Bill Zentgraf, and Alan Engelberg. Everyone but Hunter returned for 1962.

Brooks had other weapons beyond the freestylers. Fred Elizalde was a butterfly record-holder, and in John Pringle the coach had one of the most versatile swimmers the

Freestyle ace Bruce Hunter '61, a local product from Cambridge Latin High School, competed for the United States at the 1960 Olympic Games in Rome.

school had ever produced. In the end, it was Pringle's versatility that made all the difference against Yale.

When the two undefeated squads met in New Haven on March 3, the Harvard following whispered, as it had for nearly 25 years, "This is the year." And when Harvard led by 40-39 with just two events remaining, one event stood in the way of those fans being redeemed.

That was the 200-yard breaststroke. Brooks had already used his top freestylers to the point that the day's final event, the freestyle relay, was being conceded to the hosts. Harvard had to take first and second in the breaststroke to end another Yale streak.

First place was generally given to Harvard sophomore Bill Chadsey. It was the second spot that had Brooks worried. It looked as if Yale's Jerry Yurow would grab those crucial points. Enter John Pringle. The junior had not swum the breaststroke all year and had just completed a winning backstroke less than ten minutes earlier. Yet he was still Harvard's best shot at a second.

Through 150 yards, amazingly, it was Pringle by four or five feet. But the day's work started to tell at that point. And with ten yards to go, the lead over Yale's Yurow was just inches. As they touched at the finish, Pringle appeared

Above: *He had not swum the event all year, but John Pringle managed a second-place finish in the 200-yard breaststroke to help beat Yale in 1962. The two-time All-American was selected as Harvard's top athlete in 1963.*

to have held on. And he had, by a tenth of a second. That was good enough to propel Harvard to a 48-47 win, its first over Yale in 24 years and just the second Yale loss in 220 meets.

Pringle's success continued into his senior year, when he was named Bingham Award winner, only the second swimmer so honored. Brooks would coach a third such honoree in Bob Corris, a backstroke champion, who won the award in 1967.

1971–77: No more titles came Brooks's way in his last eight years at Harvard. When the league mark reached 2-5 in 1970–71 the coach decided to step down; he had served Harvard for 25 years. His departure ended the first major phase of Harvard swimming, the Ulen-Brooks period. As intercollegiate swimming began to demand recruiters as well as teachers, a new era would begin.

Ushering in this new era was Don Gambril, whose selection as head coach raised an eyebrow or two in Cambridge. Gambril, who came to Harvard from California's Long Beach State, was considered big time. He had been named an assistant coach of the U.S. Olympic team for 1972 and had earned a reputation as an aggressive recruiter. Specifically, Gambril had been criticized for bringing world-class foreign swimmers to Long Beach, and in 1971 his team had included just four Americans.

More than 40 years of varsity coaching are represented in this picture of Harvard's first two swim coaches, Bill Brooks (left) and Hal Ulen, who returned to Harvard for the dedication of the Blodgett Pool in February of 1978.

When this former football coach arrived in Cambridge with his crew cut and reputation as a taskmaster, Harvard-watchers expected a clash of cultures. Harvard's antiquated IAB pool housed more than a few long-haired activists who had grown to like a program short on discipline. As one friend wrote to Gambril upon his accepting the job, "You going to Harvard is like putting peanut butter on caviar."

While a few veterans summarily gave up swimming, most of the Harvard swimming community took to Gambril. He had made a conscious effort to adapt to his new setting, and that keyed his success.

"I was the nonconformist here, not my swimmers," said the coach his first year. "There is a different motivation here. You can't lay down ultimatums. Every step I've taken has been fair and firm, yet I haven't set down rigid rules—only guidelines."

The moderate approach worked. Gambril stayed just two years at Harvard, but he ended the slide and launched Harvard into a new world of swimming. His first team, with 12 of 15 participants either freshmen or sophomores, finished 6-3. More important for the future, the coach attracted 61 applications from swimmers.

The next season the turnaround was complete, and victory over Yale left the two schools tied atop the Eastern League standings. New school records were set in 16 of 17 events, as this seniorless team produced four All-Americans in sophomores Dave Brumwell and Tim Neville and freshmen Hess Yntema and Tom Wolf.

Gambril had done the job and was ready for new challenges. So after his second year at Cambridge, he accepted a greater challenge at the University of Alabama, where no one doubted big-time aspirations. And in 1984, when Gambril was named head coach of the U.S. Olympic swim team, he was back to his old tricks. Sixteen of his Alabama swimmers participated in the Los Angeles games, but none of them swam for the United States.

Gambril's successor, Ray Essick, continued Harvard's forward march. The former Southern Illinois coach inherited Gambril's numbers, brought in talent of his own, and raced off to a 19-0 record in his first two seasons. The first of those was highlighted by an 82-31 splashing of a Princeton team described in its own press releases as the school's best ever.

Fred Mitchell, the captain of that 1973–74 team, had a unique four-year career. Mitchell swam for three different head coaches and was a stabilizing force for the swimmers, as evidenced by his being elected freshman captain and twice being chosen as varsity captain. As a

A new era for Harvard swimming was launched when Don Gambril (above) came to Harvard from Long Beach State in 1971. Before he left for Alabama in 1973, Gambril and such talent as (below, clockwise from front) Fred Mitchell, Tim Neville, Dave Brumwell, and Rich Baughman turned Harvard swimming around.

senior, he received Harvard's Bingham Award as top athlete in the school.

Essick's three years produced two outright league championships and a third shared with Princeton. In addition, Harvard swimmers took 13 individual Seaboard titles, led by breaststroke phenom Ted Fullerton (five titles), butterfly ace George Keim (two), and the incomparable Hess Yntema.

The versatile Yntema took the 200-meter butterfly, 200-meter freestyle and 200-meter individual medley at the 1974 Eastern Seaboards. Including relays, he claimed six victories in Seaboard competition and might have accomplished more were it not for his balanced perspective on the sport. When asked about possibly making the Olympics in 1976, he said, "It would require much more training than any of us have time to do here. I came to Harvard for more than swimming; I don't want to be just a swimmer and nothing else when I graduate."

In the fall of 1976 Ray Essick made an abrupt departure from Harvard to take an administrative post with the Amateur Athletic Union. His three-year mark of

Harvard dominated eastern swimming during the tenure of head coach Joe Bernal. Through his first eight seasons at Harvard, Bernal was 75-4 with seven straight Eastern Seaboard titles after a near miss his first year.

26-1 had included everything but a team title at the Seaboards. He had even seen ground broken for a new pool at Harvard.

Assistant Coach Pete Orscheidt, later a head coach at Syracuse and Cornell, became acting head coach and along with diving coach John Walker led Harvard to a respectable 6-2 record and an even more respectable second at the Eastern Seaboard championships. With that 1976–77 season Phase II, the transition phase, came to an end for Harvard swimming. When a new facility and a new coach arrived the next season, Phase III was under way.

1978–85: When the Indoor Athletic Building opened in 1930, Harvard joined the eastern intercollegiate swimming world. Nearly 50 years later, when the Blodgett Pool opened in 1978, Harvard began to leave that world behind.

It didn't happen all at once. But the 1977–78 season was the launching pad for the next dominant power in eastern swimming. First, it was Yale. Then came Princeton. Beginning in 1978, it would be Harvard. And the Crimson haven't been caught yet.

Along with Blodgett Pool, Harvard welcomed a new coach and a new superstar who arrived together from New York in 1977. Joe Bernal had been head coach at Fordham and at the same time had worked with a kid from Fordham Prep named Bobby Hackett. On Hackett's broad shoulders, Harvard would make its move to the top.

Hackett arrived in Cambridge with more advance billing than any previous Harvard swimmer. In fact, one had to go back to Yale's Don Schollander in 1964 to find such a buildup for an easterner. An Olympic silver medalist in the 1,500 meters at Montreal, Hackett lived up to all expectations at Harvard.

In his first Harvard event, he set a school record in the 200-meter freestyle against Navy, breaking Schollander's New England mark as well. In his second meet, he set an NCAA record of 9:02.05 in the 1,000 meters against Army. That mark was an incredible 33 seconds better than the existing Harvard and New England records. Later in that same meet, he set similar records in the 500.

These early meets understandably focused on Hackett. Lost in the Hackett watch were the efforts of freshman imports like Mike Coglin (Libya) and Tuomo Kerola (Finland). In that blazing 1,000 meters against Army, Coglin's second-place time also bettered the existing Harvard record.

With each meet Hackett and Harvard made new headlines, amazed new fans. Still, the reigning eastern power was Princeton, and headlines and hype weren't going to drown the Tiger. But maybe Hackett and company could.

The showdown took place on February 4, 1978. Not coincidentally, the meet was the occasion for Blodgett Pool's dedication. Harvard president Derek Bok was there. Retired businessman and benefactor John W. Blodgett, Jr., '23 was there. Former coaches Hal Ulen and Bill Brooks were there. And, of course, that other VIP was there, Robert W. Hackett '81. In the end, his presence would make all the difference.

Bobby Hackett

Following the 1976 Summer Olympics Swimming World *magazine ran a feature story on 17-year-old Bobby Hackett, the freestyler from Yonkers, New York, who had won the silver medal in the 1,500 meters. The young Hackett was preparing his college applications at the time of the story, and in outlining his future he told the magazine, "I want to be remembered." Five years later, his Harvard career completed, he had made sure that he would never be forgotten.*

Bobby Hackett and his silver medal were known commodities in Cambridge even before the modest young man registered for his freshman year in September of 1977. The Harvard swimming program had hovered at or, more commonly, near the top of the eastern swimming world for most of its history, but there was always a Yale or Princeton cutting into that success. The advance word was that this kid Hackett could change all that. And he did. Quickly.

The first time he ever swam for Harvard, he set a New England and school record. A week later, he set a national record. And so went the four-year story. It can easily be a story of numbers: 8 university records, 12 All-American selections, 10 Eastern Seaboard titles, and so on. He certainly did all those things.

But there's so much more to the story. First is Hackett's impact on swimming at Harvard and in the East. The 1977–78 season brought Hackett, Coach Joe Bernal, and the Blodgett Pool to Harvard. This trio, and the supporting cast that was

often overshadowed, combined to lift Harvard past Princeton as the East's top swimming program. But it was Hackett himself, and his ability to regularly pick up three victories in a meet at a variety of events, who spelled the difference between being as good as Princeton and being better than Princeton.

"He was a real team person in that sense," said Bernal. "He swam the events that we needed in order to win a meet. I'd say to him, 'We're not in control of it, Bobby. You've got to put out the fire.' And he would. In his first two years, he didn't exclude any event except diving and the breaststroke."

Hackett's presence could be intimidating. At times he could help Bernal gain the upper hand without ever dipping into the pool.

"Against Princeton in Bobby's senior year, we sent him up to the block before every event," recalls Bernal. "We knew, with maybe one exception, which events he'd be swimming. But we wanted to rattle the Princeton coach a little, keep him off guard. Sometimes, I'd just tell Bobby to be prepared to swim anything. The rest of the team was amazed. A lot of them needed to know exactly what they'd be doing so they could prepare mentally. Not Bobby."

Timing played a part in this story as well. In Hackett's first three years at Harvard, the so-called major sports of football, ice hockey, and basketball failed to record a single winning season. Into this void swam Harvard swimming and its outstanding Olympian. The program received unusual visibility and continued to improve while more people took notice.

Success begat success, as more national caliber swimmers wanted to go to Harvard. Swimmers from all over the country—and outside as well—seemed to say, "If it was good enough for a silver medalist, it's good enough for me." And Harvard began to pull away from the pack. That carried Hackett's impact to yet another level.

Said Bernal: "I think schools looked at us and said, 'If Harvard can do it, so can we.' And the caliber of swimmers around the league improved as a result. And I'm not so sure that some of it wasn't through a kind of negative recruiting. A sort of, 'Don't go to Harvard. You'll never swim there with all that talent.' "

Although joined by an increasingly talented cast as his four years unfolded, Bobby Hackett was the major reason that Harvard swimming left all challengers in its wake beginning in the late 1970s. The Yonkers, New York, native won a silver medal at the Montreal Olympics in 1976 before rewriting the Harvard record books from 1977 to 1981.

The other part of this story rarely came to light. Through most of his phenomenal four years, Hackett swam in pain. Not just the pain that normally accompanies the grueling 1,650-yard freestyle, his specialty, but pain caused by a rare blood disorder.

"Bobby suffered from a form of anemia. He could not reproduce red blood cells at the normal rate, and one effect of this was that he would grow tired sooner in competition," explained Bernal. "And so he experienced fatigue and pain earlier in an event than he normally would have."

Hackett never hid behind this condition. On many occasions, such as the 1979 Seaboards, in which he won the Phil Moriarty Award as the meet's outstanding performer, he competed while ill without anyone's being aware of the situation. When he experienced defeat more frequently as a junior and senior, those who knew of his condition assumed it was taking its toll. It is difficult to assess if those second-place finishes were the result of his health or the reality that the competition was improving.

Certainly, the supporting cast around Hackett was deeper by his junior year. As a result, Bernal

didn't always need three victories from his prize pupil. There were others around who could pick up those points and win those memorable championships.

The "others" had come to Harvard because of what Bobby Hackett started. He remains the best of them all, and that's just how he wanted to be remembered.

• • •

Joe Bernal wanted this meet badly. He pulled out all the stops. And that included bringing Hal Ulen into the locker room before the meet.

"You could sense the greatness of the man," recalled Bernal. "He was sitting in a wheelchair and you could feel the energy that he must have ignited into his own teams. Under different circumstances, his words might have seemed cornball. But that day, he got to a group of young kids from a different era."

Princeton took an early lead and held it to the final event of the day, the 400-meter freestyle relay. That Harvard still had a shot was the result of a handful of extraordinary performances. Hackett as expected took firsts in the 200 and 500, the former in record time.

But it was a pair of unexpected seconds, by Mike Coglin in the 500 and Tuomo Kerola in the 200 breaststroke, that kept Harvard's chances alive. Then, with 1,500 fans providing a deafening accompaniment, the relay began.

Princeton, which would win this event at the next three Eastern Seaboard championships, held the lead through the first half of the race. After the third leg, freshman Julian Mack handed Bobby Hackett a lead of 0.19 seconds. That was plenty as Hackett beat Princeton ace Alan Fine by a half second over the final 100 yards and Harvard took the meet, 58-55. The heir apparent had emerged.

Princeton avenged the defeat at the Eastern Seaboards, winning its sixth straight title. Individually, Hackett was named the meet's top performer for setting records in the 200-, 500-, and 1,650-meter freestyle events. And Harvard, second by just 364-356, used the occasion to reinforce the message sent earlier in February.

"They [Princeton] were in awe that we were in the meet so late," said Bernal. "They were an older team, seniors and a couple of juniors. We were making noise with our freshmen. They could see what was coming."

What was coming was a Harvard string of seven (and counting) straight Seaboard championships, which began the next year. Just as the crowd had been a factor in that dedication meet, so it was when Harvard hosted the 1979 Seaboards.

Above: *Harvard's swim team rejoices after its victory in the 1979 Eastern Seaboard Championships, the school's first ever, at the Blodgett Pool. By 1985 the Crimson had won seven straight.*

Below: *When retired lumberman John W. Blodgett, Jr., '23 read about Harvard's athletic facilities being among the worst in the country in the early 1970s, he set out to change that reputation. As a result of his generosity, Harvard built the Blodgett Pool, shown here as the site of the 1980 NCAA championships.*

"The key was the 800-freestyle relay on the second night," said Bernal. "Princeton had owned the event for five years, we won it, and walked out of the place knowing that all we had to do was swim to form the last day. The way that crowd pumped up our guys, we knew it was ours."

And it was. The score read Harvard 606, Princeton 548. Hackett repeated as the meet's top performer and Harvard, which set a record for total points, won its first Seaboard title ever.

Those two meets, Princeton '78 and Seaboards '79, established the new order in eastern swimming. Two other meets underscored just how quickly Harvard had pulled ahead of the pack.

It is February, 1980. Harvard hosts perennial Big Ten champion and national powerhouse Indiana at Blodgett. Entering the meet with a "Gee, it's great to have you here" posture, Harvard proceeds to win 10 of 11 swimming events and blows out the Hoosiers, 67-46.

Ambushing the Hoosiers

In an earlier day the college coach could afford to be primarily a teacher. But by the 1980s, coaches had to be teachers, fundraisers, psychologists, recruiters, and, to succeed in all of those roles, salesmen. Few Harvard coaches mastered these modern techniques better than swimming coach Joe Bernal.

It would be easy to see Bernal as the simple beneficiary of timing. After all, he arrived with Bobby Hackett in the fall of 1977, and a few months later he was given a new pool to work out of. But the coach didn't take these gifts and sit back to see what would happen next. He made sure that Harvard swimming would use these blessings to begin the push to the top.

Bernal was aware that Harvard—and New England—normally found its winter sports thrills in places other than swimming pools. So the salesman in Bernal went about turning the athletic community's eyes toward Blodgett Pool. What better than a major event or two?

The 1979–80 Blodgett Pool season included two such events, the more prestigious being the NCAA Division I Swimming Championships. This is always a major spectacle, even more so in an Olympic year such as 1980.

But the other event, a Sunday afternoon dual meet with Indiana, proved to be the masterstroke in Bernal's campaign for visibility. While a few Harvards might shine at the NCAAs, that was really a weekend to show off Blodgett Pool. But if Harvard could upset Indiana, that would say something about the Harvard swimming program.

Indiana was the perfect choice. Even the non-swimmer had read about the Hoosiers and their legendary coach James "Doc" Counsilman. They had been among the nation's best for years and seemed to own the Big Ten. Their lofty perch in the swimming world was being challenged by the new order of schools to the south and west. But still, when they agreed to meet with Harvard on February 10, 1980, they were riding a win streak that would reach 140 dual meets, the longest in the nation.

If this wasn't enough to grab some headlines, 58-year-old Doc Counsilman created a few of his own when he became the oldest man to swim the English Channel shortly before the Hoosiers came to Cambridge.

Everything was in place as February approached. A local television station agreed to televise the meet. The Boston papers picked up on it. Then, a couple of events threatened to take the luster off the occasion. First, Indiana's win streak was snapped by a loss to SMU. Then Harvard, whose 28-meet streak became the nation's longest, was upset by Princeton eight days before Indiana Sunday.

"We were looking ahead to Indiana. No question about it," Joe Bernal would say later. But still, the excitement was there when Indiana arrived for the weekend. And then Bernal went to work.

"These guys were not accustomed to losing dual meets. They came to swim against us, guys who did not seem to belong in the same pool, and they were probably motivated by the pool. They knew the NCAAs would be here, and I think they came out to get accustomed to the pool for later.

"We tried to hide our preparation. We wanted them to think that we were simply thrilled to have them here. And looking back, our loss to Princeton the week before probably made it even easier for them to underrate us.

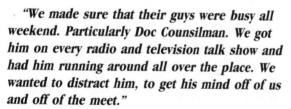
The sight of Larry Countryman's shaved head (above) got the crowd going as Harvard fashioned a 1980 upset of national power Indiana. Freestyler Jack Gauthier (right) shows the emotion that led to a 67-46 win over the Hoosiers.

"We made sure that their guys were busy all weekend. Particularly Doc Counsilman. We got him on every radio and television talk show and had him running around all over the place. We wanted to distract him, to get his mind off of us and off of the meet."

As Bernal set the scene, it became apparent that there was a personal goal in this scenario as well. He saw this as the master, Counsilman, against some young guy at Harvard.

"We were just these little guys doing something in the Ivy League. No big deal," Bernal recalled, with a trace of a smile.

Then came Sunday. And Indiana Sunday became Harvard Sunday. It wasn't just an upset. It was a drowning. Indiana's All-American divers took their events. But Harvard won 10 of 11 swimming events. Double winners included Bobby Hackett (200- and 500-meter freestyle), Brain-

tree's Jack Gauthier (50- and 100-meter free-style), and freshman David Lundberg (200-meter individual medley and 200-meter breaststroke, both university records).

But the crowd pleaser was another freshman, Larry Countryman. When the Newark, Delaware, native stepped to the blocks for the 1,650 and removed his cap, it became clear that shaving for the meet included his head. The bald Mr. Countryman proceeded to take the 1,650 in 15:35.61.

The final score was 67-46 for Harvard. This one dual meet on a Sunday afternoon reached more people outside the swimming world's inner family than all the Eastern League and Eastern Seaboard championships the Crimson would win. This victory told all the "others" about Harvard swimming.

The salesman had sold them all.

• • •

It is March, 1982. The Hacketts and Coglins and Macks and the rest from the class of '81 are gone. At Dartmouth, Harvard wins its fourth straight Seaboard title with a phenomenal 662 points, nearly 400 points ahead of second-place La Salle.

"That's when we peaked. Everything just came together for us then, and now the others have cut the gap," observed Bernal.

The rout proved what had been apparent for some time. As much as Bobby Hackett's class had meant to Harvard at the start, the program had gone past the days of needing the single star and his triple-win performances.

Standout swimmers were there in numbers, and they came from everywhere. The class of '82 had Jack Gauthier (Massachusetts), Tim Maximoff (California), Ron Raikula (Kansas), and Tom Royal (Florida). The next class brought in David Lundberg (Utah), Larry Countryman (Delaware), Ted Chappell (New Jersey), and Jim Carbone (New York).

The numbers kept coming and Harvard ran its Seaboard streak to seven in 1985. There were still superstars—Lundberg, Chappell, and Dave Barnes '85 won or shared top individual honors at the Seaboards from 1980 to 1982. But most of all there was depth and the feeling that Harvard would be on top for a long time. It was a frustrating feeling for the opposition.

Harvard appreciated that feeling. Only a few years earlier, the Crimson had been on the other side of a dynasty, watching the Yalies have all the fun. By 1985, Harvard was right where it wanted to be.

"An Established Aspect of the Team"

"I was fortunate to inherit an established aspect of the team. We didn't have to work on that part, which made it much easier to focus on the swimming."

The speaker is Harvard swim coach Joe Bernal and the "established aspect" to which he refers is the diving program. Since 1972 Harvard's divers have been in the capable hands of John Walker, a former standout diver himself at Indiana. Before his arrival, Harvard's last champion divers had been Dan Mahoney, winner of both Seaboards events in 1965, and Bill Murphy, 1-meter winner in 1967. Champion divers would wear Crimson more frequently under Walker's tutelage.

Walker's coaching career began at the high school level in Evanston, Illinois, where he had a state champion in 1965. From there, it was a six-year stint at the University of Minnesota, which peaked with the performance of Craig Lincoln.

"Craig provided my most satisfying coaching accomplishment up to that point. We started at ground zero and by 1972 he was NCAA champ at three meters and a bronze medalist at Munich," remembers Walker.

In 1972 Walker came to Harvard to work with Don Gambril, the first of three head coaches he has assisted. In his first 13 years at Harvard, Walker has consistently turned out winning divers. Some years, there has been greater depth. But there always seems to be that one diver who scores important points.

Walker has coached five Eastern Seaboard diving champions at Harvard. The first of them was David English, 1976 winner on the 1-meter board.

"I recruited him while I was still at Minnesota," recalls Walker. "He was a tough kid who bounced back from a torn muscle in his neck to win that title in 1976 when he could barely raise his left arm. I've always felt that his win was the start of our diving program."

The next winner was Mike Toal at 3 meters in 1978. Walker saw Toal as a rebellious type, battling himself as much as anyone. "When he finally got a hold on his self-confidence, it was enough to make him a champion."

Cornell seemed to rule the diving world at this time. The Big Red's Paul Steck won three straight on the 1-meter board from 1977 to 1979, and in 1981 it was Cornell's John Krakora. But sandwiched in between, in 1980, was Harvard's Steve Schramm.

"The kids called him Bomar, as in Bomar the Brain. He was always calculating things. He had memorized the intricate score chart that computes one's score from a dive's degree of difficulty and the judges' points awarded. People would say, 'Hey, Bomar, what was the score on that one?' And instantly, he'd have it figured."

He also figured out how to score those points himself and won the 1980 title, doing so in some pain.

"He was doing a reverse one-and-a-half somer-

Harvard produced a string of consistently outstanding divers under diving coach John Walker from 1972 on. The best of them all was Dan Watson '85, a three-time Eastern Seaboard champ who, at his peak, was bettered only by Olympic legend Greg Louganis.

lined, with no butt at all. I only say this because it was a big part of why he could rip his entries with the best of them.

"Second, he had an unbelievable kinesthetic sense. Whether he was upside down or twisted or whatever, he always knew where he was. You can teach awareness to a point but not the kind of sense he had.

"And finally, he trained very, very hard."

Watson won a U.S. indoor title as a freshman and went on to sweep both diving events in the three Eastern Seaboards that he competed in (1982, 1983, and 1985). Harvard's diving depth was on display that first year as Crimson divers took first, second, sixth, and seventh on the 1-meter board and first, second, fourth, and seventh on the 3-meter. Their point totals alone would have been good for tenth place in the meet's team standings.

During the Olympic year of 1984, Watson was third at the Olympic trials behind Greg Louganis and Bruce Kimball, who won the gold and silver respectively in the platform diving (Louganis added the gold in the springboard competition as well). In 1985 at the U.S. Platform Championships, Watson finished ahead of Kimball and just behind Louganis to take a silver medal.

Joe Bernal gave his supreme stamp of approval to Watson. "In terms of performance, he was the Bobby Hackett of divers."

And Bernal as much as anyone appreciated what John Walker's divers as a group meant to Harvard's overall success.

"There's no doubt that we depended on the divers. Our strategy was often based on the assumption that they would bring in points and then we could use our personnel in a certain way to get the other points we would need. It's a tribute to John that he can consistently keep his divers at that productive level."

sault with one-and-a-half twists and hit his head on the board the night before the meet," recalled Walker. "The next day, sporting stitches and some sponge rubber under his cap, he went out and won the title anyway."

The next year Jeff Mule became Harvard's fourth Seaboard champ, capturing the 1981 three-meter event. Mule won his title to cap off a strong sophomore year in which he frequently swept both diving events. But Mule's time in the limelight would be limited. The very next year, a freshman from Ashland, Kentucky, would redefine the standards of diving in the East.

Dan Watson had the perfect combination. He was gifted and he worked hard. That made him tough to beat.

"The first thing about Danny was his physical makeup," noted Walker. "He was slender, stream-

• • •

WOMEN'S SWIMMING: PIONEERS AT THE START

1923–75: One of the major problems in chronicling women's athletics at Harvard is semantic. It is a matter of determining when Radcliffe athletics ended and Harvard women's athletics began.

For sports in which intercollegiate play began in the late 1970s or early 1980s, there is no problem. But for other sports, in which athletes wore the letter R long before Harvard paid attention to them, there are too many chances for historians to shortchange the Radcliffe past.

Swimming is one of these sports, one whose history dates back to 1923, when Radcliffe met Sargent College in the country's first women's intercollegiate swim meet (Sargent won). For nearly half a century, swimming continued on a fairly casual basis at Radcliffe, the campus pool occupied more by recreational swimmers than intercollegiate athletes.

By the early 1970s the first signs of a more competitive intercollegiate program had emerged. And though still called Radcliffe at the time, the 1973–74 team was the first to compete under the auspices of Harvard's Department of Athletics. The swimmers were coached by Alice McCabe, who had taken charge of women's swimming in 1961 and remained as head coach through 14 seasons.

It was a world different from the one women swimmers would know a decade later. Although the top swimmers might gain access to a couple of lanes at the IAB, most of the program operated out of the small pool in the lower level of the Radcliffe gym. It was a four-lane, 20-yard facility that would later seem comical compared to Blodgett Pool's splendor. But it was somewhat less startling in its time.

"People forget that next to the IAB, just about every pool in the area was a small, twenty-yard pool," said Alice McCabe. "People forget that it was still a fairly effective place to train at that time."

Others took a slightly different view, suggesting that the pool wasn't even 20 yards long, which made regulation meets difficult to guarantee. "It was a bath tub," said one swimmer. "Lousy, terrible, a travesty," said another. "Effective" must be in the eye of the beholder.

Still, McCabe molded a competitive program throughout her years at Harvard-Radcliffe and was able to produce some of her best talent toward the end of her tenure. That is when the usual group of casual, country club swimmers was supplemented with a few more competitive types who had trained at YMCA or AAU clubs with sights on more national goals.

RoAnn Costin, Connie Cervilla, Jean Drew, and Jean Guyton were among the more talented personnel in this time, swimmers who watched the athletic transition from Radcliffe to Harvard in its earliest phase. Their performances keyed Radcliffe successes that have received minimal attention over the years.

"In 1971, we went out to Arizona and competed at the second national championships ever held," recalled McCabe. "And we finished eleventh in the country. Individually, our relay teams were in the top five nationally and RoAnn Costin had a fourth in the 200-yard freestyle."

Costin, an All-American from Lynn, Massachusetts, was one of the new breed of swimmers who had competed at the national level on YMCA and AAU club teams. Not only did she compete, but she held YMCA records for five years in the 100-, 200-, and 500-yard freestyle and New England and Eastern AAU records in those events plus the mile.

"Alice did a great job making us competitive," recalled Costin, whose younger sister Maura would follow as swimmer and head coach at Harvard. "We had a few people who had trained competitively before Radcliffe, but we still had to round out our relays with the country club sort of swimmer. And I remember that our budget my first year [1970–71] was just six hundred dollars. That meant paying our own way to Easterns and nationals."

The transition years from Radcliffe Pool to IAB to Blodgett were not without conflicts. "We had some problems but we managed," McCabe would say. Some people were more helpful than others. Men's coach Don Gambril was supportive during his two Harvard seasons (1971–72 and 1972–73), opening up opportunities for the top women. Another friend was diving coach John Walker, who began his magic with Radcliffe divers before he was officially charged with the task.

Walker was particularly supportive of Nancy Sato, a swimmer turned diver whose story mirrored the growth of women's athletics in that period. Sato had come to Radcliffe from St. Louis, where she had been a swimmer and, at best, a casual diver. ("I had one lesson when I was eleven.").

Arriving in Cambridge in the fall of 1971, Sato took one look at the conditions of the Radcliffe Pool and decided to try diving. That may have seemed a curious decision in

Despite injuries through most of her Harvard career, Maura Costin still managed to set school records in both the 100- and 200-meter butterfly. The 1980 graduate returned to Harvard in 1984 as head coach of the women's swim team.

light of the fact that the pool's depth could not accommodate divers at all.

"I would go to the Indoor Athletic Building from eight to eight-thirty in the morning, three days a week, and work with Harold Miroff, whose job it was to work with what few divers there were," recalled Sato.

And prevailing policy demanded that she exit precisely at 8:30 since the IAB was not yet coed and more than a few male swimmers chose to dip into the pool sans bathing suit in those days. So with little background and an hour and a half of training per week, Sato set out to become an accomplished diver.

John Walker arrived from the University of Minnesota at the start of Sato's sophomore year. With Alice McCabe's encouragement, and after a month of self-doubt, Sato finally approached the new men's diving coach and sought out some help.

"I figured that I should take his introductory diving course rather than try to work out with his male divers on their time," said Sato. "But when I first worked with him, he insisted that I join his men at the IAB. I guess I undersold myself."

Walker agreed. Sato had a great deal of potential but had to start believing in herself before she would get anywhere.

"She was doing a baby list at the time," said Walker. "Very limited, no reverses. But you could see she had talent. She just didn't realize it."

Working out with Dave English, Walker's first Eastern

Seaboard champion, proved valuable to Sato. By the end of her first year with Walker, she was the top female diver in New England. That was also the year that she competed in the men's JV meet against Williston Academy and won her event handily.[*]

Sato would remain New England's best for the rest of her career and eventually went from 20th in the East to 4th, from 59th in the nation to 16th. And as a senior, she became the recipient of the first Radcliffe Alumnae Association Award as the best female athlete in the school.

This progress in the pool was only half the story. Sato was a leader in the never-ending battle for better conditions for women athletes. Before the so-called merger of athletic interests, Harvard had no stated responsibility in providing for women athletes. The fact

---

[*] At the time it was reported that Sato was the first woman to compete for a Harvard team. In fact, a classmate, Betsy Inskeep, was a member of the varsity rifle squad that same year (1972–73) and became the first woman to receive a varsity H, other than three female managers who had previously. Because of Ivy League and Association of Intercollegiate Athletics for Women (AIAW) regulations, Sato had to choose between men's and women's competition and chose to stay with the women's team.

that the best swimmers got a lane at the IAB or a Nancy Sato got to work with the men's divers was only because a Don Gambril or John Walker was open to such a gesture.

But after Harvard assumed that responsibility, equal treatment of the women was slow to come around. And that's where undergraduates like Nancy Sato and RoAnn Costin led the fight for better practice times, more realistic budgets, and more.

"Nancy's fight over practice times told a lot about her," recalled Walker. "One effect of the women getting decent hours at the IAB was to cut the divers' time from four hours to an hour and a half a day. And these were times when we were literally dodging swimmers in the pool. To gain better times for her entire squad, she cut down the amount of time she herself would have access to. But she was determined to do what was right."

1976–85: Stephanie Walsh succeeded Alice McCabe as head coach beginning with the 1975–76 season. It was during Walsh's time that Harvard women's swimming entered a new world, one affected by two developments: the growth of Ivy League competition and the opening of Blodgett Pool. Walsh had been a successful swimmer herself, ranked as high as eighth in the world in the 200-meter butterfly in 1966. She knew what the program would need.

The first Ivy League champion in women's swimming was crowned in 1977, when Princeton took the first of five titles it would win over a six-year period. All of these were won by capturing the Ivy League Championship Meet. Beginning in 1983, the Ivy champ was determined by round-robin league competition. Brown has dominated league play since, with Harvard's best finish a second in 1985.

Even with the arrival of the spectacular, Olympic-sized Blodgett Pool in 1978, Harvard was unable to fashion that first Ivy title. Neither Stephanie Walsh nor her successor, Vicki Hayes, was able to beat Princeton, and the last win over Brown came in 1978.

To focus on what the program didn't do is to shortchange all that it did. The talent seemed to arrive in waves, so to speak. Coach Walsh had four swimmers from the classes of 1979 to 1981 who held nearly all the individual school records at one time. They were Laurie Downey '79 (backstroke), Maura Costin '80 (butterfly), Jane Fayer '80 (freestyle), and Liz Kelly '81 (freestyle).

"We placed fourth at the small college nationals with just six kids in 1978," recalled Walsh. "Janie, Liz, Laurie,

Diving coach John Walker had a gem in Pam Stone, 1979 National Small College Champion and top woman athlete in the school as a senior in 1982.

and Sherry [Lubbers] did most of the scoring. But Gina Stuart and Katie Kelley were part of that group, too. Each good individual helped attract others down the line."

The next wave of record-breakers arrived in 1979–80, Walsh's final season, and graduated four winning years later when former Stanford swimmer Vicki Hayes was in charge. Norma Barton (butterfly), Shelby Calvert (freestyle and backstroke), Maureen Gildea (freestyle), and Janie Smith (freestyle and butterfly) were all members of the class of '83 and together set 11 individual and 4 relay records.

Of equal importance were the record-breaking efforts of Adele Joel '82 in the breaststroke and Debbi Zimic '84 in both the 200- and 400-meter individual medleys. And of course, there were John Walker's divers.

Beginning in 1979 Walker-coached divers won virtually everything in sight through 1984. First came Pam Stone, winner of four Ivy titles on the 1-meter and 3-meter boards from 1979 to 1981. Then it was Adriana Holy winning on the 1-meter board in 1981, Jennifer Goldberg on both in 1982, and Shannon Byrd taking the Eastern Seaboard 1-meter championship in 1984.

Each new diver seemed to arrive at Harvard with greater experience than the last and go on to pile up more and more points. But the most significant accomplishment came from the pride of Louisville, Kentucky, Pam Stone. As a freshman in 1979, Stone exceeded all expectations by winning the AIAW National Small College Championships.

"We didn't even figure her to be a factor at Easterns," said Coach Walker. "But by January, she had come farther than her age group background would have led us to predict."

When former Harvard record-holder Maura Costin left a coaching position at Alabama to return to Harvard in 1984, the goals for Harvard women's swimming were well defined. The new coach wanted to chalk up Harvard's first win ever against Princeton, challenge reigning Ivy powerhouse Brown, and make a respectable showing in the Eastern Swimming Championships, the new showcase event at season's end. After one season at Blodgett, Costin had pulled off two out of three.

"Princeton had gotten the jump on everyone back when league play started by accepting good swimmers right away," according to the young coach. But by the time she returned to Cambridge, Harvard's third wave of talent had caught up with the Tiger.

Freshmen Lisa Shauwecker, Molly Clark, and Karen Dehmel were the big names when Harvard defeated Princeton by 76-64 in February of 1985. Shauwecker's contributions were as a freestyler even though her specialty was the breaststroke.

"We didn't have the distance people we would have liked so we switched around a lot," said Costin, whose season-long juggling of personnel was a custom first mastered by Alice McCabe in even leaner years. Costin had to continue creative use of people throughout the year, and the selfless acceptance of this by the team became a source of pride for the rookie coach.

So too was Harvard's finishing third out of 27 teams at the Eastern Swimming Championships, fulfilling another goal for the Harvards. All that was left was dethroning Ivy champ Brown. That didn't happen, but getting past Princeton did leave Harvard closer to the Ivy summit than ever before. All that was needed was one more wave to push Harvard to the top.

CHAPTER 9

Soccer

An American tourist in Italy turns on a television set on a fall Sunday afternoon. The screen reveals a soccer game being played before a large and boisterous crowd. The tourist's host discusses the "football game" being played, and the American laughs. "You call it 'football' here? That's funny."

Only an American would find it odd that the rest of the world calls a game played almost exclusively with the foot football. At the same time, we see nothing unusual about taking the foot out of our own game of football with any number of rules changes over the years.

Harvard had a lot to do with some of those changes in the years when two games emerged from what was referred to as association football. In fact the word "soccer" is derived from this term.

By the middle of the 19th century, sometime after William Webb Ellis of England's Rugby School picked up the ball and ran with it during a soccer game, a new game was taking hold at Harvard and elsewhere. The lines were drawn. There was association football, soccer as we know it, and there was the "Boston game," a modification that would evolve into American football.

Colleges in the Northeast rallied behind one game or the other, and the matter came to a head in 1873 when college representatives met to draw up a single set of rules. Harvard refused to attend the meeting, and the resulting set of rules closely resembled those of soccer. That's what you would have seen at the first "football" game between Princeton and Rutgers in 1869.

But Harvard held firm in its desire to play the Boston game, which allowed players to use their hands. They took on McGill University in 1874 under that set of rules and have since claimed theirs to be the first "real" football game. The implied message is that considering how the sports developed, the Princeton-Rutgers game might have been more appropriately termed the first soccer match.

As Morton Prince of the Harvard class of 1875 said in *The H Book of Harvard Athletics,* "If Harvard had not refused to attend [that 1873 meeting], it is highly improbable that the modern game [of football] played today would ever have evolved. Instead, all of the universities, colleges and schools today would be playing association [soccer] rules."

Indeed, association football at Harvard faded into the

background as the new brand of football took hold at the end of the 19th century. Little is known of soccer at Harvard from 1874 to 1903 despite the fact that the game was played in one form or another for nearly 100 years before football emerged.

MEN'S SOCCER: THOSE CHAMPIONSHIP SEASONS

1903–47: It was during the 1903–04 academic year that the modern era of Harvard soccer was born. Much of the credit for early progress must go to Dr. Richard Gummere, Haverford '02, Harvard PhD '07, and later Harvard's director of admissions. Dr. Gummere had organized the first Haverford teams while an undergraduate there and was in a position to do the same as a graduate student at Harvard.

According to Gummere, soccer in 1903–04 was informal, more of an intramural pastime among undergraduates and graduates both. "Compared with the quality of play now prevalent, their efforts were crude and no attempt was made that year to do more than choose up sides and belt the ball down the field as far as possible," said Gummere. "Short passing was definitely a courteous and unselfish action."

Joined by a couple of undergraduates, Alfred Kidder '08 and Charles Osborne '07, Gummere helped set up Harvard's first intercollegiate contests. As recalled by Kidder, finding opponents wasn't easy.

"We organized one of the first teams to play here but had great difficulty digging out opponents. The only team in the easily reachable neighborhood was the Lowell Textile School. Our first really outside game was with Haverford, which we lost, 1-0, the closeness of the score being due to the heroic efforts of one Beaton H. 'Beet' Squires '06, who was a guard or tackle on the [football] varsity. I played goal on the Harvard team and scored the single one which led to our defeat myself, by kicking the damned ball so hard on a slant that it only bounced a few yards in the proper direction but, on landing, had such a twist on it that it buzzed right back into the net."

That first game took place on April 1, 1905, at Soldiers Field, and the 1-0 loss was followed several weeks later by another loss to Haverford, this time by a 2-1 score. Finally, on May 6 of that year, Harvard recorded its first intercollegiate victory, 2-1 over Columbia.

At this time, soccer was played during the winter and

spring, which allowed football players to participate. Until the sport became a fall event in 1914, this factor added a certain roughness to the playing style.

One stabilizing influence in the early years was Harvard's first soccer coach, a Scot named Charles Burgess. His ten-year tenure took Harvard up to World War I and included the 1913 championship squad. The title won was that of the Intercollegiate Association Football League, the first of many college organizations to be set up. Pacing this team were four All-Americans: goalie Brayton Nichols '15, fullback Elwyn Barron '13, right halfback Eugene McCall '13, and outside right Daniel Needham, '13.

After the war Harvard went through a decade without the continuity a single coach could provide. A procession of men took on the assignment, and the results suffered accordingly. That changed with the arrival of John F. Carr in 1929.

Carr had been the Harvard captain in 1927, his senior year. Moving on to the law school after graduation, Carr decided to try a hand at coaching as well and ended up staying aboard for 12 seasons.

At first it was a bit awkward for the young mentor, who had to coach many athletes he had played with just two years earlier. It couldn't have been too awkward, though, because Carr's first team went 7-2-2 and his second 8-1, losing to Yale, 1-0, after winning eight straight.

The big names on those early teams were John Bland '31, a three-year All-American, and Harvard Broadbent '32, a scoring wizard whose 29 career goals remained a Harvard standard for 30 years. Carr continued his winning ways throughout his dozen years and enjoyed his most successful campaign in 1938, when he led the Crimson to their first undefeated season at 8-0-1.

More important than the wins were the many ways Carr developed enthusiasm and interest in soccer throughout the campus. That he kept the sport fun as well as competitive is borne out by the fact that the school fielded varsity, junior varsity, freshman, and sometimes second freshman teams during Carr's tenure. At one point, as many candidates turned out for soccer as signed up for varsity football. In addition to all of this, Carr was instrumental in organizing the intramural soccer program.

No small part of this success was derived from two coaching appointments made within Carr's time. In 1934 Jim MacDonald became freshman coach. An excellent teacher, "Mac" remained as freshman coach until succeeding Carr as head coach in 1941.

Also influential was Andrew "Poley" Guyda, a member

From 1931 to 1961, the record for career goals at Harvard was held by Harvard H. Broadbent (left), seen here with head coach John Carr, who served from 1929 to 1940.

of the 1936 U.S. Olympic team who became junior varsity coach in 1938. Guyda later served as Harvard's freshman coach until his untimely death in 1956.

1948–59: Jim MacDonald served as head coach of Harvard soccer for four years, a pair of years before and a pair after World War II. In 1948 Harvard turned to a young coach who, like Charley Burgess and Mac MacDonald, had ties to Scotland.

Bruce Munro was born in Scotland, came to America as a boy, and attended Springfield College, where he earned All-American status in both soccer and lacrosse. After serving in the air force, he began his coaching career at Trinity College. In 1948 he began a 26-year career at Harvard.

After dropping his opener to his alma mater Spring-

field, 1-0, Munro led Harvard to eight wins, seven by shutouts, in the season's final ten games. The new coach had wasted little time in leaving his mark. As his first captain, Phil Potter, once said, "Whereas Mac taught me how to play soccer and handle the ball individually, Bruce Munro taught me how to cooperate on the short passing game. He ran his insides ragged. The switch from Coach MacDonald to Munro was markedly one from a game of individual polish to one characterized by a short-passing group effort."

The Munro teams of the early 1950s were always well coached, and although their overall records were not impressive, these teams were never to be taken lightly. In 1952 Yale found that out in a big way.

Harvard had won only 1 of its first 7 games that year, just 3 of its first 11. By contrast, Yale was unbeaten and untied. To make matters worse, Harvard had not defeated Yale since 1949, and the Harvard seniors had not scored a single goal against the Elis in their freshman, sophomore, and junior years.

Just to add a Hollywood touch to the story, note that Harvard's starting goalie, Henry Briggs, had to sit out the game because of an arm injury. All of this, of course, is background to one of Harvard's greatest wins from that era. It was a 3-2 overtime affair, finally won on Dana Getchell's penalty shot.

The upset knocked Yale out of contention for the national championship and gave the Harvard seniors a moment to cherish after four fairly tough years. It was particularly rewarding to captain Charlie Ufford, a squash and soccer standout, who performed well in hard times for Munro and Harvard.

Not until 1955 did a new resurgence begin for Harvard soccer. That was the year that formal Ivy League soccer was born, and Harvard responded by sharing the league title with Pennsylvania. When Harvard also won the New England championship, the athletic department elevated soccer to major sport status.

The next two years brought no championships but served as an incubating period for one of Harvard soccer's golden eras. In the 1958 and 1959 seasons, Harvard put on a show, on and off the field.

These teams were molded around the class of 1960, which is not to slight the efforts of Karim "Aga" Khan and Roger Tuckerman, seniors on the first of these great squads. The 1958 team went 10-2-1, captured the Ivy title, and set a school mark of 36 goals in 13 games, the longest schedule in Harvard history.

The following season produced a repeat performance

on the field, which was equaled in certain respects by the seniors' efforts off the field. As captain Lanny Keyes would later recall, "The team was a pretty amazing group of individuals. With nine of the starting eleven writing theses, a member of the Bach Society, a stage director for one of the house plays, two members of the glee club, and several winners of fellowships and scholarships all in the same group, it made for quite an interesting season—and not just because of the games played."

Again there were 13 games, and Harvard's 9-1-3 record showed what these singers and actors and writers were made of. Keyes was named All-American along with teammates Marsh McCall and Tom Bagnoli, and the team won the Ivy title for a third time, the second straight to come after a 1-0 season-ending win over Yale.

While all the seniors could savor a four-year record of 40-4-3, goaltender Bagnoli must have taken special satisfaction from the events of his final season. The All-American played 12 games and recorded 6 shutouts and 6 one-goal games, losing none of them. When a fractured wrist kept him out of the Princeton game, Harvard fell 1-0, its only loss of the year.

Returning for the final two games, cast and all, Bagnoli beat Brown and blanked Yale in the finale to preserve Harvard's championship season.

Chris Ohiri

The record books seem to tell us a lot. He set Harvard and Ivy League records for goals in a game (5), in a season (17 and 11), and in a career (47 and 29). All-Ivy, All–New England, and All-American. A member of the 1960 Nigerian Olympic team. Chris Ohiri must have been a pretty good soccer player.

But the record book only shares with us his domination of the game of soccer. It can't preserve his smile, his grace, or his warmth. It doesn't tell us about Ohiri the scholar and Ohiri the gentleman. And it doesn't tell us why, at the age of twenty-seven, he fell victim to cancer.

Christian Ludger Ohiri, a native of Emekuku Owerri, Nigeria, came to Harvard in the fall of 1960 as one of 24 African students chosen for Ivy League schools. Four years later, he graduated

When Chris Ohiri '64 (left) took the soccer field, crowds were certain to gather. This gifted athlete from Nigeria, perhaps Harvard's greatest soccer player, succumbed to leukemia while still a young man.

magna cum laude and won a Corning Fellowship to study government and economics in Japan, India, and Nigeria. His graduate studies were never completed.

According to his coach, Bruce Munro, Ohiri was "a gem in a coalfield. And he was pretty much by himself those days. If he had played on one of the later, championship teams, nobody would have beaten us."

All the words used to describe great athletes have been directed toward Ohiri. And they still fall short. Professor John Finley, master of Eliot House, added a new perspective when he referred to Ohiri as "a lion . . . living with noble strength and by a noble code."

In October of 1983 the soccer and lacrosse field by the Harvard Business School was named Chris Ohiri Field. The plaque at the field provides another attempt to capture in words what this man was all about. It says:

CHRIS OHIRI FIELD
IN AFFECTIONATE MEMORY OF
CHRISTIAN LUDGER OHIRI, A.B. 1964
THIS FIELD IS NAMED

EAGER SCHOLAR—LOYAL TEAMMATE—SKILLED ATHLETE
IN SOCCER, TRACK AND FIELD

HIS COLLEGE GENERATION REMEMBERS HERE A MAN
GENEROUS IN FRIENDSHIP WHO LOVED GOD AND
HUMANKIND
AND FACED THE CONFLICTS OF LIFE
WITH HONESTY, ENTHUSIASM
AND COURAGE

1960–63: The 7-2-1 record that followed in 1960 was a pleasant surprise. With nine regulars lost to graduation the previous spring, few expected this squad of sophomores and reserves from the previous two seasons to accomplish much. Two one-goal losses meant the difference between third place and another piece of the Ivy title.

While the varsity forged a few headlines, the freshman team was attracting even greater attention. The reason for the interest in the Yardlings was the presence of one Christian L. Ohiri of Nigeria. This flashy athlete was the main reason that the frosh averaged a goal every 15 minutes, and word of this awesome attack spread quickly.

It is little wonder that the fall of 1961 was met with unparalleled anticipation. When Ohiri scored five goals in

each of his first two games, soccer interest was at an all-time high at Harvard. For the second of those two games, a 9-1 demolition of Cornell, the Harvard grounds crew had to position restraining ropes to keep the crowd from surging onto the field.

Ohiri was the best of a handful of African student-athletes attending Harvard at the time. The soccer team rosters of the early 1960s included two other Nigerians, Onwechekwa "Chuck" Okigwe and Azinna Nwafor (via Bowdoin College), and three players from Ghana, Fred Akuffo, Emmanuel "Mama" Boye, and Ebenezer "Klu" Klufio.

"Around this time, the Ivy League had a special program to attract outstanding individuals from Africa, not just athletes but strong individuals. Some of these guys could have just as easily ended up at another Ivy school," said Munro.

At a time when the national average of foreign students at an American university was 1.3 percent of total enrollment, Harvard's figure was slightly over 10 percent. The benefits of this fact to Harvard's soccer team cannot be overstated.

From 1961 to 1963 Ohiri and his teammates compiled a mark of 16-4-1, winning one Ivy title outright and sharing two more. That gave Harvard a piece of six Ivy crowns in nine years of league competition.

Along the way, Ohiri set every Harvard and league scoring record possible. Through his junior year, he already held game, season, and career marks, despite suffering a thigh injury in the mud against Amherst as a sophomore that bothered him the entire season.

And it wasn't just a matter of padding his numbers with four- and five-goal efforts against the lesser opponents. This is clear from the final two games of his senior year. The league standings read Brown 6-0 and Harvard 4-1. Harvard had to win its last two games, one of which was Brown's final game of the year. The results were 1-0 and 3-2 wins against Brown and Yale respectively, with Ohiri scoring the game-winner in each contest.

1964–72: With the graduation of Chris Ohiri and his classmates, Harvard soccer slipped a notch from championship caliber to just plain successful. From 1964 to 1968 Harvard compiled a record of 34-15-6 in five winning seasons. But the Ivy League finish ranged from second place to fourth in that period, as the title eluded the Crimson.

If that kind of success failed to satisfy the Harvard

Solomon Gomez gets in a kick against Boston University in a 1968 contest. A mainstay of the 1969 NCAA semifinalists, Gomez led the Ivy League in scoring that year.

following, what happened over the next four seasons was unlike anything the soccer people in Cambridge had ever seen. And not surprisingly, it was another foreign invasion that keyed the new success.

Munro's 1969 roster included the likes of Chris Wilmot of Middlesex, England (twice an All-American); Russ Bell of Kingston, Jamaica; Richie Hardy of Tunis, Tunisia; and Solomon Gomez and Charlie Thomas of Bathurst, Gambia. Of course, the same roster also included some talent from exotic places like Andover, Massachusetts, and South Norwalk, Connecticut. Together, this imported and domestic blend produced Harvard's first perfect regular-season record of 12-0.

Gomez and Thomas, with 16 and 15 goals respectively, were the big guns offensively for this powerhouse. But a handful of Americans played key roles as well. Goalie Bill Meyers (Andover) had eight shutouts in those first 12 games, six of them in a row at one point. With two more in postseason play, Meyer set a school mark of ten that still stands.

The playmaking of sophomore Phil Kydes (South Norwalk) recalled memories of his older brother Andy '67, twice an All-Ivy selection. Phil, who had 13 assists in his first varsity season, would equal his brother's Ivy accolades.

It remained for a rather unheralded American to provide the single biggest moment of the 1969 season. Following the regular-season perfection, Harvard entered its first NCAA tournament. A 4-0 win over Brown gave the Crimson the NCAA District I title and matched them up with tiny Hartwick College, a not-so-tiny name in college soccer, for the championship of the East.

A coin toss gave Harvard the right to host the affair, and some 4,000 strong turned out on a November Saturday to witness the big game. The contest was scoreless into its second sudden-death overtime period when the Gomez-Thomas tandem went to work.

It was Gomez moving the ball down the field and feeding it to Thomas who, as usual, drew a crowd of defenders. That left John Gordon all alone in front of Hartwick goalie Frank van der Sommen. Thomas sliced the ball to Gordon, and the senior from New York sent everyone home with his first goal of the season.

That goal also sent Harvard to San Jose, California, for the national championships. But there would be no further glory, as eventual champion St. Louis handed Harvard its only loss of the season, 2-1, in the semifinal round.

With only two seniors claimed by graduation, Harvard expected great things again in 1970, and no one was disappointed. Another undefeated regular season brought Harvard into postseason play once more.

Scoring star Charlie Thomas was the standout for Harvard down the stretch. In the season finale, it was Thomas's goal that beat Yale, 1-0, to keep Harvard's regular season perfect. In the NCAA tournament Thomas had four goals and then two in 6-0 and 2-1 wins over Worcester Tech and Brown respectively.

That brought Harvard face to face with Hartwick again. This time the script was different. It was a high-scoring contest and the winner was Hartwick, 4-3.

In 1971 Harvard had some new heroes but old results. There was goalie Shep Messing, the self-proclaimed flake who posed for *Playgirl* magazine and later played on the 1972 U.S. Olympic team. There was a sophomore forward from Nigeria, Felix Adedeji, who set a new Harvard record with 18 goals on the year. And there was another remarkable record. Everything was the same . . . sort of.

After 27 consecutive regular-season victories, Harvard traveled to Pennsylvania for a midseason night game on Franklin Field's artificial surface. Some 11,000 fans were on hand as well, and they watched the host Quakers end that streak with a 5-2 victory.

That would be Harvard's only loss until the NCAA semifinals. To get that far, the Crimson had to battle through the rest of their schedule and then sweep NCAA regional matches against Southern Connecticut (5-0), Brown (3-0), and, again, Hartwick (4-1).

Then it was a trip to Miami to fight for the national championship. As had happened two years earlier, the eventual champ stopped Harvard in the semifinals. This time it was Howard University by a 1-0 margin.

For the nine seniors, it was the end of perhaps Harvard soccer's most successful three-year period ever. The

It's all over, and the hero is hoisted high. This particular hero is John Gordon, whose goal gave Harvard a 1-0 double-overtime victory over Hartwick College in the 1969 Eastern final at Harvard.

veterans like Wilmot, Kydes, Bell, and Thomas forged a 39-4 mark overall, a phenomenal 32-1 in regular-season play.

The big numbers and the shouting would last one more season. In 1972 the Crimson went 10-2-1 and advanced as far as the NCAA quarterfinals, where league rival Cornell knocked them off. Penn again took the league crown despite Ivy record-setting performances by Harvard's Chris Papagianis (13 goals, 21 points) and Bent Hinze (9 assists).

For Bruce Munro it marked his 22nd winning season in 25 years at Harvard. Number 26 would be his last and, unfortunately, a less than memorable finale.

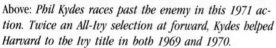

Above: *Phil Kydes races past the enemy in this 1971 action. Twice an All-Ivy selection at forward, Kydes helped Harvard to the Ivy title in both 1969 and 1970.*

Top right: *He once posed in* Playgirl *magazine, but his real strength was playing goal. And Shep Messing, shown here as a member of the New York Cosmos, played that position well for Harvard, the U.S. Olympic team, and then the Cosmos.*

Bottom right: *Chris Ohiri holds plenty of Harvard soccer records, but the one for most goals in a season belongs to another Nigerian, Felix Adedeji, who had 18 in 1971, when he was just a sophomore.*

1973–81: Seven of 11 starters from the 1972 team were gone. But when Bruce Munro's final team started out at 2-1-1 in 1973, a successful season seemed possible. The team could win only one of its last eight games and finished at 3-7-2.

For Munro it meant the end of a varsity career that produced a record of 192-85-25 in 26 seasons. All-American Lanny Keyes, captain of the 1959 Ivy champions, remembered Munro this way:

"Bruce Munro was a great coach. No one could have been better for the type of people who turned out for soccer. He was low pressure, objective, and never lost sight of the fact that the most important part of soccer and athletics was to provide an opportunity for a group of people to come together and work and play hard, and benefit from each other as much as they did from the sport itself."

Munro's successor was George Ford, a former professional player and coach from England who came to the United States in 1964. Ford, who played professionally in the North American Soccer League, entered collegiate coaching at Bryant College in Rhode Island.

The eight-year Ford era never quite put it all together. The closest Harvard could come to back-to-back winning seasons was in Ford's first two years, when a 7-4-2 season in 1974 was followed by a 6-6-1 mark. After that, Harvard experienced winning years in 1977 and 1980 but losing records in the four other years.

The best year was 1980, when the squad went 10-4-1. But six of the wins were against the likes of MIT, Williams, Bowdoin, Wesleyan, Amherst, and Haverford. In defense of the coach, Harvard was not getting the soccer talent, particularly the foreign players, that previous teams had enjoyed. Columbia was the new Ivy soccer power, and much of its success was due to talented imports.

Still, Harvard did come up with All-Ivy performers such as Lyman Bullard (1974), Mike Smith (1978–80), John Sanacore (1979), and Mauro Keller Sarmiento (1980), one of three Keller Sarmiento brothers from Argentina.

Bruce Munro

"I liked the psychological challenge of bringing athletes together. Getting them to talk to each other, play with each other. Getting them to work together. I think that's what I liked the most."

The speaker is J. Bruce Munro, Harvard's soccer and lacrosse coach from 1948 to 1974. In his

Coach Bruce Munro rejoices at Penn, where victory led to the 1969 Ivy title. In 26 years as soccer coach, Munro was 192-85-25.

26 years in Cambridge, he brought all sorts of athletes together. But it wasn't always easy.

"The great teams of the late sixties and early seventies were the least enjoyable to work with. They were too intent on national championships. They were too intense. And some of them had egos that made it a constant battle," observed Munro.

"I liked to win as much as anyone, but these guys were too intense, almost professional. It was more fun with earlier teams that may not have had as much natural talent but enjoyed themselves more, partly from developing their talent."

The foreign flavor of some of his later teams created unique problems in bringing players together. "Some of the African players came from different countries that were at war back home. If players weren't speaking to each other, it could have been egos or it could have been the war."

While remembering both sports fondly, Munro enjoyed soccer a bit more than lacrosse. He was more comfortable, and successful, with soccer but also recalls a greater variety of personalities.

"Soccer attracted prominent people back then. It was a moneyed sport. We had the son of David Niven, the actor. Another player came from royalty. And then there was the day the Aga Khan showed up at practice with his bodyguards, complete with machine guns. I had never heard of him."

Part of the reason Munro recalls these individuals fondly is the way they handled themselves. "It seems that the more notoriety they had, the less attention they demanded."

By 1974 the burden of coaching both sports, particularly the recruiting, had changed the experience for Munro. He spent a year with the freshmen, where his teaching skill could be put to use.

"I don't think I ever wrote a recruiting letter the whole time I coached. But college athletics have changed."

Yes, they have. In too many places, salesmen have replaced teachers. And the Bruce Munros are no longer bringing people together.

. . .

1982–84: With soccer success rapidly becoming a thing of Harvard's past, a change was sought. And so in 1982, George Ford was followed by Jonathan "Jape" Shattuck. The youthful Shattuck had played at Syracuse before graduating in 1976 and then began a coaching career, first at his alma mater and later at Hartwick College.

After opening with a 3-0 blanking of MIT, Shattuck experienced hard times. The team lost 7 of its next 9 games and finished the year at 5-10. With only 18 goals in 15 games—8 by Lance Ayrault—offense proved to be a problem, and the team was shut out six times.

First-year blues behind him, Shattuck began putting the house in order with very visible results the second time around. Looking at a mediocre 3-4-3 record in November, the 1983 edition of Harvard soccer won its final five games to finish above .500. Sophomore John Catliff emerged as an offensive threat, and his 13 goals led the team and earned him All-Ivy status.

What made 1983's late-season success particularly important was that it included wins against Ivy foes Penn

and Yale as well as national power Hartwick. What would follow in 1984 would be even more impressive.

When the 1984 squad lost its first two games, including one to Division III's Brandeis, it seemed for a moment that the team's progress had been reversed. Then came the home opener against Connecticut, and all the fears were put to rest.

Harvard's 2-0 victory over UConn marked the first time since 1969 that the Crimson had prevailed over the Huskies. In the interim the Huskies had outscored Harvard by 17-5 in chalking up a 5-0-2 record. With this history and Harvard's poor start, the word "upset" seemed in order.

"That game wasn't a fluke," Coach Shattuck would offer immediately after the contest. The team's success over the remaining weeks of the season would even challenge the use of "upset."

A loss to Boston College put the team at 1-3 and momentarily slowed Shattuck's progress. The team responded by winning 11 of its next 12 games to forge the most successful season since 1971. The 4-2 Ivy mark left Harvard a game behind league champ Columbia. But the combined efforts of this talented squad were enough to land Harvard a somewhat controversial berth in the NCAA tournament.

At the time of the selection committee's decision, the New England rankings, in order, read Connecticut, Providence, Yale, and Harvard. When the tournament selections were announced, Providence was the only team among the four not to be invited.

As it turned out, Harvard made the selection committee look good as it beat third-ranked Yale in the season finale and repeated its earlier domination of UConn with a 1-0, double-overtime victory in the NCAA District I championship.

But that's where the story ended. At the NCAA quarterfinals in Los Angeles, UCLA brought to a close Harvard's best season in more than a decade. The score was 2-0, but Harvard stood tall.

John Catliff (10-5-25) and Lane Kenworthy (11-2-24) provided a strong one-two punch offensively, but the attack was really team oriented as indicated by the five players who scored in double figures. Senior goalie Matt Ginsburg, playing his first full season, was equally impressive and nowhere more so than during Harvard's six-game win streak, during which he recorded four straight shutouts.

Like the strong teams of the early 1970s, this squad had an international flavor. Catliff was a member of the 1984

A. Y. Ake (above), *Nigerian ambassador to the United States, speaks at the 1983 dedication of the soccer field as Chris Ohiri Field.*

there is evidence that no team since then could rival the 1984 edition. One knowledgeable observer of this period, All-Ivy forward Lyman Bullard '77, had this to say about the squad:

"There is no comparison between this team and our 1974 NCAA participant. We were both strong defensively, but this team was so much more talented at midfield and forward. And John Catliff is one of the most talented soccer players I have ever seen.

"The other thing this team did extremely well was that they won the individual battles. They hustled, they tackled well, and they beat the other team to the ball consistently."

Harvard soccer was back.

Harvard returned to the NCAA play-offs in 1984 thanks to the play of John Catliff and others. Catliff was a member of the Canadian Olympic team as well.

Canadian Olympic team that played at Harvard Stadium in the summer of 1984. Nick Hotchkin, who scored the overtime goal that beat UConn, had played on junior national squads in England. Paul Nicholas and Mark Pepper had similar backgrounds in Scotland and West Germany respectively.

While the 1969–71 teams may have been stronger,

WOMEN'S SOCCER: EARLY WINNERS

In professional sports, expansion teams have always needed heroes. The teams and their followers recognize that one superstar can lift a franchise to instant respectability.

In the world of college athletics, the women's teams of the 1970s—and in many respects still today—were expansion teams. They were the new kids on the block who needed heroes to increase their visibility and, in the process, give them legitimacy.

The heroes, let's forget "heroines," could have been individuals or full teams. The need was for some athlete or team to emerge as a shining example of what could be for the many women breaking new ground.

At Harvard, this shining example appeared in a handful of women's soccer teams that excelled in the late 1970s. They were talented, they were attractive personalities, and they were winners at a time when winners were scarce among Harvard's fall teams. And that helped their visibility.

Support for this premise came along in November of 1979, as the women were wrapping up their second straight Ivy League championship. On the same weekend, Harvard's football team was losing its sixth straight game. When the women received top billing on the front page of "News and Views," the weekly newsletter produced by the Harvard Varsity Club, a few of the old boys grumbled. That had never happened before.

But at the athletic department and elsewhere the theory prevailed that winners should be recognized, all winners. And so the headline and story proved to be one small step for women's soccer and one giant leap for women's athletics at Harvard.

Like many of the women's sports at Harvard, the soccer program owes its existence to a small group of individuals who gave a little extra at the start. The record books don't mention Karen Fifer and Jackie Schlenger, but without their efforts in the spring of 1976, the others whose names are remembered would never have been heard from.

All the smiles indicate a championship feeling. This time it's the 1979 Ivy League soccer title for Harvard's women.

Fifer and Schlenger approached Bob Scalise at that time and made their pitch for the formation of a women's soccer program. Scalise, coach of men's freshman soccer and varsity lacrosse at the time, hardly needed a new assignment. But with the athletic department's blessing, he added one more.

And so in the fall of 1976, Fifer, Schlenger, and Scalise had rounded up 30 soccer candidates, and a club program was born. Scalise ran the show like a varsity, demanding a "varsity commitment from the start." As he would later comment, "It was obvious from the start that their desire wouldn't allow for anything less."

The first team was 4-5 against college opponents, 0-4 against Ivy foes, most of whom had been organized a year or two longer. But the commitment displayed by the athletes encouraged the department to raise the team to Level II status, just short of full financial support, for 1977.

It was at this point that the program took off. Successive seasons of 9-2-1, 13-1, and 15-1-1 made soccer the paragon for other women's programs. The teams were successful, they had fun, and they brought attention to the women's athletic program in general.

Much of that attention was directed toward Sue St. Louis, a freshman forward who scored 18 goals in 1977. When she upped the total to 20 as a sophomore, St. Louis, clearly the fastest and strongest player on the team, was on her way to becoming the first superstar in Harvard women's athletics.

The other members of the team were equally responsible for the success of the early years. Most notable were Cat Ferrante, Jeanne Piersiak, Ellen Jakovic, and Ellen Hart, a world-class distance runner after graduation. Then there was the playmaker who emerged from Sue St. Louis' shadow in her final two seasons.

While St. Louis got the early attention for her goal-scoring prowess, it was Julie Brynteson who lifted the program to championship heights. In both the 1978 and 1979 Ivy League tournament championship finals, Brynteson scored hat tricks to lead Harvard to titles. She was tournament MVP both times.

Further recognition came to Brynteson when *Soccer America* magazine selected her for one of its annual MVP awards, the first woman to be so honored. The two-year record for 1978–79 was 28-2-1 with two Ivy championships. The only losses were to Massachusetts, 2-1 in 1978 and 4-3 in overtime in 1979. The tie, an extended 1-1 overtime affair with Cortland State in 1979, resulted in a shared Eastern AIAW title.

One of the major reasons that Harvard was an immediate Ivy power in women's soccer was the scoring prowess of Sue St. Louis.

Success continued in 1980 with a 14-7 mark, as St. Louis wrapped up her career with virtually every Harvard scoring record. The first wave of soccer talent had passed, and it seemed that the opposition was catching up. Enter the second wave.

The 1981 All-Ivy soccer team featured five Harvard players, all freshmen. These honors were bestowed after those freshmen paced Harvard to a 17-2 season that included another Ivy championship. Harvard was also crowned Eastern AIAW champion by virtue of tough 2-1 victories over Massachusetts and Connecticut. The latter win was particularly sweet, as it was a double-overtime battle in the final and avenged Harvard's only regular-season loss, a 4-2 decision to the Huskies.

Making all of this possible was a mix of veterans from

Early in the 1984 season, her senior year, Kelly Landry established virtually every offensive record in Harvard women's soccer.

Harvard's earlier success and those five freshmen. The newcomers—Kelly Landry, Alicia Carillo, Jenny Greeley, Inga Larson, and Deb Field—reflected the new kind of athlete entering women's programs at the college level.

"Our first championship teams simply had great all-around athletes. This next group featured skilled soccer players, products of soccer programs that never existed for our earlier players," said Scalise.

It would be tough to pick the best of the lot. Four of the five All-Ivy freshmen also earned All–New England honors. Landry's 24 goals and 31 points were new records. Greeley was MVP of the Ivy tournament and an all-tournament player at the AIAW nationals.

That's where Harvard's 1981 season ended. The Crimson were stopped by Central Florida, 2-0, in the opening game. But in subsequent rounds, wins over Texas A & M and Oregon lifted Harvard to a fifth-place national ranking.

In 1982 the opposition gave signs of catching up. The

record was 8-6-2, which included six overtime games and three one-goal losses in regulation. The last of the losses came in the AIAW (now NCAA) nationals, against Missouri-St. Louis, a 2-1 heartbreaker that ended the season.

While Landry and Greeley repeated All-Ivy honors, three veterans who bridged Harvard's championship years were also honored. Earning first team status as seniors were Jeanne Piersiak, Kelly Gately, and Laura Mayer.

Injuries colored the next two seasons, both very successful campaigns just the same. The most costly were two separate knee injuries to Alicia Carillo that kept her out of both seasons.

The 1983 record was 10-5, outstanding by most standards. But without an Ivy title or playoff appearance, it was not quite what the Harvards were accustomed to. Greeley, Larson, and particularly Landry continued their individual heroics.

That left 1984, the final year for the amazing class of '85. In addition to high hopes for the team, more than a little attention would be focused on Kelly Landry's assault on Sue St. Louis' scoring records.

Landry, like classmate Greeley, was a coach's dream. Both brought a blend of skill and desire that produced inspired performances. Landry's natural athletic ability allowed her to take up ice hockey as a sophomore and become a 16-goal scorer as a junior and team captain as a senior. Greeley simply took her soccer skills to the lacrosse field each spring and remained a moving force in two of the school's most successful programs in her four years at Harvard.

Freshmen Tracee Whitley in goal and Karin Pinezich up front joined these veterans to create one more memorable year for Harvard soccer. The record stood at 14-2-1 after a thrilling 2-1 win over Vermont in the opening game of the NCAA play-offs. Only Massachusetts stood in the way of a Final Four berth.

But the old nemesis from Amherst, 1-0 losers to Harvard in the regular season, turned the score around in the NCAAs. And the injury factor played a key role again. The year began with Alicia Carillo's knee injury ending her season. The finale saw Jenny Greeley break her hand, removing her leadership from the Harvard lineup. It was too much to overcome.

With Greeley and Landry earning their unprecedented fourth All-Ivy berths, another era in Harvard soccer was wrapped up. Landry succeeded in catching and destroying all of Sue St. Louis' scoring records, as Harvard women's soccer approached the end of its first decade.

CHAPTER 10

Lacrosse
and
Field Hockey

Football claims to be the toughest game. Ice hockey, the fastest. And what about lacrosse? Could it be the oldest game in America? North American Indians played a form of lacrosse long before English settlers brought any of their favorite pastimes across the Atlantic. And that was certainly a good many years before college lacrosse was born in the late 19th century.

Today when college lacrosse is discussed, one is likely to hear the names of Johns Hopkins, Maryland, North Carolina, and other Mid-Atlantic institutions. Or perhaps the talk will focus on New York schools like Cornell and Syracuse.

Such conversation not only does an injustice to today's revived Harvard lacrosse program, it also ignores what history tells us of Harvard's role in the origins of the college game. In the late 19th and early 20th centuries, Harvard was a big name, if not the biggest, in college lacrosse. To this day, only Johns Hopkins and Navy have won more national titles.

To be fair, the history books also show that the initial

success has never quite been equaled. Changes in the game, on and off the field, have created new powers over the years. And changes at Harvard in recent years may have just caught up with the new game.

MEN'S LACROSSE:
FROM NATIONAL CHAMPION
TO IVY POWER

1878–1945: Lacrosse at Harvard dates back to 1878, when the Harvard Lacrosse Association was formed and a team was put together for the following spring. The leader of this effort was Charles F. Squibb '81, who received ample help and encouragement from the Union Lacrosse Club of Boston.

In these formative years, the many lacrosse clubs along the East Coast were influential in developing college

lacrosse. Many of the clubs predated the college programs and were in need of both competition and a steady source of players. Union, formed in 1871, was one of these. The Baltimore Lacrosse Club had a similar relationship with lacrosse at Johns Hopkins University, one of the early and continuing lacrosse powers.

As was so often the case in other intercollegiate sports, the first schools to prosper in lacrosse were Harvard, Yale, and Princeton. The earliest recorded intercollegiate championships were won by Harvard in 1881 and 1882, Yale in 1883, and Princeton in 1884 and 1885.

Gradually colleges to the south began fielding teams and, of equal importance, preparatory schools and high schools in the Middle Atlantic states began to nurture lacrosse programs after the turn of the century. This development, fostered by the lacrosse clubs in that region, would make the Mid-Atlantic the center of the sport in this country.

Two college leagues were formed early, the Intercollegiate Lacrosse Association in 1888, and the Inter-University League, of which Harvard was a member, in 1894. The two combined to form the United States Intercollegiate Lacrosse League in 1906.

Harvard, a member of the league's Northern Division, won six league titles and shared another in the 19-year existence of the organization. The first title came in 1908, when lacrosse at Harvard was still an interclass activity, teams being made up of members of the same class. It wasn't until 1910, when Harvard won another Northern Division title, that the sport shifted fully to an interuniversity pastime.

Two more titles were added in 1913 and 1915 before World War I interrupted play for the 1917 and 1918 seasons. After the war lacrosse was revived at Harvard without missing a step.

The first two postwar seasons were successful in terms of the number of students out for the squad and results on the field. In 1920 Harvard went 5-1 behind the coaching of Paul Gustafson '12, a former Crimson laxman who instilled a rough-and-tumble attitude among the team members. He couldn't maintain his early success as indicated by the 2-15 record of his final two years.

Those disappointing seasons launched a dark period for Harvard lacrosse. With the exception of 1925, when Coach Irving Lydecker forged a winning campaign, Harvard lacrosse suffered losing seasons under a parade of head coaches up through 1929. There were Gustafson from 1920–1923, Harry Hubert from Syracuse in 1924, Lydecker from Syracuse in 1925 and 1926, Talbot Hunter from Toronto in 1927, and H. W. Jeffers from Princeton in 1928.

It remained for another son of Harvard to stem the tide and make long-lasting changes over a four-year period. Madison "Maddy" Sayles, a former standout player from the class of 1927, took over as head coach in 1929. Much as the Syracuse tandem of Hubert and Lydecker had done, Sayles continued efforts to change Harvard lacrosse from a free-for-all attack to a more organized system of play.

During his four years with the Crimson, Sayles developed freshman and junior varsity teams, received a new field behind the business school, and developed the first real coaching staff with the addition of former players Ernie Gamache and J. Hamilton Lane.

This period also saw the emergence of Harvard's first lacrosse superstar, All-American Nelson Cochrane. Cochrane earned that honor as a junior in 1931, an odd 3-6 season in which Harvard scored as many goals as the opposition. In Cochrane's senior year, Sayles's last as coach, Harvard posted an outstanding 7-2-1 mark.

After Sayles's departure Harvard turned to St. John's graduate Robert Poole, who coached the club for three years. His tenure produced Harvard's first New England League champion in 1935, a team led by All-American Jonathan England. England, who had played goal for both the soccer and lacrosse teams as a sophomore, was converted to attack for his last two years. It was there that the gifted athlete earned his All-American status.

In 1936 Poole was replaced by assistant football coach Neil "Skip" Stahley. It was a time when budget cuts made in the athletic department severely hampered the lacrosse program. It was also a time when New England prep schools were starting to send more seasoned players to Harvard and the other Ivy schools. Among the best of these were the Hunsaker brothers, Jerome and Pete, out of Exeter, and Harold van B. Cleveland from Andover.

Stahley fought the financial restrictions and produced two good seasons in 1936 and 1937, the latter a championship year behind All-American John Witherspoon. But two more rough years followed, and the

stability seemingly brought to the program a decade earlier by Maddy Sayles was lost.

Witherspoon, three years out of college, became head coach in 1940 and led Harvard to a three-way tie among New England's best. That quickly became a 2-10 overall record in 1941 and an 0-6 New England mark in 1942. After a 4-4 season in 1943, formal play was suspended for two years, and the 1944 and 1945 seasons were informal.

1946–67: After the war the lacrosse program was revived by a small but enthusiastic contingent that doubled as both the varsity and junior varsity in 1946. Over the next two seasons, the numbers grew and the program got back to its prewar status.

In 1948 Harvard lacrosse turned 70 years old. And although great individuals and great teams dotted that history, a distinct period of domination had never really

Dexter Lewis '56 led the country in scoring in 1955, when he set a Harvard record with 58 goals, a mark he still holds, tied by Mike Faught in 1978.

been established after the success of the initial years. Perhaps more distressing than the lack of a modern glory era was the sense that steady, uninterrupted progress seemed impossible to maintain.

Such progress had been made in other sports at Harvard. Not surprisingly, most of those programs had benefited from one or more excellent coaches whose influence had been felt over a long period of time. Up through the 1940s, Harvard lacrosse had not enjoyed the presence of that one stabilizing individual.

In 1949 the lacrosse program got the chance to change all of that. Bruce Munro, a former All–New England in lacrosse and All-American in soccer while at Springfield, became the new head coach of Harvard lacrosse. Given similar responsibilities in soccer at the same time, Munro guided the fates of both programs for the next 26 years.

The Munro era is difficult to label. Off the field, he proved successful in ultimately leading Harvard lacrosse to stable ground. But that did not come easily. As late as 1959 financial support was withdrawn from the program, and only Munro's optimism and scrambling alumni kept the sport from fading away.

On the field, Munro never did forge a powerhouse that could be a major force in the East year after year. Each decade had its team or teams that raised the level of play for a brief period. But they were quickly followed by teams that hovered near .500 or worse.

Munro made it clear from the start that he would not tolerate haphazard play. In his first season he made the team discard the long sticks they had been using in favor of shorter sticks. These, thought Munro, would help restore the finesse so lacking in the sloppy Crimson game.

After a 6-6 start in 1949, Munro returned the longer sticks to the players, and in 1950 the first of his strong periods unfolded. The key player in this era was Dick Hudner '51, a clever ballhandler up front who twice recorded eight assists in a game, a Harvard record (later tied by Grady Watts '62).

The record was 6-5-1 in 1950, and with only four seniors graduating, chances for an even better year in 1951 seemed strong. And no one was disappointed. With Hudner setting up Ned Yost—he had seven goals in an 18-1 rout of Penn—Harvard enjoyed an 11-2 season that included a record nine-game win streak.

The success could not be maintained, as a 5-6-1 record followed in 1952. Further slippage was prevented by the emergence of a scoring machine in the person of Phil Waring. Joining the varsity as a sophomore in 1952, Waring took a year to get revved up. But as a junior in

1953, he scored 50 goals in 14 games, more than double the total of any previous Harvardian.

Too often, it seems that fate has an infuriating habit of keeping exceptional athletes at least four years apart within a given athletic program. When an aberration occurs, and two great players get a chance to perform together, the results are usually fun to watch.

Bruce Munro was the beneficiary of such a scenario in 1954, when senior Phil Waring was joined by sophomore Dexter Lewis. With two gunners up front, Munro put together a 9-2 season, the first winning record in three years.

Lewis returned in 1955 and came through with a phenomenal individual effort. His 58 goals led the nation that year and set a Harvard record that still stands. But Lewis was the only bright spot on a team that allowed 227 goals in a 4-11 season.

The losing ways continued through 1959, when Harvard looked back on a five-year mark of 23-49-1. In fairness to all involved with the sport, the program was battling to survive both on and off the field. In 1958 the southern trip was canceled. Following that season, financial support was withdrawn by the athletic department.

Jerry Pyle, captain of the 1959 squad, recalled the experience for *The Second H Book of Harvard Athletics:*

> After exams in June of 1958, the Athletic Department announced that it was withdrawing financial support from lacrosse, as well as several other minor sports. As school was over, no real plans could be made until the next fall. At that time, a large group of undergraduate lacrosse players, supported heavily, both morally and financially, by a group of graduates led by Charles E. Marsters '07, attempted to persuade the Athletic Department to reverse its ruling. This failing, the sizable number of undergraduates interested in lacrosse, encouraged by graduate support and Bruce Munro's optimism, notified all their 1959 opponents that the Harvard team would honor its schedule. In the won-lost column, the result was mediocre (5-8); however, as a demonstration of graduate and undergraduate desire for lacrosse at Harvard, the season was a success. Seniors such as Charlie Devens, Bob Hurlbut and Mike Adair drove the team to all the away games, which included such mileage-makers as Princeton and Cornell.

The experience of 1959 returned dividends a lot sooner than anyone would have predicted. The spring trip was restored the next year, and Harvard responded with wins over Stevens Tech, City College of New York, Duke, and North Carolina. Strangely, it was in defeat that this

Two of Harvard's greatest lacrosse players at work: Grady Watts (20) passes to Dave Bohn (30) in a 17-11 win over Oxford-Cambridge in 1961.

team's mettle was best revealed. Against Cornell, a team that had soundly trounced the Crimson in 1959, Harvard trailed early, 6-0 and then 7-3. Suddenly, in the third period, the score was 10-10. The game ended in Cornell's favor, 13-12, Harvard's only Ivy loss of the season.

The success continued in 1961, an 11-1-1 season helped by the restoration of financial support from the athletic department. This team, ranked seventh in the nation, scored 215 goals and won ten straight, Harvard's longest winning streak ever. The offense was paced by Grady Watts, the playmaker, and Dave Bohn, the scorer. Watts, a junior, had set Harvard assist and point standards the previous year. Bohn, a senior, finished his career with 132 goals, still a Harvard record.

"Watts was a great player," Munro would recall later. "But Bohn made him in those first two years."

In June of 1961, Harvard's Faculty Committee on Athletic Sports voted to elevate lacrosse from a minor sport to a major sport. While the on-field efforts of the 1961 team made them worthy of lacrosse's first major H awards, a tip of the hat was in order to the members of that 1959 team, which paved the way both on and off the field.

Harvard enjoyed its third straight banner year in 1962. Not coincidentally, it was the third and final year for Grady Watts, the small but talented terror on attack from lacrosse-mad Manhasset, New York. In 1960 Watts had set Harvard marks for assists in a game (8) and season (63) and for points in a game (11) and season (100).

In 1962, without Dave Bohn to feed, Watts was named to the All-American team for his role in leading Harvard to a 10-4 finish and eighth-place national ranking. Munro was named coach of the year by his peers and Watts established Harvard career records for assists (145) and points (241). No one has come close to him since.

Harvard dropped to 6-6 in 1963, the year that Princeton won its seventh straight Ivy title. The Crimson and the Tigers had fought for championships in the game's early years, each team with a degree of success. Unfortunately, while Princeton continued to collect banners, decades had passed since Harvard's last title of note. That would change in 1964.

Despite the influx of lacrosse talent in the 1970s and 1980s, Grady Watts '62 remains Harvard's all-time point-getter. The All-American attack set records for assists in a game (8), season (63), and career (145), as well as points in a game (11), season (100), and career (241).

That was the year that Princeton, after 38 straight wins in eight seasons, finally lost an Ivy League game. The Tigers lost two, in fact, but neither of them to Harvard, whom they handed a 7-6 loss before 2,000 fans at the Business School field.

Still, when this wild, anybody-could-beat-anybody season came to a close, Harvard's 4-2 league record was good for a share of the Ivy title. To be exact, it was good for a third of the pie, Dartmouth and, of course, Princeton grabbing the other two pieces.

The final overall mark was 11-3, an impressive record produced by a well-balanced attack that saw four men—Dick Ames, Tink Gunnoe, Lou Williams, and Ted Leary—each score between 19 and 23 goals.

Though Leary continued to score goals, winning Ivy scoring titles in 1965 and 1966, it would not be enough. The team was 3-10 and 5-9 in those years, 1-5 and 0-6 in the league.

The 6-7 record of 1967 wasn't much better, but the year finished with four straight wins. That signaled something better just around the corner.

1968–74: In 1968 Harvard finally solved the puzzle that was Princeton. It wasn't just that the Tigers had shared in 10 of the last 11 Ivy titles. It was worse than that. Harvard had not beaten Princeton since 1925 and had only six wins in a series dating to 1883.

Finally, on April 27, 1968, the drought ended. Revealing a sense of history, the team posted a simple sign in its locker room on that day. It said, "43 years—a long time." When the Tigers led by 9-6 late in the game, it appeared even longer. But then the Maryland Connection went to work.

Three different Baltimore natives—Marty Cain, Bruce Regan, and Jim Kilkowski—scored for Harvard in rapid succession, Kilkowski's goal coming with 15 seconds left in regulation time. It remained for a product of another lacrosse hotbed, Garden City, New York, to cap the rally. At 1:36 of overtime, sophomore John Ince, the eventual Ivy scoring champ, tallied the game-winner and the streak was history.

The late-game barrage may have eventually won this game. But the play of reserve goalie Ed McCrea was of equal importance. McCrea came off the bench to replace starter Kirby Wilcox after Wilcox fractured his collarbone making a save earlier in the game.

Over the next two seasons, Ince was the big story. Well, actually he was a small story, at 5 feet 10 inches and 130 pounds. But his scoring exploits made for big news. After a 20-26-46 sophomore year, Ince was 29-27-56 as a junior, in 1969. He earned All-Ivy status along with teammates Regan and Mike Ananis. Princeton was defeated once more, again in a wild game, 13-12, after the Tigers led 12-10.

That 6-8 team of 1969 was followed by a "6-7*" team in 1970. The "*" came about from a pair of games, against Dartmouth and Yale, forfeited when Harvard players chose to respect the national strike organized in response to the war in Southeast Asia. With a 17-23-40 finish, John Ince completed his Harvard career with 142 points, 1 point shy of second place on the all-time Harvard list. Undoubtedly, he would have ranked second to Grady Watts had those two Ivy games been played.

In 1971 both the strike and John Ince were history. Harvard lacrosse turned to new leaders like Charlie Kittredge, the defender, and Phil Zuckerman, the scorer. Perhaps the driving force behind this team was captain and midfielder Rick Frisbie.

Frisbie led the squad to an 8-3 overall record, 4-2 among the Ivies. Those results included a fourth straight win over Princeton. Unfortunately, Princeton was no longer the team to beat. And those results also included the second of ten straight losses to Cornell, the new team to beat.

The Big Red, like the rest of the Ivies, had grown tired of the Princeton dynasty of the 1960s. But unlike the others, Cornell went out and did something about it. Under the leadership of Coach Ned Harkness, and later Richie Moran, Cornell reached a new level of dominance. A 1-5 last-place finisher in 1965, Cornell rebounded with a 6-0 championship season in 1966. After finishing second to Princeton in 1967, Cornell proceeded to win or share the Ivy crown every year but one (1973) through 1983.

Cornell became the standard for Harvard to reach. Behind the Big Red's success was the wizardry of Harkness, coach of national champions in both lacrosse and ice hockey at Cornell. Of all his contributions to lacrosse, perhaps the most influential was the introduction of systematic recruiting to the sport.

It was apparent by the early 1970s that Harvard could not challenge the top lacrosse powers with the regular stream of prep school players who traditionally were the majority of the Harvard roster. The best prep players were very good. But they were not enough.

A quick look at the peak years of Harvard lacrosse revealed teams led by players from the lacrosse breeding grounds of Maryland and Long Island. As competing schools stepped up their recruiting pace in the 1970s, Harvard paid a price.

Munro's final three years at Harvard were 3-8, 3-10, and 3-7 seasons. The major reason for the disappointing records: The Harvard talent, particularly in terms of depth, was no match for the opposition.

Those final campaigns, after such a successful tenure, nearly cost Bruce Munro a winning career record. With three games to go in the 1974 season, Munro's last, his career mark stood at 171-169-7. But his troops came through with two wins in those last games to keep the coach on top.

When Harvard ended a 43-year drought against Princeton, it was John Ince's overtime goal that beat the Tigers in 1968. Ivy scoring champ that year as a sophomore, Ince was first-team All-Ivy in each of his three varsity seasons.

Bruce Munro's record at Harvard was not simply one of longevity. Through 26 seasons, Munro battled shifting departmental support off the field and, quite often, superior enemy personnel on the field. Still, he put the program on firm ground, was named the best coach in the country in 1962, and won a piece of the Ivy League title in 1964, the first of only two such finishes since 1955, when league play began, to the present.

Perhaps the best statement on Munro's reputation was the establishment of the J. Bruce Munro Award in 1976. This honor, instituted by the New England Lacrosse Club, is bestowed annually on the top intercollegiate lacrosse player in the Greater Boston area. It is a fitting tribute to someone who has done so much for the game.

• • •

1975–80: To face the challenges of modern college lacrosse, Harvard turned to a product of the new game. Bob Scalise, a three-time All-Ivy and two-time All-American selection at Brown, became head coach in 1975, just four years after his graduation in Providence.

Scalise knew a little bit about the specific problem at hand: battling the Big Red. In his playing days, Scalise's teams tied Cornell once (1969) and finished second by a game twice (1970–71). After graduation, Scalise assisted veteran Brown coach Cliff Stevenson and helped the Bruins finally wrest the title away from the Big Red in 1973.

But to change the direction of Harvard lacrosse was going to take some time. In 1975 Scalise's first team won just 2 of its first 11 games. But when the season ended with 2 wins, there was a sense of accomplishment and optimism. Even the biggest optimist could not have expected what followed in 1976.

Scalise remembers the turning point. "It was the Princeton game. For the first time since the new teams to

The one-two punch in 1978's 10-4 season: Mike Faught (top left), whose 58 goals tied Dexter Lewis's 23-year-old record, and Steve Martin (12 below), who won the 1978 Bingham Award as Harvard's top male athlete.

beat had established themselves, we won a tough, close game that by most standards we should have lost. We beat them 11-10 and started to believe that we belonged with the best."

The team finished with a 10-5 mark, three losses coming at the hands of teams ranked in the top eight nationally (Brown, Cornell, and Massachusetts). Captain Kevin McCall was the inspirational leader of this club. A midfielder from Connecticut, home of gunners Chico MacKenzie and Mike Faught as well, McCall had seen the lean years and enjoyed this success as much as anyone.

Beyond that Connecticut trio, Harvard's roster was starting to show the effects of greater penetration into traditional lacrosse breeding grounds. There were Jim Michaelson, Bill Forbush, and Bill Tennis from Baltimore, Hank Leopold from upstate New York, and Steve Martin from Long Island.

The final record for 1977 read 4-8. But no one panicked. Those in the know saw what was to come. And that was a pair of 10-4 seasons that paved the way for the championship season of 1980.

The first of the 10-4 years belonged to the dynamic duo of Steve Martin and Mike Faught. Martin was the all-purpose attack man whose 30-45-75 season led Harvard in scoring. Faught was the scoring machine whose 58 goals tied Dexter Lewis's 23-year-old record.

When the Ivy season was launched with a 17-4 upset of then eighth-ranked Penn at Franklin Field, Harvard was immediately taken seriously. A few more people stood up and took notice when Harvard won games by scores of 27-2, 23-5, 29-3, and 23-7.

But two scores went the other way and left the team a little less than satisfied. Cornell's 18-10 victory was Harvard's only Ivy loss of the season, and a 12-11 heartbreaker to Massachusetts gave the Minutemen bragging rights for New England.

Still, when it was all over, Harvard had its best record in more than a decade and had definitely turned the corner. Perhaps the most significant event of the year took place when all the games had been completed. At the June awards dinner, senior Steve Martin became only the second lacrosse player ever to win the Bingham Award (Lanny Keyes '60, also a soccer standout, was the first). The significance of this honor was not lost on those who recalled how Harvard lacrosse nearly died less than 20 years earlier.

While the impressive numbers run up by Martin and Faught had captured the headlines in 1978, Coach Scalise

knew where an equal amount of credit belonged: back with the defense.

"What Haywood Miller and Frank Prezioso did on defense was every bit as important as our guys up front, maybe more so," said Scalise. Also important was the fact that Miller, from Annapolis, and Prezioso, from Uniondale, New York, represented the type of player that Harvard had to get to compete with the best.

The 1979 season was almost a carbon copy of 1978. The team again finished 10-4 overall, 4-2 in the Ivy League, tied for second with both Dartmouth and Princeton, a game behind Cornell. Faught had another banner year on the attack, scoring 49 goals and completing his career with 123 goals, 9 shy of the Harvard record.

Also making his mark in 1979 was midfielder Peter Predun, perhaps the best all-around player on the squad. As a sophomore in 1978, he found his efforts dwarfed by the offensive show put on by Martin and Faught. In 1979 a broken thumb hampered his results, yet he still made All-Ivy along with Faught and Miller. The spotlight would be his in 1980.

The year began with some questions. Sure, Predun was back. And defensive anchors Miller and Prezioso were ready for their third trip around. But who would replace goalie Ken First? Would a gunner emerge to take Faught's role up front?

The questions were still unanswered after a 13-3 opening-game loss to Johns Hopkins. An 8-7 win over Delaware followed, and things started to look a little brighter. Then came Cornell, and all the questions were answered.

On a cold afternoon in late March, the type of day all too common for spring sports in New England, the 1980 Harvard lacrosse team did something that no Harvard team in the 1970s could do. It beat Cornell.

Trailing 7-4 midway through the game, the Crimson saw the afternoon, the season, and maybe the program turn around. Harvard scored the next eight goals en route to a 12-8 upset of the defending league champs. It was Harvard's first win over the Big Red in 11 years and launched what was arguably the Crimson's best season ever.

The defense lived up to all expectations and got unexpected help from senior goaltender John Lechner, a first-year starter whose 24-save effort against Cornell was the first of many brilliant games. There would be no single big gun up front but a shared attack instead. Impressive

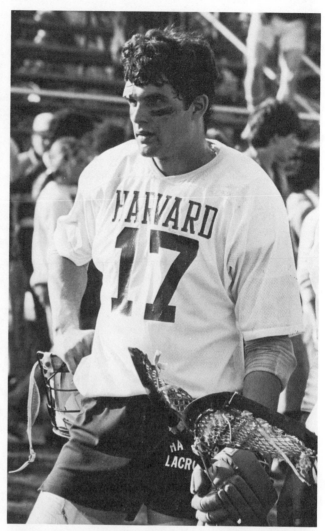

Key players in Harvard's 1980 Ivy title were these All-Ivy performers: goalie John Lechner (top left), whose 24-save effort beat Ivy power Cornell; defenseman Haywood Miller (top right), cited by Coach Bob Scalise as a key to the team's success; and midfielder Peter Predun (bottom right), the school's top male athlete that year.

freshmen like Brendan Meagher joined veterans like Predun to pace the offense.

When it was over, the Crimson were 11-3 overall, 5-1 in the league. All that was good for Harvard's second shared Ivy title and its first ever berth in the NCAA postseason tournament. Only a 9-8 loss to Princeton kept the team from its first outright league title. The third loss came when seventh-ranked Harvard faced second-ranked Johns Hopkins in the NCAAs. Even in defeat, an evenly fought 16-12 decision, did Harvard show how far it had come from its one-sided opening-day loss.

Predun, like Steve Martin two years earlier, made the lacrosse program proud by winning the Bingham Award, along with squash star Mike Desaulniers.

1981–84: The success forged by the 1978–80 teams, 31-11 over three years, could not be maintained. A roller coaster pattern returned over the next five seasons, as Harvard alternated between winning and losing records.

"That 1982 season was one of my most satisfying," said Scalise. "It was a real team effort following a rough year and two bad losses at the start of the year."

That team won 9 of its last 11 games and earned a more than respectable 12th place in the national rankings.

Each team had its heroes. There was the steadiness of Gary Pedroni and Norm Forbush, the big day from Brendan Meagher or Steve Bartenfelder, and the goaltending of Tim Pendergast and Mike Bergman.

Pendergast played the first three of these seasons and ultimately earned All-American mention. His departure at the end of the 1983 season was supposed to mean big trouble for Harvard. But Bergman came along and was named the Ivies' top rookie for his performance in 1984.

Although lacking the one superstar, these teams had as many solid players as any period in Harvard lacrosse history. But the game was growing fast, and the competition was never better.

The future of lacrosse in the Ivy League may turn on a new factor: artificial playing fields. Harvard players, under both Bruce Munro and Bob Scalise, have been known to shovel snow off the tennis courts to have a place to practice in the New England spring. The teams with artificial surfaces have eliminated this problem and get outside earlier.

Scalise has identified this development as a key to the new powers of Ivy lacrosse. "Cornell's rule was brought to a close by Pennsylvania in 1984 after both tied in 1983. Finishing second both years was Brown. What they all have

in common is an artificial playing field that allows them to get out earlier for full-field practice."

Another change has taken place on the field, where greater specialization leads to more substitution in the game and a need for more players. No longer is a player simply a midfielder, for example. Now he is an offensive midfielder or a defensive midfielder.

What remains the same is that if you are among the Ivy League's best, you are among the nation's best. That is one constant linking today's college lacrosse with the game of the late 19th century. Bridging those decades are the men of Harvard. They were the first collegiate lacrosse power and they remain a competitor today.

Finding the Talent

There once was a time when a college lacrosse coach could turn to New England prep schools for the talent that would make him a winner. For the top programs, Harvard's included, those days are over.

"The best players coming out of prep schools in the eighties are still good players and they'll make their contribution," says Harvard coach Bob Scalise. "But those players alone won't make you competitive in the Ivy League or nationally. You've got to draw from those few pockets where lacrosse is the major sport."

For the record, those pockets are the areas around Baltimore, upstate New York, and Long Island. And, not coincidentally, Harvard's best lacrosse teams over the years have been paced by individuals from these areas.

From 1960 to 1962 Grady Watts established scoring records that still stand. He learned his lacrosse in Manhasset, New York, on Long Island. When Harvard first won a piece of the Ivy title in 1964, Towson, Maryland's Tink Gunnoe was the heart of the team.

In 1968 Harvard beat Princeton for the first time in 43 years. The win was forged by Marty Cain, Bruce Regan, and Jim Kilkowski, all Baltimore natives, and John Ince of Garden City, New York.

When Harvard lacrosse reached new heights in the period from 1978 to 1980, the Maryland-New York influence peaked. Bingham Award winners

Steve Martin (1978) and Peter Predun (1980) hailed from Bethpage and Greenlawn, New York, respectively. The four leading scorers in 1980, apart from Predun, were Norm Forbush, Brendan Meagher, Gary Pedroni, and Mike Davis. All of them were from the Baltimore area.

"Lacrosse is a lot like ice hockey in that a few distinct regions of the country produce almost all the talent," says Scalise. "But in hockey the local area, Greater Boston high schools and New England prep schools, produces the best players in the country. The local area is not as good to lacrosse."

And so the recruiting wars are that much tougher for lacrosse coaches. But what makes these areas so different?

"To the kid coming out of those areas, lacrosse is his main sport. Not football, not baseball, but lacrosse," says Scalise. "He is not concentrating on other sports first or perhaps at all."

What also distinguishes lacrosse from other sports is that its participation pattern is inverted from so many other sports. Baseball has its Little League. Football has Pop Warner Football. Hockey has youth programs from age seven or even younger. Youth lacrosse programs are rare.

Norm Forbush (21), who followed his brother Bill to the Harvard lacrosse program, was one of many talented players to come out of the Baltimore area.

"It is like an inverted pyramid. The largest group of players is at the older ages, colleges and clubs. The fewest people play at the youngest ages," says Scalise. And this limits the amount of information available on recruits.

"Since most of our potential players take up the game late, we really have just one year to judge them on, their junior year in high school. Before that, they are just learning fundamentals. As seniors, their fates have already been decided."

Harvard has attracted more and more of these players in recent years. An upgraded schedule, improved facilities, and the institution of fall lacrosse practice has made the program more attractive to the blue-chip prospect.

"Harvard has made a real commitment to excellence," says Scalise. "The young players understand this, and we've enjoyed the results over the past decade."

• • •

Bob Scalise, a former All-Ivy player at Brown, succeeded Bruce Munro as head coach of lacrosse. He won Ivy titles as both men's lacrosse and women's soccer coach at Harvard.

WOMEN'S LACROSSE: STAYING AT THE TOP

The first decade of women's athletics at Harvard was one of steady growth, punctuated by a handful of exceptional teams that stepped up the pace of progress. First it was a national championship in rowing in the early 1970s. Then it was Ivy domination in soccer in the late 1970s. Then, in perhaps the most convincing fashion, came the championship lacrosse teams of the 1980s.

Lacrosse for Harvard women dates back to the spring of 1975. The early teams played basically a Greater Boston and Ivy League schedule, winning against the former and struggling with the latter. Results ran from a low of 1-10 to a high of 9-2-2 in the first five years. The common denominator: trouble with Ivy rivals.

What would be a rather stunning turnabout began in 1979. Carole Kleinfelder, coach of the U.S. national

lacrosse team in 1978 and already Harvard's women's basketball coach, became the school's new lacrosse coach. At the same time, Harvard lacrosse received a new agenda.

"When you want to build a program, you must find out who the good teams are in your sport and schedule them," said Kleinfelder. "That first spring trip was a key to what followed."

The spring trip of 1979, to the Philadelphia area, was the first for women's lacrosse, and it brought Harvard face to face with the good teams of the sport, such as Ursinus and West Chester State, Kleinfelder's alma mater.

These were national powers from Pennsylvania, where women's sports had an established tradition in terms of years and quality. Replacing a Wellesley, whom Harvard had played four years earlier, with a West Chester was the equivalent of a men's basketball team dropping Bentley in favor of Georgetown.

That Ursinus and West Chester won those games by 14-2 and 15-5 scores was not important. Their presence on the schedule sent a message that the Harvard lacrosse program was heading in a certain direction. That Harvard would play those teams again in postseason play-offs, losing by 13-11 and 6-4, showed how quickly Kleinfelder was bringing the team along.

Another step toward the top came in 1980, when Harvard tied Yale, a team that would eventually share the league title. "I remember Sarah [Mleczko] saying after that game. 'Why can't we beat them?' But I knew we were just about there."

For Mleczko and 1980 captains Stefi Baum and Julie Cornman, the program would get "there" one year late. They were the first wave and had established the foundation for the Ivy titles that followed. Mleczko set all the offensive standards, Baum was the defender. And Cornman, one of the team's few experienced lacrosse players from the Philadelphia area, provided inspiration. Battling injuries throughout her field hockey and lacrosse careers, she became the first female recipient of Harvard's John P. Fadden Award, given each year to an athlete who overcomes physical adversity.

In 1981 everything came together. It was a matter of the second and third waves hitting the opposition at the same time. The second wave was the class of 1981, led by Chris Sailer and Ann Velie, the cocaptains. The third wave consisted of a pair of sophomores up front who put on an offensive show that may never be equaled.

Francesca DenHartog and Maureen Finn were the dominant lacrosse players in the Ivy League from 1981 to

1983. There was DenHartog, out of nearby Weston High School, scoring goals at a record pace and being named Ivy League Player of the Year two seasons in a row. And there was Finn, perhaps the more complete player, from Malvern, Pennsylvania, setting up DenHartog and eventually being the Ivy's top player as a senior.

"Maureen had an understanding of how to make Fran a scorer and in some respects had to swallow her pride a little bit," said Kleinfelder. "And we were also fortunate that we had the defensive players who could get the ball to them. What Sailer, Velie, and Jeanne Piersiak were able to accomplish can't be overlooked."

Together, they were able to bring three straight Ivy titles to Harvard, sharing 1982's honors with Pennsylvania. Beyond the Ivy success, Harvard established a name for itself nationally. That 1981 season saw Harvard take a 17-0 record into postseason play, losing two of three playoff games by 8-6 to Temple and 5-3 to eventual national champ Maryland.

"We left that tournament knowing we had something going," said the coach. "And we kind of said, 'Let's hold on to it.'"

At season's end the program received more visibility when cocaptains Chris Sailer and Ann Velie were honored. Sailer was selected as the school's top female athlete, while Velie was named to the U.S. national squad.

By the time DenHartog and Finn were graduated in 1983, the two All-Americans had piled up some astounding offensive numbers. Scorer DenHartog finished at 249-66-315; partner Finn was 190-124-314.

The athletes were piling up the points and getting the job done on the field. But the central figure in this success story remained Carole Kleinfelder. Her extensive background in the sport gave her an edge. She knew how to line up the opposing teams needed to upgrade the schedule. She could locate the talent, like a DenHartog or a Finn.

"We got a jump on the others and it was fairly easy because I was in the network. I knew how to get those games. I knew where the talent was. And lacrosse wasn't like basketball, where Division I schools were offering scholarships to the best players. We didn't have to deal with that problem."

Two players who led Harvard to three straight Ivy lacrosse titles from 1981 to 1983: three-time All-Ivy and 1983 player of the year Maureen Finn (top right) and four-time All-Ivy and 1981 and 1982 player of the year Francesca DenHartog (bottom). Both were first-team All-American performers.

Kleinfelder felt that timing had a lot to do with Harvard's success. And this may well be true. But someone had to take advantage of the situation, and she did just that. No small part of her success has been her ability to develop players who had never played the game before. Experienced players like DenHartog and Finn were exceptions.

In 1984, when Harvard won its fourth straight Ivy title, all but four players learned their lacrosse while at Harvard. One of these newcomers, senior Maggie Hart, became Ivy League Player of the Year and an All-American.

"She was an excellent athlete who became an excellent lacrosse player," Kleinfelder said of Hart, whose older sister Ellen had been a soccer and track standout at Harvard four years earlier.

And that's the way the coach wanted it. She put considerable effort into finding those good athletes on campus and enjoyed a stream of two-sport players, particularly soccer players, who came out for lacrosse in the spring.

"I know we can make lacrosse players out of the right type of kid, the good athlete. It used to be the field hockey player. Now it's the soccer player, like Jenny Greeley (Ivy Player of the Year in 1985), Alicia Carillo, and Jeanne Piersiak. That sport is producing some of the best athletes."

The arrival of former U.S. national team coach Carole Kleinfelder lifted Harvard to the top of the Ivy League lacrosse standings.

The other ingredient provided by the coach was very simple. She was demanding. Not simply demanding of her athletes but, more significantly, of the athletic department. If equipment was second-rate or a field wasn't properly lined or practice times were unsatisfactory, she spoke up. She wanted reasons. She wanted results.

This unbending approach did not always win friends. But it was no small part of Harvard lacrosse's becoming a first-class program almost overnight. Now Harvard was one of those teams you wanted on your schedule, to make it more attractive. That's what had happened since 1979. Six years later, the coach could see it.

"When I talk to young athletes now and say 'Harvard lacrosse,' they react," she said. "They know all about us."

FIELD HOCKEY: MISS APPLEBEE'S GIFT TO RADCLIFFE AND AMERICA

The record books say that Harvard women's field hockey began in the fall of 1974. But if you look elsewhere, you'll find that the game of field hockey was introduced not only to Radcliffe College but to America in 1901.

That was the year that Constance Applebee, a young student from Devonshire, England, came to study with Dr. Dudley Sargent. Professor Sargent was the director of Harvard's Hemenway Gymnasium and a true friend to the women who wished to participate in athletic activities.

At that time, women were hardly encouraged to take up athletics, particularly team sports, while studying in college. It was into this climate that Miss Applebee arrived.

While sitting in on a discussion of women's exercises, she heard mention of such activities as musical chairs and drop the handkerchief. To this, Miss Applebee responded with, "We play those games at parties. For exercise, we play hockey."

And so, on a hot August afternoon outside the Radcliffe Gymnasium, Constance Applebee gathered a collection of improvised equipment—men's ice hockey sticks, brooms, and a white-painted baseball—and demonstrated to her hosts what field hockey was all about.

At a time when women's games were limited to croquet or a mild game of lawn tennis, field hockey seemed quite revolutionary. It was the first game to demand stamina, coordination, and team effort for women. Not surprisingly, the game met early opposition. But thanks to Constance

Applebee and others, it survived the critics and became popular throughout the country.

When Harvard assumed control of Radcliffe women's athletics in 1974, field hockey was one of a handful of sports that had prospered at Radcliffe for decades. The 1974 field hockey team retained vestiges of the old days. The schedule included the likes of Pine Manor, Wellesley, and Wheaton, teams that would soon be dropped in favor of a more complete Ivy and stronger New England flavor.

That 1974 team compiled a 1-10-2 record, the only victory coming against Pine Manor. With the 1975 hiring of Debi Field, a former college performer of U.S. national team caliber, the program took its first step toward greater legitimacy. But the process would take time.

In 1975 the team was only 2-10-3. Field had to juggle people around in the lineup, for instance moving one of her best athletes, Carlene Rhodes, from forward to goaltender. The move was made possible by the play of Karen Linsley up front. Linsley, one of the school's best athletes in this pioneering period, was the top scorer on this team and earned All–New England status.

Field took little time in turning things around. That first year was her only losing season, as she produced three winning teams before leaving Cambridge at the close of the 1978 season. The best of these was the 1976 team, which went 11-1-2 and featured a blend of strong athletes from all four classes.

Seniors such as Linsley and Ann Dupuis enjoyed the

More than 70 years before the Harvard field hockey team competed for Ivy League honors, a group of Radcliffe students were among the first women in the country to learn the game. They were taught by Constance Applebee, who introduced it to the U.S. during a visit from Great Britain.

addition of younger players who were appearing on the scene with more experience than many of their contemporaries. Freshmen like Sarah Mleczko and Stefi Baum were keys to the offense and defense respectively. Mleczko, for example, scored 9 goals in her first 5 games. By contrast, it had taken the entire team 13 games to score 9 goals the year before.

Perhaps the real key defensively was goalie Ellen Seidler. Her 9 shutouts, 6 coming in a row, established a single-season mark that still stands. She would author 21 such games in all before graduating in 1979.

With Gwill York, Jenny Stone, and others lending their support, the team outscored the opposition 24-5. Of the three games that got away, two came against Ivy opponents, as Princeton prevailed 1-0 and Brown salvaged a 0-0 tie.

The inability to establish Ivy supremacy would haunt Field and her successor, Edie MacAusland Mabrey. In Field's final years, 7-4-4 and 8-4-1 teams, the record against Ivy opponents was 5-7-2. Mleczko continued her offensive heroics with 10 and 12 goals respectively, tying

LACROSSE AND FIELD HOCKEY

One of the early record-setters in field hockey was Sarah Mleczko '79 (above), who earned 11 letters in field hockey, squash, and lacrosse. Her field hockey marks were equaled by Kate Martin '83 (right, No. 25), three-time All-Ivy forward.

and breaking her original season mark. Despite passing up her senior year, she set a career mark of 32 goals.

Meanwhile, fresh talent had arrived on the scene. Players like Chris Sailer, Ann Velie, and Elaine Kellogg represented an improved, more experienced athlete arriving at the college level. The record books may omit many of these names because defense, not goal-scoring, was their strong suit.

The teams of 1977 and 1978 parlayed their winning records into playoff appearances at the tournament sponsored by the Eastern Association of Intercollegiate Athletics for Women. One of these had historical overtones, as Harvard hosted Yale at Harvard Stadium in 1977, the first women's athletic event staged in the 74-year-old landmark. However, Yale won, 2-0.

Another milestone occurred in 1978, when the squad,

ably led by captain Lucy Wood, enjoyed a preseason trip to England and Scotland. That represented a sizable jump from the days of playing Pine Manor.

Edie Mabrey's tenure began in 1979, and her early teams struggled to get past the .500 mark. With Sailer and Velie leading the way, the team defense was generally strong. Finding scoring help for Kate Martin, Mleczko's offensive successor, seemed to be the problem.

Sue Field served the role through 1980. And then came Jenny White, a likable multisport athlete who brought a special presence to ice hockey and lacrosse as well as field hockey. White joined Martin on the 1980 All-Ivy team, but it wasn't until the fall of 1982 that the pair proved to be a much more devastating one-two punch.

Things finally came together for Mabrey and Harvard that year, as the squad posted an 11-2-3 record and, with

Chris Sailer '81 earned three All-Ivy selections in field hockey and lacrosse and was named the top female athlete in the school in 1981.

great satisfaction, a 4-1-1 Ivy record. That left Harvard in second place behind undefeated Princeton, a team that nipped the Crimson, 1-0.

This was a tough defensive team as indicated by its Ivy statistics: In six league games, the team scored seven goals and allowed just one. Other than a 4-0 win over Cornell, all other league games featured one goal or less.

Goaltender Juliet Lamont tied Seidler's record of nine shutouts in a season. And the Martin-White tandem finished first and second in scoring, with White's 11 goals one shy of the record shared by Martin and Mleczko. All-American Kate Martin finished her career with a new Harvard standard of 33 career goals and became only the fifth player in Ivy League history to be named to the All-Ivy team three times. She was joined in 1982 by Harvard midfielder Lili Pew.

It is difficult to assess what the loss of Lili Pew to injury meant to the 1983 season. The team finished at 8-6-1 and again played well in the league. This could have been Harvard's first championship season, and it looked that way when eventual champ Penn was beaten early, 3-1.

But the 4-0 league record became 4-1-1 when the squad stumbled late at Brown (2-0) and at Yale (0-0). A victory against a weaker Yale team would have meant a share of the title with 5-1 Penn. But it was not to be.

All-Ivy status was conferred upon Beth Mullen, Andy Mainelli, and Ellen O'Neil in this near-miss effort.

If lack of offensive production had been a problem in the past, it took on new meaning in 1984. In each loss of a 5-10 season, Harvard failed to score a goal. Still, the season provided Mabrey's first win over perennial power Massachusetts and featured the fine play of Bambi Taylor, injured early when the team went into a tailspin that it never seemed to shake.

There will come a day, possibly in the near future, when Harvard does enjoy its first Ivy field hockey championship. When the champagne pours that day, a glass should be raised to the Linsleys and Seidlers and Martins who set the stage. And let's hope one glass will be for Constance Applebee as well. She made it possible for everyone.

CHAPTER 11

Squash and Tennis

When asked to consider greatness in Harvard athletics, the average sports fan might be forgiven if he recalls a particular football game at the Stadium or a Beanpot hockey moment. Thousands of people see those events annually.

But if that fan is asked which of Harvard's athletic programs has been the most consistently successful and dominant in its sport, he might be stumped.

Since 1922 one sport at Harvard has compiled a record of 523-129-2 and has earned 27 national championships. And all of this has come under just three coaches. This well-kept secret is the unique success story of Harvard squash.

Millions of people play racquet sports in this country, but relatively few have access to squash courts. So it is understandable that public knowledge of the game in general and of one program in particular is limited.

But anyone who has ever played squash or tennis or racquetball can appreciate what has happened at Harvard since Harry Cowles started this success story back in

1922. It is arguably the most consistently successful program in the history of college athletics.

There was a time when the heroes of squash and tennis were the same, at Harvard and elsewhere. Those days have been replaced by a world of specialization, in which the very best choose one sport or the other at an early age. What follows is a look at both worlds.

MEN'S SQUASH:
A UNIQUE SUCCESS STORY

1922–37: To play squash you need squash courts. And from the beginning, Harvard has been blessed with facilities of quality and quantity. At its peak, in 1937, Harvard had 71 squash courts on campus, nearly three times the number of any other institution in the world.

From 1922 to 1937 Harry Cowles was Harvard's squash and tennis coach. A peerless teacher in his day, Cowles led his teams to five national squash titles and coached 13 individual champions.

In the first half of the 20th century, competitive squash, as a rule, was found in amateur clubs, not at universities. Until 1937 Harvard's only intercollegiate opponents were Yale and Princeton. Gradually, other colleges in the Northeast took up the game, and Harvard was able to make the transition to a full college schedule.

The story of Harvard squash can be neatly divided into three parts, one for each of its three coaches. Harry Cowles served from 1922 to 1937. He was followed by one of his former players, Jack Barnaby '32, who served for 36 seasons before being replaced by one of his former players, Dave Fish, in 1976. All three coached both squash and tennis.

Under Cowles, Harvard squash teams compiled a record of 100-27-2, won five national team titles, and produced 13 national individual champions. The national team titles won under Cowles, and later Barnaby, were the only national titles ever won by a college team until Yale earned the 1959 title. (All the others were won by amateur clubs.)

Cowles was a man of unbending character. As Barnaby described him. "He stood very straight, he had a

penetrating blue eye, and an uncompromising sense of right and wrong which admitted to no gray areas. If something was at all gray, then it was pure black to Harry."

As a coach, Cowles was an innovator for his time. He brought intelligence and touch to a game that had been dominated by power. Yet, among the best of Cowles' pupils, there was no particular type. He let each player develop his own strengths.

There was W. Palmer Dixon '25, national champion in 1925 and 1926, who was the master of positioning on the

W. Palmer Dixon '25 was national squash champion in 1925 and again in 1926. One of the most generous benefactors to racquet sports at Harvard, Dixon made possible Harvard's first indoor tennis center, the Palmer Dixon Courts at Soldiers Field.

court. There was Herbert Rawlins '27, who won in 1928 and again in 1930. His trademark was his deft touch. There were the Pool brothers, Lawrence '28 and Beekman '32, and Myles Baker '22, who won four titles between them as power players. And there was Germain Glidden '36, possibly the best of all of them, whose gifts of speed and anticipation earned three titles from 1936 to 1938.

"His champions were never 'molded,' they grew," said Barnaby. "There was rather that uncanny understanding of the pupil coupled with an imagination that enabled Cowles to envision this particular person, in his own particular way, playing championship squash."

Another Cowles gift to Harvard and the game of squash was a strict code of ethics. Harvard teams have been known as much for their sportsmanship as their talent through the years.

"Harry believed that you should never want any point that your opponent didn't think you should have," said Barnaby. "And when he played the game, he lived this creed. You could play him for hours and he would never once get in your way."

1938–75: In 36 seasons as head coach of Harvard squash, Jack Barnaby ran up a 355-95 record and produced 20 national team champions and nearly as many individual titlists. His program struggled just once, immediately following World War II, and then returned to the top, where he remained for most of his career.

Barnaby's philosophy on the coach's role is defined by two comments he made while writing the squash and tennis chapters in *The Second H Book of Harvard Athletics.* He said, "There is no such thing as poor material. There is green and ignorant material," and, "Boys will fight like mad and go an incredible distance if they are properly led."

Once the Harvard machine got in gear, Barnaby by his own admission rarely had "green and ignorant material." When he didn't, and even when he did, he usually took the teams that "incredible distance."

The postwar rebuilding of Harvard squash was completed with the undefeated national champion team of 1951. The championship final was an all-Harvard affair, with senior Henry Foster defeating sophomore Charlie Ufford.

The grandson of a former football letterwinner, Charles H. W. Foster '81, Henry Foster followed brothers Rockwood and Hugh as Harvard captain and No. 1 racquetman. Their contributions to the program recalled

the Glidden brothers of the 1930s and 1940s, Germain, Nathaniel, and John. This all-in-the-family routine was hardly unique in Harvard sports. And the pattern continued through the 1980s, when Montreal's Desaulniers brothers—Mike and Brad—played championship squash for Coach Dave Fish.

Though 6-foot 5-inch Charley Ufford lost that 1951 national final, he twice won national intercollegiate titles, as did Ben Heckscher. Heckscher followed his intercollegiate titles of 1956 and 1957 with national individual titles in 1959 and 1963. As more schools developed squash programs, the intercollegiate championships replaced the nationals as the primary goal of the undergraduate squash player.

Barnaby could take pride in the fact that many of his great players were also outstanding students. Ufford, winner of the Burr Scholarship as top scholar-athlete in 1953, passed up a legitimate shot at a national title to complete his thesis. Another intercollegiate champ, Vic Niederhoffer in 1964, actually won his title while shuttling back and forth from his hotel room, where he completed his thesis.

Niederhoffer, one of the greatest thinking players the game has seen, was a source of tremendous pride for Barnaby. When he arrived at Harvard in 1960 he had never played a single game of squash, and by the time he was a senior, he was the intercollegiate champion.

At the conclusion of the 1964–65 season, Harvard had

Though he had never played a single game of squash before coming to Harvard, Vic Niederhoffer was intercollegiate champ as a senior in 1964.

No one had ever won three straight intercollegiate titles until Anil Nayar did from 1967 to 1969. No one has done so since.

put together four straight undefeated campaigns and captured four straight intercollegiate team championships. The win streak went to 47 matches before Princeton snapped the string in 1966. Still, Harvard took another team title that year as well.

An unprecedented individual streak began in 1966–67, when a sophomore from Bombay, India, won the first of three consecutive individual titles. By the time Anil Nayar was a senior, he gave his sport tremendous visibility as the first squash player to win the Bingham Award as the school's best athlete.

"He was the smoothest, most fluid player ever on the court," said Barnaby. "The first time I saw him play, I said, 'national champion.' And a few years later, he was."

With the 1969–70 season, a new format was introduced for championship play that divided the competition into A, B, and C divisions. Harvard's strength was reflected in the fact that it won all three divisions, placing five men among the six finalists.

Larry Terrell's win in the A Division gave Harvard its fourth straight individual titlist, and left-hander Peter Briggs's back-to-back titles in 1972 and 1973 brought the record to six individual championships in seven years.

How dominant was Harvard in the 1960s and early 1970s? From December 2, 1961, through the 1972–73 season, Barnaby's teams were 120-3, winning 11 team championships in 12 years.

By 1974 another lengthy undefeated streak had been fashioned. This time it was 49 match victories in a row, and again Princeton brought the Crimson down to earth. The Tigers would remain Harvard's chief rival through the decade and into the next.

1976–85: Dave Fish followed a familiar path. After playing both squash and tennis for Jack Barnaby, Fish served as assistant coach for five seasons. In the fall of 1976, the fate of those two programs was placed in his hands.

Through his first three seasons, Fish experienced success but not Harvard success. That is, he compiled a 24-5 record and produced a two-time individual champ in Mike Desaulniers. But in each of those seasons, the national team title went to Princeton.

Nobody said it would be easy following a legend. But the young coach took a big step in carving out his own niche in Harvard squash history with the happenings of the 1979–80 season. Harvard and Princeton had swapped roles. This time it was Princeton with the gaudy win streak and Harvard out to turn the tide. And that's exactly what happened.

It was the last time around for the remarkable Desaulniers, the senior from Montreal who had never been beaten in three years of competition. For all the great players who had preceded him, Mike Desaulniers was being called the greatest.

"He was the most exciting player ever," said Coach Fish. "He used the whole court and kept attacking his opponents relentlessly."

Watching Desaulniers play, one was first drawn to his incredible quickness. But his game was so complete that to attempt to characterize it by a single attribute was an injustice.

It is not surprising that when Princeton came to Hemenway Gymnasium, the tiny gallery was packed to see if the old power could dethrone the new. The Tigers, who had twice stopped Harvard streaks of better than 40 wins in earlier decades, came to town having won 43 in a row.

The match lived up to all expectations and was ultimately decided at the No. 4 position, where Harvard's Chip Robie battled Princeton's Jason Fish (no relation) through a 12-15, 15-11, 15-6, 15-16, 15-13 marathon. In

The major reason that Harvard was the country's best squash team in 1983 and 1985: Kenton Jernigan, individual titlist both years.

the end, Harvard won 5-4 and went on to Coach Fish's first national nine-man title.

During the next two seasons, Harvard was unable to hold on to its nine-man title but captured the six-man championships for the first time in ten years. The second of these six-man titles was paced by the play of freshman David Boyum in 1982.

With the arrival of Kenton Jernigan for the 1982–83 season, Fish had his next superstar and the catalyst for new championships.

"Kenton had the physical skills of Desaulniers with even greater power," according to Fish. "In fact, he possessed so much talent that his only weakness was his ability to harness that talent. That's the only thing that kept him from reaching a Desaulniers' status."

In Boyum, Fish had perhaps the best No. 2 player in Harvard history.

"He had the most accomplished squash mind since Niederhoffer," said the coach. "Were it not for the presence of Jernigan, he would easily have been the top name in intercollegiate squash."

In 1983 and 1985, the Jernigan-Boyum combination led Harvard to a sweep of all major titles: six-man and nine-man intercollegiates and five-man nationals. This last title was particularly rewarding, as it marked the first time that a competing Mexico squad was defeated for top honors.

Mike Desaulniers

It was a brief discussion between two men who knew a little bit about squash. Germain Glidden '36, a former national champion known for incredible quickness, asked Jack Barnaby '32, former champion coach, what this kid Desaulniers was like.

The coach responded: "He plays more like Glidden than Glidden."

That was one man's tribute to this unique talent from Montreal who set new standards in the game of squash. Mike Desaulniers was one of a kind.

"Michael dealt with tempo but in a way that no one else had ever done. To him a change of pace was to go from fast to faster, and when he did that, no one could keep up with him."

Only an injured foot kept Mike Desaulniers '80 from becoming the first four-time intercollegiate squash champion. Desaulniers, who became a successful professional after Harvard, won his intercollegiate titles as a freshman, sophomore, and senior.

That was how his coach, Dave Fish, saw him. When Desaulniers arrived at Harvard in the fall of 1976, Fish was Harvard's 25-year-old rookie head coach. He had been 10-0 as a junior for one of Jack Barnaby's intercollegiate championship teams and captain of another. He had seen the best of the modern talents, and then he met Desaulniers.

"He was so quick and incredibly precise. He had this kind of telescoping last step, always enabling him to get to the ball."

Desaulniers would have been the first player to win four straight intercollegiate titles had a foot injury not sidelined him at the end of his junior year. Still, this young man, who won the Canadian, U.S. and intercollegiate titles as a freshman without losing a single game, graduated without ever losing an intercollegiate match.

After leaving Harvard Desaulniers tackled both the professional squash circuit and the New York Stock Exchange, working for another Harvard champion, Vic Niederhoffer '64. Despite the pressures that accompanied that 40-hour week and the injuries that plagued the postgraduate athlete, Desaulniers was able to make his mark among the pros. A year after leaving college, he was simply the No. 1 squash player in the world.

• • •

WOMEN'S SQUASH: CONTINUING THOSE WINNING WAYS

The winning tradition of squash teams at Harvard has been continued by the women. Since the first squad went 7-7 back in 1974–75, the program has never suffered a losing season. The struggle has been to reach the top.

Under coaches Eric Cutler (a Harvard Hall of Fame swimmer) and Paul Moses, the program enjoyed four strong seasons, with records running from 8-4 to 11-2. Players like Julia Moore, Jenny Stone, Becky Tung, and Sarah Mleczko found success just about every time out.

The "just about" was the doing of Princeton and Yale, whose success kept Harvard from earning championship status. The championship they all coveted was the annual Howe Cup competition, which always seemed to escape the Harvards.

In 1979 Harvard decided to play hard ball. The cavalry

was summoned in the form of Jack Barnaby, who returned to Harvard three years after stepping down as coach of the men's program.

The result was not terribly surprising. In 1982, in his third season with the women, Barnaby and Harvard won the Howe Cup. Another addition to the program, freshman Mary Hulbert, keyed the victory.

"Mary was really the first superstar in the program," said Priscilla Choate, Barnaby's assistant, who took over the program following that Howe Cup win. "Before her, Harvard had plenty of athletes of lesser skills who did an extraordinary job in getting the most out of their ability."

Choate's first two teams were successful, 5-2 and 7-0, but were unable to retain the Howe Cup title. Finally, in 1985, everything came together again. It was a deep squad with four All-Ivy performers: Hulbert, Diana Staley, Ingrid Boyum (sister of men's team star David), and Diana Edge.

Still, beyond the depth, the key to the victory, as she

Three years of promise paid off with an individual title for Mary Hulbert in 1985. Hulbert led Harvard squash teams to Howe Cup titles as a freshman and again as a senior.

had been in her freshman year, was senior Mary Hulbert.

"The only thing that delayed Mary's final success was her tremendous humility," observed Choate. "Our whole aim was to convince her that she was really that good a player. She didn't fully believe it for the longest time."

At the 1985 individual championships, everyone believed it. Seeded third, the 5-foot 11-inch Hulbert used her tremendous range and touch to knock off the first and second seeds in the semifinals and final respectively. The victories made her the indisputable champion of college squash. And she believed it at last.

MEN'S TENNIS: THE ONCE AND FUTURE POWER

1880–1922: The British may have given lawn tennis to America. But it was Harvard that gave American tennis its early leadership. The Harvard Lawn Tennis Association was formed in 1880, a year before the U.S. Lawn Tennis Association came into being. And the list of early national champions reads like a list of early Harvard tennis greats.

One of America's first influential tennis coaches was Dr. James Dwight '74 who, along with Richard Sears '83, won five national doubles titles. Sears, Dwight's pupil as well as partner, captured seven national singles titles.

In addition to these open national events, the intercollegiate championships were launched in 1883. As Jack Barnaby described the competition (won by Harvard's Joseph Clark '83), being first wasn't the only memorable feature of this event: "The first Intercollegiates were held at an insane asylum in Hartford. With delighted inmates functioning as unpredictable ball boys, this first tournament ranks among the more extraordinary in the history of tennis."

Harvard continued to produce national champions in both singles and doubles until the competition caught up with the Crimson in the 1920s. By 1921 the likes of Robert Wrenn '95, Malcolm Whitman '99, Dwight Davis '00, William Clothier '04, Norris Williams '16, and Colket Caner '17 had earned for Harvard 33 of a possible 80 titles—16 in singles and 17 in doubles.

Today's Davis Cup performers have these Harvard alumni to thank. The international competition grew from their efforts in 1899. From left: Dwight Davis, Beals Wright, George Wright, Holcombe Ward, and Malcolm Whitman.

Although Harvard's supremacy ended, Harvard's influence didn't. Dwight Davis' desire to foster international competition resulted in the formation of the Davis Cup competition, which still prospers today. In the beginning, it was simply Davis and teammates Whitman, Beals Wright, and Holcombe Ward successfully challenging a talented British team. Today, Davis Cup competition includes countries from throughout the world.

Another international competition began in 1921 when a combined Harvard-Yale team met a group from Oxford and Cambridge. Four years later, with a trophy donated by Bernon Prentice '05, this competition became known as the Prentice Cup, a trophy battled for every two years.

1923–36: While Harvard's national domination may have lapsed, the Crimson still prospered against the ever growing intercollegiate ranks. No small part of this success was the selection of Harry Cowles as tennis coach in 1923.

Before Cowles' appointment, there was no systematic coaching system for Harvard tennis players, and team selection was left to the team captain. Cowles introduced both expert teaching and a competitive "test match" system, which established a clear-cut way to rank team members.

As a result of Cowles' influence, Harvard teams in the 1920s and 1930s were virtually unbeatable, with the exception of a few Yale teams in the early seasons and an occasional stumble against the warm-weather teams to the south.

One of the Yale matches provided a memorable yet unusual meeting between Harvard's Richard Dorson and Yale's Howard Stevens in 1937. The score was 6-0, 6-0, in favor of Dorson over the Elis' No. 1 man. But the contest was hardly a breeze, as it took over two hours to complete. Though evenly matched, Dorson simply would not be denied that day and gained the upper hand.

Despite his victory, Dorson was snubbed when the top seed was announced for that summer's combined Harvard-Yale Prentice Cup team. When asked his opinion of the matter, Dorson replied, "Well, I guess I didn't beat him badly enough."

The New England weather proved to be the toughest opponent to Cowles and the coaches who followed him. The spring season in the Northeast was so short and the weather so unpredictable that it is remarkable that Cowles' players improved as much and as quickly as they did.

1937–75: When Jack Barnaby took over the tennis program in 1937, the primary opponents remained the earliest opponents, Yale and Princeton. The rivalry among these schools is underscored by Eastern Intercollegiate Tennis Association (Ivies plus Army and Navy) results kept since 1940. The top three records, in order, belong to Princeton, Harvard, and Yale.

Also belonging in the upper echelon is Pennsylvania. From 1950 to 1985, all but two league titles were won by these four schools.

Harvard did not win its first Eastern title until 1956, when it swept through its league schedule undefeated. It repeated that accomplishment two years later, and a key member of both squads, particularly 1958's, was captain Dale Junta.

"Junta was a big guy with a big strong serve," Barnaby recalled. "But what I remember most is how he would get everyone else so charged up."

Junta was instrumental in one of Harvard's most celebrated victories, a 6-3 upset of Yale at New Haven in 1958. The favored Elis squad was led by Donald Dell, later a Davis Cup player and today a successful attorney and

One of the best tennis players in the Barnaby era was 1958 captain Dale Junta.

agent for professional athletes. This was a deep Yale team whose No. 4 player, Gene Scott, qualified to play at Wimbledon.

But once the matches got under way, it was Harvard's day. Junta, trailing Dell 1-3 in the third set, won five straight games to win the match. Later, teaming with Larry Sears, Junta bested Dell in doubles. Another key to victory was Tim Gallwey's win over Yale's Gene Scott. (Gallwey would later author *The Inner Game of Tennis*.)

Junta was perhaps the best individual in the first half of Barnaby's 36-year tenure. But there was also Charlie Ufford '53, an all-around athlete who was a soccer All-American, national squash champ, and twice tennis captain. Another two-time captain was Paul Sullivan '63, New England champ in 1963. The biggest difference between these standouts was size: Ufford stood 6 feet 5 inches, Sullivan, 5 feet 8 inches.

Harvard won back-to-back EITA titles in 1965 and 1966 and then took three straight from 1968 to 1970. All but the 1966 title were shared.

These were the closing years of the period in which multisport stars were ranked on the tennis team. The squash-tennis double was a natural. But there were also gifted athletes like hockey All-American Joe Cavanagh, who was 12-0 playing No. 4 on the 1970 team. As tennis became open and professionals became millionaires, changes were felt in the college game.

"First came the better tennis players who chose to concentrate on that one game at an early age," said Dave Fish, No. 2 in both squash and tennis for Jack Barnaby before succeeding Barnaby as coach. "Then, as the good squash player who was a marginal tennis player realized he couldn't compete with these improving tennis players, we got specialization in squash."

From 1937 to 1976, Jack Barnaby won more than 700 squash and tennis matches at Harvard. No Harvard coach, in any other sport, ever came close to that figure.

Jack Barnaby

Of the 16-year Harry Cowles era, Jack Barnaby once observed, "There will never be another period like it." The pupil held great respect for his teacher. And then the pupil went out and did him one better.

The Barnaby era covered 36 seasons in which Harvard squash and tennis teams won more than 700 matches and close to 30 league or national titles. There was frequently—but not always—deep talent on those Harvard squads. But more than any- thing else, there was Barnaby the teacher, who got the most out of all his athletes.

Harry Cowles was generally conceded three major contributions to the game. He was an exacting technician, he let each player develop within his own limits, and he was a vocal advocate of fair play. Barnaby emulated Cowles and then went a step further.

"I consciously tried to imitate Harry," said Barnaby. "If I added anything new, I think it was that I was able to develop more players faster."

That Barnaby developed more players is evident from Harvard's perennial strength at the No. 7, No. 8, and No. 9 spots as well as at the top. The notion of developing players faster came from one particular Barnaby theory.

"Of all the skills, finesse takes the longest to learn. It is the most exacting technical job you've got as a player. Yet normally, those finer points

of touch were introduced late in a player's training. I felt that if it takes longer to learn, it should be introduced earlier. And as a result, we developed players fully by the start of their junior year as opposed to other places, where players didn't complete their game until the middle of their senior year."

And that became the hallmark of Barnaby's reputation: Players improved more and faster at Harvard than anywhere else. The importance of this was underscored by the fact that through the mid-1960s, half of the average squash team had never played the game before arriving at Harvard.

Two stories that Barnaby enjoyed telling reveal what the coach liked most about his days at Harvard. One involved the squash player who was struck with infantile paralysis before his sophomore year, leaving him without the use of his right hand. Approached by the youngster, Barnaby made a deal that he'd teach him to play left-handed if the boy agreed to a rigorous rehabilitation program beyond the normal practice hours.

The youngster, Gene Nickerson '41, was beaten by everyone as a sophomore, won a few matches at No. 9 as a junior, and was eventually playing No. 1 as a senior.

The other story involved Ned Weld '59, a tennis player who was No. 4 on his freshman team and who, according to Barnaby, "arrived with no backhand, no serve, and no net game."

Weld joined the Boston Badminton and Tennis Club that winter to work on his game. He would also track down Barnaby at Hemenway Gym, where the two of them would step into a squash court and work on Weld's tennis game.

As a sophomore Weld was playing at No. 6 on the varsity. The next year he was No. 3. By the time he was a senior, he was captain of the team and No. 1 in both singles and doubles. But Weld's improvement did not stop there. In 15 of the next 18 years after graduation, Weld was ranked the No. 1 tennis player in New England.

As Barnaby learned from Harry Cowles, Dave Fish learned from Barnaby. And like Barnaby, Fish added a wrinkle or two of his own.

"Dave did not stand still," said Barnaby. "He instituted a conditioning program, which I never had. Our guys just played themselves into shape."

Reminded of his comment that there would never

be another period like that of Harry Cowles, Barnaby was asked if there would ever be another period like his own. The coach smiled and paid his former pupil the ultimate compliment.

"Dave may have already started one."

• • •

Captain of both squash and tennis in 1972, Dave Fish was head coach of both four years later.

1976–85: Harvard surprised people by upsetting Princeton and winning a piece of the EITA in 1976, Jack Barnaby's last year. It was the only time from 1974 through 1980 that Princeton didn't own the league.

There was little satisfaction in Cambridge that a former Barnaby captain, Dave Benjamin '66, was coaching the Tigers to this success. So it remained for another Barnaby captain, Dave Fish '72, to bring Harvard back to the top.

That happened in 1981, when Harvard ended the Princeton streak and began one of its own. Behind the play of Howard Sands and Don Pompan, Harvard took the first of three straight EITA titles and hinted at even greater achievements down the road.

With the success of Californians Pompan and Sands, other standouts from the junior tennis world started looking at Harvard as a strong alternative to some of the warm-weather tennis schools.

Howard Sands, more than anyone else, represented the rebirth of Harvard tennis. Sands became Harvard's first tennis All-American, earning that honor three times from 1981 to 1983. At one time, he was ranked as high as second in the country, and twice he led Harvard upsets of seeded teams in the NCAA tournament.

Harvard tennis joined the nationally ranked squads when Howard Sands took the court from 1980 to 1983.

"The 1983 season helped our identity tremendously," noted Fish. "Howard beat then number one Rodney Harmon of SMU, and at season's end we beat number nine Clemson, 5-4."

Eastern League battles with Princeton and others continued. But Harvard tennis was also getting closer to the days of James Dwight and Dwight Davis when Harvard *was* tennis in America.

WOMEN'S TENNIS: REACHING NEW HEIGHTS

In the tennis office at Harvard there are photographs depicting Radcliffe women attired in hats and long dresses enjoying a game of lawn tennis in the early 20th century. Women played the game in Cambridge long before the Harvard women's program challenged the national tennis powers in the 1980s.

It was a different game then, played for the sheer fun of it. Yet there was also competitive tennis, and one Radcliffe student, Frances Jennings '23, was winning area championships more than 50 years before Harvard fielded a women's varsity.

"Athletics in my day was a natural part of living," said Jennings in 1981. "Games were played for the fun of it—recreation was the whole thing."

There was still plenty of fun and recreation in 1975, but there was also a varsity program coming together at Soldiers Field. The early teams played schedules that included familiar opponents such as Vassar as well as new, more competitive programs such as North Carolina. The bulk of the matches still came against Ivy League and Greater Boston opponents.

From the beginning the program enjoyed excellent teaching. First there was Corey Wynn '40, Jack Barnaby's freshman coach for 30 years, who helped get the program off the ground. He was followed by Peter Felske, a 1976 graduate of Arizona, who served four successful seasons and laid the foundation for new levels of success.

Building upon that foundation was Don Usher, an experienced coach of both amateurs and professionals, who inherited a growing program and took it to new heights.

"Harvard was successful from the start," said Usher. "People like the Roberts sisters [Martha and Sally] were good and demanded that the program develop. There was Betsy Richmond, the best player up to that time. But still, the program didn't have the players that could beat Princeton and Yale."

To break that Princeton-Yale domination, Harvard needed to attract another level of talent. And in the fall of 1979, the first of those great players arrived.

"Tiina Bougas was the first Harvard player of national caliber who had played in national events before and during her time at Harvard," said Usher.

Bougas' presence seemed to attract other skilled players who kept getting better and better. Bougas was No. 1 as a freshman in the spring of 1980. The next year freshman Maria Pe was No. 1. And in 1982 the No. 1 spot went to freshman Elizabeth Evans.

The Massachusetts-bred talent, like Richmond and Bougas, was being supplemented by California products like Pe, Evans, and 1984 freshman Kathy Vigna. And in that 1984 season, Harvard enjoyed new success.

Matches with the Vassars and Wellesleys were replaced with contests against the likes of USC, Stanford, and Texas. The gap with Princeton and Yale was closed as Harvard beat Princeton for the first time in 1983 and swept both opponents for the first time in 1984, taking the Ivy title in the process.

Individually, Elizabeth Evans earned All-American honors in both singles and doubles, joined in the latter by Robin Boss, another talented freshman. With Evans ranked 3rd and the team 18th nationally, the program reached new competitive heights. But Coach Usher and Harvard had not lost sight of the values of participation. When asked to identify what made Harvard tennis special, the coach didn't hesitate.

"We have the largest and most extensive B Team in the country. Never have more people been able to take part in the program."

And that would please Frances Jennings most of all.

Elizabeth Evans was the last and best in a line of No. 1 players from the late 1970s, when Harvard was a club team, to the mid-1980s, when Harvard was a nationally respected varsity.

CHAPTER 12

Wrestling

The question put before Harvard wrestling coach Johnny Lee could have taken him a while to answer. He was asked to select the most important quality Harvard wrestling embodied over the years. He didn't even hesitate.

"Opportunity. We've provided opportunities for all kinds of people to participate," said Lee. "As I have told people in the past, we've had blind kids, deaf kids, and little kids. There aren't too many intercollegiate sports that can say that."

One cannot count the number of Harvard students who have enjoyed the opportunities of which Lee speaks. Although the intercollegiate program struggled to develop in the 1920s, some form of intramural wrestling existed at Harvard as far back as 1780. Sophomore wrestlers would issue an annual challenge to the freshman class, and after the ensuing competition the winners would be treated to a dinner by the losers.

Not until 1916 did wrestling move from the intramural world to that of intercollegiate competition. Despite the effect of World War I, Coach Samuel Anderson attracted 25 candidates for wrestling in 1916 and nearly twice that number the next year.

Anderson's 1917 team placed second in the intercollegiate championships, and L. C. Davidson '17 became Harvard's first individual wrestling champion. After the war, the program came into its own.

WRESTLING COMES INTO ITS OWN

1921–45: Harvard wrestling really blossomed in the 1920s. Under Coach William Lewis, Harvard won five straight New England Intercollegiate titles from 1924 to 1928. The first year of this streak, with 80 men out for the squad, produced three intercollegiate champions in George Karelitz '24 (145 pounds), Carl Stearns '26 (125 pounds), and Bernard Goldberg '26 (115 pounds).

As was the case in so many sports, Yale proved to be an early nemesis, as Harvard won only 6 of the first 39 matches with the Elis. That included a 22-match streak in favor of the enemy from 1935 to 1957.

Cliff Gallagher followed Lewis as coach and enjoyed winning seasons from 1929 to 1936. In that time Gallagher picked up three wins over Yale. Those victories played a role in the 1930 squad's being the first to receive the minor H. As manager Henry C. Speel '30 recalled, it wasn't easy. "To win the minor sports H, we had to win three-quarters of our meets and the Yale meet. Indeed, until then wrestling was a minor, minor sport, feared by the football coaches as detrimental or dangerous for a football player."

The team went 6-1-1 and beat Yale to meet the challenge. The early 1930s produced some of Harvard's greatest wrestlers. Joe Solano '30 (158 pounds) lost twice as a sophomore and never again. Pat Johnson '33 (135 pounds) became Harvard's first All-American when he finished second in the 1933 NCAA championships. And Richard Ames '34 (175 pounds) finished four years of dual meet competition without ever being defeated.

It was also in this period, during the 1930–31 season, that the Indoor Athletic Building opened and Harvard wrestling found a permanent home. This, and the success of the program, boosted wrestling's popularity.

In 1936 Coach Gallagher was succeeded by former All-American Pat Johnson. Under Johnson's guidance, Harvard's second All-American emerged when John "Chip" Harkness captured the 175-pound title at the 1938 NCAAs. No Harvard wrestler since has been able to match this accomplishment.

In fact, Johnson coached the last Harvard men to win Eastern Intercollegiate titles until Jim Phills did so in 1983. The men were Harkness, at 175 in 1938, and Clarence "Chief" Boston at heavyweight in 1939. Wrestling's popularity was at an all-time high at this point, as the 1930s produced nine winning seasons and individuals who still rank among the best ever at Harvard. Only the advent of war would stop the show.

1946–68: After the war Chief Boston took over as head coach. He brought with him an enthusiasm for the sport that was contagious, not only attracting candidates to the program but also bringing crowds. At one time wrestling trailed only football and ice hockey in attendance at its contests.

One of Coach Boston's better wrestlers, and 1948 captain, would go on to make a name for himself in the world of sports some 40 years later. That was Peter Fuller, second-place finisher in the 1947 Easterns in the unlimited class. Fuller, whose father Alvan was governor

One of Harvard's best wrestlers in the 1940s was Peter Fuller (standing), *captain of the 1948 team. Fuller went on to make sports headlines as owner of Dancer's Image, the original winner of the 1968 Kentucky Derby whose victory was later taken away.*

of Massachusetts, was the owner of Dancer's Image, the original winner of the 1968 Kentucky Derby. The horse was the "original" winner because a postrace urine test revealed the presence of an illegal drug, which cost Dancer's Image the victory.

Boston's two years as coach were followed by a similar stint for Forest Jordan. In contrast to these brief tenures, the next two Harvard coaches served longer than anyone who had preceded them.

In 1950 Harvard tabbed Bob Pickett as its new wrestling coach. Pickett, a former Eastern Intercollegiate (195 pounds) and AAU champion, had attended Yale prior to the war and eventually finished at Syracuse, where he captained the Orangemen. He would serve Harvard wrestling for 18 seasons before stepping down in 1968 to become executive director of the Harvard Varsity Club.

Pickett inherited a program that was facing two problems. Interest on campus was beginning to wane, and the talent pool within the program was small. The crowds of the early years had diminished and they would never come back. As for the talent, there was one bright light.

As Bob Pickett would later recall, "I was fortunate to

have Johnny Lee in those first years. He was the most outstanding wrestler I ever had, at any weight."

John H. Lee, Jr., '53 rates with Harvard's best. In fact, it is doubtful that anyone else has meant more to Harvard wrestling in the program's history. Wrestling at 125 pounds, Lee twice earned All-American status by finishing fourth and third in the 1952 and 1953 NCAA tournaments respectively. He also won the 1951 AAU 123-pound competition.

Following graduation Lee returned to Harvard to assist Bob Pickett as Harvard's first full-time wrestling assistant. Pickett's appreciation of Lee's role was always up front.

"Johnny was young, single, and dedicated at that time," said Pickett. "He would stay until eight o'clock at night working with kids and he really helped me tremendously. We may have been the first Ivy program to have a full-time assistant, and he did a great job."

While no one would equal Lee's level of achievement for some time, Pickett coached several individuals who stood out from the rest. Heavyweight Pete Morrison '56 finished second in the Easterns as a senior. Bob Foster '59 lost only once during his undergraduate dual meet career. Nick Estabrook '61 had a ten-meet winning streak his final year. And George Doub '62, a three-year standout, compiled a 22-2-7 record in his career.

Pickett's biggest victory came outside the IAB, when wrestling was given major sport status after the 1956–57 season. It had long been the most major of minor sports

at Harvard. That season also produced the first win over Yale since 1935.

Formal Ivy League play came into being at this time, creating a new goal for the six Ivy schools that had wrestling. Five of the six have reached that goal. Harvard has not.

In the early years Cornell ruled the Ivies. And by the 1965–66 season the Big Red had won 58 of their last 60 Ivy contests. Harvard kept getting closer, losing by 20-16 in 1966. That squad, one of Pickett's best, got strong years from Ed Franquemont (152 pounds) and Tack Chace (heavyweight). Both went 9-1, Chace undefeated until the season's final match.

The 1966 record of 7-3 overall, 5-1 in the league, was Pickett's best. With a strong nucleus returning, there were preseason hopes that 1967 would finally bring Harvard an Ivy title. That appeared to be not just a dream when the Crimson matmen beat Cornell for the first time in 20 years, 20-14. Two sophomores won key matches, Howie Freedman at 190 pounds and Danny Naylor, defeating a veteran Cornell captain, at 130 pounds.

The dream became a nightmare a month later when Princeton, trailing 11-14, rallied to beat Harvard, 17-14. The Crimson finished with the same record as the year

A Saturday afternoon at the Indoor Athletic Building, home of Harvard wrestling.

before, one match from the coveted title. Key to the two-year run at the top was Ed Franquemont, 9-0-1 as a senior and 26-2-3 for his career.

Following the 1967–68 season, his 18th, Bob Pickett stepped down from his coaching duties to begin an equally long relationship with the Varsity Club. His tenure, more than double that of any previous coach, produced a mark of 86-86-2.

CLOSING IN ON THE TITLE

1969–80: There was little difficulty in selecting a successor to Pickett. John Lee, one of Harvard's greatest wrestlers and an assistant for 14 years, took over as head coach in 1968–69. His first year featured a win over Cornell and winning records both overall and in the league.

The Ivy League title remained as elusive to Lee as it had been to Bob Pickett. While the overall record hovered near .500 for the next 12 seasons, only two of those years featured winning records in Ivy competition. The first came in 1971, when Harvard was 14-5-1 overall, 5-1 in the league.

There were early signs that 1971 would be a special year. The year before, an undefeated Mark Faller had made All-Ivy as a junior at 167 pounds. Classmate Pat Coleman was a two-year standout at 150, and this tandem would be joined by Ritchie Starr, the Eastern freshman champ at 177 in 1970.

When Springfield was knocked off early in the 1970–71 season, Lee knew he had something special. It was Springfield's first loss in New England in ten years and only the 9th time in 36 tries that Harvard had beaten them. Only a 22-12 loss to Princeton kept Harvard from its first Ivy title.

Still, the second-place finish matched Harvard's best ever, and the trio of Faller, Coleman, and Starr was named to the All-Ivy team. Starr joined an elite group when his fifth-place finish at the NCAA championships made him Harvard wrestling's fourth All-American.

While Starr earned two more All-Ivy berths, the succeeding teams could not equal 1971's accomplishment. In fact, Lee's talent remained thin through the end of the decade, and Harvard was a combined 14-31-1 from 1972 to 1979. The best of the post-Starr wrestlers was Dan Blakinger, an All-Ivy selection in 1973 at 118 pounds.

"The talent in the mid-seventies wasn't the equal of either the 1971 team or the great teams of the early eighties," Lee would later observe. "From 1974 to 1978, there were ten kids each year we wanted to get into the college. We ended up zero for forty."

The man officiating this Harvard match watched Crimson wrestlers from another perspective for 18 seasons in Cambridge. He's Bob Pickett, head coach for Harvard from 1950 to 1968 before assuming duties as director of the Harvard Varsity Club.

Opportunities for All

John Lee's comment that the Harvard wrestling program had "blind kids, deaf kids, and little kids" was not a remark offered lightly. The coach spoke with great pride.

"One of the highlights of my career was coaching Ed Bordley. He was a bright light in our program," said Lee of his blind wrestler.

"You should have seen his legs, how bruised they were. He knew his way around our place, but when we went on the road he got banged up quite a bit from being unfamiliar with a gym or a locker room.

"But that was about all that bothered him. He was an inspiration, a tremendous person. And you can imagine what he meant to me as a coach. The other guys saw what he was accomplishing, and it pushed them a little more."

Bordley was not just a member of the team. He was a winner, earning his first Ivy victory against perennial league power Cornell in 1976.

Harvard's celebrated deaf wrestler was Andy McNerney, perhaps the best wrestler Harvard ever had. He arrived known as much for his handicap as his talent. By the time he graduated, he was simply known as one of the country's best wrestlers.

"I never had anyone so into their wrestling as Andy," said Coach Lee. "He had an unusual, unorthodox style we called a crab style. It was difficult to learn, but he had the dedication to do so."

Lee's words about McNerney sound similar to what Lee's coach, Bob Pickett, once said about him.

"The thing that made Johnny Lee so good was his dedication. I never saw anyone who loved wrestling so much, and he carried that over into his coaching."

. . .

1981–84: The situation changed for the better with the new decade. The 1980–81 season saw Harvard run up a 17-4 record, 15-1 outside the Ivy League. The team beat archenemy Yale for the first time since 1972 and saw the emergence of two sophomores who would key a resurgence in Harvard wrestling.

A profile in courage: Ed Bordley '79 celebrates victory, overcoming blindness—and his opponent.

Heavyweight Jim Phills compiled a 23-3-1 record, while classmate Andy McNerney was 16-6 at 142 pounds. These two, and veteran Paul Widerman (118 pounds), were the heart of this squad that won more matches than any Harvard team before or since. Still, the 2-3 league mark kept the title from Cambridge.

Then came 1982 and the title that got away. This team had four wrestlers who were first team All-Ivy choices at one time or another. They were Widerman, who would be an alternate on the 1984 Olympic team, Phills, McNerney, and Sean Wallace (117 pounds).

The leaders of the 1983 team, one of Harvard's best, were heavyweight Jim Phills (left) and 142-pound All-American Andy McNerney (right).

The team finished at 15-4 and, for a while, 4-1 in the league. When it was discovered that a weigh-in before the Columbia match had not been properly witnessed, a Harvard victory over the Lions was taken away. The result was that Columbia finished at 4-1, one match ahead of 3-2 Harvard.

"I'd have to say that 1983 was possibly the best year we've ever had." That's how Johnny Lee assessed the happenings of the 1982–83 season. The year became a showcase for the heroics of his two seniors, Jim Phills and Andy McNerney.

Phills had a 23-0 season until he was beaten at the NCAA tournament. His Eastern title in the heavyweight class gave Harvard its first Eastern champ since Chief Boston in 1939. Through four years, Phills was 71-7-1.

Andy McNerney arrived at Harvard known as the deaf student who wrestled. He left with the recognition as one of Harvard's greatest wrestlers. When McNerney finished fourth at the NCAAs in 1983, he became the fifth Harvard wrestler to earn All-American status. That fourth-place finish was the highest for any Harvard wrestler since Johnny Lee's third-place showing in 1953. Through his college career, McNerney was beaten only twice and both times by NCAA champions.

Without Phills and McNerney doing their magic, Johnny Lee's 16th varsity relied on the likes of Sean Wallace and Brian Bausano to produce a fifth straight winning season. The 11-8 record wasn't as impressive as its immediate predecessors but was a success just the same.

"Phills and McNerney have had an effect even after their graduation," according to Coach Lee. "They gave great visibility to the program that has made it attractive to other wrestlers."

And perhaps those other wrestlers will pay back that duo by winning Harvard's first Ivy title, one that can't be taken away.

• • •

The Title That Got Away

The 1981–82 Harvard wrestling team thought it could make history. No Harvard team had ever won an Ivy wrestling title, but the talent on the 1982 squad seemed deep enough to change all of that. And it did. Sort of.

Johnny Lee's 1982 squad did indeed compile the best Ivy record on the mat. But when a victory over Columbia was overturned on a technicality, the Ivy crown went to the Lions.

"Andy McNerney wrestled at 150 on Friday at Cornell," recalled Lee. "We lost, 21-20, in one of the best matches I had ever seen. After the match, we found that Fritz Campbell was hurt, couldn't go at 142 the next day at Columbia, so I had to go with Andy."

McNerney, who had wrestled most of the year at 142, was weighed in before the Columbia match and made the proper weight. What wasn't proper was the fact that no one officially witnessed the weigh-in.

"I should have made sure it was properly witnessed, but I figured that [Columbia coach Ron] Russo wouldn't raise a question on it, and he didn't," said Lee.

"What I didn't figure was that Cornell coach Andy Noel would. Noel, whose Big Red team was still in contention for the title, noticed that McNerney had wrestled at two different weights and on further inspection discovered only one witnessed weigh-in. So he made an issue out of it and succeeded in overturning Harvard's victory over Columbia."

When Cornell subsequently lost its match to Columbia, Noel's efforts came up short. He didn't get his title but he effectively cost the Harvard wrestlers theirs.

Columbia accepted its good fortune somewhat reluctantly. As Johnny Lee would say in January of 1985, nearly three years after the incident, "Do you realize that Columbia still hasn't put its name on the Ivy trophy yet for 1982?"

• • •

A former Harvard All-American, Johnny Lee followed Bob Pickett as head coach in 1968 and entered his 17th season in the fall of 1985.

CHAPTER 13

Fencing

Ask your average sports fan to tell you all he knows about fencing. He may recall a Douglas Fairbanks movie. Or an episode of Zorro. Or maybe the word "épée" was an answer on his morning crossword puzzle.

His ignorance is easily forgiven. In America, little boys and little girls grow up with plenty of chances to run and swim and throw and catch and do all sorts of things with all sorts of balls. Rarely are the saber, the foil, and the épée components of the toy box.

Despite these facts of life, intercollegiate fencing has survived for nearly a century, and at Harvard that century has held more than a few moments of glory. While the public has rarely stopped to take notice, the dedicated fencers and coaches have built a program that has been consistently competitive and frequently brilliant.

• • •

MEN'S FENCING: FLASHES OF BRILLIANCE

It was in the 1880s that Harvard fencing was born. Unorganized activity became less so when the Harvard Fencing Club first met on January 8, 1889. Two weeks later the club received its first fencing instructor, Allen Lowe, whose previous experience had been with the Montreal Athletic Club and the Toronto Fencing Club.

Similar events were transpiring at Columbia and Yale and by 1894, when these schools adopted the French rules of fencing already in use at Harvard, the Intercollegiate Fencing Association was formed. The IFA championships remain one of fencing's postseason highlights today.

The first IFA championship was won by Harvard on May 5, 1894. In fact, Harvard won six of the first seven titles and produced three individual champions. They were Melvin Green '96, Archibald Thacher '97, and George

Breed '99. No Harvard fencer would equal their efforts until John Hurd took the 1934 foil championship.

Harvard fencing in the 20th century has been molded by a handful of dedicated coaches. Their devotion to the sport and to the undergraduates has more than made up for the lack of recognition from the masses.

1901–30: While championship events were held before the turn of the century, it was not until the 1901–02 season that the first dual meets took place. In that year Harvard split a pair of matches, defeating Yale, 5-4, and losing to Army, 9-0.

The fortunes of the fencing program suffered in the first two decades of the 20th century. But what followed was perhaps the most successful and certainly the most colorful period in Harvard fencing history.

Three fencers in this period were among the best ever. They were Burke Boyce '22, acknowledged as Harvard's

Coach Rene Peroy (right) demonstrates for his 1951 captain Winfred Overholzer. Peroy coached Harvard fencers from 1931 to 1952, compiling a 105-43-3 record and winning the 1931 intercollegiate team championship.

greatest stylist, and the Lane twins, Edward and Everett, whose athletic styles were as contrasting as their looks were similar. Guiding their fortunes was the coach, or master—or, as this particular coach was called, Le Maître d'Armes de l'Equipe d'Escrime de Harvard College, Monsieur Jean Louis Danguy.

This was an exciting time for fencing. Boyce was a dashing figure who followed his Harvard tenure with a stint on the U.S. Olympic team. Then came the Lane twins, who led Harvard to consecutive intercollegiate titles in 1923 and 1924 (the school's first since 1899), at a time when the championships were held at the Grand Ballroom of New York's Hotel Astor. And then there was the coach.

"Monsieur was a technical perfectionist," Roland Fleer

'24 once said. "Learning to fence under him was like trying to learn the violin under Fritz Kreisler, or conducting from Toscanini."

The short, rotund Danguy was a colorful character, made all the more so by his difficulty with the English language. One of his better-remembered advisories on how to hold a foil was, "You hold heem like a bird and not so tight you keel him and not so loose he fly away."

1931–51: Danguy's tenure was followed by that of Rene Peroy. This beloved coach served for 21 years and compiled a record of 105-43-3, his greatest moments coming early in his Harvard career.

In 1931, led by seniors Henry Wesselman, Henry Cassidy, and Joseph Allen, Harvard again won the intercollegiate team championship. That victory was more than equaled in 1934 when Harvard scored a rare double, winning individual and team events in different weapons. The victors were individual foil champion John Hurd and team épée champions Edward Langenau and Webster Williams, Jr.

No individual or team efforts in the remainder of Peroy's time would match these accomplishments. And when Edo Marion took over as head coach in 1952, Harvard fencing was a struggling program. After a handful of subpar seasons, Marion turned things around and returned Harvard fencing to winning ways.

1952–84: Edo Marion, an aeronautical engineer and member of the 1936 Yugoslavian Olympic team, continued the tradition of dedicated teaching and caring that Harvard fencers had enjoyed for years. In his 24 years he added new devices to keep the program growing.

First was the establishment of the George H. Breed Competition. Breed, a former champion at Harvard as well as an Olympian in 1912, 1920, and 1924, left an endowment to Harvard fencing in 1956. Two years later, on Marion's suggestion, an intrasquad competition was established in Breed's name. That competition, which runs from October through January, is still used to determine the makeup of the squad from week to week.

In 1966 Marion instituted an annual competition between alumni and members of the varsity squad. With the so-called minor sports often feeling financial pressure, this link to the alumni proved valuable to the fencers.

Away from intrasquad and alumni battles, Marion's teams were often strong, with the Ivy League offering the

most competition. Typical of this reality were the 1965 and 1966 seasons. The squads compiled overall records of 12-4 and 11-5 but struggled with 2-3 and 1-4 Ivy seasons.

Marion earned his only share of an Ivy League crown in 1974, when his 10-5 team finished in a three-way tie for first among the Ivies with a 3-2 record. That was the year that half the league was 3-2 and the other half 2-3. Key to Harvard's top-half finish was a 14-13 win over Columbia, Marion's only win over the Lions in his 24 years. The title could have been all Harvard's except for two 14-13 losses to Cornell and Yale, the former after Harvard had led 12-7.

One of Marion's best moments came at the 1969 NCAA championships, when Harvard finished second in a field of more than 50 schools. The key to this finish was the depth provided by Geza Tatrallyay (épée), Larry Cetrulo (saber), and Tom Keller (foil). Keller was a three-time All-American.

Individually, Marion coached 23 fencers who earned first team All-Ivy recognition at a time when the Ivy schools were the nation's best. Twelve times from 1951 to 1971, the NCAA champion was an Ivy League school.

One of the best of the All-Ivy fencers was Larry Cetrulo '71, a first team choice in the saber for three years. Jonathan Kolb '65 and Ron Winfield '69, both saber standouts, were two-time All-Ivy selections. The other two-time winners were Geza Tatrallyay '72 in épée and Phillippe Bennett '75 in foil.

Though he only earned one All-Ivy berth, Terry Valenzuela '73 gained added recognition for the fencing program when he earned a Rhodes Scholarship as a senior.

By the end of his tenure, Marion was as proud of the program's level of participation as he was of these standouts.

"My philosophy of what a college sport should be was to give an opportunity for large participation to students, nonathletes," said Marion after leaving Harvard. "During my coaching period, I kept three full varsity teams and two freshman teams. And I never recruited."

When Marion stepped down after the 1975–76 season, Harvard turned to another former Yugoslav Olympian, Branimir "Ben" Zivkovic. Zivkovic's tenure continued the success of his predecessors and also included supervision of the women's program, which was inaugurated in 1976.

Zivkovic enjoyed immediate success in his first season. The 1976–77 Harvard team finished at 10-2 and, more significantly, won another share of the Ivy title. Harvard's

Above: *Harvard's 1968–69 fencing team placed second in the national collegiate championships with these representatives* (from left): *Geza Tatrallyay, épée; Coach Edo Marion; Larry Cetrulo, saber; and Thomas Keller, foil. Both Cetrulo and Keller placed second individually in their weapons.*

Left: *Coach Edo Marion talks with 1973 captain and Rhodes scholar Terry Valenzuela. Marion coached for 24 years and won more than 150 matches.*

league mark, best ever for the Crimson, came after a combined 1-9 Ivy record over the previous two years.

The program's successes were more modest over the next three years, but beginning with the 1980–81 season Harvard forged four years of results that recalled the early 1930s.

In 1981 Harvard took the IFA foil title for the first time in 50 years. Key performers were the Merner brothers, Mike and Dave; Stanlake Samkange, a Rhodes scholar; and Dave Hanower, an All-Ivy choice with Dave Merner.

After an 8-2 season in 1982, the Merner brothers led Harvard to a third-place finish at the 1983 IFAs, Harvard's best in more than 50 years. Dave Merner's personal

Above: *Fencing coach Ben Zivkovic stands proudly among his Ivy League and IFA foil champs. From left, Mike Merner, captain Steve Biddle, Zivkovic, David Hanower, Stanlake Samkange, and David Merner. Samkange also became a Rhodes scholar.*

Left: *Nearly 40 years of fencing excellence are represented in this photo. Larry Cetrulo '71 (left) tied for the 1969 NCAA saber title. John Gavin Hurd '34 (right), shown here on the evening of his induction into the Harvard Hall of Fame in 1981, was the 1934 national foil titlist.*

record for the year was 21-7; his younger brother Mike's was 26-7.

Then came another banner year in 1984. Harvard was 11-3 and captured Ivy League team épée honors and the IFA individual épée crown. That winner was Steve Kaufer, an All-Ivy choice along with Mike Merner, whose third place in the IFA foil competition was Harvard's best finish since John Hurd won the event in 1934.

WOMEN'S FENCING: TOILING IN OBSCURITY

The women's program has not had the flashy performances that the men have had during this period. But the women have developed a strong, competitive program in their first decade of existence.

With the exception of the 1977–78 season, when the team was 9-1 in dual matches and fourth at the Eastern Intercollegiate meet, the women's team has hovered near the .500 mark. Two individuals have stood out in the program's first eight years.

Kathy Lowry was the mainstay of the first three squads. As a sophomore, she compiled a 22-10 record while the team struggled to reach .500. She certainly would have been an All-Ivy choice had the selections been instituted for women at the time.

Vivi Fuchs became the first bona fide All-Ivy selection for Harvard women when she earned that honor in 1982. A New England champion the year before, Fuchs ran up a 31-7 record in her All-Ivy season.

. . .

CHAPTER 14

Skiing, Golf, and Sailing

There has been no conspiracy. But over the years certain sports at Harvard have gone relatively unnoticed by the masses. Heading the list of the underappreciated are the ski, golf, and sailing programs.

The simplest explanation is that none of these programs competes on campus, unless you extend the campus to include the Charles River Basin. The skiing and sailing programs include both men's and women's teams. Golf has been a men's sport with the exception of the appearance of Leslie Greis '80 in the late 1970s. Without a women's team to play on, the Holden, Massachusetts, native earned a spot on the men's team coached by Bob Carr '68. At the same time, she entered women's championship events and won the 1979 Massachusetts women's intercollegiate title.

...

SKIING: BATTLING THE ELEMENTS AND THE OPPOSITION

When asked who his toughest opponent was, one semiserious Harvard basketball coach once answered, "Our admissions director." Recruiting battles aside, most Harvard programs have been able to focus their competitive energies on one opposing team or another in an attempt to define their season's goals.

Now consider the plight of the Harvard skier. As if the Dartmouths and Vermonts and Middleburys weren't enough, there are the matters of finding some snow, getting to the snow, and securing a coach who can bring some structure to the whole enterprise. For most of its touch-and-go life, the Harvard ski program has battled to survive as often as it has battled to win on the slopes.

The challenges built in to the Harvard ski experience have, in a perverse way, afforded some of its best moments. But they are moments that can best be appreciated when an undergraduate has finished a season or a career and been able to look back at the obstacles that were overcome. That has been the story of Harvard skiing from the start.

The start was in 1931, when a member of the lightweight crew named Bob Livermore traded his oar for ski poles and entered the Dartmouth Carnival. The diminutive blond won the slalom, and Harvard had entered the world of intercollegiate skiing.

This was still just one man's foray into the young sport. It wasn't until the next year that Harvard had anything that could be called a ski team, if one could be generous with the term. Brad Washburn '33 and Bob Balch '31 composed that first "team," which accepted an invitation to the 1932 Dartmouth Carnival.

The invitation came about due to the efforts of four Harvard men—Livermore, Alec Bright '19, Rupert Mac-Laurin '29, and John Sherburne '24—who had finished first, third, fourth, and seventh at the Mount Moosilauke Down Mountain Race in March of 1931. On the strength of that showing, Dartmouth welcomed Harvard's first team to its 1932 event.

The key names in Harvard's skiing infancy were undergraduates Livermore and Washburn and graduate Bright. Livermore's skill lent legitimacy to Harvard efforts. Washburn's contributions were both as a skier and an organizer. And Bright, the best friend Harvard skiing ever had, was simply the chief catalyst in launching a program and, for decades, maintaining it.

It was Alec Bright urging Harvard to enter this new athletic world from the start. It was Alec Bright making the U.S. Olympic ski team in 1936 at the age of 39. It was Alec Bright who would pick up the phone and call Harvard students from the White Mountains, urging them to get in their cars and drive north because the team needed an extra competitor or two. And it was Alec Bright who found a way to tap a hidden resource to make sure the funds were there to keep Harvard skiing alive.

Ironically, for all that he did for skiing, Bright's name remains forever connected to his other passion, ice hockey. A prime mover in the formation of the Friends of Harvard Hockey and the building of Harvard's first hockey rink, the Watson Rink, Bright's efforts were formally recognized when the Alexander H. Bright Hockey Center was dedicated in 1979.

Harvard granted official status to the ski team in 1934, when its first recognized captain, Herbert S. Sise '34, was joined by Bud Ritchie '34, Andrew Marshall, Jr., '34,

Edward Davis, Jr., '34, and Charles Lawrence '36. Ritchie holds the distinction of earning the first minor H given to Harvard skiers.

Another first was the luxury of a coach, albeit a volunteer coach, in the person of Charles O. Proctor. Over the years Harvard would turn to any number of sources for its coaches, the most unusual being Norwood Cox, manager of the ski equipment department at the Harvard Coop.

The 1940–41 season brought Bill Halsey, a former Dartmouth skier who was a student at the Harvard School of Design. Academia was good to the skiers, as Theodore Lockwood, a member of the MIT faculty, was coach in 1957–58, and Charles Gibson, a former Williams skier, coached while pursuing an MS (1959) and an MBA (1962) at Harvard. He would remain through the 1966–67 season.

By 1935 the program's main concern was the personal safety of its skiers. Under captain H. Adams Carter '36, the team earned the nickname Carter's Ski Smashers. Carter himself claimed to have broken both the Wildcat Trail record and his arm at the same time. The extent of the danger was brought to light in 1936 when captain Peter Brooks filed this report to Harvard officials:

At present, several hundred undergraduates go out each year, see good skiers run fast, and try to do the same. They develop a technique of running fast and then falling down because they do not know how to turn a corner.... Harvard skiers have developed the desire for speed rather than skill [which] results in numerous serious accidents. Here are some facts compiled by the Harvard Hygiene Department for December, January, February, and March: three fractures, three bad knees, three large hematomas in the muscle, one broken thumb, four sprained ankles and twisted knees each week.... What is the significance of this accident record? It means that Harvard skiers have developed a dangerous and costly technique of running out of control.

Harvard, hoping a responsible, paid head coach would make a difference, responded with $600 for the hiring of Norwood Cox in 1937. It was around this time that an energetic group of undergraduates set out to solve another problem that plagued the program: the lack of an effective headquarters in the New Hampshire–Vermont area.

Brad Washburn had engineered Harvard's first cabin project on Mount Washington in 1932. In the spring of 1939, captain Bill Hinton and captain-elect Tom Winship sought out the help of Washburn and Alec Bright to make a more complete cabin a reality.

The project got off the ground when Washburn provided three acres of land in Jackson, New Hampshire, and Bright launched a fund-raising drive. It remained for Winship, later the celebrated editor of the *Boston Globe*, to round up undergraduates for the actual construction, which took place in the summer of 1939.

By the end of its first decade, Harvard skiing had established a foundation for the future. At the same time, it was becoming clear that any future the skiers might have would depend on their success on two battlefields.

The first battlefield was financial. The program was heavily dependent on the skiers' own fund-raising efforts, and although Harvard support would grow, this remained a fact of life throughout the program's history. While a football team might fly to a game and others let a bus driver take the risks, members of the ski team became accustomed to getting themselves to the mountains. This resulted in a few dented automobiles, and it was alleged that Spike Holden '61 even rode a motorcycle through a snowstorm to the Middlebury Carnival.

Even as late as 1985, the ski team received only half of its $20,000 budget from the Department of Athletics. And that budget had to cover coaches, meals, lodging, equipment, and the renting of two vans for a three-month period. (The coaching arrangement had changed in the late 1970s, when Harvard turned to the Pat's Peak Educational Foundation in Henniker, New Hampshire. This was a type of coaching co-op, which directed more than one ski team at a time. By 1985 the coaching situation had changed again; the Alpine program was under a co-op at Okemo Mountain in Ludlow, Vermont, and the Nordic program was under George Weir of Williamsville, Vermont.)

The remaining battles were on the slopes. Because of the low-budget operation and the realities of geography, good skiers had good reasons not to come to Harvard. But because of the type of person it attracted in general, Harvard inherited its share of talented people who happened to be good skiers.

Ben Steele earned his place in the Harvard record books in 1973, when he became the first Crimson skier ever to win the EISA Alpine combined championship at Middlebury College. Not only did Steele win the title, he forged a margin of victory of a second and a half in an event normally decided by tenths and hundredths of seconds.

These were people who came from ski country. People such as Del Ames '43 from Hanover, New Hampshire; Finn Ferner '43 from Norway; Steve Blodgett '67 from Stowe, Vermont; Ben Steele '74 from Littleton, New Hampshire; Eric Klaussen '81 from Olympic Valley, California; and Per-Arne Weiner '88 from Uppsala, Sweden.

But there was no way to guarantee this level of talent, so Harvard's competitive record is inconsistent. The Ames-Ferner combination brought success in the early 1940s, but their victory at the Williams Winter Carnival in 1940 was the last such accomplishment for decades.

Traditionally, when Harvard teams have done well, they have been strong in Alpine events (slalom and downhill) and suffered in Nordic events (jumping and cross-country). The other tradition has been a never-ending battle to remain at the top levels of eastern skiing. That meant finishing high enough at key meets to remain first an A-Rated as opposed to B-Rated program, and later Division I instead of Division II.

Since the late 1960s, Harvard has frequently lost its

Division I status, only to win the Division II championship and return to the higher division once more. This also became the annual challenge for the women's program, which was initiated in the late 1970s.

Sometimes it has taken extraordinary efforts to stave off imminent demotion, such as in 1971 when senior jumper Chris Ferner was talked out of retirement to save the day. Harvard needed to finish in the top eight at the Eastern Intercollegiate Skiing Association championships to remain in Division I. Ferner, a native of Oslo, Norway, who had established himself as a consistent scorer as a freshman, earned enough points to move Harvard into sixth place and keep its desired status intact.

Considering all the extra baggage the program carries, it is that much more remarkable when a Harvard skier is successful over the best that the schools to the north have to offer. And perhaps the most remarkable of all was Ben Steele '74. At 5 feet 7 inches, 145 pounds, the pride of Littleton, New Hampshire, was not the most imposing figure in the world. But that didn't stop him from becoming the only Harvard man to win the EISA's Alpine combined championship in 1973. In winning the slalom, Steele won both runs and beat the second-place skier by a second and a half. As his coach Peter Carter pointed out, "Ben was in a class by himself. Those races are usually won by tenths and hundredths of seconds."

Steele's junior-year performance earned him a trip to the NCAA championships, for which he also qualified as a senior. No other Harvard skier would qualify for the nationals until Eric Claussen did as a senior in 1981.

GOLF: IN SEARCH OF A HOME

Playing golf at Harvard has never been easy. Between the New England weather and the lack of a course to call their own, Harvard golfers have had more than the game's own frustrations to battle. All things considered, they have done remarkably well.

Records indicate some formal play as early as 1896, and the first significant success arrived two years later. That's when James F. Curtis '99 earned the 1898 national intercollegiate championship. Curtis was the first of eight Harvard men to win that honor between 1898 and 1916. The others were Halstead Lindsley '02, H. Chandler Egan '05, Alverse White '06, Henry Wilder '09, Frank Davison A.M. '14, Edward Allis '15, and James Hubbell '17.

Harvard won six national team titles in this period as well, the last of them in 1904. Rarely did the Crimson have the depth to challenge in later championships.

The long-lasting relationship between golf and ice hockey blossomed in the 1920s when three hockey players—Clark Hodder '25, Jim Hutchinson '28 (later JV hockey coach under Cooney Weiland), and Joe Morrill, Jr., '28—were among the golf team's best. Not only did JV and varsity hockey players frequent the golf roster from time to time, but the coaching duties were often left to a member of the hockey coaching staff.

Hodder was the first of these, assisting head coach Bert Nicholls at golf before assuming head hockey duties. Ralph "Cooney" Weiland was head coach of both sports in the 1950s and 1960s. And later a string of hockey assistants, beginning with Tim Taylor '63 (later head hockey coach at Yale) in 1974, took over golf's top post, frequently serving more as administrator than coach.

While Messrs. Hodder, Hutchinson, and Morrill may have played Harvard's best golf in the 1920s, none of them qualified as the best golfer at Harvard. That honor was reserved for Robert T. "Bobby" Jones, 1923 U.S. Open champion. Jones was already a graduate of Georgia Tech when he arrived at Harvard to pursue a bachelor of science degree. As a result, he was ineligible to compete for Harvard.

Jones was attending Harvard at the time of his Open victory in 1923. As a result, he was awarded a special H by Harvard and served as the golf team's unofficial coach so he could accompany the team on its trips. At one point, an informal Harvard tournament was set up that matched Jones against the six members of the golf team. Playing against all six at once, Jones won handily.

It has been suggested that the fate of Harvard golf was decided in the late 1930s when the university passed up a chance to purchase the Belmont Country Club. Such a transaction would have given Harvard its own course, a luxury enjoyed by such Ivy opponents as Yale, Princeton, and Dartmouth. It didn't happen, and Harvard continued to practice out at Myopia, Belmont, and most significantly, The Country Club in Brookline.

Bob Carr '68, an outstanding hockey defenseman for Harvard and one of the hockey assistants to coach the golf team, summarized the effect of not having a home course.

"First of all, because of the weather, the kid in the East who is a good golfer first and then a good student will opt for a Duke or a North Carolina. The kid who is a good student and then a good golfer will look at the Ivy League schools and is more likely to choose a Yale or Princeton or some other place with its own course."

John Arnold '54, the longtime president of the Friends of Harvard Golf and father of golfer George '80, said it another way.

"Good golfers will come to Harvard, but they won't come to play golf. Golf happens to be one of many things they do well."

Still, all this being true, Harvard lands the occasional gem. One of the best—maybe *the* best—was Ted Cooney '55. He captured top individual honors at the Eastern Intercollegiate Golf Association championships twice and New England Intercollegiate meet once. Said teammate John Brophy of Cooney, "Ted Cooney was one of the finest amateur golfers New England has ever seen. He was a fine, devoted, and meticulous golfer with an intense desire to beat golf."

Just how good Cooney could have been was never determined, for he died in an auto accident shortly after graduating from Harvard Business School.

The average Harvard golf season was divided into three parts: the Friends-financed spring trip, the regular season against Greater Boston and Ivy opponents (and frequently

Harvard's undefeated 1924 golf team poses for the camera. Front (from left): Clark Hodder, Robert Clough, Wallace Soule. Rear: Harris Kempner (manager), James Mapes, Rollie Parker.

snow), and the postseason tournaments. The last consisted of the Eastern Intercollegiate Golf Association tournament from 1928 to 1978, the Ivy tournament since 1975, and NCAA play when qualified.

Harvard's only EIGA championship came in 1968. That season belonged to Arlington's Bob Keefe, but at the Easterns it was sophomore Yank Heisler leading the way. Keefe had been a multisport star at Arlington High School and Exeter before coming to Harvard. He had played a little golf with his father at the Winchester Country Club but didn't take up the sport in earnest until a shoulder injury prevented him from playing his specialties, football, basketball, and baseball.

In 1967 Keefe won the Greater Boston title as a junior. He repeated as a senior and at that point had a 17-6 record since reacquainting himself with the game at age

One of Harvard's better golfers in recent years was Alex Vik '78, a resident of Spain's Grand Canary Islands. Vik sharpened his game on Europe's junior circuit before coming to Harvard, where he won back-to-back Ivy and Greater Boston championships.

19. After leaving Harvard, he developed into one of the finest amateurs in the Boston area.

Harvard's only Ivy title came in 1975, the first year of the Ivy League tournament. The hero of this squad was a seasoned golfer when he arrived at Harvard from Spain in the fall of 1974. Alex Vik won individual honors at that inaugural Ivy tournament as a freshman, just as he had led the way at the Greater Bostons earlier that year. His totals: 77-70-147 at the Ivy tourney, 69-73-142 at the Greater Boston meet.

Vik's background made him a unique entry to the Ivy golf world. His father was Norwegian, his mother from Uruguay, and he was born in Sweden. At age 14 he moved to Spain's Canary Islands, where he took up golf while serving as his father's caddy. The senior Vik had once been president of the Norwegian Olympic Committee and

had a varied sports background. With his backing, Alex joined the European amateur golf circuit and won the Norwegian Amateur and Junior championships and finished second in the European Amateur championship. Twice he was named to the All-Continental European golf team.

Despite these credentials, Vik arrived in Cambridge as a walk-on in 1974. Active recruiting has never been part of Harvard's golf program. And while he was unknown at the start of that freshman year, the whole league was well aware of his talents by the spring.

As a sophomore Vik repeated his double, although Harvard was unable to defend its Ivy team title. That went to Princeton, and the event has been a Princeton-Dartmouth-Yale exclusive since.

Before Vik graduated he had become one of just two golfers to earn All-Ivy status four times. The other was Princeton's Steve Loughran.

Two other Harvard golfers managed to earn All-Ivy status twice. They were Art Burke (1973 and 1974) and Glenn Alexander (1979 and 1981). The most recent All-Ivy choice came in 1982, when Carroll Lowenstein, Jr., son of Harvard's football hall of famer, earned the honor, finishing second at the Ivy tournament to Princeton's Loughran.

Future Harvard golfers may be busier in the fall than the spring, as the sport considers a switch to autumn's more favorable conditions. As one golfer put it, "Yeah, spring golf in New England is something. I competed at the Greater Bostons three straight years, and the temperature never got above fifty degrees."

SAILING: A WELL-KEPT SECRET

Harvard's skiers and golfers weren't the only athletes in Cambridge who grew accustomed to performing without a permanent home. For more than four decades of intercollegiate competition, Harvard sailors shared this same burden. Sure, the Charles River Basin provided a natural and convenient place to compete. But for those 40-odd years, Harvard was without a boat-house of its own, not to mention its own fleet, which didn't materialize until 1962.

In April of 1962, fifteen fiberglass 12-foot dinghies were delivered to the MIT boat house, Harvard's adopted home since intercollegiate sailing took off in the late 1920s. Ten years later, Harvard sailing finally got its home.

The acquisition of a facility had been discussed since the mid-1950s, along with the purchase of a fleet. With former skipper James Rousmaniere leading the way, funds were collected to take care of the fleet, and then Harold Vanderbilt spearheaded a drive to bring about the facility.

That effort resulted in the opening of the Harvard Sailing Pavilion on June 6, 1972. Harvard president Derek Bok joined Radcliffe president Mary Bunting at the dedication ceremonies, which launched a new era in Harvard and Radcliffe sailing.

"Having the facility has given the program a visible focus and an identity," said Mike Horn '63, a former sailor who has served as head coach since the 1965–66 season. "It provided a sense of belonging, and allowed alumni to return and have a place to return to."

Harvard's sailing alumni can look back on a program that dates to the late 19th century. The Harvard Yacht Club was formed in 1894, and from that point up through the birth of modern intercollegiate yachting in 1928, Harvard men have left their mark on all aspects of the sailing world. Some of the more notable figures are:

- Clinton H. Crane '94, a noted designer of yachts and president of the North American Yacht Racing Union from 1942 to 1949.
- George E. Hills '97, one of the world's leading authorities on racing rules.
- W. Starling Burgess '01, designer of three successful America's Cup defenders: *Enterprise, Rainbow,* and *Ranger.*
- Harold S. "Mike" Vanderbilt '07, a three-time defender of America's Cup.
- Leonard M. Fowle '30, beloved Boston sportswriter, who never sailed for Harvard but as secretary of the Intercollegiate Yacht Racing Association, (ICYRA) was instrumental in writing the rules for intercollegiate dinghy competition (along with George Nichols, Jr., '43).
- George F. O'Day '45, the 1960 Olympic gold medal winner in the 5½ meter class.
- Hilary H. Smart '47, winner of the 1948 Olympic gold medal for Stars at Torquay on the English Channel coast. Sharing this gold medal effort was his father, Paul '17, who became the oldest American gold medal winner in the history of the games.
- Robbie Doyle '71, a 1968 Olympian. Doyle was a three-time All-American, three-time New England single-handed champion and, as a junior, North American single-handed champion. After graduation, the Marblehead native became one of the most important figures in the design and production of sails.

• • •

Surrounding the McMillan Cup hardware are members of Harvard's victorious crews in the 1938 competition. Front (from left): N. H. Batchelder, Robert Burnett, Edward Hutton. Rear: Joseph Kennedy, James Rousmaniere, John Kennedy.

The list regretfully omits such names as F. Gregg Bemis, William Cudahy, Carter Ford, Charles Hoppin, and Mike Horn, all Harvard men who have entered the Intercollegiate Sailing Hall of Fame. And there are those former Harvard sailors who have gone on to greatness outside the sailing world, such as Franklin D. Roosevelt '04 and John F. Kennedy '40.

The best account of Harvard sailing's earliest period can be found in *The Second H Book of Harvard Athletics*. It is there that Leonard Fowle pinpoints intercollegiate sailing's start.

Modern college yachting commenced June 13–14, 1928, after a revival of the Yale Corinthian Yacht Club, when Harvard, Princeton, and Yale crews raced off the Pequot Yacht Club at Southport, Connecticut. The new start was hardly modest, for the collegians raced 50-foot One-Design Eight-Meter Sloops. Arthur Knapp of Princeton sailed the winner, outdistancing Harvard in this series for the Oliver May Cup, which was retired by Princeton with three wins in 1931.

Harvard fared better in another major competition of that day, the McMillan Cup, which was introduced the same year. This event, still sailed each fall in the navy's 44-foot yawls, went to Harvard four times between 1932 and 1944. Two key contributors to the 1938 victory off Osterville, Massachusetts, were the Kennedy brothers Joseph P. '38 and John F. '40. After the 1944 triumph, Harvard's next McMillan Cup victory came in 1971.

By the mid-1930s dinghy racing had taken hold among the colleges. Princeton took the first step in 1935 with a fleet of student-owned dinghies. The following year MIT and Brown set the example of college-owned fleets. Meanwhile, Harvard students purchased their own dinghies or took advantage of the generosity offered by MIT's Jack Wood at Tech's boat house.

Prior to World War II the ICYRA had grown to 35 member colleges that found a series of intersectionals and cup races in which to compete. By 1948 membership had expanded to 50 schools, as new associations grew outside the hotbeds of New England and the Mid-Atlantic.

Up to the 1950–51 season, Harvard's had been a respectable program but not a championship one. That changed dramatically during the next decade, with two periods of domination.

The first came from 1951 to 1953, when Harvard won both the New England dinghy championships and the New England team racing championships three straight years. More significantly, the Crimson won consecutive national titles in 1952 and 1953 behind the brilliance of Charley Hoppin.

The first of these major victories was the New England dinghy title of 1951. Forging that upset of MIT were Frank Scully, John Gardner, John Bishop, and Tom Carroll.

Then came Hoppin's incredible two years. Fowle captured Hoppin's greatness in this *H Book* excerpt:

His abilities were the more remarkable as polio in childhood had left Charley with virtually no strength in his right arm and hand—barely enough to grasp a tiller, much less properly play a mainsheet, which most dinghy skippers deem highly important. Relying on well-trained crews, Hoppin did his best to conceal this physical disability, and he never asked quarter from any opponent. Yet he was a splendid sportsman, never taking undue advantage of his rivals and not suffering a single disqualification for rule infractions during four years of competition. On the two occasions Hoppin fouled an opponent, he instantly withdrew."

In both national championship victories Hoppin, who would graduate summa cum laude, finished as high point skipper. He accomplished the first of these despite battling infectious mononucleosis at the time.

Harvard's 1959 national championship may not have been as dramatic but was no less significant. Chief architects of this victory were seniors Hanson Robbins and William Saltonstall. Robbins had enjoyed success throughout his Harvard career, but the emergence of Saltonstall as a partner brought him his greatest intercollegiate victory.

While new events were added to the traditional schedule over the next 25 years, Harvard's chief goal remained the same. That was to finish in the top two at the New England Intercollegiates in order to qualify for the North American championships.

Harvard was particularly successful in reaching this goal in the early 1960s, qualifying four straight years from 1961 to 1964. With more schools competing, and more participants at each school, Mike Horn has kept Harvard competitive since he became the first full-time coach in 1965.

Horn's teams have qualified four times (1970, 1974, 1975, and 1983) and won the championship in 1974 behind All-Americans Terry Neff and Chris Middendorf. The 1970 group included two All-Americans in Robbie Doyle and Abbott Reeve, a finalist for College Sailor of the Year. Doyle, a three-time All-American, was part of a brother act that year, as his brother Rich was an All-American at Notre Dame.

His Harvard sailing career began with a stint as skipper in the class of 1963. By 1985, Mike Horn was finishing up his second decade as coach of Harvard-Radcliffe sailors. His 1985 seniors honored his efforts by establishing the Horn Trophy, which, fittingly, was captured by Harvard in the first year of competition.

Harvard's own brother act surfaced in 1983 when Cohasset's Brian and Jon Keane earned All-American honors. It was Brian who articulated a concern of all Harvard sailors in regard to the timing of championship events, which usually coincided with Harvard's exam period. Speaking of a recent disappointment in the 1981 season, Keane said, "We have got to learn to overcome our biggest late-season disadvantage—lack of sleep."

In 1983 Brian Keane received the Senior Trophy. This award, voted by all sailing seniors in New England, recognizes competitive excellence and sportsmanship.

Harvard produced two other All-Americans during Horn's tenure, Jim Hammitt in 1978 and Steve Strittmatter in 1980. Although these individual and team honors are symbols of the program's excellence, the coach will just as quickly point out other signs of what Harvard sailing has accomplished.

"Between four hundred and five hundred recreational

sailors use our facility each year," says Horn. "We have sixty-five out for the team, and there may be fifty at any given practice. Where we used to have twenty people in the whole program when I was here, we now have twenty competing on a single afternoon."

Horn is also proud of the reputation that the Charles River Basin is building as a site for competition. It is simply one of the best places to host a regatta.

"People like coming here. Good teams know they can get good competition here, and we are attracting the major regattas," says Horn.

One of those is the Boston Dinghy Club Challenge Cup. The race for the 56-year-old trophy is the oldest continuous competition of its kind, and after years of rotating throughout New England, it has found a permanent home on the Charles.

Horn's pride over involvement at the Pavilion also includes the Radcliffe program. There was a time when women could crew with the men. But all that changed in the early 1960s.

"The University of Rhode Island complained about the practice, and at the time people were upset with the change. In retrospect, it was the best thing that ever happened to women's sailing because it put them on their own and gave New England a head start on the others."

While New England and the Mid-Atlantic compete as the strong areas in men's sailing, New England is the area for women. Consequently, it is that much tougher for New England crews to qualify for national and North American championships.

Radcliffe has been strong from the start. The women at Harvard continue to use the name Radcliffe because four national championships were won under that name long before Harvard entered the women's athletics business. Those titles came from 1968 to 1970 and again in 1972.

Jane Chalmers and Martha Fransson captured the first two titles. In 1970 the winners were Sandy Storer, later an assistant to Radcliffe president Matina Horner, and Lisa Fulweiler.

But the most extraordinary individual effort came in 1972, when Barbie Grant and Janice Stroud brought a fourth title to Cambridge. Stroud's 14-race performance included 12 firsts and 2 seconds, a level of consistency unheard of in championship competition.

Although the women have not won any further national titles, they have remained among the most consistent programs in the country. And a number of individuals have brought greater visibility to the program. In 1979 Laura Brown received the Radcliffe College Alumnae

Association Award, given each year to the top female athlete in the school. In 1981 this honor went to Lauren Norton, who also excelled as an All-Ivy ice hockey player.

The New England sailing community recognized two other sailors when the Outstanding Woman Sailor Award, voted on by the undergraduate sailors, went to Rony Seebok in 1983 and Jamie Jenkins in 1984.

Perhaps the honor that best tells the story of Harvard sailing over the past two decades was one bestowed upon Coach Mike Horn by the seniors in 1985. Through their efforts, a new event for men and women was added to the fall schedule, the Horn Trophy. And most fittingly, the first Horn Trophy was captured by the sailors of Harvard-Radcliffe.

CHAPTER 15

New Sports

Have pity on today's sports publicist. It used to be that a college sports information director could do a masterful job by knowing a lot about football, hockey, baseball, basketball, and track, and knowing a little about crew, squash, soccer, and a handful of other sports.

That is no longer the case. In 1970–71 Harvard athletics encompassed 19 men's varsity sports. They were cross-country, soccer, and football in the fall; basketball, fencing, hockey, skiing, squash, swimming, track, and wrestling in the winter; and baseball, heavyweight and lightweight crew, golf, lacrosse, sailing, tennis, and track in the spring. In 1984–85 the list was up to 41 men's and women's varsity sports.

"If a group of people want to do something here, we give them that opportunity," says Director of Athletics Jack Reardon. "They can form a club and then, if they show interest and show that they can maintain numbers, we can move them along to Level II varsity status."

The Level II label means that the Department of Athletics does not necessarily have to provide full financial support. It has been a way of moving a sport along quickly to the varsity level yet keeping certain controls on the operation of that sport. It is not simply a financial matter, for often a Level II sport shares a facility with a Level I sport (women's and men's ice hockey, swimming, and water polo), and priority in the use of facilities becomes a factor.

At the club level the undergraduates must be willing to work and prove that they are serious about their sport. "We don't encourage them at first," says Floyd Wilson, former head basketball coach and director of the Department of Intramurals, Physical Education, and Recreation since 1968. "Somebody has to show the interest, be willing to do all the legwork, and then we try to open doors for them and let them use the Harvard name."

As a result of this arrangement, club activity is often sporadic, depending on the presence of undergraduates who have a keen interest and will work for it. There will be a movement for a gymnastics team for a while and then, when graduation claims a certain organizer, the interest will die down. Polo, not water polo, is another of the sports that has surfaced at Harvard from time to time.

"What has frequently happened is that a club team will get pretty good, want to increase its schedule, and find that certain schools won't play them or they can't enter a tournament because they have that club status. Then they seek varsity status," says Wilson.

Another factor in deciding to move a sport to varsity status is what is happening in that sport throughout the Ivy League. If there is league-wide interest, then it becomes more desirable to field a varsity team in a given sport.

Five varsity teams emerged in the late 1970s and early 1980s in men's and women's volleyball, men's and women's water polo, and women's softball. The concern over what the league is doing doesn't always dictate what Harvard might do. As late as the 1984–85 season, only softball and women's volleyball among these had enough league interest to crown legitimate Ivy champions.

VOLLEYBALL (1980–85)

The origin of the volleyball program can be traced to its years as a club team under the control of Harvard's Department of Intramurals, Physical Education, and Recreation. The Indoor Athletic Building was volleyball's home then and remained so when varsity status was finally achieved.

The men's team has been consistently competitive since its inaugural campaign in 1980–81. The most successful season was 1982's 31-2 campaign, highlighted by winning the Ivy League tournament behind MVP David Twite. Again in 1985 Harvard bested its Ivy competition. However, the Ivy League has not recognized these as true Ivy championships, as only four Ivy schools have varsity men's volleyball programs.

The league has formally recognized women's volleyball, since six of the eight Ivy schools fielded varsity teams by 1983, with Yale and Dartmouth offering club entries. Harvard's team became a varsity in 1981 and immediately produced a two-time All-Ivy performer in Margaret Cheng (1981 and 1982).

WATER POLO (1980–84)

Another new varsity sport that emerged from longtime club status was water polo. This was one of the club sports

that went through peaks and valleys of undergraduate popularity.

Finally, in the fall of 1980, Coach Steve Pike and the men's varsity water polo team brought its act to Blodgett Pool. Three things became apparent right away. When NCAA runner-up UCLA came to town and took a 29-5 decision, it was reaffirmed that Harvard wasn't national caliber. When Harvard went 8-3 against New England competition, the Crimson proved to be one of the best teams in the area. And finally, when Brown won by 12-8, Harvard's chief nemesis had been identified. By the fall of 1984, with swim coach Joe Bernal directing Harvard fortunes, the record against the Bruins had reached 0-13.

While men's competition took place in the fall, the women took to Blodgett in the spring. Steve Pike got this program going in 1984 and was followed by women's swim coach Maura Costin '80 a year later. Blodgett Pool wasn't the only thing these programs shared. Through two seasons, the women were also looking for their first win over Brown.

SOFTBALL (1981–85)

"We have had some good people, some All-Ivy performers, but we haven't had that one pitcher who could make the difference. And that's what makes champions at this level."

That, according to Harvard softball coach John Wentzell, is what has kept his program from crossing that line from being marginally successful to challenging for championships.

Wentzell, a 1977 University of New Hampshire graduate, took over the program in its second varsity season, following Kit Morris, a former varsity ballplayer at Mississippi. (After leaving Harvard, Morris became an associate athletic director at Yale and then, in 1985, director of athletics at Davidson. One of his first moves there was to hire former Harvard football great Vic Gatto '69 as head football coach. Gatto, captain of Harvard's famed 1968 team, had been a succesful coach at Bates and Tufts and at one time a rumored successor to Harvard's Joe Restic.)

Both Morris and Wentzell served as an assistant to Director of Athletics Jack Reardon at the same time they carried out their spring coaching duties. These administrator-coaches directed teams that more often than not were winners against New England competition and near .500 in Ivy play. Both also coached Pat Horne, a

Above: *Harvard's philosophy of athletics for all is reflected in the 41 varsity sports offered by 1985. One of the newest was water polo, a sport in which Harvard quickly became second only to Brown among Ivy schools.*

Right: *Softball joined the varsity ranks in the spring of 1981, and third baseman Pat Horne immediately distinguished herself by earning two first team All-Ivy selections.*

hard-hitting third baseman whose two All-Ivy selections made her Harvard's best individual.

The best individual accomplishment came in the 1985 season, when freshman second baseman Mary Baldauf hit .488 to lead the nation in hitting.

Ivy softball crowned its champion through an annual tournament rather than through round-robin league play. This was as much a concession to spring weather in the Northeast as for any other reason. Harvard's best finish was third in 1982, when the weekend record was 3-3. Such is the fate of teams without the fastballer on the mound.

• • •

Harvard Senior Award Winners

William J. Bingham Award

Awarded annually to that (male) member of the graduating class of Harvard College who, through integrity, courage, leadership, and ability on the athletic fields, has best served the high purpose of Harvard as exemplified by William J. Bingham '16 (Harvard's first athletic director) in his years of loyal service to the College.

1954	T. Jefferson Coolidge '54, football and hockey
1955	Robert Rittenburg '55, track
1956	James P. Jorgensen '56, swimming
1957	John A. Simourian '57, football and baseball
1958	Dale W. Junta '58, tennis
1959	R. Dyke Benjamin '59, cross-country and track
	Robert R. Foster '59, football and wrestling
1960	Langley C. Keyes '60, soccer and lacrosse
1961	Perry T. Boyden '61, heavyweight crew
	Charles D. Ravenel '61, football and baseball
1962	Mark H. Mullin '62, cross-country and track
1963	John Pringle '63, swimming
1964	Eugene Kinasewich '64, hockey
1965	Paul Gunderson '65, heavyweight crew
1966	Anthony Lynch '66, track
1967	Robert Corris '67, swimming
1968	James Baker '68, cross-country and track
1969	Anil Nayar '69, squash
1970	Keith Colburn '70, cross-country and track
1971	Joseph V. Cavanagh '71, hockey and tennis
1972	Vincent McGugan '72, baseball
1973	Kevin F. Hampe '73, baseball and hockey
1974	Frederick L. Mitchell '74, swimming
1975	Richard M. Cashin, Jr., '75, heavyweight crew and squash
1976	Melvyn C. Embree '76, track
1977	Thomas P. Winn '77, football
1978	Steven C. Martin '78, lacrosse
1979	Geoffrey M. Stiles '79, track
1980	Michael Desaulniers '80, squash
	Peter S. Predun '80, lacrosse

1981   Robert W. Hackett '81, swimming
1982   Donald R. Fleming, Jr., '82, basketball
1983   Donald J. Allard, Jr., '83, baseball and football
        Mark E. Fusco '83, hockey
1984   Joseph K. Azelby '84, football
1985   Joseph D. Carrabino '84–5, basketball

Radcliffe College Alumnae Association Award

Awarded annually to that senior woman letter-winner who, through outstanding ability on the playing field and dedication to her sport or sports and qualities of leadership, best reflects the purposeful achievement of Radcliffe alumnae in every field around the world.

1975   Nancy Sato '75, diver
1976   Alison Muscatine '76, basketball and tennis
1977   Karen L. Linsley '77, field hockey
1978   Lucy E. Wood '78, field hockey
1979   Laura J. Brown '79, sailing
1980   Juliette D. Brynteson '80, soccer
1981   Lauren I. Norton '81, ice hockey and sailing
        Christine A. Sailer '81, field hockey and lacrosse
1982   Pamela Stone '82, diver
1983   Francesca S. DenHartog '83, lacrosse
        Maureen A. Finn '83, field hockey and lacrosse
1984   Margaret L. Hart '84, lacrosse and track
1985   Kate M. Wiley '85, cross-country and track

Francis H. Burr Scholarship

A scholarship fund established in memory of Francis H. Burr by his friends, to be awarded to a senior "who combines as nearly as possible Burr's remarkable qualities of character, leadership, scholarship, and athletic ability."

1918   William B. Snow '18, football
1919   Not awarded
1920   Wesley G. Brocker '22, football
1921   Not awarded
1922   Not awarded
1923   Joseph S. Clark '23, baseball
1924   Charles J. Hubbard, Jr., '24, crew and football
1925   Henry T. Dunker '25, football and track
1926   John J. Maher '26, football
1927   Ellsworth C. Haggerty '27, track
1928   John P. Chase '28, baseball and hockey
1929   Not awarded
1930   Francis J. Mardulier '30, track
1931   Vernon Munroe, Jr., '31, track

1932   W. Barry Wood, Jr., '32, baseball, football, hockey, and tennis
1933   Carl H. Hageman, Jr., '33, baseball and football
1934   Richard G. Ames '34, wrestling
1935   Chester K. Litman '35, football
1936   Robert C. Hall '36, track
1937   Charles W. Kessler '37, football
1938   Vernon H. Struck '38, baseball and football
1939   David R. V. Golding '41
        Richard H. Sullivan '39, basketball
1940   Thomas V. Healey '40, baseball and football
1941   Not awarded
1942   Loren G. MacKinney '42, football
        Paul Burton Rail '45
1943   David E. Allen '46
        F. Barton Harvey, Jr., '43, baseball and football
1944   Not awarded
1945   Not awarded
1946   Not awarded
1947   Not awarded
1948   Not awarded
1949   Paul W. Knaplund '49, crew
1950   Howard E. Houston, '50, heavyweight crew and football
        Paul C. Shafer '50, football
1951   A. Dwight Hyde, Jr., '51, football
1952   Dustin M. Burke '52, football, golf, and hockey
        Richard T. Button '52, world champion figure skater
1953   Charles W. Ufford, Jr., '53, soccer, squash, and tennis
1954   William W. Geertsema '54, crew
1955   Roger J. Bulger '55, basketball
1956   Arthur G. Siler '56, track
1957   H. Chouteau Dyer '57, swimming
1958   W. French Anderson '58, track
1959   Robert R. Foster '59, football and wrestling
1960   Lawrence B. Ekpebu '60, soccer
        Harold J. Keohane '60, football
1961   William P. Schellstede '61, swimming
1962   Robert E. Kaufmann '62, swimming
1963   David L. G. Johnston '63, hockey
1964   Robert P. Inman '64, basketball
1965   John F. O'Brien '65, football
1966   Barry L. Williams '66, basketball
1967   Dennis M. McCullough '67, hockey
1968   Thomas S. Williamson, Jr., '68, football
1969   Robert T. Bauer '69, hockey

1970	Gary L. Singleterry '70, football
1971	Michael K. Cahalan '71, swimming
1972	Geza P. Tatrallyay '72, fencing
1973	John B. Hagerty '73, football and lacrosse
1974	David P. St. Pierre '74, baseball and football
1975	Stephen H. Dart '75, football and track
1976	J. Hovey Kemp '76, heavyweight crew
1977	William B. Kaplan '77, squash
1978	Paul J. Halas '78, baseball and football
1979	Glenn A. Fine '79, basketball
1980	Richard A. Horner '80, football
1981	Robert J. Woolway '81, football
1982	Michael H. Davis '82, lacrosse
1983	James E. Johnson '83, track
1984	Kenneth S. Code '84, hockey
1985	Brian D. Bergstrom '85, football

Mary G. Paget Prize

Awarded annually by the presidents of Radcliffe and Harvard to that senior student who has contributed the most to women's athletics.

1975	Jean M. Guyton '75, basketball
1976	Nova Carlene Rhodes '76, field hockey and lacrosse
1977	Susan M. Williams '77, basketball
1978	Katherine N. Fulton '78, basketball
1979	Mary T. Howard '79, field hockey and track
1980	Kathryn A. Taylor '80, cross-country and track
1981	Elizabeth A. Ippolito '81, field hockey and softball
1982	Marlene T. Schoofs '82, soccer, softball, and volleyball
1983	Jennifer White '83, field hockey, ice hockey, and lacrosse
1984	Nancy W. Boutilier '83–84, basketball, crew, lacrosse, and softball
1985	Joan E. Pew '85, field hockey, lacrosse, and squash

John P. Fadden Award

Awarded annually to a senior student who has overcome physical adversity to make a contribution to his/her team (varsity, junior varsity, or intramural).

1966	Richard St. Onge '66, football
1967	David Davis '67, football
1968	Carleton Goodwin '68, football
1969	John Ignacio '69, baseball and football
1970	John Cassis '70, football

1971	Joseph V. Cavanagh '71, hockey and tennis
1972	Peter Sutton '72, heavyweight crew
1973	Richard Bridich '73, baseball and football
1974	Bernard Bach '74, intramural basketball
1975	Leigh P. Hogan '75, baseball and hockey
1976	David English '76, diver
1977	James P. Kubacki '77, football
1978	Christopher J. Doherty '78, football and lacrosse
1979	Gordon A. Gardiner '79, heavyweight crew
1980	Julie Cornman '80, field hockey and lacrosse
1981	John O. Murphy '81, cross-country and track
1982	Valerie L. Romero '82, basketball, softball, and volleyball
1983	Maureen V. Gildea '83, swimming
	Brendan A. Meagher '83, lacrosse
1984	Andrew Nolan '84, football
1985	Joseph D. Carrabino '84–5, basketball
	Jennifer J. Hale '85, heavyweight crew and skiing

Carroll F. Getchell Manager of the Year Award

Awarded each year to the manager who demonstrates excellent qualities of leadership and ability as well as making significant contributions to the Harvard managerial system.

1972	Hollis McLoughlin '72, baseball
1973	Steven Berizzi '73, swimming
1974	Ronald D. Thorpe '74, football
1975	Robert Drucker '75, basketball, football, and lacrosse
1976	Mark Maloney '76, football and lacrosse
1977	Alan S. Dawes '77, baseball
1978	Carlos A. Cordeiro '78, crew
1979	Yuki A. Moore '79, hockey
1980	David Shultz '80, cross-country and track
1981	Barbara B. Keenan '81, football
1982	Susan A. Barton '82, track
1983	John M. Fenton '83, baseball and basketball
1984	Frances Hochschild '84, football
1985	Christina L. Covino '85, cross-country and track

• • •

Harvard Varsity Club Hall of Fame

Harvard's athletic Hall of Fame is supervised by the Harvard Varsity Club. To be eligible for the Hall of Fame, an athlete must be at least 25 years out of college. As a result, there are no female letter-winners in the Hall through 1985. There is one female who was not a letter-winner, Dr. Tenley Albright, Radcliffe '53–55, the Olympic gold medal winner in figure skating (in 1956) who was inducted in 1980. She follows Dick Button '52, another champion figure skater, who became the first inductee from a non-varsity sport.

All-Around Performance
Robert P. Kernan '03
George P. Gardner '10
Richard B. Wigglesworth '12
George Owen '23
Isadore Zarakov '27
W. Barry Wood, Jr., '32
Charles W. Ufford, Jr., '53
Richard J. Clasby '54

Baseball
Frederick W. Thayer '78
William H. Coolidge '81
Edward H. Nichols '86

George W. Foster '87
John A. Highlands '93
William T. Reid '01
Orville G. Frantz '03
Walter Clarkson '03
Henry L. Nash '16
Richard Harte '17
George E. Abbot '17
Robert W. Emmons '20
Arthur J. Conlon '22
John N. Barbee, Jr., '28
Howard W. Burns '28
George E. Donaghy '29
Edward H. McGrath '31

Charles Devens '32
Richard Maguire '36
Thomas H. Bilodeau '37
Ulysses J. Lupien, Jr., '39
Warren S. Berg '44
Walter Coulson '48 ocC
John G. Caulfield '50
Clifton D. Crosby '50
Ira F. Godin '50
Robert Hastings '57
John Simourian '57

Basketball
Saul W. Mariaschin '47
George J. Hauptfuhrer '48

Boxing
Walter L. Crampton '36
William A. Smith '36

Crew
William A. Bancroft '78
Fred W. Smith '79
Robert P. Perkins '84
James J. Storrow '85
Francis L. Higginson '00
Oliver D. Filley '06
John Richardson '08
Roger W. Cutler '11
Alexander Strong '12
Charles C. Lund '16
Richmond K. Kane '22
Geoffrey Platt '27
John Watts '28
Forrester A. Clark '29
Malcolm Bancroft '33
Gerard J. Cassedy '33
Edward H. Bennett, Jr., '37
James F. Chace '38
Dudley Talbot '39
David Challinor, Jr., '43
Darcy Curwen '43
Robert G. Stone, Jr., '45 ocC
Justin E. Gale '48
Michael J. Scully '48 ocC
Paul W. Knaplund '49
Frank R. Strong '49
William T. Leavitt '50

Louis B. McCagg, Jr., '52
Townsend S. Swayze '59,

Fencing
George H. Breed '99
Burke Boyce '22
Edward L. Lane '24
Everett H. Lane '24
John G. Hurd '34

Football
Bernard W. Trafford '93
Marshall Newell '94
Charles Brewer '96
Benjamin H. Dibblee '99
Percy D. Haughton '99
Charles D. Daly '01
David J. Campbell '02
Francis H. Burr '09
Hamilton Fish '10
Lothrop Withington '11
Charles E. Brickley '15
Huntington R. Hardwick '15
Stanley B. Pennock '15
Edward W. Mahan '16
Edward L. Casey '19
Arnold Horween '20
Thomas S. Wood, Jr., '20
Charles J. Hubbard '24
Arthur E. French '29
David Guarnaccia '29
Eliot T. Putnam '29
Benjamin H. Ticknor II '31
Edmund A. Mays, Jr., '32
Irad B. Hardy, Jr., '33
David E. Kopans '34
Joseph F. Nee '38
Vernon H. Struck '38
Clarence E. Boston '39
Clifford W. Wilson '39
Torbert H. Macdonald '40
Francis M. Lee '42
Loren G. MacKinney '42
Endicott Peabody II '42
John W. Fisher '45 ocC
Philip K. O'Donnell '49
Thomas H. Gannon '50
Howard E. Houston '50

Carroll M. Lowenstein '52 ocC
T. Jefferson Coolidge '54
John C. Culver '54
William M. Meigs '56
Theodore N. Metropoulos '57
Robert T. Shaunessy '59

Golf
Henry C. Egan '05
Walter E. Egan '05
Robert T. Jones '24
Charles L. Peirson '25
Edward S. Stimpson II '27
James A. Hutchinson, Jr., '28
Edward A. Cooney, Jr., '55

Hockey
Alfred Winsor '02
Daniel A. Newhall '06
S. Trafford Hicks '10
Frederick D. Huntington '12
William H. Claflin '15
John I. Wylde '17
Edward L. Bigelow '21
Jabish Holmes '21
John P. Chase '28
Joseph Morrill, Jr., '28
Rene F. G. Giddens '30
John B. Garrison '31
Paul deB. deGive '34
Frederick R. Moseley, Jr., '36
George S. Ford '37
George F. Roberts '38
F. Austin Harding, Jr., '39
Goodwin W. Harding '43
Richard W. Mechem '45
William J. Cleary, Jr., '56
Charles B. Flynn '56
Robert B. Cleary '58
E. Robert Owen '58

Lacrosse
Charles E. Marsters '07
Fred C. Alexander '10
Paul Gustafson '12
Nelson N. Cochrane '32
Philip B. Waring '54
Dexter S. Lewis '56

Sailing
Hilary H. Smart '47 ocC
Hanson C. Robbins '59
William G. Saltonstall, Jr., '59

Skating
Richard T. Button '52
Tenley E. Albright '53–55

Soccer
Walter W. Weld '16
John F. Carr '28
Harvard H. Broadbent '32

Squash
Myles P. Baker '22
W. Palmer Dixon '25
J. Lawrence Pool '28
Beekman H. Pool '32
Germain G. Glidden '36
Benjamin H. Heckscher '57

Swimming
Charles G. Hutter, Jr., '38
Elisha R. Greenhood, Jr., '39
Eric Cutler '40
Francis C. Powers '41
Forbes H. Norris, Jr., '49
David F. Hawkins '56
James P. Jorgensen '56
H. Chouteau Dyer '57
Francis X. Gorman '59 ocC
William T. Murray '59
James D. Stanley II '59

Tennis
Richard D. Sears '83
Robert D. Wrenn '95
Malcolm D. Whitman '99
William J. Clothier '04
Richard N. Williams '16
George C. Caner '17
Dale W. Junta '58
Edward W. Weld '59

Track
Evert J. Wendell '82
William H. Goodwin '84

Wendell Baker '86
George R. Fearing '93
John L. Bremer '96
Ellery H. Clark '96
William A. Schick '05
William M. Rand '09
William J. Bingham '16
Edward O. Gourdin '21
Willard L. Tibbetts, Jr., '26
John N. Watters '26
Ellsworth C. Haggerty '27
James L. Reid '29
N. Penrose Hallowell, Jr., '32
Eugene E. Record '32
John H. Dean '34
Milton G. Green '36
Alexander C. Northrup '38
James D. Lightbody, Jr., '40
Samuel M. Felton, Jr., '48
Robert Rittenburg '55
Arthur G. Siler '56
Peter C. Harpel '57
Richard G. Wharton '57
Arthur E. Reider '58

R. Dyke Benjamin '59
Joel R. Landau '59

Wrestling
Pat O. Johnson '33
Richard G. Ames '34
John C. Harkness '38
John H. Lee, Jr., '53

Harvard Varsity Club Award
1965   John P. Chase '28
1966   Richard P. Hallowell II '20
1967   David A. Mittell '39
1968   Alexander H. Bright '19
1969   Wilbur J. Bender '27
1970   William J. Bingham '16
1971   Albert H. Gordon '23
1972   Samuel S. Drury '35
1973   John P. Fadden '27
1980   Forrester A. Clark '29
1981   John W. Blodgett, Jr., '23
1982   Leroy Anderson '29
       John M. Barnaby '32

INDEX OF MAJOR H WINNERS

This index contains the names of all the men and women who are listed by the Harvard Department of Athletics and the Harvard Varsity Club as having been awarded major letters between the years 1852 and 1985.

The symbols for various sports are as follows:

B	Baseball	G	Golf	Sl	Sailing	TI	Indoor Track
Bb	Basketball	H	Hockey	Sk	Skiing	TO	Outdoor Track
C	Crew (for years 1852–1963)	HC	Heavyweight Crew	S	Soccer	V	Volleyball
CC	Cross Country	L	Lacrosse	So	Softball	WP	Water Polo
Fc	Fencing	LC	Lightweight Crew	Sq	Squash	W	Wrestling
FH	Field Hockey	R	Rifle	Sw	Swimming		
F	Football	Rb	Rugby	Te	Tennis		

1852–1922

Abbot, George Ezra, '17. B '15, '16
Abbott, Edward Gardner, '60. C '59, '60
Abbott, John, L.S. B '93
Abeles, Alfred Taussig, '13. C '11, '12, '13
Abeles, Charles Taussig, '13. C '11, '12, '13

Abercrombie, Daniel Putnam, 66. B '65, '66
Abercrombie, Ralph, '03. T '00
Acton, Robert, M.S. F '93. C '92
Adams, Arthur, '99. B '99

Adams, Charles Francis, '88. C '86
Adams, George Caspar, '86 and L.S. F '82, '83, '86
Adams, Henry, '98. C '96, '98
Adams, Ivers Shepard, '95. B '95

Adams, Schuyler, '14. H '14

Adams, William Bradford, '13. T '12, '13

Agassiz, Alexander, '55 and G.S. C '55, '56, '57, '58

Alexander, Walter, '87 and L.S. C '85, '87, '88

Alger, Horace Chapin, '79 and M.S. B '78, '79, '80

Allen, Edward Ellis, '84. T '84

Allen, Frederick Hobbes, '80. C '77, '78, '79

Allen, Frederic Stevens, '16. T '16

Allen, Horace Russell, '92. T '89, '90

Allen, Herbert Tufts, '86. B '83, '84, '85, '86

Allen, Otis Everett, '72. B '71

Allen, William Sylvester, '88. F '86

Allis, Edward Phelps, '15. G '14

Alsop, Edward Hussey, '15. B '13

Alward, James Herbert, L.S. B '90, '91. F '90

Ames, Adelbert, '03. F '02

Ames, Frederick Lothrop, '98. C '96

Ames, James Barr, '68. B '66, '67, '68

Ames, Leroy Allston, '96. B '94

Angell, James Waterhouse, '18. C '18

Angier, Donald, '22. H '20, '21, '22. F '21

Annan, William Howard, '75. B '71, '72, '73

Apollonio, Carlton, '08. F '07

Applegate, William Augustus, '01. T '00

Appleton, Francis Randall, '75. C '75

Appleton, George Miller, '22. C '21, '22

Appleton, James Waldingfield, '88. F '87

Appleton, Randolph Morgan, '84. F '81, '82, '83

Appleton, William Channing, '17. H '17

Arai, Yoneo, '12. B '12

Armstrong, Joseph Jerome, '14. T '13

Arnold, Robert Veazie, '08. C '06, '07

Aronson, Ralph Harris, '10. B '08, '09

Aspinwall, George Lowell, '14. C '14

Atkinson, Charles Heath, '85. T '83, '84, '85

Atkinson, Edward Williams, '81. C '80. F '80

Atkinson, Henry Morrell, '84. F '81

Atkinson, Henry Morrell, '15. F '14

Atkinson, Henry Russell, '21. C '21

Austin, Francis Boylston, '86. F '83

Austin, Percy, '71. B '69, '70, '71

Austin, Perry Gwynne More, '13. T '12

Austin, William Russell, '79 and L.S. F '76, '77, '79

Avery, Thomas Morris, '21. H '19, '20

Ayer, James Bourne, '03. C '01, '02, '03

Ayers, Howard, '83s. F '82

Ayres, Daniel Roe, '05. T '04

Ayres, Russell Romeyn, '15. B '13, '14

Babson, Richard Cedric, '12. B '10, '11, '12

Bacon, Daniel Carpenter, '76. F '75. C '73, '74, '75

Bacon, Elliot Cowdin, '10. C '08, '09, '10

Bacon, Francis McNiel, '21. H '19, '20, '21

Bacon, Gasper Griswold, '08. C '07, '08

Bacon, Robert, '80. F '77, '78, '79. C '80

Bacon, Robert Low, '07. C '05, '06, '07

Badger, Sherwin Campbell, '23. C '22

Baker, Charles William, '84. B '81, '82, '83, '84

Baker, Charles William, '22. H '20, '21, '22

Baker, Edwin Osborne, '17. H '15, '16, '17

Baker, Myles Pierce, '22. B '21

Baker, Wendell, '86. T '83, '84, '85, '86

Baker, William Francis, '93. T '93

Balch, Franklin Greene, '88. T '88. C '87

Balch, Gordon Henry, '12. C '10, '11, '12

Baldwin, Charles Handy, '88. T '88

Baldwin, David Alonzo, '03. F '01

Baldwin, George Storer, '21. H '21

Baldwin, Robert, '17. H '15, '16, '17

Ball, George Gill, '08. C '06

Bancroft, Guy, '02. C '00, '02

Bancroft, Hugh, '97 and L.S. C '99, '00, '01

Bancroft, William Amos, '78 and L.S. C '76, '77, '78, '79

Bancroft, Wilder Dwight, '88. F '87

Bangs, Francis Reginald, '91 and L.S. F '91

Bangs, Lester Walton, '08. T '08

Banker, Benson Beriah, '66. B '65, '66

Bardeen, Charles Russell, '93. T '92, '93

Barker, Albert Damon, '11. T '10

Barker, William Torrey, '73. B '73

Barnard, Charles Arthur, '02 and L.S. F '00, '01, '02

Barnes, Albert Mallard, '71. B '70, '71

Barney, Harold Bryant, '08. F '05

Barr, John Lester, '10. T '09, '10

Barron, William Andros, '14. T '12, '13, '14

Barrows, Albert Armington, M.S. H '00

Bartholf, John Charles Palmer, '13. B '12

Bass, George, '71. C '71

Batchelder, Charles Foster, '20. C '18, '19, '20

Batchelder, Ferdinand Winthrop, '85. T '83

Batchelder, George Lewis, '92. T '91, '92

Batchelder, George Lewis, '19. C '19. F '16

Batchelder, Roland Brown, '13. T '12

Bates, Harry Wakefield, '91 and '92. B '88, '90, '91, '92

Bates, Waldron, '79. B '79

Battelle, Harold Munro, '93. C '90, '91

Bauer, Frank Robert, '04. T '03, '04

Beal, Jarvis Thayer, '17. B '16

Beale, Arthur Messinger, '97. B '94, '97. F '93, '95, '96

Beaman, Harry Clayton, '85. B '83, '85

Bean, Karl Albert, '84. B '81, '82

Beardsell, William Lee, '00. H '00

Behr, Gustave Edward, '03 and G.S. T '01, '02, '03

Belknap, Waldron Phoenix, '20. F '19

Bell, William Appleton, '73. C '72

Belshaw, Charles Mortimer, '83. C '81, '83

Bemis, Harry Haskell, '87. T '85, '86, '87

Bemis, John Wheeler, '85. F '84

Bettens, Thomas Simms, '74. B '74

Bettle, Griscom, '14. F '13

Biddle, Alexander, '16. T '15, '16

Biddle, Louis Alexander, '84. F '83

Biddle, Nicholas, '00. C '98, '00

Bigelow, Edward Livingston, '21. B '19, '21. H '19, '20, '21

Bigelow, Francis Horace, '98. T '96, '97, '98

Bigelow, John Lawrence, '16. F '14

Bingham, Isaac Edward, '89. B '87

Bingham, Norman Williams, '95. T '93, '95

Bingham, William John, '16. T '14, '15, '16

Bird, Charles Sumner, '77. B '76

Bird, Francis William, '04. T '02, '03, '04

Blackall, Robert Murray, '12. H '10, '11, '12. F '11

Blackman, Floyd Horace, '14. T '13

Blagden, Crawford, '02. F '01

Blagden, Francis Meredith, '09. C '06, '07, '08, '09

Blagden, Linzee, '96. C '96

Blaikie, William, '66. C '65, '66

Blair, Austin Benedict, '22. B '20

Blake, Charles Arthur, '93. T '93

Blake, Robert Fulton, '99 and G.S. C '98, '99, '01

Blake, Robert Parkman, '94. C '93

Blakemore, Arthur Walker, '97 and L.S. T '00

Blanchard, Benjamin Seaver, '79. F '75, '76, '77, '78

Blanchard, John Adams, '91. F '89

Blanchard, Wells, '16. F '15

Blanchard, Webster Sanderson, '17. T '17

Bloss, Edward Buell, '94. T '91, '92, '93, '94

Blumer, Thomas Spriggs, '10. T '08, '09

Blythe, Hugh, '01. F '00

Boal, Walter Ayres, '00 and L.S. F '97, '98. T '99, '00, '01

Boardman, Edwin Augustus, '99. C '97

Bolan, Joel Carlton, '76. C '76

Boles, William Joseph, '17. F '15

Bolton, Irving Castle, '12. B '12

Bond, Charles Lawrence, '20s. T '20

Bond, Carroll Taney, '94. C '92

Bond, Rufus Hallowell, '19. B '19. F '16

Bonsal, Leigh, '84. F '82, '83

Borden, Alfred, '96. F '95. C '95.

Bordman, John, '94 and L.S. T '96

Borland, William Gibson, '86. C '83, '84

Bothfeld, Henry Soule, '17. B '16

Bouvé, George Winthrop, '98. F '96, '97

Bowditch, Edward, '69. B '68

Bowditch, Edward, '03 and L.S. F '00, '01, '02, '03

Bowditch, John Perry, '05. C '04

Bowen, Richard Howard, '20. C '18

Boyd, Alexander, '82. F '80, '81

Boyd, Robert Saint Barbe, '14. T '11, '12, '13, '14. H '14

Boyden, Robert Wetherbee, '10. T '09

Boyden, Roland William '85 and L.S. F '86, '87. B '86, '87, '88

Boyer, Sidney Clarke, '10. B '10

Boynton, Eleazar Bradley, '02. T '01, '02

Brackett, Sewall Caroll, '91. T '91

Bradbury, William Francis, '06. B '05

Bradford, Standish, '24. C '22

Bradlee, Frederick Josiah, '15. F '12, '13, '14

Bradley, Everett, '13. F '13

Bradley, John Dorr, '86. T '84, '85, '86

Brandegee, Edward Deshon, '81. C '79, '80, '81

Bremer, John Lewis, '96 and M.S. T '94, '95, '96, '98

Brennan, Daniel Clarke, '07. B '07

Brewer, Arthur Harris, '96 and '99. F '93, '94, '95, '96

Brewer, Charles, '96. F '92, '93, '94, '95

Brewer, Edward Slocum, '19. C '19

Brickley, Charles Edward, '15. F '12, '13, '14. T '13, '14, '15. B '15

Briggs, Templeton, '09. B '07, '08, '09. H '07, '09

Brigham, Dwight Stillman, '08. B '08

Brigham, Nat Maynard, '80. C '77, '78, '79, '80

Bright, Alexander Harvey, '19. H '19. B '18

Brill, Karl Friedrich, '08. F '04, 8

Brinsmade, Chapin, '07. T '06

Brocker, Wesley Goodwin, '22. F '20, '21

Brooks, Lawrence, '91. C '90

Brooks, William Allen, '87. F '84, '86. C '85, '86, '87

Brown, George Franklin, '92. T '92

Brown, Holcombe James, '02. T '99, '00

Brown, John Fiske, '22. F '20, '21. T '21, '22

Brown, Joseph Mansfield, '53. C '52, '53

Brown, Lathrop, '04. F '01

Brown, Randolph Randall, '17. C '16

Brown, Reginald Woodman Plummer, '98. F '95, '96

Brown, Stanley Noël, '24. C '22

Browne, Gilbert Goodwin, '10. F '07, '08, '09

Browne, Thomas Quincy, '88. C '85, '86, '87

Brownell, Morris Ruggles, '02. C '01, '02

Bryant, John, '73. C '72

Bryant, William Sohier, '84. C '84

Buchman, Julius, '83. C '81

Buell, Charles Chauncey, '23. B '21. F '20, '21

Buffum, Fred Stephen, '04. T '04

Bull, Charles Caldwell, '98. C '96, '97

Bullard, Frederick Keil, '20. B '19

Bullard, Harold, '02. C '00, '01, '02

Bullard, John Richards, '96. C '94, '95, '96

Buntin, Roger Williams, '21. H '19, '21

Burbidge, Norman Elwell, '17. F '16

Burchard, Leeds, '06 and '07. C '05, '07

Burden, James Abercrombie, '21. C '20

Burden, William Armstead Moale, '00. F '98, '99

Burgess, Edward Guyer, '98. B '95, '96, '97, '98

Burgess, George Ebenezer, '93. C '93

Burgess, James Atwood, '04. F '01

Burgess, Theodore Phillips, '87. C '85, '86. F '84, '86

Burke, Francis, L.S. F '79

Burke, John William, '23. T '21, '22

Burke, Thomas Edmund, sp. T '99

Burnett, Francis Lowell, '02. F '98, '99, '00

Burnett, John-Torrey, '91. B '90

Burnham, Arthur, '70. C '69

Burnham, Bradford Hinckley, '24. C '22

Burnham, Stanley, '19 and ocC. F '19

Burr, Francis Hardon, '09. F '05, '06, '07, '08. B '06

Burt, Charles Dean, '82. B '81, '82

Bush, Archibald McClure, '71. B '68, '69, '70, '71

Bush, Henry Keneth, '11. F '10[1]

Bush, Stephen Hayes, '01. T '98, '99

Busk, Frederick Wadsworth, '16. C '16

Butler, Alfred Munson, '02. T '00

Butler, Arthur Pierce, '88. C '86, '87. F '86, '87

Cable, Arthur Goodrich, '09. B '09

Cable, Theodore, '13. T '11, '12, '13

Cabot, Arthur Tracy, '72 and M.S. F '74

Cabot, Edward, '20. H '19

Cabot, Edward Twisleton, '83 and L.S. F '79, '80, '81, '82, '83. C '81

Cabot, Henry Bromfield, '17. C '15, '16

Cabot, Norman Winslow, '98. F '94, '95, '96, '97

Callaway, Trowbridge, '05. H '04, '05

Cameron, Alexander Abbot, '17. C '16

Cameron, Winfield Henry, '95. C '94

Camp, Jay Beidler, '15. T '13, '14, '15

Campbell, David Bell, '22. C '22

Campbell, David Colin, '02. F '99, '00, '01

Campbell, Francis Augustine, L.S. B '87, '88

Campbell, Rolla Dacres, '17. T '16

Campbell, Thomas Joseph, '12. F '10, '11

Caner, George Colket, '17. F '16, LT '16

Capper, Francis Whittier, '15. T '13, '14, '15

Carlisle, Walter Gordon, '08. B '08

Carnochan, Gouverneur Morris, '14. H '14

Carpenter, Charles Cummings, '24. T '22

Carpenter, George Albert, '88 and L.S. F '88, C '88

Carr, Frank Fletcher, M.S. T '91, '92

Carr, John Preston, '11. B '10

Carr, Proctor, '04. H '02, '03, '04. B '02, '03, '04

Carr, Willard Zeller, '06. F '05

Carson, William Henry, L.S. T '94

Carter, Bernard Shirley, '15. T '13

Cary, George, '83s. T '82

Casey, Edward Lawrence, '19 and ocC. F '16, '19

Castle, Alfred Lowrey, '06. B '06

Cate, Karl Springer, '09. H '09

Cate, Martin Luther, '77. F '74, 75

Chadwick, Oliver Moulton, '11. H '10, '11

Chalfant, William, '82. C '80, '81, '82

Chamberlain, David Blaisdell, '86. T '86

Chandler, Whitman Mitchell, '98. B '96, '97, '98

Chaney, George Carter, '94. T '91, '93

Chanler, Lewis Stuyvesant, '14. C '12, '13, '14

Chanler, William Chamberlain, '19.   C '19

Chapin, Vinton, '23.   F '21

Chase, Alfred Endicott, '05.   C '04, '05

Chase, John Denison, '22.   T '22

Chase, Percy, '88.   T '86, '88

Chase, Samuel Thompson, L.S.   LT '90

Chatman, John Edwin, '97.   C '95

Cheney, George Locke, '78.   C '76

Chisholm, Henry Arnott, '74.   B '72

Choate, Charles Francis, '88.   B '86, '87

Church, Frederick Cameron, '21.   H '19. F '19[2]

Churchill, Asaph, '88.   F '87[3]

Churchill, Winthrop Hallowell, '23.   F '20, '21

Chute, Richard, '22.   T '20, 21

Claflin, Adams Davenport, '86.   B '85

Claflin, William Henry, '15.   H '13, '14, '15

Clapp, Channing, '55.   C '55

Clark, Charles Arthur, '20.   F '19. H '19. T '19, '20

Clark, Clarence Sewell, '16.   H '16

Clark, David Crawford, '86.   T '85

Clark, Edward Henry, '66.   C '65

Clark, Ellery Harding, '96 and L.S.   T '96, '97, '99

Clark, Franklin Haven, '84.   F '82, '83

Clark, George Crawford, '01.   B '98, '99, '00

Clark, Harold Benjamin, '01.   T '98, '01

Clark, Herbert Lincoln, '87.   T '86, '87

Clark, Henry Wadsworth, '23.   F '21

Clark, John Dudley, '03.   F '00, '02

Clark, Joseph Sill, '83.   L T '83

Clark, Joseph Sill, '23.   B '22

Clark, Louis Monroe, '81.   F '79, '80

Clark, Philip MacLean, L.S.   T '06

Clark, Sydney Proctor, '14.   B '12, '13, '14. H '14

Clark, William Carroll, '03.   T '03

Clarke, Edmund Arthur Stanley, '84.   C '82, '83

Clarke, John Gray, '98.   T '97, '98

Clarkson, Thomas Henry, '99.   B '96

Clarkson, Walter, '03s. and '04s.   B '01, '02, '03, '04

Clement, Frederic Percival, '16.   T '16

Clerk, William Graham, '01 and G.S.   T '00, '01, '03

Clifford, Robert Clifford, '12.   B '11

Clothier, William Jackson, '04.   F '02, '03. H '03, '04. L T '02

Cobb, Augustus Smith, '07.   T '06

Cobb, Frederick Woodburn, '93.   B '91, '92

Cobb, Robert Codman, '15.   C '15

Coburn, Philip Fairbairn, '23.   F '21

Coburn, Paul Naylor, '02 and L.S.   B '03, '04, '05

Cochrane, Francis Douglas, '99.   F '97, '98

Codman, John, '85.   F '83

Cogswell, George Proctor, '88.   T '88

Cohen, Alfred Henry, L.S.   B '79

Coleman, John Stanley, '19.   C '18

Collamore, Gilman, '93.   T '92, '93

Colony, John Joslin, '85 and L.S.   C '85, '86

Colwell, William Arnold, G.S.   T '03, '04

Condon, Edward Beach, '18.   H '17

Conlon, Arthur Joseph, '22.   B '20, '21, '22. F '21

Converse, Joseph Henry, '02 and M.S.   T '99, '01, '02, '03

Cook, Benjamin, '92 and L.S.   B '91, '92, '93, '94

Cook, John Sheerer, '92.   T '91, '92

Coolidge, Amory, 17.   C '16

Coolidge, Charles Allerton, '17.   F '14, '15, '16

Coolidge, Edward Erwin, '01 and L.S.   B '00, '01, '02, '03

Coolidge, Frank Pelham, '16.   B '15, '16

Coolidge, Frederic Shurtleff, '87.   C '86

Coolidge, John Gardner, '20.   B '18

Coolidge, Julian Lowell, '95.   T' 94

Coolidge, Thomas Jefferson, '84.   T '81. B '83

Coolidge, Thomas Jefferson, '15.   F '14

Coolidge, William Henry, '81 and L.S.   B '79, '80, '81, '82, '83, '84. F '82

Coon, James Hathaway, '13.   B '12

Coonley, Avery, '94.   T '94

Copeland, Frederick Winsor, '13.   T '11, '12, '13

Corbett, Hamilton Forbush, '11.   F '08, '09, '10

Corbett, John, '94.   B '92, '93, '94. F '90, '91

Corbin, John, '92 and G.S.   T '92, '93

Corlett, William Wellington, '06.   C '05

Corning, Henry Wick, '91.   B '89

Costigan, Henry Dunster, '20.   T '18

Cowdin, John Elliot, '79.   F '78. T '79

Cowen, Rawson Richardson, '16.   F '13, '15

Cowling, John Valadon, '87.   F '83

Cozzens, George Freeman, '98.   F '96. B '98

Crane, Aaron Rogers, '84.   F '82, '83. T '83, '84

Crane, Joshua, '90.   T '90

Crane, Roy Elwood, '05.   T '05

Cranston, John Samuel, '92.   C '89. F '88, '89, '90

Crocker, Adams, '85.   B '82, '83, '84

Crocker, Alvah, '79.   C '77, '78

Crocker, Douglas, '10.   B '09

Crocker, Frank Weyman, '22.   B '21

Crocker, John, '22.   F '20, '21

Crosby, Maunsell Schieffelin, '08.   T '06, '07, '08

Crosby, Steven Van Rensselaer, '91.   F '88, '89

Crosby, William Edgar, '24.   H '22

Crowley, Charles Francis, '11.   F '08

Crowninshield, Benjamin William, '58.   C '55, '56, '57, '58

Crowninshield, Casper, '60.   C '58, '59, '60

Crowninshield, Frederic, '66.   C '65

Cummin, John White, '92.   B '91

Cummings, Charles Kimball, '93.   C '91, '92, '93

Cummings, Harry Irving, '91.   B '89, 90

Cummings, John Brennan, '13.   T '11, '12, '13

Cumnock, Arthur James, '91.   F '87, '88, '89, '90

Cunniff, John, '07.   F '04

Cunningham, Alan, '16.   H '15

Cunningham, Lawrence, '15.   B '15

Cunningham, William Henry, '53.   C '52

Currier, Edward Putnam, '09.   B '06, '07, '08, '09

Curtis, Charles Pelham, '83 and L.S.   C '81, '82. T '84, '85

Curtis, Horatio Greenough, '65.   C '64

Curtis, James Freeman, '99.   G '98

Curtis, Laurence, '16.   F '15. H '14, '15

Curtis, Louis, '14.   C '14

Curtis, Nathaniel, '77.   F '75, '76

Curtis, Richard Cary, '16.   F '14, '15

Curtis, Thomas James, '52.   C '52

Cushing Hayward Warren, '77 and M.S.   F '75, '76, '77, '78, '79

Cushing, Livingston, '79 and L.S.   F '76, '77, '78, '79

Cushman, Paul, '13.   H '13

Cutler, Elliott Carr, '09.   C '08, '09

Cutler, John Wilson, '09.   F '08

Cutler, Roger Wilson, '11.   C '09, '10, '11

Cutler, Walter Salisbury, '75.   B '73, '74

Cutting, Hayward, '59.   C '58

Cutts, Harry Madison, M.S.   B '81. F '80

Cutts, Oliver Frost, L.S.   F '01

Dabney, Alfred Stackpole, '09.   L T '07

Dabney, Ralph Pomeroy, '82.   F '80

Dadmun, Harrie Holland, '17.   F '15, '16

Daland, Tucker, '73.   C '73

Daly, Charles Dudley, '01.   F '98, '99, '00. T '99, '00

Daly, Leo Jameson, '03. B '02. F '02

Damon, Lindsay Todd, '94 and G.S. C '95

Damon, Sherman, '21. C '20, '21

Dana, Edmund Trowbridge, '09. B '07, '08, '09

Dana, Paul, '74. C '73

Dana, Payson, '04. T '04

Dana, Richard Henry, '74. C '72, '73, '74

Dana, William Butler Duncan, '14. F '13

Davenport, Charles Albert, '90. T '87, '88

Davidson, Frederick Coolidge, '13. G '12

Davis, Charles Bridge, '84. C '84

Davis, Dwight Filley, '00. L T '99

Davis, Edward Perkins, '99. B '97

Davis, Fellowes, '95. C '94

Davis, Harry Ransom, '23. T '22

Davis, John Tilden, '89. F '88. C '87, '88

Davis, Lincoln, '94. C '93, '94

Davis, Philip Whitney, '93. T '90, '92, '93

Davis, Robert Howe, '91 and L.S. T '88, '90, '91, '92

Davis, Samuel Craft, '93. C '92

Davis, Wendell, '21. C '19, '20

Davis, William Franklin, '67. B '65

Davison, Robert Howell, '17. T '16

Day, Paul, '96. C '94

Dean, Arthur Lyman, '00. T '00

Dean, Dudley Stuart, '91. B '89, '90, '91. F '88, '89, '90

Dean, Frank Lincoln, '88. T '85

Dean, James, '97. B '95, '96, '97

Denholm, William James, '97. T '96, '97

Dennis, William Andrew, '11. T '11

Denniston, Arthur Clark, '83. T '80. F '82

Denny, George Parkman, '09. C '09

Derby, Augustin, '03. T '03

Derby, George Strong, '96 and M.S. C '96, '98

Derby, Richard, '03. C '01, '02

Derby, Roger Alden, '05. F '03, '04. C '05

Desha, John Rollin, '12. B '11

Desmond, John Kenneth, ocC. F '19

Devens, Arthur Lithgow, '74. C '73, '74

Devens, Arthur Lithgow, '02. B '00, '01. F '00

Devereux, John Corish, '14. H '14

deWindt, Heyliger, '12. F '10

Dexter, Samuel, '90 and L.S. F '91. C '89

Dexter, Wallace Dunbar, '07. B '05, '06, '07

Dibblee, Benjamin Harrison, '99. B '99. F '96, '97, '98

Dickinson, Alexander, '94. B '91, '92, '93, '94

Dillingham, Harold Garfield, '04. C '03, '04

Dives, Edward Josiah, '06. T '03, '04, '05, '06

Dobyns, Fletcher, '98. C '98

Dodge, Laurence Paine, '08. T '05, '06, '07, '08

Doherty, John Andrew, '16. F '15

Dole, Richard Emerson, '10. H '09

Donald, Malcolm, '99 and L.S. F '95, '97, '98, '99

Doty, Augustus Flagg, '16. H '15, '16

Doucette, Allan Edward, '95 and L.S. F '94, '95, '96, '97

Dow, Herbert George, '77. B '76, '77

Downer, Charles, '89 and L.S. B '89, '90

Downs, Daniel Frederick, '03s. C '03

Downs, William Charles, '90. T '89, '90

Doyle, John Francis, '07. T '06

Draper, Charles Dana, '00. T '98

Drew, Charles Davis, '97. T '94, '95

Driscoll, Gerard Timothy, '13. F '12

Duane, William North, '92. T '92

Dudley, Albertus True, '87. F '86

Duffy, James Patrick Bernard, L.S. C '03, '04

Duggan, Daniel Joseph, '20. T '18

Duncan, Robert Fuller, '12. H '10, '11, '12

Duncan, Samuel Augustus, 22. C '21, '22

Dunlap, Charles Edward, '11. F '08

Dunlop, John William, '97. F '93, '94, '95, '96

Durfee, Randall Nelson, '19. C '19

Dutcher, Pierpont Edwards, '08. F '07

Dwight, Jonathan, '52. C '52

Eager, Howard, '12. C '12.

Easton, James Hamlet Bolt, '83 and L.S. T '84, '85, '86

Eaton, William Dearborn, '02. F '98, '99, '00

Eckfeldt, Thomas Hooper, '17. H '16, '17

Eddy, Spencer Fayette, '96. C '93

Edgell, Calvin Sumner, '99. T '99

Edgerly, Walter Howard, '86. B '85, '86

Edmands, Thomas Sprague, '67. C '67

Edmands, William Otis, '83. F '80, '81, '82. T '82

Edmunds, John Winthrop, '98. B '98

Edwards, Harry Ransom, '83. B '80, 81

Eggleston, Richard Henry, '09. F '08

Eldridge, Frederick Larnac, '82. F '78

Eliot, Charles William, '53. C '58

Elliot, Frederic Sherwood, '95. T '94, '95

Elliott, John, '12. H '12

Elliott, William Henry, '57. C '55, '56, '57

Ellis, Arthur Blake, '75. F '74

Ellis, Richard, '09. C '08

Ellis, Shirley Gregory, '01. T '98, '00, '01. F '99, '00

Ellison, James Harris, '59. C '57, '58, '59

Emerson, Guy, '08. T '08

Emerson, Haven, '96. T '95

Emerson, William Forbes, '06. C '06

Emery, Frederick Ingersoll, '02. H '02

Emmet, Richard Stockton, '19. C '18

Emmons, Arthur Brewster, '98. T '96, '97

Emmons, Nathaniel Franklin, '07. C '06

Emmons, Robert Wales, '95. F '91, '92, '93, '94

Emmons, Robert Wales, '21. B '19, '20, '21. H '20, '21

Endicott, Arthur Lovett, '94. T '91, '92, '93

Endicott, Henry, '97. B '97

Endicott, Laurence, '01. C '99

Enright, William Fairleigh, '16. H '16

Ernst, Harold Clarence, '76 and M.S. B '75, '76, '77, '78, '79

Erving, John, '53 and L.S. C '55

Erving, Langdon, '55. C '55

Estabrook, John Albert, '73. B '72, '73

Eustis, William Ellery Channing, '71 and G.S. B '69, '70, '71, '72, '73

Evans, Dwight Durkee, '01. C '99

Evans, Leland Brown, '20. B '18

Evans, William Henry, '90. B '89, '90

Everett, Francis Dewey, '11. T '11

Evins, Samuel Nesbitt, L.S. T '91, '92

Fairchild, John Cummings, '96. F '94, '95

Farley, Eliot, '07. C '05, '07

Farley, John Wells, '99. F '98

Farnham, Edwin, '66. C '64

Faucon, Gorham Palfrey, '75 and '77 C.E. F '74, '75, '76

Faulkner, Richard Manning, '09. C '07, '08, '09

Faulkner, William Edward, '87. F '86

Faxon, Henry Hardwick, '21. F '20

Fay, Joseph Story, L.S. C '69

Fearing, George Richmond, '93. C' 93. T '90, '91, '92, '93. F '89

Feibleman, Edward William, '21. L T '21

Felton, Samuel Morse, '13. B '13. F '10, '11, '12

Felton, Samuel Morse, '16. C '16

Felton, Winslow Bent, '19 and ocC. B '19, '20. F '16, '19

Fennessy, Edward Henry, '96. C '93, '94, '95, '96

Fenno, Edward Nicoll, '66. C '65, '66

Fenno, Edward Nicoll, '97. T '97

Fenno, John Brooks, '21. L T '21

Fenton, David Wakeman, '95. T '93

Ferguson, Robert Dennis, '00s. T '99

Fernald, Walter Hunt, '12. T '12[1]

Fessenden, James Deering, '80.   B '78, '80
Filley, Oliver Dwight, '06.   C '03, '04, '05, '06. F '04
Fincke, Reginald, '01.   B '99, '00, '01. F '00
Finlay, James Ralph, '91.   C '88, '89. F '90. T '91
Finley, Robert Lawrence, '21.   F '20
Finney, John Miller Turpin, M.S.   F '84
Fischel, Ellis, '04.   B '04
Fish, Hamilton, '10.   F '07, '08, '09
Fish, Henry Hudson, '99.   T '97, '98
Fish, Sidney Webster, '08.   C '06, '07
Fisher, Charles Edward, '01 and G.S.   T '02
Fisher, Robert Thomas, '12.   F '09, '10, '11
Fisher, Thomas Knight, '17.   H '15, '16, '17
Fiske, Frederick Augustus Parker, '81 and L.S.   T '84
Fitts, Roscoe William, '23.   F '20, '21. T '21, '22
Fitz, Walter Scott, '99.   B '98, '99
Fitzgerald, Joseph John, '23.   F '20
Flagg, George Augustus, '66 and L.S.   B '65, '66, '67
Fleek, John Sherwood, '15.   H '15
Fletcher, Jefferson Butler, '87.   F '86
Flint, Philip Witter, '06.   C '04, '05
Flower, Henry Cowin, '19.   F '16. T '19
Floyd, Richard Clark, 11.   T '11
Fogg, Francis Brinley, '85.   T '85
Foley, John Leo, '15.   T '14, '15
Folsom, William Howard, '81.   B '80, '81
Foote, Henry Wilder, '97 and D.S.   T '00
Forbes, Francis Murray, '96.   C '94
Forbes, William Cameron, '92.   C '91
Forbes, William Hathaway, '61.   C '59
Force, Horton Caumont, '01 and L.S.   F '02
Ford, Francis Joseph William, '04 and L.S.   T '05, '06
Ford, Shirley Samuel, '09.   H '08, '09
Forster, Henry, '11.   C '09, '10
Fosdick, Paulding, '04.   H '02
Foster, Charles Henry Wheelwright, '81.   F '80
Foster, Frederick William Choate, '03.   C '02, '03
Foster, George Waldo, '87.   B '85, '86, '87
Foster, Hatherly, '07.   F '05, '06. H '07
Foster, Herbert Ira, '98.   B '98
Foster, John Winthrop, '03.   H '02, '03
Foster, Joseph, '02.   T '01
Foster, Newton Hinckley, '11.   H '10, '11
Foster, Reginald Candler, '11.   T '09, '11
Fox, Allan James, '21.   T '21
Fox, Francis Bird, '96 and L.S.   T '97, '98, '99

Francis, Richard Standish, '02.   C '01, '02
Francke, Hugo, '15.   F '14
Frantz, Orville Gish, '03.   B '01
Fraser, Somers, '07.   F '06
Freedley, Vinton, '14.   F '13
Freeland, Wiliam, '81.   C '80
French, Amos Tuck, '85.   F '84. C '84
Fripp, Frank Giles, '16.   B '14, '15, '16
Frothingham, Channing, '02.   B '02
Frothingham, Louis Adams, '93.   B '90, '91, '92, '93
Frothingham, Lawrence Potter, '02.   T '02
Frothingham, Theodore, '12.   F '09, '11
Frothingham, Thomas Harris, '13.   F '12
Frothingham, William Bainbridge, '21.   B '19, '20
Frye, Russell Brigham, '15.   B '13, '14, '15
Fuller, Henry Holton, '23.   C '22
Fuller, Kenneth Eliot, '16.   T '15
Fuller, Richard Buckminster, '83.   F '81
Fuller, Samuel Lester, '98.   F '97
Fuller, Thomas James Duncan, '15.   C '13

Gaddis, Hugh Lawrence, '12.   T '12
Gage, Walter Boutwell, '94.   F '91
Galatti, Stephen, '10.   F '09
Galbraith, Archibald Victor, '99.   B '99
Gallivan, James Ambrose, '88.   B '88
Gammack, Thomas Hubbard, '20.   B '18, '20
Gannett, Robert Tileston, '15.   B '13, '14, '15
Garcelon, William Frye, L.S.   T '93, '94
Gardiner, William Tudor, '14.   C '13, '14
Gardner, George Peabody, '10.   B '10. H '08, '09, '10. T '08, '09, '10. L T '07
Gardner, Henry Burchell, '13.   F '10, '11, '12. H '12, '13
Garrison, William Lloyd, '97 and L.S.   F '97
Garritt, Walter Grant, '17.   B '15, '16
Gaston, John, '22.   F '20. H '20
Gehrke, Erwin Lawrence, '24.   B '22
Gelston, Robert Bruce, '58.   C '58
George, Ernest, '03 and G.S.   C '03, '05
George, Frank William, M.S.   B '00
Gerould, Richard Dodge, '24.   T '22
Gerrish, Thornton, '01.   T '01
Gibson, Howard Berrs, '88.   T '85, '88
Gibson, Henry Thomas, '12.   B '11, '12
Gierasch, Walter Siegfried, '02.   F '00
Gilder, Rodman de Kay, '99.   C '98
Gill, Austin Goddard, '06.   C '05, '06
Gilman, Charles Freeman, '85.   F '82, '83, '84. C '83
Gilman, Joseph Atherton, '16.   F '13, '15
Glass, Gordon Goldwin, '08.   C '06
Glidden, Nathaniel Frank, '03.   T '00

Goddard, Homer Lehr, '10.   T '10
Goddard, Josiah Holmes, '92.   C '90
Goldsmith, William Gleason, '57.   C '55, '56, '57
Gonterman, Madison Gillham, '96.   F '93, '94, '95. T '95
Goodale, Alfred Montgomery, '13.   H '13. C '11, '12, '13
Goode, Edward Francis, '22.   B '20, '21, '22
Goodell, Roscoe Harris, '02.   C '00, '01
Goodell, Warren Franklin, '21.   T '20, '21
Goodhue, Albert, '04.   F '03
Goodhue, Francis Abbot, '06.   F '05
Goodrich, Arthur Lewis, '74.   F '74
Goodrich, Clinton Burr, L.S.   B '99
Goodrich, David Marvin, '98.   C '96, '97
Goodridge, Frederick James, '98 and M.S.   H '00, '01
Goodwin, John Cheever, '73.   B '70, '71, '72
Goodwin, Wendell, '74.   C '72, '73, '74
Goodwin, William Hobbs, '84.   T '82, '83, '84
Goodwin, William Hobbs, '20.   T '20
Gordon, Lewis, '24.   B '22
Gorham, John Dwight, '90.   C '88
Gould, Alfred Henry, '96.   F '95
Gourdin, Edward Orval, '21.   T '19, '20, '21
Gozzaldi, Richard Silvio de, '13.   T '12
Grant, Alexander Galt, '07.   T '06, '07
Grant, Dick, '97 and M.S.   T '96, '97, '98
Grant, Henry Rice, '74.   F '74
Grant, Patrick, '08.   F '07
Gratwick, Mitchell, '22.   F '19, '20, '21. H '22. T '22
Graustein, Edward Adolf, '13.   F '12
Graves, William Grant, '06.   T '06
Gray, Francis Calley, '12.   T '10
Gray, George Arthur, '94.   F '92, '93
Gray, Reginald, '75.   F '74
Gray, Thomas Herbert, '67.   B '65
Graydon, Thomas Hetherington, '03s.   F '00, '01, '02
Greeley, Morris Larned, '15.   T '15
Green, Andrew Hugh, '92.   T '91, '92
Green, Edward James, '97 and L.S.   T '98
Greene, Elbridge Howe, '02.   F '01
Greene, Gardiner Frank, '07.   B '06
Greenidge, Ralph Malcolm Clarke, E.S.   T '22
Greenleaf, William Bainbridge, '92s.   T '89
Greenough, Henry Vose, '05.   B '04, '05
Greenough, James, '15.   T '15
Greenough, John, '65.   C '64
Grew, Henry Sturgis, '24.   F '21

Grilk, Louis, '04. T '04

Gring, Rudolph Brainerd, '05. T '04

Gross, Robert Ellsworth, '19. H '19. B '18

Guild, Horace, '10. T '11²

Guild, Robert Francis, '06. F '05

Hadden, Harold Farquhar, '09. T '07

Haigh, John Edward, '03. T '00, '02, '03

Hale, Herbert Dudley, '88. C '87

Hale, Robert Sever, '91. T '91

Hall, Edward Cunningham, '76. F '75

Hall, Frederick Stanley, '82. B '81, '82

Hall, John Howe, '03. T '03

Hall, Nathan Lord, '07. F '06

Hall, Richard Walworth, '10. B '08

Hallock, Leonard Avery, '22. B '20, '21, '22

Hallowell, Frank Walton, '93. B '91, '92, '93. F '89, '90, '91, '92

Hallowell, John White, '01. F '98, '99, '00. T '98, '99, '00, '01

Hallowell, Norwood Penrose, '97. T '97

Hallowell, Robert Haydock, '96. F '94, '95

Hallowell, Richard Price, '20. B '18, '19, '20

Hamilton, Arthur Dean, '21. F '20

Hamlin, Edward Everett, '86. C '84

Hammond, Charles Mifflin, '83. C '81, '82, '83. F '82

Hammond, Samuel, '81. C '81

Hanks, Charles Stedman, '79. T '78

Hanley, William Augustine, '07. T '06

Hann, Charles, '11. B '11

Hanson, Donald Rea, '14s. H '13

Hapgood, William Powers, '94. B '93

Harbeck, Charles John, '00. T '97

Hardell, Everett Sterns, '21. B '19

Harding, Benjamin Fosdick, '78. B '75

Harding, Charles Lewis, '00. C '98, '99, '00

Harding, Francis Austin, '09. B '08

Harding, George Franklin, '92. F '88

Harding, Victor Mathews, '89. F '86, '87, '88

Hardwick, Huntington Reed, '15. B '13, '14, '15. F '12, '13, '14. T '13, '15

Hardy, Everett Clarkson, '13. B '12

Hardy, Roger Sumner, '01. H '00, '01

Harrington, Francis Bishop, M.S. F '77, '78

Harrington, James Taylor, '99. T '99

Harris, Duncan Gilbert, '00. T '00

Harris, José Calderon, '17. F '15, '16

Harrison, Charles Learner, '18. B '16

Harrison, Walter Thacher, '06s. F '02

Harte, Richard, '17. B '15, '16. F '15, '16. L T '14, '15, '16

Hartford, Newton Keith, '09. B '07, '08, '09

Hartley, Joseph Milton, '23. F '21

Hartley, Roland English, '86. F '83

Harvey, Alexander, '81. B '81

Harvey, Curran Whitthorne, '09. B '06, '07, '08, '09

Harwood, Bartlett, '15. C '13, '14, '15

Harwood, Richard Green, '09. T '07, '08, '09

Harwood, Robert Walker, '21. T '19, '20, '21

Haskell, Guy Butler, '98. F '97

Hastings, Edmund Trowbridge, '76. C '76

Hastings, Robert Paul, '78. B '78

Hauers, Carl Richard, '23. T '21, '22

Haughton, Percy Duncan, '99. B '96, '97, '98, '99. F '96, '97, '98

Havemeyer, Charles Frederick, '21. F '19, '20

Hawes, Oscar Brown, '93. T '91

Hawes, Oliver Kingsley, '92. T '91

Hawley, Edward Welles, '89. B '89

Haydock, George Guest, '16. T '15, '16

Haydock, Robert, '10. B '09. H '10

Hayes, Bartlett Harding, '98. B '98

Hayes, John Joseph, '96. F '94. B '94, '95

Hellman, Robert Richard, '06. B '06

Henderson, Harry Peters, '01. C '00

Hennen, William Davison, '98. T '96, '98

Henry, Barlie McKee, '24. C '22

Henry, William Alexander, '85. F '81, '83

Henshaw, Arthur, '89. B '86, '87, '88, '89

Herrick, Edwin Hayden, '77. F '74, '75, '76. T '77

Herrick, Robert Frederick, '90. C '89

Herrick, Robert Frederick, '16. C '16

Herrick, William Hale, '82. T '80, '81

Hibbard, Ford, '20. B '19

Hicks, Samuel Trafford, '10s. B '08, '09, '10. H '08, '09, '10

Higgins, Lawrence, '18. B '18

Higgins, Richard Robertson, '22. F '21. H '22

Higginson, Francis Lee, '00. C '98, '99, '00

Highlands, Andrew Albert, '95. B '93, '94, '95

Highlands, John Ashley, '93s. B '92, '93

Hildreth, Loring Townsend, '96. T '94

Hill, Edward Burlingame, '94. T '94

Hill, Francis Sherburne, '24. H '22

Hill, Lewis Dana, '94. B '93

Hitchcock, Harvey Rexford, '14. F '11, '12, '13. B '13, '14

Hoar, Samuel, '09. F '07, '08

Hobbs, Edmund Sanderson, '21. B '21

Hodges, Amory Glazier, '74. B '72, '73, '74

Hodges, Benjamin Deland, '10. T '10

Hodges, Thorndike Deland, '57. C '56, '57

Hofer, Philip, '21. H '21

Hoffman, Robert, '19. B '18

Holden, Albert Fairchild, '88. F '86, '87. B '86, '87

Holden, Francis Marion, '81. B '78, '79, '80. F '77, '79

Holder, Daniel Stewart, '24. F '21. C '22

Holdredge, George Ward, '69. C '67, '68

Hollister, Evan, '97. T '94, '95, '96, '97

Hollister, Paul Merrick, '13. F '12

Hollister, Stanley, '97. C '96, '97

Holmes, Arthur Brewster, '96. T '93

Holmes, Jabish, '79. F '77, '78

Holmes, Jabish, '21. H '19, '20, '21

Holmes, John Russell, '78. B '77

Holt, Edgar Garrison, '98s. F '95

Holt, Frank Herbert Ford, '99. T '97

Homans, John, '58. C '55

Homans, William Parmelee, '85. F '84

Hood, Donald Tucker, '14. B '14

Hooper, Sewall Henry, '75. B '73, '74, '75

Hooper, William, '80. C '79. F '79

Hopkins, Stephen Tullock, '14. H '13, '14

Hornblower, Ralph, '11. H '09, '10, '11

Horween, Arnold, '21. F '19, '20

Horween, Ralph, '18 and ocC. F '15, '16, '19

Houghton, Amory, '21. C '20

Houston, Francis Augustine, '79 and L.S. F '76, '77, '78, '79, '80, '81

Houston, Francis De Hart, '10. F '09

Houston, Philip Kingsland, '12. H '12

Hovey, Frederick Howard, L.S. B '91, '92, '93. L T '90, '91

Hovey, Frederick Howard, '22. F '21

How, James Eads, '91. T '89

Howard, Herbert Burr, '81. C '80

Howard, Luther Damon, '14. T '12

Howard, Oscar Shafter, '85. F '84

Howard, William Gibbs, '07. T '05, '07

Howe, Everett Chase, '93. B '90, '91

Howe, Lawrence, '07. B '07

Howe, Percival Spurr, '17 and ocC. C '17,² '19

Howe, Reginald Heber, '01. C '99, '00, '01

Howe, William Addison, '81. B '78, '79

Howes, Kenneth, '08. C '08

Howland, Leonard Paul, L.S. B '88, '89, '90

Hoyt, Henry Reese, '82. F '80

Hoyt, William Welles, '98 and M.S. T '95, '97, '98, '00

Hubbard, Charles Joseph, '24. F '21. C '22
Hubbard, Wynant Davis, '22. '19, '20
Hubbell, Chauncey Giles, '93. T '93

Hubbell, Frederick Winsor, '13. B '13
Hubbell, James Windsor, '17. G '16
Hudgens, Seymour Isaac, '84. C '81, '82, '84
Huidekoper, Reginald Shippen, '98. C '97
Huling, Ray Greene, '13. T '12
Humphrey, Richard Sears, '21. F '19, '20. H '21
Hunneman, Roger Defriez, '17. H '17
Hunnewell, Arthur, '68. B '65, '66, '67, '68
Hunnewell, Henry Sargent, '75. C '72
Huntington, Frederic Dane, '12. F '11. H '10, '11, '12
Hurd, Charles Henry, '53. C '52
Hurd, Charles Otis, '86. F '84
Hurley, Daniel Joseph, '05 and M.S. F '02, '03, '04, '05
Hutchins, Constantine, '05. H '05
Hutchinson, James Dana, '20. T '19
Hutchinson, James Pemberton, '90. C '89, '90. F '89
Hutchinson, Samuel Ingersoll, '84. C '83

Iasigi, Augustus Dromel, '78. F '74
Inches, Henderson, '08. F '07
Irving, George, '75 and L.S. C '76
Iselin, Oliver, '11. C '11
Ivy, Malcolm Hyde, '04 and L.S. C '02, '03. H '04, '06

Jackson, Alexander Louis, '14. T '12, '13, '14
Jackson, Edward William Cecil, '02. C '01, '02
Jacobs, Martin Reiley, '79. C '76, '77, '78, '79
Jaffrey, Percy Malcolm, '99. F '95, '98
James, Montgomery, '77. C '75, '76
James, William, '03. C '01, '02
Jameson, Herbert Wendell, '95. T '93, '94
Janin, Henry Covington, '22. B '20, '21, '22. F '21[1]
Jaques, Herbert, '11. T '08, '09, '10, '11
Jenkins, Percy, '24. T '22. B '22.
Jenney, Charles, '97. F '96
Jenney, Reginald, ocC. and '21. C '20
Jennings, Albert Toof,[2] '98s. C '95
Johnson, Frank Jewett, '22. F '20, '21
Johnson, Richard Newhall, '22. T '21
Johnson, Walter Sydney, '94. C '93
Johnstone, John Oliver, '16. T '14, '15, '16

Jones, Boyd Nelson, '12s. T '12
Jones, Daniel Fiske, '92. C '90, '91
Jones, Gilbert Edward, '11. B '11
Jones, George Irving, '71. C '69, '70, '71
Jones, Guy Lincoln, '03. F '01
Jones, Lucius Paine, '20. B '20
Jordan, Eben Dyer, '80. F '76
Jordan, Wallace Bishop, '06s. T '05

Kales, Albert Martin, '96. C '94
Kane, Richmond Keith, '22. F '19, '20, '21. C '20, '21
Keane, John Francis, '21. T '20
Keene, Francis Bowler, '80. T '80
Keep, Wallace Irving, '84. B '83, '84
Keith, Arthur, '85. C '84
Keith, George Paul, '83. F '79, '80, '81, '82
Kelley, Herbert Willis, '11. T '09, '10, '11
Kelley, Nicholas, '06. B '06
Kelly, Arthur James, '12. B '10, '11
Kelton, George Howard, '93. C '90, '91, '92
Kemble, Francis Walker, '08. B '05, '08
Kemp, George William, '84. T '83

Kendall, Edward Hale, '02. B '00. F '99, '00
Kendall, Louis Wilmer, '84. F '80, '81, '82, '83
Kennard, Victor Parry, '09. F '06, '08
Kennedy, Joseph James, '22. H '22
Kennedy, Joseph Patrick, '12. B '11
Kent, Edward, '83. F '80
Kent, John Fuller, '75. B '72, '73, '74, '75
Kent, Warner Williams, '16. T '15
Ker, William Henry, '62. C '60
Kernan, Hubert Dolbeare, '05s. B '03, '04, '05. F '04
Kernan, John Devereux, '00. C '98, '99
Kernan, Robert Peebles, '03s. B '00, '02, '03. F '01, '02. T '02, '03
Kersburg, Harry Edwin, '06 and '07s. F '05, '06. T '06, '07
Keyes, George Thomas, '89. C '88
Keyes, Henry Wilder, '87. C '85, '86, '87
Keys, John Baker, '77. F '75, '76
Kimball, Marcus Morton, '86. F '83, '84
King, Archibald, '03 and L.S. T '03, '04
King, George Anderson, '18. T '16
King, Henry Parsons, '21. B '19
King, McGregor Adams, '10. C '08, '09, '10
King, Richard Stuart Cutting, '16. F '14, '15
Kip, Charles Hayden, '83. T '82, '83
Kirk, Alexander Edgar, '20. B '20

Kissel, Rudolph Hermann, '17. H '17
Knowles, Henry Swift, '02. T '00, '01
Knowles, James, '18 and ocC. B '16, '19
Knowlton, Daniel Waldo, '03, G.S., and L.S. F '02, '03, '05
Knowlton, Herbert Eugene, M.S. B '88
Koch, Theodore William, '14s. T '12
Kreger, Henry Ludwig Flood, '16. C '14, '15, '16
Krogness, Christopher George, '21. T '19, '21
Krumbhaar, Edward Bell, '04. B '04
Kubli, Kaspar Karl, L.S. T '95, '96

Lacey, Walter Hamer, '12. T '12
Ladd, Alexander Haven, '23. C '21. F '21
Ladd, William Edwards, '02. C '00
Laird, David Sidney, '19 and ocC. T '20
Lake, Everett John, '92 and '93. F '90, '91, '92
Lakin, Herbert Conrad, '94. T '93
Lane, Daniel Winn, '94. F '93
Lanigan, Charles Leo, '10. B '08, '09, '10
Lanman, Ludlow Thomas, '21. H '20
Laroque, Joseph, '23. H '22
Latham, Aaron Hobart, '77 and L.S. B '75, '76, '77, '78
Laverack, William Harold, '01. H '00, '01
Lawless, Harvey Platt, '13. T '10, '11, '12
Lawrence, James, '01. F '99, '00. C '99, '01
Lawrence, Richard, '02. F '01
Lawrence, Samuel Crocker, '10. T '09, '10
Lawson, Carl, '05s. C '03, '04, '05
Lawson, Douglas, '13. F '12
Leary, Leo Henry, '05 and L.S. F '04, '05
Leatherbee, George Henry, '82. F '79, '80
Leavitt, Heyward Gibbons, '82. B '80, '82. F '81
Leavitt, Robert Greenleaf, '89. T '89
Lee, Charles Carroll, '23. B '22
Lee, Joseph Howard, '00. F '96
Lee, James Parrish, '91. F '88, '89, '90. T '89, '90, '91
Lee, William George, '01 and M.S. F '00, '01
Lee, William Henry Fitzhugh, '58. C '57
Leeds, Herbert Corey, '77. F '74, '75. B '74, '75, '76 '77
Lefurgey, Alfred Alexander, L.S. T '93
Legate, Burton John, '77 and G.S. C '77, '78
Leighton, Delmar, '19. C '19
Leland, Joseph Daniels, '09. T '09
LeMoyne, Henry, '07s. F '03. T '04
LeMoyne, Louis Valcoulon, '84. B '82, '83, '84

LeMoyne, William Murray, '78. C '76, '77

Leonard, Charles Reginald, '08. B '05, '06, '07, '08. H '07

Leonard, Edgar Welch, '03. L T '02

Leonard, Laurence Barberie, ocC. T '19

Leroy, Herman Stewart, '79. B '79

Leslie, Freeland Huston, '12. T '11, '12. F '11

Leslie, Howard Clifford, '11. F '08, '09, '10. H '09, '10, '11

Lewis, Burnham, '20. T '19

Lewis, Jacob Kingsland, '11. T '10, '11

Lewis, Kenneth Hastings, '96. C '94, '95

Lewis, Richard Plimpton, '13. F '10

Lewis, Samuel Watts, '00. B '98. F '96

Lewis, William Henry, L.S. F '92, '93

Liebmann, Charles Joseph, '98. T '96

Lightner, Milton Turnley, '03. T '01, '02, '03

Lincoln, Carl Erlund, '08. F '06

Lincoln, Edwin Clapp, '22. B '20, '21, '22

Linder, John Farlow, '19. C '18, '19

Lindsley, Halstead, '02. G '01

Lingard, Eric Adrian Alfred, '13. F '12

Linn, Philip Billmeyer, '90. B '87, '88, '89, '90

Litchfield, Bayard Sands, '03s. C '03. H '03

Litchfield, Everett Starr, '87. B '85

Littauer, Lucius Nathan, '78. F '77. C '77, '78

Little, Clarence Cook, '10. T '08, '09, '10

Little, Leon Magaw, '10. T '10

Livermore, Charles Frederick, '53. C '52

Livermore, Robert, '00. F '96

Lloyd, Robert McAllister, '19. B '18

Lloyd, William James, '73. C '72

Lockwood, Benoni, '22. F '21

Lockwood, Philip Case, '08. T '06, '07, '08. F '05, '07

Logan, Malcolm Justin, '15. F '13, '14

Lombard, Frederick Howard, '74. F '74

Lombard, Warren Plimpton, '78. F '75, '76, '77

Long, Elmer Ebert, '21. C '21

Long, Earl Van Meter, '10. F '09.[1] B '10

Long, James Parker, '11. T '09, '10

Longworth, Nicholas, '91. C '89

Loring, Alden Porter, '69. C '66, '67, '68, '69

Loring, Caleb, '10. C '10

Loring, William Caleb, '72. C '71

Lothrop, Francis Bacon, '21. C '19, '20

Loughlin, Edward Francis, '00. B '98, '99, '00

Lovering, Joseph Swain, '03. H '02, '03

Lovering, Reuben Whittle, '84. B '81, '82, '83

Lowell, Guy, '92. T '91, '92

Lowell, James Arnold, '91. F '89

Lowell, John, '77. B '77

Lowell, Ralph, '12. C '12

Lowery, Jenner, '04. H '04

Lucas, Edwin Earle, '19. T '18

Lund, Charles Carroll, '16. C '14, '15, '16

Lund, Edward Griffing, '23. T '22

Lund, Fred Bates, '88. T '88

Lunt, Lawrence Kirby, '09. C '07, '08, '09

Lyman, Arthur Theodore, '16. T '16

Lyman, Frank, '74. F '74.

Lyman, Francis Ogden, '71. C '69, '70

Lynam, Frank, M.S. C '91, '92

Lynch, Wilbur Henry, '99. B '97, '98, '99

McBurney, Charles Heber, '66. C '65, '66

McBurney, John Wayland, '69. C '68

McCagg, Louis Butler, '22. C '20, '21

McCall, Henry, '09. B '06, '07, '08

McCarthy, Frederick, sp. B '94

McCarthy, Joseph Anthony, '22. T '22

McCarty, Arthur Eugene, '07. B '04, '05, '06

McCobb, James Selden, '71. C '70

McConnell, George Malcolm, '01. C '00

McCornick, Willis Sylvestre, '00. B '98

McCouch, Eric Alan, '20. B '18

McCoy, James Chester, '90. B '89

MacDonald, Charles Ambrose, '01. B '00

McDonald, James Fox, '08. F '05, '06, '07

MacDougall, Albert Edward, '18. H '18

McDuffie, Charles Henry, '99. C '97

McFadon, Donald, '06. F '04

McGrew, Dallas Dayton Lore, '03. C '01, '02, '03

McKay, Robert Gordon, '11. F '08, '09, '10

McKean, Frank Bowers, '91. B '89

McKim, Charles Follen, L.S.S. B '67

McKinlock, George Alexander, '16. F '14, '15

McLaughlin, Charles Bernard, '11. B '09, '10, '11

MacLeod, Eldon, '06. H '03, '04, '06

MacLeod, Willard Wise, '19. B '19

MacLure, Henry Goldsborough, '15. T '13, '14

MacNider, Hanford, '11. H '11

McVey, John Rankin, '98. B '95

MacVicar, Guy Mortimer, '15. C '13

Mackie, William Charles, '94 and M.S. F '91, '92, '93, '94

Macomber, Charles Clark, '22. F '20, '21

Macomber, Frank Gair, '04. C '04

Mahan, Edward William, '16. B '14, '15, '16. F '13, '14, '15

Mahar, John Burton, sp. B '05

Mahon, Henry Macleod, '23. T '21

Manahan, Thomas James, '96s. F '93

Mandell, George Snell, '89. T '88, '89

Mandell, Henry Fauntleroy, '84. T '84

Mann, Clarence Churchill, '99. C '99

Manning, John Brown, '03s. and M.S. H '01, '02, '03, '05

Manning, Robert Franklin, '04. C '04

Manning, William Hobbs, '82. F '78, '79, '80, '81

Mansfield, Walter Ralph, '97. T '95

Manson, Thomas Lincoln, '04. T '01

Markoe, James Brown, '89. F '87. C '88

Marshall, Andrew, L.S. F '02, '03

Marshall, Carl Bertrand, '04. F '01, '02, '03

Marshall, Lewis Keith, E.S. T '22

Marshall, Napoleon Bonaparte, '97. T '94, '95

Marshall, Ralph Stevens, '10. B '10

Martin, Alan Rhys, '18. H '17

Martin, John Morrison, '22. H '21, '22

Marvin, George Decker, '99. C '97, '98

Mason, Austin Blake, '08. T '07

Mason, Albert Gardner, '00s. T '00

Mason, Francis, '96. T '96

Mason, Frank, '91 and L.S. B '90, '91, '92, '93. F '92

Mason, Frank Atlee, '84. F '81, '82, '83

Matthews, William Clarence, '05. B '02, '03, '04, '05. F '04

Mealey, Edward Windsor, '67. B '66, '67

Meehan, Thomas Jefferson, '21. B '19

Meier, Theodore Gerhardt, '04 and G.S. C '04, '05. F '03

Merrihew, Edward King, '10. T '08, '09

Merrill, James Edward, '24. T '22

Merrill, Sherburn Moses, '94. T '92, '93, '94

Merwin, Davis, '21. T '21

Metcalf, George Pierce, '12. C '10, '11, '12

Meyer, George von Lengerke, '13. C '11

Meyer, Henry Hixon, '15. C '14, '15

Middendorf, Henry Stump, '16. C '14, '15, '16

Middendorf, John William, '16. C '14, '15, '16

Mifflin, Samuel Wright, '01 and L.S. F '01

Miles, Charles Appleton, '53. C '52

Miles, Harry Roberts, '88. T '88

Milholland, John Angus, '14. B '14

Miller, Herbert Fletcher, '08. T '08

Miller, Ralph Gifford, '93. C '93

Miller, William Victor, '23. T '22

Mills, Charles Henry, '95. F '94. C '94

Mills, Edwin Walter, '02s.   T '01, '02
Mills, Lewis Hunt, '14.   F '13. C '12
Mills, Philip Overton, '05.   F '02, '03, '04
Mills, Samuel Frederic, '99s.   T '98. F '97
Milne, George Parker, '01 and G.S.   B '00, '02
Minot, Henry Whitney, '17.   F '16. T '17
Minot, William, '07.   T '06, '07
Minot, Wayland Manning, '11.   B '10. F '09, '10
Moën, Edward Calvin, '91.   T '88, '89, '91
Moffatt, Alexander White, '13.   T '12, '13
Montgomery, James Mortimer, '06.   F '03, '04, '05
Montgomery, John Robb, '06.   C '04, '05
Moore, Fred Wadsworth, '93.   F '91, '92
Moore, William, '18 and ocC.   T '19
Morgan, Charles, '08.   C '06
Morgan, David Percy, '16.   C '14, '15, '16
Morgan, Edwin Denison, '77.   C '76
Morgan, Edwin Denison, '13.   C '11, '12, '13
Morgan, Henry Carey, '14.   H '13, '14
Morgan, Henry Sturgis, '23.   C '21
Morgan, John Edward Parsons, '17.   H '15, '16, '17
Morgan, James Hewitt, '94.   C '93
Morgan, Lewis Henry, '89.   B '87
Morgan, William Fellowes, '10.   H '09, '10
Morgan, William Otho, '18.   H '16, '17
Morison, George Burnap, '83.   F '80, '81, '82. T '82, '83.
Morrison, George Ernest, '12.   F '10
Morse, Eugene Dorr, '19.   H '19[2]
Morse, George Ferderick, '81.   F '78, '79
Morse, Henry Lee, '74 and M.S.   F '74, '75. C '72, '73, '74

Morse, Samuel Vining, '99.   B '98, '99
Morse, William Gibbons, '99.   T '97, '98, '99
Mosle, Johann Ludwig, '20.   B '18
Motley, John Lothrop, '02 and L.S.   F '02
Moulton, John Babcock, '98.   F '96, '97. C '96
Movius, Hallam Leonard, '02.   H '01
Mullins, Edwin Stanton, '93.   T '91
Mumford, George Saltonstall, '87.   C '85, '86
Mumford, Norman Winthrop, '90.   B '87, '89
Mumford, William Woolsey, '84.   C '82, '83
Munroe, Vernon, '96.   T '94, '96
Munson, Samuel Lyman, '00.   T '97
Murdock, Harris Hunnewell, '01.   B '01
Murphy, Foye Melvin, '03 and L.S.   T '02, '03, '04

Murphy, Jeremiah Daniel, '22.   B '21, '22
Murphy, Thomas Francis, '04.   B '01
Murray, Allan Kennedy, '23.   T '22
Murray, Cecil Dunmore, '20.   F '18[3]
Murray, Henry Alexander, '15.   C '13, '14, '15
Murray, William James, '18 and ocC.   F '16, '19

Nash, Henry Lamb, '16.   B '14, '15, '16
Neilson, Alexander Slidell, '13.   C '13
Nelson, George Lewis, '93.   C '90
Nelson, Nils Victor, '18 and ocC.   F '19
Nelson, Thomas, '66.   C '64. B '65, '66
Nesmith, Fisher Hildreth, '06.   F '04
Newell, Gerrish, '98.   F '95
Newell, Marshall, '94.   C '91, '92, '93. F '90, '91, '92, '93
Newhall, Campbell, '24.   T '22
Newhall, Daniel Allerton, '06.   H '03, '04, '05, '06. C '05, '06
Newhall, Morton Lewis, '08.   F '05, '06, '07. H '06, '07, '08
Newton, George Frederick, '12.   C '10, '11, '12
Newton, Paul, '11.   T '10
Newton, Philip Converse, '20.   B '18
Nichols, Charles Prosser, '83.   B '80, '81, '82, '83
Nichols, Edward Hall, '86.   B '83, '84, '85, '86
Nichols, Harold Willis, '07.   H '07
Nichols, John Donaldson, '06.   B '04. F '03, '04, '05
Nichols, James Osgood, L.S.   T '91
Nickerson, Albert Lindsay, '01.   T '98
Nickerson, Joshua Atkins, '22.   C '22
Nickerson, Thomas White, '80.   F '79
Niles, Nathaniel William, '09.   L T '07, '08
Norton, Eliot, '85.   T '82
Norton, John Leonard, '95.   T '92
Nourse, Charles Joseph, '09.   F '08
Nourse, Frederic Russell, '99.   F '98
Noyes, Stephen Henley, '03 and '05s.   F '04
Nunn, Charles Pierce, '79.   B '78, '79

Ober, Harlan Foster, '05.   C '03, '04
O'Brien, Francis Joseph, '14.   F '12, '13
O'Connell, Dennis Francis, '21.   T '19, '20, '21
O'Flaherty, Daniel Vincent, '11.   F '09
O'Keefe, Daniel Joseph, '18.   B '18
Olmsted, Marlin Edgar, '22.   C '19, '20, '21
Olmsted, Oliver Allen, '82.   B '79, '80, '81, '82

O'Malley, Walter John, '96.   B '94
Oñativia, José Victor, '08.   T '07
Orr, George Mason, '08.   F '06
Orton, Grosvenor Porter, '98b.   C '98
Osborn, Robert Palmer, '14.   B '13, '14
Osborne, Charles Glidden, '07.   F '06
Otis, James, '81.   C '79, '80
Otis, Walter Joseph, '76s.   C '74, '75
Oveson, Raymond Hansen, '05 and L.S.   T '06. F '04
Owen, George, '23.   F '20, '21. H '21, '22. B '21, '22

Page, Richmond, '23.   T '22
Page, William Hussey, '83.   T '83
Paine, Charles Jackson, '53.   C '52
Paine, Charles Jackson, '97.   B '95, '96, '97. T '94, '95
Paine, John Adams, '09.   H '07, '08, '09
Paine, René Evans, '94.   B '92, '94
Palmer, Bradley Webster, '88.   F '87
Palmer, Franklin Hall, '13.   H '12, '13
Parker, Bartol, '08.   F '04, '05, '06, '07
Parker, Franklin Eddy, '89.   C '87
Parker, Gurdon Saltonstall, '00.   F '97, '99
Parker, Haven, '22.   B '22
Parker, Henry Boynton, '67.   B '65, '66, '67
Parker, James, '78.   C '78
Parkinson, John, '06.   F '03, '04
Parkman, Francis, '19.   C '18
Parkman, Samuel Breck, '57.   C '55, '56, '57
Parmenter, Derric Choate, '13.   F '11, '12
Parson, Kenneth Barnitz Gilbert, '16.   F '14, '15. C '14, '15
Parsons, George Ayer, '17.   B '17
Parsons, Theophilus, '70.   C '69
Parsons, William Barclay, '10.   F '09
Pavenstedt, Edmund William, '20.   H '19
Peabody, Francis, L.S.   C '79
Peabody, Francis Greenwood, '69.   B '68, '69
Peabody, Harry Earnest, '87.   F '83, '84, 86
Peabody, Robert Swain, '66.   C '64, '66
Pease, Edward Allen, '88.   T '85, '86, '88
Peirce, Waldo, '08.   F '05, '06, '07
Peirson, Edward Lawrence, '21.   C '19, '20, '21
Pell, Clarence Cecil, '08.   H '05, '06, '07, '08
Pendleton, Elliott Hunt, '82.   B '81
Penhallow, Dunlap Pearce, '03s.   H '01, '02
Pennock, Stanley Bagg, '15.   F '12, '13, '14
Pennypacker, Henry, '88.   T '88

Pennypacker, Thomas Ruston, '16. T '16

Penrose, Richard Alexander Fullerton, '84 and G.S. C '85, '86

Percy, George Almy, '18. B '16. H '16, '17

Perin, Edmund Sehon, '82. F '80, '81

Perkins, Arthur, '20. T '19

Perkins, Edward Cranch, '66. C '64

Perkins, John Forbes, '99. C '97, '98, '99

Perkins, James Gerritt Bradt, '11. F '10

Perkins, James Handasyd, '98. C '96, '97, '98

Perkins, Keneth Wheeler, '20. B '19, '20

Perkins, Robert Forbes, '89. C '87

Perkins, Robert Patterson, '84. C '82, '83, '84

Perkins, Stephen George, '56. C '55

Perkins, Thomas Nelson, '91. C '89, '90, '91

Perrin, Willard Taylor, '70. B '69, '70

Perry, Frederick Gardner, '79. F '77, '78

Perry, Gardner, '89. C '89

Perry, Nelson Williams, '76. B '73

Pfeiffer, Emil Charles, '89. C '87

Pfeiffer, Oscar Joseph, M.S. C '81

Philbin, Philip Joseph, '20. F '19

Phillips, James Duncan, '97. T '94, '95, '96, '97

Phillips, Morgan Brigham, '15. H '13, '14, '15. B '13, '15

Phillips, Walter Brigham, '86. F '84. B '83, '84, '86

Phinney, Morris, '19 and ocC. F '16, '19

Pieper, Louis Peter, '03. B '07

Pierce, Edward Peter, '12. H '12

Pinkham, Edward Warwick, '92 and M.S. T '92, '93

Piper, Louis Allison, '90. F '87

Piper, William Thomas, '03. T '02, '03

Plimpton, George Faulkner, '14. F '13

Pond, Thomas Temple, '21. C '20, '21

Pope, Ruel Putnam, '10. T '08, '09

Porter, Charles Allen, '88 and M.S. F '86, '87, '88

Pote, Leonard Holden, M.S. B '96

Potter, Allen, '17. C '16

Potter, Albert Bailey, '87. B '86

Potter, Robert Sturgis, '12. B '10, '11, '12. F '10, '11

Pounds, James Dee, '08. B '06, '07

Powers, John Craig, '92. C '90, '91

Prado, Plinio da Silva, '95. T '94

Pratt, Frederick Sanford, '94. T '91

Preble, Blanchard Mussey, '12. T '11, '12

Preble, William Pitt, '75. F '75

Presbrey, Palmer Ellis, '85. L T '83

Preston, Thomas Webb, '79. C '77

Prince, Morton, '75. F '74

Pritchett, Leonard Waller, '08. B '07

Prouty, Charles Newton, '00. T '00

Pruyn, Frederic, '06. F '04

Pruyn, Robert Dunbar, '02s. H '01, '02

Purdon, James, '95. C '94

Purdon, John Rogers, '88. T '86

Putnam, Eliot Thwing, '01 and '03s. F '01, '02

Putnam, Goerge Thwing, '01. B '01

Putnam, William Edward, '96. T '93, '95, '96

Quackenboss, Alexander, M.S. B '88, '89

Quigley, William Alonzo, '06. B '03

Quimby, Horace Alonzo, '18. C '16

Quinlan, James Francis, L.S. T '99

Rand, James Henry, '08. F '07

Rand, Waldron Holmes, '98. B '95, '96, '97, '98.

Rand, William Henry, '88. B '87

Rand, William McNear, '09. T '06, '07, '08, '09

Randall, Clarence Walter, '05. B '02, '03, '04, '05. F '04

Randall, Frank Eldridge, '74. F '74

Ranney, Dudley Porter, '12. T '10, '12

Rantoul, Neal, '92. C '90, '91, '92

Rawle, Francis, '69. B '68, '69

Read, Harold Wilson, '03. H '03

Read, Nathaniel Goodwin, '71. C '69, '70, '71

Redpath, Léon Wallace, '98. T '95, '96

Reece, Franklin Augustus, '09. C '08

Reed, Benjamin Calvin, '74. B '71, '72

Reed, Clarence Searles, '17. B '15, '16

Reed, Stephen Alexander, '11. T '10

Reeves, Henry Everett, '12. B '11, '12

Reid, William Thomas, '01. B '98, '99, '00, 01. F '98, '99

Reidy, David Dillon, '23. T '22

Remington, Franklin, '87. F '86. C '85, '86. T '85

Reynders, Charlton, '20. C '18

Reynolds, John, '71. B '69, '70, '71

Reynolds, John, '07. F '06

Reynolds, Kenneth, '14. B '12. F '11

Reynolds, Quentin, '14. C '12, '13, '14

Rice, Arthur Noble, '00. T '97, '98, '99, '00

Rice, George Tilly, '96s. F '95

Rice, Paul Moseley, '15. T '15

Rice, Theodore Holton, '17. H '16, '17

Richards, Lyman Gilder, '16. T '14, '15

Richards, Thomas Kinsman, '15. F '14

Richards, William Whitlock, '68. C '67, '69

Richardson, Frederic Leopold William, '99. F '97

Richardson, Herbert Augustus, '82. B '80

Richardson, Henry Hyslop, '95. C '93

Richardson, John, '08. C '06, '07, '08

Richardson, Otis Weld, '99 and L.S. T '00, '01

Ristine, Albert Welles, '02s. F '99, '00, '01. T '01, '02

Rives, Arthur Landon, '74. F '74

Robb, Hampton, '18. F '17[2]

Roberts, Edward Reese, '16. T '16

Roberts, Henry Knowlton, '04s. F '00

Robinson, Arthur Weeks, '01s. T '98

Robinson, Chester Haven, '04. T '01, '02, '03, '04

Robinson, John Kelly, '01. B '98

Robinson, Miles Pratt, '15. T '15

Robinson, William Farr, '18. F '15, 16

Roche, James Thomas, '99s. T '96, '99

Rock, John Charles, '15s. T '13, '14

Rogers, Emery Herman, '87. T '86, '87

Rogers, Harold Alton, '11. B '10, '11. F '09

Rogers, Orville Forrest, '08. T '05, '06, '08

Rogers, William Bowditch, '96. F '95

Rollins, Frank Waldron, '77. F '76

Rollins, Wingate, '16. F '15

Roosevelt, George Emlen, '09. T '06, '07

Ropes, Francis Codman, '57. C '56

Ropes, Henry, '62. C '60

Rotch, Charles Morgan, '01. T '00, '01

Rowe, Henry Stuart Payson, '22. T '22

Rowe, John Jay, '07. T '07

Rowse, Arthur Edward, '18. T '16

Rumsey, Charles Cary, '02. H '00, '01, '02

Rumsey, Laurence, '08. H '07, '08

Russell, Fred Adams, '99 and L.S. H '00

Russell, Harlan Smyth, '22. B '21, '22

Russell, Henry Sturgis, '60. C '59

Russell, James Savage, '87. C '85

Russell, Robert Shaw, '72. C '70

Russell, William Eustis, '77. F '76

Rust, Edgar Carter, '04. T '01, '02, '04

Rust, Paul Drummond, '98. C '95, '96

Ryan, Joseph Francis, '20. F '19

Ryan, William Francis, '11. T '11

Ryley, George William, '10. T '10

Safford, Truman Henry, '16. B '16

Saltonstall, John Lee, '00. C '00

Saltonstall, Leverett, '14. H '14. C '13, '14

Sampson, Thompson Sawyer, '09. H '06, '07, '08, '09

Sanders, William Huntington, '97. B '96

Wetherbee, James Allen, '78 and '79. F '74, '75, '76, '77, '78

Wetmore, Charles Whitman, '75. C '75

Wharton, Bayard, '22. T '21.

Wheeler, Charles Nathan Brooks, '86. T '86

Wheeler, Stuart Wadsworth, '98. F '94, '96, '97

Wheeler, William Asa, '74. C '73

Wheeler, Walter Heber, '18. F '16

Wheelwright, Henry May, '94. T '91, '92, '93, '94

Whitbeck, Brainerd Hunt, '99. C '97

Whitcher, Warren Faxon,[1] '09. T '08

White, Alverse Lysander, '06. G '04

White, Alexander Moss, '92. T '90, 91

White, DeLancey Pierrepont, '01. T '99

White, Frederic Hall, '06. F '04

White, Henry Kent, '20. H '19

White, Henry Preston, '99. T '98

White, Horatio Stevens, '73. B '70, '71, '72, '73

White, James Clarke, '17. C '16

White, Norman Hill, '95. B '95

White, Robert Vose, '09. F '08

Whitelock, William Marshall Elliott, '13. F '11, '12

Whiting, William Austin, '77. F '74, '75, '76

Whitman, Arthur Holmes, '11. T '11

Whitman, Frederic Bennett, '19. C '18, '19

Whitman, Hendricks Hallett, '06. T '05, '06. F '04

Whitman, Malcolm Douglass, '99. L T '96, '97, '98

Whitney, Edward Herbert, '14. L T '11

Whitney, George, '07. C '07

Whitney, James Edward, '89. C '88, '89

Whitney, Myron Henry, '09. T '08

Whitney, Richard, '11. C '09, '10

Whitney, Richard Skinner, '22. T '20, '21, '22

Whitney, Wilmot, '16s. B '14, '15, '16. F '15

Whittemore, Parker Williams, '95. B '94, '95. F '94

Whittren, Jacob Potter, '95s. T '93

Whitwell, William Scollay, '03. F '02

Wiestling, Frank Beecher, '87. B '85, '86, '87

Wiggin, Joseph, '93 and L.s. B '91, '92, '93, '94

Wiggin, Morrill, '18. F '16

Wiggins, Charles, '08. C '07

Wiggins, John Gregory, '12. C '11

Wigglesworth, Frank, '15. F '12

Wigglesworth, Richard Bowditch, '12. B '11, '12. F '09, '10. H '10

Wilder, Enos, '06. H '04, '05

Wilkinson, Edward Tuckerman, '66. C '65, '66

Willard, Gardner Goodrich, '69. B '67, '68, '69

Willard, Josiah Newell, '57. C '55

Willard, Sidney, '52. C '52

Willard, Waldo Wickham, '87 and L.s. B '85, '86, '87, '88, '89. F '84

Willcox, Westmore, '17. T '15, '16. F '16

Willetts, Joseph Prentice, '09. H '06, '08, '09

Willetts, William Prentice, '14s. H '12, '13, '14. F '13

Williams, Harvey Ladew, '97. T '96, '97

Williams, James Hunt, '94. B '94

Williams, Richard Norris, '16. L T '13, '14, '15

Willis, Grinnell, '70. C '69, '70

Willis, Joseph Grinnell, '02. T '00, '01, '02

Williston, Samuel, '82. T '81

Wilson, George Bennett, '94. C '94

Wilson, William Reynolds, '86. C '85

Wingate, Dana Joseph Paine, '14. B '12, '13, '14

Winslow, Andrew Nickerson, '96. B '94, '95

Winslow, Frederick Bradlee,[2] '95. L T '92

Winslow, Samuel Ellsworth, '85. B '83, '84, '85. F '84

Winsor, Alfred, '02. H '01, '02

Winsor, Robert, '80. B '78, '79, '80. F '77, '78, '79

Winthrop, Frederic Bayard,[3] '91 and L.s. C '90, '92

Withington, David Little, '20. C '18

Withington, Frederic Burnham, '15. T '15. F '14.

Withington, Lothrop, '11. F '09, '10. C '09, '10, '11

Withington, Paul, '09 and '10. F '08, '09. C '08, '09

Withington, Paul Raymond, '12. T '09, '10, '11, '12

Wolcott, Samuel Huntington, '03. C '03

Wolverton, John Boyd, '20. B '18

Wood, Clement Biddle, '98 and L.s. C '99, '00

Wood, John Walter, '88. C '86, '87. F '86, '87

Woodbury, Thornton, '89. B '88

Woodman, Francis Call, '88 and L.s. F '86, '87, '88

Woods, Thomas Smith, '22. F '19, '20

Woodward, Calvin Milton, '60. C '60

Woodward, Harry Reamer, '84. C '82. F '81

Woodward, William, '98. C '97

Wrenn, Robert Duffield, '95. B '95. F '94. L T '91, '92

Wright, Cushing Frederic, '03. F '01, '02

Wright, Edward Clarence, '86 and L.s. T '86, '87, '88

Wright, Frank, '66. B '65, '66

Wright, James Anderson, '79. B '76, '77, '78, '79

Wright, William Hammond, '92. T '90, '91, '92

Wrightington, Edgar Newcomb, '97. F '93, '94, '95, '96. C '95, '97

Wylde, John Irton, '17. H '15, '16, '17

Wyman, Philip, '10. B '10

Yocom, James Reed, '85 and M.s. C '84, '85, '86

Young, Benjamin Loring, '07. T '06, '07

Young, Edward Lorraine, '06. T '04

Young, Henry Bateman, '03 and G.s. T '04

Young, William Bartholomew, '13. B '10, '12, '13

1923–1963

Aadalen, Richard J. '61   F'60

Aaron, Robert F. '46 ocC   Sw '43, '47

Abbot, David M. '50   H '48, '49, '50

Abbot, Henry W., Jr. '59   T '58, '59

Abbott, Gordon, Jr. '50   Sk '50

Abell, Carlisle '35   T '33, '35

Abramson, David H. '65   Sw '63

Acheson, Donald T. '57   T '57

Acker, Earle D. '44   H '42, '43

Adams, Arlon T. '53   W '53

Adams, Francis W. W. '28   H '27

Adams, John II '63   S '60, '61

Adams, John Q. '45 ocC   LC '46

Adams, Myron J., Jr. '62   F '61

Adams, Samuel II '50   F '48

Adams, Stirling S. '33   B '33

Adams, Thomas W. '53   C '53

Adelman, Gary W. '63   T '61, '62

Batt, Robert R. '41 Fc '41
Bauer, Karl J. '48 B '46
Bauer, Ronald L. '62 B '61, '62
Beadie, David M. '58 G '58; H '58
Beal, Robert L. '63 Sw '62, '63
Beale, Benjamin '34 F '33; H '32, '33, '34
Beals, Edward M., Jr. '25 F '24; H '23, '25
Beane, Arthur '36 C '36
Beaver, Donald DeB. '58 S '55, '56
Beck, Paul '55 CC '54
Beckett, William H. M. '62 H '60, '61, '62
Beckwith, Martin J. '62 T '59, '60, '61, '62
Beebe, Marcus, Jr. '44 H '42, '43
Beer, Walter E., Jr. '26 C '26
Beery, James R. '63 F '62
Beizer, Richard L. '64 F '61, '62; L '62
Belisle, Eugene L. '31 C '29
Bellknap, Michael H.P. '63 Te '62, '63
Bell, Dudley '28 F '26, '27
Bell, James D. '59 F '56
Bellows, Charles S. '37 H '37
Bemis, Grosvenor '24 B '23
Bender, Paul '54 Sw '54
Bender, Ralph H. '50 F '48, '49
Benedict, Raymond T. '38 Sw '37
Benedix, August F., Jr. '41 L '41
Benjamin, John T. '62 CC '59, '60; T '61
Benjamin, R. Dyke '59 CC '57, '58; T '57, '58, '59
Benner, Allen R. II '33 B '33
Bennett, Edward H., Jr. '37 C '35, '36, '37
Bennett, George E. '27 B '27
Bennett, Henry S. '49 Sw '46
Bennett, William McG. '61 Fc '61
Bentley, Robert L., Jr. '36 Te '36
Berenberg, Jeffrey L. '63 W '62
Berg, Warren S. '44 B '42, '43
Bergantino, Thomas S. '58 B '56, '57, '58
Berger, Robert L. '52 S '51
Berglund, Paul T. E. '26 T '24, '25, '26
Berizzi, Dario C. '38 Sw '37, '38
Berke, Robert N.J. '51 Sw '49, '50, '51
Berman, Elihu H. '44 T '42
Berman, Ronald S. '52 T '50, '51, '52
Bernheim, Thomas O. '58 S '56, '57
Bernstein, Philip '62 B '60, '61, '62
Berresford, Richard C. '28 B '28
Bertelsen, Viggo C, Jr. '58 LC '58
Best, David B. H. '50 T '49
Bezanson, Richard B. '50 L '49
Bickford, Albert C. '24 T '24
Bickford, Robert C. '56 S '55
Biddle, Oliver C. '43 LC '41
Bigelow, Albert S. '29 H '28, '29
Bigelow, Chandler, '24 H '23

Bigelow, Hugh W. '29 H '28, '29
Billings, Franklin S., Jr. '44 B '43
Bilodeau, Thomas H. '37 B '35, '36, '37; F '34, '35
Bilodeau, Thomas H., Jr. '65 B '63; F '62
Bingham, Charles W. '55 F '54
Binney, Peter A. '61 C '59, '60
Birch, David L. '59 L '59
Bird, Benjamin L. '40 Bb '39
Bird, Jackson '38 Bb '38
Bishop, John, Jr. '52 Sl '52
Bissell, Dwight M., Jr. '62 Sw '60, '61, '62
Bissell, H. Hamilton '33 C '31, '32, '33
Bixler, Frank D. '45 occ Bb '43
Black, Dwight P. '53 T '52, '53
Blackwood, George W. '37 F '34, '35
Blake, Francis, Jr. '61 LC '60, '61
Blake, George B. '39 Sq '39
Blake, Robert I. '56 T '54
Blakey, Richard B. '63 H '63
Blanchard, Albert N. '39 L '39
Blanchard, Walter S. '25 C '25
Blanco, Carlos A. '48 S '47
Bland, Robert P. '62 H '60, '61, '62
Bliss, Anthony A. '36 T '34
Bliss, Edward P. '55 C '54; H '53, '54, '55
Bliss, William L. '52 C '51, '52; H '50, '51, '52
Blitz, Jerome H. '53 F '50, '52
Blodget, Alden S., Jr. '38 H '38
Blodgett, Thomas N. '61 S '58; T '59, '60, '61
Blodnick, Edward K. '54 Bb '52, '54
Blohm, Henrik '56 S '55, '56
Blotner Norman D. '40 L '40
Blumberg, Benjamin M. '63 R '63
Bodden, Paul H. '52 Bb '52
Bodiker, David H. '56 F '54
Boeckeler, William C. '60 Sw '58
Boersma, Frederick L. '62 Fc '62
Bohlen, Edwin U. C. '51 C '50, '51
Bohn, David C. '61 L '61
Bohn, Lewis C. '45 occ C '46
Bolster, Phillips E. '51 F '48
Bolton, Charles P. '64 F '62
Bolton, Oliver P. '39 F '38
Bonner, John F. '43 T '42
Boone, Thomas H. '62 B '60, '61; F '60, '61
Booth, Kenneth L. '39 F '36, '37, '38
Booth, Roy H., Jr. '27 B '26, '27
Borchard, Gary C. '62 Bb '60, '61, '62
Borden, Spencer IV '63 C '61, '62, '63
Borkenhagen, David M. '60 B '60, '61
Bornheimer, Allen M. '65 Bb '63
Bossart, Donald E. '54 Te '54
Boston, Clarence E., Jr. '39 F '36, '37, '38; W '39

Boston, George F. '46 F '42
Bosworth, Arthur S., Jr. '41 Sw '40, '41
Bosworth, Frank M., Jr., '35 L '35
Botsford, Matthew W., Jr. '57 B '55, '56, '57; F '54, '55, '56
Bottenfield, Carl D. '51 F '49
Boulris, Chester J. '60 occ B '59; F '57, '58, '59
Bourneuf, Henri J. '33 H '33
Bowditch, Patrick F. '48 W '48
Bowditch, Robert S., Jr. '61 Bb '59, '60, '61 Te '59, '60, '61
Bowman, Robert A. '56 Bb '54, '56
Boyce, Peter B. '58 Fc '58
Boyda, Robert J. '62 F '59, '60, '61
Boyden, Perry T. '61 C '59, '60, '61
Boyden, Walter L. III '53 C '51, '52, '53
Boye, Emmanuel M. '63 S '61, '62
Boynton, Elwood D. '35 P '34
Boynton, Thomas W. '43 C '41, '42
Boys, Richard C. '35 Bb '35
Brackett, Charles E., Jr. '41 B '39
Bradbury, John D. '63 Te '61
Braden, George D. '25 occ F '25
Bradford, Charles H. '26 F '25; T '26
Bradford, Edward H. '26 F '25; T '26
Bradford, Robert F. '23 C '23
Bradford, Standish '24 C '22; F '23
Bradlee, Douglas H. T. '50 F '48, '49
Bradley, Joseph C. '39 S '38; T '39
Brandling-Bennett, Anthony D. '64 Sw '62, '63
Brady, William J., Jr. '48 Bb '47, '48; F '47
Braggiotti, Dorilio C. '35 B '34, '35
Braggiotti, Rama A.B. '33 H '33
Brahms, David M. '59 T '58, '59
Brainard, Snelling R. '48 occ Sw '48
Braisted, Richard C. '50 Sl '50
Bramhall, Robert R. '49 occ Bb '49, '50, '51; Te '51
Bray, John R. '54 H '52, '53, '54
Bray, Philip V. '35 C '35
Bray, Robert C., Jr. '60 W '59
Brayton, Lincoln D. '28 T '28
Brayton, Richard A. '37 T '35, '37
Brayton Roswell '39 T '37, '39
Breasted, James H. III '60 Sk '60
Breckinridge, John C. '61 C '59, '60, '61
Brennan, Stephen H., Jr. '38 T '36, '37, '38
Brewster, Galen '65 C '63
Bridges, Robert S. '62 C '61, '62
Briggs, Alden, Jr. '60 Sq '60; Te '58, '60
Briggs, Peter G. '59 F '56, '57, '58
Briggs, Winslow R. '50 Sw '50
Brigham, David L. '58 B '57, '58

Brignall, James T. '63 H '63
Britton, Stanley J. '53 F '50
Brokaw, Caleb, Jr. '43 LC '42
Bronstein, John B. '61 T '59, '60, '61
Brooke, Peter A. '52 L '52
Brookings, Robert S. II '35 F '34; T '35
Brookings, Walter DuB. '37 T '35, '36,' 37
Brooks, Benjamin R. '65 W '63
Brooks, John W. '39 H '39
Brooks, Peter C. '66 Sq '63
Brooks, Peter T. '38 C '37
Brooks, Reginald L. '26 T '24
Broome, Joseph H. '26 T '24, '25
Brophy, John J. '54 G '54
Brown, Bradford S. '53 Sw '53
Brown, Dudley B. W. '32 C '32
Brown, Earl L. '24 B '24
Brown, Ernest B. '50 T '48
Brown, Everett H. III '42 C '42
Brown, Gordon K. '28 F '27, '28
Brown, Harold O. J. '53 C '53
Brown, Henry MacP. '59 CC '56, '58
Brown, Philip S. '30 T '28, '29
Brown, Robert A. '55 Sq '54, '55
Brown, Robert P. '39 C '39
Brown, Shepard '50 Sw '50
Brown, Stanley N. '24 C '22
Brown, Sumner E. '30 T '28
Brown, Thornton '36 H '35, '36
Brown, Timothy M. '54 Sl '53, '54
Brown, William P., Jr. '41 F '39, '40
Brownell, Lawrence D. '54 C '53, '54; Sq '53, '54
Brownell, Morris R., Jr. '30 C '29
Bruce, Roger G. '55 T '55
Bruck, Norman '56 T '54, '55, '56
Bryan, Mario E. '59 LC '58, '59
Bryant, John W. '36 T '36

Buckley, Edward T., Jr. '42 B '40, '41; Bb '40, '41, '42
Buell Charles C. '23 B '21, '23; F '20, '21, '22
Bulger, Roger J. '55 Bb '53, '54, '55
Bullard, Frederic K., Jr. '46 ocC Te '49
Bullard, Lyman G. '55 H '43
Bullard, Robert P. '24 B '24
Bullard, Walter L. '50 Sw '47
Bunker, John P. '42 T '40, '41, '42
Bunker, Laurence E. '26 T '24
Burbank, Bouldin G. '28 T '26, '27
Burbank, Daniel E., Jr. '37 S '36
Burditt, George M., Jr. '44 Bb '42, '43
Burgess, George W. '25 B '25; H '24, '25
Burke, Dustin M. '52 F '50, '51; G '52; H '50, '51, '52

Burke, Edmund J. '26 T '25
Burke, John R. '27 F '26
Burke, John W. '23 CC '21, '22; T '21, '22, '23
Burnaman, Phillip R. '56 W '56
Burnap, Larry R. '61 CC '60
Burnett, Robert M. '39 F '38
Burnham, Bradford H. '24 C '22, '24
Burnham, Frederic B. '60 LC '59
Burns, Howard W. '28 B '26, '27, '28; F '27
Burns, Samuel C. '29 F '27, '28, '29
Burr, Francis H. '35 F '34
Burr, Sturtevant '31 T '31
Burrage, William S. '33 F '33
Burt, David S. '40 Te '40
Burton, John C. '44 H '42, '43
Burton, Wilton S. '36 F '34, '35
Burwell, Edward L. '41 CC '39, '40
Butler, Paul F. '44 ocC B '46
Butler, Samuel C. '51 F '48, '49
Butters, Donald H. '55 B '53, '54, '55
Butterworth, George W. III '60 H '59, '60
Butzel, Albert K. '60 S '57, '58
Buzby, Jesse M., Jr. '47 ocC Sw '47, '48
Byrne, George P., Jr. '38 Sw '38
Byrne, James J. '52 L '52

Cabot, Charles C., Jr. '52 B '52
Cabot, David '53 Sl '53
Cabot, Frederick C. '59 LC '58, '59
Cabot, Samuel, Jr. '33 F '33
Cabral, Manuel J. '59 Fc '59; L '59
Cahn, Arthur S. '60 T '58, '59, '60
Cahners, Fulton I. '39 T '37
Cahners, Norman L. '36 T '34, '35, '36
Cairns, David D. '52 CC '51; T '50, '51, 52
Cairns, James J., Jr. '57 CC '54; T '55, '56, '57
Calhoun, John D. '43 S '42
Calkins, Wendell N. '39 Sw '39
Callanan, Gerard J. '43 B '42, '43
Callanan, William S .'62 H '61
Callaway, John MacI. '37 H '35, '36, '37; T '37
Callaway, Leigh L. '64 T '62
Callaway, Samuel R. '36 H '34, '35, '36
Calvin, Edwin E. '35 T '33, '34, '35
Cameron, James R. '59 Te '58, '59
Campana, John P. '36 B '36
Campbell, Rolla D., Jr. '41 ocC T '41
Campbell, Thomas '24 B '24
Campion, Thomas B. '38 L '38
Canavarro, Kim deS. '40 Sq '40
Canepa, John C. '53 B '53
Canfield, Maynard M. '57 Te '56

Canning, Elisha, Jr. '26 C '26
Cannistraro, Nicholas, Jr. '61 C '60, '61
Canty, Robert D. '57 Bb '55, '56, '57
Caploe, George M. '46 ocC T '46, '47
Cappiello, David L. '60 F '58, '59
Caputo, Bruce F. '65 L '63
Carden, John G. D. '57 F '56
Carman, John J. '51 J '49, '50
Carpenter, Charles C. '24 T '22, '23, '24
Carr, Charles E. '35 ocC B '35
Carr, Louis B. '37 H '35, '36, '37
Carroll, Tom J. '52 Sl '52
Carson, Barry A. '49 H '46
Carstein, Lawrence W. '39 H '39
Carswell, Robert '49 S '48
Carter, Albert B., Jr. '50 C '50
Carter, David N. G. '58 S '57
Carter, David R. '50 T '48, '49, '50
Carter, Edward P. '56 T '54, '55, '56
Carter, Forest L. '51 Fc '51
Carver, John J. '30 B '30
Casale, Frank J. '35 F '34
Case, John McM. '37 T '37
Casey, Warren A. '34 F '33
Cass, Donald J. '52 F '49, '51
Cass, Edward H. '51 Sw '51
Cassedy, Gerard J. '33 C '31, '32, '33; F '32
Cassidy, Henry C. '31 Fc '31
Caulfield, John G. '50 B '47, '48, '49, '50
Cavanaugh, Thomas F., Jr. '51 B '49, '50, '51
Cavicke, David C. '48 T '47, '48
Cavin, William B. '64 W '62
Cavin, W. Brooks, Jr. '37 W '37
Celi, Mario J. '56 H '55, '56
Chace, Arthur F., Jr. '34 C '34
Chace, J. Fletcher '38 C '36, '37, '38
Chadsey, William L. III '64 Sw '62, '63
Chalfant, Henry, Jr. '31 T '31
Challinor, David, Jr. '43 C '41, '42
Chambers, Michael T. E. '55 C '55
Champion, Paul W. '47 Bb '46; F '45
Chandler, Carl V. '23 T '23
Chandler, Hugh P. '54 W '54
Chang, Albert '63 S '60, '61, '62
Chanler, Bronson W. '45 ocC C '46, '47
Channing, Hayden, Jr. '37 CC '35, '36
Chapin, Aldus H. '52 B '52
Chapin, Vinton '23 F '21, '22; T '23
Chapin, Walter L., Jr. '25 T '24
Charat, Philippe M. '60 Fc '60
Chase, George W. '53 H '53
Chase, John P. '28 B '26, '27, '28; H '26, '27, '28
Chase, John R. '50 H '48, '49, '50
Chase, Philip W. '25 F '24; H '24, '25; T '25

Chase, Robert M. '43   T '41, '42

Chase, R. Kingsbury '59   LC '58, '59

Chauncey, Henry '28   B '26, '27; F '25, '26

Chauncey, William E. '55   B '53, '54, '55

Cheek, David B. '34   F '33; T '32

Cheek, Marion A., Jr. '26   B '24; F '23, '24, '25

Chiappa, Keith H. '65   T '63

Chick, David S. '53   B '53

Choate, Arthur O., Jr. '34   F '33; H '34

Choate, Thomas H. '37   C '37

Christensen, Boake W. '61   LC '60

Christensen, Jon H. '61   F '59, '60

Christian, Michael W. '60   LC '58, '59, '60

Christman, George III '44   Sw '43

Chun, Kenneth K-H. '48   S '47

Church, Herbert, Jr. '44   C '43

Churchill, Edward D., Jr. '56   S '55; Sk '56

Churchill, Frederic E. '63   S '62

Churchill, Winthrop H. '23   F '20, '21, '22

Chute, Richard S. '60   Sq '60; Te '58, 60

Claflin, Richard M. '36   H '35, '36

Claflin, Robert '50   W '49

Claflin, William H. III '41   H '39, '40, '41

Clapp, David P. '64   S '61, '62

Clark, Christopher T. '62   Te '61

Clark, Clarence S. '45   occ   C '47

Clark, David C. '49   LC '47, '49

Clark, Eben C. '26   F '25, '26; H '26, '27

Clark, Eugene V. '40   CC '38, '39; T '38, '39

Clark, Forrester A. '29   C '27, '28, '29; F '27, '28

Clark, Forrester A., Jr. '58   F '57; H '58

Clark, Francis B. '28   T '26, '27, '28

Clark, George B., Jr. '55   F '53

Clark, Henry W. '23   F '21, '22

Clark John D. '47   Bb '46, '47

Clark, John R. '28   C '36, '38

Clark, Joseph S., Jr. '23   B '22, '23

Clark, Joseph S. III '51   Sq '51

Clark, Percy H., Jr. '30   LC '29

Clark, Philip M., Jr. '51   H '49

Clark, Raymond S. '36   C '34, '35, '36

Clark, Robert T. '47   T '46

Clark, Sherman H. '46   B '43

Clark, Sydney P., Jr. '51   L '51

Clark, Warren H. '52   C '51, '52

Clarke, Samuel M. '25   T '25

Clasby, Richard J. '54   B '52, '53, '54; F '51, '52, '53; H '52, '53, '54

Clay, Landon T. '50   B '49

Clay, Louis M. '42   B '40, '41, '42

Clayman, Loren Z. '63   T '61, '62, '63

Cleary, Richard S. '59   H '59

Cleary, Robert B. '58   B '56, '57, '58; H '56, '57, '58

Cleary, William J., Jr. '56   B '54, '55; H '54, '55

Cleland, Hugh J. '61   F '59

Clement, Robert B., Jr. '63   LC '62

Cleveland, Harold Van B. '38   L '38

Clifton, Roger L. '57   Sw '56, '57

Clos, Delavan C. '35   S '34

Coady, Clement D. '27   F '24, '25, '26; H '26, '27

Coan, John T., Jr. '50   F '45, '48, '49; H '46

Cobb, David '31   T '29, '30, '31

Coburn, Arthur L., Jr. '24   T '24

Coburn, Frederick R. '51   L '51

Coburn, Lawrence H. '56   L '56

Coburn, Philip F. '23   F '21, '22, '23

Cochran, Moncrieff M. III '64   S '62

Cochran, Robert N. '55   F '52, '54

Cochran, Thomas C., Jr. '58   Sw '56, '57, '58

Cochran, William D. '45   occ   C '46

Coffman, Amos J., Jr. '62   Sw '60, '61, '62

Cogan, John F., Jr. '49   T '48, '49

Coggeshall, Timothy '44   T '43

Cohen, Joel H. '57   T '55, '56, '57

Cohen, Myron L. '39   F '38

Cohen, Stephen B. '61   F '60; T '59, '60, '61

Cohodes, Eli A. '50   Bb '49

Coker, Peter H. '55   T '53

Coleman, Franklin W., Jr. '38   Sw '37, '38

Coleman, Joseph G. III '29   T '29

Coleman, William C., Jr. '40   F '38, '39; H '39, '40

Collins, Herbert F. '55   T '53, '54

Collins, Joseph R. '32   T '32

Collins, Richard, Jr. '26   LC '26

Collins, William E. III '59   H '59

Colloredo-Mannsfeld, Franz F. '32   C '30

Colony, John J., Jr. '37   Sw '37

Colpak, Edward A. '29   B '29

Colwell, Alfred H. '38   B '36

Combs, James J. '63   B '62, '63

Combs, James L. '26   occ   F '23, '27

Combs, Lee '26   T '24, '25, '26

Combs, Preston C. '50   Te '50

Comeford, John C., Jr '46   F '42

Comfort, George V. '36   F '34

Condon, Edward G. '54   Bb '52, '53, '54

Connell, Michael J. '61   G '61

Connelly, Arthur P., Jr. '51   F '49, '50

Connolly, Paul F. '36   B '36

Connolly, Thomas D., Jr. '45   occ   B '47

Connor, David G. '62   H '62

Conzelman, Joseph H., Jr. '55   F '53

Cook, Howard A. '37   T '37

Cook, Wallace L. '61   B '59

Cooke, Goodwin '53   T '53

Cooke, John E. '54   B '54

Cooledge, W. Scott III '55   H '53, '54, '55

Cooley, Frederick B. II '61   Sw '59, '60

Coolidge, Nicholas J. '54   C '54

Coolidge, Thomas J. Jr. '54   F '51, '52, '53; H '52, '53, '54

Coolidge, Thomas R. '55   B '55

Cooney, Edward A., Jr. '55   G '54, '55

Cooper, Paul F. Jr. '52   T '52

Cooper, William G., Jr. '33   Bx '33

Copeland, John T. '58   F '55, '57; H '56, '57

Coppinger, John E., Jr. '48   B '46, '47, '48

Corbin, Thomas E. '62   T '60

Cordes, Carl B. '56   B '56

Cordingley, Robert F. '25   B '25; F '23

Cordingley, William A., Jr. '40   G '40

Corning, Nathan E. '53   H '51, '52

Cortesi, Alexander C. '62   S '60, '61

Cortesi, Henry B. '58   Sq '58

Cortesi, Roger S. '56   Sq '56

Cotter, Paul J. '58   L '58

Couch, William M., Jr. '42   T '41

Coughlin, William G. '55   LC '55

Coulson, Walter '48   occ   B '47, '48, '49; F '46, '47, '48

Coulter, Charles J., Jr. '49   H '47, '48, '49

Covey, Richard B. '50   Bb '49, '50

Cowen, Charles T. '44   F '42; H '42, '43

Cowen, Robert II '47   F '45, '46; H '46

Cowles, Robert R. '55   F '52, '53, '54

Cowperthwaite, William J. '55   S '54

Cox, Howard A. '53   F '52

Cox, Louis A. '49   C '48, '49

Cox, Robert H. II '41   H '40, '41

Coyne, Peter M. '51   F '48

Craig, John E. II '56   Fc '56

Crain, William C. '65   CC '62; T '63

Crampton, Walter L. '36   Bx '36

Crane, Francis J. '34   F '32, '33

Craven, Richard '52   S '51

Crawford, David C. '36   T '34, '35

Crawford, George '28   F '28

Creery, Philip A. '60   Sk '60

Crehore, Joseph F. '56   F '55; H '54, '55, '56

Cretzmeyer, Charles H., Jr. '38   occ   T '36

Crickard, John W. '32   F '30, '31, '32

Croach, J. William, Jr. '40   Fc '40

Croasdale, Olney R., Jr. '65   T '63

Crocker, Frederick G. '34   F '33

Crocker, John, Jr. '46   occ   H '46, '47

Crocker, Julian '44   H '43

Crocker, Prescott B. '64   H '63

Crocker, Seth C. '41   LC '41

Cronin, George R., Jr. '57   Sl '57

Crook, Robert W. '59   W '57

Crosby, Clifton D. '50   B '48, '49, '50; Bb '48, '49, '50

Crosby, David B. '61   H '59, '60, '61

Crosby, Joseph P. '28   F '25, '27

Crosby, William E., Jr. '24   F '23; H '22, '23, '24

Crosby, William E. III '56   B '56; F '55

Crosby, Wilson H. '32   H '30, '31, '32

Cross, John '30   H '29, '30

Crowe, John C. '59   Te '59

Crowley, Paul J. '53   B '52; F '50, '51, '52

Crowther, William E., Jr. '55   C '54, '55

Crump, Julian T. '55   L '57

Cuffe, Edward W. '61   Bb '60

Culbert, Alan H. '56   F '53; W '57

Culbert, Kenneth B. '55   W '55

Cullen, Albert F., Jr. '60   F '57, '58, '59

Cullen, John P. '34   F '33

Culolias, Nicholas G. '53   F '50, '52, '53

Culver, John C. '54   F '51, '52, '53

Cumings, Thayer '26   H '24, '25, '26

Cummin, Graham '38   Sw '37, '38

Cummings, Charles K., Jr. '23   C '23

Cummings, Francis E. '30   T '28, '29, '30

Cummings, Leonard '44 ocC   F '42, '46

Cunningham, Charles C. '32   F '29, '31; H '30, '31, '32

Cunningham, Francis, Jr. '44 ocC   C '47

Cunningham, John H., Jr. '39   H '39

Cunningham, William J., Jr. '60   B '60

Curran, Peter F., Jr. '53   T '51, '53

Curran, Robert L., '53   T '51, '52, '53

Curtin, Neal J. '65   F '62

Curtis, Edward B. '54   L '54

Curtis, Frazier '40   F '39

Curtiss, Harold M., Jr. '39   B '37, '39

Curwen, Darcy '43   C '41, '42; Sw '41, '42, '43

Curwen, Henry A. '40   Sw '38, '39, '40

Curwen, William L. '50   C '48, '49

Cushing, Howard G., Jr. '55   C '54, '55

Cushman, Allerton '29   C '29

Cushman, John G. '25   H '25

Custer, Benjamin S., Jr. '58   Te '59

Cutcheon, Byron R. '25   CC '24; T '23, '24, '25

Cutler, Eric '40   Sw '39, '40

Cutler, Philip '41   H '39

Cutler, Robert B. '35   C '35

Cutler, Roger W., Jr. '37   C '36, '37

Cutler, William W. III '63   B '62, '63

Cutler, Edward L., Jr. '38   H '36, '37, '38

Cutts, Frank B. '28   B '26, '27, '28

Daley, Leo F. '27   F '26, '27

Daley, Leo H. '57   F '54, '55

Dall, Mark H. '37   LC '37

Dalrymple, Willard '43   T '43

Daly, John S. F. '65   H '63

Damis, James J. '57   F '56

Damis, John J. '62   F '61

Dampeer, John L. '38   Bb '38

Dana, Allston F. '33   B '32

Dana, George W. '40   Sw '39

Dane, Ernest B. III '55   Sk '55

Daniels, John L., Jr. '65   W '63

Danner, Bryant C. '59   Bb '57, '58, '60

Danner, William D. '62   Bb '60, '61, '62

D'Arcy, John P. '65   CC '62

Darlington, Charles F., Jr. '26   C '25, '26

Darrell, Richard W. '55   C '53, '54, '55

Daughaday, William H. '40   W '40

Daughters, Donald L. '39   F '36, '37, '38

Davenport, S. Ellsworth III '34   Te '34

David, Charles N. '62   S '59, '60, '61

Dow, Peter B. '54   T '51, '52, '53, '54

Dow, Richard A. '35   H '33, '34, '35

Dow, William M. '29   T '28

Dowd, William R. '44 ocC   LC '46, '47, '48

Downer, Gerald W. '36   T '36

Downes, Gregory '61   H '59, '60

Downes, James E. II '63   H '63

Downes, Philip G. '40   H '40

Downes, Robert C. '38   F '37

Downey, Frank L., Jr. '39   L '39

Downey, James F. III '52   T '51, '52

Downing, George A. '40   F '39; T '38, '39, '40

Downing, Walter L. '42   Sw '42

Downs, Robert C. S. '60   T '58, '59, '60

Doyle, Joseph T. '39   Fc '39

Doyle, Paul K. '38   B '37, '38

Drake, Ervin T. III '44   B '42

Draper, Charles D. '32   H '30

Draper, George, Jr. '64   S '61, '62

Draper, Thomas F., Jr. '57   L '57

Dreher, George R. '42   H '40, '41, '42

Drennan, Robert M. '46 ocC   F '46, '47

Driggs, H. Perry, Jr. '58   G '58

Drill, Frederick E. '52   F '51

Driver, William R. III '61   S '58, '59, '60

Drohan, Thomas E. '49   Sw '46, '47, '48, '49

Droller, Michael J. '64   Te '63

Drucker, William R. '43   Sw '41, '42, '43

Drummey, Michael F., Jr. '62   B '60, '61, '62

Drury, Samuel S., Jr. '35   C '34, '35

Drvaric, Emil J. '49   F '46, '47, '48

Duane, George E. '40 ocC   F '40; H '40, '41

Duane, Morris '23   Te '22

Duback, Richard T. J. '53   F '50, '51, '52

Dubiel, Emile '37   F '34, '35; T '35, '36

Du Bois, Philip M. '53   C '51, '52, '53

Ducey, James G. '42 ocC   C '43

Duchin, Ralph I. '27   B '27

Dudley, James D. '30   B '29

Duffey, Arthur F., Jr. '36   H '34, '35, '36

Duffey, John G. '36   L '36

DuMoulin, John '58   T '57, '58

Dunbar, Robert P. '58   H '58

Duncan, Leslie R. '59   H '58, '59

Dunker, Henry T. '25   F '22, '23, '24; T '23, '24, '25

Dunker, Henry T., Jr. '51   F '48

Dunlap, Charles E. '30   T '29, '30

Dunn, John M. '48 ocC   B '48, '49

Durant, John B. '27   H '27

Durant, Weston J. '48 ocC   B '49

Durkee, Ralph E., Jr. '29   B '29

Durwood, Stanley H. '43   F '42

Dwinell, James F. III '62   B '60; H '60, '61, '62

Dyer, H. Chouteau II '57   Sw '55, '56, '57

Eager, John M., Jr. '58   C '57, '58

Earle, M. Mark, Jr. '59   LC '58

Eastling, John R. '59   W '57

Eastman, Charles A.C. '24   F '22, '23; T '23, '24

Eaton, Charles F. III '58   F '56

Eaton, David C. '40   H '39, '40

Eaton, Donald K., Jr. '51   H '51

Eaton, Peter K. '45 ocC   H '46

Ecker, Leo A. '37   F '34, 35; H '35, '36, '37

Eckert, Richard N. '44   Bb '43

Edelman, John A. '46 ocC   T '46

Ederer, John H. '53   F '51, '52

Edgar, William, Jr. '41   S '38, '40

Edmonds, Hugh W. '49   F '48

Edmunds, Edward P. '41   L '41

Edwards, Charles W., Jr. '54   L '54

Edwards, Frederick B. III '50   T '49

Edwards, John '55   Sw '55

Egan, Charles J., Jr. '54   Sw '52, '53, '54

Ehrlich, Nathaniel J. '61   Te '59, '60, '61

Eikenberry, Ronald G. '57   F '56

Eisenbrey, Norris H. '63   Sw '60

Eisinger, Irwin J. '56   T '56

Ekpebu, Lawrence B. '60   S '57, '58, '59

Elbel, Donald R. '41   G '41

Elfast, Royal A., Jr. '50   R '49

Eliades, Peter G. '60   F '57, '58, '59

Eliel, Leonard P. '36   C '34, '35, '36

Elizalde, Fred J. '62   Sw '60, '62

Elken, Richard G. '44   Bb '42

Elkins, William L. '29   H '28

Ellefson, John O. '58   C '59

Elliott, Calvin H., Jr. '40   LC '40

Elliott, Charles J.F.W. '55   Sq '53

Elliott, John, Jr. '42   H '42

Elliott, Osborn '46   H '43

Ellis, Gordon K. '50   B '49

Ellis, Harwood '31   H '30, '31

Ellis, William S. '44 ocC   T '46

Ellis, William V., Jr. '42 ocC   F '42

Ellison, William P. '27   B '25, '26, '27; H '25, '26, '27

Elsas, Frederick J. '64   F '62; LC '63

Elsas, Louis J. II '58   CC '57

Elser, Peter F.D. '41   F '40

Elwell, Edwin S., Jr. '39   Bb '39

Emerson, Ashton '36   H '35, '36

Emerson, Eugene '38   H '36, '37, '38

Emerson, Kenneth '53   Sw '51, '52, '53

Emmet, Grenville T. III '60   B '58; Sq '58, '59, '60

Emmet, Richard S., Jr. '46 ocC   C '47, '48

Emmet, William T. '29   C '28, '29

Emmons, George B., Jr. '51   F '48

Emory, Richard W. '35   W '35

Enders, Anthony T. '59   Fc '59

Engelberg, Alan D. '63   Sw '61, '62, '63

England, Jonathan S. '35   L '35; S '34

Enos, George E. '37   G '37

Erhard, Henry E. '46 ocC   LC '47

Erhard, John W. '38   CC '37; T '37, '38

Erickson, Douglas '38   C '36, '37, '38

Erickson, Josiah M. '32   C '30, '31, '32

Ervin, Henry N. '40   H '38, '39, '40

Erskine, John M. '42   C '41, '42

Essayan, Armen K. '49   B '46, '49

Estabrook, James M. '34   T '34

Estabrook, James M., Jr. '61   W '59, '60, '61

Esterly, James D. '33   F '31, '32

Estes, Bay E., Jr. '32   CC '29, 30; T '30, '31, '32

Estes, Richard F. '34   T '32

Estin, Hans H. '49   L '48

Eusden, John D. '44   Sw, '42, '43

Evans, Augustus E. '33   T '32

Evans, Earl '25   F '23

Everett, Horace D., Jr. '31   H '30, '31

Everett, Torrey III '60   C '58, '59, '60

Everett, Walter C. '33   H '32

Everts, Albert P., Jr. '44   B '43; H '42, '43

Evjy, Jack T. '57   F '56

Faber, Robert H. '45 ROTC   F '45

Falk, David '58   Sw '57

Falk, Sigo '57   Sw '55, '56, '57

Fallon, Robert A. '51   F '50

Fallon, Robert D. '33   Sw '33

Fanning, Charles F., Jr. '64   H '63

Fansler, Michael D. '46 ocC   Bb '48

Farnham, Edwin '27   B '27

Farnsworth, Frederick E. '29   LC '29

Farrell, David J. '45 ocC   F '46; H '43, '47

Fastov, Robert S. '64   W '62, '63

Faulkner, Charles S. II '57   C '57

Faxon, Robert M. '32   F '31

Fearon, James B. '39   F '38

Feinberg, James E. '48   F '46, '47

Feloney, Robert J. '46   H '46, '47

Felstiner, Louis J., Jr. '58   S '56, '57

Felt, Donald M. '49   C '48, '49

Felt, Gaelen L. '43   Sq '43

Felt, Thomas R. '48   F '46, '47

Felton, Edgar C.II '56   B '54, '56

Felton, Samuel M., Jr. '48   T '47, '48

Fenn, Abbott T. '42   H '40, '41, '42

Fenollosa, George M. '33   T '33

Ferguson, Donald R. '62   CC '61; T '61, '62

Fernald, Mason '40   T '37, '38

Ferris, Benjamin G., Jr. '40   L '40

Ferris, Joel E. II '41   F '40

Field, Henry F. '58   L '61, '62

Fields, Jerry L. '58   T '56

Filley, Oliver D., Jr. '45 ocC   C '47

Filoon, John W., Jr. '59   H '59

Fincke, Reginald, Jr. '32   B '30, '31, '32

Finegan, John C. '42   Bb '40, '41, '42

Finkelstein, Elliot M. '57   S '55, '56

Finlayson, Ian E. '61   Sw '60, '61

Finlayson, Murdoch J. '32   F '31; T '31, '32

Finley, John H. III '58   C '57

Finn, George R., Jr. '63   B '63

Fiorentino, John A. '49   F '46, '47, '48

Fischer, Frederick C. '56   Te '56

Fischer, Lindsay E. '56   S '55

Fischer, Richard S. '59   H '57, '58, '59

Fiscina, Salvatore F. '63   F '62

Fisher, John W. '45 ocC   F '42, '46; T '46, '47

Fisher, Richard E. '56   S '55

Fisher, Richard T., Jr. '36   Sw '36

Fisher, Richard W. '57   B '56, '57

Fisher, Robert T., Jr. '43   F '42

Fisher, Rollin B. II '44 ocC   F '46

Fisher, William O. '45 ocC   F '42, '45; T '43, '46

Fiske, Francis '23   C '23

Fitchen, Douglas B. '57   Fc '57

Fitts, Roscoe W. '23   F '20, '21, '22; T '21, '22

Fitz, Reginald H. '42   C '42

Fitz, William R. W. '46 ocC   B '46, '47; F '46, '47

Fitzgerald, Jared E. '61   CC '58, '59, '60; T '59, '60, '61

Fitzgibbons, Edward S. '44   B '42, '43

Fitzpatrick, John A. '35   B '34, '35

Flagg, Washington A., Jr. '52   Sq '51, '52

Flaksman, Leslie '29   CC '27, '28; T '27, '28, '29

Flamand, Paul J. '42   Bb '42

Flanagan, Thomas A. '63   C '63

Fletcher, Jefferson '27   T '24

Fletcher, Richard G., Jr. '35   B '35; Bb '35; F '34

Flint, John G. '23   H '23

Flint, Weston '45 ocC   T '47

Flower, John '39   T '39

Flynn, Charles B. '56   H '54, '55, '56

Flynn, Leo M '46 ocC   F '42, '46, '47

Flynn, Wallace J. '46 ocC   B '43; F '42, '46, '47

Fobes, Joseph W. '32   T '29, '30, '31

Fogelberg, Lawrence E. '63   LC '61

Foker, John E. '59   Bb '59; F '57, '58

Foley Francis F. '39   B '38; F '37, '38

Folger, Lee M. '56   Sq '56

Foote, Arthur '33   CC '30, '31, '32; T '31, '32, '33

Forand, Paul G. '55   Fc '55

Forbes, Alexander C. '32   T '31, '32

Forbes, C. Stewart '61   H '59, '60, '61

Forbes, Robert B. '39   P '38

Forbush, Lothrop M. '39   Sw '37

Forbush, Robert B. '61   S '59, '60

Ford, Carter G. '63   Sl '63

Ford, Edmond J., Jr. '40   T '39, '40

Ford, George S. '37   F '34, '35, '36; H '35, '36, '37

Ford, Lincoln E. '60   LC '58

Ford, Richard '36   Fc '35

Ford, Truman M. '43   T '41, '42

Fordyce, Allen O. '28   F '27

Fordyce, Clifton P. '23   B '23

Fordyce, John R., Jr. '26   F '24

Forster, Richard H. '45 ocC   Bb '43

Forsyth, Robert B. '49   L '49; T '48, '49

Forte, Donald '43   F '41, '42

Forte, Donald, Jr. '64   T '62, '63

Forte, John H. '46 ocC   B '46, '47; H '46

Foster, C. Henry W. II '51   Sq '51

Foster, Howard S. '48   F '45

Foster, Hubert C. '50   B '50

Foster, Hugh K. '50   Sq '50

Foster, Robert R. '59   F '57, '58; W '57, '58, '59

Fouquet, Richard J. '53   Sw '51, '52, '53

Fowler, Robert L. III '41   C '39, '40

Fox, Joseph M. '50   Sw '48, '49, '50

Fox, Joseph M. '32   CC '31; T '30, '31, '32

Foynes, Edward N., Jr. '51   B '49, '50, '51

Framke, Carl A. III '60   F '57

Francis, Edward L., Jr. '59   F '57

Francis, John M. '64   Sq '62, '63

Francisco, Leon A. '33   F '31, '32, '33

Frankel, Harold '34   W '34

Frankmann, Raymond W., Jr. '50   Fc '50

Frate, William A. '54   F '53, '54

Freedley, Vinton, Jr. '40   H '38, '39, '40

Freedman, Harold J. '23   T '23

Freedman, Melvin '50   F '47, '48

Freeman, Lee A., Jr. '62   W '60

Freeman, Malcolm T. '30   B '30

Freienmuth von Helms, Johann C. '62   W '61

Fremd, George, Jr. '33   B '33

Fremont-Smith, Thayer '53   F '52

French, Arthur E. '29   F '26, '27, '28; T '27, '28, '29

French, Arthur E., Jr. '53   F '51, '52; Te '53

French, Jonathan A. '61   LC '59, 60, 61

French, Joseph D. '56   CC '53, '54, 55; T '54, '55

Frey, John M. '50   Te '50

Friberg, Eric G. '64   C '63

Frieden, Roy A. '65   T '63

Fritts, Herbert R. '47   F '45; T '46

Fritze, Gunther E. A. '58   LC '58

Frothingham, Channing, Jr. '31   H '31

Frothingham, Thomas E. '47   H '46

Frothingham, William B., Jr. '52   F '51

Fryer, William J. '64   H 63

Fuess, John C. '35   B '35

Fuld, James J. '37   Te '37

Fullam, Paul A. '31   F '30

Fuller, Henry H. '23   C '22

Fuller, Peirce '35   F '34

Fuller, Peter '46 ocC   W '48

Fulton, Paul '44 ocC   B '47

Fulton, Robert '40   B '38, '39, '40

Fulton Robert E., Jr. '31   T '31

Fyock, Samuel H. III '55   F '52, '54

Gabler, James D. '51   Bb '49, '50, '51

Gaffney, James J., Jr. '37   F '35, '36

Gaffney, James J. III '64   W '62, '63

Gagnebin, Charles L. III '63   F '61, '62

Gaidis, James M. '62   F '60

Gale, James L. '57   L '57

Gale, Justin E. '48   C '47, '48

Gallagher, James F., Jr. '45   B '43

Gallagher, Rollin McC., Jr. '34   B '34

Gallwey, W. Timothy '60   Sq '59, '60; Te '58, '59, '60

Galston, Clarence E. '30   T '30

Gamache, Ernest F. '27   F '24, '26

Gammons, Robert W.M.P. '39   T '39

Gannett, Robert T. II '39   B '37, '38, '39

Gannon, Thomas H. '50   B '48; Bb '47, '48, '49; F '46, '47, '48

Gantt, John W. '47   Bb '46

Gardella, Joseph W. '41   F '38, '39, '40

Gardiner, John H. '38   C '37, '38

Gardiner, Sylvester '46 ocC   C '46

Gardiner, Thomas '42   F '40, '41

Gardner, Allan L. '61   Fc '61

Gardner, Douglass S. '57   Te '56

Gardner, Harrison '24   H '24

Gardner, Harrison, Jr. '54   Sk '54

Gardner, James E., Jr. '36   C '34, '35, '36

Gardner, John B. '51   Sl '51

Garfield, Michael R. '63   H '63

Garibaldi, Richard A. '63   B '61, '62, '63

Garland, Peter II '45 ocC   F '42, '46; T '46, '47

Garrigue, Paul, Jr. '54   Sq '54

Garrison, John B. '31   H '29, '30, '31

Garrison, William D. '59   B '58; R '59

Garrity, William L., Jr. '50   H '49, '50

Garver, Richard P. '63   LC '63

Garvey, Ronald F., Jr. '49   F '46, '48

Gaston, Thomas L. '62   F '60, '61

Gately, David K. '59   T '57

Gates, Donald C. '26   C '25, '26

Gates, Frederick L. '65   L '63

Gates, Otis A. III '56   T '55, '56

Gay, John H. III '49 ocC   Fc '49

Gebelein, George C., Jr. '43 ocC   H '41, '42, '47

Geer, William D., Jr. '56   Sw '54, '55

Geertsema, William W. '54   C '52, '53, '54

Gehrke, Erwin L. '24   B '22; F '22, '24

Geick, Harold W. '52   T '49, '50, '51, '52

Genieser, Werner R. '56   Sq '56; Te '56

Genn, Gerald Y. '48 ocC   Sk '49

Gentry, Willard M., Jr. '44   Sw '43

George, Joseph A. '58   F '57

Gerety, Donald C. '59   F '57, '58

Gerould, Richard D. '24   T '22, '23, '24

Gerrity, James F. II '39   P '38

Gerry, Edward H. '36   P '34

Gerry, Harold J.C. '54   CC '53; T '52, '53, '54

Gerry, Henry A. '36   P '34, '36

Getch, John S. '56   B '56, '57, '58

Getchell, Dana H. '53   S '52

Gianelly, Anthony A. '57   F '54, '55, '56; T '57

Gianetti, Ian M. F. '57   Te '56, '57

Gibbs, Braman '36   B '34, '35, '36

Giddens, Rene F.G. '30   H '28, '29, '30

Gifford, Benjamin C. '39   LC '39

Gifford, Douglas G. '64   S '62

Gifford, George H., Jr. '52   C '50, '51, '52

Gifford, Richard P. '43   S '42

Gifford, Stephen W., Jr. '44   F '42

Gilbert, William H. '50   S '49

Gildea, Joseph H. '31   F '29, '30

Gilder, Richard W. '36   Sq '36

Gilkey, James G., Jr. '39   LC '39

Gilkey, Langdon B. '40   Te '40

Gillette, Howard F., Jr. '35   H '35

Gillie, Bruce L. '60   H '58

Gilligan, Thomas W. '31   B '29

Gllis, Daniel J. '57   Fc '56

Gilman, Peter A. '62   Sw '62

Gilmor, Robert, Jr. '57   W '57

Gilmor, W. Gavin '63   B '62, '63

Gilmore, Thomas N. '65   W '63

Ginman, William K. '32   F '31

Glaser, Howard H. '57   H '57

Gleason, Francis H. '34   B '32, '33, '34; F '32; H '33, '34

Gleason, Gerald K. '62   Sw '62

Gleason, Jay W. '43   B '41, '43

Gleason, Sarell E., Jr. '27   T '27

Glendinning, William T. '38   W '38

Glidden, Germain G. '36   Sq '35, '36; Te '36

Glidden, William T. III '45 ocC   H '46

Glueck, David S. '38 ocC   F '38

Glynn, Charles R. '50   F '46, '47, '48, '49

Goddard, Samuel P., Jr. '41   C '40, '41

Godfrey, Henry P. '61   L '61

Godin, Ira F. '50   B '47, '48, '49, '50

Goethals, Henry W. '44 ocC   F '42, '46

Gold, Robert N. '62   B '60

Goldfeld, Stephen M. '60   T '60

Goldman, Allan B. '58   Te '56, '58

Goldman, Carl A. '55   T '53, '54, '55

Goldman, Steven M. '62   T '62

Goldstein, Robert V. '59   C '59

Goldthwait, David A. '43   F '41

Goodman, Anthony A. '61   LC '59, '60, '61

Goodman, Frank I. '54   Te '54

Goodman, William III '52   Te '52

Goodrich, Donald C. '39   S '38

Goodrich, George W., Jr. '50   F '47, '48

Goodwin, George M. '39   Te '39

Goodwin, Robert B. '62   C '61, '62

Goodwin, Todd '54   L '54

Goodwin, Walter C. '29   F '26

Gorczynski, John S. '49   F '47

Gordon, Albert F. '59   CC '57; T '57, '58, '59

Gordon, Donald H. '39   Te '39

Gordon, Lewis '24   B '22, '23, '24; F '22, '23

Gordon, Melvin J. '41   F '40

Gorham, Robert S. '40   H '40

Gorman, David N. '51   G '51

Gorman, Francis X. '59 ocC   Sw '57, '58, '60

Gorman, Jeremy W. '49   Sw '47, '48, '49

Gosse, M. Roy '60   LC '58, '59

Gottlieb, Stephen '57   Te '56, '57

Gould, John S. '60   L '60

Graae, Michael J.F. '65   W '63

Grady, John C. '33   T '32, '33

Grady, John C. '47   F '45, '46

Graff, Robert D. '41   Sw '41

Graham, James M. III '49   L '48

Graham, Philip L., Jr. '65   Sw '63

Graham, William G. B. '51   L '51

Grana, William A. '64   F '61, '62

Grand, Paul R. '55   T '53

Graney, Michael '60   H '58, '59, '60

Grannis, David L. III '62   H '60, '61, '62; L '61, '62

Grant, Gordon D. '62   W '61

Gravem, Hamish C. F. '56   Te '56

Graves, Robert B. '40   G '40

Graves, Sidney C. '24   H '24

Gray, Ernest A., Jr. '37   Bb '37

Gray, John C., Jr. '64   F '62; L '62, '63

Gray, Sherman '41   C '39, '40, '41; H '39, '40, '41

Gray, Wyndol W. '46 NROTC   Bb '46

Grayer, David I. '60   Bb '58, '59, '60

Graziano, Alfred J. '33   L '33

Greeley, Joseph M. '25   T '25

Greeley, Richard S. '49   H '46, '47, '48, '49

Greeley, Samuel S. '36   F '35

Greeley, Sidney F., Jr. '47   H '47

Greeley, Walter F. '53   B '51, '53; F '52; H '51, '52, '53

Greelish, William T. '61   F '59, '60

Green, Milton G. '36   T '35, '36

Green, Robert L., Jr. '39   F '36, '37, '38

Greenacre, Martyn D. '64   LC '62, '63

Greenhood, E. Russell, Jr. '39   Sw '37, '38, '39

Greenidge, Ralph M. C. '24   T '22, '23, '24

Greenough Malcolm W. '25   F '22, '23, '24

Gregg, Charles N., Jr. '49 ocC   L '49

Gregg, Kenneth W. '61   C '59, '60, '61

Gregory, David P. '52   CC '51; T '51, '52

Greitzer, Edward M. '62   W '61, '62

Gremp, Robert K. '54   B '53; Bb '52

Grew, Henry S., Jr. '24   F '21, '22, '23

Grew, Joseph C. II '62   Sq '61, '62

Griffin, Lawrence L. '48 ocC   Sk '49

Griffith, Charles A., Jr. '42   H '42

Grondahl, Reino R. '39   B '37, '38, '39

Groper, Earle '54   B '53

Groshong, David L. '49   T '46

Gross, Courtlandt S. '27   H '25, '26, '27

Grover, Melvin G. '35   S '34

Grover, Thomas '41   F '40

Grunig, James K. '42   F '41

Grutzner, Edward E. '52   T '50, '51, '52

Guarnaccia, David '29   F '26, '27, '28; T '27, '28

Gudaitis, Charles B. '45 ocC   F '42, '46

Guidera, Richard T. '50   F '47, '48, '49

Guild, George C. '23   H '23

Gullette, David G. '62   Sw '60

Gummere, Richard M., Jr. '34   S '34

Gund, Gordon '61   H '61; LC '60

Gunderson, Paul E. '65   C '63

Gundlach, Herman W., Jr. '35   F '32, '33, '34

Gunnoe, Charles E. '64   L '62, '63

Gurley, Franklin L. '47   T '47, '48

Gustafson, James P. '63   Te '62, '63

Guthart, Leo A. '58   Te '58

Guttu, Lyle R. '58   H '56, '57, '58

Habicht, Ernst R., Jr. '60   F '58

Hackett, George H. '43   H '42

Hadik, John B. '56   S '55

Hadley, Edward L. '44   Bb '42

Haegler, Alex H. '55   Te '55

Hageman, Carl H., Jr. '33   Bb '33; F '30, '31, '32

Hager, Alan '62   C '61, '62

Haggerty, Ellsworth C. '27   T '25, '26, '27

Halaby, Samuel A., Jr. '60   F '57, '58, '59; T '58, '60

Halaby, Theodore S. '62   F '60, '61; T '60

Hale, Matthew '32   H '32

Haley, John R. '35   F '33, '34

Hall, Arthur P. '47 ocC   LC '46, '47, '48

Hall, Donald R. '39   B '38

Hall, George A. '47 ocC   LC '46, '47, '48

Hall, Howland P. '48   LC '46, '47

Hall, Robert C. '36   T '34, '35, '36

Hall, William P. '45 ocC   F '46

Hallett, Moses D. '40   F '38, '39

Hallowell, Alfred B. '34   T '33, '34

Hallowell, Benjamin H. '36   H '34, '35, '36

Hallowell, John W. '31   C '30, '31

Hallowell, N. Penrose, Jr. '32   CC '29, '30, '31; T '29, '30, '31, '32

Hallowell, Robert H., Jr. '25   T '24, '25

Hallowell, Roger H. '33   C '32, '33; F '31, '32

Halstead, David G. '40   L '40

Hamblett, David C. '50   T '47, '48

Hamilton, William L. '63   LC '62, '63

Hamlen, Nathaniel '27   F '26; H '25, '26, '27

Hamlen, William T. '45 ocC   B '47; H '47

Hamlin, Edwin M., Jr. '63   CC '60, '61, '62; T '61, '62, '63

Hamm, Charles J. '59   Sq '58, '59

Hammond, Charles P. '39   L '39

Hammond, John S. III '59   Sw '57, '58, '59

Hammond, John W. '25   B '23, '24, '25; F '22, '23, '24; H '23, '24, '25

Hammond, Ormond W. '65   L '63

Handy, John L., Jr. '43   B '42

Haneman, William F. '42   H '42

Hanford, George H. '41   L '41; S '38, '40

Hanlon, Alfred J., Jr. '39   T '39

Hansen, Forest W. '53   Bb '51, '52, '53

Hanson, Harlan P. '46 ocC   C '48

Harde, Dudley M. '61   LC '61

Hardie, Walter S. '30   B '28

Hardenbergh, Nelson K. '40   S '38

Harding, Charles L., Jr. '26   H '26

Harding, Francis A. '30   H '30

Harding, F. Austin, Jr. '39   F '36, '37, '38; H '37, '38, '39

Harding, George R., Jr. '43   H '42, '43

Harding, Goodwin W. '43   H '43

Harding, Victor M., Jr. '31   F '29, '30; T '29, '31

Harding, William G. '46   H '43

Hardy, Irad B., Jr. '33   F '31, '32

Hardy, Robert B. '54   F '51, '52, '53

Hardy, Rodney D. '60   Sw '59, '60

Hardy, Stuart G. '29   B '29

Hare, Michael J. '61   S '60

Harford, William J. '47   B '46; Bb '47

Harkness, John C. '38   W '38

Harnden, Frank R. '39   S '38

Harpel, Peter C. '57   T '56, '57

Harper, Wallace R. '30   F '27, '28, '29

Harrigan, John E., Jr. '49   T '46, '47, '49

Harrington, Frederic, Jr. '46   LC '46, '47

Harrington, George N. '59   B '59; Bb '57, '58, '59

Harris, A. Brooks '56   Te '56

Harris, Melvyn H. '53   Sw '53

Harris, Nathaniel L., Jr. '52   H '51, '52

Harris, Richard G. '42   Sw '41

Harris, Robert W. '58   F '56

Harrison, Bernard J. '29   C '29

Harrison, Carter H. '57   C '56

Harrison, Joseph III '56   C '56

Harrison, Randolph '55   C '54, '55

Harrison, William S. '43 ocC   F '47

Harshbarger, L. Scott '64   B '62; F '61, '62

Harshman, Donald C. '51   S '50

Hart, Alex W. '62   F '60, '61

Hart, James E. '61   Bb '60

Hart, John H. '52   Sk '52

Hartford, George H. II '34   Te '34

Hartley, Joseph M . II '23   F '21, '22

Hartranft, John C. '64   F '62

Hartstone, George D. '37   L '37

Hartung, Frank E. '63   F '62

Hartwell, Harold H., Jr. '45   Sw '43

Hartwell, Hugh B. '52   Sw '51, '52

Harvey, F. Barton, Jr. '43   B '41, '42; F '42

Harwood, Charles C. '50   T '48

Harwood, John H. Jr. '27   C '27

Harwood, Peter G. '48   F '45; T '46, '47

Haskins, Stanley G. '35   Sq '35

Haskins William C. '37   C '36, '37

Hasler, Wyndham '34   H '32, '33, '34; T '33, '34

Hastings, Robert A. '57   B '55, '56, '57; Bb '55, '56, '57

Hatch, Morgan P. '52   H '51, '52

Hatch, William H. III '63   F '60, '61, '62; T '61, '62, '63

Hathaway, Kent S. '58   B '58

Hauck, Hubert H. '38   Te '38

Hauge, Christopher W. '60   F '57, '58

Haughey, Philip C. '57   B '56, '57; Bb '55, '56; F '56

Haughie, Glenn E. '61   F '58, '59, '60

Hauptfuhrer, George J., Jr. '48   Bb '47, '48; T '47

Haussermann, Oscar W., Jr. '42   B '41

Haveles, Harry P. '48   LC '46

Hawes, John B. '32   T '31, '32

Hawkins, David F. '56   Sw '53, '54, '55, '56

Hawkins, Richard B. '63   T '63

Hayden, Jay G. '62   Sw '60, '61

Haydock, Francis B. '46 ocC   T '46, '47

Haydock, George G. '41   F '40

Haydock, Robert, Jr. '39   T '37, '38, '39

Hayes, John J., Jr. '34   T '33, '34

Hayes, Richard C. '36   T '34

Hayes, William K. '34 ocC   B '35

Hazard, Peter H. '41   LC '39, '40

Healey, John J., Jr. '34   F '32, 33; T '32, '33, '34

Healey, Thomas V. '40   B '38, '39, '40; F '38, '39

Healey, William D., Jr. '52   F '50, '51

Heard, Charles S. '25   C '25

Heard, Nathaniel '40   T '39, '40

Hearne, Roger W. '56   C '54

Heath, Brooks N. '56   B '42, '43

Heath, Melville F., Jr. '34   G '34

Heath, Milton S., Jr. '49   Sq '48

Heck, Peter J. '63   L '62, '63

Heckel, Frederick W. III '39   B '39; Bb '38, '39

Heckscher, Benjamin H. '57   Sq '56, '57; Te '56, '57

Heckscher, Martin A. '56   Sq '56

Hedberg, David L. '53   G '53; Sw '51, '52, '53

Hedberg, Stephen E. '52   C '50, '51

Hedblom, George G. '37   F '34, '35, '36

Hedblom, Richard P. '39   F '37

Héder, Lajos S. '62   Fc '61

Hedreen, John C. '60   S '57, '58, '59

Heiden, George W. '42   F '39, '40, '41

Heidtmann, Richard H. '53   F '50

Heintzman, Thomas G. '62   H '60, '61, '62

Henderson, John W. '61   H '60

Henderson, Lee W. '53   C '53

Hennessy, Dean McD. '45   Bb '43

Hennessy, Vincent L. '30   T '29, '30

Henry, Barklie McK. '24   C '22, '23, '24

Henry, William L. '50   Bb '47, '48; F '48, '49

Henshaw, Paul C. '36   C '36

Herberich, Edward A. '41   Bb '41

Hermance, Nelson F., Jr. '44   C '43

Herndon, James H., Jr. '60   C '59

Herr, Robert W. '28   C '28

Herrick, John H. '38   Bb '38; T '36, '37, '38

Herrmann, Edmund C.F. '25   B '25

Herscot, James '58   L '58

Hershon, Stuart J. '59   F '56, '57, '58

Herskovits, Monroe E. '43   T '42

Herter, Frederic P. '42   C '41

Hessel, John H, '56   R '56

Hewes, William L., Jr. '44   Sw '43

Hibbard, George A. '44   F '41, '42

Hibbert, George W., Jr. '43   C '42

Hickey, John W. '52   F '51

Hickey, William K. '50   F '48

Hickey, William M. '52   Bb '50, '51, '52

Hicks, Samuel T., Jr. '38   H '36, '37, '38

Higginbottom, George H. '59   H '57, '58, '59

Higgins, Richard A. '54   C '52, '54

Higginson, John '62   C '60, '61, '62

Hildreth, Edward W. III '60 ocC   CC '57, '59, '60

Hill, Francis S. '24   B '23, '24; H '22, '23, '24

Hill, George H. '50   F '47, '48

Hill, Kenneth N. '24   B '23; F '22, '23

Hill Thomas E., Jr. '59   F '57; W '58

Himmelhoch, Jonathan M. '60   S '58

Hinckley, Frank L., Jr. '41   C '41

Hines, Philip W. A. '34   B '33

Hitzig, William M. '65   S '62

Hoadley, Alfred W. '57   Sw '55

Hoagland, James VanF. '56   CC '58

Hoague, George, Jr. '26   F '24, 25

Hoar, Samuel, Jr. '51   Sq '51

Hobbs, Peter W. '57   C '55

Hobson, Arthur L., Jr. '24   C '23, '24; F '23

Hocutt, Hubert E. '57   Fc '57

Hodder, Clark '25   H '24, '25

Hodder, Melville T. '60   H '60; LC '59

Hodges, Arthur C. '57   C '55, '56, '57

Hodges, John A. '62   C '61, '62

Hodnett, Grey '57   S '55, '56

Hoefer, Richard W. '63   R '63

Hoelzer, Hiram H. '49   Sw '46, '47, '49

Hoffman, John P. '65   W '63

Hoffman, Mark, Jr. '59   LC '58, '59

Hoffman, Richard M. '55   B '54, '55

Holbrook, Guy C., Jr. '30   H '28, '29, '30

Holbrook, John G. '49   T '46, '48, '49

Holcombe, Arthur N. II '62   C '61

Holcombe, Robert C. '37   S '36

Holcombe, Thomas W. '64   T '62, '63

Holcombe, Waldo H. '33   C '31, '32, '33

Holden, John C. '60   Sk '61

Holder, Daniel S. '24   C '22; F '21, '22, '24

Hollands, Fayette R. '40   T '38

Holleran, Romer '62 ocC   Sq '60

Hollister, Clay H. '24   C '23

Holmes, David U. '57   H '57

Holmes, Dunbar '35   H '34, '35

Holmes, F. Stacy, '31   C '30, '31

Holmes, Francis S. II '56   S '55

Holmes, Henry C. '57   S '55, '56

Holmes, King K. '59   W '59

Holmes, Robert L. '57   CC '54, '55, '56

Holt, James R. '47 ocC   LC '46, '47

Holton, Robert V., Jr. '63   G '63

Holyoke, Thomas C. '44   T '42, '43

Holzschuh, Richard J. '57   F '55, '56

Hooper, Donald C. '64   CC '61

Hooper, Robert C. '41   LC '41

Hooper, Roger, F., Jr. '39   T '39

Hooper, Thomas B. '58   F '55, '56, '57

Hoover, John R. '24   C '24

Hopkins, Stephen '56   C '56

Hoppin, Charles S. '53   Sl '52, '53

Hoppin, Frederic G., Jr. '56   Sl '56

Horn, Michael S. '63   Sl '63

Horner, Henry C. '52   Sk '52; Sl '52

Horton, Wesley W. '64   Sq '63

Horvitz, Paul S. '64   W '63

Horween, Arnold, Jr. '53   F '51, '52

Hough, Jerry F. '55   Bb '55

Houghton, Charles G., Jr. '39   H '38, '39

Houghton, Robert B. '42   T '41, '42

Housen, Stanley X. '34   L '34

Houser, John G. '50   Sk '52

Houston, Howard E. '50   F '46, '47, '48, '49

Hovenanian, Michael S. '36   H '34, '35, '36

Hovey, Chandler, Jr. '39   C '39

Hovey, Charles F. '32   C '32

Howard, Frederic K. '61   CC '60; T '59, '60, '61

Howard, Godfrey G. '50   H '50

Howard, Leavitt '36   L '36

Howard, Thomas P. '48   T '46

Howard, Willard '27 ocC   H '25, '27, '28; B '28

Howe, Alan T. '55   T '53, '54, '55

Howe, Nathaniel S. '26   F '25; H '24, '25, '26

Howe, Reginald H. II '62   H '62

Howe, Stephen W. '50   B '48, 49; H '49

Howell, A. Harold, Jr. '63   H '61, '62, '63

Howell, Hampton P. III '63   Sq '61

Howell, Henry L. '55   Sw '55

Howes, Kenneth, Jr. '46   H '46

Hoye, Robert G. '39   B '38, '39

Hoyt, Alfred M. '57   S '55

Hoyt, Barrett, '30   H '30

Hubbard, Charles J. '24   C '22; F '21, '22, '23

Hubbard, Charles W. III '37   T '37

Hubbard, E. Amory '53   H '51, '52, '53

Hubbard, James DeW. '29   C '28

Hubbard, John P. '25   C '25, '26

Hubbard, Russell S. '24   F '23

Hudepohl, David H. '63   F '60, '61, '62

Hudner, Richard R. '51   L '51

Hudock, Emanuel B., Jr. '56   F '55

Hudson, Barclay M. '62   Sk '63

Huebsch, Ronald E. '53   L '53; Sw '51, '52, '53

Huff, Warren E. '59   F '58

Hughes, Hilliard W., Jr. '50   Te '50

Huguley, Arthur W., Jr. '31   F '28, '29, '30

Hull, Morton D. II '50   Sw '50

Hulse, Stacy B., Jr. '41   H '39, '40, '41

Humenuk, William A. '64   F '61, '62

Humes, William B. '40   Bb '38

Hunneman, John R., Jr. '46   C '43

Hunnewell, Francis O. '60   C '58, '60

Hunnewell, Walter, Jr. '39   H '39

Hunter, Andrew A. '51   H '50

Hunter, Dennis A. '64   Sw '62

Hunter, John C. '46   T '46

Hunter, R. Bruce '61   Sw '59, '60, '61

Hunter, Robert C., Jr. '36   G '36

Hunter, Robert L., Jr. '61   F '60

Hunter, Thomas H. '35   C '35

Huntington, Francis C. II '53   C '52, '53

Huntington, Howard W. '34   T '33, '34

Huntington, Lawrence S. '57   C '55, '56

Huntington, Myles D. '50   B '48, '49, '50; H '48, '49, '50

Huntington, Samuel '61   C '61

Huppuch, Winfield A. II '33   Bb '33

Hurd, John G. '34   Fc '34

Hurd, Lee K. '55   T '54, '55

Hurley, Edmund M. '56   T '56

Hurley, Joseph M., Jr. '44 ocC   L '47

Hurley, Richard K. '57   Bb '55, '56, '57

Hurley, William T. III '61   W '61

Husband, Thomas B. '37   F '35

Hussey, Stewart H. '58   C '56

Hutchinson, Forney III '64   LC '63

Hutchinson, John W., Jr. '63   H '63

Hutter, Charles G., Jr. '38   Sw '36, '37, '38

Huvelle, Peter R. '64   CC '62; T '63

Huxtable, Howard L. '30   B '30

Hyatt, Robert L. '24   T '23, '24

Hyde, Arthur D., Jr. '51   F '48, '49, '50

Hyde, Hugh M. '44   Bb '42, '43

Hyde, Maclay R. '57   L '57

Hyslop, Newton E., Jr. '57   B '57

Ierardi, William J. '41   L '41

Ikauniks, Romuald '64   H '62, '63

Ingalls, Edmund F. '38   B '36, '37, '38

Ingalls, Theodore S. '61   H '60, '61

Ingalls, Willard E., Jr. '35   Te '35

Ingraham, William W. '25   Te '22

Ingram, John D. '50   H '49

Inman, Robert P. '64   Bb '61, '63; Te '62, '63

Innes, Hiller '25 ocC   F '26

Irvine, Glenn M. '58   F '57

Iselin, Charles O. III '51   C '49, '50, '51

Iselin, Columbus O. II '26   C '25

Isenberg, Phillip L. '51   F '48, '49, '50

Israel, Michael '59   T '58, '59

Ives, David O. '41   S '38, '40; T '40, '41

Jackson, Donald E., Jr. '36   F '34, '35

Jackson, Orton P. '29   H '29

Jackson, William J. II '47   F '45, '46; T '46, '47

Jacobs, J. Ethan '62   F '60, '61

Jacobson, Bernard J. '39   S '38

Jaffe, Robert H. '57   Sw '57

James, George B. '59   Bb '59

James, Robert A. '41   Bb '39, '40, '41

Jameson, Arthur G. '37   Sw '37

Jameson, John D. '24   C '23, '24

Jameson, Thomas H. '33   Sw '33

Jameson, Winthrop S., Jr. '39   F '37, '38; H '37, '38, '39

Janien, Cedric J. '36   F '33

Jantzen, Eugene A.L. '32   B '32

Jaros, Arthur C., Jr. '41   Fc '41

Jay, Robert D. '42   T '41

Jenkins, Marvin C. '47 ocC   F '45; T '48

Jenkins, Percy '24   B '22, '23, '24; F '22, '23; T '22

Jenks, Chester W., Jr. '43   C '42

Jenney, Robert M. '41   H '41

Jenney, Warren '26   LC '26

Jennings, John J. '53   F '50, '52

Jennings, Ronald C., Jr. '63   L '62, '63

Jeppson, John III '62   S '60

Jerome, Frederick W. '38   F '37

Jertson, Jan E. '53   Fc '53

Johansen, John MacL. '39   S '38; T '37

Johanson, Ronald J. '59   F '57, '58

Johns, Arthur L. '39   B '37, '38, '39

Johnson, Belden C. '65   L '63

Johnson, Berkeley D., Jr. '53   S '52

Johnson, Byron J. '59   B '58, '59

Johnson, David G. '60   Fc '60

Johnson, Eric H. '61   Sw '59, '60

Johnson, George R. '25   C '24

Johnson, Howard A., Jr. '39   H '38, '39

Johnson, James P. '51   S '50

Johnson, John G. '56   Sw '54, '55, '56

Johnson, Laurence M. '61   Fc '61

Johnson, Melvin M., Jr. '31   C '29, '30

Johnson, Pat O. '33   W '33

Johnson, Richard C. '36   T '34, '35, '36

Johnson, Richard C. '58   Fc '58

Johnson, Robert K. '61   B '61

Johnson, R. Bruce, Jr. '49   Sw '47, '48

Johnson, Russell E. '53   B '51, '52, '53

Johnson, Vahe D. '60   T '58

Johnson, Wayne, Jr. '44   F '41, '42

Johnston, David L. '63   H '61, '62, '63

Johnston, Hulburd '29   C '29

Johnston, Renner M. '60   B '60

Johnstone, C. Bruce '62   G '62; S '59, '60

Jones, Cranston E. '40   Fc '40

Jones, Frank S. '50   F '49

Jones, Frank W., Jr. '35   Te '35

Jones, Freeman F. '34   LC '34

Jones, George H., Jr. '63   T '63

Jones, Gilbert E. '38   C '38

Jones, James E. '55   G '55

Jones, Jerry H. '61   C '59, '60

Jones, John G., Jr. '61   Sq '61

Jones, Paul E., Jr. '54   L '54

Jones, Richard P. '64   T '62

Jones, Robert S. '37   F '35, '36

Jones, Samuel B. '26   T '25, '26

Jones, Thomas DeV. '56   F '55

Jones, Vincent W., Jr. '45 ocC   H '47, '48

Jones, William B. '28   B '26, '27, '28

Jordan, Gerald R., Jr. '61   F '60

Jorgensen, Gerald W. '63   H '61, '62, '63

Jorgensen, James P. '56   Sw '54, '55, '56
Joslin, James L. '57   F '54, '55, '56
Judkins, John B., Jr. '47 ocC   F '47
Julian, Joseph W. '60   CC '57
Junkin, Peter D. '36 ocC   P '36
Junta, Dale W. '58   Te '56, '58
Juvonen, Ronald J. '62   F '61

Kaden, Lewis B. '63   Te '62
Kagan, Arnold M. '56   Bb '56
Kairis, Nicholas G. '64   L '63
Kales, Francis H. III '31   F '30, '31
Kaltreider, H. Benfer '60   T '58
Kamp, Walter B. '43   F '42
Kane, Frank P. '26   T '24, '26
Kann, Clifton F. von '37   B '37
Knater, Jerry '51   F '48, '49, '50; T '51
Kantrowitz, Warren '56   Bb '56
Karp, Fred '62   B '62
Kasarjian, Levon, Jr. '59   B '58, '59
Katz, Howard S. '59   CC '58
Kaufmann, Robert E. '62   Sw '60, '61, '62
Kay, Stephen B. '56   Te '56
Kayser, Robert B., Jr. '41   H '41
Kean, Kelvin L. '60   T '59, '60
Kean, William L. '65   L '63
Kearney, John F., Jr. '62   LC '61, '62
Keating, Frederick J. J. '63   Bb '61
Keating, James P. '59   F '58
Keegan, Raymond H. '23   B '23
Keeler, Peter R. '64   W '62
Keenan, Edward L., Jr '57   Bb '57
Keene, Philip '25   B '25
Keene, Thomas V., Jr. '45   Bb '43
Keever, Charles J. '51   F '50
Keith, Charles C., Jr. '51   T '49, '50, '51
Keith, Osmund O., Jr. '48   F '47
Keller, Albert R. '60   LC '58
Keller, Barnes D. '59   T '57
Keller, Orrin C. '39   Sw '37
Kelley, Paul M. '59   H '57, '59
Kelley, Peter S. '63   Bb '61, '62
Kelley, Sylvester B. '25   C '23, '24, '25
Kellogg, Frederic R. '64   LC '62
Kellogg, Howard, '37   H '37
Kelly, Bartow '40   F '39
Kelly, Dana J. '28   F '27
Kelly, Gerald C. '59   Fc '59
Kelly, Lawrence E. '53   Sw '53
Kelly, Shaun, Jr., '36   F '33, '34, '35
Kelso, John G. '53   F '53
Kemble, William T., Jr. '63   G '63
Kenary, James B., Jr. '50   B '48; F '47, '48, '49
Kendall, William E. '40   Sw '38
Keniston, Kenneth '51   C '50, '51
Kennedy, Edward M. '54 ocC   F '55

Kennedy, John P. '63   Fc '63
Kennedy, Robert F. '48   F '45, '46, 47
Kennel, Charles F. '59   H '59
Kenny, Charles '50   B '49
Keohane, Harold J. '60   F '57, '58, '59
Kern, Kenneth L. '62   Sk '62
Kernan, Francis '24   F '22, '23; T '23, '24
Kernan, Reginald D. '36 ocC   C '37
Kernan, Walter N. II '40   C '38, '39, '40
Kessler, Charles C. '64   F '62; L '62, 63
Kessler, Charles W. '37   F '35, '36
Kessler, Robert R. '56   B '55, '56
Ketchum, Richard R. '29   B '29
Kevorkian, Alexander, Jr. '38   F '36, '37; H '38
Key, Albert L. II '50   H '48, '49
Key, David McK., Jr. '49   H '47, '48, '49
Keyes, Frederick A, Jr. '41   B '39, '40, '41
Keyes, George T. '35   C '35
Keyes, Langley C., Jr. '60   L '60; S '57, '58, '59
Keyes, Peter B. '60   Sq '60
Khan, K. Aga '58   S '58
Kidder, Alfred II '33   T '32, '33
Kidder, J. Norton '37   H '37
Kidder, Randolph A. '35   F '34
Kiernan, Robert D. '33   B '33
Kilgour, Bayard L., Jr. '27   F '25, '26
Kimball, Richard '31   LC '29
Kimbrough, Richard L. '33   G '33
Kinasewich, Eugene '64   H '62, '63
King, Appleton '54   Te '54
King, Chester H., Jr. '34   T '34
King, Francis R. '39   T '37, '38, '39
King, Franklin, Jr. '42   F '41
King, Gilbert, Jr. '45   Sw '43
King, Harry C. '49   W '49
King, Samuel G. '49   C '48
King, William E. '61   S '60
Kingman, Lauren C., Jr. '39   C '39
Kinnell, George N. '54   C '54
Kinney, Douglas McB. '52   Sw '50, '51
Kipp, David A. '60   B '60
Kirk, Paul G., Jr. '60   F '59
Kirkland, Charles McM. '34   H '34
Kirkland, Donald N. '62   CC '61; T '60, '61, '62
Kitchel, Frederick H. '64   LC '62
Kittredge, Joseph B. '51   H '49, '50, '51
Klapper, Michael H. '58   Fc '58
Klein, George T. '38   F '37
Kludt, Carl J. '61   W '59
Klufio, Ebenezer S. '63   S '61, '62
Knaplund, Paul W. '49   C '46, '47, '48
Knapp, Bruce C. '64   W '63
Knapp, Robert H. '36   F '34, '35
Knapp, Robert V. '62   CC '59, '60, '61; T '60

Knowles, John H. '47   B '46; H '46
Kobes, Herbert R. '26   T '26
Kobusch, Richard B. '50   B '49
Koch, Richard J., Jr. '55   F '53, '54
Koch, Walter R. '29   T '29
Koeniger, Peter J. '41   C '41
Kohla, Donald S. '64   Sw '62
Kohrman, Soloman L. '49   Bb '48
Kolden, K. Mark '62   Bb '60
Kollmyer, Hamilton F. '33   T '31
Kolodney, Robert B., Jr. '63   W '61, '62, '63
Kolodny, Edwin H. '57   CC '56
Komenda, Robert F. '61   Sw '59, '60
Konrad, Erich B. '62   LC '60
Kopans, David E. '34   F '31, '33
Koufman, Joseph M. '41   F '40
Kozol, Robert D. '60   W '58
Kraetzer, John F. '58   LC '58
Kramer, Michael '63   S '60, '61, '62
Kraus, Max W. '41   Sw '41
Krayer, Frank A. '47   Sw '46
Krinsky, Edward M. '54   B '52, '53, '54, Bb '52, '53, '54
Krogh, Peter F. '58   Te '56, '58
Krumbhaar, George D. '26   C '25
Krumbhaar, George D., Jr. '58   LC '58
Kuehl, Walter M. '61   F '59, '60
Kuehn, George W. '32   F '29; T '29, '30, '31, '32
Kumpel, George F. II '50   T '49
Kunhardt, Philip B. '23   F '22
Kurth, Harold R., Jr. '46   T '43

Labastie, Albert H. '40   Fc '40
Lacey, Thomas II '41   T '41
LaCroix, William P. '42   B '42; F '41
Ladd, Alexander H., Jr. '23   C '21, '23; F '21
Ladd, Robert W. '27   C '25, '27
Ladd, William C. '26   C '26
LaFrance, Jacques E. '61   CC '58
Lagarenne, Walter R. '47   Sw '47
Lage, William P. '30   F '29
Laimbeer, George M. '26   T '25
Lake, William A. K. '61   Sq '59, '60, '61
Lakin, Charles B. '30   H '28, '29, '30
Lamarche, F. William '64   H '63
Lamb, Marshall A. '34   Bx '34
Lamont, Nicholas S. '60   L '60; S '59
Lamp, Peeter '64   T '63
Lamson, Paul D., Jr. '43   C '42, '43
Landau, Joel R. '59   T '57, '58, '59
Lane, Arthur L. '60   LC '60
Lane, Francis J. '36   F '33; T '33
Lane, William H., Jr. '37   F '34
Lange, Robert B. '49   L '48

Langenau, Edward E. '35   Fc '34, '35
Langworthy, Asher C., Jr. '56   Sl '56
Lanier, David S. M. '28   C '28
Lapsley, John W. '57   C '55, '56, '57
Larcom, Guy C., Jr. '33   Sw '33
Larkin, David J. '61   B '61
Larkin, Richard F. '64   S '61, '62
Larner, Edward B. '40   LC '40
Larocque, Joseph, Jr. '23   H '22, '23
Larrabee, Leonard C. '24   B '23, '24
Laskin, Paul L. '46   T '43
Lavalle, John E. '46 ocC   H '47, '48
Lawrence, James, Jr. '29   C '28, '29
Lawrence, Robert S. '60   C '58
Lawrence, William G. '50   T '47, '49
Lawson, Thomas E. '59   F '58
Lazzaro, Paul '46 ocC   F '46, '47
Leaf, Andrew M. '60   L '60
Leaf, James G. '63   L '61, '62, '63
Leahy, Michael A. II '65   L '63
Leamy, Charles D. '60   B '59; F '57, '59
Leary, Daniel L., Jr. '59   W '60
Leath, James F., Jr. '64   F '61; T '62
Leavitt, Alan J., Jr. '58   W '57
Leavitt, Kent '26   C '25, '26
Leavitt, Peirce H., Jr. '50   F '49
Leavitt, William T. '50   C '49, '50
LeBart, Frank T. '47   F '45
Lebovitz, Marvin E. '58   F '55, '56
Lee, Charles C. '23   B '22
Lee, Francis M. '42   F '39, '40, '41
Lee, James J. '24   F '22, '23
Lee, John H., Jr. '53   W '51, '52, '53
Lee, Roger I., Jr. '41   C '41
Leeming, Joseph III '50   T '49
Lefkowitz, Alan L. '53   C '51, '52, '53
Legg, Chester A., Jr. '40   Bb '38, '39, '40;
   Te '40
Lehmann, Paul M. '63   Sl '63
Leland, Oliver S., Jr. '54   LC '54
Lemann, Jorge P. '61   Sq '60; Te '59, '60
Lemay, Albert L. '53   F '50, '51, '52
Lenane, Gerald '44   T '42
Leness, Anthony V. '61   T '61
Leness, John G. '56   R '56
Lenzer, Terry F. '61   F '58, '59, '60
Leonard, James B. '59   C '57, '59
Leonard, James R. '33   F '32
Leonard, Laurence B., Jr. '52   S '51
LeRoy, Harris G. '63   F '62; L '62, '63
Lessig, William R., Jr. '34   L '34
Levin, Marshall M. '59   F '57
Levine, Stuart L. '58   B '56
Lewis, Dexter S. '56   F '53, '55; L '56
Lewis, Edward W., Jr. '49   T '46
Lewis, H. Finlay '60   H '60
Lewis, Howard H. '56   C '54

Lewis, John L., Jr. '52   F '50, '51
Lewis, Richard E. '40   L '40
Lewis, Richard W. B. '39   S '38
Lewy, Jeffrey R. '63   Sw '61, '62, '63
Lidgerwood, William van V. '39   LC '39
Liebeskind, John C. '57   R '57
Light, Charles R. '63   L '61, '62, '63
Lightbody, James D., Jr. '40   CC '39; T '38,
   '39, '40
Liles, Patrick R. '60   T '57, '58, '59, '60
Lilienthal, Philip E. '36   Fc '36
Lincoln, Albert L., Jr. '42   LC '41, '42
Lincoln, Richard K. '53   LC '53
Lincoln, William A. '35   B '34, '35; H '33, '35
Lind, Jon R. '57   Sw '55, '56, '57
Lindner, Carl M. '27   F '24, '25, '26; T '27
Lingelbach, William E. III '56   S '55
Linn, Jack T. '65   W '63
Lion, Donor M. '45   T '43
Lionette, Frank J. '50   Bb '49
Lionette, Richard A. '53   Bb '51, '52, '53
Lipsky, Allan G. '61   G '61
Lipton, Charles '48   LC '46, '47
Litchfield, Edward S. '34   C '33, '34
Litman, Arnold S. '38   Bb '38
Litman, Bertram M. '38   T '36, '37, '38
Litman, Chester K. '35   F '33, '34
Little, Dennis G. '56   H '55, '56; S '55
Little, Stephen '49   C '50
Little, Warren M. '55   T '53, '54, '55
Littlefield, Frank R. '35   F '34
Livingood, John M. '62   G '62
Livingston, John C. '56   Fc '56
Livingston, Peter D. '62   F '61
Livingston, Ralph E. '39   L '39
Lloyd, Demarest '42   H '41, '42
Lloyd, Henry '37   C '36
Locke, Edwin A. III '60   C '59, '60
Locke, Geoffrey G. '58   C '56
Locke, Henry W. '38   C '38
Locke, Thomas F. '35   F '33, '34; T '33
Locke, William P. '27   T '26, '27
Locker, Alan N. '61   G '61
Lockett, Andrew M. III '50   T '48, '49, '50
Lockwood, Charles C. '61   B '60
Lockwood, John M. '34   F '33
Lockwood, Luke B. '24   F '23
Logan, Sheridan A. '23   C '23
Lomasney, David A. '28   T '27
Lombard, James M. '61   H '60, '61
Long, Winfield S., Jr. '39   Fc '39
Lord, William W. '28   B '27, '28; F '27
Loring, Caleb, Jr. '43   H '41, '42, '43
Loring, George G. '50   H '48, '49
Louchheim, Harry A. '61   L '61
Loughlin, Edward F., Jr. '34   B '32, '33,
   '34

Louria, Donald B. '49   L '48; S '47; W '48
Lovett, Eugene T. '41   B '39; F '39
Lowe, Keith D. '60   S '58
Lowe, Robert L. '34   F '33
Lowenfels, Lewis D. '57   Bb '56
Lowenstein, Carroll M. '52 ocC   F '49, 50,
   51, 53
Lowman, George F. '38   Bb '38; Te '38
Lown, Robert G. '53   T '51
Lowry, Donald I. '41   F '38, '39, '40
Lowry, Edward G. III '53   C '53
Lozeau, Richard C. '64   F '61
Lubetkin, Alvin N. '56   Bb '56
Luby, Meade J. '47 ocC   C '48
Lucas, Charles P. '50   B '49
Lucas, Kenneth B. '23   B '23
Lund, Edward G. '23   T '22
Lund, Gordon G. '63   Sw '61, '62
Lund, Peter B. F. '59   Sq '58, '59
Lund, Skiddy M. '51   Sk '51
Lundell, Carl G. T. '27   T '25, '26, '27
Lunder, Leonard S. '49   B '47
Lupien, Albert J. '32   B '30, '31, '32
Lupien, Ulysses J., Jr. '39   B '37, '38, '39;
   Bb '38, '39
Luttmann, Ralph G. '28   T '26, '28
Lutz, Charles D., Jr. '40   Bb '38, '39, '40
Lutz, Roger A. '23   CC '22; T '23
Luxemburg, Marc J. '60   H '59
Lyell, Rosslyn A. '41   Te '41
Lyle, William G., Jr. '43   F '40, '41, '42; T
   '42
Lyman, Arthur T., Jr. '42   C '41, '42; F '40,
   '41
Lynch, Dennis J. '63   Bb '61, '62, '63
Lynch, James D. '42   B '40
Lyons, Champ, Jr. '62   F '60, '61
Lyons, Robert D. '38   T '37

MacDonald, George L., Jr. '55   B '54, '55
MacDonald, Jack D. 47   F '45
Macdonald, Torbert H. '40   B '40; F '37,
   '38, '39; T '39, '40
MacGowan, Peter '42   G '42
MacGregor, Caswell E., Jr. '31   H '31, '32
MacHale, William H. '31   B '29, '30, '31
Machanic, Roger '55   T '53, '54, '55
MacIntosh, David B. '37   B '36
MacIntyre, Bruce B. '61   F '58, '59, '60
MacIsaac, Frederick M. '40   T '38, '39, '40
MacKenzie, Michael V., Jr. '64   LC '62, '63
MacKinney, Loren G. '42   F '39, '40, '41
MacKinnon, John D., Jr. '43   T '42, '43
Mackinnon, Richard A. '58   L '58
Mackintosh, David D. '47   F '45
MacKusick, Meredith H., Jr. '29   LC '29
Macky, Peter W. '57   Sw '55, '56, '57

MacMahon, James R. '64   LC '62, '63
Macmillan, Alexander S., Jr. '44   H '43
Macomber, William B. '26   F '25
MacShane, Frank S. '49   C '46, '48
MacVeagh, Charlton, Jr. '57   S '55, '56; Sq '56, '57
MacVicar, William M. '49   Sw '47, '48, '49
Madeo, Laurence A. '63   Bb '63
Madey, Stephen L. '40   T '39, '40
Maesaka, Ray K. '54   B '52, '54
Magie, William A. 28   F '27
Magowan, Robert A. '27   B '27
Magowan, Robert A., Jr. '58   S '56, '57
Maguire, Hubert C., Jr. '54   CC '53; T '52, '53, '54
Maguire, Lawrence E. '58   F '57
Maguire, Lawrence E. '58   F '57
Maguire, Richard '36   B '34, '35, '36
Magurn, Joseph J. '38   L '38
Mahaney, John A. '64   T '63
Maher, John J. 26   F '24, '25
Maher, John T. '56   B '54; F '53, 54, '55
Mahon, Henry MacL. '23   T '21
Mahoney, Daniel D. '65   Sw '63
Mahoney, Francis X. '55   H '53, '54, '55
Mahoney, George G. '37   H '37
Mahoney, John H. '37 ocC   B '38
Malick, John S. '27   T '27
Malin, Seamus P. '62   S '60, '61
Mallonee, Charles G. II '58   L '58
Malloy, Howard P. '44   S '43
Mamana, John P. '65   W '63
Manchester, Douglas C. '55   H '53, '54, '55
Manheim, Frank T. '52   Sw '51
Manheimer, Leon H. '36   S '35
Mann, Eugene L. '54   Te '54
Manning, George W. B., Jr. '54   Bb '53
Manning, Richard J. '55   Bb '53, '54, '55
Mannino, Ernest N. '46 ocC   B '49
Manos, Eli '53   F '51, 52
Mantel, Samuel J., Jr. '44 ocC   C '48
Marcy, Henry O. III '37   T '36
Mardulier, Francis J. '30   T '29, '30
Marglin, Stephen I. '62 ocC   Sw '62
Margoluis, Arnold '61   L '61
Mariaschin, Saul N. '47   B '46 '47; Bb '46, '47
Markham, Dean F. '48   F '46, '47
Markos, William G. '56   F '55
Markus, William E. '60   T '60
Marland, Sidney P. III '64   T '62
Marmar, Kenneth A. '60   S '57, '58
Marmor, Theodore R. '60   F '57
Marsh, Jerry R. '55   F '53, '54
Marsh, John S. '32   T '32
Marshall, Harold T., Jr. '51   H '50, '51

Marshall, John K. '63   Sl '63
Marshall, Lewis K. '23   T '22, '23
Marshall, Randolph L. '42   C '42
Martin, Allan L. '61   B '59, '60, '61
Martin, Christopher '52   Fc '52
Martin, Christopher B. '62   S '60, '61
Martin, Edward H. '60   CC '57, '58, '59; T '57, '58
Martin, Francis A. '32   H '30, '31
Martin, Francis H. '64   Bb '63
Martin, Keith D. '62   Te '60, '61 '62
Martin, Robert D. '56   CC '55
Martin, Roger H. '34   H '32, '33
Martindale, James D. '28   T '23
Martinez, Edward L., Jr. '40   B '40
Maser, Francis E. '38   F '35
Masland, Richard H. '64   LC '63
Mason, Benjamin L. '63   H '62, '63
Mason, Charles E., Jr. '30   C '28
Mason, Henry B. '45   T '43
Mason, Thomas F. '30   F '27; T '28, '29, '30
Massari, Anthony T. '58   Bb '56
Masters, Parke W. W. '40   C '40
Masterson, Thomas A. '49   Fc '49
Matlack, David R. '44   T '42
Matthews, Edwin S. '23   C '23
Mauran, Duncan H. '50   L '50
Mavor, Huntington '48   S '47
Maw, Carlyle E., Jr. '60   Sw '59
Maynard, John '62   C '61, '62
Mays, Edmund A., Jr. '32   B '30, '31, '32; F '29, '30, '31
Mazzone, Armando D. '50   F '47, '48, '49
McAfee, William G. '65   T '63
McAnulty, Michael A. '63   Sw '61, '63
McCaffrey, James P. '33   B '31, '32, '33
McCagg, Edward K. II '57   C '55, '56, '57
McCagg, Louis B., Jr. '52   C '50, '51, '52
McCall, Marsh H., Jr. '60   S '58, '59
McCartney, Douglas '60   Sw '58, '59, '60
McClellan, S. Griffen III '59   Bb '57, '58, '59
McClennen, Charles E. '64   LC '62, '63
McClennen, James C. A. '59   C '57, '58, '59
McClung, Merle S. '65   Bb '63
McConaughy, Robert T. '53   Fc '53
McCormick, Patrick B. M. '50   T '47, '48, '49, '50
McCornack, Stuart G. '58   Sw '58
McCoy, Robert W., Jr. '62   H '60, '61
McCurdy, Walter R. '50   Bb '48, '49
McCutcheon, Howard S. '43   Sw '41
McDaniel, William H. '47   Bb '46; F '45, '46
McDonell, Alexander A. III '62   Sq '61, '62, '63

McElroy, Charles A., Jr. '51   Sl '51
McElroy, Lowell R. '58   LC '58
McElroy, Peter E. '59   T '59
McFarlan, Franklin W. '59   F '58
McGarrity, George W. '57   B '57
McGarry, Robert J. '49   T '49
McGinnis, Robert F. '57   B '57
McGlone, Joseph C. '26   F '23
McGoodwin, Robert R., Jr. '35   B '35
McGoodwin, Robert R., Jr. '35   B '35
McGowan, Lewis A., Jr. '38   G '38
McGrath, Edward H. '31   B '29, '30, '31
McGrath, Gordon R. '42   H '41, '42
McGrath, Joseph B. '44   T '43
McGrath, Thomas J. '52   T '50, '51, '52
McIntosh, John R. '61   S '58, '59, '60
McIntosh, Kenneth, '58   S '55, '56, 57
McIntosh, Rustin C. '55   S '54
McJennet, John F. III '62   Sw '61, '62
McJennett, John F., Jr '33   B '33
McKay, Donald N. '38   Sw '37, '38
McKean, Quincy A. S., Jr. '50   H '47, '48
McKeeman, Lloyd C. '59   LC '59, '60
McKhann, Serge N. '60   W '58, '60
McLaughlin, Richard M. '59   F '57, '58; H '57, '58, '59
McLaughlin, Robert J. '57   C '57
McLaughlin, Thomas C. '61   F '60
McLean, David G. '57   CC '54, '55, '56; T '55
McLoughlin, Joseph R. '41   CC '39, '40
McMeekin, Herbert T., Jr. '42   Sw '42
McNair, George N., Jr. '53   Fc '53
McNamara, John J., Jr. '53   Sw '51, '52, '53
McNeil, Donald D. '58   S '57
McNicol, Donald E. '43   F '40, '41
McNitt, Edward W. '41   Sw '41
McPherson, Stephen M. '59   H '59
McSweeney, William D. '41   Bb '41
McTernen, Malcolm B., Jr. '37   B '36, '37; F '36
McVey, Robert P. '58   H '56, '57, '58
Meadows, Robert W. '29   F '26
Meahl, Robert K. '61   H '60
Mebel, Peter E. '60   LC '58
Mechem, John S. '38   H '36, '37, '38
Mechem, Richard W. '45   H '43
Mechling, Jerry E. '65   F '62
Meehan, Edward '64   CC '61, '62; T '62, '63
Meigs, William M. '56   F '53, '54, '55
Mellen, Nicholas '39   F '38
Mello, Robert C. '53   T '51, '52, '53
Mendel, Howard P. '40   S '38, '39; T '38, '39, '40
Mercer, Charles B. '63   H '63

Merchant, Bruce M. '56   Sw '56

Merriam, Bernard F. II '36   Sw '36

Merrill, Dudley '26   LC '26

Merrill, Ernest S., Jr. '40   B '40

Merrill, James E. '24   T '22

Merwin, Gaius W., Jr. '45   C '43

Messenbaugh, Robert L. '61   F '58, '59, '60

Messer, Ronald J. '54   F '52

Metcalf, Michael P. '55   C '54, '55

Metropoulos, Theodore N. '57   F '54, '55, '56

Meyer, Jan H. H. III '56   F '53, '54, '55

Meyers, Philip M., Jr. '54   T '52, '53, '54

Michelman, Irving S. '39   T '37, '38, '39

Middendorf, William K. B. '48   F '47

Mielke, William E. '47 NROTC   F '45

Miklos, Frank J. '48   F '47

Milde, Walter J. '25   C '25

Millard, John B. '54   Sw '52, '54

Millard, Malcolm S. '36   T '34, '35, '36

Miller, Alfred H. '27   F '24, '25, '26; T '25, '26, '27

Miller, Daniel '62   R '62

Miller, Elliot S. '64   Sw '62, '63

Miller, Halbert B. '62   B '60

Miller, Harold I. '37   T '35

Miller, Harold S. '49   F '45

Miller, James V., Jr. '63   LC '61, '62

Miller, John B. '65   T '63

Miller, Richard M. '47 ocC   T '48

Miller, Richmond P. Jr. '49   S '49

Miller, Vern K. '42   F '39, '40, '41

Miller, William V. '23   F '22; T '22, '23

Millett, Francis N., Jr. '54   F '53

Milton, Robert C., Jr. '56   C '56; Sq '56

Minot, George R. II '49 ocC   H '46, '48, '49, '50

Minotti, Joseph F., Jr. '64   F '62

Minturn, Robert B., Jr. '61   B '61; H '60, '61

Mischner, Ronald P. '58   Sw '56, '57, '58

Mitchell, Robert W. '62   R '62

Mittell, David A. '39   H '38, '39

Mittell, Kenneth C. '34   H '34

Mobraaten, William L. '50   Bb '48, '49

Moffie, Harold J. '50   B '49; F '47, '48, '49

Moley, Malcolm '46   Bb '43

Molloy, Ernest L. '29   B '29

Moloy, Floyd M. '59   S '57, '58

Monks, Robert A. G. '54   C '54

Montague, William P. III '52   T '51

Monteith, William E., Jr. '53   F '51, '52

Montgomery, Charles M. '59   Sw '59

Montgomery, Johnson C. '55   Sw '55

Moore, Craig '41   Sw '39

Moore, David F. '61   Te '60, '61

Moore, Henry J. '57   T '56

Moore, John L., Jr. '51   T '50

Moore, Thomas G. '29   T '27, '28, '29

Moravec, Vincent P. '48   F '46, '47

Morgan, Charles F. '50   C '49

Morgan, Henry S. '23   C '21, '23

Morgan, John C., Jr. '52   LC '52

Morgan, John W. '43   F '40, '41

Morgan, Richard III '36   Fc '36

Morgan, Thomas L. '61   S '58, '59, '60

Moriarty, Vincent C. '47 ocC   T '46

Morrill, Joseph, Jr. '28   H '27, '28

Morris, William B. '65   Sq '63

Morris, William F. '57   CC '54, '56; T '56 '57

Morrison, Eliot F. '59   Fc '59

Morrison, Peter F. '56   T '54, '55; W '56

Morrison, Robert E. '56   F '53, '54, '55

Morse, David G. '62   B '60, '61, '62; H '60, '61, '62

Morse, John M. '34   T '31, '32, '33, '34

Morse, Malcolm '24   T '23

Morton, Byron B., Jr. '52   Fc '52

Moseley, Frederick R., Jr. '36   F '34, '35; H '34, '35, '36

Moseley, Thomas C. '46 ocC   H '47, '49

Motley, Edward, Jr. '36   S '35

Moushegian, Vahan '32   F '30, '31

Moynihan, James E., Jr. '55   H '54

Mrkonich, Edward J. '55   H '53, '54

Mudd, John H. '60   S '57, '58, '59

Muellner, Robert L. '60   Sq '59

Mugaseth, Jehangir J. '52   Sq '51, '52

Mullen, James L., Jr. '63   B '61, '62, '63

Mulligan, George G. '63   Sw '61, '62

Mullin, Mark H. '62   Cc '59, '60, '61; T '59, '60, '61, '62

Mullins, Robert O. '54   B '54

Mulvey, Donald J. '54   Sw '52, '53, '54

Mumford, George S. '25   C '23

Muncaster, Neil K. '57   Bb '55, '57, '58; T '57, '58

Munroe, James S. '38   Sw '37

Munroe, Vernon, Jr. '31   T '29, '30

Murchie, Guy, Jr. '29   C '27, '28

Murmes, Wilbert S. '33   B '33

Murner, Duane J. '58   Sw '56

Murphy, Francis D. '33   CC '30, 31; T '32

Murphy, Gerald D. '52   Bb '50, '51, '52; Te '52

Murphy, Henry R. '42 ocC   S '42

Murphy, James S. '25   T '25

Murphy, John G., Jr. '58   T '56

Murphy, Louis R. '35   L '35

Murphy, Richard A. '60   R '60

Murphy, Timothy C., Jr. '50   Sw '50

Murray, Allan K. '23   T '22

Murray, David H. '35   C '35

Murray, I. Gillis '54   T '53

Murray, James J., Jr. '56   B '55

Murray, William T. '59   Sw '57, '58, '59

Myers, Robert A., Jr. '58   Bb '58

Myerson, Henry M. '32   F '29, '30, '31

Myerson, Morton '42   S '41

Nahigian, Franklin R. '55   CC '54; T '54

Nahigian, John M. '49   B '49

Nash, Bradley DeL. '23   H '23

Nash, Edward R. '26   F '25

Nash, Nicholas D. '61   H '61

Nathanson, James E. '54   Sl '52, '53, '54

Nawi, David R. '62   T '62

Nawn, Hugh, Jr. '51   Sq '51

Nazro, Thomas W. '34   F '31 '32, '33

Neal, Herbert W. '44 ocC   B '49

Nee, Joseph F. '38   F '35, '36, '37

Nelson, Glen D. '59   F '56

Nelson, James A. '61   F '59, '60

Nelson, James A. '61   F '59, '60

Nelson, K. Eric '61   F '58, '59, '60

Nelson, Theodore C. '52   H '52

Nevin, Charles J. '34   B '33, '34; F '31, '32, '33

Newell, Franklin S. II '59   F '58

Newell, Henry H. 29   H '29

Newell, John L. '26   H '24

Newell, John L., Jr. '57   F '56

Newhall, Campbell '24   T '22

Newhall, John B. II '54   Sl '54

Nicholas, Frederick S. '33   P '33

Nicholas, Frederick S., Jr. '57   H '55

Nichols, Henry G., Jr. '52   C '52

Nichols, John D., Jr. '53   F '50, '51, '52

Nichols, Louis R. '24   F '23

Nichols, Robert B. '41   T '40

Nichols, Rodney W. '58   Te '56

Nichols, Sargent '59 ocC   T '60, 61, 62

Nickerson, Albert L., Jr. '33   C '32, '33

Nickerson, Thomas '25   B '25

Niederhoffer, Victor B. '64   Sq '62, '63; Te '61, '63

Ninde, Richard C. '39   C '38, '39

Nishimura, Dwight K. '49   F '48

Nissen, Frederick V. '30   T '30

Noble, John III '59   LC '59; W '57, '58, '59

Noble, John H., Jr. '47   Bb '47

Noon, Theodore W., Jr. '40   CC '39

Noonan, James F. '50   F '47, '48, '49

Noonan, Ronald P. '53   F '52

Noone, Richard S. '41   H '41

Nordblom, Rodger P. '50   Sk '50

Norling, Parry McW. '61   Sq '60

Pierce, Laurence A. '52   Sq '51

Pierskalla, William P. '56   Fc '56

Pike, C. Davis '62   LC '62

Pildner, Gary '60   Sw '58, '59, '60

Pillsbury, Robert L. '61   F '58, '59, '60

Pirnie, Douglas D. '43 ocC   T '41, '46

Pirnie, Warren B., Jr. '41   C '39, '40, '41

Pitchford, A. Lester '42   B '40

Pitts, Beverly L., Jr. '65   Sw '63

Place, David E. '43   F '42

Place, Henry C. '57   Sq '56, '57; Te '56

Plath, Warren J. '57   T '57

Platt, Geoffrey '27   C '25, '26, '27

Platt, Henry N., Jr. '44   C '43

Playfair, Robert S. '36   CC '33, '34, '35; T '34, '35

Plissner, William A '51   L '51

Plotkin, Theodore '38   T '36

Pochop, Jeffrey L. '64   F '62, '63

Poindexter, Joseph B. '57   Sk '57

Poletti, Charles E. '60   Sq '58, '59

Pollen, Kalman '62   Te '61

Pollock, Harry W. '64   C '62, '63

Pollock, Thomas E. III '65   C '63

Pool, Beekman H. '32   Sq '32

Poole, Frank H. '43   Bb '43

Poole, J. Douglas '61   Sq '60, '61

Poor, Daniel S. '42   S '41

Pope, Frederick, Jr. '42   H '42

Pope, Ralph L., Jr. '38   F '37; H '36, '37, '38

Popell, Floyd H. '54   F '51, '52, '53

Porter, Cedric W., Jr. '60   H '60; LC '60

Porter, Robert P., Jr. '29   T '27, '28, '29

Post, Michael St. A '49   Sl '50

Post, Richard St. F '51   L '51

Potter, Brooks '24   H '24

Potter, John M. '26   T '25

Potter, John T. '45   C '43

Potter, Josiah W. '30   F '27; T '28, '30

Potter, Philip C., Jr. '48   S '48

Powel, John H. '42 ocC   LC '41

Powell, Frank H. '46 ocC   F '48

Powell, Richard G. '38   S '37

Powers, Francis C. '41   Sw '39, '40, '41

Powning, Maynard W. '53   H '53

Prahl, Joseph M. '63   L '61, '62, '63

Pratt, Charles A., Jr. '28   F '25, '26, '27; T '26, '27, '28

Pratt, Harold I., Jr. '59   B '58, '59; H '58, '59

Pratt, Laurence O. '26   H '25, '26

Pratt, Laurence O., Jr. '59   H' 59; Te '58, '59

Pratt, Philip G. '53   Sw '51, '52; T '51, '52, '53

Preston, John McA. '28   C '28

Preston, Lewis T. '50 ocC   H '47, '49, '50, '51

Price, David L. '58   C '58

Price, Robert J. '64   Sw '62

Prichard, Michael, '58   F '56

Prince, George N. '43   C '42

Pringle, John R. '63   Sw '61, '62, '63

Prior, John A. '29   B '28, '29; F '27, '28

Prior, William A. '50   Bb '48, '49, '50

Prout, William W. '36   F '35

Prouty, Donald '38   B '37, '38

Prouty, Gardner E., Jr. '36   B '34, '35, '36

Provensen, H. Christian '59   S '56, '57

Pruyn, Milton L. '35   H '33

Puffer, Robert W., Jr. '26   B '25; F '25

Purnell, Karl H. '56   Te '56

Pusey, James R. '62   Fc '62

Putnam, Augustus L. '49   Sl '50

Putnam, Eliot T. '29   F '26, '28, '29; H '29, '30

Putnam, Eliot T., Jr. '61   H '61

Putnam, John W. '33   H '31, '32, '33

Putnam, William B. D. '41   B '41

Pyle, Jerry H. '59   L '59

Quattlebaum, Edwin G. III '64   C '63

Quartarone, Samuel F. '56   F '55

Quinby, William C., Jr. '36   H '35, '36

Quirk, David J. '26   T '24

Rabb, Irving W. '34   F '34; L '34

Radcliffe, Daniel M. '64   Lc '63

Ragle, Thomas B. '49   S '47

Rahal, James J., Jr. '55   B '54

Ransom, Donald C. '65   Bb '63

Ranz, Jules '62   F '60

Rapp, William E. '60   S '57, '58, '59

Rapperport, Alan S. '55   Sw '53, '54,'55

Rate, Henry A. '53   F '50, '51, '52

Rauh, John D. '54   Sq '53, '54; Te '54

Ravenel, Charles DuF. '61   B '59, '60, '61; F '58, '59, '60

Ravreby, Fred A. '52   F '49, '50, '51; T '50, '51, '52

Rawls, Walton H. '55   Fc '55

Ray, Daniel B. '49   W '48

Ray, John F. '34   Te '34

Ray, Robert W. '52   F '49, '50; T '51, '52

Raymond, Edward H. '58   W '57

Raynolds, Ronald G. '60   LC '58, '60

Read, David W. '44 ocC   T '47

Read, John B., Jr. '57   CC '56

Reardon, John P., Jr. '60   F '58, '59

Reckler, Jon M. '62   Fc '62

Record, Eugene E. '32   F '30, '31; T '29, '30, '31, '32

Redmon, James J. '42   W '42

Redmond, Ambrose J., Jr. '52   Bb '51, '52

Reece, Franklin A., Jr. '35   H '35

Reed, Charles L., Jr. '62   F '59, '60, '61

Reed, Howard S. '49   T '49

Reed, John G. '51   C '51

Reed, Joseph '42   C '42

Reese, John R. '62   L '61, '62

Regan, Robert F. '41   B '40, '41

Reich, David L. '59   LC '58

Reid, James L. '29   CC '26, '27, '28; T '27, '28, '29

Reider, Arthur E. '58   CC '55, '56, '57; T '56, '57, '58

Reidy, David D. '23   T '22, '23

Reidy, John S. '60   B '59, '60

Reilly, Brendan J. '45 ocC   B '43, '47

Reilly, Kevin P. '51   B '49, '51

Reilly, Richard M. '59   H '57, '59

Reisen, David A. '64   Sw '62, '63

Relyea, Peter S. '64   C '63

Relyea, Richard J. III '62   C '61, '62

Renouf, Edward von P. '28   T '26, '27

Repetto, Dominic '57   B '56, '57

Repetto, Robert C. '59   Bb '58, '59

Repsher, Lawrence H. '61   F '58, '59, '60; T '59, '60, '61

Rex, Justin L. '31   B '31

Reynolds, Brian F. '54   F '51, '52, '53; T '52, '54

Reynolds, Edward, Jr. '50   C '48, '49

Rhoades, Stephen S. '58   S '57

Rich, Harry E. '62   T '60, '61, '62

Richard, John F. '63   LC '62

Richards, Charles F. '31   F '29, '30

Richards, David K. '61   LC '59, '60, '61

Richards, Donald G. '56   T '54, '56

Richards, Donald W. '45   B '43; Bb '43; F '42

Richards, John II '54   T '52, '53, '54

Richards, John P. '49   Bb '49

Richards, John R. '40   C '38, '39, '40

Richards, Reuben F. '52   C '52

Richards, Tudor '38   T '37, '38

Richardson, Arthur W. '28   H '28

Richardson, Donald L. '60   LC '60

Richardson, E. Bradley '53   H '51, '52, '53

Richardson, John, Jr. '43   C '42

Richling, William I. '61   Bb '59; Te '60

Richmond, Richard A. '53   F '51

Rickenbacker, William F. '49   G '48

Riecken, Henry W., Jr. '39   L '39

Rient, Peter F. '60   H '60

Ries, David P. '60   LC '58

Rigby, John D. '42   Bb '40

Riggs, William R. '56   Bb '56

Righter, Volney '26   C '25

Riley, Robert S. '27   C '27

Rimmer, Charles P., Jr. '50   C '50

Rinella, Richard A. '61   B '61

Ripley, Frank C. '64   Te '62, '63

Rittenburg, Robert '55   T '53, '54, '55

Robb, Leonard L. '25   F '24; T '24, '25

Robb, Philip H. '25   F '24

Robbins, Hanson C. '59   Sl '59

Robbins, Henry B. '36   H '36

Robbins, Theodore B. '60   W '58, '59, '60

Robbins, Warren D., Jr. '34   C '34

Roberts, George F. '38   F '36; H '36, '37, '38

Roberts, James M. '60   Fc '60

Roberts, James A. '36   H '35, '36

Roberts, Thomas N. '65   Sw '63

Robertson, Alastair D. '33   C '33

Robertson, A. Douglas, Jr. '63   C '62, '63

Robertson, Gordon F. '36   Te '36

Robertson, Kenneth D., Jr. '29   F '28

Robertson, Michael S '57   T '55, '56, '57

Robie, Theodore P. '38   S '37

Robinson, Edward T. '65   Sq '63; Te '63

Robinson, John N. '27   F '26

Robinson, Ralph L. '52   B '50, '51, '52

Roche, Charles D., Jr. '50 ocC   B '49; F '45, '47, '48, '49

Rockwell, John R. '50   Bb '48, '49, '50

Rodd, Fellowes M. '62   S '60, '61

Rodgers, William H., Jr. '61   B '60, '61

Rodis, Nicholas '49   B '46; F '46, '47, '48

Rodman, Sumner '35   Te '35

Rodriguez, Juan M. '54   S '53

Rogers, Alan S. '24   B '24

Rogers, Arthur G. '26   B '24

Rogers, Eddy J. '34   F '31, '32, '33; L '34

Rogerson, Alexander G. '45   T '43

Roland, John F. '25   B '25

Romano, Joseph F. '42   Bb '40, '41

Rood, Armistead B. '31   C '31

Roosevelt, Franklin D., Jr. '37   C '36

Roosevelt, Jonathan '62   Te '61

Roosevelt, Theodore III '36   S '35

Roosevelt, Theodore IV '65   LC '63

Rose, Donald W. '62   Sw '61, '62

Rose, Edward A., Jr. '54   Sq '54

Rose, William A., Jr. '60   Sw '58, '59

Rosen, Gerald P. '33   T '33

Rosenau, William W. '51   F '48, '49, '50

Rosenfeld, Huna '49   CC '46; T '47, '48

Rosenstein, James A. '61   C '61

Rosenthal, David S. '59   T '57, '58

Rosenthal, Edward '56   F '55

Rosenthal, Paul S. '56   T '54

Rosinus, Gunther K. '49   Bb '48

Ross, Harvey M. '39   W '39

Ross, John C. '23   B '23

Ross, Joseph C., Jr. '55   F '52, '53, '54

Rossano, Kenneth R. '56   B '54, '55, '56

Rossow, Alfred W., Jr. '55   CC '54

Rothschild, Edward I. '42   Bb '40, '41, '42

Rothschild, Walter N., Jr. '42   LC '41

Rouillard, Francis '23   F '22

Rouner, Arthur A., Jr. '51   C '50, '51

Rouner, Leroy S. '53   C '51, '52, '53

Rousmaniere, James A. '40   S '38, '39; Sq '40

Row, Richard C. '42   F '41

Rowe, Warren C. '31   T '29, '30

Rowe, William S. II '39   C '38, '39

Rowley, Edward D. '40   LC '40

Roy, John L. II '50   Bb '50

Rubin, Richard H. '52   T '50

Ruby, Albert F., Jr. '50   T '49

Rudman, Sidney S. '27   F '26

Rudnick, David L. '62   G '62

Ruml, Treadwell '39   Bb '39

Rumsey, Bronson H. '39   P '38

Runnels, Douglas C. '58   Fc '58

Russell, Henry E. '39   F '37, '38

Russell, Robert M. '63   LC '62, '63

Russman, Barry S. '59   S '58

Ryan, Leo W. '26   T '25

Ryland, G. Neal '63   H '61, '62, '63

Sacks, Harry P. '55   Bb '53, '54

Sagenkahn, Chester F. '40   Sw '40

Saia, Frank R. '58   B '58

St. George, Robert M. '64   B '62, '63

Saltonstall, Henry '35   C '35

Saltonstall, Robert, Jr. '33   C '31, '32, '33; H '31, '32, '33

Saltonstall, William G. '28   C '26, '27, '28; F '26; H '28

Saltonstall, William L. '49   C '49

Samborski, Adolph W. '25   B '24, '25

Samborski, Edmund B. '31   B '30

Sandler, Marvin '54   Sw '52, '53, '54

San Soucie, Emil R. '54   CC '53' T '52, '53

Santmire, Harold P. '57   Sw '55

Sargeant, Ernest J. '40   F '39

Sargent, E. Rotan '36   Sq '36; Te '36

Sargent, George L., Jr. '64   B '63

Sargent, Hugh A. '56   S '55

Savage, Peter V. '61   S '58, '59, '60

Sawhill, John E., Jr. '43   S '42

Sawyer, Henry B., Jr. '36   B '36

Sayles, Madison '27   F '24, '25, '26

Sayre, Richard W. '57   S '56

Scaife, Roger M. '39   H '39

Sceery, Robert T. '42   Sw '42

Schafer, Roger S. '41   T '39, '41

Scheer, Richard A. '54   B '53, '54

Schein, David S. '58   F '55, '56, '57

Schellstede, William P. 61   Sw '59, '60, '61

Scherer, Lester B. '54   Fc '54

Schereschewsky, John F. '32   F '30, '31

Scheu, John P. '35   CC '34; T '34, '35

Schlaeppi, James E. '59   CC '56, '57, '58

Schmidt, William H. II '37   T '36, '37

Schneider, Steven J. '56   Fc '56

Schnitz, Paul J. '63   W '61, '62

Schoenberg, Theodore E. '41   W '41

Schoenfeld, Marcus '54   Sq '54

Schreiber, William M. '57   Bb '57

Schultz, Stephen '62   W '60

Schumacher, Alan T. '33   S '33

Schumacher, August T. '61   T '59, '60, '61

Schumann, Francis '35   F '33, '34; T '33, '34, '35

Schwartz, David T. '59   Fc '59

Schwartz, Peter A. '62   W '61

Schwartzman, Robert J. '61   Sq '61; T '60

Schwarz, Frederick A. O., Jr. '57   C '56, '57

Schwarz, Henry M. '58   S '56, '57

Schwarz, Robert D. '65   C '63

Schwede, John P. '41   B '40, '41

Scott, David R. '60   Te '60

Scott, Richard S. '27   H '25, '26, '27

Scott, Robert L. '31   C '31

Scott, Robert W., Jr. '38   S '37

Scott, Stuart, Jr. '33   F '33

Scully, Arthur J., Jr. '43   B '41, '42; Bb '41, '42

Scully, Francis P., Jr. '51   Sl '51

Scully, Leo J. '65   Bb '63

Scully, Michael J. '48 ocC   C '46, '47, '48, '49; S '49

Scully, Robin '40   S '38

Seager, Samuel N. '50   G '50

Seagren, Stephen L. '63   Sw '61, '62, '63

Seamans, F. Augustus '49   S '47

Sears, Lawrence B. '58   Sq '56, '57, '58; Te '58

Sears, Walter E. '46 ocC   H '47, '48

Seaton, Edward L. '65   Sw '63

Seaton, Frederick D. '61   Sw '59, '60

Seaton, Richard H. '59   Sw '57, '58, '59

Sedgwick, Henry D. II '51   F '48, '49; H '50, '51

Seed, Randolph W. 54   LC '54

Seligman, Carl B. '43   C '43

Senior, John L., Jr. '38   C '38

Sewall, Stephen P. '64   S '62

Shafer, Paul C., Jr. '50   F '47, '48, '49

Shallow, William J. '40   T '38, '39, '40

Shapiro, George I. '28   T '27, '28

Share, Neil E. '64   Bb '63

Sharf, Frederic A. '56   L '56

Shattuck, John R. '43   T '41, '42

Shaunessy, Robert T. '59   F '56, '57, '58
Shaw, David C. '29   F '28
Shaw, Joseph H. '52   F '51
Shea, Andrew F. III '63   B '63
Shea, John J., Jr. '52   R '52
Shean, David W., Jr. '38   B '37, '38
Sheats, Paul D. '54   T '52
Sheffield, Thomas C., Jr. '58   LC '58
Sheldon, John E. '32   B '30, '31, '32
Shelton, John W. '64   Sw '62
Shepley, Henry R., Jr. '42   LC '42
Sherburne, John H., Jr. '24   F '23
Sheridan, C. Michael '62   F '59, '60, '61
Sheriff, Mohamed A. '54   T '54
Sherman, Allan W. '34   F '32, '33
Shields, Daniel R. '46   Bb '43
Shima, Richard J. '61   B '59, '60, '61
Shipman, John S. '62   F '59
Shirk, William W. '38   T '36
Shortlidge, George H. '40   C '39, '40
Shrewsbury, Thomas B. '41 ocC   Sw '42
Shue, James W. '58   B '58; S '55, '56, '57
Shuttleworth, Paul '51   R '51
Sibley, Hiram W. '31   B '31
Sibley, Russell A. '44   C '43
Sidd, James J. '55   T '55
Sieglaff, Peter M. '62   L '61, '62
Siler, Arthur G. '56   T '54, '55, '56
Silverman, David M. '53   Bb '53
Simboli, David R. '40   T '39
Simmons, Bradford '34   C '33, '34; F '33
Simmons, Edward B. '37   C '35
Simonds, Daniel '28   F '26, '27
Simonds, Peter K. '54   C '52, '54
Simourian, John A. '57   B '55, '56, 57; F
    '54, '55, '56
Simpson, Francis M., Jr. '41   Bb '40, '41
Simpson, Howard K. '49   Sw '46
Singal, Arnold H. '58   Bb '58
Singer, Stephen L. '57   T '57
Sinnott, John, Jr. '39   S '38
Sisler, Glenn E. 57   Sw '57
Skalinder, Gregg L. '65   Sw '63
Skates, Ronald L. '63   F '62
Skeels, David M. '59   W '57, '58, '59
Skowronski, Eugene A. '65   F '62
Slade, Howard II '27   H '27
Slansky, Richard C. '62   CC '59
Slattery, Robert B., Jr. '46   B '43
Slayton, Hovey E., Jr. '26   B '26
Slingerland, Dorraine W. '44   T '42, '43
Sloan, Phillip L. '61   C '60, '61
Slocum, James E. '52   C '50, '51, '52
Smails, Robert A. '54   Sw '53, '54
Smart, Hilary H. '47 ocC   T '48
Smith, Albert O. '40   T '40
Smith, Baldwin, Jr. '65   H '63

Smith, Benjamin A. II '39   F '38
Smith, Charles C. '41   T '39
Smith, David L. 51   W '51
Smith, David W. '45 ocC   Sw '47
Smith, Edward B. '51   Bb '49, '50, '51
Smith, Edward J., Jr. '63   F '61, '62
Smith, Frederic P. '58   T '54
Smith, George W. '29   T '27
Smith, John W. '52   Fc '52
Smith, Kilby P. III '56   T '54, '55, '56
Smith, Langdon M. '57   Te '59
Smith, Lawrence G. '59   Bb '59
Smith, Norman T. '54   T '52
Smith, Owen R. '43   Sw '42
Smith, Peter H. '61   Sq '59, '60, '61; Te
    '59, '60, '61
Smith, R. F. Walker '30   C '30
Smith, Robert J. '53   B '52, '53
Smith, Sidney O., Jr. '45 ocC   F '42, '46
Smith, William A. '36   Bx '35, '36
Smith, William M. '59   W '62
Snow, Crocker, Jr. '61   H '59, '60, '61
Snow, James M., Jr. '39   C '39
Snow, Robert B., Jr. '49   L '48
Snow, Robert L. '49   Sw '46
Snow, William R., Jr. '44   T '42
Snyder, Frank V. '43   C '43
Snyder, Roger A. '61   Bb '60
Snyder, William F. '44   Bb '42
Sollee, Eric T. '52   Fc '52
Soltz, Joseph B. '39   B '38, '39
Sommers, Davidson, '26   B '26
Sonnabend, Stephen '54   Sq '53
Soper Michael R. '65   C '63
Sorgi, Walter V. '46   B '43
Sorlien, Richard C. '44   Bb '43
Sorlien, Robert P. '38   T '38
Southall, Henry '62   Sw '60, '61, '62
Southmayd, William W. '64   F '61, '62
Souvaine, Henry D. '47   Bb '46
Spalding, Hobart A. '34   F '33
Spalding, Philip '25   B '24, '25; F '22, '23
Spence, William J. '52   L '52
Spencer, Donn N. '54   Te '54
Spencer, George H. '38   T '38
Spinney, David C. '59   T '57, '58
Spitzberg, Jack W. '64   T '62, '63
Spivak, Jonathan M. '50   S '49; T '49
Splaine, Edward F., Jr. '60   B '60
Sprague, Edwin D. W. '32   B '32
Sprague, Howard B., Jr. '46 ocC   C '47
Spreyer, Frederick C. '42   F '39, '40
Spring, Graham K. '37 ocC   F '34
Spruance, Spotswood L. '62   L '61, '62
Staber, Ernest C. '42   S '41
Stabler, Warwick B. '40   P '40
Stade, Francis S. von, Jr. '38   P '38

Stafford, Alfred H. '26 ocC   F '24, '26
Stahura, Walter J., Jr. '58   B '56, '57; F
    '55, '56, '57
Stanley, James D. II '59   Sw '57, '58, '59
Stanley, Malcolm N. '29   H '27, '29
Stanley, Peter vonS. '61   W '60
Stannard, Russell B. '43   F '41, '42
Stanton, John K. '46   B '42
Staples, Oscar S., Jr. '30   LC '29
Staples, Philip C., Jr. '37 ocC   F '36
Stargel, Robert N. '53   F '50, '51, '52
Stebbins, Albert H., Jr. '32   C '30
Stedman, William E. '41   H '41
Steedman, Christopher L. '63   H '63
Steele, Charles N. '60   S '57, '58, '59
Steele, Chauncey D. III '65   Te '63
Stein, Arthur O. '53   Sq '53
Steinert, Alan R. '58   G '58
Steinhart, John S. '51   Sw '49, '50, '51
Steinzig, Richard M. '60   W '60
Stensrud, Gordon B. '50   F '48
Stephens, Bradford A. '64   F '62
Stephenson, Donald B. '59   Sk '59
Stephenson, Thomas F. '64   B '63; F '62
Steuart, Charles D. '56   L '56
Stevens, Edward W. D. '48   B '48
Stevens, Robinson '40   C '38, '39, '40
Stevenson, John M. '52   Bb '51, '52
Stewart, Guilford '27   F '26
Stewart, John G. '40   Te '40
Stewart, Ralph A. '30   F '27
Stetz, Joseph J., Jr. '64   Sw '62, '63
Stiles, Quentin R. '51   Bb '49
Stillman, John S. '40   H '40
Stimpson, Wallace I. '59   Sq '58, '59
Stoddard, Howland B. '36   W '36
Stohn, Alexander C., Jr. '41   H '41
Stokes, James W. '61   S '60
Stone, Alan A. '50   F '47, 48
Stone, Allen B. '54   Sq '54
Stone, Christopher D. '59   L '59
Stone, David B. '50   Sw '50
Stone, Donald H. '48   F '47, '48
Stone, Galen L. '43 ocC   H '42, '46
Stone, Gregory B. '58   Sw '56, '57, '58
Stone, Herbert S. III '54   Te '54
Stone, Peter L. '39   H '37, '38
Stone, Robert G., Jr. '45 ocC   C '47
Storey, Richard C., Jr. '24   C '22
Stork, George F. '35   S '34
Stowell, Colles C. '39   Sw '39
Stowell, E. Esty '34   Sw '32, '34
Stowell, Harley L., Jr. '38 ocC   Sw '37, '38,
    '39
Stowell, Lonsdale F. '41   Sw '40, '41
Strand, Vernon F. '63   Bb '61, '63
Straus, Albert K. '63   L '61, '62, '63

Straus, David A. '64   LC '62, '63
Straus, Edward K. '31   H '31
Strauss, Leonard, Jr. '64   Bb '61, '63
Striker, Paul S. '59   W '57
Stringer, Robert A., Jr. '64   F '61, '62
Stromsted, Erik A. '51   T '50
Strong, Barton H. '27 ocC   F '26, '27
Strong, Frank R. '49   C '47, '48, '49
Stroud, Robert M. '52   Sw '50, '51, '52
Struck, Vernon H. '38   Bb '38; F '35, '36, '37
Stuart, Harborne W. '44 ocC   C '47
Stuart, Robert C. '38   F '36
Stubbs, Frank R., Jr. '32   H '30
Sturges, Hale II '60   B '60
Sturges, Harry W., Jr. '30   C '30
Sturgis, Warren '35   T '35
Subrin, Stephen N. 58   B '58
Sullivan, Frederick R. '27   C '26, '27
Sullivan, James T. '36 ocC   B '35, '36, '37
Sullivan, Paul W. '63   Sq '61, '62, '63; Te '61, '62, '63
Sullivan, Ralph C. '28   B '26, '28
Sullivan, Richard F. '59   W '58, '59
Sullivan, Richard H. '39   Bb '38, '39
Sullivan, Thomas Q. '46 ocC   B '48
Sulloway, Alvah W. '38   Sq '38; Te '38
Summers, James G. '45   H '43
Summers, M. Greely, Jr. '42   F '40, '41; H '40, '41, '42
Summers, Peter '56   H '55, '56
Sundqvist, John C. '54   C '53, '54
Sutermeister, Oscar '32   T '30, '31, '32
Sutton, Edmund H. '60   S '58, '59
Swaim, Stanley W. '31   C '30
Swan, William D., Jr. '45 ocC   H '47
Swanberg, Kenneth G. '63   B '63
Swanson, Richard W. '43   LC '43
Swartzman, Howard L. '47 ocC   Te '49
Swayze, Francis J. '33   C '32, '33
Swayze, Townsend S. '59   C '58, '59
Sweeny, Tadhg '61   L '61; S '59, '60
Swegan, Donald B. '46 NROTC   B '46; Bb '46; F '45
Swinford, William S. '62   F '59, '60, '61
Switzer, Alan A., Jr. '52   B '52
Symmes, David '52   Sq '51

Taggart, Robert D. '50   C '49
Tague, Peter F. III '61   B '60
Talbot, Dudley '39   C '37, '38, '39
Talbot, George N. '31   F '29, '30, '31
Tangeman, Frederick T. '62   Bb '61, '62
Tarlov, Edward C. '60   L 60
Tarre, Michael A. '65   Te '63
Tate, Albert C., Jr. '60   C '60
Tatlock, Hugh '34   B '34

Taylor, Brainerd R. '26   F '25
Taylor, Charles W. '63   F '61, '62
Taylor, Fenton, Jr. '44   H '43
Taylor, Graham R., Jr. '49   Sk '49
Taylor, Harold W. '33   B '33
Taylor, Louis S. '41   T '41
Taylor, Timothy B. '63   H '61, '62, '63
Telfer, James S. '54   L '54
Tennant, Thomas E. '47   F '45, '46
Terner, Ian D. '61   C '60
Terrell, Allen M., Jr. '65   Sq '63; Te '63
Tews, Thomas D. '64   LC '63
Thacher, Hamilton, Jr. '33   B '32, '33
Thayer, A. Bronson '61   L '61
Thayer, Duncan F. '23   B '22, '23
Thayer, Edward C. II '51   H '51
Thayer, Harvey H. '50   T '47, '48, '49, '50
Thayer, Richard W. '29   T '29
Thayer, Robert F. '23   T '23
Theopold, Philip H. '25   F '24
Thielens, Alexis O. '56   T '56
Thomas, Bruce R. '64   H '60, '63
Thomas, Grant F. '43 ocC   C '46
Thomas, Landon, Jr. '56   Sq '56
Thomas, Mitchell, Jr. '58   Fc '58
Thomas, Richard H. III '52   L '52
Thomas, Richard N. '42   W '42
Thompson, Beverly T. '28   T '28
Thompson, Robert H. '52   F '51
Thompson, Samuel '65   S '62
Thompson, Wiliiam T. III '59   CC '56, 57, '58; T '57, '58, '59
Thomson, Ronald P. '63   H '62, '63
Thorndike, John '64   S '61, '62; Sq '62, '63
Thorndike, John L. '49   T '48, '49
Thoron, Samuel G. W. '38   B '38
Thurmond, George B. '55   G '55
Tibbetts, Willard L., Jr. '26   CC '24; T '24, '25, '26
Tice, Orville M. '56   F '53, '54, '55
Ticknor, Benjamin H. II '31   B '29, '30, '31; F '28, '29, '30
Ticknor, William D., Jr. '30   F '28, '29
Tilghman, George H., Jr. '48   H '46, '47
Tilney, Nicholas L. '58   C '56, '57, '58
Timpson, Carl W., Jr. '52   H '50, '51, '52
Timpson, Lawrence L. '63   C '61
Timpson, Richard L. '57   LC '57
Tingle, Donald E. '59   Fc '59
Tittmann, George F. '36   B '36
Tobe, Phineas '32 ocC   B '33
Tobias, Paul H. '51   Te '51
Tobin, James E. '27   B '25, '26, '27
Todd, C. Lee, Jr. '26   B '24, '25, '26
Todd, Edward B. L. '60   Bb '59
Todd, Eveleth R. '29   B'29

Toepke, Henry T. '53   F '50, '51, '52
Tolf, Robert W. '51   Sw '50
Tomes, Alexander H., Jr. '54   Sq '53, '54
Tootell, Goeffrey H. '48 ocC   T '49, '50
Torgan, Jackson L '44   Bb '42, '43
Torrey, Owen C., Jr. '47 ocC   T '46, '47, '48
Toulmin, Paul R. '59   W '58
Toulmin, Peter N. '50   B '49
Townsend, Benjamin R. '37   C '37
Townsend, Rodman '41   F '40
Tracy, James J., '50   Sw '49
Trafford, William B. '32   F '30
Trainer, John N., Jr. '31   F '28, '29, '30
Trainer, John N. III '59   Sw '58, '59
Trask, Frederick K. III '60   Sq '58
Travis, William P. '54   Sw '53, '54
Treadwell, Barry L. '64   H '63
Trebilcock, William A. '59   Fc '59
Trimble, Donald E. '50   T '47, '49, '50
Tripp, Borden C. '28   F '27
Tsavaris, Louis J. '52   T '50
Tubman, William S., Jr. '58   S '55
Tucker, Walter I. '33   L '33
Tuckerman, Edward M. '43   G '43
Tuckerman, Roger W. '59   S '57, '58
Tudor, John '29   H '27, '28, '29
Tulenko, John F. '54   F '51
Tulloch, Peter H. '59   C '57
Tully, William r. '41   B '39, '41
Tupper, George A. '29   T '27, '28, '29
Turner, Harry W. '64   Sw '62
Turner, Howard M., Jr. '40   LC '40
Turner, John M. '52   T '52
Turner, LeBaron '50   B '49, '50
Turner, Ralph W. '28   F '25, '27
Tuttle, Mark '46   T '43
Tuttle, William P., Jr. '40   CC '38, '39
Twitchell, Robert S. '53   T '51, '52, '53
Tyler, Michael E. '63   H '63; L '61, '62, '63
Tyler, Robert O. '58   LC '58

Ufford, Charles W., Jr. '53   S '52; Sq '51, '52, '53; Te '53
Ulbrich, Konrad A. '60   Sw' 58, '59, '60
Ulcickas, Frank S. '65   F '62
Ulen, Donald M. '46 ocC   Sw '43, '48
Ulin, Richard O. '38   B '38
Ullman, Leo S. '61   L '61
Ullman, William '27   B '25, '26, '27
Ullyot, Daniel J. '58   H '56, '57, '58
Upton, Thomas G. '31   F '30

Valentine, Eugene J. '62   W '61, '62
Vander Eb, Henry G. '42   F '39, '40, '41
Van Schaik, Govert K. '62   LC '60

Wilcox, Benjamin, Jr. '40   L '40
Wilcox, James B. '44   B '43
Wildes, James O. '29   CC '27, '28; T '27, '29
Wile, Darwin C. '63   F '59, '60, '61
Wilkinson, John B. '35   Te '35
Willard, Holland L. '40   L '40
Willetts, Joseph P. '41   H '39, '40, '41; S '38, '40
Williams, Bruce D. '54   C '54
Williams, Harold P., Jr. '39   S '38
Williams, Louis E. '64   L '62, '63; S '61, '62; Sq '62, '63
Williams, Philip M. '57   CC '54; T '55, '56, '57
Williams, Richard L., Jr. '59   T '58, '59
Williams, Roy E. '62   F '61
Williams, Thomas B., Jr. '63   Sk '63
Williams, Webster F., Jr. '35   Fc '34, '35
Wills, Arthur A. III '56   CC '54, '55; T '54, '55, '56
Wills, Richard H., Jr. '38   Bb '38
Wilson, Bennett C. '50   Bb '49
Wilson, Clifford W. '39   F '36, '37, '38
Wilson, James D. '62   Te '61, '62
Wilson, John G. '41   C '39, '40, '41
Wilson, Kenneth G. '56   CC '55; T '55, '56
Wilson, N. Allen, Jr. '51   F '49; T '50, '51
Wilson, Orme, Jr. '42   Te '42
Wilson, Roger K. '61   F '59; T '60, '61; Te '60
Wilson, Walter C, Jr. '44   F '41, '42
Wing, Richard L. '40   CC '39
Winig, Paul I. '62   Fc '62
Winship, Thomas '42   Sk '42
Winslow, Francis E., Jr. '47   C '46; LC '46
Winslow, Walter T., Jr. '65   S '62
Winslow, Warren '40   H '38, '39, '40
Winter, Gibson '38   F '36
Wintersteen, Prescott B. '34   T '34
Winthrop, Adam '61   H '61
Winthrop, Griffith J., Jr. '58   Sw '56, '58

Winthrop, Robert '26   C '24, '25, '26
Wise, Stephen A. '46 ocC   Sw '47
Wise, Timothy J. W. '53   B '51, '52, '53
Wister, William R., Jr. '55   Sq, '53, '54 '55
Witherspoon, John J. '37   L '37
Withington, Frederic B., Jr. '45 ocC   T '47
Withington, Henry R. '35   T '34
Witkin, Richard '39   S '38
Wolcott, Robert S. '36 ocC   C '36, '37
Wolcott, Samuel H., Jr. '33   C '33; F '32; H '33
Wolcott, Samuel H. III '57   C '55, '56, '57
Wolf, Albert E. '51   S '50
Wollan, Dennis E. '63   G '63
Wolle, Charles R. '58   Bb '58
Wood, Benton S '33   Sw '31, '33
Wood, Frank E. '64   Sw '62
Wood, Frank E., Jr. '35   B '35
Wood, Harcourt '49   H '48
Wood, Henry F., Jr. '53   L '53
Wood, James A. E. '37   L '37; S '36
Wood, M. Wistar, Jr. '52   Sq '51, '52
Wood, Peter H. '64   L '62, '63
Wood, R. Norman '54   H '52, '53, '54
Wood, W. Barry, Jr. '32   B '30, '31, '32; F '29, '30, '31; H '30, '31, '32
Wood William B. III '59   Te '58, '59
Wood, W. Godfrey, '63   H '61, '62, '63
Woodard, Charles F. '35   CC '33; T '33, '34, '35
Woodberry, John D. '35   T '35
Woodbury, Mark III '62   Te '60, '61, '62
Woodfield, Anthony W. '61   W '61
Woodruff, Craig D., Jr. '35   B '33, '34, '35
Woods, Thomas S. III '50   Sw '48, '49, '50
Woodward, Harper '31   LC '31
Woodward, Robert D. '37   T '35, '36
Woodworth, Alfred S. '29   H '29
Woodworth, Arthur V., Jr. '33   C '33
Woodworth, Kennard '26   H '26
Woolf, Michael A. '59   Fc '59
Woolston, Richard K. '58   Bb '57, '58

Worthen, Thomas B. '57   H '55
Wright, Thomas W. D. '41   Fc '41
Wright, William H., Jr. '38   T '38
Wulf, Richard '61   W '60
Wykoff, James H. '52   H '51
Wylde, Cecil I. '27   H '27; T '27
Wylde, John '58   H '58
Wylde, John H. '60 ocC   Te '61
Wylie, Warren D. '52   F '50, '51
Wyman, Edward L. '48   T '46
Wynne, Robert '57   F '59; W '60

Yarbro, Alan D. '62   B '60, '61, '62
Yatsevitch, Gratian M. '33   Fc '33
Yazejian, George M. '53   F '52
Yeomans, Edward, Jr. '33   C '32, '33
Yeomans, Frank S. '61   T '59, '60, '61
Yetman, William E. '49   H '47, '48, '49
Yoffe, Franklin M. '55   F '52
Yost, Edward DuR. '52   L '52
Young, Edward L. III '37   T '37
Young, Hamilton '33   F '32
Young, Henry A., Jr. '52   B '52
Young, John H. '65   LC '63
Young, L. Josselyn '23   B '23
Young, Patric J. '63   F '62
Young, William C. B. '55   W '56
Young, William H., Jr. '42   T '41
Youngman, William S. '29   F '28
Yuh, Jai K. '62   Fc '62

Zani, Ralph L. '54   Sw '52, '53, '54
Zarakov, Isadore '27   B '25, '26, '27; F '25, '26; H '25, '26, '27
Zeeb, Robert C. '60   C '58
Zemo, Peter L. III '58   Sw '58
Zentgraf, William L. '62   Sw '60, '61, '62
Zezza, Carlo F., Jr. '57   C '55, '56, '57
Ziel, Harry K. '53   Fc '53
Zissis, Ernest J. '64   F '61, '62
Zuege, Robert H. '55   F '52
Zuromskis, J. Michael '60   C '58

1964–1985

Abate, Joseph Anthony III '83   F '82
Abbot, William Robert '74   L '72
Abbot, Steven Warren '85   F '83, '84
Abott, James Milton '70   W '68, '70
Abbott, Preston Holliday '70   Fc '68, '69
Abecassis, Max '73   S '73
Abelon, Michael Hugh '68 (MGR)   Bb '67, '68
Abely, Kristin Marie '88   FH '84; So '85
Abkowitz, Suzanne Jill '80   Sw '77

Ablow, Gail Nan '84   Sl '81, '82, '83, '84
Abouchar, Susan Elizabeth '81   Bb '78, '79
Abrams, Peter Joseph '70   Sq '68, '69, '70
Abrams, Robert Elihu '65   HC '63, '64, '65
Abrams, Stanton Van '64   G '63, '64
Abramson, David Harold '65   Sw '63, '64, '65
Acacia, Marie '85   TI '82, '83, '84; TO '82, '83, '84
Acheson, Raymond James '82   F '80, '81; L '80

Ackerman, Ashley Dealy '88   Sk '85
Ackerman, Gary Neil '78   Bb '76, '77, '78
Ackermann, Albert John '72   Sw '70, '71
Acorn, David Paul '77   S '74, '75, '76
Acosta, Daniel Griljalva '79   Handball '79
Adair, Fred Lawrence '73   L '73, '74
Adams, Alison Mary '77   S '76
Adams, Caroline Rule '83   Sw '80
Adams, Earl Leonard III '75   Bb '74, '75

Baer, Allan Tucker '64   HC '63

Baer, Bryan Gordon '82   W '79, '80, '81, '82

Baer, David Alan '82   W '79, '80, '81, '82

Bagger, Paula Marie '80   Sw '77, '78

Baggott, Robert Charles '78   F, '76, '77, '78

Bailey, Adam Olney '80   LC '80, '81

Bailey, Ian James '79   TO '79

Bailey, Robert Behrens '77   F '75, '76

Bain, R. Clark '80   Sq '78, '80, '81

Bain, Virginia Roe '84   Sq '83, '85

Baird, Charles Fitz Jr. '75   Te '73, '74, '75

Baird, Stephen Warner '74–'75   Sw '72, '74, '75

Bakalar, Steven David '82   Sq '81

Baker, Ann Fitzpatrick '86   S '82, '83, '84

Baker, Barbara Alison '84   WP '84

Baker, Charles Duane '79   Bb '78

Baker, Frank Calvin '66–'67   F '65, '66

Baker, George Arthur '76   W '73, '74, '76

Baker, Henry Scott '72   LC '70, '71, '72

Baker, James Victor '68   CC '65, '66, '67; TI '65, '66, '67, '68; TO '65, '66, '67, '68

Baker, John Charles '72   HC '71, '72

Baker, Katharine Kinsman '84   S '83

Baker, Robert Denio Jr. '68   LC '67, '68

Baker, Rust; Lyn '84   V '81

Baker, Steven Harold '83   G '81, '82, '83

Baker-Albanese, Elizabeth Anne '85   Fc '84, '85

Bakkensen, John Reser '65   TO '63, '64, '65

Baldauf, Mary Christine '88   Bb '85; So '85

Balko, John Francis Jr. '76   F '75

Ball, Christopher Rusell '79   G '78

Ball, Colin Peter '81   TI '79, '80, '81   TO '79, '80, '81

Ball, Russell Conwell '88   Sq '85

Ball, William Austin '70   Te '69, '70

Ballantyne, Garth Hadden '73   L '71, '72

Ballantyne, John Ainslie '69–'70   F '68, '69

Ballentine, Bruce Davis '78   Sk '75, '76, '77, '78

Ballmer, Steven Anthony '77 (MGR)   F '75, '76

Baloff, Steven Nicholas '77–'78   Ba '77, '78

Baney, Richard Neil Jr. '84   LC '84

Banks, Brian Leonard '77   Bb '75, '76, '78

Bannish, Peter James '78   Ba '76, '77, '78

Bannon, Cynthia Jordan '84   LC '83, '84

Barakett, Timothy Robert '87   H '84, '85

Barber, Peter Kennard '70   L '68, '69

Barber, Robert Cushman '72   L '71, '72

Barbiaux, Lawrence '74   Ba '72, '74

Bargar, Richard Michael '72   Fc '70, '71, '72

Bargar, Robert J. '78   Fc '77

Barker, George Lincoln '73   CC '71

Barker, James Sherman '65 (MGR)   H '63, '64

Barnard, Robert Nichol '69   Fc '67, '68

Barnes, Benjamin Ayer '68   Sk '66, '67

Barnes, David Moore Victor '85   Sw '82, '83

Barnes, Kevin Douglas '76 (MGR)   TI '76; TO '76

Barnett, Randel Gale '73   Te '71, '72, '73

Baron, Bruce Gaynor '65 (MGR)   L '63, '64

Barresi, Gia Elizabeth '87   Bb '84; So '84, '85; FH '84

Barrett, Mary Jeanne '85   CC '81; TI '82, '83; TO '82, '84

Barrett, Robert Gene '66   F '63, '64, '65

Barrett, William Sisson '64   CC '63, '64

Barringer, Paul Anthony '65   F '63, '64

Barrington, Samuel Cheney '83   LC '80, '81, '82

Barron, Eric Adam '85   TO '85

Barry, Edward Thomas Jr. '73   G '71, '72, '73

Barry, Lori Ann '88   S '84

Barry, Michael Edward '75   H '75

Barsness, Zoe Irene '87   Sk '85'

Bartels, Kenneth Gilbert '73   Fc '72, '73

Bartenfelder, Steven Edward '85   L '82, '83

Bartlett, Alfred Victor III '66   LC '65, '66

Bartlett, John Patrick '85   Sw '85

Barton, Frederick Durrit '71   Te '69, '70

Barton, Joseph Edward '64   L '63

Barton, Norma Lynn '83   Sw '80

Barton, Susan Adelaide '82 (MGR)   TI '81, '82; TO '81, '82; CC '80, '81

Baskauskus, Edward Leon '72   TI '70, '71, '72; TO '70, '71, '72

Bassett, Michael Howes '64   F '61, '62, '63; L '62, '63

Bator, Thomas Ewing '83   Sq '81, '83

Batter, Kathryn Ann '80   S '77, '78

Battle, Richard Vernon '72   W '70

Bauer, Bradley Joel '83   Ba '80, '81, '82, '83

Bauer, Dean James '67   Te '65, '66, '67

Bauer, Mark Eugene '74   F '71, '72, '73

Bauer, Robert Theodore Jr. '69   H '67, '68, '69

Baughman, Richard Emery '75   Sw '72, '73, '74, '75

Baum, Carl Alan '69   W '67

Baum, Stefi Alison '80   FH '76, '77, '79; S '78, L '77, '78, '79, '80

Bauman, Andrew Jay '75   Sk '74

Baumgart, Stephen Michael '71   Sw '69, '70

Bausano, M. Barry '85   W '82, '83, '84, '85

Bayley, Richard Brinton '76 (MGR)   Bb '74, '75, '76

Bayliss, Elizabeth Ardys '82   LC '82

Bayliss, George Palmer '82   LC '82

Beach, Murray MacDonald '76   HC '75

Beal, Hannah Freeman '85   S '81

Beal, Raymond Howard '73 (MGR)   LC '72, '73

Beals, Whitney Austin '68   R '66, '67, '68

Bean, Lawrence Francis '86   F '84

Beardsley, Larry Noble '67 (MGR)   H '65, '66

Beasley, Jerry Lynn '66   F '65

Beati, Stephen Anthony '86   W '83

Beatrice, Thomas Eugene '80–'81   F '78, '79, '81

Bechtold, Timothy Matthew '84   W '82

Beck, Cari Lyn '88   S '84

Beck, Scott David '88   W '85

Beckett, Scott Wilkins '72   Fc '70

Beckford, Darlene Francis '83–'84   CC '79, '80, '81; TI '80, '81, '82; TO '80, '81, '82

Beckman, David Leo '85   Te '82, '83, '84, '85

Beckman, Sharon Lynn '80   Sw '77, '78, '80

Bedell, Kevin Bryan '86   LC '85

Behrens, Eric Kindler '70 (MGR)   W '69, '70

Beilenson, John Peter '84   Rb '84

Beizer, Richard Lawrence '64   F '61, '62, '63

Beling, Craig Thomas '79   L '76; W '77, '78; F '76, '77, '78, '79

Bell, Alison Jane '79   H '79

Bell, David Scott '77   H '75, '76

Bell, David Sheffield '67   TO '65; TI '65

Bell, George deBenneville Jr. '80   Sq '77, '79, '80

Bell, Russell Alexander '72   S '69, '71

Beller, Frederic Roy '84   W '81, '82, '84

Beller, Robert '68   Bb '66, '67, '68

Belmont, Howard Michael '76   L '74, '75, '76

Belshe, Sharon Kimberly '82   Bb '79, '80

Bemis, John Gordon '68   H '68

Benca, Ruth Myra '75 (MGR)   Sw '74, 75

Bender, Robert Jacob '73   L '71, '72

Bengel, Richard James '79   Bb '77, '78

Benjamin, David A. '66   Sq '65; Te '63, '64, '65

Benjamin, Kevin Anderson '73   TI '71, '72; TO '71, '72

Benka, Richard William '69   TI '67, '68, '69; TO '67, '68, '69

Bennet, John Daniel '75   F '75

Bennett, Amanda Patricia '75 (MGR)   W '74

Bennett, Daniel John '85   F '83, '84

Bennett, Mark Robert '82 (MGR)   F '80, '81

Bennett, Patrick Mulvey '85   LC '84, '85

Bennett, Philippe '76   Fc '73, '74, '75, '76

Bennett, William Craig '67   Ba '67

Bennett, William Lauriston '71   L '69, '70, '71

Benning, Mark Kenneth '86   H '85

Benninger, Michael Steven '77   F '74, '75, '76

Bennion, Lynn Jacobsen '63–'66   Bb '65, '66

Benson, Donald Owen '88   WP '84

Benson, Richard Duane '81   H '78, '79, '80, '81

Benton, Anne Frances '81   HC '78, '79, '80, '81

Benton, Lauren Ann '78   L '76, '77

Berdik, Richard Frederick '66   F '64, '65

Beren, Adam Ephraim '83   Te '80, '81, '82, '83

Berg, Donald Lavern '75   TI '72, '74, '75; TO '72

Berg, Peter Calvin '68   F '67

Bergen, Charles Samuel '77   Bb '77

Berger, David Lawrence '86   LC '85

Berger, Michael Stuart '74–'75   F '71, '72, '73

Berger, Paul Steven '68   Sl '68

Berggren, Kirsten '88   Sk '85

Bergman, Stephen Joseph '66   G '65

Bergmann, Michael Roger '87   L '84, '85

Bergstrom, Brian Daniel '85   G '84; F '82, '83, '84

Berizzi, Steven Stanford '73 (MGR)   Sw '72, '73

Berkman, Richard Alan '83   S '80, '81

Berkoff, David Charles '88   Sw '85

Berkowitz, Ethan Avram '83   Sl '81, '82, '83

Berle, Adolf Augustus '85   TO '84, '85

Bermingham, Yamilee Odile '86   TI '85; TO '85

Bernard, David Mark '86   Bb '83

Berne, Richard Smith '70   F '68, '69

Bernhard, Peter Charles '71   Ba '69, '70, '71

Bernieri, Louis Michael '77   F '75, '76

Bernson, Henry Blair '69   TO '67, '68, '69

Bernstein, David Paul '69   TI '68; TO '69

Bernstein, Lisa Beth '81   Bb '79; SO '81

Bernstein, Ronald Mark '73   Fc '71

Berry, Pamela Jean '80   HC '77; S '77

Bersin, Alan Douglas '68   F '66, '67

Bertagna, Joseph Dennis '73   H '71, '72, '73

Berthold, Megan '84   H '81, '82, '83, '84

Bertoli, Pamela St. John '85   Sk '83, '84

Bertozzi, Edward Joseph '64 (MGR)   Bb '63, '64

Beske, Kirsten A. '87   Te '84, '85

Beslity, James Mark '75   L '73

Better, Steven Jay '82   H '82

Beuche, James Richard '69 (MGR)   G '69

Beusman, Thomas Jeffrey '76   Sk '73

Bianucci, John Steven '82   F '81

Bickley, Ian Martin '86   G '83, '84, '85

Biddle, Robert Whelen '82   LC '82

Biddle, Stephen Duane '81   Fc '79, '80, '81

Biello, Carl David '75   W '72, '73, '74, '75

Biemann, Betsy '86   HC '83

Bienstock, Anthony Revell '85   W '83

Bierer, Michael Frederick '79   Fc '77, '79, '80

Bigelow, Eve Marie '85   Sk '83, '84

Bihrle, William III '73   TI '71, '72; TO '71, '73

Bilodeau, Thomas Herbert '65   Ba '63, '64, '65; F '62, '63, '64, '65

Bilodeau, Timothy William '72   Ba '71, '72; F '72

Bindelglass, David Fred '81   F '80

Bingham, Clara York '85   Sk '82, '83, '84

Bingham, Mark Leonard '80   Ba '77, '78, '79, '80

Binney, Geoffrey Gage Jr. '87   LC '85

Binning, Daniel Paul '79   F '77, '78

Birch, Alan Jeffrey '68   Sw '67, '68

Bird, William George '88   Sw '85

Birnbaum, Julian R. '70 (MGR)   F '68

Bixby, David Michael '76   HC '74, '75, '76

Bixby, Thomas David '78   W '75, '76, '77, '78

Black, Gordon McKellar '68   Sq '66, '67

Black, Lisa Mincha '85   L '82, '83, '84, '85

Black, Steven Hodgkinson '84   L '81

Black, Thomas Everett '66   CC '63; TI '64, '66

Black, Timothy Seymour '75   Sl '73, '74, '75

Black, Tracy Elizabeth '86   Sw '83, '84

Blades, Edmond William '78 (MGR)   TI '77; TO '77, '78

Blair, Grant Alexander '86   H '83, '84, '85

Blair, Peter Heyliger Jr. '74   HC '73, '74

Blair, Sally L. '76   Sq '75, '76

Blair, William MacLean '78   TO '76, '77

Blais, Joline Jeannine '82   LC '80, '81, '82

Blake, Robert Orris Jr. '79   Sq '77, '80

Blakinger, Dan Allan '74   W '72, '73, '74

Blasier, Peter Cole '75   Sq '73, '74, '75

Bleakie, John Maxwell Jr. '71 (MGR)   H '70, '71

Block, Huntington MacDonald '75–'76   TI '76; TO '75, '76

Blodget, Dudley French '67   S '65, '66; Te '65, '66

Blodgett, Joanne Washington '87   TO '84

Blodgett, Stephen Sargent '67   Sk '65, '66, '67

Blood, William Marshall '80   Ba '77, '78, '79, '80; S '77, '78, '79

Bloom, Paul '70   L '68, '70

Blount, Karen Marcella '81   TI '81; TO '80, '81

Bluestone, Hanya Harris '88   Bb '85; So '85

Blum, Lauren, '81   HC '81

Blye, Kenneth Bruce '84   S '80, '81, '82

Boak, Jeremy Laurence '74   LC '73, '74

Boepple, Paul A. '75   L '75

Boeschenstein, William Wade Jr. '77   L '75

Bogden, Philip Stuart '82   LC '80, '82

Boghossian, David Mark '78   HC '77, '78

Bogovich, Peter Mario '71   S '68, '69, '70

Bohlen, Charles Eustis Jr. '69   HC '68

Bohn, Roger Eric '75   LC '73

Boit, Christopher Sprague '78   HC '78

Bojanowski, Alice Mary '81   Sk '78

Boland, James Peter Jr. '77   F '76

Boland, Mary Elizabeth '85–'86   HC '85

Bolduc, Daniel George '76   H '74, '75

Bollinger, Jan Anders '66   L '63, '64, '65

Bolster, Marshall Grant Jr. '68   LC '65, '66, '67, '68

Bolton, Charles Payne '64 (MGR)   F '62, '63

Bond, Gary Paul '73   F '72

Bone, Jeffrey Weston '74   F '72, '73

Booker, Carl Edward '76   L '74

Booker, Cyrus Lucius '78   Bb '76, '78

Booker, Lewis Thomas Jr. '80   LC '80

Boone, Louise Lawrence '87 (MGR)   L '84, '85

Booth, Ralph Harman '76   S '73, '74, '75

Borden, Diana Kimball '78   Sw '75, '78

Bordley, William Edward '79   W '76, '77, '78

Borgmann, Andrea Jo '85   HC '83

Bornheimer, Allen Millard '65   Bb '63, '64, '65

Boslego, Robert Philip '75   Sw '73

Bosnic, Gary Michael '79   F '76, '77, '78

Boss, Robin Lisle '87   Te '84, '85

Boteler, Diane Louise '82   So '81, '82

Bott, Julian Mark '84   Sw '81, '82, '83, '84

Bott, Victoria Ann '79   Sw '76

Bottomley, Kevin Taylor '74   Te '72

Boudreau, Jacqueline Marie '86   TI '83, '85; TO 83, '84, '85

Bougas, Tina Maria '83   Te '80, '81, '82

Bouley, Laurent Henry '83   F '82

Boulris, Jacqueline Marie '86   TI '85; TO '85

Boulris, Mark Johnson '84   F '83

Bourgois, Nicole A. '76   Sk '75, '76

Bourgois, Phillipe Irwin '78   Sk 75

Boutilier, Nancy W. '83   Bb '80, 81, '83, '84; LC '84; HC '84; So '81; L '80

Bowditch, Nathaniel Hale '66   S '63, '64, '65

Bowen, Joseph D. '84   TO '81, '82, '83, '84

Bowens, Monte Alan '74   F '71, '72

Bowers, John Thomas '72   Sl '70, '71, '72

Bowes, Warren Winslow '67   S '66

Bowie, Jonathan Munford '73   LC '73

Bowles, Daniel Lee '81   Ba '80, '81; F '80

Bowyer, Matthew Gordon '79   S '75, '76, '77

Boyan, Craig Lawrence '85   HC '85

Boyd, Douglas Phillips '86   TI '83, '84, '85; TO '83, '84, '85

Boyda, Kenneth Leo '66   F '63, '64 (CAPT), '65

Boyer, Alan Barry '75   TO '74

Boyer, Landya Marie '84   So '81, '82, '83, '84

Boyle, Edward Anthony '87   TO '85

Boyle, John Lennox '71   Sk '70, '71

Boyle, Kevin, '85   Bb '82, '83, '84

Boyum, David Anders '85   Sq '82, '83, '84 '85

Boyum, Ingrid Anne '87   Sq '84, '85

Bozek, Matthew Joseph '72   Bb '70

Bracewell, Joseph Searcy III '69   LC '68, '69

Brack, Glenn Douglas '85   S '83, '84

Bradlee, Robert Gardner '79   Sk '78, '79

Bradshaw, Charles Robbins '73   LC '71, '72, '73

Bradshaw, William Henry '78   Ba '78

Bradt, George Benet '80   Sl '78, '79, '80

Brady, Patrick Dennis, '78   F '75, '77

Bragg, John Kendal Jr. '69   Sw '67, '68, '69

Brams, David Mendel '83   LC '83

Brandeberry, Mike Emmett '72 (MGR)   LC '71, '72

Brandling-Bennett, Anthony David '64   Sw '62, '63 (CAPT)

Branowitzer, Sandra Eileen '77 (MGR)   LC '75

Braun, William Howard '68   LC '67, '68

Brayton, Roswell, Jr. '73   Ba '71, '72, '73

Brea, Cesar Augusto '85   Sl '83, '84, '85

Breeze, James Bert '69   S '67

Brennan, Paul Joseph '67 (MGR)   LC '66, '67

Brewster, Galen '65   LC '63, '64, '65

Bridgeland, John Marshall '82   Te '79

Bridich, Richard John '73   Ba '72, '73; F '72, '73

Briggs, Peter Sheffield '73   Sq '71, '72, '73; Te '73

Briggs, Richard Stuart '65   TO '63, '64

Bright, Cameron Stark '83   Fc '82, '83

Brissette, Mary Elizabeth '83 (MGR)   S '82; L '82, '83

Britz, Gregory Joseph '83   H '80, '81, '82, '83

Broad, Richard Michael '75 (MGR)   LC '73, '74, '75

Brock, John Meigs '77   HC '75, '76, '77

Brock, William Justus '71   S '68, '69, '70; Te '69, '70, '71

Brockett, Francesca Lane '82 (MGR)   F '81

Brockmeyer, Douglas Lee '82–'83   HC '83

Broderick, James Baldridge '76   R '76

Brody, Edward Aaron '83   Fc '81, '82

Brog, Spencer Marland '84   Sq '81, '82, '83, '84

Brokaw, Jeffrey Johnson '73–'74   CC '71, '74; TO '71

Brommer, Lois Elaine '86   CC '82, '83; TI '83; TO '84

Brooks, Arthur Oakley Jr. '67   H '67

Brooks, Benjamin Rix '65   W '63, '64, '65

Brooks, Bruce Morgan '80   TI '78, '80; TO '77, '79, '80

Brooks, Geoffrey Robinson '78   LC '76, '77

Brooks, Peter Campbell '66   Sq '63, '64, '65

Brooks, Robert Thomas '68   F '66, '67; TO '65

Brooks, Roger Angus '71   HC '71

Brooks, Stephen Harrington '70   HC '68, '69, '70

Brooks, Tony Dean '72   LC '70, '71, '72

Brooks, William Blair '75   HC '74, '75

Brottman, Andrea Jill '82   So '81

Brown, Anna Maria '84 (MGR)   S '80

Brown, Duncan Leo '74 (MGR)   S '72, '73

Brown, Gregory Thomas '83   Ba '81, '82, '83; F '80, '81, '82

Brown, James Talmadge '73   Bb '71, '72, '73

Brown, Jeffrey David '79   LC '78, '79

Brown, Laura Jennings '79   Sl '77, '78, '79

Brown, Lawrence Leonard '79   Ba '76, 77, '78, '79; F '77, '78

Brown, Michael Gaetan '80   F '78, '79

Brown, Patricia Jean '87   Bb '84, '85; So '84, '85

Brown, Paul Brooks '72   Sq '70

Brown, Robert Stephen Jr. '85   Sl '85

Brown, Ronald Dwayn '83–'84   L '82, '84

Brown, Steven Anthony '77   TI '76, '77; TO '74, '75, '77

Browne, Charles Billings '71 (MGR)   Sk '70

Brownlee, David Bruce '73   Sl '72, '73

Brownsberger, William Nordyke '78   CC '76

Broyer, Bert Kenneth '73   F '72

Bruce, John Stuart '79   Sw '76

Bruckmann, Bruce Cameron '76   L '74, '75, '76

Bruener, R. Joseph '82   HC '82

Brumwell, David Kendall '75   Sw '72, '73, '74, '75

Brush, Thomas Hamilton '78   Sl '78

Bryan, Anne Virginia '79   TI '78, '79; TO '78, '79

Bryan, Benjamin Fiery '75   S '73, '74

Bryan, Kerry Lamb '81   S '79, '80; L '80, '81; TI '80

Bryan, Virginia Anne '79   L '76

Brynteson, Juliette Drought '80   S '77, '78, '79; L '78, '79, '80

Bryson, Thomas Layton '70   Sw '68

Buchanan, James Galloway III '65   G '65

Buchanan, Michael Clifford '82   F '79, '80, '81

Buckley, Brian Joseph '80–'81   F '77, '80

Buckley, Randy John Gordon '75   TI '74; TO '73

Bucknell, Sarah Harlan '77   FH '76

Bui, Clara LeLam '85   LC '84, '85

Bulard, David Virgil '78 (MGR)   S '75

Bull, Nicholas '67   L '65, '66

Bullard, Lyman Greenleaf Jr. '77   S '75, '76, '77; H '77

Bulloch, Steven Nolen '68   Sw '65, '66

Bunney, Edward Bradshaw '84   TI '81, '82, '83, '84; TO '81, '82, '83, '84

Bunis, Alvin Woodrow Jr. '79   Te '77

Buntic, Rudolf Fabian '86   TI '83, '84; TO '83

Burbank, Stephen Bradner '67 (MGR)   Sq '66, '67

Burke, Arthur Edmund '74   G '73, '74

Burke, Charles Joseph '77　H '77

Burke, David Michael Jr. '82–'83　H '79, '80, '81, '83

Burke, George William III '74　LC '73

Burke, John Vincent '82　H '79

Burke, Kevin Frances '76　H '74, '75, '76

Burke, Kevin Michael '66　H '65

Burlage, David Allen '75　F '75

Burnaman, Phillip Ross '81　W '80

Burnes, Andrew Phillip '72　H '71, '72

Burnes, Daniel Carney '68　H '68

Burnes, Gordon MacGregor '88　Sl '85

Burnes, Kennett Farrar '65　H '63, '64, '65

Burnett, Howard David '72　LC '70, '71

Burnett, Howard David '72　LC '70, '71, '72

Burnham, Petrina Marie '85　FH '82, '83, '84; L '84, '85

Burns, Christine Alvina '88　H '85

Burns, Christopher Jon '68　F '66, '67, '68

Burns, Lindsay Harriet '87　LC '85

Burns, Robert Allan '83　H '80, '81

Burns, William Wesley III '68　CC '66; TI '65, '66, '67, '68; TO '66, '67, '68;

Burr, Robert Steven '81　L '79, '80, '81

Burris, John Edward '71　Sw '69, '70, '71

Burrus, Lisa Celeste '79　TI '77; TO '77, '78, '79

Burwell, Langdon Gates '66　CC '63

Busby, Kathryn Ann '84　TI '82, '83, '84; TO '81, '82, '83, '84

Busch, Peter Alan '64　Fc '63, '64

Busconi, Brian David '85　H '82, '83, '84, '85

Buster, Robert Anthony '68　Sw '65, '66

Butler, Katherine Mary '82　HC '80, '81, '82

Butler, Lawrence Michael '64　Fc '63, '64

Butler, Samuel Coles Jr. '76　TI '73, '74, '75, '76; TO '73, '74, '75, '76

Buttenwieser, Carol Helen '81　LC '81; H '80, '81

Butterworth, Scott Christopher '73　F '72

Button, Adam Gilmour '85　WP '82, '83, '84

Byrd, Leverett Saltonstall '74　H '72, '73, '74

Byrd, Shannon Lyn '86　Sw '83, '84, '85

Byrne, Denis Patrick '65　H '65; L '65

Cabot, Edmund Billings '65　Sk '63, '65

Cadenhead, Bruce Anthony '86　V '85

Cahalan, Michael Kermit '71　Sw '69, '70, '71

Cahill, William Aloysius '73 (MGR)　HC '73, '74

Cahners, Andrew Philip '67　TI '65, '66; TO '65, '66, '67

Cahoon, Edward Charles '80　Sw '78, '79, '80

Cain, James Edward '72　W '70, '71, '72

Cain, Martin Harrison '68　L '66, '67, '68

Calder, William Musgrave '83　LC '82, '83

Calderwood, Daniel Beaven '66　F '64, '65; L '64, '65, '66

Caligor, Eve '78　Sq '76, '77

Caligor, Eve '78　Sq '76, '77

Call, Newel Branson '70　Bb '70

Callahan, Thomas Robert '69　TO '67

Callinan, James Laurence '82　F '79, '80, '81

Calvert, Shelby Lynn '83　Sw '82, '83

Cameron, Matthew Fitzpatrick '85　S '83, '84

Cammett, John William '84　Rb '84; F '83

Camp, John McKesson II '68　S '67

Campbell, Andrew Morton '74　CC '73, '74; TI '74, '76

Campbell, Frederick Bonsal '73　L '71

Campbell, Fritz '83　W '80, '81, '82, '83

Campbell, Jeffrey Scott '77　CC '73, '75, '76; TI '74, '75, '76, '77; TO '74, '75, '76, '77

Campbell, Rebecca Ellen '84　Sl '82, '84

Campbell, Walter Joe '67　TO '65, '66, '67

Campen, James Temple '65　G '63, '64, '65

Campisano, Mark Stephen '75 (MGR)　F '73

Canaday, John Harwood '74　HC '72, '73, '74

Canales, Francisco Luis '78　Sw '75, '76, '77, '78

Cancian, Mark Franklin '73 (MGR)　R '71, '72, '73

Canning, Curtis Ray '68　HC '66, '67, '68

Cantor, Michael Cary '77　Bb '76

Caplan, Lincoln Walter '72　L '70, '71, '72

Caprio, Frank Thomas '88　Ba '85

Caputo, Bruce Faulker '65　L '63, '64, '65

Carbone, James Joseph '83　Sw '80, '81, '82, '83

Carden, Guy '66　Sl '65, '66

Carey, Daniel Hugh '88　Sk '85

Carey, Richard Adams '73　L '71, '72, '73

Carey, Robert Matthew '77–'78　S '76

Carey, Timothy Babcock '80　Bb '78

Carey, William Rae '76　Bb '74, 75, '76

Carfagna, Peter Alphonso '75　F '74

Carle, Wendy Catherine '80　Bb '77, '78, '79, '80; S '79; TI '77; TO '79

Carley, Natalie '84–'85　F '85

Carney, Karen Elizabeth '88　H '85

Carney, Susan Mary '83　S '79; So '82, '83

Caron, Roger Eugene '84　F '83, '84, '85

Carone, Nicholas Edmund '88　H '85

Carpentier, Judith Anne '81　Sw '78

Carr, Kevin Michael '76　Ba '76; H '74, '75, '76

Carr, Robert Harkin Jr. '68　H '66, '67, '68

Carr, Stephen Emery '74　HC '72, '73, '74

Carrabino, Joseph Dominic Jr. '84–'85　Bb '81, '82, '84, '85

Carreon, Patrick Anthony '81　F '79, '80

Carrico, Matthew John '80　LC '79, '80

Carrillo, Alicia Louise '85　S '81, '82, '83, '84; L '82

Carrillo, Elizabeth Jane '84　S '80

Carrion, Wesley Vanwye '83　W '80, '81

Carroll, Deborah Jean '82　Sl '81, '82

Carroll, Kathleen Louise '84　H '82, '83, '84

Carroll, Leslie Seton, 85　FH '81, '82, '83, '84

Carter, Graham Murray '81　H '79, '80

Carter, Lawrence Adams '70　Sk '68, '69, '70

Carter, Peter Hobart '69　Sk '67, 68, 69

Carthy, Ray Derek '87　Fc '84, '85

Carty, Arthur Gerard '69 (MGR)　F '67, '68

Cary, Trumbull '74　LC '72, '73, '74

Cashin, Richard Marshall '75　HC '73, '74, '75; Sq '73, '74, '75

Casey, Edward John '80　F '80

Cash, Harold Cochise '82　F '80, '81, '82

Cass, Leo Maxwell '65　LC '63, '64, '65

Cass, Penny Lynn '84　WP '84

Cassis, John Langstroth '70　F '69, '70

Castaneda, Marina '78　Sq '77

Castellano, Thomas John '73 (MGR)　F '72

Castillo, Alida Josefina '83　TI '81; TO '80

Castle, Gilbert Howard III '72　Fc '70

Casto, JohnFrederick '80　F '78, '79

Castro, Antonion DaSilva '80　S '77, '78, '79

Cathcart, Dolita Dannet '81　So '81

Catinella, Paul Elbridge '70　W '68, '69, '70

Catliff, John Terence '86　S '83, '84

Cavanagh, David Joseph '72　H '70, '71, '72

Cavanagh, Richard Edward '84　H '84

Cavanaugh, Joseph Vincent Jr. '71　H '69, '70, '71; Te '70, '71

Cavanaugh, William Condon '84　Rb '84

Cavin, Thomas Jeffrey '76　Sk '73, '74, '75, '76

Ceko, Peter '84　F '82, '83

Cetrulo, Lawrence Gerald '71　Fc '69, '70, '71

Chace, James Fletcher Jr. '66　W '63, '64, '65

Chadsey, William Lloyd II '64   SW '62, '63

Chafee, John Hubbard '79   TI '76, '77, '78, '79; TO '77, '78, '79; CC '78

Chafee, Jonathan Knowlton '66   Sk '64, '65; CC '64, '65

Chaffee, George Keen Jr. '64   Sk '63, '64

Chaffee, Orison Young III '83   HC '83

Chaffin, Ellen Marcia '82   LC '80, '82

Chaikovsky, Andrew Leo '79   Te '76, '77, '78, '79

Chalfie, Martin Lee '69   Sw '67, '68, '69

Chalmers, Gregory Rolland '85   H '82, '83, '85

Champi, Frank Kenneth '70   F '69; TO '67, '68, '69, '70

Chandler, Douglas Newell '69 (MGR)   F '68

Chandler, Elizabeth Anne '88   Bb '85

Chang, Lisa Frances '80   L '77

Chang, Mark Wan Soo '83   V '83

Chao, David Jee-Wei '86   WP '82

Chapman, Kirk Emery '85   Rb '84

Chapman, William Howard '77–'78   LC '77, '78

Chappell, Theodore Clifford '83   Sw '80, '81, '82, '83

Chapus, Jean-Marc '81   TI '80, '81; TO '78, '79, '80, '81

Chase, Jonathan David '77   G '77

Chase, Michael Christopher '84   F '82, '83

Chase, Philip Seton '68   Sw '65, '66

Chase, Robin '77   HC '76

Chatterton, Howard Treat '69   W '67, '68, '69

Cheek, Douglas S. F. '65   HC '63, '64

Cheever, Roger Pierce '67   LC '65, '67

Chenevey, James Paul '87   Ba '84, '85

Cheng, Margaret Susan '83   FH '80; V '81, '82

Cheng, Sheilah '83   Sq '83

Chernin, Niki '85   LC '84

Cherry, William Edward '70   Ba '69

Chessin, Paul Norman '75   LC '75

Chetin, Timur Claude '73   Sw '71

Chew, Robert David '72 (MGR)   Fc '70, '71, '72

Chiappa, Keith Henry '66   CC '64; S '63, '64, '65; TI '63; TO '63, '64, '65

Chiarelli, Peter Eugene '87   H '84, '85

Chicarello, Paul Andrew '82   Ba '80, '81, '82

Chien, May Elizabeth '81   Sk '79

Child, Margaret Harrison '78   L '76

Childs, John Norris III '67   S '65

Ching, Dora Chung Yee '85   FH '83

Chiofaro, Donald Joseph '68   F '65, '66, '67

Chipman, John Miguel '78   FC '76, '77, '78

Choquette, Thomas Albert '67   F '65, '66; TO '65

Christensen, Loretta Lynn '80   Bb '77, '78; S '78, '79

Chu, Leeland Jerome '71   HC '71

Chubb, Lucy Alsop '86   L '84

Chubb, Sarah Caldecot '82   S '81; FH '78, '79

Chvany, Peter Andre '85   Fc '83

Cibotti, Nancy '88   Bb '85

Cicchetti, Giancarlo '86   Fc '83, '84, '85

Cicchetti, Maria Giulia '85–'86   Fc '85

Ciepiela, Marie Carolyn '87   Sw '84, '85

Cimmarrusti, Anthony Blaine '81   W '78, '79, '80, '81; F '78, '79

Ciota, Frank Richard '86   F '83, '84

Cirillo, Vicki Ann '84   Sw '82, '83, '84

Clabby, Martha Louise '82   CC '80; TI '80, '81; TO '79, '80, '81

Claflin, William Henry IV '65   LC '63, '64, '65

Clapacs, Brent Daniel '85   F '83, '84

Clapp, Cynthia Grace '84   Bb '83

Clapp, David Payne '64   S '61, '62, '63

Clapp, Wayne George '72   Bb '70

Claps, William Robert '85   W '82

Clareman, Lloyd Samuel '73   Sq '73

Clark, David Pape '87   Te '84, '85

Clark, Dennis Paige '68   H '66, '67

Clark, Geoffrey Burton '78 (MGR)   Te '77, '78

Clark, Harold Robert '76   Sl '75, '76

Clark, Jane Rogers '77   LC '76, '77

Clark, Janet Frances '77   Te '77

Clark, Jeffrey '88   W '85

Clark, John James Jr. '81   F '79, '80

Clark, Luther Theopolis '71 (MGR)   F '69; L '69, '70

Clark, Michael Thomas '79   TO '76; F '76, '77, '78

Clark, Molly Helen '88   Sw '85

Clark, Robert Lee '66   H '63; '64, '65

Clark, Robert Lee Jr. '86   L '83, '85

Clark, Thomas Spencer '82   F '80, '81

Clarke, John Kennedy '75   F '73, '74; TI '72

Clarke, Terry Bradley '79   Te '77, '78

Clarke, Thomas Patrick '82   Bb '79, '80, '81, '82

Clasby, Michael Patrick '79   H '79

Clayton, Robert Lloyd '73   TI '71, '72, '73; TO '71, '72, '73

Cleary, William John '85   H '84

Clemow, Brian '66   HC '63, '64, '65

Clemson, Gordon Scott '77   L '75

Clendenning, Joy Marie '88   Sk '85

Clermont, Kimberly Jean '79   TI '77, '78, '79; TO '77, '78, '79

Cleveland, William Edward '87   Sw '84, '85

Clifford, Timothy Joseph '79   Ba '76, '77, '78, '79

Clifton, Alicia Gorham '86   FH '83, '84; L '83, '84

Clifton, Theodore Eccleston III '85   Sl '84, '85

Cline, Marsha C. '78   LC '75

Coatsworth, David Scott '82   Bb '79; V '81

Cobb, Julianne '80   HC '77

Cobb, Roy Calhoun Jr. '65   CC '64

Cobb, William Stafford '68   Ba '67, '68; F '65, '66, '67; TI '68

Coburn, Broughton Alexander '73   Sk '71, '72

Coburn, Lawrence Stockton '65   S '62, '63, '64

Cocalis, Mark William '80   W '79, '80

Cocalis, Reid Alexander '78   F '75, '76, '77

Cochran, Susan Evarts '73 (MGR)   Sk '71

Cochrane, John Gregory '79   H '77, '78, '79

Code, Kenneth Stuart '84   H '81, '82, '83, '84

Codel, Alisa Hermine '88   Sw '85

Cody, David Marshall '81   F '79, '80

Coffey, Timothy Anthony '84   CC '83; TO '84

Coffin, Barbara Ellen '81   H '79, '80

Coffman, Linda Jean '76   LC '76

Coglin, Michael John '81   Sw '78, '79, '80, '81

Cohen, Sheila Beth '85 (MGR)   S '82, '83, '84

Coit, Craig Irwin '73   L '71

Colbourne, Edward Jack '88   Sq '85

Colburn, Keith Whiting '70   CC '68, '69; TI '68, '69, '70; TO '67, '69, '70

Colburn, Oliver Call '84   LC '84

Cole, John Arthur '75 (MGR)   R '72, '73, '74, '75

Coleman, James Earl '70   TI '68, '69, '70; TO '68, '69, '70

Coleman, Patrick Raymond '71   W '69, '70, '71

Coleman, Robert Michael '66   H '65

Coleman, William Caldwell III '66   G '65, '66

Colker, Ruth '78   HC '76, '77, '78

Collar, Keith Jeffrey '86   Te '85

Collatos, William Peter '76   F '73, '74, '75

Collins, Anna Rose '86   Bb '83, '84, '85; V '82

Collins, Michael Hmer '71   Bb '69

Collins, Morris Hollowell '74   F '73

Collins, Philip '71   Ba '70, '71

Collins, Scott Charles '87   F '84

Colombo, Armond Celeste '84   F '83

Combs, Frank Marion Gifford '80 (MGR)
F '77, '78, '79

Colony, George Forrester '77   Sq '77

Colony, John Joslin III '67   L '67

Cominsky, Michael David '80   LC '78, '79,
'80

Compton, Richard Carlton '72   Sk '70, '71,
'72

Conant, Howard Rosset '73   Te '71

Conant, Jon Frederick '79   H '79

Condry, Ian Richard '87   Sw '84, '85

Confer, Gary Bruce '80   F '77

Congdon, Gordon Hall '77–'78   Bb '76

Conley, Brian James '66   W '63, '64

Conley, Jonathan C '75   S '75

Connell, Christian Lee '85   W '83

Connolly, James Gerard '82   F '81

Connolly, Mark Collins '73   CC '70; TI '72

Connolly, Melissa Lynn '81   Bb '79

Connolly, William Dwyer '87   L '84, '85

Connors, David Michael '83–'84   H '80,
'81, '83, '84

Connors, Paul Francis '81   F '78, '79, '80

Considine, Terence Michael '69   LC '67,
'68

Constantikes, Patricia Sophia '85   FH '81,
'82, '83, '84

Constantine, Sandra '79   LC '76

Conway, James Francis '75   H '75

Conway, Patrick Anthony '67–'68   F '64,
'67

Coogan, Philip Gerlach '84   S '82, '83

Cook, Bryan Walter '78   H '76, '77, '78

Cook, Joseph Edward Jr. '68   F '66

Cook, Michael Joseph '70   Sk '68

Cook, Michael Lewis '74   Sw '73

Cook, Robert Edward '68   TI '66, '67; TO
'66, '68

Cooke, Brian William '85   F '83, '84

Cooley, Beth Ellen '84   TI '81

Cooley, Jeffrey Whitman '79   LC '77, '78,
'79

Cooley, Mark Andrew '82   W '79, '80, '81,
'82

Coolidge, Charles Allerton III '77–'78   Sl
'78

Coolidge, R. Scott '78   F '76, '77

Cooper, Arthur '71   HC '71

Cooper, Ellen Alice '75 (MGR)   G '75

Cooper, Lawton Shaw '78   F '77

Cooper, Leslie Karen '86   CC '82, '83, '84

Cooper, Malcolm '79   Sw '76, '77, '78, '79

Cooper, Nancy Achbar '78   Fc '77, '78

Cooper, Raphael Mason '79   W '79

Coplan, Robert Brooke '74   L '72, '73

Coppinger, Peter Michael '82   F '79, '80,
'81

Corbat, Michael Louis '83   F '80, '81, '82

Corcoran, James J. '78   W '75, '76, '77,
'78

Corcoran, Thomas Patrick '86   L '83, '84,
'85

Cordeiro, Carlos Antonio '78 (MGR)   HC
'78; LC '76, '77, '78

Cordeiro, Peter Gabriel '79   LC '77, '78,
'79

Cordova, Frederick Benedict III '79   F '77,
'78

Corey, David Reid '85   HC '85

Coric, Marko '81   F '78

Corkery, William John '73   H '71, '72, '73

Corman, Julie '80   FH '76, '77, '79

Cornman, Julie '80   L '77, '78, '79, '80

Corrado, Richard Francis '82   W '79, '80

Correia, Joaquim Jose Caldas '82   S '80, '81

Corrigan, Jacqueline Anne '83   Sq '80, '81,
'82, '83

Corris, Robert Bennett '67   Sw '65, '66,
'67

Corry, Charles Rober '83   S'82

Corwin, Howard James '73   TO '71, '72,
'73

Cosentino, John Arthur Jr. '71   L '69, '70,
'71

Cosentino, Paul Batchelder '75 (MGR)   H
'74

Cosgrove, John Morgan '79   F '77, '78

Costa, Jonathan Leeds '64 (MGR)   Sw '63,
'64

Costello, Alexander Steven '75   F '73, '74;
H '75; L '73, '74, '75

Costin, Maura Patrice '80 (MGR)   S '77,
'79; L '78, '79, '80; Sw '77, '78, '79

Cote, William Bertrand '78   Ba '76

Countryman, John Edgar '72   W '70

Countryman, Lawrence Richard '83   Sw
'80, '81, '82, '83

Covello, Nancy Jean '87 (MGR)   Sw '84,
'85

Covino, Christina Louise '85 (MGR)   TI
'82, '83, '84, '85; TO '82, '83, '84, '85;
CC '82, '83, '84, '85

Cowen, Robert Bradford '66   H '65, '66

Cox, Arthur Joseph '73 (MGR)   Bb '71, '72

Cox, Cecil C. III '86   Ba '84

Cox, James Edward '68   Ba '68

Cox, Hannah '83   TI '80; TO '80

Cox, Katherine Eddy '86   LC '83, '85; S '82

Cox, Katherine Mary '82   HC '82, '83

Cox, Roosevelt McKinley '78   Bb '78

Coy, Stephen Lawrence '68   Sw '65, '66

Coyne, Patrick Paul '85   F '84

Craig, Elizabeth Jane '80   Bb '77; Te '77

Craig, John Morgan '76–'77   Sw '73, '74,
'76, '77

Craig, Nona Marie '82   Fc '82

Crain, William Christopher '65   CC '62,
'63, '64; TI '63; TO '63

Cramer, John Francis '70   F '68, '69

Crane, Daniel Christopher '72 (MGR)   H
'71, '72

Crane, Hugh Michael '69   LC '69

Craven, William Moten '73   F '70, '71, '72

Crawford, David Mackay '72   F '71; L '70,
'71, '72

Creedon, Roy Phillip '67   Ba '67

Crim, Guthery Doyle '70   F '68, '69

Crim, Paul Douglas '73   F '72

Crnkovich, Paul Richard '82 (MGR)   LC
'81, '82

Croasdale, Olney Rowland '65   TI '63; TO
'63, '64, '65

Crocker, John Franklin IV '68   HC '65, '66

Crocker, John III '77   LC '76, '77

Crocker, Lauren Margaret '85   HC '85

Crockett, Courtney Caren '88   Te '85

Crone, Eric Robert '73   F '70, '71, '72

Cronin, Barry Michael '76   Ba '75, '76

Cronin, Edward Joseph Jr. '75   F '72, '73,
'74

Cronin, Francis Xavier '76   Ba '74, '75; F
'73, '74, '75

Cronin, Michael Jeremiah '83   F '82, '83

Cronin, William Richard '76   R '76

Crosby, Laura Hastings '86   Sk '83

Crosby, Stephen Patrick '67   F '66

Cross, Alan Stephen '66   Ba '65, '66

Crotty, Kenneth Brian '84   F '82, '83

Crowley, Cynthia Ann '82   FH '78, '79

Crowley, Peter Jeremiah '81   Ba '79, '81

Crudo, Timothy Paul '84   TO '81

Cuccia, Ronald Daniel E.M. '82–'83   F '80,
'81, '82

Cukier, Jody Ann '79 (MGR)   Sw '79

Culig, Carl Albert '76   F '73, '74, '75; W
'73

Cummins, Carl William III '69   Sw '67, '68

Cunningham, Caroline Cromwell '81   Sq
'78, '80; L '78

Cunningham, Eleanor Lamont '81   Sq '78,
'79, '80, '81

Cunningham, Joan '85   So '82, '83, '84,
'85

Cunningham, Kevin Richard '78   LC '76,
'77, '78

Cunningham, Robert Thomas '68   Ba '67

Cunningham, Van Buren '65 (MGR)   F '63,
'64

Ehrman, James William '71   HC '69, '70, '71

Eichner, Reed Allen '80   CC '77, '78, ' 80; TI '78; TO '77, '78

Eisenberg, Brian '72 (MGR)   F '71

Eisenberg, Richard David '71   Sw '69, 70, '71

Ekama, Emmanuel Erhieyovwe '73   S '70, '71, '72

Elbaum, Daniel '87   Sl '84, '85

Eldridge, Elizabeth Sansford '88   Sk '85

Elkins, Lorren Ray '81   Sw '78, '80, '81

Ellen, David Edward '86   W '83, '84

Elliott, Charles Wharton '79   Sq '78, '79

Elliott, David Arthur '73   TO '71

Elliott, Joan Theresa '84   S '80, '81, '82, '83; L '81

Elliott, John Douglas '73   H '71, '72, '73

Elliott, Lori Susan '87   Sw '85

Ellis, Dwight Holmes III '69 (MGR)   H '68, '69

Ellis, Jonathan Perry '75   G '75

Ellis, Russell Todd '76–'77   Fc '77

Ellis, Tracy Ann '82   S '78

Elsas, Frederick John '64   LC '63

Elser, Marco Maximilian '81   Sk '81

Emberling, Geoffrey Alan '87   LC '85

Embree, Melvyn Charles '76   TI '73, '74, '75, '76; TO '73, '74, '75, '76

Emerson, Geoffrey Webster '67   H '67

Emerson, Rebecca Field '81   HC '81

Emery, John Clinton '69   Ba '68; F '66, '67, '68

Emery, Patrick William '69   TO '67

Emmett, Tucker John '66   Sl '65, '66

Emory, Benjamin Riegel '66   HC '65

Emper, William David '77   F '74, '75, '76

Endicott, William Thorndike '68   LC '67

Eng, John '70   W '68

Engh, Michele Jan '88   Sw '85

Engel, Thomas Edward '67   L '66, '67

Engle, Arthur Knapp '88   Te '85

English, David Russell '76   Sw '73, '74, '76

Engstrom, Frederick William '70 (MGR)   Sq '68, '69

Enriquez, Juan Cabot '81   WP '80

Enscoe, Robert Jon '71   CC '68; TI '69; TO '70, '71

Epstein, Daniel James '84   V '82, '83

Epstein, David Alexander '83   Sl '81

Erburu, Lisa Ann '82   LC '80, '81, '82

Erickson, Silvanus Osborn '71   LC '69

Ernst, Anthony Michael '83   F '80, '81, '82

Ernst, Bruce Richard '83   L '80, '81

Ernst, Steven Roy, '84   F '82, '83

Ersek, Cynthia Marie '88   L '85

Erulkar, Benjamin '82   S '80, '81

Esch, Michael David '76   Sw '73

Eskow, Lisa Royce '87   V '84

Esmonde, Christopher Andrew '82   L '79, '80, '81, '82

Esserman, James Neal '73   Te '71, '72

Eustis, Augustis William '71 (MGR)   H '70, '71

Eustis, Frederick Augustus III '72   LC '70, '72

Evans, Arthur Thompson III '69   HC '68, '69

Evans, David Durkee '76   Sq '75, '76

Evans, Elizabeth '85   Te '82, '83, '84, '85

Evans, Frederick Maxwel '66   F '65

Evans, Michael Richard '73   F '72

Evans, Peter John '83   H '80, '81

Evans, Philip Robert '81   H '78

Evensen, Brynjulf '74   Sk '72

Everett, Nicholas Shethar '73   L '71, '73, '74

Everett, Oliver Shethar '66   L '65

Everist, Brian Douglass '73   L '73

Ewing, Eberle A. '78   Sk '75, '76

Ewing, John Garver '82   Sw '82

Ezeji-Okoye, Stephen Chukwuma '85   TI '82, '83, '84, '85; TO '82, '83, '84, '85

Fabry, Stephen Corvin '86   W '84

Faden, Arthur Ames '75   S '73, '74

Fadule, James John '84   F '83

Faecher, Elizabeth Jeanne '88   L '85

Fajtova, Vera Tatano '80   S '77, '78, '79; Sk '77, '78, '79, '80

Falcone, Philip Alan '84   H '81, '82, '83, '84

Falcone, Vincent Robert '65   Ba '63, '64, 65

Faller, Mark Andrew '71   W '69, '70

Fanikos, David William '85   F '83, '84

Fanning, Charles Frederick '64 (MGR)   H '63

Farber, Seth Charles '86   V '85

Farden, Richard Scott '88   H '85

Fargo, James Frederick '83   HC '83, '84

Farley, Claire Todd '85   L '84

Farley, Felipe Jose '86   Bb '83, '84

Farmer, Elspeth Lanham '79   Sw '77

Farneti, Gary William '71   F '68, '69, '70

Farrell, Edward John '83   Ba '80, '82, '83; F '82

Farrell, Robert William '70   H '70

Farrell, Stephen Charles '87   W '84, '85

Farrish, Kenneth Robert '78   H '78

Fasi, David Francis '84   WP '80, '81, '82, '83

Faught, Michael Flynn '79   L '76, '77, '78, '79

Faulkner, Bradford William '80   Sk '77

Faust, Philip Stocklen '73   F '71

Fayemi, Bamidele Omowunmi '88   TI '85; TO '85

Fayer, Jane Carolyn '79   Sw '77, '78

Fearnett, Brian Jeffrey '74   S '71, '72, '73

Fearon, James Dana '84   G '82, '84, '85

Feder, Leslie Margaret '81   Fc '79, '80

Federico, Bruno Joseph '77 (MGR)   H '77

Fee, Matthew Guertin '82   L '79, '80, '81, '82

Fegley, Harry William '66   Bb '63, '64, '65

Feldman, Emily '82   Sw '79

Feldman, Michael Frederick '75   R '75

Fellows, David Munro '74   HC '72, '73, '74; R '72

Felson, Katherine McClintock '88   L '85; FH '84

Feng, Sandy '83 (MGR)   S '79

Fenton, Bradley Wayne '71   F '69, '70

Fenton, John Martin '83 (MGR)   Ba '81, '82, '83; Bb '80, '81, '82, '83

Ferguson, James Joseph '75   HC '73; S '73, '74

Ferguson, Marc Kendric '73   F '70, '71, '72

Ferguson, Scott Sherwood '79   TI '78

Ferner, Christian Donald '71   S '69, '70; Sk '69, '70, '71

Ferrante, Catherine '82   S '78, '79, '80, '81; L '79, '81

Ferry, Angela '86   So '84

Ferry, Charles Mansfield '72   R '71

Ferry, Robert Dean '85   Bb '82, '83, '84, '85

Ferry, William Paul '74   F '71, '72, '73

Fertig, Lamar Hamilton '66   W '63, '64

Ferullo, John Albert '72   F '69, '70, '71

Feyerick, Steven Jeremy '85   Sw '82

Fichter, David Jonathan '73   Fc '72, '73

Fiechter, Jacques Poindexter '67   HC '66, '67

Field, Debora B. '85   S '81, '82, '83, '84

Field, John Christopher '80   Sl '79, '80

Field, Susan Louise '81   Bb '78, '79; FH '78, '79, '80

Fierke, David Marland '70   Ba '70

Fifer, Karen Fern '78   S '77

Filpi, Robert Alan '66   TO '65

Finan, Anthony Gerard '81   F '79, '80

Finch, Diana Secor '76   FH '75; L '76

Fine, Anne Deborah '80   TI '78

Fine, Glenn Alan '78–'79   Bb '76, '78, '79

Fine, Peter Arnold '64   L '63, '64, '65

Finglass, Brian '80   L '77

Fingleton, Anthony James '67   Sw '65

Finkowski, Michael Joseph III '69   L '67, '68

Graber, Arnold Steven '75 (MGR) Bb '73, '74

Graff, Robert Leonard '87 L '84, '85

Graham, Dean Christopher '88 L '85

Graham, Gordon Charles '78 F '77

Graham, James Brian '85 WP '82, '83, '84

Graham, Russell Dale '76–'78 Fc '77

Graham, Stuart William '67 (MGR) Bb '66, '67, '68

Grana, William Anthony '64 F '61, '62, '63

Grand, Gordon III '70 L '68, '69

Granger, Michael LeMoyne '83 F '80, '81, '82

Granger, R. Matthew '79 F '77, '78

Grant, Douglas Augustus '85 H '84, '85

Grant, Jeffrey Morton '67 W '65, '66, '67

Grant, Patrick Jr. '70 G '70

Grant, Robert Gourlay '77 S '76; H '77

Grant, Walter Warren '66 F '63, '64, '65; L '65

Grassby, George Edward '77 S '75, '76

Grate, Donald Jeffrey '68 Ba '66, '68; Bb '65, '66, '67, '68

Gratwick, Geoffrey Mason '65 HC '63, '64, '65

Gravallese, David Marshall '75 R '72, '73, '74

Gray, Austen Townsend Jr. '68 L '66, '67

Gray, John Chipman Jr. '64 F '62, '63; L '62, '63

Gray, Karen Johanna '83 TI '80, '81, '82, '83; TO '81, '82, '83

Gray, Robert Forsythe '70 S '67, '68, '69

Gray, William '74 G '74

Gray, William Barton '64 Sk '63, '64

Greacen, James Robertson '79 Sw '76, '77, '78 '79

Greeley, David Foote '75 (MGR) Te '73, '74

Greeley, Jennifer '85 S '81, '82, '83, '84; L '82, '84, '85

Green, Meredith '88 CC '84; TO '85

Green, Robert Belknap '72 L '71, '72

Greenacre, Martyn Douglas '64 LC '62, '63

Greenberg, Jerry Alan '87 W '84, '85

Greenberg, Mark David '76 TO '76

Greenberg, Richard '73 Te '72, '73

Greene, Carol Ann '87 Bb '84

Greenidge, Stanley Ernest '68 F '66, '67

Greer, Boyce Ingram '78 S '76, '77

Greer, Richard Alden '80 Sw '77, '78, '80

Gregg, Lauren '82 S '80; L '81

Gregory, George Bradford '84 HC '84

Gregory, James Barnum '85 TO '82

Greis, Allison Ann '86 Sw '83, '85; WP '84, '85

Greis, Leslie Endres '80 Bb '77, '78; G '78, '79, '80

Greyson, Clifford Russell '80 Sl '79, '80

Griffin, Brian Colvert '74 Te '73

Griffin, Corey Anthony '84 H '84

Griffin, Michael Kevin '75 Bb '74, '75

Griffith, Stephen Loyal '67 S '66

Grim, Jane Marie '88 To '85

Grimble, Donald Louis '68 H '67, '68

Grimm, David Charles '85 Rb '84

Grinstead, Eugene Andrews III '67 Sw '65, '67

Griswold, James Bradford '68 Bb '65, '66, '68

Grogan, Richard Henry '75 HC '74, '75; LC '73

Groome, Evelyn Salisbury '87 L '84

Groper, Scott Douglas '79 F '78, '79

Grossi, Marina Emma '79 (MGR) F '77, '78

Grossman, Richard William '68 Hc '68

Grossman, Warren '83 Te '80, '81, '82, '83

Grottkau, Brian Edward '85 Sw '82, '83, '84 '85

Grout, Daniel Alan '87 HC '85

Guarino, Rose Ann '83 Bb '81

Guerra, Frank Salvatore '73 F '72

Guerra, Ricardo '83 WP '80, '81, '82

Guilfoyle, Kathleen Marie '81 LC '81

Gulya, Brigitta Rianna '86 Sl '84

Gunderson, Paul Einar '65 HC '63, '64, '65

Gunn, Donald Kenneth '66 F '65

Gunnoe, Charles Edward '64 L '62, '63

Gurel, Ogan '86 LC '85

Gurry, Christopher Jude '70 H '68, '69, '70

Gustavson, Eric David '69 Bb '67, '68, '69

Gustafson, Robert Charles '87 TI '84, '85; TO '84, '85

Gutschow, Todd William '83 W '80, '82

Guyton, Jean M. '75 Bb '75

Guzzi, Paul Henry '64–'65 F '64

Gwathmey, Archibald Llewelyn '74 Sq '72, '73, '74

Gwozdz, R. Scott '87 Sq '84

Gwynne-Timothy, Kenneth Gordon '87 HC '85

Haase, Brian Kent '78 (MGR) F '77

Hackert, Timothy John '75 LC '73, '74, '75

Hackett, Robert '85 Rb '84

Hackett, Robert William '81 Sw '78, '79, '80, '81

Hadley, Mark Anthony '80 Bb '78

Hadley, Nancy A. '76 HC '75, '76

Hadsel, Jane Latimer '78 Sq '76

Hagebak, Robert Waldo '64 F '63

Hagedorn, Charles Henry '82 Sl '80, '81, '83

Hagerty, Henry Fleming '78 TO '77

Hagerty, John Brady '73 F '71, '72; L '71, '72, '73

Hagerty, Thomas Gibbes '76 F '74, '75; L '74, '75

Haggerty, Francis Joseph Jr. '68 TI '65, '66, '67, '68; TO '65, '66, '67, '68

Halas, Paul Joseph '78 Ba '76, '77, '78; F '75, '76, '77

Hale, Allan Lemont '79 Sk '76, '77, '78, '79

Hale, Jennifer Jill '85 HC '83, '84, '85; Sk '82, '83, '84

Haley, Paul Richard '76 H '74, '75, '76

Haley, William Joseph '76 W '73, '74, '75

Hall, Allison B. '77 HC '75

Hall, David Lynn '69 LC '68

Hall, Frenesa Kaye '83 Bb '80, '81, '82 '83; HC '82, '83

Hall, George Houston '82 WP '80, '81

Hall, Gerard John '81 F '80

Hall, Jeffrey Rudolph '67 Ba '67

Hall, Jonathan King '75 F '74

Hall, Matthew Warren V '66 Sq '66, '67

Hall, Peter Edward '67–'69 F '64, '67, '68

Hall, Shawn Richard '82 TI '80, '82, '83; TO '80, '82, '83

Hall, Stephen Padney '73 F '70, '71, '72

Hallo, Ralph Ethan '78 (MGR) CC '76, '77

Hallock, Michael Eldred '69 TO '69

Hamelin, Marcia Jean '80 S '77, '78, '79

Hamlin, Charles Borden '70 HC '69, '70

Hammit, James Knoderer '78 Sl '76, '77, '78

Hammond, Ormond Willson '65 L '63, '64, 65

Hammond, Richard Edwin '67 S '64, '65, '66

Hampe, Kevin Frances '73 Ba '71, '72, '73; H '71, '72, '73

Hancock, Christopher Michael '82 Sw '79, '80

Hands, David '74 H '72, '73, '74

Handy, Susie S. '76 Sq '75, '76

Hanes, Stephen Andrew '77 TI '76; TO '74

Haney, Richard Warren '87 H '85

Hannemann, Muliufi Francis '76 Bb '75, '76

Hanower, Lee David '81 Fc '79, '80, '81

Hanrahan, Michael Joseph '88 W '85

Hansen, John Cyril Jr. '81 WP '80

Hanson, Eric Cotter '70 Sw '68, '69

Harden, Craig Winslow '80 Sw '77

Hardin, Douglas Ray '69   CC '66, '67, '68; TI '67, '68, '69; TO '67, '68

Hardington, Ian Jonathan '86   S '82, '83, '84

Hardy, Ernest Benson '70   Bb '69, '70

Hardy, Richard Evelyn Whittelle '70   S '67, '68, '69

Hare, Noel Edwin Jr. '70   TI '68, '69, '70; TO '68, '69, '70

Hargadon, Geoffrey Lancaster '76   F '73, '74, '75

Harlan, John Woody '75   LC '74

Harman, Andrew John '86   Sk '85

Harman, David Brainerd '71   LC '69, '70, '71

Harnice, John Douglas '84   Bb '82, '83

Harper, Elizabeth Warren '81   LC '81

Harper, James McKell Edwin '68   Sl '68

Harper, Richard Charles '75   LC '74

Harper, Robert Straube Jr. '85   G '84, '85

Harper, Susan Norma '80   TI '77, '78, '79, '80; TO '77, '78, '79, '80

Harrell, James Earl '75   Ba '74, '75

Harring, Maryann '87   TI '85; TO '84

Harrington, Alden Clark '66   H '65, '66

Harrington, Allan Crane '79   TI '79; TO '79

Harrington, Anne '82   LC '82

Harrington, Justin Laurence '74   F '73

Harrington, Mark Henry III '68 (MGR)   HC '66, '67, '68

Harrington, Samuel Parker '73   L '72

Harris, Jonathan Miller '76   H '76

Harris, Mark Christopher '81   Bb '79, '80, '81

Harris, Sarah Newton '85   HC '82

Harris, Stephen Joseph '73   H '73

Harris, Susan Louise '87   Sw '84, '85

Harrison, Elise Kenyon '83   Sq '80, '81, '82, '83

Harrison, Philip Leonard '86   Sk '83

Harrison, Stephen Francis '72   F '69, '70, '71

Harrower, Norman III '72   S '69, '70, '71

Harshbarger, Luther Scott '64   F '61, '62, '63 Ba '62

Hart, Ellen Mary Gerarda '80   Bb '77; S '77, '78, '79; TI '80; TO '80

Hart, Joan Marie '78   TI '77, '78

Hart, Margaret Laurian '84   L '82, '83, '84; TI '84; FH '80

Hart, Timothy John '86   H '84

Harting, Donald Markham '78   LC '77, '78

Hartman, Russell William '73   HC '73

Hartmann, Ralph Peter '86   L '83, '84, '85; H '84

Hartnett, Paul John '75   F '73, '74

Hartranft, John Charles '64   F '62, '63

Hartung, Amy Elizabeth '88   H '85

Harvey, Frederick Barton III '71   W '69, '70

Harvey, Tobin Neil '72   Ba '70, '71, '72; F '72

Harwood, John Henry II '67   Sq '66, '67

Hassell, Suzanne '82   LC '80, '81, '82

Hassine, Eliezer '75   W '75

Hastings, Dan Thomas '69 (MGR)   Sw '68, '69

Hatch, George Merck '81   HC '78, '80, '81

Hatfield, Timothy Lynn '67   TO '65, '66, '67

Hathaway, Fred William '79   LC '77

Hauck, Michael Arthur '67   S '64; TO '65

Haughey, Philip Carberry Jr. '84   W '83

Haveles, Harry Peter Jr. '76 (MGR)   Sq '73, '74, '75, '76

Havens, John Paul '79   Sq '76, '77, '78, '79

Havens, Peter Hessenbruch '76   Sq '75, '76

Havern, Robert Anthony '72   H '70, '71, '72

Hawke, George Gardner Whitaker '78–'79 (MGR)   F '76

Hawkins, Anita Elaine '88   Fc '85

Hawkins, Charles John III '66   G '64, '65

Hawkins, John Douglas '75   Fc '73, '74, '75

Hawley, Andrew James '87   HC '85

Hawley, Robert Daniels '85   L '82, '83, '84, '85

Hay, Glen Orr Jr. '68   L '68

Hayes, Neville Ronald '67   Sw '65

Hayes, Robert Dixon '71   L '69, '70, '71

Hayes, Sharon Marie '88   Bb '85; So '85

Hayward, James L. '70 (MGR)   HC '70

Hayward, Paul Stewart '87   TI '85

Haywood, Brent Dennis '77   Sw '74, '75, '76

Hazard, Rowland Gibson '71   Sk '69, '71

Healey, Martin Frances '77   Bb '77

Healey, Sean Michael '83   W '81, '82, '83

Healey, Stephen James '85 (MGR)   Sq '84, '85

Healy, Mary Elizabeth '87   S '83

Heckel, Blayne Ryan '75   TI '73, '74, '75; TO '72, '73, '74, '75

Hedendal, Bruce Eric '69   TI '67, '68; TO '67, '68, '69

Hedges, Patricia Helen '88   Bb '85

Heffelfinger, Joan Perry '78   Te '77

Heffernan, David John '84   Rb '84

Hehir, Brian Patrick '75   F '72, '73, '74

Heisler, Robert Bauman '70   G '68, '69, '70

Heiszek, Stephen Charles '84   WP '83

Heller, John Gaylord '79   Sq '78, '79

Heller, Kate Lawrence '80–'81   LC '81

Heller, Richard '74 (MGR)   Sw '74

Heller, Steven McArthur '76   LC '74, '75, '76

Hemphill, Gary '78 (MGR)   Bb '76

Henderson, Jeremy Davenport '78   Sl '76

Henderson, Joseph Welles III '67 (MGR)   Sq '65

Henderson, Nina Teresa '85   V '81, '82

Henderson, Robert Alan '84   CC '84; TO '84

Hendricks, Martha Jane '77   Sw '76, '77

Henjyoji, Howard Shinje '67   W '65, '66, '67

Henkel, Hugh Garret '74   W '73

Henriques, Elizabeth Werner '82 (MGR)   Sq '81

Henriques, Horace Fuller III '77   L '75

Henry, Mark Warren '84–'85   TI '81, '82, '83, '85; TO '81, '82, '83, '85

Henry, Paul Shala '65   LC '63, '64

Henson, Josiah Douglas '72   W '71, '72

Herberich, James F. '85   TI '82, '83, '84, 85; TO '84, '85

Herbert, Walter Beull '76   F '73, '74, '75

Herbig, Peter Karl '86   LC '85

Herlihy, Mary Margaret '82   CC '81; TI '81, '82; TO '81, '82

Herman, Nancy Elizabeth '78   HC '76, '77

Hern, Christopher John '81 (MGR)   Fc '79; F '79, '80

Hernandez, Mary Teresa '85   S '83

Hernstein, Max Govinlock '85   S '84

Herold, Frederick George '78   S '75, '76, '77

Herrick, Sarah Elaine '76   Sl '75, '76

Herron, Allison Lynne '80   LC '80

Herter, Eliot Miles '75   Sk '73

Hetzler, Kenneth Alf '72   Fc '71, '72

Hevern, Gerard Joseph '72   F '70, '71; TO '70

Hewitt, Charles Colby III '71   LC '70, '71

Hewitt, Susan Hill '79   Bb '76, '77, '78; TI '79; TO '79

Hewlett, Walter Berry '66   CC '63, '64, '65; TI '63, '64; TO '63, '64, '65

Heyburn, John Gilpin '70   CC '67, '68, '69; TI '69, '70; TO '70

Heyman, David Jonathan '83   Fc '80, '81, '82, '84

Hickman, Dewey Caul '73   TI '71, '72, '73; TO '71, '72, '73

Hickman, Diane N. '78   HC '75, '76, '77, '78

Hickman, Diane Nadine '77–'78   HC '77

Higgins, David Dillon '69   HC '67, '68, '69

Higgins, Robert Francis '68   H '68

Higgins, Robert Joseph '83   TI '82, '83; TO '79

Higginson, Stephen Andrew '83   S '80, '81, '82

Hildebidle, John Jermon Jr. '67 (MGR)   F '65, '66

Hill, Alice Eddy '81   H '79, '80

Hill, Alison P. '76   HC '75, '76

Hill, Jeffrey William '77   Bb '75, '76, '77

Hill, Renee '85 (MGR)   L '84

Himelman, Ronald Barnet '79   G '77, '78, '79

Hines, Jerome Laurence '74   CC '71, '73

Hines, Stephen Paul '76   S '73, '74, '75

Hines, Walter Peyton '77   Bb '75, '76

Hing, Roberta Ong '86   Te '83, '84, '85

Hingeley, James McCarrell '69 (MGR)   F '67

Hinkle, Stephen Currier '70   Sk '68, '69, '70

Hinton, Andrew Jay '82   F '80, '81

Hinton, Juliann Marie '80   HC '80

Hinze, Bent Frederik '76   S '72

Hirschfeld, Edward Babcock '72   HC '72

Hirschfeld, John Duskin '76   Fc '73, '75, '76

Hirschler, Charles '76   Sk '76

Hissey, Mark Anthony '84   Rb '84

Hitzig, William Maxwell '65   S '62, '64

Ho, Vincent Yuan-Cheng '84   TI '83; TO '84

Hobart, Robert '85   F '84

Hobbs, Franklin Warren IV '69   HC '67, '68, '69; Sq '67, '68, '69

Hobbs, Fritz Warren '70   Sq '70

Hobbs, Jill Elaine '84 (MGR)   Fc '82

Hobbs, Steven Henry '75 (MGR)   Fc '73, '74, '75; F '73

Hobbs, William Barton Rogers '70   HC '69, '70, '71

Hobdy, Lawrence Edward '78   F '75, '76, '77

Hocevar, Richard Alan '70   R '68, '69, '70

Hochberg, Brenda Joan '81   CC '77

Hochschild, Frances Sewall '84 (MGR)   F '82, '83

Hodakowski, George Tadeusz '80   F '79

Hodder, Elizabeth Espy '84   Sl '82

Hodder, Holly Elizabeth '82   LC '82

Hodges, David Chetwoode '67   Te '65, '66, '67

Hodgkins, Kristin '80   Sk '78, '79

Hoeppner, Lutz Juergen '68   S '65, '66, '67

Hofer, Timothy Philip '79   Sk '77, '78, '79

Hoffman, John Parker '65   F '64; W '63

Hoffman, Joseph Louis '77 (MGR)   Bb '76, '77;L '77, '78

Hoffman, Paul '68   HC '66, '67, '68

Hoffman, Robert Michael '68   F '66, '67

Hoffman, Steven Geoffrey '64 (ASST MGR)   LC '63, '64

Hogan, Leigh Paul '75   Ba '73, '74, '74; H '73, '74, '75

Hogshead, James Andrew '82   HC '81, '82

Holbrook, Noel Michele '82   Sk '79, '80

Holcombe, Thomas Wood '64   TO, '62, '63

Holland, Isable Beatriz '84   V '81

Holland, Mary Susan '81   Fc '79

Holland, Michael Francis '66   F '65

Holleran, Romer '65   Sq '63, '64, '65

Holley, William Arthur '83   F '82

Hollingsworth, Amor '75   S '75

Hollingsworth, Arthur Woods '85   HC '84, '85

Hollingsworth, Jonathan '80   F '78, '79

Hollman, Steven Paul '80   F '78, '79

Hollomon, Jonathan Bradford '66   LC '65, '66

Holmes, Boris Dessau '75   W '72

Holmes, Graham '75   H '75

Holmes, Peter John '88   W '85

Holpuch, Elaine '82–'83   Bb '79, ' 80, '81, '83; So '81

Holt, Milton Addison Ikaika '75   Ba '73, '74, '75; F '72, '73, '74

Holy, Adriana Kay '83   Sw '80, '81, '82, '83

Holtzworth, Anne Stuart '84   LC '83, '84

Holzinger, Richard George '79   Sw '76, '77

Hom, Louise '82   V '81, '82

Homer, Robert Joseph '79   Fc '78, '79

Honaker, Richard H. '73   F '71

Honick, Eric '71   F '70

Honick, Jonas Ian '77   Bb '75, '76, 77

Hooft, Robert Craig '79   Bb '77, '78, '79

Hooks, Todd Gordon '77   Bb '75; TI '76, '77; TO '75, '76, '77

Hooper, Jay Gordon '84   S '82, '83

Hootstein, Daniel David '67   Ba '65, '66, '67

Hopkinson, Reginald Ronald '84   Sk '81, '82, '83, '84

Horn, John Richard '77   Te '74, '75

Hornblower, John Greenwood '84   HC '84

Hornblower, Ralph III '70   F '67, '68, '69; TO '68

Horne, Patricia Michele '83   Bb '80, '81, '82, '83; So '81, '82, '83

Horne, Robert Alan '81   Te '78, '79, '80, '81

Horner, Richard Alan '80   F '77, '78, '79

Hornig, Christopher Wayne '76   Sl '74, '75, '76

Hornig, James Allyn '70   H '69

Horton, Douglas Lloyd '81   H '80

Horton, Michael Keith '76   TI '74; TO '73, '74, '75

Horton, William Russell Jr. '77   H '76, '77

Horvitz, Paul Fisher '72   Sw '70, '71, '72

Hosea, Timothy Michael '74   HC '73

Host, Niels George '74   LC '72, '73

Hotchkin, Nicholas Paul '88   S '84

Houlihan, Arthur Thomas III '82   V '81, '82

Houston, Kenneth Mapes '78   Sk '76, '77, '78

Houston, Neil John Jr. '67   Ba '65, '66, '67; TI '65

Howard, Mary Thomas '78   FH '75, '76, '77, '78; TI '78; TO '78

Howard, Peter David '69   L '67, '68

Howard, Todd Kevin '75–'77   LC '73, '74, '75

Howe, Elizabeth Bigelow '84   Sq '82, '83, '84

Howe, Mark Peter '76   LC '76, '77

Howe, Peter Fairfax '76   Sl '75

Howe, Richard Turner '68–'69   CC '65, '66, '67; TI '68; TO '66, '67, '68

Howe, Roger Evans '66   HC '65

Howe, Thomas Andrew '78   HC '76, '77, '78

Howes, Thomas Andrew '78   HC '76, '77

Howkins, Jefrey Paul '84   F '81, '82, '83

Howland, Charles Child '65 (MGR)   W '63, '64, '65

Howland, John MacLure '72   TO '70

Howland, Kinnaird '66   HC '65, '66

Hozack, William James '77   H '75, '76, '77

Hrabchak, Robert Blount '85   Sw '82, '83, '84, '85

Hsiao, To Yao-Hin '79   S '77, '78

Hubbard, Jonathan Van Hook '69 (MGR)   W '69

Huber, Tania Mills '81–'82   FH '77, '78, 81; H '79

Hudak, Richard George '66   F '65

Hudson, Jay Alan '84   TI '81, '82, '83, '84; TO '81, '82, '83 , '84

Hudson, John Morgan '66   S '63

Huebner, Bernard Converse '65   S '63, '64

Huff, Andrew Gregory '72   Sw '70, '71

Hughes, James Francis '79   CC '79; TO '79

Hughes, James Richard '75   CC '72; TI '72, '73

Hughes, John Francis '80   H '77, '78, '79

Hughes, John Mather III '74   TI '72, '73, '74; TO '72, '73, '74

Hughes, Justin Peter '67   F '65, '66 (CAPT)

Hughes, Noreen Elizabeth '81   LC '81

Hughes, Robert Everett Jr. '69   Sw '68, '69

Hughes, Scott Richard '75   Sq '75

Hughes, George Sylvester '79   H '76, '77, '78, '79

Hughes, William Henry III '85   Rb '84

Hugon, Jacques Loouis '82   Sw '80, '81, '82

Hulbert, Mary Winifred '85   Sq '82, '83, '84, '85

Hull, Jeffrey Stephen '86   Ba '85

Humenuk, William Anzelm '64   F '61, '62, '63

Humphreville, Edward Taylor '76   Sq '76

Humphreys, Tatyana Roberta '85   WP '84, '85; Sw '82

Hundahl, Scott Alfred '77 (MGR)   Sl '75

Hung, Judy Wei Ming '85   Sq '84, '85

Hunley, Wayne Patrick '86   F '84

Hunnewell, George Lyman '87   HC '85

Hunnewell, Jane Peele '84   FH '82

Hunt, Margaret Rose '76   LC '75, '76

Hunter, Dennis '64   Sw '62, '63, '64

Hunter, John Greenleaf '77   Sk '74, '75, '76, '77

Hunter, Thomas Scott '76   L '74

Huntoon, Christopher Lindsey '71   HC '71

Huntsman, Peter Randolph '74   LC '72, '73, '74

Hurlbut, Robert Satterlee '86   L '84, '85

Hurley, Cornelius Joseph Jr. '70   Ba '69, '70; F '68, '69

Hurley, Dianne Patricia '84   S '80; H '81, '82, '83, '84

Hurty, Craig Wesley '83   F '81, '82

Hurwitz, Eliot '72   Fc '70

Huskey, James Lee '71 (ASST MGR)   F '69, '70

Hutchison, Elizabeth Quay '86   S '84

Hutchison, Keith Randall Jr. '67   L '65, '66, '67

Huvelle, Jeffrey George '68   TI '66, '67, '68; TO '66, '67, '68

Hyde, Hugh Musgrave '75   Te '73, '74, '75

Hyland, William Vincent '85   F '83, '84

Hynes, David Edward '73   H '71, '72, '73

Hynes, John Bernard '80   H '78, '79, '80

Iafrati, Mark David '85   W '83

Ignacio, David Anthony '72   Ba '70, '71; F '69, '70, '71

Ignacio, John Joseph '69   Ba '68, '69; F '69

Ikauniks, Romauld '64   H '62, '63, '64

Illig, Karl Armistead '84   Sw '81, '82, '83, '84

Imrie, John Brookings '71   W '69

Ince, John Frederic '70   L '68, '69, '70; Sq '69, '70

Ingard, John Uno '75   Te '72, '73, '74, '75

Ingari, John Victor '82   Sw '81

Ingber, Audrey '76   Bb '76

Ingersoll, Raymond Vail II '69   Sk '67, '68

Inman, Robert Paul '64   Bb '62, '63; Te '62, '63

Innes, Richard Craig '78 (MGR)   H '78

Inskeep, Betsy Dawn '75 (MGR)   R '73, '75

Intrater, Keith Mitchell '74   LC '74

Ippolito, Alphonse '79   F '77, '78

Ippolito, Elizabeth Anne '81   FH '79, '80; So '81

Ippolito, Jon Cooper '84   Fc '83, '84

Ippolito, Joseph '84   F '82, '83

Ippolito, Michele Terese '86   FH '83, '84

Irion, Steven Mark '78   Bb '76, '77

Irving, Ronald Scott '73 (MGR)   HC '72, '73

Irvings, Mark Lewis '71   Fc '69, '70, '71

Irwin, Charles Fayette III '66 (MGR)   F '64, '65

Isaacson, Daniel Rufus '67   Fc '65

Isackson, Kristin Ann '85   Sw '82, '84, '85

Iselin, Josephine Lea '84   Sq '82, '83, '84; Sl '81

Iselin, William Duane '87   Sq '84

Israel, Susan Jill '81   Sl '78, '79

Istvan, Rudyard Lyle '72   Sl '70, '71, '72

Iwakuni, Eri '85   Ba '84, '85

Iwasawa, Takashi '67   Fc '65, '66, '67

Jackenfelds, John Eduards '79   TO '79

Jacker, Michael Howard '76   Sl '74, '76

Jackmauh, Gregory John '76–'77   L '74, '76, '77

Jacks, Tyler Edwards '83   W '80

Jackson, George Anthony '80   F '79

Jackson, Lawrence Vincent '75 (MGR)   Bb '74

Jackson, Pamela L. '78   Sw '75

Jackson, Richard John '85   Sq '83, '84, '85

Jackson, Richard Montgomery Jr. '66 (MGR)   F '64

Jacobs, Michael Matthew '81   F '78, '79, '80

Jacobs, Paul Schafran '81   CC '80; TO '81

Jacobs, Steven Craig '86   TI '84

Jacobson, Diane Kay '80   CC '79

Jacobson, Michael Richard '75 (MGR)   HC '74, '75

Jadick, Theodore Spencer '76   F '74, '75

Jahncke, Redington Townsend '72   H '70

Jakobson, Patrick Ulf '82   Sw '79, '80; WP '80, '81

Jakovic, Ellen Marie '82   S '78, '79, '80, '81; So '81, '82

James, Alexander Long '79   Bb '77

James, Hamilton Evans '73   S '72

James, Rafael Rivera '74 (MGR)   TI '72, '73

James, Thomas Alan '64   Te '63, '64

Janczewski, Micjael John '71   Bb '69, '70

Janfaza, Andrew Edward '88   H '85

Jang, Curtis Chaochun '87   Sw '84, '85

Janicek, Steven Augustine '75   H '74, '75

Jannino, Robert William '69   F '68

Jarvis, John Willard '69   Te '67, '68, '69

Jason, Joseph Francis '78   F '75, '76, '77, '78

Jayne, Parker Hilton '69   Sl '69

Jean-Louise, Pascale Lyne '87   V '84

Jefferies, Bradley Clinton '83   Fc '81, '82, '83

Jeffrey, Paul Murray '82–'83   HC '83

Jeffries, William Quincy '82   Sl 80, '81, '82

Jelley, Peter Collins '85   C '82, 83, '84, '85; TI '83, '84; TO '84

Jellison, Ronald Alan '80   F '79

Jen, Lillian C. '77   LC '75, '76

Jenkins, Jamie Rachel '85   Sl '83, '84, '85

Jenkins, Robert Chauncey '80   Ba '77, '78

Jenkins, Robert Maxwell III '69   LC '67

Jenkins, Willie Anthony '74   Bb '72, '73, '74

Jennings, Katherine Dana '82   Sl '80

Jensen, Cynthia Lund '79   L '78, '79

Jensen, Kelly T. '74–'76   W '75, '76

Jensen, Mark Alfred '66   Sk '64, '65

Jensen, Samuel James '85   F '83, '84

Jergesen, Harry Everett '68   Fc '66, '67, '68

Jernigan, Kenton LeRoy '86   Sq '83, '84, '85

Jernigan, Kevin Marc '87   Sq '83, '84, '85

Jewett, Eric David '77   Sk '74, '75

Jewett, Theodore Thomas '66 (MGR)   H '65

Jewett, William Ramsey '69   TI '67; TO '67, '68

Jiggetts, Danny Marcellus '76   F '73, '74, '75; TI '75, '76; TO '75

Jiggetts, Kevin Bernard '77   S '74, '75, '76

Joel, Adele Marian '82   Sw '79

Johannigman, Roger Thomas '77   Sw '74, '75, '76, '77

Johnsen, Thomas Christopher '73   L '71, '72, 73

Johnson, Anne Carter '77   L '75, '76, '77

Johnson, Anne Mary '78   LC '78

Johnson, Barry Frederick '69   H '67

Johnson, Brian Lee '71   HC '69, '70, '71

Johnson, Bruce Evan '75   W '72, '73, 74, '75

Mahoney, Solabunmi David '80   TI '78, '79; TO '77, '78, '79, '80

Mahoney, William Thomas '73   HC '71, '72, '73

Mahony, Devin-Adair '86   HC '84, '85

Mainelli, Andrea Louise '85   Bb '82; FH '81, '82, '83, '84; L '83, '84, '85

Major, John Frederick '77   Fc '75, '76, '77

Makaitis, Algirdas Bronius '66   Fc '65

Makari, Grace '77   S '76

Malenbaum, Roxanne Fay '76   LC '75, '76

Malinowski, Barry Charles '73   Ba '71, '72, '73; F '70, '71, '72

Mallory, George Kenneth Jr. '67   S '64, '65, '66

Malmquist, Derek Phillip '83   H '80

Malone, Joseph Daniel '78   F '77

Maloney, Mark Daniel '76   L '74, '75, '76; S '75; F '74

Malugen, William Bernarr Jr. '68   W '65, '66

Mamana, John Philip '65   W '63

Mamarchev, Steven Mark Ford '75 (MGR)   Sw '75

Manchester, Richard Ellery '68   Ba '67, '68; F '67

Mandelbaum, Eric Jay '78   Fc '77, '78

Mangano, Mary Ellen '80   Sw '77

Mangano, Paul Stephen '80   H '80

Mangrum, Richard Collin '72   W '70, '71, '72

Manna, Timothy John '74   F '71, '72, '73

Mannix, Thomas William '81   Bb '79, '80, '81

Manuelian, Martin Der '82–'83   S '83

Maneulyan Atinc, Tamar '79   Bb '78

Maranto, Anthony Rosario '78   R '77

Marcello, David Edward III '81   HC '80, '81

Marchand, John Raymond '79   H '79

Marchese, Charles Robert '85   Ba '82, '83, '84, '85

Marchok, Christopher Robert '87   Ba '84, '85

Marcin, Donna Marie '85   Sw '82, '85

Marcis, Theodore James '85   G '82

Marcus, Paul Bernard '84   F '83

Mares, David Richard '76   R '76

Margolis, David Michael '81   LC '81

Margolis, Joseph David '83   F '80, '81, '82

Marino, Angelo '72   W '71, '72

Marino, Consuelo '87 (MGR)   WP '84

Marino, Gerald Edward '69   F '67, '68

Marion, Mark Douglas '82   F '80, '81

Mark, Jonathan Baird '74   G '74

Mark, Ronald Edgar '70   H '68, '69, '70

Marks, Andrew Harold '73   G '71, '72, '73

Marks, Anthony John '67   S '64, '65, '66

Markson, Deborah Elizabeth '83   Sw '80, '81, '82, '83; TO '81, '83

Marquez, Carol Madellaine '83 (MGR)   W '80, '81, '82, '83

Marshak, Daniel Robert '79   HC '79

Marshall, Charles Tedrick '81   Ba '78, '79, '80, '81; F '78, '79, '80

Marshall, Nina Townsend '82   S '78, '79

Marshall, William Lawrence '82   Fc '81, '82

Marson, Judith Ilene '87   S '83

Martell, Daniel '69   Bb '67

Martelli, Vincent Albert '83   Ba '80, '81, '82, '83

Martin, Bradley Paul '83   V '81, '82, '83

Martin, Clare Marion '85 (MGR)   F '83, '84

Martin, Francis Hall '64   Bb '63

Martin, Constance Lillian '82 (MGR)   F '81

Martin, Gary Bradford '84   H '81, '83, '84

Martin, Harold Hamman '78   S '75, '76, '77

Martin, James William '66   Bb '65, '66

Martin, Kathryn Ann '83   Bb '80, '81, '82, '83;   FH '79, '80, '81, '82; L '82, '83

Martin, Neil William '77   Sw '74, '75, '76

Martin, Stanley Wade '82   F '82

Martin, Steven Carey '78   L '76, '77, '78

Martin, Terry Dean '85   V '83, '84

Martineau, Belinda Marie '80   Bb '77

Martucci, Frederic James '71   F '69, '70

Masaracchio, Paul Peter '71   F '70

Masland, Richard Harry '64   LC '63

Mason, Douglas Richard '80   W '78, '79, '80

Mason, John Homans '67 (MGR)   Ba '66, '67

Mason, Maureen Clare '78   FH '75

Maspons, Miguel Angel '85   Ba '83, '84, '85

Massey, David Reid '67 (MGR)   F '65, '66

Masterson, Harris Frederick II '74   Te '72

Masterson, Thomas Gerard '79   F '77, '78; L '78

Masterson, Thomas Marshall '80   HC '80

Mastronardi, Janet Anthony '82 (MGR)   F '80, '81

Mather, Jane Elizabeth '79   Sk '77, '78; Sl '79

Mathews, Kathleen Watts '85 (MGR)   Te '83, '84

Matson, Barbara B. '75   FH '75; L '75

Mauel, John Gregory '82   WP '80

Maughan, Delray '72   TI '72; TO '70

Mauro, Teresaa Nicole '81   LC '79, '80, '81

Maximoff, James Timothy '82   Sw '79, '80, '81, '82; WP '80, '81

Maybank, Joseph '85   L '84

Mayberg, Marc Robert '73   F '72

Mayer, Laura Jeanne '83   S '79, '80, '81, '82

Mayer, Paul Overton '88   TO '85

Mayfield, James Clifton '79 (MGR)   Sw '77, '78

Mazzone, Carolyn Cook '85   Sw '82, '83, '84, '85

Mazzone, Robert Joseph '85   H '84, '85

Mazur, Janet E. '78   LC '75

McAlpine, Howard Hugh '72   H '70

McAndrews, Brian Patrick '80   TI '78, '80; TO '80

McAndrews, Christopher Lee '86   Ba '84, '85

McAree, Julia Kathleen '82   Sw '79

McArthur, Jocelyn Natasha '85   HC '84, '85

McAuley, Clyde Edward '75   L '73

McAuliffe, E. Anthony '80   LC '78, '79

McBride, Kelly Anne '87   Bb '84; L '85

McBride, William Alan '70   TI '69

McCabe, Robert William '83   Bb '81, '82

McCabe, Scott Christopher '83   F '80, '81, '82

McCafferty, Kevin Michael '76   F '73, '74, '75; TI '74, '75, '76; TO '73, '74, '75, '76

McCaffrey, Timothy Warren '86   L '83, '84, '85

McCall, Kevin '76   L '74, '75, '76

McCandlish, James Edward '67   Ba '65, '66, '67

McCarron, Brian George '78   Sw '75, '76

McCarthy, Denise Marie '85   Sq '85

McCarthy, John Steven '77   F '75, '76

McCarthy, Kevin Francis '87   Fc '84, '85

McCarthy, Mary Wiley '83   CC '80, '81, '82; TI '82; TO '80, '81, '82, '83

McClain, Mark Anthony '78   TO '75, '76

McClain, Rollin Clark '71   S '68

McClees, David Lachlan '78   Fc '76, '77, '78

McClennen, Charles Eliot '64   LC '62, '63

McClennen, Walter '67   LC '65

McClew, Katharine Elizabeth '84   LC '83, '84

McCloskey, Kathleen '83   Sw '80, '81, '83

McCloskey, William '85   Sw '82, '83, '84, '85

McClung, Merle Steven '65   Bb '63, '64, '65

McCluskey, John Asberry '66   F '64, '65

McCollom, Marion Ewing '72 (MGR)   Sk '72

McConaghy, Raymond Joseph Jr. '75   LC '75

McConnell, Stephen A. '75   G '73, '74, '75

McCormish, Robert Allan '80   F '79

McCrea, Edward Franklin '69   L '68

McCree, Paul Ingrid '80   LC '79, '80

McCulloh, John Russell '76   TI '74, '75, '76; TO '74, '75, '76

McCullough, Dennis Michael '67   H '65, '66, '67

McCune, Susan Kellogg '78   FH '76, '77, '78

McDermott, Robert Francis Jr. '67   Sw '65

McDermott, Robert Michael '77   F '74, '75, '76

McDevitt, Thomas Francis '79   TO '76, '78; F '76, '77, '78; TI '77

McDonald, James Scott '74   Sq '74

McDonald, Robert Charles '81   H '78, '79, '80

McDougall, Christopher Jude '85   HC '84, '85

McDonough, Paula Marie '86   So '83, '84

McDowell, Carter Nelson '75   L '73, '74

McDowell, Robert LeRoy Jr. '70   L '68, '69, '70

McEvoy, Richard Michael '86   H '83, '84

McGagh, William Terrence '85   F '84

McGee, Timothy Edmund '79   HC '78, '79

McGill, Paul Lawrence '75 (MGR)   W '75

McGinty, Kevin Michael '87   W '84, '85

McGivern, Thomas More '81–'82   L '79, '81, '82

McGlade, Margaret Francesca '80   Sq '77, '78; S '77

McGlone, William Michael '82   F '79, '80, '81

McGowan, Michael Paul '85   G '83, '84, '85

McGrath, James '77 (MGR)   H '72; HC '76; LC '76

McGrath, Joseph Charles '69 (MGR)   Ba '68; F '69; H '68, '69

McGregor, Bernard Joseph '73   Ba '73

McGugan, Timothy Shannon '84   F '82, '83

McGugan, Vincent John '72   Ba '70, '71, '72

McGuinn, Brian James '67   G '65, '66, '67

McHugh, Kevin John '82   F '80, '81

McHugh, Margaret '82   HC '82   .

McHugh, Michael Joseph '73   F '70, '71, '72

McInally, Patrick John '75   F '72, '73, '74

McIntosh, D. Steven '80   Bb '78

McIntyre, Angus Philip '74   Sl '73, '74

McIntyre, Rebecca Pomeroy '80   L '77

McKelvey, David Scott '68   TI '66, '67, '68; TO '66, '67, '68

McKenna, Paul Martin '74   LC '73, '74

McKenna, Timothy Mark '76   H '76

McKennan, James Thomson '76   S '73

McKetta, John J. III '69 (MGR)   CC '67; TI '68; TO '68

McKinney, Joe Clayton '69   F '68

McKinnon, Bruce Fahey '78   F '75, '76, '77

McLane, Deborah '75   Sk '75

McLaughlin, Kevin Michael '76   Bb '74

McLaughlin, Lori '85   Fc '83, '84, '85

McLaughlin, Teresa Ellen '79   HC '77

McLean, Alexander Stokes '69   F '69

McLean, Daniel Norman '75   L '72, '73, '74, '75

McLeod, Caroline Clagett '83   HC '81

McLeod, Creighton Scott '80   F '78, '79

McLeod, Gary Alan '82   LC '81

McLoone, Timothy Thomas '69   CC '66, '67, '68; TI '67, '68, '69; TO '68, '69

McLoughlin, Hollis Samuel '72 (MGR)   Ba '70, '71, '72

McMahon, James Joseph '75   H '73, '74, '75

McMahon, Kevin C. '66   L '65

McMahon, Stacie Jeanne '81   Bb '80

McMahon, Timothy Michael '86   H '84

McManama, George Benson Jr. '70   H '68, '69, '70

McManama, Robert Spang '73   H '71, '72, '73

McManus, Patricia Ann '80 (MGR)   Fc '79

McMillan, Katherine Jane '78–'79   Sk '78

McMonagle, Charles Edward '66   Bb '65, '66

McMullen, Hugh Sinclair '68 (MGR)   Ba '66, '68; H '67, '68

McMurchy, Kevin Weiss '79   LC '79

McNamara, Jane '79   Sw '76, '77

McNamara, Joseph Patrick '85   Ba '83, '84, '85

McNealy, Scott Glenn '76   G '75, '76

McNerny, Andrew Patrick '83   W '80, '81, '82, '83

McNulty, Paul Michael '84   CC '80, '81, '82, '83; TI '82; TO '81

McNulty, Thad Larson '80   TI '77, '78, '79, '80; TO '77, '78, '79, '80; CC '77, '78, '79

McOsker, Paul Lyne '79   Ba '77, '78, '79

McPherson, Joseph Warren '70   LC '68

McRoskey, Guy William '79   CC '78; TI '78; TO '79

McWhirter, Maurice John '77 (MGR)   R '77

Mead, Edward Scott '77   L '75; Sq '76, '77

Mead, Mark Cooper '84   F '82, '83

Mead, Stephen Jr. '75   S '72, '73, '74; Sq '73, '74, '75

Meade, Michael Spencer '87   W '84, '85

Meagher, Brendan Arthur '83   L '80, '82, '83

Meagher, Cecilia Charity '85   V '82

Mears, John Willis '71   Bb '69, '70, '71

Mechem, Richard Thomas '68   H '68

Mechling, Jerry Eugene '65   F '62, '63, '64

Medalie, Daniel Alexander '85   W '82, '83, '84, '85

Medlar, Michael James '73 (MGR)   H '72; L '73

Mee, Daniel Owen '81   F '79, '80

Mee, Peter Joseph '76   F '74, '75

Meehan, Edward '64   CC '61, '62, '63; TI '62, '63; TO '62, '63

Mehra, Sanjeev '82   G '80, '81

Meier, Anthony Philip '84   Sw '81, '82

Meisel, Wayne W. '82 (MGR)   FH '79, '80, '81

Meiselman, Abby Sue '82   Te '79, '80

Melfa, Lawrence Anthony '67   Ba '67

Mellen, Arthur William '76   L '74

Mellen, Robert Lind '78   L '76, '77, '78

Melvoin, Richard Irwin '73   TO '71

Mena, Demetrio Jr. '73   S '70, '72

Mende, Paul Frederick '83   LC '83

Mendelman, Eric Bruce '82   L '79, '80, '81, '82

Mendelman, Joel Timothy '88   L '85

Menichella, Daniel Leoard '81   Sw '78, '79, '80

Menichella, Lee Paul '82   Sw '79

Mercer, Charles Douglas II '66 (MGR)   G '64, '65

Meredith, Robert Rollyn '66   Sw '63, '64, '65

Merkin, Arthur Jay '85   Sk '83, '84, '85

Merner, David Robert '83   Fc '80, '81, '82, '83

Merner, Michael Dennis '84   Fc '81, '82, '83, '84

Mertz, Kristen Jean '82   Te '79, '80, '82

Messer, Karen Sue, '79   LC '76, '77, '78

Messing, Shep Norman '72   S '70, '71

Messinger, Miriam Sara '87   Sk '84

Metzger, John Mackay '70   TI '68, '69; TO '68, '69

Meyer, John Hornblower Jr. '71   LC '69, '70, '71

Meyer, Laurence Rolnick '87   LC '85

Meyer, Margaret Ann '81   Te '78, '79, '80, '81

Meyer, Mark '79   CC '76, '77, '78; TI '79; TO '77, '78

Meyers, Hildy '79   Bb '76, '77, '78, '79

Murray, Robert Steven '79   F '77, '78

Murray, Thomas '81   H '78, '79, '80, '81

Murrer, Herbert Scott '83   TI '80, '81, '82, '83; TO '81, '83; F '81, '82

Muscatine, Alison '76   Bb '75, '76; Te '75, '76

Muse, Robert Francis '73   H '71, '72, '73

Musliner, Thomas Allen '67   Fc '65, '66, '67

Musselman, Jeffrey Joseph '85   Ba '82, '83, '84, '85

Mustoe, Thomas Anthony '73   Bb '71, '72, '73

Muxlow, Douglas Berton '70 (MGR)   Bb '69

Myers, Christopher David '84   F '81, '82

Nadkarni, Mohan Moreshwar '85   V '83, '84, '85

Nahl, Angela Beatrice '85   WP '84

Nakamoto, Jon Masao '80   Fc '79

Nakamoto, Karen Junko '84 (MGR)   V '83, '84

Nakatsukasa, Laura Lynn '82 (MGR)   WP '81

Nance, Frederick Richard '75   TO '74

Nanula, Peter Joseph '84   G '82

Narva, Andrew Steven '73   LC '71, '72, '73

Nastala, Chet Lawrence '85   G '82, '83, '84, '85

Natterson, Paul David '85   LC '84, '85

Naughton, Joseph Mathias '73   TI '71, '72; TO '71

Nawrocki, Leon William '78 (MGR)   Sk '76, '77, '78

Nayar, Anil '69   Sq '67, '68, '69; Te '69

Naylor, Danny Alan '69   W '67

Nazir, Tarek Fuad '85   S '82, '83

Neal, Dale Kent '70   F '68, '69

Neal, George David '71 (MGR)   Sq '69, '70

Neal, John Eric '72   F '70, '71

Needle, Howard Marc '84 (MGR)   F '82, '83

Needleman, Arnold Elliot '75   Bb '74, '75

Neefe, John Robert Jr. '65 (MGR)   Te '63, '64

Neff, Taylor Eugene '76–'77   Sl '74, '76, '77

Neilson, Johanna Knorr '88   H '85

Nelson, Gordon Lyle Jr. '79   L '76, '77, '78, '79

Nelson, Lee William '78–'80   S '76, '77, '78

Nero, Nicholas Anthony '88   L '85

Nesto, Richard William '71   S '68, '69, '70

Neubert, Stephen Faulkner '67   L '65, '66, '67

Neuenschwander, Jack Lynn '64   F '63, '64

Neuhauser, Alice Perry '84   TI '81, '82, '83, '84; TO '81, '82, '83, '84

Neville, George '66   Ba '63, '64, '65; Bb '65, '66

Neville, Timothy David '75–76   Sw '72, '73, '74, '76

Nevin, Janice Elizabeth '81   LC '78, '79, '80

New, Thomas Lyon '73   CC '70, '71

Newell, Susan Milliken '84   H '81, '82, '83, '84; So '84

Newhouse, George Braxton Jr. '76   F '73, '74, '75

Newkirk, William Lee '72   Bb '70

Newman, Frederick Samuel '67   F '66

Newman, John Hughes '67   TI '65, '67; TO '67

Newman, Martha Gay '80   HC '77

Newman, Virginia Isette Santos '83   HC '83

Newmark, Brian Elliott '72   Bb '70, '71, '72

Newnham, Paula Margaret '82   CC '78; TI '82; TO '82

Newton, Dexter Jr. '66   H '65, '66; L '63, '64, '65, '66

Newton, Martha Louise '79 (MGR)   TI '77, '78; TO '78, '79

Nicholas, Gerrit Jaap '84   L '81

Nicholas, Jonathan Seth '87   L '84

Nicholas, Paul '87   S '83, '84

Nichols, Philip Martin '82   LC '82

Nichols, Richard Frederick Fuller '86   G '83, '84

Nickel, Jeffrey David '85   LC '84, '85

Nickens, Jacks Clarence   Ba '69, '70, '71

Nicodemus, Christopher Farley '79   TI '78, '79; TO '78, '79

Nicosia, Thomas Arnold '69   L '67, '68, '69

Niederhoffer, Victor Barry '64   Sq '62, '63

Nieland, Todd Allan '76   H '74, '75, '76

Nielsen, John Christopher '71   Te '69, '70, '72

Nielsen, Paul Jackson '82   LC '82

Niemi, Steven Matthew '75   TI '73, '74, '75; TO '73, '74, '75

Nierman, Eliot Hillel '71   F '70

Niles, Barbara Lindsay '82   LC '82; Sw '79

Niles, John Lindsay '76   HC '76

Nilsen, Nils '75   Ba '75

Nixon, Clarence Bovaird III '79   Sq '77, '78

Njoku, Charles Achilike '67 A.S.   S '64, '65; TI '65, '66

Noback, Roger Allen '66   F '64, '65

Noble, James Alexander '71   Bb '69

Noble, John Harmon III '75 (MGR)   CC '72, '73

Nolan, Andrew Robert '84   F '81, '82, '83

Nolen, William Dennis '78   H '77, '78

Nomizu, Yvonne '81   Sk '80

Noona, Everett Mark '74   H '72, '73, '74

Nordell, Eric Peter '80   Sk '78, '79, '80

Nordlund, Randall Ravall '82   S '79

Norlander, Michael Lewis '70   Bb '68

Norris, Barbara Ann '77   HC '75, '76; LC '77

North, Jay Robert '84   H '81, '82, '83, '84

Norton, Lauren Inness '81   Sl '78, '79, '80, '81;   H '79, '80, '81

Norton, Robert Joseph '67   F '65, '66, '67; L '67

Nosal, Edward Robert Jr. '71   TI '69, '70; TO '69, '70, '71

Novis, Bruce Kevin '86   WP '83, '84

Nowygrod, Roman '66   LC '63, '64, '65, '66

Noyes, Frederick '66   Sk '65

Nsiah, Peter '81   TI '80, '81; TO '80, '81

Nullet, Joseph James '84   L '81, '82

Nwafor, Azinna '64   S '63

Nwokoye, Godwin Nonyelum '67   TO '66, '67

O'Brien, Daniel Francis '84   TI '84; TO '84

O'Brien, John Francis '65   F '63, '64

O'Brien, John Lawrence '84   F '82, '83; TO '81, '82

O'Brien, Stephen James '77   F '75, '76

O'Connell, Kenneth Drew '69   Ba '68; F '68

O'Connell, Kevin Barrett '78   Sw '75, '76, '77

O'Connor, Austin James '74   TO '72, '74

O'Connor, Brian Patrick Wright '78   S '77

O'Donnell, John Emmett Jr. '84   G '83, '84

O'Donnell, Joseph James '67   Ba '65, '66, '67; F '65, '66

O'Donnell, Linus Charles '81   F '79, '80, '81

O'Donoghue, Kevin Joseph '78   H '76, '77, '78

O'Hare, Robert Michael '74   F '71, '72, '73

O'Konski, Mark Steven '79   HC '79

O'Leary, Francis Xavier '73   LC '72

O'Leary, Paul Hennessey '85   CC '84; TI '84; TO '83

O'Malley, Cormac Kevin Hooker '65   S '62, '63

O'Malley, Michael Joseph '74   Ba '72, '73, '74

O'Marah, Meave Gately '86   S '82, '83

O'Neil, Ford Edward '85   L '84

O'Neil, Gerald Thomas '70   Bb '68

Shemitz, Leigh Addison '86   Sk '85

Shepard, Richard Kesniel '82   TO '82

Shepley, Robert Gardiner '76   H '76

Sheppard, Dean '71   W '69, '70, '71

Sherlock, Robert Francis '84   L '81, '82, '83, '84

Sherman, Frederick Scott '71   G '70, '71

Shevlin, John Booth '67   F '66

Shields, Sara Grace '84   LC '84

Shirey, Charles William '86   F '84

Shlimbaum, Terry Earle '75   Ba '75

Shofner, Stewart Robert '79   F '78

Shofner, William Emory '73   F '71, '72

Shoumatoff, Alex '68   Sq '68

Showerman, Earl Roy '66   Sw '63, '64

Shrout, William Clay '68   Sw '66, '67, '68

Shulman, Hal Mitchell '75 (MGR)   LC '75

Shultz, David Victor '80 (MGR)   CC '77, '79

Sicher, Michael Atwood '69   S '67, '68

Sideropoulos, Henry '73   S '71, '72

Sidman, Peter Alan '81   Sq '78

Sieber, Mark Christopher '76   LC '74, '75

Siegel, Craig Owen '80   Sw '77, '78

Sigal, Robert Keith '81   LC '79, '80, '81

Sigillito, Jon Michael '78   F '75, '76, '77

Sigward, Eric Hall '68   HC '66, '67

Sikora, Mitchell Joseph Jr. '66   Ba '65, '66

Silk, Paul Michael '68   HC '66, '67

Silver, David Gray '72   Sw '70, '71, '72

Silver, Louis Grant '75   Bb '73, '74, '75

Silvey, Brian Everett '79   F '77, '78

Silverman, Mitchell Sheldon '75   W '73, '75

Simbeck, John David '87   Bb '84

Simkowitz, Daniel Aaron '87   Sw '84, '85

Simmons, Geneva Ann '86   H '83, '84, '85; L '83, '84, '85

Simmons, Joseph Paul '80   F '77

Simmons, Matthew Clay '77   Fc '75, '76, '77

Simon, Amy Rebecca '85   CC '83, '84; TI '82, '85; TO '84, '85

Simon, Daniel Ira '83   HC '81, '82, '83

Simon, John Gregory '84   Te '84

Simpson, Michael '81 (MGR)   Ba '81

Simpson, Stephen Whittington '66   Sq '65

Sims, Leslie Mosell '81   TI '79; TO '79

Sinclair, Robert Lindsay '67   G '66, '67

Sinek, Jeffrey Scott '85   Bb '82

Singer, Carlyle Heath '78   L '77, '78; Sk '75, '76, '77

Singer, Margaret Worthington '82   So '82

Singer, Pamela Joanne '86   Sk '83, '84

Singh, Nikhil Pal '87   S '84

Singleterry, Gary Lee '70   F '68, '69

Singleton, Andrew Seth '84–'85   Sk '84

Singleton, David Joseph '79   Ba '76, '77

Sirlin, Claude B. '87   HC '85

Sise, James Gallison '67   Sk '65, '66, '67

Sismanidis, Roxanne D. '77   Bb '75

Skaff, Daniel Lawrence '82   Ba '79, '80, '81

Skalinder, Gregg Lewis '65   Sw '63

Skartvedt, Virginia Ann '84–'85   Sl '81, '82, '83, '84, '85

Skelly, Kevin Andrew '83   Te '80

Skinner, Dirk Eliot '75   CC '73, '74; TO '75

Skowronski, Eugene Anthony '65   F '62, '64

Skowronski, Theodore Edwin '69   F '68

Slutzker, Michael Laurence '71   W '69, '70, '71

Small, William Stuart '72   Sw '70

Smart, Jonathan '69   LC '69

Smart, Michael William '84   Sk '82, '83, '84

Smerczynski, Michael Thomas '82   Ba '81, '82; F '79, '80

Smith, Baldwin Jr '65   H '63, '64, '65

Smith, Benjamin Atwood III '68   H '66, '67, '68

Smith, Christopher Kelly '88   Sw '85

Smith, David Brian '66   W '63, '64

Smith, David Stephen '70   F '69

Smith, Diane Carol '85   Sw '82

Smith, Elizabeth '84   WP '80

Smith, Erika Bamford '86   Te '83, '84, '85

Smith, Fred Douglas Jr. '73   F '71, '72

Smith, Frederick Theodore '78   W '76, '77, '78

Smith, Harold Francis '73   Ba '71, '72, '73; Bb '71, '72, '73

Smith, James Christopher '76   Sw '73

Smith, James Ferrell '67   CC '64, '65, '66; TI '65, '66, '67; TO '65

Smith, James Wesley '77 (MGR)   H '77, '78

Smith, Jay Bradford '80   HC '79, '80, '81

Smith, John '83   HC '81, '82, '83

Smith, Joseph Edward '66   TO '63, '64, '65

Smith, Karen Louise '82   Bb '79, '80

Smith, Kimberly Ann '87   Bb '85

Smith, Kirk Charles '86   F '84, '85

Smith, Layle Kipland '77   W '74, '75, '76, '77

Smith, Lewis Conrad III '69   Sw '67, '68

Smith, Leslie Jane '83   Sw '80, '83

Smith, Marian Guyon Purchas '80   LC '77, S '77; TI '78; TO '78

Smith, Mark Griffin '79   LC '79; Sk '78

Smith, Michael '81   S '77, '78, '79, '80

Smith, Patrick Sean James '86   Bb '83, '84, '85

Smith, Paul Andrew '81   Fc '79

Smith, Paul Quentin '74   G '72, '73, '74

Smith, Peter Pembroke '78   G '76, '77, '78

Smith, Philip Joseph '68   Ba '67

Smith, Richard Kent '67   Sw '65, '67

Smith, Richard Warren '74   HC '72, '73, '74

Smith, Roger Stanley '66   CC '63, '64,

Smith, Timothy Stanley '86   H '83, '84, '85

Snavely, Stephen Vant '73   F '71, '72

Snook, Curtis Pendleton '82   HC '81

Snowden, Frank Martin III '68   TO '67

Soderberg, Leif Gallup '76   LC '74, '75

Soghikian, Gregory Will '82   LC '80, '81, '82

Sollee, Joseph Rainer '86   L '83

Sollee, William Lawrence '85   L '82, '83

Solomon, William Julius '87   F '84

Somers, Joseph Vincent '81   Sq '79, '80

Sonnabend, Wendy '81   Sq '78, '79, '80, '81; S '79, '80; L '78, '79

Sontag, Anne Burnett '78 (MGR)   W '76, '77, '78

Sorbara, George James '87   Ba '84, '85; F '85

Sorich, John Micjael '82   Ba '81, '82

Southmayd, William Webster '64   F '61, '62, '63,

Spalding, Amy McKean '83   H '80, '82, '83

Spalding, Andrew Pratt '78   H '78

Spagnola, Lawrence John '77   F '75, '76

Spanos, Gus Boonos '84   Rb '84; TO '81

Spears, Sally A. '78   Fc '75, '76

Spence, Sarah Jane '84   WP '84

Spencer, Charles Hutton '66   LC '65, '66

Spencer, Frank Phillip II '71 (MGR)   F '69, '70,

Spencer, Karen Elizabeth '80   HC '77, '78, '79, '80

Spengler, Thomas Matthew '71   CC '68, '69, '70; TI '69, '70; TO '69, '70, '71

Sphire, Raymond Daniel '81   L '81

Spiegel, Eric Allan '80   F '80, '81

Spitzberg, Jack Wolf '64   TI '62, '63; TO '62, '63

Spitzer, Nicholas Canaday '64   Fc '63, '64

Sprague, James Baird '65 (MGR)   Sk '65

Sprague, Phineas Jr. '72   LC '70, '71, '72

Springate, James Edward '76   TI '73, '75, '76; TO '74

Springer, Jenny '84   Sl '84

Springer, Sandee Alice '84 (MGR)   S '80, '81

St. George, Robert Martin '64   Ba '62, '63

St. Goar, Janet Treat '77–'78   Te '77

St. John, Judson Burke '80   Ba '77, '78, '79; F '79

St. Louis, Jennifer Ann '88   TO '85

St. Louis, Peter '80   Sw '79, '80

St. Louis, Susan Marie '81   S '77, '78, '79, '80; L '78, '79; TO '80

St. Onge, Richard Arhur '66   F '64, '65

St. Pierre, David Philip '74   Ba '73, '74; F '72, '73

Stabler, Edwars Amesbury '81   LC '81

Stack, James Otto Jr. '72 (MGR)   Sq '71, '72

Stack, Robert William '68   G '68

Stafford, Benjamin Thomas '65 (MGR)   F '63

Stafford, Linda Montague '81 (MGR)   FH '78

Staggers, Daniel Casey '75   F '73, '74

Staggers, Harley Orrin '74   F '73

Staley, Diana Victoria '85   Sq '84

Standaert, Christopher John '87   WP '84

Standish, Myles Erwin '77   Sw '74, '75, '76, '77

Standley, Timothy Kyle '85   Bb '82, '83, '84

Stanislaw, Joseph Andrew '71   Bb '69, '70

Stanley, William Reid '87   Te '84, '85

Stanton, Cynthia Joyce '82   Sq '79

Stanton, James Locke '67   Sw '65

Stapleton, Craig Roberts '67   L '65, '67; Sq '65, '66, '67

Starbuck, Robert Burnham '84   H '82, '83

Starck, Walter Joseph '72   F '70, '71

Stargel, Willard Rough '69   F '68

Starkey, Kathleen Meghan '87   Sw '84

Starr, Enid Luella '85   H '82, '83, '84, '85

Starr, Julie Maslon '82   H '79, '80, '81, '82

Starr, Richard Marc '73   W '71, '72, '73

States, Katherine Pierson '79   Sk '76

Stearns, Marshall Jr. '70 (MGR)   G '70

Steele, Benjamin Belknap '74   Sk '72, '73, '74

Steele, Chauncey Depew III '65   Te '63, '64, '65

Steele, Eugenie Marie Frances Poole '77   LC '75

Stein, Laurence J. '82   G '81, '82

Steinberg, Robert Mark '86   F '83, '84

Steiner, Mark Edward '72   F '69, '70, '71

Steketee, Scott Nelson '68   HC '66, '67, '68

Stelling, Meredith Taylor '82   Sl '80, '81, '82

Stempson, Robert Duncan '68   CC '65; TI '66, '67, '68; TO '66, '68

Stenhouse, Michael Steven '80   Ba '77, '78, '79; Bb '78

Stephens, Bradford Archibald '64   F '61, '62, '63

Stephens, David Kimbro '83–'84   TI '80, '81, '82, '84; TO '80, '81, '83, '84

Stephenson, Thomas Fleetwood '64   Ba '63; F '61, '62, '63

Steponaitis, Vincas Petras '74 (MGR)   S '72, '73

Stern, David Gennet '68 (MGR)   W '67, '68

Stern, David Thomas '84   SL '82

Sterne, Richard Justin '68   Sq '65, '66, '67, '68; Te '65, '66, '67, '68

Stetz, Joseph John Jr. '64   Sw '62, '63

Stevens, John Emerson '66   H '63, '64

Stevens, Margaret Katherine '81   HC '80, '81

Stevens, Ruth S. '75   Sq '75

Stevenson, Bruce Richard '66   LC '63, '64, '65

Stevenson, Robert Hooper '75 (MGR)   H '73

Steward, Lorelee Sharon '86   So '83

Stewart, Lorelee Sharon '86   Bb '83

Stewart, Michael Wesley '79   TO '76, '78, '79

Stewart, Ronald Mark '80   Ba '77, '78, '79, '80

Stich, Laura Coela '85   S '82; H '85

Stiles, Geoffrey Martin '79   TI '76, '77, '78, '79; TO '76, '77, '78, '79

Stimpson, Courtney Sutton '82   Sq '79, '80, '81, '82

Stinn, Bradley John '82   F '79, '80, '81

Stockman, Paul Keidel '88   Sw '85

Stockman, Robert Bernard '76   H '76

Stoeckel, James William '74   Ba '72, '73; F '72, '73, '74

Stokes, Mary Elizabeth '78   LC '75, '77, '78

Stokes, Wade Leeger '88   WP '84

Stone, Alfred Douglas '76   S '75

Stone, David Smart '80   S '79

Stone, Jennifer Page '80   FH '76, '77, '78; HC '77; Sq '77, '78, '79, '80

Stone, Pamela Gertrude '82   Sw '79, '80, '81, '82

Stone, Robert Gregg '75   HC '73, '74, '75

Stookey, David Wood '64   Sl '63, '64

Storer, Jeffrey Burton '70   Sl '70

Storey, Charles Mills '82   HC '80, '81, '82

Stoviak, John Francis '73   G '71, '72, '73

Strandemo, Gary Allan '68   F '67

Strassman, Eric Harold '85   Fc '83, '84

Strathmeyer, James Merle Jr. '76   W '73, '74, '75, '76

Strauss, David Aaron '73   Sw '71

Strauss, Marshall Bruce '72 (MGR)   Sw '71, '72

Strauss, Robert Elliot '86   WP '82, '83, '84

Streeter, Cornelia Van Rensselaer '85   LC '82, '83, '84, '85

Streeter, Margaret Montgomery '79   H '79

Strehler, Allen Evans '81   TO '81

Stricker, Jenny Anne '85   CC '81, '82, '84; TI '82, '83; TO '82, '83, '84, '85

Stringer, Robert Arthur '64   F '61, '62, '63, '64

Strittmatter, Stephen Mark '80   Sl '78, '79, '80

Strnad, Nina Phelps '78 (MGR)   FH '76, '77

Strominger, Matthew Brandt '79–'80   Sk '79

Strong, Cynthia Huddleston '79   HC '76, '77, '78, '79

Stuart, Claire '74 (MGR)   Te '72, '74

Stuart, Harborne Wentworth Jr. '78   HC '78

Stuart, Regina Kathryn '81   Sw '78, '79, '80

Stubbs, John Delano Jr. '80   Sq '77, '78, '79, '80

Sudduth, Andrew Hancock '83–'85   HC '82, '83, '85

Sugrue, Erin Elizabeth '87   Bb '84, '85; TO '84, '85

Sujansky, Walter Vladimir '86   Sk '83, '84

Sullivan, Anne Louise '81   CC '77, '78

Sullivan, Barrett Eugene '81 (MGR)   H '80

Sullivan, Brian Deming '68   LC '66, '67, '68

Sullivan, Daniel John '78   TI '75, '76, '77, '78; TO '76, '77, '78

Sullivan, David William '79   CC '78

Sullivan, Deidre Mary '79 (MGR)   LC '78, '79

Sullivan, Denis Paul '72   F '70, '71

Sullivan, John Steven '74 (MGR)   F '73

Sullivan, Matthew Joseph Jr. '85   Rb '84

Sullivan, Nicholas Peter '72   L '70

Sulloway, Frank Jones II '69   CC '68

Sundlun, Stuart Arthur '75   W '74

Sung, Bing '66   W '65, '66

Sunstein, Cass Robert '76   Sq '74, '75, '76

Sutton, Alexander Leather '88   Sl '85

Sutton, Douglas Kendall '86   Ba '84, '85

Sutton, Peter Campbell '72   HC '72

Sviokla, Sylvester Charles III '67   F '64, '65, '66

Swan, D. Turner '84   F '81, '82

Swansey, John David '82   HC '82

Sweeney, Donald Clarke '84–'85   H '85

Sweitzer, Brandon Weller '64   H '63, '64

Swift, Phelps Hoyt Jr. '76   H '74, '75, '76

Switzer, Alan Alexander III '86   LC '85

Swords, Deirdre Helen '86   Sk '83

Sykes, Gene Tiger '80   LC '78, '79, '80

Sylvester, Thomas Oliver '80   Ba '80

Symington, John Fife III '68   L '65, '66

Szaro, Richard Julian '71   F '69, '70; TO '69, '70, '71

Sze, Deborah Yung-Ning '78   Fc '77, '78

Szeremeta, Wasyl '84 (MGR)   Bb '82; Sw '83, '84; WP '84

Sztorc, William Adam '84   H '84

Taber, Kelley Morgan '88   Sw '85

Tabler, William Benjamin Jr. '65 (MGR)   Ba '63, '64, '65

Tabor, Charles Sumner '78   Sl '77, '78

Taft, David Robert '66   S '63, '64, '65

Taft, Deborah Gamble '84   H '81, '82, '83, '84

Tague, Peter Winston '65   G '63, '64, '65

Talbert, Phillip Allen '84   LC '84

Talbot, Samuel Spring '69   HC '68, '69

Taliaferro, John Christopher '73   L '72, '73, '74

Tanaka, Jon Tamio '84   V '81, '82, '84

Tang, Cha-Nan Michelle '76   FH '75

Tanner, Suzanne Marie Flavia '85   H '82, '85

Tarczy, Kenneth Allen '86   F '83, '84

Tarlow, Elliot Stanley '78–'79   HC '79

Tarre, Michael Alan '65   Te '65

Tate, Cheryl Jean '84   H '81, '82, '83, '84

Tatrallyay, Geza Paul '71   Fc '69, '71, '72

Taubes, Gary Alan '77   F '75, '76

Taylor, Bambi Lynne '86   FH '82, '83, '84; L '84, '85

Taylor, Daniel Mark '77   Sw '74, '75, '76

Taylor, Kathryn Ann '80   CC '77, '79; TI '77, '78, '79; TO '78, '79, '80

Taylor, Mark Sherman '77   F '74, '75, '76

Taylor, Randall Louis '87   H '84, '85

Taylor, Richard Manley '77–'78   LC '77

Taylor, Robert Lee '82   Bb '79, '80, '81

Tecce, Pamela Mary '87 (MGR)   L '84, '85

Teaford, Stephen Dale '66   Sw '65

Tellez, Trinidad L. '85   V '82

Temple, Harry Thomas '80   F '78

Templeton, Paul Whitfield '79   HC '77, '78, '79

Tennant, Alexander Thomas '74   F '71, '72, '73

Tennis, William James '76   L '74, '75, '76

Tepe, Nicholas Allen '76   Fc '75, '76

Terner, Michael Adam '82   Te '80, '81

Terranova, William Anthony '69   LC '67, '68, '69

Terrell, Allen McKay Jr. '65   Sq '63, '64, '65; Te '63, '64, '65

Terrell, Lawrence Peters '70   Sq '68, '69, '70; Te '68, '69

Terry, Crystal Dionne '80   FH '77

Terry, Lawrence Jr. '68   HC '68; LC '66, '67

Teske, Kurt Frederick '81   HC '80, '81

Teske, Robert Thomas '70   F '69

Tetirick, Bruce Lyle '74   F '71, '72, '73

Tetlow, Peter Wayne '77   Sw '74, '75, '76

Tew, Adrian Douglas Christopher '74   TO '72, '73, '74

Tew, David Stewart '74   LC '73; Sl '74

Tew, James Dinsmore III '66   HC '63, '64, '65

Tews, Thomas '64 (ASSOC. MGR)   HC '63, '64

Thal, Denise Ann '77   Bb '75, '76; Te '75, '76, '77

Thayer, Lisa Bissell '83   HC '81

Theodore, William Harold '69   Fc '68

Thio, Benjamin Pok-Ay '85   F '83, '84

Thom, James Richard '79   F '78

Thomas, Charles Whitfield '72   S '70, '71

Thomas, Christopher Gerard '75 (MGR)   H '74, '75

Thomas, Harvey Lowell III '67   TI '65; TO '65

Thomas, James Hardwick '75   Ba '73, '74, '75; H '73, '74, '75

Thomas, Michael Francis '73   Ba '70, '71, '72

Thompson, Daniel Otha '69   Sw '68

Thompson, Douglas Samuel '79   H '77

Thompson, John Apthorp '80   G '80

Thompson, LeRoy Jr. '75   L '74, '75; S '74, '75

Thompson, Robert Torrey '76   G '74, '75, '76; S '75

Thompson, Samuel '65   S '62, '63, '64

Thompson, Willaim Joseph '82   F '81

Thompson, William Randolph '68   TO '67

Thornbrough, Wayne Dole '66   G '64, '65

Thorndike, John '64   S' 61, '62, '63; Sq '62, '63

Thorndike, Theodore Baker '75   H '73, '74, '75

Thornton, John Lawson '76   Te '75

Thorpe, Ronald Dale '74 (MGR)   F '72, '73

Tibbetts, Joseph Vincent '70   G '68, '69

Tice, Alan Douglas '66   LC '63, '64, '65

Tiffany, Thomas Dougald '71   HC '69, '70, '71

Tighe, Francis William '69 (MGR)   HC '68, '69; LC '67

Tilles, Stephen Andrew '82   Ba '79; HC '82

Tillman, Robert Reiff '78   Fc '77

Tilly, Kathryn Louise '78   Sl '77, '78

Tilton, Samuel Odin '66 (MGR)   H '65

Timberlake, Alan Harrington '68   L '66, '67

Timmins, Edward Patrick '77   LC '75

Timpson, William Michael '68   F '67

Tivnan, Terrance '69 (MGR)   H '69

Toal, Michael Arthur '78   Sw '75, '76, '77, '78

Tobin, James Joseph '88   Sw '85

Tobin, James Robert Jr. '66   Ba '63, '64, '65

Todd, John Joseph '71   Ba '70, '71

Tolbert, Richard Vacanerat '72   Fc '70, '71

Tom, Roslyn '85   H '82

Tomford, John Walton '71 (MGR)   S '69, 70

Tompkins, Richard Floyd '67   Sw '67

Tonks, Philip Estabrook '67   LC '67

Torg, Elisabeth '84   FH '80, '81, '82, '83

Torhorst, James Bruce '68   G '65, '66

Toth, Katalin Elizabeth '85   WP '84

Townley, Alison '87   HC '84, '85

Townsend, Heather Mary '86   LC '83

Toy, Lisa Stephanie '85   Fc '85

Trainor, James Vichael '79   H '76, '77, '78, '79

Trakas, Christopher John '81   WP '80

Treadwell, Barry Lincoln '64   H '63

Treidman, Johon Knapp '79–'80   Sk '79

Trembowicz, Richard Lawrence '78   Ba '77

Tria, Alfred Jacques Jr. '68 (MGR)   H '67, '68

Tripp, Thomas William '71   W '69, '71

Tron, Lanny Mark '82   TI '80, '81, '82; TO '79, '80, '81, '82

Trout, Monroe Eugene '84   Bb '81, '82, '83, '84

Troy, James Lawrence '71 (MGR)   F '70

True, Lawrence Dashiell '67 (MGR)   F '66

Trumbull, Constance Hunt '85   V '81, '83, '84

Trumbull, Walter Henry Jr. '81   V '81

Trusty, Terry Lorenza '80   F '78, '79; L '78, '79, '80

Tsigdinos, Karl Andrew '76   CC '73, '74

Tsitsos, Alkinos '75   F '72, '73, '74

Tsomides, Theodore '82   HC '80, '81

Tu, Lawrence Paul '76   Fc '74, '75, '76

Tuck, Gary Leonard '69   R '69

Tucker, Curtis John '71   Ba '69

Tuke, John Patrick '78   F '75, '76, '77

Tung, Rebecca Lillian '80   Sq '77, '78, '79, '80

Turco, John Harvey '70   Ba '68, '69, '70; H '68, '69, '70

Turner, Harry Vincent '64   Sw '62, '63, '64

Turner, James Bernard '83   H '80, '81, '82, '83

Tutun, Theodore Eric '86   Ba '84
Twite, David Leif '84   V '81, '82, '83, '84
Tyler, David Armistead '69   LC '68, '69
Tyler, Robert Stephen '84   Sw '82, '83, '84; WP '80, '81
Tyng, James '65   S '63, '64
Tyson, John Dormer '69   F '66, '67, '68
Tyson, Neil DeGrasse '80   W '80

Udo, Augustine Francis '83   TI '80, '81, '82, '83; TO '80, '81, '82, '83
Uecker, Jeffrey Craig '84   F '82, '83
Ueda, Karen Aiko, '82   TI '81; V '82
Uhl, Lawrence Edmund '73   L '71, '72, '73
Ulcickas, Frank Stanley '65   F '62, '63, '64
Underwood, Charles Marshall II '64   Te '63, '64
Unkovic, John Clark '65   HC '63, '64, '65
Updike, David Hoyer '79   S '76, '77
Upjohn, Emily Dawes '82–'83   So '82

Vagelos, Randy Herodotus '79   LC '78, '79
Valentine, Donald Wallace '73   Fc '71, '72
Valenzuela, Terence David '73   Fc '71, '72, '73
Vallone, Paul Ernest '86   Ba '83, '84, '84
Van Den Broek, Richard Albertus '88   L '85
Van Dyke, Melinda Agard '85   Te '82
Van Niel, Anthony '74   S '72, '73
Van Oudenallen, Harry '66   F '63, '64, '65; L '65
Van Ryn, Debbir Maria '80   Sw '77, '78
Vanderpoolwallace, Vincent Samuel '75   TI '72, '73, '74, '75; TO '72, '73, '74, '75
VanDissell, Bart Jan '75   W '74, '75
Vanelli, Mark Reid '79   Sk '77
Vann, Thomas James '75   L '74
Vargas, Jaime Ernesto '69   S '66, '67, '68
Varney, Richard Frederick Jr. '71   Ba '69, '70, '71; F '68, '69, '70
Varsames, Louis John '82   F '80, '81, '82
Vassallo, Susan Anne '79   Sw '76, '77, '78
Vastola, Eugene Luca '79   Fc '76, '77, '78, '79
Vavassis, Denis '86   F '84
Vecchi, Dennis Joseph '85   F '84
Velie, Ann Elizabeth '81   FH '77, '78, '79, '80; L '78, '79, '80, '81
Velie, Ellen Mary '85   S '82; Sw '82, '83, '84, '85
Vena, Edward Francis '73   F '70, '71, '72
Ventley, Erics A. '84 (MGR)   Fc '84
Vera, George Amero Jr. '65   LC '63, '64, '65
Verdin, Thomas Edward '83   Sw '80, '82, '83

Verlin, Howard Evan '83   W '81
Veteran, Frank Anthony '72   F '70, '71
Vierra, Scott Gerard '85   Ba '82, '83, '84, '85
Vigna, Katherine D. '87   Te '84, '85
Vignali, Mark Patrick '85   F '82, '83, '84
Viita, Paul Sears '70   Fc '68, '70
Vik, Alexander Mikael '78   G '75, '76, '77, '78
Villa, Anthony Gambrill '72   S '71
Villanueva, James Jay '84   F '81, '82, '83
Villar, Alberto Jose '81–'82   S '77, '78, '79, '81
Vincent, E. Christopher '78   LC '77
Vincent, Gilbert Tapley '67   LC '65, '66, '67
Vine, Suzanne Ellen '82   L '79, '80, '81
Vinton, John Thayer '64   Sq '62, '63
Visone, Anthony '84   H '81, '82, '83, '84
Vita, Mark Robert '86   L '83, '84
Vitale, David John '68   F '67
Voelkel, John Stephen '85   L '82, '83, '84, '85
Vogel, Deborah Ruth '80   TI '77
Vogel, Deborah Ruth '80 (MGR)   CC '77; TI '77, '78; TO '78, '79
Vogt, Eric Edwards '70   L '68
Vogt, Evon Zartman III '68   L '66, '67
Voit, Leslie Stewart '83   CC '79
Voltz, Michael Allerton '85   L '82, '83, '85
Voros, Arpad Peter '74–'75 (MGR)   F '74; Te '75; S '75
Vosters, Francis Adrian Cornelius '73   Sq '71, '72, '73
Vujovic, Dragan '75   S '73

Wade, Julie G '75   Sw '75
Wagener, David Paul '76   HC '76
Wagner, James Peter Wisloh '88   Sl '85
Wagner, Robert Anthony '76   F '75
Wahl, Dieter Hermann '66   TI '63, '64
Waickowski, Paul Stanley '69   Bb '68, '69
Wald, Barry Michael '78   H '78
Waldfogel, Jane L. '76   L '75
Waldinger, Carl Peter '67   H '65, '66, '67
Waldman, Daniel Robert '77   Te '75, '76, '77
Waldstein, John Douglas '75   H '75
Waldstein, Thomas Gordon '71   F '69, '70
Wales, Roger Martin '68   G '67
Walker, Allan Elliott '64   Te '62, '63
Walker, Frederick Burgess II '73   HC '72
Walker, Janet Shakuntala '81   Sk '78
Walker, Joseph Monroe '73   L '71, '72
Walker, Peter Fitz-Randolph '65 (MGR)   H '63, '64, '65
Walker, William Scott '79   Te '77, '78, '79

Wallace, Michael Brunson '73   F '72
Wallace, Sean Robert '85   W '82, '83, '84, '85
Wallace, Thomas Joseph '72   Sw '70, '71, '72
Walsh, Eric Wyatt '72   L '71
Walsh, Fraser MacFarland '67   LC '65, '66
Walsh, Norman Joseph '74   Ba '72, '73, '74
Walsh, Peter Feely '82–'83   S '78, '80, '81
Walther, Douglas Lynn '69   Sw '68
Walton, David Albert '78   F '75, '76, '77
Wanta, Erik Dirk '88   Bb '85
Ward, Elizabeth Damon '85   H '82, '83, '85
Ward, Michael Rodthur '79   L '77, '78, '79, '80
Wardenburg, Elizabeth Blair '86   L '83, '84, '85
Ware, Dwight Allen '69   H '67, '68, '69
Wark, Joseph Arthur '81   Ba '78, '79, '80, '81
Warren, Caleb Thomas '72   L '70
Warren, Dana Ann '82   Bb '80; S '80, '81
Wartel, Scott Major '77   Sw '74
Washauer, William Warner '71   Te '69, '70, '71
Washburn, Edward H. '64   HC '63, '64
Wasserstrom, William Ross '70   W '69
Waters, Margaret Mary '84   Sk '82, '83, '84
Watson, Alan Fraser '71   Sk '69, '70, '71
Watson, Daniel Lee '85   Sw '82, '83
Watson, Donald Clarke '73   LC '72, '73
Watson, Michael Dennis '82   H '79, '80, '81, '82
Watson, Peter Thacher '72   H '70
Watson, Welcom Henry '73   Sw '71
Wattles, Kevin Scott '86   W '83, '84
Watts, Diana Beth '87   Sw '85
Watts, James Darrell '65   TO '65
Waugh, Daniel Charles '77 (MGR)   HC '76, '79
Webb, Bucknell Chapman '78   Sl '76, '77, '78
Weber, Bruce William '83–'84   CC '79, '80, '81, '83; TI '80, '82; TO '80, '81, '82, '84
Webster, Keith William '87   Bb '84, '85
Weckstein, Leslie Ellen '82   Sl '81
Weeks, Charles Sinclair '85   Rb '84
Weinberg, David Leslie '74   HC '72, '73, '74
Weiner, Per-Arne '88   Sk '85
Weinfurtner, Edward Lamar '80   S '78, '79, '80
Weintraub, Joshua Lorin '87   Fc '84
Weir, James Ronald '64   L '62, '63

Weisheit, Bowen Pattison Jr. '71   HC '69, '70

Weiss, Ellen Suer '80 (MGR)   Fc '80

Weiss, Frederick Lincoln '75   S '74

Weiss, Howard Carl '74   Fc '73, '74, '75

Weiss, Thomas George '68   F '67; L '66

Weissent, Alexander Bruce '73   Ba '71, '72, '73

Weissman, Arthur Bruce '70   Fc '68, '69, '70

Weissman, Lisa Beth '77   S '77

Welch, Bernard Charles Jr. '88   L '85

Welch, Charles Alfred '66   HC '63, '64

Welch, Henry Gilbert '76   LC '75, '76

Welch, Leighton Bridge '83   S '80, '81, '82,

Welch, Miles Parker '86   S '83, '84

Welch, Patricia Anne '81   S '78, '79, '80

Welch, Robert Warren '67   TO '65, '66

Welch, Thomas Cary '79 (MGR)   Bb '77, '78

Welch, Wade Mark '65   H '63, '64, '65

Weller, Bruce Mark '84   Ba '81, '82, '83, '84

Welz, Robert Gerard '68   Ba '65, '66; F '65, '66

Wen, Patrici Poo '80 (MGR)   Te '77, '78

Wendel, William Collins '77   F '75, '76; TI '77

Wendland, Christopher Scott '87   LC '85

Werbowski, Andrew Paul '86   G '84

Werly, James Patrick '78   Ba '76, '77

Westlake, Lisa Marie '80   TI '79; TO '80

Westra, James Richard '73   F '71, '72

Whalen, Giles Francis '76   L '74, '75, '76

Whatley, Lowell McKay Jr. '77 (MGR)   Sq '77

Wheeler, Edward Adams '70   Te '68

Wheeler, Jeanne Huse '78   Sk '76

Wheeler, Mark Alfred '73   F '72

Wheeler, Robert Jerome '84   Te '81, '82; H '83, '84

Whelchel, Henry Jerd '66   Sw '65

Whiston, Mark Bradley '84   H '81

Whitbeck, John Van Husan '68 (MGR)   Sq '68; Te '66, '67, '68

White, Brian Joseph '86   F '83, '84

White, Dennis Craig '69   Sw '68

White, Edward Spaulding '86   S '84

White, Eugene Nelson '74   Fc '72, '73, '74

White, George Francis '83   Bb '80, '81, '82, '83

White, Jennifer '83   FH '79, '80, '81, '82; L '80, '81, '82, '83; H '81, '82, '83

White, Jennifer Lee '81   S '77, '78

White, Jonathan Robertson '77   HC '75, '76, '77

White, Lawrence Henry '77   Fc '75

White, Richard Price '74   Sl '72, '73, '74

White, Samuel Giltinan '68   LC '68

White, Sumner Wheeler '77   L '75, '76, '77

White, Virginia '86   V '84

Whitehead, Bradley Wayne '82   HC '81, '82

Whiteside, Alexander II '66   HC '63, '64, '65

Whittington, Justin '81–'82   F '79, '80, '81

Whitley, Lona Tracee '88   S '84

Whitman, Charles Seymour III '64   S '62, '63

Whitman, Glenn Joseph Robert '74   Sq '72, '73, '74

Whitman, Hugh Jr. '74   R '73, '74

Whitman, Stephen Laurence '74   L '72

Whitman, Stephen Van Rensselaer '69   Sq '69; Te '68

Whitman, Sylvia Choate '83–'84   Sq '83

Whitney, Robert Bacon '65   HC '63, '64, '65

Whitney, Wallace French Jr. '64   L '62, '63; S '61, '62, '63, '64

Whittemore, Gilbert Franklin Jr. '72 (MGR)   F '70, '71

Wickens, Christopher Thomas Dow '67   W '65, '66, '67

Widerman, Paul Martin '83   W '79, '80, '82, '83

Wiedemann, Harden Hull '75   F '73, '74

Wiegand, Andrew '73   Sq '71, '72, '73; Te '71

Wiegand, Bruce '69   Sq '68, '69; Te '67, '68

Wiegand, Jeffrey Phillips '76   Sq '74, '75, '76

Wiesen, Paul John '87   W '85

Wigdor, E. Mitchell '77 (MGR)   H '75, '76, '77

Wiggin, Charles Everett '68   L '67, '68

Wigglesworth, David Trecartin '80   L '77, '78, '79, '80

Wilbanks, Thor Miller '86   Fc '84, '85

Wilcox, Maurice Kirby Collerre '70   L '68, '69, '70

Wilde, Deirdre Atwood '82   Sl '82

Wilder, Elisabeth Johnson '86   LC '85

Wildes, Gregory George '86   Bb '83, '84, '85

Wiley, Kate Margaret '85   CC '81, '82, '83, '84; TI '82, '83, '84, '85; TO '82, '83, '84, '85

Wiley, Robert Leroy III '78   HC '78

Wilinsky, John Francis '76   Fc '73

Wilkins, Ronald Wayne '65   LC '65

Wilkinson, James Brent '85–'86   F '83, '84

Wilkinson, Jean Mishell '73   Bb '71, '72, '73

Wilkinson, Todd Scripps '66   Sq '65; Te '64, '65

Wilks, Donald Kenneth '71   TI '69

Willard, Robert Bruce W. '66   L '65

Williams, Barry Lawson '66   Bb '63, '64, '65

Williams, Daniel Paul '75   Ba '73, '74, '75

Williams, Denise Darcel '82   So '81

Williams, Gregory Brian '85   LC '84, '85

Williams, Hadley Cogswell '66   L '63, '64

Williams, John J. '79   W '77, '79

Williams, Katherine Colwell '83   FH '79, '81, '82; H '80

Williams, Louis Gerry '64   S '61, '62, '63; Sq '62, '63; L '62, '63

Williams, Marjorie Curtis '79   FH '75; L '76

Williams, Roberton Capell Jr. '68 (MGR)   Ba '67

Williams, Sumner Randall '68 (MGR)   LC '67, '68

Williams, Susan M. '77   Bb '75, '76, '77

Williamson, Denise Darcel '82   Bb '81, '82

Williamson, Thomas Samuel Jr. '68   F '65, '66, '67

Willis, Kenneth Walter '74   Sk '72

Wills, Elizabeth Shewell '84   S '81

Wilmot, Christopher Albert '72   S '69, '70, '71

Wilson, Ann Roberta '86   Sw '83, '84, '85; WP '84, '85

Wilson, Ann Terese '85   So '82, '83, '84, '85

Wilson, Bradley Page '75   H '75

Wilson, Daniel Bennett '69   F '68

Wilson, David Raymond '73 (MGR)   F '72

Wilson, Howard Eugene '72   TI '72; TO '70, '71

Wilson, Larry James '72   R '70, '71, '72

Wilson, Lenora '76   Sk '75, '76, '77

Wilson, Orme III '75   Te '73, '75

Wilson, Ronald Alfred James '66   L '65, '66

Wilson, Ronald Thomas '68   TI '66, '67, '68; TO '66, '67, '68

Wilson, Thomas George Jr. '72   HC '72

Wimberly, Floyd Stephen '70   TO '69

Winfield, Ronald Paige '69   Fc '68, '69

Winig, Hugh Richard '65   Fc '65

Winn, Thomas Paul '77   F '75, '76

Winnick, Martha Ann '85–'86   Sq '84, '85

Winslow, Walter Thacher Jr. '65   S '62, '63, '64

Wise, Andrew Edmund '82   W '81, '82

Wise, Erich Paul '70   Te '68

Wisentaner, Richard Albert '85   HC '85

Withy, Kelley Marie '87   WP '84, '85

Witten, Mitchell Ross '77   TO '75, '76; F '75, '76

Wolbach, William Wellington II '68   HC '66, '67

Wolcott, William Prescott '67   H '67

Woel, Gerard Marie '84   L '81, '84

Wolf, Scott Allen '88   Bb '85

Wolf, Thomas Charles '76–'77   Sw '73, '74, '75, '77

Wolfe, Kenneth Ira '74   Bb '72, '73, '74

Wolff, James Alexander Jr. '69   S '68; Sk '68, '69

Wolff, Robert Lee Jr. '69   LC '68, '69

Wolff, William Edward Grand '88   WP '84

Wolovic, David Alan '65   Ba '63, '64

Wolz, John Frederick '71   LC '69, '71

Wong, Catherine Jane '85   V '82, '83, '84

Wong, Gloria Chu '85 (MGR)   V '84

Wood, Christopher Robinson '75   HC '74, '75

Wood, Clement Biddle '74 (MGR)   Sl '72, '73, '74

Wood, David Mark '88   Sk '85

Wood, Douglas Earl '79   HC '78, '79

Wood, Lucy Eaton '78   FH '75, '76, '77

Wood, Maude Hunnewell '76   Bb '75, '76; FH '75; Te '75

Wood, Martha Augusta '84   WP '84

Wood, Peter Hutchins '64   L '62, '63

Wooddell, Jennifer Sarah '83   Fc '81, '82, '83

Woodhouse, Edward James '75   HC '73, '74, '75

Woodruff, Jon Allen '84   Rb '84

Woodruff, Kathryn Morrell '86   LC '85

Woods, Robert Soutter '72   S '71

Woodward, Scott Revello '78   Sk '75

Wool, Stephen Cornelius '81   F '79, '80

Woolery, Dorris Ann '82   Bb '79, '80

Woolsey, David Dean '82   Sl '78, '79, '82

Woolway, Robert Joseph '81   F '78, '79, '80

Worcester, David Lee '66   W '65, '66

Worrell, Mark Daniel '80   LC '78, '79, '80

Worsley, Charlotte Cheston '82   L '79, '80, '81, '82

Worsley, Cornelia Sibley '79   HC '76, '78, '79; H '79

Worth, Joseph Christopher III '71   Sl '70, '71

Worth, Robin Marie '81 (MGR)   Te '78, '79; H '80

Worthen, Hilary Goddard '69   S '67, '68

Wright, Alyce Anne '87   L '85

Wright, Conrad Edick '72 (MGR)   L '71, '72

Wright, David Griffith '68   S '66, '67

Wright, Edward James '84   L '81, '82, '83, '84

Wright, Robert John '76   HC '75, '76

Wright, Sarah Elizabeth '80   S '77

Wu, George '85   CC '84; TO '84, '85

Wulsin, Lawson Reed '74   S '71, '72, '73

Wyatt, Oswald Silvanus '76   H '74, '75, '76

Wylie, David Stiles '71   S '70

Wylie, James Chilton '83   L '80, '81

Wynne, Davis Ann '83   Sw '80

Wynne, James Jeffrey '64   Sq '63, '64

Wynne, Robin French '75   G '74, '75

Wynne, Terry Frank '72   G '71, '72

Wynne, Thomas Duncan III '69   F '67, '68; G '67, '68, '69

Wyzanski, Charles Max '66 (MGR)   W '65, '66

Yajima, Lenny Sae '83   TI '80, '81, '82; TO '80, '81

Yakopec, Stephen Jr. '80   S '77, '78, '79

Yale, Phyllis Robn '78 (MGR)   Sw '77

Yalouris, Eleftherios '71   LC '69, '70, '71

Yanelli, Kathleen Marie '85   V '81, '82

Yannopoulos, Aris Demetrios '77   S '76

Yastrzemski, Stanley Leon Jr. '65   F '62, '63, '64

Yasunaga, Milton Minoru '77   W '74, '75, '76, '77

Yates, Adlop Joseph '80   F '79

Yates, Carlan Kent '77   LC '75, '76

Yates, George David '71   Bb '69, '70

Yeadon, George Henry '75 (MGR)   TI '75; TO '75

Yeager, Linda Renee '84   CC '80, '81; TO '81

Yedinsky, Sarah Elizabeth '83   FH '79

Yehia, Ahmed Emin '69   S '66, '67, '68

Yellin, Thomas Gilmer '75   G '73, '74, '75

Yntema, Hessel Edward '74   Sw '73, '74, '75

York, Gwill Elaine '79   L '77

York, Gwill Elaine '79   FH '75, '76, '77

You, Harry Lee '79   HC '79

Young, Michael Alan '79   TI '78, '79; TO '77, '78

Ysrael, Catherine Zeien '86   WP '84, '85

Yue, James Joseph '88   L '85

Yunick, Suzanne Marie '82   H '79, '80, '81, '82

Zachariasen, Judith Ann '86   So '83, '84

Zager, Eric Louis '77   S '74, '75, '76

Zakotnik, John Michael '74   Sw '72, '73, '74

Zakula, Steven Donald '71   Bb '70

Zaslavsky, Alexander '86 (MGR)   S '83, '84

Zebal, Stephen Francis Jr. '69   F '67, '68

Zeeben, Wendy Lynn '87   S '83, '84

Zehnder, Dominik E.D. '83   Sk '83

Zeller, Martin Ellsworth '68   Sk '68

Zellner, Edward Arnold '67   H '65

Ziegler, Margaret Danna '81   HC '78, '79, '80, '81

Zimering, Mark Bernard '77   S '75, '76

Zimic, Deborah Lee '84   Sw '81, '82, '83, '84

Zimmerman, Richard Samuel Jr. '68   F '65, '66, '67

Zinn, William Michael '69   W '67, '68

Zischkau, Herbert Stuart III '74   S '73

Zizka, Robert John III '85   Rb '84

Zolcosky, John Theodore '87   W '85

Zuckerman, Laura Julie '82   H '81

Zuckerman, Phillip '71   L '69, '70, '71

Zukerman, Martin '66   F '65

Zumbrum, Jerry Alan '82   F '80, '81

Zurawel, Mark Steven '79   Ba '77, '79

Zurkow, Peter '75   G '75

Zweng, Nancy Ann '76   L '76

Zygas, Kestutis Paul '64   Fc '63, '64

Index

Italics indicate pages on which illustrations appear.

PHOTO CREDITS

Morse Photography: pp. 4 (bottom), 7, 11, 26 (bottom), 29 (bottom right), 42 (right), 56, 58, 59, 60 (top), 85, 86 (bottom right), 42 (right), 56, 58, 59, 60 (top), 85 (bottom two), 88, 89, 92, 112, 113, 142, 143, 144, 145, 147, 148, 167, 168, 169, 181, 186 (right), 195, 196, 198, 200, 202, 215, 216, 217, 217, 226 (top), 231, 232 (bottom), 233, 241 (top), 242, 246, 247, 255, 260 (top), 274. **Jet Photo:** pp. 31, 34, 37, 77, 82, 91 (bottom), 110, 121, 135 (bottom right), 138, 144 (bottom left), 158 (left), 163, 183, 186 (left), 203, 225, 235 (left), 240, 241 (bottom), 245, 254, 259 (bottom), 160 (bottom). **Dick Raphael:** pp. 35, 36, 39, 46, 50 (bottom), 52, 53, (top), 54, 55, 76, 107 (bottom), 109, 135 (bottom left), 136 (top), 159, 176 (right), 178, 179, 192 (top). **Fred Kaplan:** pp. 133 (top), 176 (left), 224, 239. **Richard Mills:** pp. 180, 191 (bottom), 253. **Walter Fleischer:** pp. 100, 129. **Joe Wrinn:** pp. 57, 236. **Amateur Hockey Association of the United States:** p. 70. **Steve Babineau:** p. 91 (top). **H. S. Berman:** p. 233. **Boston Globe:** p. 26 (top). **Charles Carey:** p. 73. **Tim Carlson:** p. 264. **Cincinatti Bengals:** p. 48 (right). **Stuart Cohen:** p. 140. **Paul Donahue:** p. 86 (top). **Geoffrey Fulton:** p. 107 (top). **Bruce Kluckhohn/Harvard Crimson:** p. 182 (left). **Joseph Kovacs/*Harvard Crimson*:** p. 182 (left). **Joseph Kovacs/ *Harvard Crimson*:** p. 259. **Lenscraft Photos:** p. 101 (top). **Gary Mottola:** p. 210. **McDaniel Photo:** p. 75. **Charles Olchowski:** p. 80. **C. W. Pack:** p. 235 (right). **Alex Rhinelander/*Harvard Crimson*:** p. 182 (right). **Peter Southwick/*Harvard Crimson*:** p. 212 (bottom). **Brian Sullivan/*Harvard Crimson*:** p. 230. **Wilcox Photo:** p. 24. **Bruce Wood:** p. 144 (top). All other photos courtesy of the Harvard University Sports Information Office.

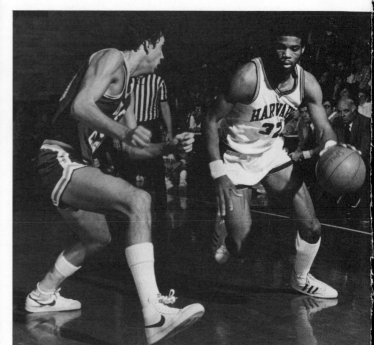